Cautious Hearts

A Trust-After-Heartbreak Romance
Collection

Alison Reid

Cautious Hearts – A Trust-After-Heartbreak Romance Collection

by Alison Reid

ISBN: 978-1-7644837-1-1

Independently published

Introduction to…

Cautious Hearts

A Trust-After-Heartbreak Romance Collection

Some hearts don't stop believing in love—they simply become more careful with it.

The stories in **Cautious Hearts** were written for readers who understand that love isn't always fearless. Sometimes it's hesitant. Sometimes it comes after heartbreak, betrayal, or disappointment. And sometimes, the bravest thing a heart can do is try again.

Each romance in this collection explores the quiet vulnerability of trusting someone when past wounds still ache. These are stories about women who have learned to protect themselves and men who must prove that love can be patient, steady, and worth the risk. Whether shaped by misunderstandings, hidden truths, or years of emotional distance, every relationship here unfolds slowly—allowing trust to be earned, walls to fall, and love to grow stronger because of what it's survived.

Written in the spirit of classic Mills & Boon with a modern emotional depth, these standalone romances focus on connection, healing, and the moment when guarded hearts finally choose love. There is no cheating, and every story promises a deeply satisfying happily-ever-after.

If you believe love is most powerful when it's chosen with open eyes and a cautious heart, I hope these stories stay with you long after the final page.

Table of Contents

Blueprints of the Heart

Alison Reid

A complete standalone romance

Previously published individually

Prologue

Elliott and Marie sat together in the sterile, white-walled office; their hands intertwined tightly as they waited for the doctor's arrival. Their daughter, Sophie, just fourteen years old, sat beside them, her feet barely touching the floor, swinging nervously as she glanced between her parents. She didn't fully understand why they were there, but the tension in the room was palpable.

The door finally opened, and the doctor entered, carrying a clipboard and wearing a gentle but serious expression. After a few pleasantries, he took a seat across from them and began explaining.

"Marie, based on your symptoms and the test results, we've confirmed that you have primary progressive multiple sclerosis," the doctor said carefully, pausing to let the words sink in.

Elliott's grip on Marie's hand tightened, his jaw clenched, but he remained silent. Marie's face paled, her breath catching as she processed the diagnosis. Sophie, sitting between them, looked up at her parents, sensing the gravity of the situation but still unsure what it meant.

The doctor continued, his voice calm but direct. "Primary progressive multiple sclerosis is a form of MS where symptoms gradually worsen over time. Unlike other forms of MS, there are fewer periods of remission. Over the coming years, you may experience increasing difficulty with mobility, fatigue, and coordination. The disease can affect your ability to walk and may cause muscle weakness and stiffness. While the progression can vary from person to person, it is generally steady."

Marie's eyes filled with tears as she listened, and Elliott leaned in closer, wrapping his arm around her as though trying to shield her from the harsh reality they were facing. Sophie, still unsure, tugged at her mother's sleeve, whispering, "Mom, what does this mean?"

The doctor softened his tone, looking at Sophie. "It means that your mum is going to need some help in the future, Sophie. She'll still be the same person, but she may get tired more easily, and there will be times when she needs help walking or moving around."

Marie swallowed hard, her voice trembling as she spoke. "How long... how long before things get worse?"

The doctor sighed, clearly wishing he had better news. "It's hard to say. The disease progresses at different rates for everyone. Some people manage for years with only mild symptoms, while others may see faster changes. We'll work together to manage the symptoms and find the right treatments to help slow it down as much as possible."

Elliott finally spoke, his voice rough with emotion. "What can we do? How do we prepare for this?"

The doctor nodded, his expression understanding. "It's important to start planning early. Physical therapy can help maintain strength and mobility for as long as possible. Occupational therapy can assist with learning how to manage daily tasks as things change. There will be medications to manage pain, muscle stiffness, and other symptoms as they come."

Sophie stared at the doctor, then looked at her mother, trying to comprehend what was happening. "Will you be okay, Mum?" she asked, her voice small.

Marie looked down at her daughter, her heart breaking for the burden this would place on her. She forced a brave smile, though tears shimmered in her eyes. "Yes, sweetheart, I'll be okay. We'll get through this together."

Elliott nodded, kissing Marie's forehead gently. "We're going to take care of you," he whispered, though there was a mix of fear and determination in his voice.

The doctor gave them time to absorb the news, offering support and resources, but the weight of what was to come loomed large. As the family left the office, Elliott and Marie held each other a little tighter, while Sophie, still young and innocent, began to realise that their world was about to change forever.

The house was unusually quiet as Elliott descended the stairs. It had been nine months since Marie's MS diagnosis, and each step felt heavier than the last, as if they were carrying him toward an inevitable, unspoken decision. Marie sat at the kitchen table, staring out of the window. She was lost in her thoughts, her gaze distant, but her posture spoke of exhaustion. Sophie was in her room, probably reading or doing homework, blissfully unaware of the tension building between her parents.

Elliott hesitated by the doorway, his heart pounding in his chest. For months, he had tried to convince himself that he could handle it, that he could be the supportive husband Marie needed. But every time he saw her struggle with the simplest tasks, saw the toll the MS diagnosis was already taking on her body, something inside him recoiled. He felt helpless, overwhelmed, and ashamed of the resentment he couldn't seem to shake. This wasn't the life he had imagined for them.

Marie, sensing his presence, turned to look at him. She could read the emotions on his face before he even spoke. She had seen this coming; she knew Elliott was struggling, but she had hoped, somehow, that he would stay. That their love, their family, would be enough to keep him by her side.

"Elliott?" she said softly, her voice laced with a mixture of fear and resignation. "What's wrong?"

He couldn't look at her directly, his eyes dropping to the floor as he gathered the courage to speak. "I... I don't think I can do this, Marie," he muttered, his voice barely audible. "I can't handle this."

Her breath caught in her throat, the words hitting her like a punch to the chest. She knew it was hard; her illness had changed everything but hearing him say it out loud made it all the more real. "You mean... you can't handle *me*," she said, her voice cracking. She struggled to stand, her legs wobbling beneath her, but she managed to stay upright, her hands gripping the table for support.

Elliott looked up then, meeting her gaze for the first time. The pain in her eyes was unbearable, but it wasn't enough to change his mind. "I'm sorry," he whispered, guilt tearing at him. "I just... I'm not strong enough for this. I'm not strong enough for what's coming."

Marie felt the sting of his words settle deep in her heart. Tears welled up in her eyes, but she refused to let them fall. "What about Sophie?" she asked, her voice trembling. "You're just going to leave us? Leave her?"

His expression crumpled at the mention of their daughter, but he didn't back down. "I'll still be her father. I'll still see her," he said, though the words felt hollow. He knew this wasn't something you could walk away from and still expect to stay involved. "But I can't stay here, Marie. I can't pretend everything's okay when I'm falling apart."

Marie shook her head, disbelief washing over her. "You think I'm not falling apart too? You think I don't need you now more than ever?"

There was silence between them, thick and heavy with everything left unsaid. Elliott's shoulders slumped, defeated, and he ran a hand through his hair, unable to offer her anything more than an apology. "I'm sorry," he repeated, as if those words could fix the damage he was causing.

Finally, Marie spoke again, her voice soft but laced with bitterness. "If you leave now, Elliott, don't expect to come back. Not to me."

He nodded, knowing the truth of her words, but still unable to stay. He turned and walked out of the kitchen, the sound of the front door closing behind him echoing through the house. Marie stood alone in the kitchen, her body trembling, her heart shattered.

Upstairs, Sophie heard the door slam and hurried to the window. She watched in confusion as her father walked down the driveway, suitcase in hand, and drove off without looking back. A sinking feeling settled in her chest. Something had shifted, and deep down, she knew things would never be the same. She rushed downstairs, her voice shaky as she asked her mother, "Where's Dad going? How long will he be gone?"

Chapter One

Sophie Highland was the kind of beautiful that turned heads, though she seemed determined to avoid attention. Her long, dark brown hair, rich as mahogany, was most often tied back in a simple ponytail, loose strands framing her face with an almost unintentional elegance. She exuded a quiet confidence, as though she was too preoccupied with more pressing matters to give her looks a second thought. Her beauty was effortless, understated, and all the more striking for it.

Her doe-brown eyes were her most captivating feature. Wide and expressive, they held a depth that spoke of both resilience and vulnerability. There was kindness in her gaze, a warmth that made people feel seen, but there was also an undercurrent of sadness—an invisible weight she carried alone. Those eyes lit up when she smiled, transforming her entire face, but smiles were a rare luxury Sophie reserved for the people she cared about, particularly her mother.

Her natural lips, full and subtly upturned at the corners, added an air of softness to her focused expression. She rarely wore makeup, a reflection of her practicality, but her beauty required no enhancement. Her petite frame was slender but strong, a testament to years of discipline and quiet endurance. Her wardrobe, filled with muted tones and functional pieces, seemed to echo her resolve to keep things simple. Yet no amount of practicality could mask the grace with which she moved—a grace born not of privilege but of quiet strength and determination.

At twenty-five, Sophie bore the weight of her world with remarkable composure. Her days were a delicate balance of caring for her mother, Marie, who had battled multiple sclerosis for a decade, and working two part-time jobs to make ends meet. Her nights were often spent studying, sketching, and dreaming of a better future, though she rarely allowed herself the luxury of imagining it for her own sake.

Life had tested Sophie early and often. When she was fifteen, her father, Elliott, walked out, unable to face Marie's diagnosis. His absence had left a scar, not just on their family but on Sophie's perception of trust and dependency. It was a wound she never spoke of; one she channelled into an unwavering resolve. From that day, Sophie had become the rock of her family, promising herself she'd never let anyone down the way her father had.

Despite the hardships, she had managed to excel academically, completing both her bachelor's and master's degrees in architecture within seven gruelling years. Her journey had been anything but easy. Between long shifts at a coffee shop on weekdays and managing the front desk at a gym on weekends, Sophie's time had been stretched impossibly thin. Yet she had graduated at the top of her class, not just because of her talent but because of her need to succeed—for herself, for her mother, and for the future she had vowed to build.

Architecture became her sanctuary, a place where she could create order and beauty in a world that often felt chaotic. It was her way of reclaiming control, of designing spaces that felt safe, enduring, and full of possibility. In her designs, Sophie saw a reflection of the life she hoped to construct—one where the walls she'd built around herself could finally come down, piece by piece, revealing a woman who had weathered every storm and emerged, quietly, victorious.

But even now, with her degrees in hand, life hadn't slowed down. Sophie's days were still an intricate balancing act, packed from morning until night. She would rise early, often before dawn, to squeeze in hours at the café, her feet already aching as she brewed coffee and served pastries to hurried patrons. On weekends, she'd rush to her second job at the gym, assisting clients and managing the front desk with her practiced, polite smile. And always, without fail, she hurried home afterward to care for her mother, Marie, who relied on her for nearly everything.

Sophie never complained. It wasn't in her nature to dwell on what she lacked or how hard things were. Her love for her mother was unwavering, and the bond they shared— born from years of struggle and mutual sacrifice—gave her strength. When she looked at Marie, she saw a woman who had once been vibrant and full of life, now trapped in a body that betrayed her. It made every ounce of effort worth it. Sophie knew she was her mother's lifeline, and she would never let her down.

Even so, the weight Sophie carried was immense. She had worked tirelessly to earn her degrees, pouring her heart into countless late nights of studying and designing, yet the reward she had hoped for—a chance to truly start her career—felt just out of reach. The mountain of student debt loomed over her like a storm cloud, ever-present and suffocating. Every paycheck seemed to disappear the moment it arrived, swallowed by rent, bills, and the never-ending stream of expenses required to keep their fragile household running.

Her dream of becoming an architect, once a bright beacon of hope, had shifted into something more urgent—a lifeline. It wasn't just about passion anymore; it was about survival, about building a future that would free her from the endless grind. Sophie had started applying for internships with a fervour that bordered on desperation. She knew the odds were slim, especially without connections in such a competitive field, but she clung to the belief that her work ethic and talent would speak for themselves.

Sometimes, late at night, Sophie allowed herself to dream of what life could look like if she succeeded. She pictured herself in a sleek office, her sketches and blueprints coming to life in sprawling buildings that stood as a testament to her creativity and perseverance. She imagined a life where she could afford small luxuries, like buying her mother a better wheelchair or taking a weekend off just to rest. Maybe one day, she could even travel, see the structures that had inspired her love of architecture—the Eiffel Tower, the Sagrada Família, the streets of Florence.

But for now, those dreams felt far away. Her reality was deadlines, rejection letters, and exhaustion. Still, she refused to give up. Sophie was no stranger to hardship, and she knew that nothing worthwhile came easily. Every long shift, every sleepless night, was a step toward something better.

On this particular morning, Sophie found herself seated in the pristine, modern lobby of Prescott Design Group, her hands tightly clutching the leather portfolio resting on her lap. The building itself was a masterpiece of contemporary architecture, with its soaring glass walls and sleek, minimalist design. Sunlight streamed in, illuminating the polished floors and casting geometric shadows that danced across the room. Sophie's heart pounded as she took it all in, the air heavy with both intimidation and possibility.

She adjusted the blazer she had bought from a second-hand store, its sleeves slightly too long for her petite frame, and smoothed her skirt with trembling fingers. This was the interview she had been waiting for—the opportunity she had worked so hard to reach. Sophie had rehearsed her answers to every possible question, her mind buzzing with facts about the firm and its recent projects. Yet, as she sat there, she couldn't help but feel a creeping doubt. What if she wasn't enough?

Shaking off the thought, she took a deep breath and straightened her posture. She reminded herself of everything she had overcome to get here. Her academic record, her relentless work ethic, the portfolio in her lap—all of it was a testament to her dedication. She had earned this moment. No matter the outcome, she would walk into that interview and give it her all.

Because Sophie Highland wasn't just a dreamer. She was a fighter, a builder—someone who knew how to lay a foundation even in the toughest of circumstances. And though the future was uncertain, one thing was clear: she wouldn't stop until she had built the life she and her mother deserved.

Her name was called, and Sophie stood, smoothing down her skirt. She took a deep breath, squared her shoulders, and walked into the conference room with as much confidence as she could muster. The space was as sleek and modern as the rest of the building, its minimalist design offset by floor-to-ceiling windows that offered a breathtaking view of the city skyline.

Behind a polished glass table stood a tall, sharp-eyed woman dressed in an impeccably tailored suit. Her presence was commanding, yet not unkind, as she extended a hand to Sophie.

"Miss Highland," she said, her tone professional but warm. "I'm Julia Winslow, Head of Talent Acquisition. Please, have a seat."

Sophie thanked her, sitting carefully in the plush chair, her leather portfolio resting on the edge of the table. Julia opened a folder and began flipping through its contents, her eyes scanning the pages with practiced efficiency.

"I must say," Julia began, glancing up with a faint smile, "your academic achievements are nothing short of outstanding. Top of your class in both your Bachelor's and master's programs. A five-year Bachelor of Architecture followed by a two-year Master's—both completed with honours. That's no small feat."

Sophie's heart thudded in her chest, but she managed a calm nod, a small, genuine smile playing on her lips. "Architecture has always been my passion. I've worked hard to stay focused and committed, no matter the challenges."

Julia's sharp gaze lingered on her, as if assessing more than just her words. She nodded approvingly and continued, "Your portfolio is equally impressive. I've reviewed it thoroughly, and I must say, your designs are remarkable—thoughtful, innovative, and incredibly detailed. You clearly have a talent for not just envisioning spaces but creating designs with purpose."

Sophie felt a surge of pride swell within her, though she kept her composure. Her hands rested clasped in her lap; her posture poised but not rigid. "Thank you," she said quietly, her voice steady despite the rush of excitement building inside her.

Julia leaned back slightly in her chair, closing the folder with a decisive motion. "Now, I'll be upfront with you. This internship is highly competitive, and we're only taking on one candidate this year. However, I can already say you've made a very strong impression."

Sophie's pulse quickened at the words, but she remained steady, nodding in acknowledgment.

Julia's expression softened into something closer to curiosity. "Let's talk more about your vision. Why Prescott Design Group? What makes you think you're the right fit for this firm?"

Sophie leaned forward slightly, her confidence growing as she spoke. "Prescott Design Group has been a name I've admired for years, not just for the beauty of its projects but for the innovation and sustainability embedded in its designs. I believe architecture is about more than creating aesthetically pleasing spaces—it's about solving problems, shaping communities, and leaving a lasting impact. Your firm embodies that philosophy, and it's a vision I share."

Julia's brows lifted, and a genuine smile spread across her face. "Go on," she encouraged.

"I've always been driven by the idea of pushing boundaries, finding new ways to make architecture functional, sustainable, and meaningful," Sophie continued. "I believe I can bring fresh, bold ideas to the table—concepts that align with Prescott's vision but also challenge it in ways that drive growth and innovation. I want to learn from the best while contributing to projects that make a difference."

Julia seemed to consider her words carefully before nodding, an expression of clear approval on her face. "Well, Sophie," she said, rising from her chair and extending a hand, "you've certainly set yourself apart today. We'll be making our decision soon, and you can expect to hear from us within the next week.

As Sophie left the office, her heart pounded with a mix of nerves and cautious optimism, but a sense of lightness followed her out the door. She had given it her all, and now it was out of her hands. As she stepped onto the bustling streets of San Francisco, the sun dipping low on the horizon, she allowed herself a fleeting smile. For the first time in a long while, she felt like she might be one step closer to the dream she had fought tirelessly for.

Still, there was no time to linger in the moment. The interview had run longer than expected, and she was cutting it dangerously close to the start of her shift at the coffee shop. Weaving through the crowded sidewalks, she dodged pedestrians and street vendors, her mind racing as fast as her feet. The hum of the city surrounded her—the clang of streetcars, snippets of conversation, the distant wail of a saxophone from a nearby corner. Normally, she loved the energy of San Francisco, but today it was just background noise to her singular focus: making it to work on time.

By the time she reached the shop, the bell above the door jingling as she hurried in, she was breathless but relieved. She quickly pulled on her apron, tying it behind her back as she flashed a sheepish smile at Beryl, the café's owner.

"Cutting it close there, Sophie," Beryl teased, her hands busy restocking the display case with freshly baked muffins.

"Sorry about that," Sophie said, brushing a stray strand of hair from her face. "The interview ran longer than I expected."

Beryl's eyes lit up with curiosity. "Oh, the big interview? How did it go?"

Sophie hesitated, her cheeks flushing slightly as she adjusted her apron. "I think it went well," she said, a small smile forming. "At least, I hope so. Fingers crossed."

Beryl paused her work to give Sophie an encouraging nod. "You've worked so hard for this, Sophie. I'm sure you made a great impression. I'll be keeping my fingers crossed too."

"Thanks, Beryl," Sophie said, her smile widening. "That means a lot."

With that, she grabbed her notepad and pen, ready to dive into the bustling rhythm of the café.

The evening rush was in full swing, and Sophie moved through the café with practiced efficiency, balancing trays of steaming coffee and plates of sandwiches. Her mind slipped into the familiar rhythm of taking orders, offering warm smiles, and making light conversation with the regulars.

Despite her exhaustion, she found comfort in the steady pace, in the small, fleeting connections with customers who offered her kind words or a moment of shared laughter.

Hours passed, and the crowd began to thin. By the time the café closed at 9pm, Sophie's feet ached, and her arms felt like lead. She wiped down the last table, her motions slow but deliberate, as the once-bustling space grew quiet around her.

"All done for the night," Sophie said, untying her apron and folding it neatly. She set it on the counter, letting out a small sigh of relief.

Beryl looked up from the espresso machine she had been cleaning, her warm smile unwavering. "You worked hard today, as always. Go home and get some rest."

"I will," Sophie promised, slinging her bag over her shoulder. "Thanks, Beryl. Goodnight."

"Take care, Sophie. And don't forget to say hi to your mum for me," Beryl called after her.

Sophie waved over her shoulder as she stepped out into the cool night air.

The walk home was quiet, the streets mostly deserted now except for the occasional car passing by. Sophie's footsteps echoed softly on the pavement, and the cool breeze carried the faint scent of salt from the bay. It was a peaceful moment, one of the few she allowed herself to savour as she moved through her busy days.

When she reached the small, worn apartment building she shared with her mother, she paused for a moment, looking up at the dimly lit windows of their third-floor unit. It wasn't much—far from the house they'd once called home—but it was theirs.

Sophie climbed the stairs, her legs protesting every step, and unlocked the door. The familiar scent of lavender greeted her, a comfort she had come to associate with home.

Her mother, Marie, was asleep on the couch, a knit blanket draped over her legs. Sophie's heart softened at the sight. Even in sleep, her mother's face bore traces of the strength and resilience that had carried them through so many hardships.

"Mom," Sophie said gently, kneeling beside her and brushing a hand over her shoulder. "It's time to get to bed."

Marie stirred, blinking sleepily as she looked at her daughter. "Sophie? You're home."

"I am," Sophie said, smiling warmly. "Come on, let's get you to bed."

Marie nodded, allowing Sophie to help her to her feet. Together, they moved slowly toward the bedroom, Sophie's arm steady around her mother's waist.

Once Marie was tucked into bed, Sophie adjusted the blankets and smoothed her hair back from her face. "Goodnight, Mum," she whispered, pressing a kiss to her forehead.

"Goodnight, sweetheart," Marie murmured, her voice soft with affection.

As Sophie closed the door and retreated to her own room, she felt the weight of the day settle over her. She sank onto her bed, too tired to do more than kick off her shoes and lie back against the pillows. Despite the exhaustion, a small flicker of hope warmed her chest.

Tomorrow would bring more challenges, more hard work—but for tonight, she allowed herself to believe that all of it might lead to something better.

Chapter Two

Damian Prescott stood tall, exuding an effortless confidence that turned heads wherever he went. His jet-black hair, always impeccably styled, framed a chiselled face, accentuating his sharp jawline and high cheekbones. His piercing green eyes, which seemed to see right through people, carried an intensity that both disarmed and intrigued. They were eyes that rarely betrayed his emotions—a skill that had served him well in both business and personal matters.

His athletic build was a testament to his disciplined lifestyle, though he was careful to maintain a balance that emphasised refinement over brute strength. Everything about him, from his tailored suits to his polished Italian leather shoes, spoke of precision and control. Damian was a man who understood the power of presentation, and he wielded it masterfully.

As the owner and CEO of Prescott Design Group, Damian had built an empire through sheer determination and an uncanny ability to anticipate trends in the architectural world. Under his leadership, the firm had become synonymous with cutting-edge innovation and sustainable design. His relentless drive for excellence, however, was not without its challenges. Employees both admired and feared him, knowing his exacting standards left little room for error.

Yet, beyond his business acumen and professional rigour, Damian's personal life was a subject of much speculation. Known as a consummate playboy, he had a reputation for short-lived relationships that rarely extended beyond a few thrilling weeks. Women were drawn to his charisma and enigmatic aura, but Damian had long since mastered the art of detachment. He enjoyed the chase, the passion, the fleeting excitement—but nothing more. Commitment was a territory he avoided, and emotional vulnerability was a concept he dismissed outright.

Still, those closest to him knew there was more to Damian than his carefully curated image suggested. Beneath the polished exterior was a man deeply loyal to the select few he allowed into his inner circle. He valued integrity in others as much as he demanded it of himself, and he harboured a quiet, unspoken yearning for something beyond the shallow connections he had grown accustomed to.

Damian leaned back in his sleek leather chair, the expansive windows of his corner office framing a panoramic view of the city skyline. The space reflected him: modern, minimalist, and uncompromisingly sharp. Floor-to-ceiling bookshelves housed meticulously arranged architectural monographs and accolades, while abstract artwork added subtle bursts of colour to the otherwise monochromatic décor.

He glanced at the clock mounted on the wall—an industrial-style piece that ticked with precision. Julia Winslow, the Head of Talent Acquisition, was due any moment. Damian respected Julia for her shrewdness and professionalism; she had an unerring ability to identify talent, and she didn't hesitate to speak her mind, even to him.

The door swung open, and Julia Winslow strode in with purpose, a leather-bound folder clutched in her hand. Her tailored navy suit and silver-streaked hair projected an air of authority that few dared to challenge.

"Good morning, Damian," she greeted, her tone brisk yet professional as always.

"Morning, Julia. I've been looking forward to discussing the intern candidates?" Damian replied, straightening in his sleek leather chair, the sunlight streaming through the floor-to-ceiling windows behind him.

"I've narrowed it down to two finalists: Sophie Highland and Michael Jones." She placed the folder on his desk and flipped it open, revealing neatly organised profiles. "Sophie brings an impressive academic record, particularly in sustainable architecture. Michael, on the other hand, has more practical experience, having completed an internship at one of our competitors, Crane & Morgan."

Damian's sharp green eyes scanned the profiles Julia handed him, his expression unreadable. He lingered on Sophie Highland's portfolio. The designs stood out—bold, innovative, and meticulously detailed. He could almost sense the passion behind her work.

He leaned back slightly, his interest piqued. "What's your take on them?"

Julia folded her arms and regarded him thoughtfully. "Michael's experience is valuable, no doubt, but Sophie's story is compelling. She's put herself through school, juggling two jobs while caring for her mother, who has significant medical needs. That kind of dedication and resilience can't be taught. And her portfolio? It's not just good—it's inspired."

Damian tapped his finger on Sophie's résumé, his gaze still fixed on the profile. "Interesting. But how does she handle pressure? You know how demanding it is here."

"Extremely well," Julia answered without hesitation. "She maintained top grades in one of the toughest programs while balancing multiple responsibilities. I believe she's more than capable of thriving in this environment."

He looked up, curiosity flickering in his green eyes. "After meeting with both candidates, if you had to choose, who would you hire?"

Julia didn't miss a beat. "Sophie Highland, without question. Michael might have the edge in practical experience, but Sophie has the potential to bring something new to

Prescott Design Group. She's hungry to prove herself, and I believe she'll rise to any challenge we throw her way."

Damian considered her words, his fingers steepled in front of him. "All right," he said decisively, leaning forward. "Let's go with Miss Highland. Make the arrangements."

Julia nodded, her professional demeanour unwavering. "Understood. I'll have the paperwork ready by the end of the day and contact her. She can start in two weeks—that should give her enough time to prepare."

"Perfect. Thank you, Julia," Damian said, offering her a rare smile of appreciation.

As Julia gathered her folder and exited the office, Damian leaned back in his chair, his gaze drifting to the cityscape outside. For a moment, he let his mind wander. Sophie Highland intrigued him. Her determination, her sacrifices, the fire in her designs—it all painted a picture of someone who wasn't afraid to fight for what she wanted.

This wasn't just about hiring the right talent for Prescott Design Group; it was about seeing if Sophie could match the expectations, he held for himself and his team. As a man who demanded nothing less than excellence, Damian found himself curious to see if Sophie Highland would rise to the occasion—or crumble under the weight of it all.

Damian's thoughts shifted to his date with Clara later that evening. She had been growing increasingly clingy, her once alluring attentiveness now bordering on suffocating. While he had initially enjoyed the thrill of her pursuit, he knew it was time to cut ties. Relationships—if he could even call this brief fling that—were complications he preferred to avoid.

He sighed, running a hand through his perfectly styled black hair as he prepared for the conversation ahead. It would be messy; women like Clara didn't take rejection lightly. Still, he owed it to himself to prioritise his freedom over an emotional entanglement that no longer served him.

Later that night, Damian pulled out Clara's chair at the upscale restaurant, ever the gentleman despite his inner turmoil. The golden glow of candlelight danced across their table, creating an atmosphere that would've been romantic under different circumstances. Clara, in a crimson dress that hugged her curves, radiated confidence. She chatted animatedly, her laughter filling the space between them as she sipped her wine.

But Damian's focus wavered. He responded politely, even smiled at the appropriate moments, but his mind was elsewhere, carefully crafting his approach. As their entrées arrived, he realised it was time. He set his fork down, his expression softening.

"Clara," he began, his deep voice steady and calm. "I need to talk to you about something."

She tilted her head, curiosity flickering in her eyes. "What is it?"

He took a measured breath. "I've been thinking a lot about us, and I feel it's best if we go our separate ways."

The change in her demeanour was immediate. Her light-hearted smile vanished, replaced by an expression of disbelief. "What?" she demanded, her voice sharper than he'd expected. "You're serious?"

Damian nodded, keeping his tone level. "I think it's for the best. We've had fun, but—"

"Fun?" she interrupted, her voice rising. Heads began to turn from nearby tables, but Clara seemed oblivious to the attention she was drawing. "You think this was just fun? Damian, I thought we were building something real!"

He exhaled; his frustration carefully concealed. "Clara, please. Let's not make a scene."

But her anger spilled over, her voice cutting through the ambient murmur of the restaurant. "You can't just decide this out of nowhere! After everything I've given to you—"

Damian leaned back in his chair, his green eyes narrowing as he fought to maintain his composure. "Clara, it's not about you. I just need space. This isn't working for me."

Her laughter was bitter, almost incredulous. "Space! That's your excuse? Unbelievable."

The rest of the dinner passed in strained silence, punctuated by Clara's pointed remarks and icy glares. Damian endured it with the same detached composure he employed in boardroom negotiations, knowing the ordeal was nearly over.

On the drive home, the tension followed them into his car. Clara's frustration bubbled over as they weaved through the busy San Francisco streets. The glow of passing headlights highlighted the tears she refused to shed, her voice laced with bitterness.

"You never cared, did you?" she accused. "I was just a way to pass the time."

Damian's grip tightened on the steering wheel, his jaw clenching. "That's not true," he replied, his tone measured but firm. "I enjoyed our time together, but I don't want to lead you on."

"Lead me on?" Clara scoffed. "You already did."

The conversation continued in circles, her anger refusing to abate. By the time they arrived at her apartment, Damian felt drained, the weight of the evening pressing heavily on his chest. He parked the car, turning to her with an expression of finality.

"Clara," he said gently, "I hope you can understand one day. I wish you the best."

She stared at him, her fury giving way to a look of hurt that almost made him hesitate. Almost. Without another word, she stepped out of the car and slammed the door behind her.

When arriving home Damian stepped into his penthouse, the quiet luxury of the space embracing him like an old friend. The city lights twinkled through the massive windows, the skyline a soothing contrast to the chaos he had just left behind. He loosened his tie, letting it fall onto the polished hardwood floor as he made his way to the living room.

Collapsing onto his plush leather sofa, Damian exhaled deeply, the tension in his chest easing with each passing moment. The sleek, modern decor of his home reflected his carefully curated life—minimalist, controlled, free of unnecessary attachments.

"Finally," he muttered to himself, reaching for the decanter of whiskey he kept on the coffee table and poured himself a glass. The amber liquid glinted in the dim light as he took a slow sip, savouring the warmth that spread through his chest.

Clara had been a distraction; one he was now free of. Tomorrow, his focus would return to what truly mattered: his career, his ambitions, and the endless possibilities waiting for him in the world of architecture.

For now, though, Damian allowed himself this moment of solitude, his thoughts already shifting to the projects that demanded his attention. Clara was behind him, and his path forward had never felt clearer.

Chapter Three

Sophie was mid-shift at the bustling coffee shop when her phone buzzed in her pocket. The faint vibrations cut through the hum of espresso machines and chatter from customers. Stealing a glance at the screen, her breath hitched. *Julia Winslow.*

She quickly scanned the café. It was a brief lull—no orders lined up, and her coworker seemed to have things under control. Taking the opportunity, she slipped into the back room, the cool metal walls of the refrigerator pressing against her as she pulled her phone to her ear.

"Hello?" she said, her voice trembling with a mix of nervousness and hope.

"Sophie! It's Julia Winslow from Prescott Design Group," came the unmistakable warm tone from the other end.

Her heart pounded so loudly she could barely hear the rest of Julia's sentence. "I have some great news for you!"

Clutching the edge of the counter, Sophie felt her knees go weak. "Oh? What is it?" she asked, though a part of her already dared to hope.

"You've got the internship! Congratulations! You'll start in two weeks on Monday."

For a moment, Sophie stood frozen, the words replaying in her mind. Then, elation hit her like a tidal wave. "I got it. Are you serious?"

"Absolutely," Julia said, her excitement mirroring Sophie's. "Your qualifications were impressive, and your dedication shone through. I have no doubt you'll be a fantastic addition to our team."

Tears pricked at the corners of Sophie's eyes, though she blinked them back quickly. She couldn't cry in the storage room of a coffee shop. "Thank you so much, Julia. This means everything to me—I can't wait to get started!"

"Bring your A-game, Sophie. We're thrilled to have you on board," Julia replied before hanging up, leaving Sophie alone with her swirling emotions.

For a moment, she stayed in the quiet of the back room, leaning against the wall as reality sank in. This was it. The break she had been waiting for—the chance to step into the world of architecture and finally start building the life she'd always dreamed of.

She thought of her late nights balancing textbooks and the café's closing shift, the countless sacrifices she and her mother had made to keep their lives afloat. This internship wasn't just a job; it was a lifeline.

Her heart swelled with pride as she imagined her mother's reaction. She could already hear her voice: See? I knew you could do it.

Taking a deep breath to steady herself, Sophie straightened and stepped back into the café. The vibrant aroma of freshly brewed coffee greeted her, and she resumed her tasks with renewed energy. Every latte she made, every customer she served, felt like a step closer to her future.

For the rest of her shift, Sophie couldn't stop smiling. Even the grumpiest customer couldn't dampen her spirits. The promise of a brighter future shimmered on the horizon, and for the first time in years, Sophie felt like she was finally on her way.

As the clock struck 9pm, Sophie let out a long, relieved sigh. The café was finally quiet, the hum of conversation and the clatter of dishes replaced by the soft hiss of the espresso machine being cleaned. She untied her apron with practiced ease, shaking off the fatigue that had weighed on her all day. The warm, familiar scents of coffee and freshly baked pastries lingered in the air, a bittersweet reminder of her countless hours spent here.

She glanced around the café, her gaze landing on Beryl, the café owner, who stood behind the counter meticulously wiping down the espresso machine. Despite the late hour, Beryl's energy was as steady as ever, her movements precise and purposeful. She looked up as Sophie approached, her face lighting up with a warm smile.

"Hey, Sophie! Another stellar day," Beryl said, her voice tinged with pride. "I don't know how you do it, but the customers love you."

Sophie returned the smile, grateful for the praise. "Thanks, Beryl. It's been a long one, but I think I survived."

Beryl chuckled. "Survived? You thrived. The place wouldn't run half as smoothly without you."

Sophie hesitated, her fingers fidgeting with the hem of her apron. This was the moment she had been dreading, though a part of her knew Beryl would understand. She took a deep breath, steadying herself.

"Actually, Beryl, there's something I need to tell you," Sophie began, her voice calm but tinged with nervous anticipation.

Beryl paused, raising an eyebrow in curiosity. "Oh? What's on your mind?"

Sophie bit her lip before letting the words tumble out. "I got an internship at Prescott Design Group. I'll be starting in two weeks. It's a full-time commitment, but I still want to help out here in the evenings if that's okay."

For a moment, Beryl just stared, her expression unreadable. Sophie braced herself, half-expecting a reprimand or a disappointed sigh. Instead, Beryl's face broke into a wide grin, and she clapped her hands together in delight.

"Sophie, that's incredible!" Beryl exclaimed, her eyes shining with genuine excitement. "Prescott Design Group? That's huge!"

Relief flooded Sophie, and she felt a grin spreading across her face. "It's been a dream of mine for so long," she admitted. "I can't believe it's finally happening."

Beryl stepped out from behind the counter, her enthusiasm infectious. "I'm so proud of you, Sophie. You've worked so hard for this. And don't worry about your shifts here—we'll work around your schedule. You focus on that internship and knock their socks off."

Sophie blinked, touched by Beryl's unwavering support. "Thank you, Beryl. I was worried about leaving you short-staffed, but this means so much to me."

"Don't you worry about a thing," Beryl said, pulling Sophie into a quick hug. "You deserve this. Just promise me one thing—don't burn yourself out trying to juggle everything, okay?"

"I promise," Sophie said, her voice filled with gratitude.

As she stepped out into the cool night air, Sophie felt an overwhelming sense of peace. The city streets stretched out before her, bathed in the soft glow of streetlights. Each step she took felt lighter, as if the weight of her struggles had lifted, leaving behind only hope and excitement.

For the first time in what felt like forever, the future didn't seem so daunting. It seemed bright, full of promise, and undeniably hers.

As Sophie walked through the door of their modest apartment, the familiar scent of home wrapped around her like a warm blanket. The soft glow of the lamp in the living room illuminated the space, casting a gentle light over the cozy furnishings. Her mother, Marie, was nestled on the couch with a blanket draped over her legs, her book resting on her lap. Her expression, a mix of fatigue and peace, softened when she saw her daughter.

"Hey, Mum," Sophie called softly, setting her bag down by the door. She walked over, her steps light as though she didn't want to disturb the tranquility of the room. "How was your day?"

Marie looked up, her face lighting up at the sight of Sophie. "Oh, you know, the usual. I read a bit, napped a bit. How was work?"

Sophie knelt beside the couch, brushing a strand of hair from her mother's forehead. Her mother's skin was cooler than she'd like, and the sight made her heart ache a little. "It was good, Mum. Actually… I have some exciting news!"

Marie's brows lifted, curiosity flickering in her tired eyes. "What is it, sweetheart?"

Sophie took a deep breath, her heart thudding in her chest. This was the moment she'd been waiting for. "I got the internship at Prescott Design Group!" she announced, her voice bubbling with excitement.

For a moment, Marie stared at her in stunned silence, and then her face broke into a radiant smile. "Oh, Sophie! That's wonderful!" she exclaimed, reaching out to take her daughter's hands. "I knew you could do it. You've worked so hard studying for this."

Sophie's grin widened; her happiness mirrored in her mother's pride. "It's such a big opportunity for me—finally, a step toward my dream."

Marie opened her arms for a hug, and Sophie leaned in, savouring the comfort of her mother's embrace. "You deserve this, darling," Marie said, her voice thick with emotion. "I'm so proud of you."

Sophie blinked back tears, the weight of her mother's words sinking deep into her heart. "I couldn't have done it without you, Mum. Thank you for always believing in me."

Later, after helping Marie settle into bed, Sophie retired to her room. But her excitement was too big to keep to herself. She grabbed her phone and immediately dialled her best friend, Lizzie.

"Hello?" Lizzie's voice came through the line, warm and curious.

"Lizzie! You won't believe what just happened!" Sophie exclaimed, unable to contain her giddy enthusiasm.

"What? Tell me!" Lizzie's tone perked up, laced with anticipation.

"I got the internship at Prescott Design Group!" Sophie said, her voice trembling with joy.

A high-pitched squeal came through the phone. "No way! Soph, that's amazing!" Lizzie cried. "I'm so proud of you. You've worked your butt off for this!"

"Thanks, Lizzie. I still can't believe it's real," Sophie admitted, her voice softening with awe. "I'm starting in two weeks."

"This calls for a celebration," Lizzie declared. "No arguments! Saturday night—we're going out, and you're going to look like the goddess you are."

Sophie laughed, her nerves surfacing despite her excitement. "You always know how to make me blush, Lizzie. But okay, let's celebrate."

As Sophie busied herself in the kitchen, the doorbell rang, its chime breaking the quiet rhythm of the afternoon. She wiped her hands on a towel, feeling the familiar warmth of the home, she'd grown accustomed to in recent months. With a quick glance toward the door, she sighed, knowing her mother would be resting for the day. Sophie walked toward the door, her heart unexpectedly picking up speed, as she wondered who could be visiting.

When she opened the door, she was met with the bright, energetic face of her best friend, Lizzie. Her tall, curvy figure was dressed casually but stylishly, radiating the confidence Sophie had always admired.

"Surprise!" Lizzie exclaimed, her eyes sparkling with mischief and excitement. "I have something for you!"

"What is it?" Sophie asked, her curiosity piqued as Lizzie stepped inside, practically glowing with energy.

Lizzie's lips curled into a mischievous grin as she reached behind her, pulling out a beautifully wrapped package. The glossy paper was adorned with silver ribbons that shimmered in the light, making it impossible for Sophie to ignore.

"Ta-da!" Lizzie said dramatically, holding the package up as if she were presenting a rare treasure. "Open it!"

Sophie took the package, feeling the gentle weight of it in her hands. A rush of anticipation swept over her, making her heart race a little. She carefully peeled away the wrapping paper, revealing a stunning black satin fitted dress. The fabric gleamed under the light, designed to hug her curves, creating a silhouette that would be both elegant and alluring. The dress had a timeless quality to it, a combination of grace and sensuality that Sophie could barely believe was now in her hands.

"Oh wow, Lizzie!" Sophie breathed, taking in the breathtaking design. She let out a soft gasp, momentarily taken aback by how beautiful it was. "It's... beautiful."

Lizzie's eyes twinkled with pride; her voice filled with genuine excitement. "I bought it for you as a congratulations for all your hard work," she insisted, her voice softer now, more sincere. "You deserve to treat yourself, especially now that you got that internship! This is your moment to shine."

Sophie's fingers lingered on the fabric of the dress, feeling its smoothness against her skin. A mix of gratitude and reluctance filled her chest. "I don't know if I can accept this…" Sophie murmured, her voice tinged with doubt.

Lizzie's playful tone returned in an instant. "Too bad! You're taking it," she interrupted with a wink, her expression firm but friendly. "And guess what? We're going out to celebrate this Saturday night! You're going to wear this dress, and we are going to have the best time. No excuses."

Sophie felt a strange thrill of excitement at the thought of it, but alongside it was a sharp pang of anxiety. She had spent so much of the past few years buried in work, only to emerge now, unsure of how to embrace something so… carefree. "I'm not sure if I'm ready for that…" Sophie confessed, her voice wavering slightly.

Lizzie took a step closer, placing her hands on Sophie's shoulders in a grounding gesture. Her smile softened as she met Sophie's eyes, her blue eyes full of warmth and understanding. "Trust me, you are," Lizzie urged, her voice gentle but confident. "You've been working your butt off for this internship. You deserve a night out. Just let loose for once. It'll be fun, I promise."

Sophie couldn't help but smile at the infectious enthusiasm radiating from Lizzie. It was impossible not to feel the energy and excitement bubble up inside her. "Okay, okay!" she relented, laughing softly, feeling her nerves start to melt away. "I'll wear the dress. But only if you promise we'll have a great time."

Lizzie clapped her hands together in delight, her joy contagious. "Deal! It's going to be amazing! Just you wait, Sophie, it's going to be a night to remember."

With the dress in hand and a plan in place, Sophie felt a rush of excitement, something she hadn't felt in a long time. The weight of her responsibilities and self-imposed limitations seemed to lift just a little, as the promise of a fun evening ahead became a welcome possibility. It was a small but meaningful step toward embracing life again, toward taking a moment for herself amidst the hustle and grind.

She found herself grinning, a genuine smile spreading across her face. The thought of the celebration with Lizzie, of stepping out and enjoying herself, filled her with anticipation. Maybe, just maybe, this was the break she had been waiting for, a chance to feel something beyond the stress and pressure that had dominated her life for so long.

As Lizzie left with a final enthusiastic hug, Sophie lingered by the door for a moment, holding the dress in her hands. A soft sigh escaped her lips, a mix of excitement and nervousness, but she knew deep down that she needed this. She needed to break free from the walls she'd built around herself. The night ahead felt like a doorway—one she was finally ready to step through.

The week passed in a blur for Sophie, each day feeling like a whirlwind of endless tasks and responsibilities. Between her shifts at the café and her job at the gym's front desk, there seemed to be little time for anything else. Every evening, she poured herself into the chaotic rhythm of the café, her smile a bright beacon in the dimly lit room as she moved through the bustling atmosphere. The clink of dishes, the murmur of conversations, and the steady hum of the espresso machine became her soundtrack.

She'd learned to push through the exhaustion, greeting each customer with the same practiced cheer, though inside, she was often running on fumes.

Saturdays, however, brought a different kind of energy. The gym was always busy, the air charged with the sound of weights clanking, machines humming, and upbeat music blasting through the speakers. Sophie always found herself energised by the sound of it all, even if the hours spent behind the front desk were long and sometimes lonely.

As she checked in members, handing out passes and offering friendly smiles, she couldn't help but notice the attention she attracted. Several of the regulars would linger at the desk a moment too long, sending her flirtatious remarks and flashing smiles that made her cheeks flush with embarrassment. Though she was used to being in the background, quietly doing her job, these moments always made her uneasy. Sophie was never one to draw attention to herself, and the extra focus, no matter how innocent, was enough to send her stomach into nervous twists.

Despite her discomfort, Sophie maintained her professional demeanour. She replied with polite smiles, all the while feeling the heat rise in her face and her heart race with a mix of embarrassment and discomfort. It wasn't that she didn't appreciate the compliments—she just wasn't used to being seen in that way.

By the time her shift ended around 2pm, Sophie was physically drained but emotionally relieved. She was grateful to have made it through another busy day without incident. As she walked home, her thoughts turned to the evening ahead. She was going out with Lizzie to celebrate her internship, a long-awaited occasion to mark her hard work and recent accomplishment. Lizzie had insisted on a night of celebration, and though Sophie had initially hesitated, she had agreed. The thought of a night out was both exciting and nerve-wracking. Sophie had spent the past few years so focused on her work that the idea of stepping out into the spotlight—of being seen—made her stomach churn.

She thought about the dress Lizzie had given her, how it shimmered under the light and promised an elegance that Sophie had never felt before. The thought of wearing something so beautiful made her heart flutter, but it was accompanied by the inevitable fear of being in a crowd, the eyes of strangers on her. She couldn't shake the feeling of vulnerability that always accompanied attention and tonight would be no different. Sophie tried to push the anxiety away, telling herself it would be a fun night, a chance to let loose and celebrate with her best friend.

As she reached her apartment building, Sophie sighed deeply, trying to quiet the nerves that had been building all day. She needed to let go of her fear and embrace the night ahead, but it wasn't easy. The invitation to step outside her comfort zone was both thrilling and daunting. She just hoped that, by the time the evening was over, she wouldn't be regretting her decision.

As the evening approached, Sophie felt her apprehension simmer beneath the surface. She slipped into the black satin dress Lizzie had gifted her, she couldn't help but feel a mixture of nervousness and excitement. The dress fit like it was made for her, highlighting her figure in a way she wasn't used to. She stared at her reflection in the mirror, her hands smoothing over the soft fabric as a small smile tugged at her lips.

"You look stunning, sweetheart," her mother said from the doorway, her voice filled with quiet pride.

Sophie turned to face her mother, a blush creeping up her cheeks. "Thanks, Mum. I'm a little nervous, though. It's been a while since I've dressed up like this."

Marie stepped closer, resting a comforting hand on Sophie's arm. "You have nothing to be nervous about. You've earned this celebration. Go out there and have fun—you deserve it."

When Lizzie arrived, Sophie couldn't help but laugh at her friend's enthusiastic reaction. "Oh my god, Soph! You look like a total knockout!" Lizzie exclaimed, practically bouncing with excitement.

"Thanks," Sophie said shyly, biting her lip. "I just hope I can handle all the attention."

"No shyness allowed tonight! We're celebrating, and you're going to have the best time," Lizzie declared, linking her arm with Sophie's and dragging her out the door.

Chapter Four

Damian sat at the sleek bar of the luxurious hotel, the ambient glow of soft lighting reflecting off polished marble surfaces, creating an aura of refinement around him. He had just wrapped up a meeting with a potential client—an evening event that had dragged on longer than he'd anticipated. The client had insisted on booking him a suite for the night, a gesture Damian appreciated but found unnecessary. He wasn't interested in mixing business with pleasure; he had learned the hard way that such entanglements only muddied the waters.

He swirled the amber liquid in his glass, watching the way it caught the light as he contemplated the evening ahead. A few drinks would help him unwind before retiring to his suite for an early night. The thought of solitude was oddly comforting after the intensity of the meeting. He took a slow sip, feeling the warmth of the whiskey slide down his throat, and glanced around the bar, observing the scene unfolding around him.

Women in stylish dresses glided through the space, their laughter ringing out, accompanied by the soft clink of glasses and the low hum of conversation. It was a familiar sight—beautiful women seeking out rich men, hoping to catch the eye of someone who could elevate their status. They came with practiced smiles, eye-catching outfits, and an unspoken expectation that wealth and charm would secure their favour.

Despite their efforts, Damian felt an overwhelming sense of boredom wash over him. The predictable game of attraction and status played out before him like a rehearsed script he had no interest in reading. He'd been in this world long enough to see through the façades, to know the motives behind the flirtatious glances and carefully crafted conversations. He wasn't looking for a fleeting connection, not tonight, and certainly not one tied to wealth or appearance. He craved something deeper, something more meaningful than the shallow exchanges he'd grown tired of.

The few women who approached him with flirtatious smiles and lingering glances were met with polite indifference. Their attempts to engage were polite but distant. He had long since mastered the art of disinterest. He wasn't rude, but he knew the dance all too well. He'd seen it a thousand times, and the charm they offered couldn't disguise the fact that it was all part of a well-worn routine.

Damian leaned back in his chair, feeling the weight of his own expectations settle in. Once, the thrill of attention from attractive women had excited him. But now, the attention seemed hollow, a distraction from his true ambitions. He wasn't interested in empty encounters; he sought a connection that transcended the superficiality of wealth and status. He had his business, his reputation, and his goals—those were the things that truly drove him.

He finished his drink and signalled the bartender for another, casting a glance around the plush surroundings. The hotel exuded luxury, a perfect reflection of his professional life, but tonight, it felt empty. There was no spark, no sense of excitement. The world of high society, despite its glittering exterior, felt shallow, as if it were all just a game, one that no longer held any appeal for him.

Damian took a deep breath, letting the warmth of the whiskey settle in his chest. He mentally prepared for the quiet evening ahead—no late-night escapades, no exciting encounters—just him, his thoughts, and the comfort of a plush hotel suite. He was used to the solitude, the quiet moments of reflection that allowed him to recalibrate and prepare for whatever came next in the pursuit of success.

Just as he was about to rise and make his way up to his suite, a movement across the bar caught his attention. His gaze shifted instinctively, and for the first time that evening, his mind was no longer consumed by thoughts of business and self-reflection. A striking sight across the room demanded his focus.

A tall blonde woman entered the bar with an air of confidence that immediately drew the attention of those around her. Her laughter rang out like music, a bright note amidst the otherwise low hum of conversation. She was undeniably beautiful, but it was the petite brunette beside her that truly caught Damian's eye.

The brunette wore a slinky black dress that clung to her exquisite figure with a subtle elegance. The fabric wrapped around her curves without being overt, highlighting her shape in a way that felt effortless and refined. Her legs seemed to go on forever, and the way she moved—fluid, graceful—exuded a magnetic presence. Her soft waves of gorgeous brown hair framed her delicate features, creating a striking contrast with her bold, dark eyes that shimmered with something deeper. She wasn't trying to impress anyone; her very presence seemed to command attention without effort.

Damian found himself studying her, intrigued not just by her appearance but by the aura she carried. She had an elegance about her, a quiet confidence that made her stand out from the others. While the rest of the room buzzed with superficiality, she seemed untouched by it, floating through the space as if she existed in a world of her own making. The way she moved, the way she held herself—it was all so… compelling.

For the first time in a long while, Damian felt his pulse quicken, not from the allure of wealth or status but from something far more interesting. This woman was different. And for reasons he couldn't quite place, he found himself eager to learn more.

As they walked further into the bar, the atmosphere shifted subtly. Damian could feel the collective gaze of the men around him drawn to the two women. Yet, while many found themselves captivated by the blonde's boldness and ease, it was the brunette who held his attention. There was something about her—a mix of elegance and mystery— that stirred something in him. She didn't seek attention, yet she commanded it effortlessly, drawing every eye without the need to perform.

Damian leaned slightly against the bar, his gaze fixed on the brunette as she laughed at something the blonde had said, her eyes sparkling with delight. It was a moment of pure enchantment, the kind of laugh that seemed to light up the room, and he found himself wondering who she was, what her story was. In a sea of predictable encounters and surface-level interactions, she felt different. She felt real. Her smile was warm but enigmatic, as though she carried with her secrets, she wasn't ready to share. And for the first time in a long time, Damian was genuinely intrigued. She wasn't just a pretty face—there was depth in her presence.

Across the bar, Sophie felt an uncomfortable rush of excitement and anxiety as she entered the hotel. The atmosphere was luxurious, exuding a level of sophistication that made her feel both out of place and exhilarated. The soft lighting, the polished surfaces, and the elegant hum of conversation made it feel as though they had stepped into another world, one far beyond her everyday life.

Her black satin dress, a gift from Lizzie, hugged her figure in a way that should have made her feel confident, yet it only seemed to highlight her insecurities. The fabric clung to her curves, accentuating her silhouette, and with each step, she felt more exposed. The dress was beautiful, but it made her feel like she was on display. She tried to focus on the excitement of the evening, but as men's eyes flicked toward her, she could sense their assessment in the way their gazes lingered.

Lizzie, ever the picture of confidence, radiated a different energy entirely. Her tall, striking frame and flowing blonde hair drew admiring glances as she breezed into the bar. She was the type of woman who commanded attention without a second thought, and tonight, she was determined to make Sophie feel special. "Tonight is all about celebrating you!" she exclaimed, clinking her glass with Sophie's, her voice infectious.

Sophie offered a smile, though it didn't quite reach her eyes. Lizzie's enthusiasm was hard to resist, but she couldn't shake the feeling that the night was moving too fast, that the bright lights and glittering atmosphere were closing in on her. As they found a spot at the bar, Sophie shifted uncomfortably in her seat, crossing her legs and lowering her head, hoping the subtle movement would help her feel less exposed.

"Can we just enjoy our drinks without all… this?" she murmured, her voice quiet but laced with discomfort. The feeling of being observed was like a constant weight on her shoulders.

Lizzie, ever perceptive, leaned closer, her smile warm and reassuring. "Don't let them ruin this night. You look stunning, and you deserve to have fun," she said, her words soft but firm, as though she were trying to erase Sophie's doubts with a wave of her hand.

Sophie managed a small smile, grateful for Lizzie's support, but the unease still lingered. She wasn't used to being the centre of attention, and tonight, it felt like the world was watching her. As they toasted to new beginnings, Sophie wished she could shake off the feeling that she was simply playing a part in a world that didn't quite fit her.

The tension that had been building in Sophie was momentarily broken when two men approached the bar, their confident strides and easy charm immediately catching Lizzie's attention. The man who spoke first flashed a disarming smile, his gaze flickering between Lizzie and Sophie.

"Hey there," he said, his tone smooth and casual, as though they had known each other for years.

Lizzie greeted him with her usual enthusiasm, her bright eyes sparkling as she jumped into conversation without hesitation. But Sophie remained quiet, watching the interaction with a mixture of curiosity and caution. She wasn't in the mood for flirty banter, especially in her current state of vulnerability. Lizzie, however, seemed perfectly at ease, enjoying every word exchanged.

The man who had spoken to Lizzie leaned in slightly, his voice dropping as he whispered something that made her laugh heartily. Sophie couldn't help but offer a polite smile, though she felt a twinge of discomfort as his gaze flicked toward her intermittently. It wasn't overt, but there was a subtle shift in the air—a calculated attempt to draw her into the conversation. She wasn't interested, not tonight.

As if sensing her discomfort, Lizzie threw Sophie a quick glance, a playful glint in her eyes. Sophie tried to relax, but the way the man's eyes roamed made her feel like she was under a microscope, like every inch of her was being analysed and scrutinised. She couldn't fully mask her unease.

The atmosphere took a different turn when the man, perhaps sensing the moment to capitalise on his flirty rapport, became a little too familiar with Lizzie. His hand brushed against her arm, lingering just a little too long. Sophie frowned, her stomach tightening as she watched the interaction. Lizzie, however, didn't seem fazed by it at all. She laughed and nudged him playfully, not the slightest bit uncomfortable.

"I'll be right back, Soph!" Lizzie called over her shoulder, her voice filled with excitement as she grabbed the man's hand.

Sophie watched Lizzie and the man walk away, a mix of relief and concern washing over her. She was grateful for Lizzie's carefree spirit and determination to make the night memorable, but at the same time, she couldn't shake the feeling of being left behind. As much as she loved Lizzie, who seemed to thrive in any social setting, Sophie often found herself feeling out of place, and tonight was no exception. The weight of her isolation in the bustling bar made her acutely aware of how vulnerable she felt in the sea of unfamiliar faces.

The man who remained beside her—a ruggedly handsome fellow in his thirties with a well-tailored suit and a smirk that could be charming under different circumstances—seemed not to sense her discomfort. He started the conversation with polite small talk, commenting on the ambiance of the bar, the lighting, and the music. Sophie responded absently, offering more polite nods than actual engagement. She tried to focus on the conversation, but with each passing moment, she felt more distant from the man and from the environment. His attempts at flirting, though subtle at first, soon became more persistent, his questions veering toward more personal topics. His curiosity about her grew obvious, and Sophie found herself mentally retreating further, hoping for the interaction to fizzle out.

She shifted uncomfortably in her seat, her fingers lightly drumming the edge of her glass. "I should probably find my friend," Sophie said, her tone polite but firm, offering a hint of finality.

The man's eyes narrowed slightly, assessing her reaction before he let out a quiet sigh. Realising she was no longer interested; he offered a resigned smile. "Sure, no problem. Enjoy your night," he said, his words polite but with an edge of frustration that didn't escape Sophie's notice. He gave her one last lingering look before he turned and walked away, blending back into the crowd.

Sophie let out a soft sigh of relief, her shoulders unwinding slightly as she watched him retreat. But as the relief settled, she was left with an odd sense of loneliness. The bustle of the bar, the laughter and conversations all around, felt distant, as though she were isolated in a world of her own. She glanced around for Lizzie, hoping to find her in the sea of faces, but there was no sign of her friend. A twinge of concern gnawed at her—Lizzie had a way of drawing people in, and Sophie wasn't sure she liked the idea of her friend being alone with a stranger, especially in a setting like this. But then again, Lizzie could handle herself.

Still, Sophie couldn't shake the feeling of discomfort that clung to her like the dress she wore, which now seemed to mock her insecurities rather than flatter her. She had never liked being the centre of attention, and tonight, despite Lizzie's best efforts, it felt like the spotlight was shining far too brightly on her.

Across the bar, Damian leaned casually against the polished wooden counter, his drink momentarily forgotten. His gaze was focused on the petite woman in black, watching her interaction with the man who had approached her. He had seen it all—how the man's charm had failed to break through her defences, how Sophie had forced a smile but seemed uncomfortable, trapped in the small talk that she didn't want. He noted the way her posture had shifted from relaxed to tense, the small but telling signs of her discomfort.

Damian couldn't help but observe her. There was something about the way she carried herself, the soft elegance of her features and the grace in the way she moved. Her dark hair cascaded in waves around her face, framing her delicate features, and her dress—tight and black, yet somehow understated—clung to her figure in a way that was both elegant and alluring. He admired her beauty from a distance, but it was the vulnerability in her eyes that intrigued him most. There was a quiet wariness there, an unease that seemed to have settled into her bones.

He watched as the man leaned in a little too close, a flirtatious attempt that was met with an imperceptible shift in her expression—a subtle flinch, a slight stiffening of her body. The man, oblivious to her discomfort, continued with his advances, but her responses became more and more distant. It was clear to Damian that the man was out of his depth, his attempts growing more insistent as he failed to read the subtle signs that Sophie wasn't interested.

Damian's protective instinct flared. He didn't know why, but something about the way she seemed so out of place in this environment—so uncomfortable—moved him. She wasn't playing the game, wasn't engaging with the superficiality that everyone else seemed so eager to participate in. The way the man was pushing her boundaries irked him, and for the first time in a long while, he felt compelled to do something about it.

When the man finally backed off, with a resigned look in his eyes, Damian saw his chance. He wasn't sure why he cared so much, but there was something about Sophie that made him want to step in, to offer her an escape from the unwanted attention. He knew he had to be subtle; she didn't strike him as the type to welcome a direct approach from a stranger.

Taking a deep breath, Damian stood, his usual confident swagger muted as he made his way over to her side of the bar. He didn't want to come off as imposing or arrogant; he simply wanted to offer a sense of comfort in an uncomfortable moment. He approached her slowly, his movements casual yet deliberate, giving her time to notice his presence without feeling rushed.

"Do you mind if I sit?" Damian asked, nodding toward the empty stool beside her. His voice was casual, yet there was an undercurrent of genuine interest. He waited for her to process the offer, his posture open and relaxed, ready to back off if she seemed uncomfortable. But he hoped—he truly hoped—that she would see he wasn't like the others that he wasn't here to add to the barrage of unwanted attention she had already endured tonight. He just wanted to offer her a bit of peace in what had clearly been a far from ideal evening.

Chapter Five

Sophie took a moment to consider him, her gaze lingering on him as if assessing whether this man was different. He had a commanding presence, no doubt—tall, with sharp features that seemed to hold both strength and warmth in equal measure. His dark hair fell effortlessly into place, adding to the allure of his angular jaw and deep green eyes. She found herself caught off guard by how attractive he was, though there was something else about him, something more subtle but equally magnetic. He was beautiful in a way that felt different—something in the way he carried himself, the kindness in his eyes that softened the confidence radiating from him. Sophie wasn't sure she'd ever thought of a man as beautiful before, but the term felt oddly fitting as she studied him.

His respectful demeanour was a refreshing change from the advances she had just endured. The man before her wasn't pushing, wasn't demanding her attention. Instead, there was an easy-going quality to his approach, an invitation rather than an imposition. It was a small gesture, but one that allowed her to relax in his presence, a shift in the air that felt almost comforting.

"Please, do," Sophie replied, her voice steadier than she'd expected. She could feel a flutter in her chest, but it wasn't the same nervous tension she had felt before—this was different. There was a quiet excitement in her, a sense that this could be the start of a more enjoyable experience than she'd initially thought. She wanted to talk to him. She wanted a conversation that felt real, without any pressure.

Damian's face lit up with a smile when she granted him permission, his relief palpable. There was something about her that intrigued him—a grounded, genuine energy that he hadn't encountered in a long time. "Would you like a drink?" he asked, his voice smooth but unassuming, as though he was simply trying to make her feel at ease.

"Yes, please," Sophie replied, her voice warm and confident. "A glass of white wine would be lovely."

Damian nodded at the bartender, placing the order with a glance, then turned his attention back to her, genuinely curious. "And what's your name?" His question was casual, but there was an unmistakable spark of interest in his eyes.

"Soph," she answered, a smile tugging at the corners of her lips, though she still felt a little shy.

"Soph," Damian repeated, the way the name fell from his lips sounding almost affectionate. "I like it. It suits you." He paused for a moment, as the bartender brought her wine and placed it in front of her. Damian studied her for a brief moment—there was something about her that made the air between them feel lighter. He hadn't expected this kind of connection, but there it was, bubbling up, and it made him want to keep talking to her, to see where this conversation could go.

Sophie took a sip of her wine, savouring the crisp taste before meeting his eyes. "What about you?" she asked, her voice soft but sincere. "What's your name?"

"Damian," he said, smiling confidently. "And it's a pleasure to meet you, Soph."

"Thank you for the drink," she said, her expression softening with gratitude. "It was really kind of you."

Damian's chest warmed at her thanks, his smile growing. He was used to compliments, but there was something different about this exchange. Soph's kindness felt genuine, and he couldn't help but admire that. The tension that had hung in the air earlier seemed to melt away, replaced by a comfortable ease that made it feel as though they had been talking for far longer than just a few minutes.

"So," Damian leaned in a little, curiosity sparking in his eyes. "What brings you here tonight?" He couldn't help but wonder about the woman who had so easily captured his attention. His question wasn't just about her being at the bar—it was more about who she was, why she was here, and what made her tick.

Sophie smiled, her eyes lighting up as she took another sip of her wine. "I just landed a new job," she said, her excitement clear. "My friend insisted that I celebrate, but as you can see," she gestured to the lively crowd around them, "she enjoys celebrating a bit more than I do."

Her laughter filled the space between them, warm and unrestrained, and Damian felt a sudden pang of admiration. It was a sound that seemed to break through the noise of the bar, soft and natural, and it made him smile. Soph's smile was infectious, and in that moment, he couldn't help but feel drawn to her. She was genuine, unpretentious, and it made her all the more captivating.

Sophie tilted her head slightly, a playful glint in her eyes as she continued the conversation. "So, what about you? What's a guy like you doing in a place like this?" Her voice was light, teasing, but her gaze was thoughtful, as if she was genuinely trying to understand what had brought him to this crowded bar.

Damian chuckled, a twinkle in his eyes. "Actually, I was here for a business meeting," he said, his tone taking on a slightly conspiratorial edge. "A potential client wanted to discuss some plans, and they put me up in this hotel to sweeten the deal." He glanced around the bar, then back at Soph, his expression softening. "But after the meeting, I decided to unwind a bit. It seems like I've stumbled upon the best part of my evening." He let that linger for a moment, a compliment disguised as casual conversation, before adding, "Celebrating your new job definitely sounds like it's worth it."

Sophie's smile widened, pleased by his light-hearted approach. "Well, I'm not going to spill all the details just yet," she said with a teasing wink. "A little mystery keeps things interesting, right?"

Damian raised an eyebrow, a playful challenge in his gaze. "I can respect that. I'm all for a little mystery." His smile deepened, a quiet admiration in his voice. "So, how's the celebration treating you so far?"

Sophie sighed, her mood shifting slightly as she glanced around the bar. "To be honest, I didn't even want to come out," she admitted, her tone becoming more introspective. "I'm more of a homebody, you know? But Lizzie insisted."

Damian nodded sympathetically, sensing the shift in her energy. "I can understand that. Sometimes you just need your space. But hey, at least you're not alone now, right?"

Sophie chuckled softly. "True. But sometimes I wish I could've just stayed home and relaxed. This whole 'celebration' thing isn't really my style."

"Well, you're certainly making my night more enjoyable for me," Damian said with a smile, leaning in just a touch. "It's nice to talk to someone who's not just here for the glitz and glam."

Sophie raised her eyebrows, intrigued. "Really? You're not one for the 'glitz and glam'?" she teased lightly, genuinely curious.

Damian laughed softly, a genuine sound that was warm and rich. "No, I'm definitely not. Honestly, sometimes I think I've been meeting the wrong people. Just the other night, I went out with this woman and let me tell you… she could talk about nothing but her skincare routine for hours. It was… well, let's just say, not the most exciting conversation."

Sophie laughed at the absurdity of it, imagining the scene. "I can imagine! That sounds like a nightmare." Her laughter rang out, carefree, and Damian found himself captivated once again by how easy it was to be around her.

"Exactly!" he agreed, shaking his head. "I need someone who actually enjoys real conversation. Someone genuine." His eyes met hers, and for a brief moment, the playful banter shifted to something more sincere. "And I think I've found that."

Sophie blushed slightly, the compliment making her feel unexpectedly warm. "You shouldn't say things like that," she replied with a shy laugh. "You'll embarrass me."

Damian smiled, leaning in a little closer. "It's the truth, Soph. You're not like anyone I've met in a long time." His voice softened, sincere in a way he hadn't expected.

Sophie smiled, a soft blush still lingering on her cheeks. "I'm just me. Maybe you should be a little pickier with the people you meet," she said, shrugging modestly.

"You might be right, Soph." Damian leaned back, studying her for a moment, intrigued by the layers he was slowly peeling away. There was something about her—something more than just her beauty—that made him want to know more. Something real. And that was more than he could say for most of the people he'd met in his life.

Lizzie breezed back to the bar, her excitement practically radiating off her as she bounced on her heels. "Soph! You won't believe it; I'm going to a club with the guy I met! You need to come with me!"

Sophie hesitated, her brows knitting together in a frown. "I don't know, Lizzie. You know those places scare me."

Damian, sitting nearby, observed their exchange with a quiet admiration. There was something so raw and real about Soph's reluctance, something he didn't often see. The women he usually met were more interested in impressing others than being true to themselves. But Soph—she was different. He found that refreshing.

Lizzie, sensing a hesitation, quickly glanced toward Damian and flashed him a bright, confident smile. "Oh, hello! I'm Lizzie," she said, her tone upbeat and flirtatious, her eyes twinkling. "Aren't you gorgeous?"

Damian raised an eyebrow, amused by her boldness. "Hello, Lizzie," he replied with a smile. "And thank you."

Sophie couldn't help but feel her cheeks heat up at her friend's forwardness, a blend of embarrassment and warmth creeping over her. She was always the quieter one in their friendship, the one who preferred the calm of a quiet evening to the hustle and bustle of clubs and crowds.

Damian, sensing Soph's discomfort, turned his attention back to her, offering a reassuring smile. "I'll make sure Soph gets home safe," he said, his voice calm and sincere. He could tell she wasn't thrilled about the idea of being alone, and he wanted to make sure she didn't feel abandoned in that moment.

Lizzie, with a mischievous glint in her eye, shot him a playful look. "I just bet you will," she teased, her gaze flicking between the two of them. "Just keep an eye on her, alright?"

Sophie exhaled sharply, trying to suppress her unease. She wanted her friend to have fun, but she also felt a pang of loneliness in the idea of being left alone. "It's okay, Lizzie. Go have a good time! I'll just grab a cab home."

Lizzie's smile faltered for a moment, concern flickering across her face as she took a step closer. "Are you sure? I don't want you to be alone if you're not comfortable. You know you can always count on me."

Sophie gave her a soft, reassuring smile, even though her stomach churned with unease. "I'll be fine, really. You deserve to enjoy your night." She knew Lizzie wasn't going to let her off easy, but Sophie didn't want to be the reason her friend missed out on the fun she was clearly excited about.

Lizzie hesitated, giving Sophie a long, searching look. Finally, she leaned in and wrapped her arms around her friend in a quick, tight hug. "Alright, but promise me you'll text me when you get home? If you don't, I will worry about you."

Sophie squeezed her back, trying to push the nervousness from her voice. "I promise."

With a final wink at Damian, Lizzie turned and dashed off, eager to join the guy she had met. Sophie watched her go, a bittersweet feeling washing over her. She didn't want to be left behind, but part of her knew Lizzie deserved to enjoy herself.

Sophie turned back to Damian, her mind swirling with a mix of anticipation and anxiety about the rest of the evening. Lizzie's bold exit had left her feeling slightly exposed, but Damian's calm demeanour and genuine interest helped steady her nerves. She wasn't sure what to expect from the night, but for the first time in a while, she felt like maybe, just maybe, it might turn out okay.

Chapter Six

As Lizzie disappeared into the crowd, Damian turned back to Soph, his green eyes sparkling with amusement. "You're not leaving me already, are you?" he asked, his tone playful yet warm, a subtle tease lacing his words.

Sophie, still feeling the lingering heat of embarrassment from her friend's audacious departure, tucked a loose strand of hair behind her ear and smiled softly. "I was thinking about it," she teased, trying to regain her composure, but her voice was light with humour. "But I'm not sure how I'd survive the trek to the door in these heels."

Damian chuckled, a rich, low sound that sent a shiver down her spine. He leaned slightly closer, his presence becoming a comforting weight. "Well, in that case, I guess you'll have to stay. Wouldn't want to risk a sprained ankle." His smile was magnetic, and Sophie found herself smiling in return, her nerves slowly easing away. The idea of leaving seemed less appealing now.

Sophie bit her lip, feeling the warmth of his gaze. "You make a compelling argument," she said, her voice teasing, but beneath the words, there was a hint of sincerity. She was no longer thinking about heading out on her own.

Just as the conversation flowed more easily, a man stumbled up to the bar, clearly drunk, and brushed past Sophie with more than a little force. His hand lingered on her back, the touch deliberate, and Sophie stiffened immediately. She tried to mask her discomfort, shifting slightly away, but the unease was clear on her face as she subtly distanced herself from the unwelcome touch.

Damian's expression darkened instantly, his jaw tightening. His green eyes narrowed, watching the man with an intensity that sent a ripple of protectiveness through him. He leaned in closer, his voice low and firm, yet still calm. "How about we move to one of the booths?" he suggested, his tone gentle but commanding. "It'll be quieter, and we won't have to deal with… that."

Sophie met his gaze, a sense of relief washing over her at his understanding and quick reaction. She felt a warmth spread through her at the thought that he'd noticed her discomfort and was so willing to do something about it. "Yeah," she said softly, her voice a little more confident. "That sounds good."

Damian stood and placed a protective hand on the small of her back, guiding her toward a private booth away from the crowded bar. His touch was reassuring, his presence grounding, and Sophie felt herself relax just a little more with each step. As they moved through the bar, she couldn't help but notice how effortlessly he seemed to take control of the situation without being overbearing. It was a comfort to have someone who respected her space but also made it clear he was there to ensure she felt safe.

Sophie settled into the booth, the tension from the bar beginning to fade as the quiet of their secluded corner enveloped them. She glanced up at Damian, her expression softening in the dim light. "Thank you," she said, her voice sincere, a touch of warmth behind her words. "That guy was… a bit much."

Damian waved it off with a casual smile, but his green eyes gleamed with a protective glint that didn't go unnoticed. "You shouldn't have to deal with that," he said, his voice firm yet easy. "Glad I could help."

As they sat down, he signalled the server and ordered her another glass of white wine. When it arrived, Sophie offered a grateful smile, the warmth of the drink already beginning to swirl in her chest, taking the edge off her nerves. "Thanks again," she said, her words tinged with appreciation. Though, deep down, she realised that the first drink had already started working its magic, the warmth from the wine spreading slowly through her body, making her feel light.

Damian noticed her slowing pace, his lips curling into an amused smile. "You're not used to drinking, are you?" he asked, his voice playful but not mocking.

Sophie shook her head, a soft laugh escaping her lips as she tucked a loose strand of hair behind her ear. "No, not really. I probably shouldn't even have this one, but… tonight's an exception." She took a small sip, her eyes meeting his for a brief moment. "I guess I'm celebrating, after all."

Damian laughed, a deep, rich sound that made her heart flutter ever so slightly. "Well, I'm glad to be part of your celebration, even if it's just for one night." His green eyes sparkled with amusement, and the warmth between them seemed to deepen as they settled more comfortably into the booth.

For the next hour, their conversation flowed effortlessly, the chatter punctuated with bursts of laughter. Damian shared stories of his travels—strange business meetings in far-off cities, hilarious mishaps with international colleagues, and an embarrassing encounter involving a goat in some remote town that Sophie found both amusing and endearing. However, he cleverly avoided giving any specifics about his business, making Sophie even more curious about his life.

Sophie, in turn, found herself loosening up, revealing little details about her own life— her passion for architecture, the part-time jobs she juggled, and her dreams of one day designing spaces that would inspire others. She laughed at his witty remarks, feeling lighter than she had in a long time. The wine seemed to open a door in her, loosening the tight hold of her usual reserve, and her earlier hesitations about the night slowly slipped away.

"I can't believe I almost didn't come out tonight," Sophie admitted, her smile soft and a little shy. "I'd be missing out on all of this."

Damian's grin widened, his expression genuine. He leaned forward slightly, his tone playful yet sincere. "It's a good thing you did. I haven't laughed this much in a while." His gaze softened as if he were seeing her in a new light. "You're something else, Soph. Really."

Sophie's cheeks flushed at the compliment, but instead of shying away, she found herself laughing again, the sound light and carefree. "I'm just me," she said with a modest shrug, though her heart picked up a beat. The connection between them, once tentative, had grown into something easy and undeniable. It was a rare thing, a conversation that felt both comfortable and exciting at the same time.

The noise from the bar seemed to fade into the background as the conversation continued to ebb and flow between them. As their words slowed, a comfortable silence hung in the air, the soft clinking of glasses and distant laughter blending into a low hum. Damian studied her face intently, his gaze warm, and there was something in the way he looked at her that made her feel both seen and cherished.

After a moment, he leaned in just slightly, his voice dropping to a low, almost hesitant tone, as though testing the waters. "Do you mind if I kiss you, Soph?"

Sophie blinked, caught off guard by the question. Her heart raced as she met his gaze, feeling the warmth from the wine and the closeness between them. For a brief moment, she hesitated, her breath catching as she processed the unexpected question.

She didn't quite know how to respond at first. She wasn't used to being asked so directly, or so respectfully. Her mind swirled with emotions, and she could feel her cheeks flush. Her breath caught in her chest as she looked up at Damian, her pulse quickening. "I—" she started, her voice shaky but honest, the vulnerability of the moment creeping in. "I haven't really done this before."

Damian's expression softened immediately, a mix of understanding and respect washing over his features. "You don't have to say yes," he said, his voice calm and reassuring, the sincerity in his tone making her feel at ease. "I just… couldn't leave without asking."

A rush of something unfamiliar, something she hadn't anticipated, swept through Sophie—trust. It was so sudden, so real, that it startled her. She felt herself nodding slowly, her lips parting into a small, tentative smile. "Okay," she whispered, the words leaving her with a surprising sense of certainty.

Damian didn't move immediately. He seemed to pause, ensuring she was ready, and when he leaned in, it was with a tenderness that spoke volumes. The kiss was soft and unhurried, a quiet promise of something more, a slow unfolding. His lips were gentle against hers, as if he was giving her all the time in the world to decide, to feel it out. It was brief but full of unexpected tenderness, a sweetness that made her heart flutter in a way she hadn't expected. When he pulled back, it wasn't far, his eyes searching hers carefully, looking for any sign of discomfort.

"Thank you," he murmured, his voice barely above a whisper, as though the kiss had been more of a privilege than a mere action.

Sophie's heart raced in her chest as she gazed into Damian's eyes. The kiss had been gentle, respectful—completely different from what she had imagined it would be. It was far more tender than she'd expected, and yet, it had left her wanting more. The feeling of his lips on hers lingered, the sweetness of it unexpectedly stirring something deep inside her, a longing she wasn't used to.

A soft blush crept across her cheeks, her gaze dropping for a moment as she whispered, her voice small but teasing, "No… thank you." Her lips curved up into a playful smile, a glimmer of warmth dancing in her tone. "You could do it again if you wanted to."

Damian's eyes sparkled with surprise and delight. His smile spread slowly, appreciating the change in her. He leaned in closer, his breath soft against her skin, and she felt a shiver run down her spine as his lips hovered near her ear.

"Well, since you asked so nicely," he murmured, his voice low and teasing, the hint of a smile in his words.

This time, when their lips met, it felt more certain, more confident. Sophie felt herself relax into it, her body responding naturally to the tenderness in his touch, to the way he was giving her space, yet pulling her in at the same time. The world around them seemed to fade away, the noise of the bar, the clinking of glasses, the murmurs of other people—everything else melted into the background. All that remained was the warm, steady connection between them, like a silent understanding shared only between two people who'd found something real.

When Damian pulled away this time, his forehead rested gently against hers, and for a moment, they just stayed there, their breaths mingling, their eyes closed in the warmth of the moment. He smiled, a slow, satisfied grin that made Sophie's heart race. "You're full of surprises, Soph."

Sophie could hardly believe the words as they left his lips. Her chest was still pounding, and the flush on her cheeks deepened. She wasn't used to this—the boldness, the teasing—but something about Damian made her feel different. Daring, even. She blushed, feeling the heat in her cheeks, but instead of retreating into herself, she met his gaze, her smile now softer, more curious.

"Do you like surprises, Damian?" she asked, her voice a mix of shyness and newfound confidence, a subtle shift that felt almost empowering.

Damian raised an eyebrow, clearly intrigued by the change in her demeanour. His green eyes glinted with interest, and the corner of his mouth curled into a playful smirk. He leaned in just a little closer, his voice dropping lower, his tone rich with amusement and admiration.

"I think I'm starting to," he replied, his voice warm and teasing. "Especially if they're anything like you."

Sophie's blush deepened, but she didn't shy away. Instead, she held his gaze, feeling a surge of something—exhilaration, maybe—run through her. She wasn't just the quiet, reserved one anymore; tonight, in this moment, she was something else, something unexpected. Something bold. She found herself revelling in it, in the way Damian made her feel alive in a way she hadn't anticipated.

This time, Sophie didn't wait for him to ask. The pull of the moment, the warmth between them, was too strong to ignore. Before she could second-guess herself, she leaned in and kissed him, her lips brushing his with a soft, hesitant touch. It was gentle at first, tentative, but there was something so real about it, something that made her heart race.

Damian, caught off guard but pleasantly so, responded slowly, savouring the unexpected boldness. His hand came to rest lightly on her waist, pulling her a little closer, and the kiss deepened, growing more confident as their connection deepened with each passing second. The world around them—everything—faded. All that existed was the space between them, their breaths, their hearts, and the soft pressure of their lips meeting.

When Sophie finally pulled away, her heart was pounding, her mind still reeling from the intensity of the kiss. She looked up at Damian, waiting for his reaction, her cheeks flushed and her breath a little unsteady. She hadn't planned it, hadn't even imagined herself being so bold, but somehow, in that moment, it felt right. She hadn't overthought it for once. She just let herself feel it, let herself be.

Damian smiled, his eyes filled with admiration and something else—something deeper. "Well," he said, his voice low, filled with both amusement and a touch of awe, "I wasn't expecting that… but I'm not complaining."

Sophie smiled, her heart still racing as she met his gaze. For the first time in a long time, she wasn't second-guessing herself. She wasn't just the quiet, thoughtful woman she always thought she was. Tonight, with Damian, she was more. She was the woman who could surprise herself, who could take a leap and land on her feet.

And for once, it felt like the world was just waiting to catch her.

Damian's gaze lingered on Sophie; his green eyes soft with warmth but edged with intent. He leaned in just slightly, his voice dropping to a quiet murmur. "What do you say we take this upstairs, Soph?" There was a pause, his words lingering between them like an unspoken question.

Sophie's heart raced at the suggestion. She had never been the spontaneous type, always cautious, always thinking things through—but something about tonight, about Damian, made her want to let go, just this once. Her cheeks flushed a deep pink as she nervously tucked a strand of hair behind her ear.

"Why not?" she whispered, a small smile playing on her lips, her voice soft but steady. The boldness of her own answer surprised her. She felt the flutter of nerves in her chest but also a strange sense of excitement, a thrill she had never allowed herself to experience before.

Damian grinned, pleased, and stood up from the booth, offering her his hand. Sophie hesitated for just a moment before slipping her hand into his. As they walked toward the elevator, her mind raced, but she couldn't stop the smile from spreading across her face. Tonight, for the first time, she wasn't going to overthink it. She was just going to live in the moment.

As soon as the elevator doors slid shut behind them, the air between Sophie and Damian shifted. The soft hum of the elevator was the only sound as Damian turned to her, his green eyes darkening with desire. Before she could think, his hand gently cupped her face, and their lips collided in a rush of passion.

Sophie responded instinctively, her hands finding their way to his chest, feeling the heat of his body through his shirt. The kiss was deep and urgent, filled with the intensity of everything unspoken between them. She pressed closer, her heart pounding in rhythm with the quick, electric energy sparking between them.

The confined space of the elevator only heightened the intensity, the world outside disappearing entirely. For that moment, it was just the two of them, lost in the heat of the kiss. Damian's hand moved to her waist, pulling her even closer, and Sophie melted into him, her mind spinning, her usual hesitations forgotten.

The elevator continued its slow ascent, but neither of them noticed, completely absorbed in each other.

When the elevator doors finally slid open with a soft chime, Damian and Sophie reluctantly pulled apart, breathless and slightly dazed. The tantalising taste of each other lingered on their lips as they stepped into the dimly lit corridor.

Damian, his heart racing, led the way down the plush carpet, glancing back at Sophie. Her cheeks were flushed, her eyes sparkling with a mix of excitement and nervousness. He couldn't help but smile; the boldness she'd shown moments before had him intrigued.

As they approached his suite, he fished out the keycard from his pocket, feeling the weight of the moment. He unlocked the door and gestured for her to enter first. The door swung open, revealing a luxurious space bathed in warm light, with elegant furnishings and a breathtaking view of the city skyline.

"Welcome to my humble abode," Damian said with a playful grin, stepping aside to let her in. Sophie glanced around, momentarily distracted by the opulence before turning her gaze back to him, her heart pounding in anticipation of what was to come.

Damian closed the door behind them, the click echoing softly in the quiet room. The atmosphere crackled with unspoken tension as they stood there, the night unfolding in ways neither of them had anticipated.

Before they knew it, the space between them vanished, and they were wrapped in each other arms once more. Damian's hands found their way the Soph's waist, drawing her closer, while her fingers curled around his neck, pulling him down to her as if they were magnetically drawn to one other.

The world outside faded into a distant memory; all that mattered was the warmth of their bodies and the intoxicating chemistry crackling in the air. Damian's lips brushed against hers gently at first, a sweet exploration the deepened as Sophie responded with an eager urgency, her heart racing with each kiss.

Their breaths mingled, and the kiss became a fervent dance, filled with the promise of everything that lay ahead. Sophie could feel the world around them disappear, leaving only the two of them in the moment of blissful intimacy. Time seemed to stand still as they melted into each other, a beautiful harmony that felt both thrilling and safe.

Chapter Seven

The next morning, as the hot water cascaded over Damian's muscular frame, he leaned his hands against the shower wall, head bowed, lost in thought. The steam enveloped him, but his mind was somewhere else, back in the soft, tangled sheets with Soph.

Last night had been unexpected. He'd known passion before, but what he felt with her was different, raw, unguarded. There was something about the way she surrendered to the moment yet held back pieces of herself, something that made him want to know more, to unravel the mystery she carried. He replayed the way her lips had tasted, the sound of her soft laughter, the way her body moved with his, fluid and natural.

Damian couldn't shake it. He'd thought it would be a fleeting encounter, one that he would forget as quickly as it happened. But standing in the shower, the memory of her lingered. He wasn't used to women like Soph, there was no pretence, no hidden agenda, just honesty and vulnerability wrapped in quiet strength.

As the water continued to run over him, Damian exhaled deeply, realising she had gotten under his skin. He was used to leaving, to detaching, but something about last night made it harder to simply let go.

Damian stepped out of the shower, towelling off as he caught his reflection in the mirror. His green eyes stared back at him, still clouded with the lingering thoughts of the night before. He shook his head, as if trying to clear it, but the memories of Soph, her softness, her unguarded innocence, kept flooding back.

He felt a flicker of something he hadn't in years: *vulnerability.*

It wasn't supposed to be this way. He'd spent years perfecting the art of detachment, of keeping his emotions at bay, especially when it came to women. They were fun distractions, fleeting encounters, but never anything that could shake him. Until now. Until Soph.

Damian's chest tightened as he realised the truth that unsettled him: an innocent like Soph, with her quiet grace and disarming purity, had brought him to his knees. *How?* He'd been with dozens of women, all confident, all knowing exactly what they wanted, but none of them had ever managed to affect him like this. None had left him thinking about them the next morning.

But Soph… Soph had done that. Without even trying. Her vulnerability, her laughter, her guarded heart, everything about her was real, untouched by the pretence he was so used to. And somehow, that innocence had a power over him he couldn't explain.

Damian wrapped the towel around his waist and began to pace the length of the room, his movements restless, his thoughts anything but steady. He was unsettled—more than he cared to admit. A woman like her, a woman who seemed almost unaware of her own power, had managed to slip past every defence he'd ever perfected. He had built his life on control, on always being the one who dictated the pace, the rules, the outcome. Yet Soph had dismantled all of that without even trying.

She'd brought him to his knees.

And the most unnerving part was that she didn't even realise it.

His mind betrayed him, replaying fragments of the night—the way she had undressed him with tentative confidence, the way she had looked at him as though he were something precious rather than powerful. He remembered thinking, with a flash of disbelief, that he might lose control completely right there, something that had never happened to him before.

When she had murmured, almost apologetically, "I haven't done this before," he'd dismissed it without thought. He'd heard those words countless times—said to soften an edge, to play coy, to create intrigue. But as the night unfolded, it became impossible to ignore the truth. There was no performance, no pretence. Soph wasn't acting.

She was innocent—in the most genuine, unguarded sense of the word.

That realisation had struck him harder than anything else.

After their first passionate encounter, Damian lay beside her, staring up at the ceiling, his thoughts tangled and unfamiliar. He turned onto his side, propping himself up on one elbow, and studied her face in the low light. She looked relaxed now, her lashes resting softly against her cheeks, but there was still a hint of vulnerability there that made his chest tighten.

"Why didn't you tell me?" he asked quietly, surprised by the softness in his own voice. "That you were a virgin?"

Soph turned to face him, colour blooming across her cheeks as she met his gaze. Her eyes were wide, honest. "I didn't think it mattered," she whispered. "I didn't want you to treat me differently."

She shifted beneath the sheets, gathering her courage before continuing. "I'm twenty-five, Damian. I'm an adult." Her voice was steady, though uncertainty flickered beneath it. "I didn't think it should define me." She hesitated, biting her lip. "I hope you didn't mind."

The question landed deeper than he expected.

"Mind?" Damian echoed, caught off guard. He searched her face, seeing not fragility, but quiet resolve. "No, Soph. I didn't mind." He paused, choosing his words carefully. "I just… wasn't expecting it."

He leaned back against the headboard, dragging a hand through his hair as he tried to make sense of the knot forming in his chest. This wasn't how he was supposed to feel. He glanced at her again, at the way her eyes searched his, waiting—not demanding, not assuming.

"I didn't expect a lot of things tonight," he admitted, his green eyes holding hers, a faint, genuine smile touching his lips. "But I'm glad. More than I thought I would be."

The sincerity in his own voice startled him. This wasn't casual. This wasn't forgettable. And for the first time in a very long while, that didn't frighten him.

Soph pushed herself up slowly, her long dark hair falling over her shoulders as she leaned in and pressed a soft kiss to his lips. It was tender, unhurried, filled with everything they weren't quite saying. Her hands rested lightly on his chest, grounding him. Damian responded instinctively, cupping her face, pulling her closer as though the space between them suddenly felt unbearable.

When they came together again, it was different. Slower. More deliberate. Soph surprised him—her confidence growing, her movements assured. She led this time, and Damian let her, captivated by the way she bloomed under her own courage. He had never felt so undone, so willing to surrender control.

As the hours slipped quietly by and the night deepened around them, they found each other once more, tangled together in the hush of early morning. Damian held her close, wide awake, realising with a strange mix of awe and certainty that something fundamental had shifted.

He didn't know what this was yet.

But he knew one thing with absolute clarity.

This woman was changing him—and he wasn't sure he wanted to stop it.

As the first rays of sunlight filtered through the curtains, Damian stirred, slowly waking. He turned to find Soph still asleep beside him, her chest rising and falling in a peaceful rhythm. Her dark hair spilled over the pillow, and her face was soft in the early morning light. For a moment, he just watched her, the innocence of her slumber drawing him in. There was something about her vulnerability that touched him in a way he hadn't expected, something that made him want to protect her, even though he wasn't one to linger after nights like this. But with her, it felt different.

Damian stepped out of the bathroom, a towel wrapped loosely around his waist, droplets of water still clinging to his skin. He rubbed the back of his neck, feeling more awake now, and glanced toward the bed, only to stop in his tracks.

It was empty.

The sheets were rumpled, and the pillow where Soph had slept was still indented, but she was gone. His eyes darted around the room, half-expecting to find her sitting quietly somewhere, but there was no sign of her. Astonishment flickered through him. Soph, the woman who had been so shy and hesitant, had left without a word.

For a moment, Damian just stood there, processing the unexpected emptiness. He wasn't used to being the one left behind. Damian's heart sank as the realisation settled in.

Soph was gone.

A frown creased his brow, and an unsettling sense of unease washed over him. He had expected her to be there, to share the quiet moments of the morning after their passionate night. But now, all he felt was disappointment and loss.

He had thought they had shared something special, a connection that went beyond the physical. The way she had looked at him, the way they had laughed and talked, made him believe there was more to explore between them. He had been drawn to her innocence, her refreshing honesty, and the way she had surprised him at every turn.

He ran a hand through his damp hair, frustration bubbling within him. He wasn't finished with her yet; there was so much left unsaid, so many paths left untravelled. She had entered his life like a whirlwind, and now, just as quickly, she had vanished.

As he stood there, wrapped in the silence of the room, Damian couldn't shake the feeling that he needed to find her, to understand why she had slipped away so suddenly. The thought of her leaving without a goodbye left a bitter taste in his mouth.

Sophie stirred awake to the sound of water cascading in the bathroom, the rhythmic splashing pulling her from the depths of sleep. Blinking against the morning light filtering through the curtains, she felt a wave of disorientation wash over her.

As her surroundings came into focus, the realisation struck her like a jolt. She was in a luxurious hotel suite, and the memories of the night before rushed back with a flood of warmth and embarrassment. Oh dear, she thought, her heart racing. What was I doing?

This was not her. She wasn't some seductive temptress who could sweep a man off his feet with a kiss. She was just plain old Sophie—awkward, earnest Sophie, who had always been the responsible one, the one who took care of others.

Sitting up in bed, she hugged the plush comforter to her chest, feeling both exhilarated and terrified. The memories of their passion danced in her mind, a stark contrast to her usual reserved nature. Had she really crossed that line? For a moment, she felt a pang of guilt creeping in, mingling with the thrill of her newfound boldness.

She couldn't help but wonder how Damian would react when he found her gone. Would he think she had regretted their night together? The thought of disappointing him made her stomach twist. No, I just need to gather myself, she reassured herself, pushing back the sheets and feeling the plush carpet beneath her feet. Today was a new day, but it was hard to shake off the lingering doubts about who she really was and what she had done.

Sophie quickly scrambled to gather her clothes, her heart racing as she slipped on her dress with trembling hands. The fabric felt foreign against her skin, a reminder of the wild night that had just unfolded. She fumbled with the zipper, her thoughts a whirlwind of confusion and excitement, knowing she needed to leave before he emerged from the bathroom.

As the sound of the shower finally ceased, she felt a surge of urgency. I need to get out of here. Taking a deep breath, she quietly tiptoed towards the door, her heart pounding in her chest. With each step, the plush carpet muted her movements, allowing her to slip into the corridor without a sound.

Once in the hallway, she practically ran toward the elevator, her heels clicking softly against the floor. The echo felt loud in the otherwise quiet corridor, but she couldn't help it; she needed to get away, to collect her thoughts and process everything. As she reached the elevator, she pressed the button with urgency, glancing over her shoulder as if expecting Damian to come rushing after her.

The doors slid open, and she stepped inside, pressing the button for the ground floor with a shaky finger. As the elevator descended, Sophie leaned against the cool metal wall, her mind racing with thoughts of what had just happened. She could hardly believe it—she was already out of breath and barely grasping the reality of last night. The doors opened, and she hurried out, ready to escape into the bustling streets below, where she could lose herself in the crowd and find some clarity.

Sophie's mind raced as she stepped out of the hotel elevator and into the bustling lobby. I have to get home, she thought, her heart heavy with the realisation that she hadn't expected to stay out all night. Her mother would be waking up soon, and she always worried when Sophie wasn't home by a certain hour.

She glanced at her phone, the bright screen illuminating her face for a moment, revealing a string of missed texts from Lizzie asking where she was. Guilt washed over her; her mother depended on her, and the thought of her waiting up in worry gnawed at Sophie's conscience.

As she hurried toward the exit, she felt a rush of anxiety. What will I say? The memory of her mother's tired smile flooded her mind, reminding her of the promise she had made to always be there for her.

Outside, the cool morning air hit her like a wave, invigorating yet grounding. She hailed a cab, the driver looking at her curiously, but she couldn't care less about the judgment. All she could think about was getting home and ensuring her mother was okay.

As the cab wove through the streets of San Francisco, she replayed the events of the night in her mind. It had been exhilarating, but now it felt like a distant dream. I need to be responsible. She resolved to talk to her mother about it later, to assure her that everything was fine.

Finally, the cab pulled up in front of their apartment building. She paid the fare quickly and rushed inside, her heart pounding with anticipation and a hint of dread. What would her mother think? How could she explain everything without revealing too much? Steeling herself, she took a deep breath and made her way up the stairs, ready to face whatever awaited her inside.

Sophie breathed a sigh of relief as she stepped into the apartment, the familiar scent of home wrapping around her like a warm blanket. She quietly closed the door, careful not to make a sound. Thankfully, her mother was still asleep, the soft rise and fall of her breathing echoing from the lounge where she often dozed off in her favourite chair.

With a sense of urgency, Sophie tiptoed into the bedroom to change her clothes, the remnants of last night's adventure still swirling in her mind. After pulling on a fresh outfit, she hurried into the kitchen, her heart racing as she replayed the events of the night. She flipped on the coffee maker, the rhythmic gurgle offering a comforting backdrop to her thoughts. As she rummaged through the fridge for eggs and bread, her phone buzzed in her pocket, pulling her back to the present.

She pulled it out and quickly typed a message to Lizzie:

"I'm so sorry I didn't text you last night! I lost track of time. Can't wait to tell you everything."

After hitting send, she took a moment to glance out the window, the sunlight streaming in and casting a warm glow over the kitchen.

She set to work, cracking eggs into a pan and toasting bread, her movements quick and efficient. As she stirred the eggs, she couldn't shake the giddiness bubbling up inside her, mingled with a twinge of anxiety about how to explain the night to her mother.

A few moments later, the coffee was ready, and she poured herself a cup, savouring the rich aroma. The routine of making breakfast felt grounding, a brief respite before the whirlwind of the day began. She was determined to make everything right, not just for her mother, but for herself too.

Sophie gently nudged her mother awake, her heart lightening at the sight of her warm smile. "Good morning, Mum," she said softly.

Her mother blinked sleepily, a grin spreading across her face. "Oh, sweetheart, you're home! Did you have a good time?"

Sophie couldn't help but beam back, the joy of the previous night still fresh in her mind. "Yes, a wonderful time," she replied, the memories filling her with warmth.

Her mother's eyes sparkled with genuine happiness. "I'm so glad to hear that, Sophie! You deserve to enjoy life a bit more," she said, her voice filled with warmth and encouragement. "You work so hard taking care of me and juggling everything else. It's nice to see you having some fun."

Sophie felt a rush of gratitude and affection. "Thanks, Mum," she replied, a smile creeping onto her face.

Chapter Eight

Sophie's week passed in a blur of activity, each day blending seamlessly into the next. The afternoons were spent working at the café, where she moved swiftly between tables, pouring coffee and exchanging quick pleasantries with the regulars. By the time Saturday arrived, Sophie found herself at the gym, managing the front desk.

In the mornings, she took care of her mother, cooking meals and chatting with her over tea or coffee, enjoying the quiet comfort of their time together. Amid all the hustle, there was a steady hum of excitement building within Sophie. Monday was drawing closer; the day she would begin her new job. Every thought of it made her heart race with anticipation. Finally, something fresh, something just for her, something in which she could excel.

On Sunday morning, Sophie was sipping her coffee, the scent of fresh toast lingering in the air, when she heard a familiar knock at the door. Lizzie.

Sophie opened the door to see her friend standing there, sunglasses perched on her head, a mischievous grin playing on her lips. "Good morning, darling," Lizzie sang, pushing past Sophie and making herself comfortable in the kitchen. "Now, tell me everything! I've been dying to catch up on the juicy gossip from last Saturday night."

Sophie hesitated, her cheeks flushing at the memory. She knew Lizzie wouldn't let her off easily, especially not after the unexpected events of that night. Lizzie leaned forward, her eyes sparkling with curiosity. "Come on, Soph. You practically vanished after I left. Spill!"

Sophie smiled nervously, pouring Lizzie a cup of coffee. "It's not as exciting as you think," she began, trying to play it down. "We talked, had a few drinks, and then… well, I left."

Lizzie raised an eyebrow, clearly not buying it. "Oh, come on! You left with that gorgeous man. You can't tell me there wasn't something more!"

Sophie bit her lip, debating how much to reveal, while Lizzie leaned back in her chair, waiting for the full story.

Sophie sighed, knowing Lizzie wouldn't let it go. She glanced down at her coffee cup, swirling the liquid around as if it would help her find the right words. Finally, she looked up at Lizzie, her voice barely above a whisper.

"I lost my virginity."

The words hung in the air between them, and Lizzie's eyes widened in surprise. "Wait—what? With that guy from the bar?!" she asked, her voice rising with shock.

Sophie nodded, her cheeks flushing with embarrassment. "Yeah... I don't know how it happened, Lizzie. One minute we were just talking, and the next, well—" She trailed off, not needing to say more.

Lizzie sat back in her chair, stunned for a moment before a smile slowly crept across her face. "Well, damn, Soph! I did not expect that. How do you feel about it?"

Sophie shrugged, her emotions still a mess. "I don't know. It was... unexpected. I didn't know who he was at the time, and honestly, I'd rather keep it that way."

Lizzie raised an eyebrow, a playful grin spreading across her face. "Oh, that's a pity," she teased. "He was gorgeous. Lucky you, Soph."

Sophie rolled her eyes, feeling a mix of embarrassment and amusement. "Yeah, lucky me," she muttered, trying to brush off the memory.

Lizzie's eyes widened in shock. "You don't sound happy about it... was he a dud?" she asked, leaning forward in curiosity.

Sophie's face flushed slightly as she quickly shook her head. "No, he wasn't a dud... We, uh, did it three times," she admitted, her voice dropping as if she didn't quite believe it herself.

Lizzie's jaw dropped. "What!" she practically yelled. "Three times! Sophie, you're full of surprises!"

Sophie sighed, playing with the edge of her coffee cup. "I left without saying goodbye," she confessed quietly.

Lizzie raised an eyebrow, incredulous. "Wait, you just... left? No goodbye? Nothing?"

Sophie nodded, feeling a twinge of guilt. "Yeah, I just slipped out while he was in the shower. I didn't know what to say, and it all felt like too much. So, I left."

Lizzie stared at her for a moment before shaking her head with a smirk. "Girl, you're something else. Most women would've stayed for breakfast at least. But I get it, you like keeping things mysterious."

Sophie rolled her eyes playfully. "Come on, Lizzie. He was a player. I could just picture him saying, 'Last night was great, see ya.' So, I figured I'd just do it first and avoid the awkwardness."

Lizzie chuckled, leaning back in her chair. "You're really not giving him much credit, are you? Maybe he would've actually cared."

Sophie shrugged, trying to dismiss the thought. "I don't know. It's better this way. I don't want to get tangled up in whatever his game is."

Sophie quickly shifted gears, hoping to redirect the conversation. "So, enough about me. How was your date at the club? Did you have fun with that guy you met?"

Lizzie's face lit up, her eyes sparkling with excitement. "Oh my gosh, it was amazing! He was so sweet and funny. We danced the whole night. I think I might actually like him."

Sophie leaned in, intrigued. "Really? That's great! Are you going to see him again?"

Lizzie nodded eagerly. "Definitely! We're planning to meet up again this week. I just hope he's not a player like some people."

Sophie laughed, relieved to hear her friend's cheerful update. "Well, let's hope he's the real deal then!"

Lizzie nodded enthusiastically, her excitement palpable. "Exactly! Fingers crossed he's a good guy. By the way, are you ready for your new job? It's starting tomorrow, right?"

Sophie felt a flutter of nerves in her stomach. "Yeah, I think so. I mean, I'm excited but also a bit anxious. It's a big change, you know?"

Lizzie grinned, trying to reassure her. "You've got this! You're going to shine. Just be yourself, and don't overthink it. You'll impress everyone, especially with all that talent I know you have."

Sophie smiled back, feeling a bit more confident. "Thanks, Lizzie. I really hope so. I just want to make a good impression."

Lizzie leaned in, her expression earnest. "Sophie, you're going to be amazing. Remember, they chose you for a reason. Just go in there and show them what you're capable of. You'll do great!"

Sophie felt a warmth spread through her at her friend's words. "Thanks, Lizzie. I really appreciate your support."

They spent a little while longer chatting, Lizzie sharing some funny stories from her recent dates, which made Sophie laugh and forget her worries for a moment. They reminisced about their college days and the crazy adventures they'd had, bonding over shared memories and dreams for the future.

Eventually, Lizzie checked the time and sighed. "I should get going, but I'll be thinking of you tomorrow! Text me and let me know how it goes, okay?"

"Will do!" Sophie said, feeling a mix of gratitude and excitement. As Lizzie headed out the door, Sophie felt a renewed sense of determination. She was ready for this new chapter, no matter what challenges lay ahead.

Monday morning arrived, and Sophie felt a mix of excitement and nerves bubbling within her. She stood in front of the mirror, slipping into tailored black pants and a crisp white blouse. She topped it off with a tailored blazer that made her feel confident and professional. With a quick motion, she pulled her hair into a neat ponytail, leaving a few strands to softly frame her face.

After ensuring everything was ready for her mother, preparing breakfast and laying out medication, Sophie tiptoed into the kitchen. Her mother was already seated at the table, a warm smile on her face.

"Good luck today, sweetheart," her mother said, eyes sparkling with pride. "You're going to do great."

"Thanks, Mum. I'll keep you posted!" Sophie replied, her voice brightening at the encouragement.

With a final wave, Sophie stepped out of the house, her heart racing as she made her way to the office. Each step felt significant, marking the beginning of a new chapter in her life.

Sophie approached the entrance of the sleek office building, her heart pounding in anticipation. The modern architecture loomed above her, exuding an air of professionalism that both thrilled and intimidated her. As she stepped inside, the scent of polished marble and fresh coffee enveloped her.

She walked up to the security desk, where a friendly guard greeted her with a smile. "Good morning! You must be Sophie Highland," he said, handing her a visitor ID badge. "Here's your ID. Julia will be down shortly to take you up and introduce you to everyone."

"Thank you!" Sophie replied, slipping the ID into her blazer pocket. She glanced around the lobby, taking in the vibrant artwork and bustling atmosphere. The guard nodded, gesturing toward the seating area. "Feel free to take a seat while you wait."

As she settled into a plush chair, her mind raced with thoughts of her new role and the people she would meet.

Soon, Julia appeared, her presence radiating warmth and enthusiasm. "Hi, Sophie! Ready to start your first day?" she asked, her bright smile putting Sophie at ease.

"Absolutely!" Sophie replied, standing up and smoothing her blazer.

Julia led her toward the elevator, continuing, "I just wanted to let you know that the owner won't be in until Wednesday, so I can't introduce you to him today. But don't worry; you'll be in good hands with Derek. He's your immediate boss, such a lovely guy, around fifty, very approachable."

Sophie nodded, feeling a bit more reassured. "That's great to hear."

Julia pressed the button for the floor and added, "Just a heads-up, you'll be working mostly with men on your floor. There are only a few women here, but everyone is friendly. You'll fit right in!"

As the elevator doors slid closed, Sophie felt a mix of excitement and nervousness. She was ready for this new chapter, even if it meant stepping into a predominantly male environment.

As the elevator doors opened, Julia stepped out first, gesturing for Sophie to follow. The office was buzzing with energy, a blend of focused conversations and the sound of keyboards clicking. Julia led Sophie to a spacious corner office, where a man with salt-and-pepper hair and a friendly smile was seated at a large desk.

"Derek, this is Sophie Highland, our new intern," Julia announced with enthusiasm.

Derek stood up, extending his hand. "Nice to meet you, Sophie. Welcome to the team!" His grip was firm, and his eyes conveyed a sense of genuine interest.

"Thank you, Derek. I'm excited to be here," Sophie replied, feeling a bit more at ease.

After the introductions, Derek motioned for Sophie to follow him. "Let me show you around and introduce you to the team."

As they walked through the open-concept workspace, Derek pointed out various desks where architects were deep in discussion or sketching designs. "These are our architects," he said, motioning to a group of men huddled around a table covered in blueprints. They looked up, offering friendly nods and smiles.

One by one, Derek introduced Sophie to the team. "This is Ryan, Alex, and Mark," he said, gesturing to each man in turn. All were in their thirties, with a mix of styles, from casual button-downs to trendy t-shirts. The air was filled with a relaxed camaraderie, but Sophie couldn't help but notice that all the men were single, laughing and chatting as they returned to their work.

"Looks like you've walked into a bachelor's den," Derek joked, his tone light. "But they're all good guys, and I'm sure you'll fit right in."

Sophie smiled, feeling a mix of excitement and curiosity about her new role among such a dynamic group.

Throughout the day, Derek kept Sophie busy with a variety of tasks. He handed her a stack of design plans, explaining, "I need you to review these and give me a summary of the key elements. It'll help you get familiar with our current projects."

Sophie nodded, diving into the work. As she focused on her tasks, she could feel the presence of her colleagues around her. Ryan was the first to break the ice, casually leaning against the desk next to hers. "So, how are you finding the place so far, Sophie?" he asked, a friendly smile on his face.

"It's great! Everyone has been really welcoming," she replied, glancing up from her notes.

Alex chimed in from a nearby workstation, "Just wait until the coffee runs out. That's when the real chaos begins around here," he teased, his eyes twinkling with mischief.

Sophie chuckled, enjoying the light banter. "I'll keep an eye on the coffee supply then," she said, feeling more relaxed in their presence.

Mark, who had been quietly observing, added, "If you ever need a coffee buddy, just let us know. We take our caffeine seriously around here."

As the hours passed, Sophie found herself immersed in conversation with the trio. They shared stories about past projects, office pranks, and even their favourite lunch spots. Each of them seemed genuinely interested in her, asking about her background and what brought her to the firm.

Derek, occasionally glancing over, noticed the camaraderie building. He smiled to himself, pleased that Sophie was fitting in so well. The more they chatted, the more Sophie felt like she was becoming a part of the team, despite the initial nerves she had felt that morning.

As the week progressed, Sophie began to notice a shift in the office dynamics. Her colleagues—Ryan, Mark, and Alex—had grown noticeably friendlier, their interactions with her taking on a more familiar and playful tone. What started as polite exchanges had transformed into frequent teasing and light-hearted jokes, often centred around Sophie's quick wit and her ability to hold her own in their banter.

It wasn't lost on her that there was a layer of subtle flirtation underlying their words, particularly from Ryan. He seemed to find reasons to linger near her desk, whether it was to ask a seemingly trivial question or to offer help with her tasks. His casual tone betrayed none of his intentions, but his actions spoke volumes—like the way his gaze would linger just a little too long or how his smile would soften whenever she laughed at one of his jokes.

Mark, ever the charmer, leaned into his playful side, constantly teasing Sophie about her 'mysterious allure' and her ability to keep the office guessing. "You know, Sophie," he said one afternoon, propping himself against the edge of her desk, "you've got this whole enigmatic vibe going on. It's dangerous—you're going to have us all competing for your attention."

Sophie rolled her eyes with a chuckle, brushing him off. "I think you're exaggerating, Mark. Besides, I'm just here to do my job."

"Sure, sure," he replied with a wink, clearly enjoying her modesty. "But don't think we haven't noticed the effect you're having around here. Even Ryan's been stepping up his game."

Her eyes darted to Ryan, who was leaning against the doorframe of the conference room, chatting with Alex. He glanced her way as if he felt her looking, and their eyes met for a brief moment. There it was again—that lingering gaze, warm and unguarded, as if he were seeing only her in a room full of people. Sophie quickly looked away, feeling a faint blush creeping up her neck.

Ryan's attempts to get closer to Sophie were more subtle but no less intentional. He'd often time his coffee breaks to coincide with hers, initiating easy conversations that made her feel at ease. On one occasion, he casually suggested they grab lunch together, framing it as a 'team bonding' moment.

"Come on, Sophie," he said, his tone light. "I think it's time you experience the best sandwich shop in town. My treat."

Alex, overhearing the exchange, smirked knowingly. "Oh, it's the best, is it? Or is this just an excuse to spend time with Sophie?"

Ryan shot Alex a mock glare but didn't deny it outright. "Hey, can't a guy share his favourite spot without being accused of ulterior motives?"

Sophie laughed, shaking her head. "I appreciate the offer, but I brought my lunch today," she said, holding up her meal container.

"Next time, then," Ryan replied smoothly, his smile never faltering. "You won't regret it."

By Wednesday, Sophie was starting to find her footing in her new role. She was adjusting to the rhythm of the office, but she couldn't shake the feeling that she was being watched—though whether out of curiosity or something else, she couldn't tell.

During a casual chat in the break room, Alex leaned against the counter, stirring her coffee. "So, how are you finding things so far?" she asked, her voice friendly.

"Not too bad," Sophie replied, though she hesitated, glancing around. "But I've noticed there's… a lot of talk about Damian Prescott."

Alex smirked knowingly. "Ah, Damian. The infamous owner of our fine establishment," he said, shaking his head. "He's got a bit of a reputation, to say the least. Total player. His longest relationship lasted three weeks, and that was with Clara."

Sophie frowned, intrigued despite herself. "Lucky Clara. Was she nice?"

"No, she wasn't 'nice'. High maintenance doesn't even begin to describe her," Alex said with a laugh. "But she knew how to get attention, and Damian? He loves the chase."

Sophie couldn't help rolling her eyes. "Sounds like he's exactly the kind of guy I'd avoid," she said, her tone dry.

"Smart girl," Alex said, flashing a grin. "But don't be surprised if he tries his luck. He has a habit of testing boundaries."

Sophie filed that warning away, determined to stay focused on her work. Still, whispers about Damian floated through the office, creating a sense of anticipation she couldn't entirely ignore.

Later that day, Mark, one of her colleagues, leaned casually against her desk, his usual playful grin in place. "Hey, just a heads-up—Damian's in today. You might get to meet him," he said, his tone light but tinged with curiosity.

Sophie raised an eyebrow. "I didn't realise he worked on-site."

"Oh, he does," Mark said with a laugh. "But he is out a lot in meetings and such. He just drops in down here now and then to remind us he owns the place. But don't worry, you'll know when he's here. He's… hard to miss."

Ryan, who had been listening nearby, joined the conversation, a warm smile lighting up his face. "You'll be fine. Besides, the office could use your kind of energy. Keeps things fresh."

Sophie glanced between them, her cheeks warming slightly under their attention. "Thanks, but I'm just here to do my job," she replied, keeping her tone professional.

Mark chuckled, clearly enjoying the dynamic. "Come on, Sophie. You're already making waves, whether you realise it or not. Just don't forget us little people when you're up there impressing the boss."

Sophie laughed, shaking her head. "I doubt I'll even speak to him."

Mark smirked, leaning closer. "Oh, you'll speak to him, alright. You're not exactly easy to ignore."

Ryan's expression shifted, his teasing grin softening into something more sincere. "Don't let Damian get to you, though. He's… not the kind of guy you're looking for."

Sophie gave him a curious look. "And what makes you think you know what kind of guy I'm looking for?"

Ryan hesitated for a beat, then shrugged, a faint smile tugging at his lips. "Just a hunch," he said lightly, though there was something in his tone that made her pause.

Alex joined them, her eyes gleaming with mischief. "Okay, Sophie, enlighten us. What kind of man would catch your attention?"

Sophie crossed her arms, her gaze thoughtful. "Someone respectful," she said after a moment. "Someone who values integrity and isn't just looking for a fling. Relationships should be built on trust and mutual respect."

Her colleagues nodded, surprised by the quiet confidence in her answer. Mark raised an eyebrow, clearly impressed. "Sounds like you've got it all figured out," he said.

Sophie smiled softly. "I just want someone who sees me for who I am—not just what I look like."

Ryan's gaze lingered on her, something unspoken flickering in his eyes. Then, with a playful grin, he leaned forward. "Well, Sophie, I might not be the big boss, but I do know how to treat someone with respect. And I promise I'm not just looking for a fling."

Sophie chuckled at his boldness, but there was an undeniable warmth in her smile. "Thanks, Ryan. I'll keep that in mind," she said, her tone light but genuine.

As the conversation shifted and laughter filled the room, Ryan's gaze lingered on Sophie.

Chapter Nine

The head architect, Derek, stood in the centre of the bustling design studio, his brow furrowed in concentration as he studied the blueprints spread across the table. The team had been grappling with how to maximise natural light in the new building for days, but every suggestion seemed to fall flat. Frustration simmered in the air, punctuated by the sound of tapping pens and the rustle of papers.

Just then, Sophie, hesitantly raised her hand. "What if we consider adjusting the facade to include angled skylights?" she suggested, her voice steady despite the tension in the room. "It could direct light deeper into the interior spaces without compromising the design."

Derek paused, looking at her intently. He studied the lines of the blueprints again, envisioning her idea in place. As the concept began to form in his mind, a spark of realisation ignited within him. "That's genius!" he exclaimed, a grin breaking across his face. "We could create a dynamic interplay of light and shadow throughout the day. Let's explore that further!"

Sophie felt a rush of pride as Ryan, Mark and Alex were all impressed, the energy in the room shifting as her idea took centre stage.

Derek mulled over Sophie's plan for a moment longer, then decided it was time to discuss it with Damian and get his perspective. With a sense of purpose, he made his way to the elevator, heading up to Damian's office.

As Derek strode confidently into the sleek office, the modern design reflecting his anticipation, he called out, "Damian, I think we've found a solution to the light problem!" His voice was filled with enthusiasm as he approached, eager to share the exciting development.

Damian looked up from his desk, intrigued. "Oh? I'm listening," he replied, leaning back in his chair, arms crossed, a glimmer of curiosity in his green eyes.

Derek stepped closer, gesturing animatedly as he explained, "We've been struggling to maximise natural light in the new building, but our new intern suggested incorporating angled skylights into the facade. This design could redirect light deeper into the interior spaces without compromising our aesthetic."

Damian raised an eyebrow, impressed. "Interesting. How would that work structurally?"

Derek elaborated, detailing the engineering possibilities and how they could create a dynamic interaction of light throughout the day. "It could also enhance the overall atmosphere of the space, making it feel more inviting."

Damian nodded thoughtfully, envisioning the potential impact on the project. "I like it. Let's see a mock-up. If it works as well as you're describing, it could elevate the entire design."

Derek felt a surge of satisfaction at the prospect of the intern's growing contribution to the company. He paused, a glimmer of curiosity in his voice. "By the way, have you had a chance to meet the new intern yet? She's something else."

Damian leaned forward slightly; his interest piqued. "Oh really? Why's that?"

Derek chuckled, shaking his head with amusement. "Well, for starters, she's stunning—those doe eyes could stop traffic. I swear, half the young bucks around here are already head over heels for her. Mark, Alex, and Ryan are practically tripping over themselves just to get her attention. But here's the thing: she's not like most young women her age."

Damian arched an eyebrow, a smirk tugging at the corner of his lips. "Oh? Let me guess. She's playing hard to get?"

"Not exactly," Derek said, leaning back in his chair. "She's… mysterious. Keeps to herself most of the time. Shy, but not in a timid way—it's more like she's carefully observing everything around her. And when it comes to her work? She's razor focused. You can tell she's here to make something of herself, not to entertain office gossip or play games."

Damian's smirk deepened, his curiosity growing. "She sounds intriguing. Should I be concerned for your wife, Derek?"

Derek burst into laughter, waving off the comment. "Trust me, my wife has nothing to worry about. If I were twenty years younger, though, maybe," he said with a wink.

Damian leaned back in his chair, his mind already wandering. "Well, now you've got me intrigued. Sophie, isn't it?"

"Yes, Sophie Highland," Derek replied, a note of admiration in his voice. "She's in a league of her own, Damian. I think you'll see what I mean the moment you meet her."

Damian's smirk transformed into a thoughtful expression, his fingers idly tapping the edge of his desk. "Sounds like I need to introduce myself. A paragon like that shouldn't go unnoticed."

Derek chuckled, standing to leave. "Just don't scare her off. She's not the type to be charmed by flashy displays or smooth talk. If anything, that might make her retreat further into her shell."

Damian gave a low laugh, a glint of challenge flickering in his eyes. "Who says I'd try to charm her? Maybe I'm just curious to see what all the fuss is about."

Derek smirked knowingly. "Oh, I know you, Damian. And for the record, the boys have already warned her about your…"—he waved his hand vaguely—"playboy existence."

Damian laughed at that, leaning back in his chair. "Have they now?"

"Oh, they have," Derek confirmed, grinning.

Damian felt a surge of curiosity; Derek didn't give praise very often, and the way he spoke of Sophie hinted at something remarkable. "Alright then," he said, a new spark of interest igniting within him. "Let's set up a meeting."

"Okay, how about tomorrow morning around ten? I'll bring her to your office," Derek suggested, a grin spreading across his face.

"Sounds good," Damian replied, leaning back in his chair with a smirk. "I'll see you then. I'm looking forward to meeting this young lady who has all the men chasing their tails," he chuckled.

As Derek left the office, Damian's thoughts lingered on the mysterious intern. A woman who could captivate a room full of admirers while staying focused and unaffected by the chaos? He couldn't help but wonder what kind of person Sophie Highland was— and why she had already managed to disrupt the careful equilibrium of his office without even trying.

During the team meeting that morning, Derek casually informed Sophie, "By the way, Mr. Prescott wants to meet you today at 10am"

Sophie blinked in surprise. "Oh, okay," she said, uncertain what to make of the news.

The reaction from Alex, Ryan, and Mark, however, was immediate. All three groaned audibly, their exasperation filling the room.

Sophie frowned, looking at them in confusion. "What's wrong?" she asked.

Ryan leaned back in his chair with a dramatic sigh. "So, it begins."

"What begins?" Sophie asked, her confusion deepening.

Alex leaned forward, his tone half-serious, half-teasing. "Damian must've heard about you."

Sophie tilted her head. "And? What's the big deal?"

Mark shook his head, giving her a look of mock pity. "Sophie, we weren't kidding when we told you he's a player. Be careful."

Derek chuckled, trying to lighten the mood. "Come on, guys, don't scare her like that. It's just a meeting."

Ryan wasn't convinced. "Derek, you know as well as we do what Damian's like. He doesn't call people into his office for nothing, especially when they're new—and especially when they're Sophie."

Sophie felt a flicker of unease at their reactions but tried to brush it off. "I'm sure it's nothing," she said, forcing a small smile.

When the time came for her meeting, Sophie stood to leave with Derek. Ryan, however, called out from across the room, his voice full of warning. "Derek, don't leave her alone with Damian!"

Sophie shot him an incredulous look. "Ryan, I'll be fine. It's just a meeting."

Ryan shook his head, a grin tugging at his lips despite his words. "Famous last words."

As they walked toward Damian's office, Sophie couldn't help but feel a twinge of nervousness. The way her colleagues had reacted left her wondering just what kind of man Damian Prescott really was—and why meeting him felt like such a momentous occasion.

Damian sat in his sleek office, the soft ambient light filtering through the large windows and casting a warm glow over the modern decor. He drummed his fingers lightly on the polished surface of his desk, his mind racing with thoughts about the upcoming meeting. The anticipation of meeting Sophie Highland intrigued him; he felt a stirring curiosity that she might offer a fresh perspective to the team.

As he glanced at the clock, he noted it was just a few minutes before ten. He leaned back in his chair, crossing his arms, and allowed himself a moment to reflect. The office was quiet, save for the faint sounds of the bustling city below. The silence only heightened his curiosity about the new intern and the unconventional ideas she might bring.

Damian could hear the faint hum of the elevator nearby and wondered if Derek was on his way up. He hoped Sophie would prove to be as remarkable as Derek had described. As he prepared for their discussion, he felt a subtle excitement building within him. He was ready to engage with someone who could potentially challenge the status quo and bring new energy to Prescott Design Group.

Derek knocked lightly on the door, a cheerful expression on his face. "Enter," Damian called, his voice steady as he straightened in his chair.

The door swung open.

The moment Derek and Sophie walked into his office; Damian's breath caught in his throat. There she was her presence strikingly different from the last time they had met. She wore a fitted blazer that hid her figure, and her hair pulled back in a ponytail. The woman who had been occupying his thoughts for days. He felt a jolt of shock ripple through him, but years of composure allowed him to hide it from Derek. His expression remained neutral, professional, though his mind raced.

Finally, I've found her, he thought, a sense of relief mingling with excitement. As she stood before him, poised and focused, Damian felt a rush of determination. This time, he wasn't going to let her slip away so easily.

"Damian, this is Sophie Highland, our new intern," Derek announced, a hint of pride in his voice as he gestured toward her. "Sophie, meet Damian Prescott."

When Sophie walked into Damian's office and saw him sitting behind the desk, her heart skipped a beat. Oh no, she thought, her mind racing as she kept her face composed, not daring to let Derek see her surprise. I didn't think I'd ever see him again.

She felt her pulse quicken, memories of their night together flashing through her mind, but she quickly pushed them down, forcing herself to remain calm. With a steady breath, Sophie plastered on a polite smile, hoping Damian wouldn't give anything away either.

Sophie smiled politely; her cheeks slightly flushed. "It's nice to meet you, Mr. Prescott," she said, maintaining her composure despite the flutter of nerves in her stomach.

Damian's green eyes narrowed slightly in surprise, his intrigue deepening. "Pleasure to meet you, Sophie. I've heard good things," he replied, his tone smooth and inviting.

As Derek continued to speak, detailing Sophie's role in the team, Damian and Sophie exchanged subtle glances, both acutely aware of the tension that lingered beneath their professional facades. It was a moment charged with unspoken words, yet they played their parts well, keeping the secret of their connection just below the surface as they moved into the formalities of the meeting.

Damian leaned forward slightly, a genuine smile crossing his face. "I wanted to take a moment to compliment you on your idea for the building yesterday," he said, his voice warm and appreciative. "The concept of integrating angled skylights was brilliant. It really shows your understanding of light and space."

Sophie felt a rush of warmth at his words, her cheeks flushing with a mix of pride and modesty. "Thank you," she replied softly, her voice a little breathless. "I was just trying to think of ways to solve the problem we were facing."

Damian nodded, clearly impressed. "Well, you certainly succeeded. I can see why Derek speaks so highly of you. Your insight will be invaluable to the team."

Sophie smiled; her confidence bolstered by his praise. "I'm excited to contribute and learn as much as I can," she said, meeting his gaze with newfound determination.

Damian's gaze shifted to Derek, his expression sharp and commanding. "Derek, would you mind giving us a moment?" he said, his tone calm but laced with authority.

Derek hesitated, his brow furrowing as he cast a glance at Sophie. He clearly wasn't thrilled about leaving her alone with Damian, but he knew better than to argue. "Alright," he said slowly, his reluctance evident. Turning to Sophie, he offered her a reassuring smile. "I'll be just down in the office if you need me."

With that, Derek exited the room, throwing one last cautious look over his shoulder before closing the door behind him.

As the door clicked shut, Damian shifted his focus entirely to Sophie, a curious gleam flickering in his green eyes. "Now, I have to ask, why did you leave so suddenly?" he inquired, leaning back in his chair with an air of casual intrigue.

Sophie met Damian's gaze, her expression a mix of shyness and candour. "It was fun, but honestly, I didn't know who you were at the time," she admitted, a hint of embarrassment colouring her cheeks. "So, it feels a bit inappropriate to even worry about it now." She shrugged lightly, trying to brush off the tension from their previous encounter while her heart raced at the memory.

Damian felt a flicker of annoyance at her response. He was the one who had been left in the morning, not her. His thoughts had been consumed by her ever since that night; the way she had laughed, how her eyes sparkled with mischief, and the undeniable chemistry they shared. "You know," he said, a hint of frustration creeping into his voice, "it's not often I meet someone who captivates me the way you did. I've been trying to figure out why you slipped away so quickly."

Sophie took a deep breath, her gaze steady on Damian. "I apologise, Mr. Prescott, but I believe we should leave the past in the past," she said, her voice firm yet polite. There was a hint of resolve in her expression, as if she were trying to distance herself from the whirlwind of emotions that night had stirred within her. She didn't want to complicate things further, especially now that they were in a professional setting.

Damian leaned forward, his green eyes locking onto Sophie's with an intensity that sent a shiver down her spine. "What if I don't want to leave it in the past?" he asked, his voice low and filled with a hint of challenge. The air between them thickened as he continued, "That night was different, and you were different. I can't just forget it." His expression softened, revealing a vulnerability beneath his confident exterior, as he searched her face for a reaction.

Sophie felt a flutter of nerves as she said, "I'm sorry, Mr. Prescott." The formality felt out of place in the charged atmosphere of the room.

Damian's expression shifted, a hint of impatience crossing his features. "Stop calling me Mr. Prescott," he replied, his tone firm yet softened by a hint of warmth. "My name is Damian, especially since we've already crossed that line." He leaned back slightly, watching her with keen interest, as if he were inviting her to step closer into his world.

Sophie felt a mix of frustration and determination as she replied, "That line would never have been crossed if I'd known who you were."

Damian's expression darkened, anger flashing in his green eyes. "Why does that matter so much to you?" he demanded, leaning forward slightly.

Sophie drew a steadying breath, her voice calm but firm. "Because you're not the relationship type, Damian. I've been warned about you—how you're a player and how your longest relationship barely lasted three weeks. I'm not interested in getting involved with someone like that."

Her gaze never wavered, her resolve clear as her words hung heavily in the air, weighted with unspoken implications.

Damian's jaw tightened at her blunt remark. The word player struck a nerve, and a flicker of something unidentifiable crossed his face—irritation, perhaps even hurt, though he masked it quickly with his usual cool demeanour.

"Is that what they've been saying about me?" he said finally, his tone measured but with an edge. "And you believe everything you hear, do you?"

Sophie raised an eyebrow, her expression unwavering. "I believe patterns speak louder than words. And yours doesn't exactly inspire confidence."

Damian leaned back in his chair; his piercing gaze fixed on her. His usual charm gave way to a quieter, sharper intensity. "If patterns speak louder than words, Sophie, did they also tell you that I have never been involved with an employee? Ever," he said, his tone soft but edged with a quiet challenge. "Maybe you're wrong. Maybe there's more to me than you—or anyone else—realises."

Sophie felt a flicker of hesitation, the conviction in his voice momentarily throwing her off balance. But she quickly steadied herself, holding her ground. "Maybe there is," she admitted, her voice firm, "but I'm not willing to take that gamble."

She paused, the weight of her own words settling over her. For a moment, her gaze dropped to the desk as she gathered her thoughts. Then she straightened, her voice softening but remaining resolute. "Actually, I'm not interested in getting involved with anyone." She cast her gaze downward, taking a moment to gather her thoughts. "I have too much on my plate right now, and the last thing I need is to complicate my life even more."

Damian leaned forward slightly, a playful yet serious glint in his green eyes. "What if I wanted to complicate your life, Sophie?" he asked, his voice smooth and teasing. "Sometimes, the unexpected can lead to the most exciting opportunities."

Sophie shook her head firmly, her expression resolute. "No. What happened last weekend can stay in the past. It was fun, but it's over now."

Damian's frustration mounted as he leaned closer, challenging her. "Why?" he pressed, unable to mask his irritation.

Sophie met his gaze, her voice steady. "Are you serious? You're my employer, and I'm your employee. That's the end of it."

Damian's eyes narrowed slightly as he replied, "I can change that in a heartbeat."

Sophie stood her ground, her determination unwavering. "Oh, now you're threatening me. Well, I'm sure I'll be open to seeing you again after you fire me... not."

Damian's voice softened as he looked at her intently. "I'm not going to fire you, Sophie. You're obviously good at what you do." He paused, gathering his thoughts. "Would you consider going on a date with me? I genuinely enjoyed spending time with you."

"Thank you, Mr. Prescott, but no." Sophie shook her head, her expression resolute. "Last weekend was an anomaly in my life; I rarely get time to myself."

Sophie took a deep breath, her voice steady as she continued, "And I'm not prepared to get tangled in a relationship that has no future. All relationships end, and I'm not interested in becoming just another statistic." She met Damian's gaze, her determination evident. "I have too much to focus on right now."

Damian leaned forward; frustration etched across his features. "You don't know what could happen in the future," he said, his tone firm yet imploring.

Sophie shook her head, her resolve unyielding. "I'm sorry, Mr. Prescott, but I'm not interested. I understand that you might not like that, but it's how I feel." She crossed her arms, standing her ground, determined not to waver.

Damian's frustration deepened as he watched her, his green eyes narrowing. He wanted to reach out, to convince her to reconsider, but the words eluded him.

Sophie stood up, her posture resolute. "If there's anything else, Mr. Prescott, I have work to do." She paused, allowing the weight of her statement to linger in the air, but Damian remained silent, his gaze fixed on her with an intensity that made her heart race.

Finally, she turned away, her head held high, determination etched into her features as she left the office, the door clicking shut behind her.

Damian sat back in his chair, running a hand through his hair in frustration. "What the hell just happened?" he muttered to himself, disbelief etched across his face. Sophie had taken him by surprise, her words cutting through his thoughts like a knife.

For the entire week, she had consumed his mind, her laughter, her innocence, the way she challenged him. He had thought he could move past their brief encounter, but instead, he found himself more intrigued than ever. He leaned forward, resting his elbows on the desk, trying to make sense of the turmoil she stirred within him.

She had dismissed him so easily, yet he couldn't shake the feeling that there was something undeniably special about her. It frustrated him to no end that she could walk away so confidently while he was left grappling with an unrelenting desire to explore whatever connection they had.

As Sophie stepped out of Damian's office, her heart raced, a mix of relief and regret swirling within her. Oh no, she thought, I didn't think I would ever see him again. The reality of their encounter weighed heavily on her mind. Now that she knew who he was, a playboy, a womaniser, her stomach twisted with unease.

He's someone who can't be trusted with anyone's heart, she concluded, the sharp edge of her thoughts cutting through the remnants of the fun they had shared. She could still feel the warmth of his gaze and the thrill of their brief connection, but it was tainted by the knowledge of his reputation.

Sophie took a deep breath, reminding herself of her earlier resolution. She had too much to focus on in her life to get entangled in something that had no future. With a determined stride, she walked down the corridor, her head held high, but inside, she wrestled with the prospect of working with him. If only he weren't who he was; the hurt in her heart refused to subside.

Chapter Ten

Damian stood outside the sleek, modern glass building, leaning casually against his polished town car. A sense of anticipation thrummed beneath his composed exterior, the late afternoon sun casting a warm glow that accentuated his tailored suit and the confident demeanour he effortlessly exuded.

As he scanned the entrance, his heart raced when he spotted Sophie stepping out. She looked radiant, her face a blend of focus and determination. But when their eyes met, she quickly averted her gaze, intent on ignoring him as she turned to walk away.

"Hey, Sophie!" Damian called out, pushing himself off the car. He noticed her determination to avoid him, but he wasn't about to let her walk home alone. "Wait! Can I give you a ride?"

Sophie hesitated, glancing back at him. The invitation hung in the air, and she found herself torn. Accepting the ride would mean more time with her mother before her shift at the café, but it also meant facing the tension that lingered between her and Damian. Ultimately, the thought of a few extra moments at home nudged her closer to acceptance.

Sophie came to a halt, turning to see Damian approaching her from behind. His presence was disarming, and she felt a mix of reluctance and curiosity as he stepped closer. "Come on, Sophie, it's just a lift home," he said, his tone warm yet persuasive.

After a moment of internal debate, she reluctantly nodded in agreement. They walked to the car together, and Damian opened the door for her with a courteous gesture. She slid into the plush interior, and he followed suit, settling into the seat beside her.

Turning to face her, he asked, "What's the address?"

Sophie took a breath and relayed the details to the driver. The car began to move smoothly away from the curb, the hum of the engine creating a comfortable atmosphere as they navigated the city streets.

As the car glided through the bustling streets, Damian turned to Sophie with a curious expression. "So, do you always walk home after work?" he asked, genuinely interested.

Sophie smiled slightly; her gaze focused out the window for a moment before meeting his eyes. "Yes, I do. I like the exercise," she replied, her tone light.

Damian nodded, impressed. "That's a good habit to have. It's nice to stay active, especially when you spend all day in an office."

Sophie shrugged, a hint of pride in her voice. "It helps clear my mind, and it's a nice way to unwind after a long day."

"Seems like you have everything figured out," he said, a playful glint in his eye. "Maybe I should take notes."

She chuckled, appreciating the light-hearted exchange as they continued their journey.

Damian glanced at Sophie, curiosity sparking in his eyes. "So, what do you usually do after work?" he asked, genuinely interested in her routine.

Sophie took a moment before responding. "Well, I organise my mother's dinner and meds first," she explained, her voice tinged with warmth as she spoke about her responsibilities. "After that, I head to the café and work until about 9pm."

Damian nodded, genuinely impressed by her dedication. "That sounds like a long day," he remarked, his tone filled with both admiration and sympathy.

"It can be, but I don't mind," she replied, a hint of resolve in her voice. "I want to make sure she's taken care of, and the café helps with the bills."

"I didn't know you had another job," he said, looking at her with newfound respect.

Sophie shrugged modestly, a small smile tugging at her lips. "Actually, I have two. I work at a gym on Saturdays as well."

"When do you find time for yourself?" he asked, concern creasing his brow.

Sophie chuckled softly. "I don't, usually. I wasn't joking when I said last Saturday was an anomaly."

Damian asked, "How long have you been juggling these two jobs?"

Sophie replied, "I've had two jobs ever since I left high school. I had to; I got a couple of scholarships, but they didn't cover all my university expenses. So, I worked while I studied."

Damian raised an eyebrow, impressed. "And you still managed to get top marks?"

Sophie said, "I had to; it's just my mum and me, and she has MS, so I had to step up. It's hard sometimes, but I cope." Her voice held a mixture of determination and vulnerability, revealing the weight of her responsibilities.

Damian asked, "Where is your dad?"

Sophie's lips pressed into a firm line as she replied, "He left when I was fifteen. He couldn't handle my mum's diagnosis, so he bailed." Her tone was steady, but there was an underlying hurt that hinted at the impact of her father's absence.

Damian frowned, his expression shifting to one of concern. "That's not good," he said softly, acknowledging the weight of her words.

Sophie smiled cheerfully, brushing off the heaviness of the conversation. "No use worrying about it. It is what it is," she replied, her tone lightening.

Damian raised an eyebrow, intrigued. "Is that what you meant when you said life hadn't been that kind?"

A blush crept across Sophie's cheeks, and she looked down for a moment, feeling slightly embarrassed. "I should not have said that," she murmured, trying to change the subject.

Damian looked at her, genuinely curious. "Why?" he asked, intrigued by her perspective.

Sophie took a deep breath, her resolve shining through. "Because life is what you make it. That's why I worked hard and still do. I believe it can all change." There was a spark of determination in her eyes, reflecting her unwavering belief in the possibilities ahead.

Damian smiled, his gaze lingering on Sophie with genuine admiration. "You really are amazing," he said, his voice filled with respect.

Sophie felt a rush of warmth flood her cheeks, and she quickly looked away, a soft, shy smile forming on her lips. "Thank you, but I'm just... me," she replied, her voice modest as she shifted her focus to the passing scenery outside the car window.

The car pulled up to her apartment and slowed to a stop. "We're here," he said, his voice a little softer now.

"Thank you for the lift."

Damian's smile deepened, though there was something almost vulnerable in it. "You're welcome. I hope you have a good night, Sophie," he said, his voice betraying a hint of something unspoken.

Sophie turned toward him, her eyes meeting his with an intensity that caught him off guard. Reaching out, she grasped his hand gently, squeezing it with a sincerity that made his heart race. "You too, Damian. Thanks again," she said, her words quiet but laden with emotion.

For a moment, time seemed to stand still. Damian felt a surge of warmth and something deeper stirring inside him. He didn't want to let go of her hand, the connection between them too palpable, too real to ignore. But with a reluctant sigh, he knew he had to.

Their hands lingered for just a moment longer, and then he slowly released her, a subtle pang of longing stirring within him. Sophie opened the door and stepped out, but not before giving him one last look, her expression soft, as though she too felt the weight of the moment.

Damian watched as she walked toward the door of her apartment, each step pulling her farther from him, yet leaving a sense of emptiness in its wake. A sense of something more that he couldn't quite name, but that he knew would stay with him long after she disappeared inside.

Sophie stepped into her apartment, greeted by the familiar warmth and comforting scent of home. She found her mother in the living room, nestled on the couch with a book in her lap. "Hey, Mum," Sophie said cheerfully, setting her bag down. "How was your day?"

"Just the same old, but I'm glad you are home," her mother replied, smiling.

Sophie quickly got to work, helping her mother settle in for the night. She prepared dinner, making sure to check that all her mother's medications were in order, and chatted about her day as they ate. With the lift from Damian, Sophie felt energised, able to dedicate more time to her mother than usual.

Once everything was sorted and her mother was comfortably settled in, Sophie grabbed her bag and headed out the door. The evening air was cool and refreshing as she made her way to the café. The walk was enjoyable, and she felt a little lighter knowing she had spent extra time with her mum.

As she walked, she reflected on her day and the unexpected joy that came from her conversation with Damian. She couldn't deny it anymore: she liked him. A lot. It wasn't just his charm or his looks, though those were impossible to ignore.

It was the moments when he seemed genuine, peeling back the layers of his reputation to reveal something deeper. The lift had not only given her time but had also brightened her mood and she couldn't help but smile as she approached the café, ready for another busy night.

As Damian entered his penthouse apartment, the familiar click of the door echoed in the stillness, amplifying the silence that enveloped him. He paused for a moment, taking in the expansive space that had always felt like a sanctuary. The floor-to-ceiling windows offered a breathtaking view of the city skyline, but tonight, the glow of the city lights did little to dispel the sense of emptiness that had settled over him.

He walked through the sleek, modern furnishings, each piece a reminder of the life he had built, yet they felt oddly uninviting now. The plush sofa sat untouched, the dining table lay perfectly set but unused, and the art on the walls, once a source of pride, seemed to stare back at him with a cold indifference.

Damian had always enjoyed his solitude, relishing the peace that came with his success. But lately, he found himself more acutely aware of the void in the space, the laughter that never filled the rooms, the conversations he longed to have, and the warmth of companionship that felt increasingly distant.

He sighed, running a hand through his hair as he contemplated the growing loneliness. The vibrant connection he felt with Sophie lingered in his mind, contrasting sharply with the quietude of his apartment. He moved to the kitchen, pouring himself a glass of wine, hoping to dull the ache of solitude that seemed to grow more profound with each passing day. For the first time, he truly recognised that the emptiness around him mirrored a deeper void within, one that he was beginning to understand he wanted to fill.

As Damian sipped his wine, he leaned against the kitchen counter, lost in thought about Sophie. He couldn't shake the feeling that winning her trust would be an uphill battle. He recalled the way she had looked at him, a mix of wariness and curiosity. It was clear to him that her past had shaped her perspective on relationships, particularly her father's abandonment when she was just fifteen. That experience had likely coloured her view of men, leaving her with a deep-seated scepticism he could easily recognise.

Damian rubbed his temples, acknowledging the challenge ahead. He was aware of his reputation, one that hardly inspired confidence in a woman like Sophie. He was known for his charm and charisma, often attracting attention for the wrong reasons. The thought of her discovering the details of his past flings and casual encounters sent a pang of regret through him. How could he convince her that he could change, be different? That he was worth the risk?

He needed to find a way to show her he was trustworthy, someone who could offer stability and sincerity instead of the fleeting connections she likely associated with men like him. The contrast between his public persona and his true self felt like a chasm he had to bridge. He wanted her to see that beneath the confident exterior lay a man capable of genuine emotion and commitment. But how could he break through the walls she had built, especially when he himself was grappling with the fear of rejection?

Damian took another sip of wine, contemplating his next move. It wouldn't be enough to simply show her kindness or charm her with his successes; he needed to be patient and allow her to see the real him, piece by piece. In that moment, he resolved to earn her trust, no matter how long it took.

Damian leaned back against the sleek marble countertop, his mind racing with thoughts about Sophie. If he was going to win her over, he realised he needed more than just surface-level information, he needed to understand the intricate details of her life, her experiences, and what truly motivated her. Each piece of information could serve as a stepping stone, helping him navigate the complexities of her heart.

He thought about her dedication to caring for her mother, the way she balanced two jobs, and the unwavering resolve that shone through her words. It was clear that her past had shaped her into a resilient individual, but he needed to dig deeper. What were her dreams? What did she truly want out of life? Did she have any hidden fears or insecurities that he could help her overcome?

Damian felt a familiar surge of determination. He couldn't approach her with the same casual confidence he typically relied on; this was different. He wanted to be someone she could trust, and that required understanding the full picture of who she was.

He picked up his phone, contemplating that reaching out to a private investigator could be a solid first step. It would be a delicate manoeuvre, but he rationalised it to himself: the more he understood about her, the better equipped he'd be to support her and, ultimately, gain her trust. Each detail, from her challenges to her dreams, could offer invaluable insight into her life.

As he pondered the potential risks of this approach, Damian knew he had to tread carefully. He didn't want to invade her privacy or make her feel like a subject of scrutiny. Instead, he aimed to gather information that would help him relate to her on a deeper level and show her that he truly cared. The thought of uncovering more about Sophie only fuelled his desire to prove to her that he was worthy of her trust, a task he was more than willing to undertake.

Damian leaned back in his sleek chair, his fingers steepled as he regarded the door, anticipation simmering beneath his composed exterior. The morning sunlight streamed through the large windows, casting a warm glow across his modern office, yet his mind was focused solely on the meeting ahead.

The soft click of the door opening caught his attention, and the private investigator stepped inside, a folder in hand and a casual confidence about him. "I've compiled all the details on your new intern, Sophie Highland," he said, flipping the folder open with a practiced ease.

Damian's interest piqued instantly, the thought of Sophie occupying his mind for weeks. He straightened in his chair, his curiosity evident. "Let's hear it," he prompted, ready to absorb every detail about the woman who had unknowingly captivated him.

"Honestly, I wouldn't mind introducing my son to this girl," the investigator remarked with a chuckle.

Damian's expression darkened, irritation flickering across his face. "Let's skip the jokes," he said, leaning forward, his interest piqued. "What did you find?"

Clearing his throat, the investigator began to detail his findings. "Sophie Highland is twenty-five and works part-time at a café and at a gym on Saturdays. She's been taking care of her mother, who has MS. Her father left shortly after the diagnosis, leaving a fifteen-year-old Sophie to shoulder the responsibility. Her life seems pretty straightforward, nothing scandalous, but she clearly holds strong values. She's intelligent; she aced all her exams and studies."

Damian listened intently, intrigued despite himself. "And?" he prompted, wanting more specifics.

The investigator continued, "She's very close to her mother, and her friends are essential to her. It sounds like she doesn't trust men much, her boss at the café was quite chatty. But everyone I spoke to had nothing but good things to say about her; they all love her."

Damian raised an eyebrow. "Nothing about her personal life? Relationships?"

The investigator shrugged. "Not much. She gets a lot of attention from men, especially at the gym she works at. Quite a few men I spoke to there are very keen on her. It seems she's never had a boyfriend. From what I gather, people think she's still an innocent."

Damian leaned back in his chair, mulling over this information. "Interesting," he murmured, a grin forming on his lips as he thought, she isn't anymore.

The investigator chuckled lightly. "I was serious earlier; if my son brought home a girl like this, I'd be a very happy man."

He then added, "Oh, and there's one more thing. The reason she has two jobs is to manage a significant amount of student debt from her studies. That's likely why she doesn't go out much. She's determined to pay off the loan as soon as she can."

Damian leaned back, processing this new layer of information. "Very interesting," he repeated, a newfound appreciation for Sophie Highland beginning to form in his mind.

Damian sat silently for a moment, absorbing the details about Sophie's life. His fingers tapped lightly on the surface of his desk, a new idea forming in his mind. He looked up at the investigator, his expression now calculated.

"How would someone go about paying off Sophie Highland's debt?" Damian asked, his tone casual but his intentions unmistakable.

The investigator raised an eyebrow, surprised by the question. "Well, that depends. If someone wanted to settle it anonymously, it could be done through her loan provider, or through a legal intermediary. She wouldn't even have to know where the money came from. Or, if they wanted her to be aware, they could pay it off directly and let her know through an official notice."

Damian nodded thoughtfully, his eyes narrowing slightly as he considered the options. "And how much are we talking about?"

The investigator flipped through the folder again. "It's a sizeable amount, around seventy thousand, give or take."

Damian didn't flinch at the number. Instead, he leaned back in his chair, a faint smile playing on his lips. "Good. I want to know the best way to handle this quietly."

The investigator nodded, realising Damian was serious. "Understood. I can look into some discreet options for you. You want it done without her knowing it's from you?"

Damian looked out the window for a moment, then back at the investigator. "Exactly. I don't want her to know, not yet anyway."

The investigator, sensing the shift in Damian's tone, nodded briskly. "I'll get back to you with the details," he said, closing the folder and tucking it under his arm. "I'll make sure it's handled quietly, just like you want."

Damian gave a curt nod, his gaze still fixed out the window. "Good. Make it quick."

The investigator offered a small smile, trying to lighten the mood. "I'll be in touch soon, Mr. Prescott. You'll have everything by the end of the week."

Without waiting for a response, the investigator turned on his heel and headed for the door, pulling it shut behind him with a quiet click.

Damian leaned back in his chair, his fingers tapping rhythmically on the desk as he thought it through. If Sophie's debt was gone, she wouldn't have to juggle three jobs. That meant less stress, more time, and fewer excuses about not going out. But he knew he was walking a fine line. If she ever found out he had meddled in her finances without her knowing, she wouldn't take it lightly. The risk was huge, she valued her independence, and if she saw this as him trying to control her, it could backfire in ways he wasn't prepared for.

Still, the thought of having her in his life more often tugged at him. He was willing to take the gamble.

Chapter Eleven

Sophie sat at the small kitchen table on Thursday afternoon, her eyes scanning the paper in front of her. Her student loan statement had arrived, but something was off, there was no balance. Her heart skipped a beat as she read and reread the number: zero. Someone had paid off her entire debt.

Confusion and disbelief flooded her as she immediately reached for her phone. She dialled the loan agency, her hands trembling slightly. After a few rings, a representative picked up.

"Hi, I'm calling to ask about my student loan balance. It says it's been paid off, but I didn't... I mean, I didn't pay it."

The agent on the other end clicked through some files. "Yes, it appears your loan has been fully paid by an anonymous donor."

"Anonymous?" Sophie repeated, her shock turning into suspicion. "There's no way to know who paid it?"

"I'm afraid not, Miss Highland. The payment was made anonymously, and that's all the information we have."

Sophie thanked the agent and hung up, staring at the statement in disbelief. Who would do this? Why? The unanswered questions swirled in her mind, leaving her feeling unsettled.

Sophie's mother, seated on the couch in the living room, noticed the perplexed expression on her daughter's face, and called out gently, "Is everything alright, honey?"

Sophie blinked, pulling herself from her spiralling thoughts. She walked over, clutching the loan statement tightly in her hand. "Mom, I… I just got this in the mail." She handed the paper over, her voice still shaky. "My student loan, someone paid it off. The whole thing."

Her mother adjusted her glasses, glancing over the document. "What? Paid off? By whom?"

"I don't know," Sophie replied, her voice filled with disbelief. "I called the loan agency, and they said it was an anonymous donor. Someone just... wiped it clean."

Her mother looked up, equally shocked but with a hint of concern in her eyes. "That's a lot of money, Sophie. Are you sure this isn't some kind of mistake?"

"I asked. It's real," Sophie sighed, running a hand through her hair. "But I have no idea who would do something like this, and it's kind of freaking me out."

Her mother, sensing her daughter's unease, reached out and placed a comforting hand on her arm. "Well, it's certainly strange. But maybe... it was your father."

Sophie paused, considering the idea for a moment. "Do you think?" she asked, her voice hesitant, though the pit in her stomach didn't ease.

Her mother gave a small shrug. "He's got the money, and maybe he felt guilty. Who else could it be?"

Sophie frowned, feeling a mix of confusion and scepticism. "But why now? After all these years?"

Her mother didn't have an answer, but her eyes softened with empathy. "Sometimes people change, sweetheart. It could be his way of trying to make amends."

Sophie nodded slowly, though her gut told her something didn't add up.

Sophie lay awake most of the night, her mind spinning over the mysterious disappearance of her debt. She couldn't shake the feeling of unease, but after hours of thinking, she finally convinced herself it must have been her father. He was the only one with the means, and maybe, after all these years, guilt had finally gotten to him.

But as she stared at the ceiling, the thought didn't bring any comfort. "It doesn't change anything," she whispered to herself. He may have paid off her debt, but it wouldn't erase the years of absence, the hurt he'd caused by walking away when her mother needed him the most. Sophie felt resolute, his money wouldn't buy back her trust or change how she felt about him.

Sophie got up the next morning, bleary-eyed from a restless night. She shuffled into the kitchen, where her mother was already seated with her cup of tea. "I've decided it must have been dad," Sophie said, her voice flat. "He's the only one who could've paid off the loan."

Her mother looked up; concern etched across her face. "Yes, I think you are right."

Sophie shrugged. "But it doesn't change anything, mum. I don't care if he's trying to make up for leaving us all those years ago. It's too late."

She leaned against the counter, arms crossed. "I just hope he doesn't try to contact me. Because I'm not interested in whatever he thinks this is supposed to fix."

Sophie sat down at the kitchen table, still turning the idea over in her mind. "I think I will give up the job at the gym," she began, tracing a finger along the rim of her coffee cup.

Her mother looked up, surprised. "Really? You've been doing that for a while now. What's changed?"

"With the loan paid off, I don't need a third job anymore," Sophie explained, her tone thoughtful. "But I want to keep working at the café. I can start saving properly now, build up something for the future."

Her mother nodded, a small smile forming. "It makes sense. You've always been careful about planning ahead. If the café makes you happy and helps you save, then why not?"

Sophie sighed in relief, grateful for the support. "Yeah, I think I'll feel more settled with just the two jobs. Besides, the café is more flexible, and I actually enjoy it there. It'll be nice to have some time back for myself too."

As Sophie sipped her coffee, the thought of finally having a weekend to herself brought a sense of excitement she hadn't felt in a long time. She envisioned two entire days free from the responsibilities of work, where she could simply relax and enjoy her own company.

Her mind drifted to possibilities, sleeping in without an alarm, reading that book she had been meaning to start, or maybe taking a long walk in the park. She could visit her favourite café; the one known for its cozy atmosphere and delicious pastries and just indulge in a leisurely brunch.

Sophie smiled at the idea of lounging in her pyjamas all day, catching up on shows she had missed or even exploring new hobbies she had pushed aside. The thought of having no obligations, no deadlines, and no pressure felt liberating. For the first time in a while, she could focus on herself and recharge, without the nagging weight of her old student debt hanging over her.

Friday morning came quickly, and Sophie found herself arriving at the office a little earlier than usual. The air was crisp with the promise of a busy day, and the quiet hum of the building greeted her as she stepped inside. She made her way up to her desk, settling in before anyone else arrived. The stillness of the office in the early morning was comforting, allowing her a moment of calm before the inevitable bustle of the day. Sophie took a deep breath, organising her workspace, mentally preparing herself to dive into the tasks ahead.

Damian entered the office, his gaze immediately drawn to Sophie, already at her desk, focused and prepared for the day. Her presence had a way of brightening the space, and he couldn't help but walk over to her.

"Morning, Sophie," he greeted, his tone warm. "How are you this morning?"

Sophie looked up, meeting his eyes with a soft smile. "Morning, Damian. I'm fine, thanks. How about you?"

"I'm good," he replied, but his attention lingered on her.

"Friday is always a happy day," she continued with a slight chuckle, "though this Friday is even happier."

Damian raised an eyebrow, intrigued. "And why is that?"

Sophie smiled, "Because I get a whole weekend off for once!"

Damian grinned back. "That definitely sounds like something to celebrate. How did that happen?"

Sophie's brows furrowed as she considered her response. "Someone paid off my student loan," she said, her voice tinged with disbelief. "The only person I can think of is my father. My mother seems to think it could have been him, too."

Damian nodded, keeping his expression neutral, though inside, he felt a wave of satisfaction. "That's... surprising. How do you feel about it?" he asked, masking his own knowledge of the situation.

Sophie sighed, her expression resolute. "Don't get me wrong, I am grateful," she began, her voice firm. "But I really hope he doesn't think this means he can just waltz back into my life because of it. That's not going to happen." Her eyes darkened slightly, betraying the hurt beneath her calm exterior. "I'm not giving him any reason to hurt me again."

Damian could see the walls she had built around herself, and it only reinforced what he already suspected, trust wasn't going to come easily for Sophie.

Damian leaned against the edge of her desk, adopting a casual tone. "So, Sophie," he began, trying to keep things light, "how about we go out for lunch on Saturday? You know, to celebrate your new freedom from the student loan. It's a big deal, and you deserve to enjoy it a little."

He gave her a relaxed smile, hoping the invitation didn't come off as too forward. "What do you say? It'll be my treat."

Sophie paused, her fingers lightly tapping on her desk as she considered Damian's offer. After a moment, she looked up at him with a soft smile. "Why not?" she said, her voice warm with appreciation. "Thank you, Damian. I would love to."

There was a flicker of excitement in her eyes, and the casualness of her agreement put both of them at ease.

Damian smiled, relieved. "Great, I'll pick you up around midday, is that okay?"

Sophie nodded, giving him a playful but firm look. "Only a casual lunch, nothing fancy. Ok?"

Damian chuckled, raising his hands in mock surrender. "Okay, casual it is."

Ryan and Alex strolled into the office, mid-conversation, when the sight before them made them pause. There was Damian Prescott, leaning casually against Sophie's desk, his posture relaxed, his expression uncharacteristically warm as he spoke to her. Sophie, for her part, seemed engaged but calm, her usual guarded demeanour slightly softened.

Both Ryan and Alex exchanged a quick glance, their eyebrows shooting up in unison. Curiosity flickered in their expressions as they took in the scene. Ryan's lips curled into a knowing smirk, his sharp eyes flickering with interest. "Well, this is new," he muttered under his breath, low enough for only Alex to hear.

Alex, always the quieter of the two, raised an eyebrow but said nothing, choosing instead to watch the unexpected interaction unfold. His surprise, however, was evident in the way his gaze lingered on Sophie. Prescott was known for being aloof, rarely indulging in casual conversations with employees, let alone taking time to stand at anyone's desk.

Both men had recently stopped pursuing Sophie on a personal level, finally accepting her polite but firm rejections—a change that Sophie had quietly welcomed. Yet, seeing Damian so effortlessly draw her into a conversation sparked a new wave of intrigue.

Ryan leaned slightly closer to Alex; his voice low but laced with amusement. "Looks like the boss is taking a shine to our Sophie."

Alex crossed his arms, a faint smile tugging at the corner of his lips. "We seen that coming, but… can you blame him?"

Sophie glanced over at Ryan and Alex as they approached. "I better get to work," she said softly to Damian. "Ryan and Alex just walked in."

Damian gave a nod, a small smile playing at the corners of his lips. "Okay, see you on Saturday," he said, his voice low but warm. Turning, he straightened his suit and addressed the approaching pair. "Good morning, Ryan. Alex," he greeted them with a nod, his composed demeanour back in place as he moved past them toward the lift.

Ryan and Alex exchanged curious glances again as Damian stepped into the elevator, his usual commanding presence effortlessly intact as he headed upstairs to his office.

Ryan raised an eyebrow, a sly grin spreading across his face. "Well, well, well," he said, nudging Alex with his elbow. "Have you ever seen Damian down on this floor talking to anyone but Derek?"

Alex smirked, glancing toward Sophie's desk. "Not once. Looks like Sophie's caught his attention."

Ryan nodded, still watching the elevator doors close behind Damian. "Yeah, and he's not the kind of guy to just stop by for a casual chat."

Alex chuckled. "Definitely not. This'll be interesting to watch."

Sophie felt her cheeks warm as she caught Ryan and Alex's teasing expressions. "Don't be silly," she said, trying to downplay the situation. "He's just being friendly."

Despite her words, a flutter of excitement danced in her stomach, but she quickly shook it off, focusing on her work instead.

As Ryan strolled back to his desk, a playful smirk danced on his lips. "Yes, very friendly," he teased, glancing back at Sophie over his shoulder. His tone was light, but there was a hint of mischief in his eyes, clearly enjoying the moment. Alex chuckled beside him, and Sophie rolled her eyes, feeling both flattered and embarrassed by their banter.

The day flew by for Sophie, each hour passing in a blur of activity and focus. She tackled her tasks with renewed energy, buoyed by the excitement of her lunch plans with Damian. Each interaction with her colleagues felt lighter, and even the usual challenges at work seemed more manageable. By the time the clock ticked closer to quitting time, Sophie felt a sense of accomplishment and satisfaction. The knowledge that she was one step closer to a more carefree weekend made the day feel especially rewarding, leaving her with a smile as she wrapped up her work.

Chapter Twelve

Sophie woke up on Saturday morning to the soft, warm light streaming through her window, the gentle sounds of the city waking up around her. No alarm jangled her peace; it was blissful to rise naturally. Stretching her arms above her head, she felt a wave of contentment wash over her as she slipped out of bed and padded to the bathroom for a refreshing shower.

Afterward, she made her way to the kitchen, the familiar aroma of coffee brewing as she prepared breakfast for herself and her mother. The rhythmic sounds of clinking plates and sizzling eggs filled the air, creating a comforting atmosphere. Once breakfast was ready, she set the table and called her mother to join her.

As they sat down to eat, Sophie looked across the table, her mother's warm smile making her heart swell. "I wanted to let you know," Sophie began, breaking the morning's tranquility, "I'm going out for lunch today."

Her mother raised an eyebrow, curious. "Oh? With whom?"

"Damian," Sophie replied, a hint of excitement in her voice. "He wants to celebrate… you know, the loan being paid off."

Her mother nodded knowingly, her smile widening. "That sounds lovely, dear. Just be yourself and have a great time." Sophie felt a rush of gratitude and anticipation, ready to embrace the day ahead.

"Thanks, Mum," Sophie said, smiling at her mother. "Do you want to go for a small walk outside? Do you feel up to it?"

Her mother's eyes brightened. "Yes, that sounds great," she replied, her voice warm with enthusiasm.

After they finished breakfast, they cleared the table together and tidied up the kitchen. Sophie gently helped her mother into a light jacket, ensuring she was comfortable. They stepped outside, and the fresh air greeted them like an old friend.

Sophie led her mother, Marie, across the road to the park, where the vibrant greens of spring filled the surroundings. The soft sound of rustling leaves and the distant laughter of children playing brought a sense of peace. They walked at a gentle pace, enjoying the beauty of the day and the simple joy of being together. Sophie kept her arm lightly around her mother's waist, offering support as they strolled along the winding path, grateful for these moments that felt so precious.

By the time they returned home, Marie was visibly exhausted but wore a content smile that lit up her face. The gentle exercise had clearly taken a toll, yet the joy of their time together was evident in her sparkling eyes. "Thank you, Sophie. That was lovely," she said, her voice filled with warmth and appreciation.

Sophie wrapped her arms around her mother, pulling her into a gentle hug. "No need to thank me, Mum. I love you," she replied, her heart swelling with affection. The bond they shared felt even stronger after their outing, and Sophie knew that these moments, however simple, were the ones that truly mattered.

As the clock ticked closer to Damian's arrival, Sophie felt a flutter of excitement in her stomach. She stepped into her bedroom and rummaged through her wardrobe, finally settling on a muted yellow sundress that perfectly suited the sunny day. The fabric hugged her waist before flaring out gently at the hips, giving the dress a lovely swing with each step she took.

She admired herself in the mirror, the soft colour complementing her features and adding a touch of brightness to her complexion. The light fabric felt comfortable against her skin, and she couldn't help but smile, feeling both relaxed and confident as she prepared for their lunch together.

Just as Sophie was adjusting her hair one last time, a knock echoed through the apartment. She walked over to the door and opened it to find Damian standing there, looking sharp and effortlessly stylish.

"Hello," he said, a warm smile spreading across his face.

"Hi, Damian!" Sophie replied, returning his smile. "Would you like to meet my mother?"

He nodded enthusiastically. "Yes, I would love to."

Sophie stepped aside, gesturing for him to come in. As he entered, she felt a mix of excitement and nervousness about introducing him to her mother, eager to see how they would get along.

Sophie led Damian into the cozy living room, where her mother, Marie, sat comfortably in her chair. "Mom, this is Damian Prescott," Sophie said, her voice filled with a hint of pride.

"Nice to meet you, Marie," Damian said, extending a hand. "I've heard wonderful things about you."

Marie took his hand with a warm smile. "Oh, it's nice to finally meet the man who's been so supportive of my daughter."

Sophie watched as Damian leaned against the doorframe, effortlessly charming her mother. He had a knack for making people feel at ease, and it showed as he shared a light-hearted story about work. Marie laughed, her eyes sparkling with amusement.

"I can see why Sophie speaks so highly of you," she said, genuinely impressed.

"Thank you! It's easy to be supportive of someone as dedicated as Sophie," he replied, glancing at her with a fond expression.

Sophie felt a wave of relief and happiness as she observed the connection forming between them. The laughter and light banter flowed naturally, and for a moment, it felt like a small family gathering—one filled with warmth and genuine interest.

Sophie wrapped her arms around her mother, giving her a gentle squeeze. "I'll be back in a couple of hours, Mum. You take it easy, okay?"

Marie smiled, her eyes softening as she returned the hug. "I will. Just have a good time, sweetheart."

Before heading out, Sophie went to the kitchen and carefully prepared her mother's medications, organising them neatly in a small pill organiser. She placed it next to the lounge, ensuring it was within easy reach for Marie.

"Here you go, all set for later," Sophie said, glancing back at her mother.

"Thank you, darling," Marie replied, a grateful smile on her face. "You're a good girl. Now go and enjoy your lunch with Damian!"

With a final wave, Sophie stepped out of the apartment, feeling a mix of excitement and anticipation for the afternoon ahead.

As they walked down the hallway, Damian turned to Sophie with a warm smile. "Your mother is delightful," he said, genuinely impressed by Marie's warmth and humour.

Sophie beamed, her eyes sparkling with affection. "I agree," she replied, then laughed softly, "but I'm biased, of course."

Damian chuckled, enjoying the light-hearted moment. "Well, it's nice to see where you get your charm from."

Sophie blushed slightly, the compliment making her feel even more connected to him as they headed toward the stairs.

As they walked down the stairs, Sophie turned to Damian with an eager expression. "So, where are we going?" she asked, curiosity lighting up her face.

Damian smiled, his eyes glinting with mischief. "Ah, that's a surprise," he replied, enjoying the playful suspense. "But I promise you'll love it."

Sophie raised an eyebrow, intrigued. "You're keeping secrets now?"

"Just a little," he teased, the anticipation making the air between them feel charged. "Trust me; it'll be worth the wait."

Damian opened the door to the sleek town car, gesturing for Sophie to step inside. As she settled into the plush leather seat, he followed suit, closing the door gently behind him. The driver, a polished professional, immediately engaged the car's engine, and they smoothly pulled away from the curb.

Inside the car, the atmosphere was relaxed yet charged with anticipation. Damian glanced at Sophie, a smile playing on his lips as he appreciated the way the muted yellow of her dress contrasted with the luxurious interior. "You look amazing," he remarked, the compliment sincere.

"Thanks," Sophie replied, her cheeks flushing slightly as she tucked a loose strand of hair behind her ear. "So, any hints about our destination?"

"Patience," Damian said, his eyes sparkling with amusement as the cityscape began to unfold outside the window.

The town car rolled to a smooth stop outside a charming bistro nestled on a quiet street lined with trees. The exterior was inviting, with warm yellow awnings and an assortment of potted flowers adorning the entrance. The soft murmur of laughter and clinking glasses wafted through the open windows, creating a lively yet intimate ambiance.

As the driver opened the door for them, Damian stepped out first, extending his hand to help Sophie navigate the small step. She took his hand, grateful for the gesture, and together they walked toward the entrance. The scent of freshly baked bread and herbs wafted through the air, heightening Sophie's anticipation.

Damian smiled down at her, his eyes glinting with enthusiasm. "Welcome to my favourite spot for lunch. I hope you're hungry."

Sophie's excitement bubbled over as they stepped inside, greeted by the warm, welcoming atmosphere and the gentle strumming of a guitar in the background. She felt a flutter of nerves mixed with thrill as she realised this was shaping up to be a memorable afternoon.

Sophie glanced around the bistro, her eyes lighting up as she took in the cozy décor and the vibrant atmosphere. "This looks lovely," she said, her voice filled with genuine appreciation. The soft lighting, combined with the rustic wooden tables and colourful art on the walls, made it feel like a hidden gem.

She turned to Damian with a smile, her excitement palpable. "And yes, I am definitely hungry!" The scent of delicious food wafting from the kitchen made her stomach rumble in agreement, and she couldn't help but feel a wave of warmth at the thought of sharing a meal with him.

Damian chuckled, his expression brightening at her enthusiasm. "I know you're going to love it." He led her to a small table by the window, where they could enjoy their meal while soaking in the charming view outside.

Damian and Sophie scanned the menu in comfortable silence, each occasionally glancing up to catch the other's expression. When they had made their choices, Damian signalled the waiter with an effortless wave.

After placing their orders, he added, "And two glasses of sparkling water, please."

Turning back to Sophie, his lips curved into a warm smile. "I think we made some solid choices," he said lightly, his tone carrying a hint of playfulness as if sharing a small conspiracy. "So, what did you do this morning?" he asked, genuinely curious. His tone was light, and he leaned slightly forward, his interest evident in his eyes.

Sophie's face lit up as she recounted her morning with her mother. "Oh, I took my mum for a little walk in the park," she said, her voice brimming with enthusiasm. "It was nice to get some fresh air together, and she really enjoyed it." A smile spread across her face as the memory warmed her heart. "After that, we just had a quiet morning at home. She gets very tired easily."

Damian nodded, his expression softening. "You really love your mum, and it's clear you enjoy looking after her."

Sophie's smile faded slightly as she reflected. "It was hard at first," she admitted. "Her symptoms started when I was fifteen. Then Dad left, so it was up to me. But you do anything for the people you love, don't you?" The conviction in her voice was palpable, underscoring the deep bond she shared with her mother.

Damian's gaze grew distant as he shared his story. "My parents passed when I was twenty-one. Car accident," he said, his voice steady but laced with an undertone of sadness.

Sophie felt a surge of empathy and instinctively reached across the table, grabbing his hand. "I'm so sorry, Damian. That's terrible," she said, her eyes reflecting her heartfelt concern. The warmth of her touch seemed to bridge the gap between their shared experiences, creating a moment of profound connection amidst their vulnerabilities.

Damian held onto Sophie's hand, feeling the warmth of her touch anchor him in the moment. She didn't pull away, allowing their fingers to intertwine gently, as if sealing a silent understanding between them.

Just then, their drinks arrived, interrupting the intimacy of the moment. The server placed the glasses on the table, breaking the tension but not the connection. Damian released her hand reluctantly, flashing her a soft smile as he picked up his drink. "Cheers to a lovely lunch," he said, raising his glass. Sophie mirrored his gesture, her heart fluttering as they clinked their glasses together, both aware of the deepening bond between them.

As the server returned with their meals, the aroma of delicious food filled the air. Damian's dish was a beautifully plated salmon, glistening with a light glaze, while Sophie had chosen a vibrant salad bursting with fresh ingredients. The colours were as appealing as the enticing scents wafting from the plates.

They dug in, the first bites met with satisfied murmurs. Laughter flowed easily between them, punctuated by playful teasing about each other's food choices. Damian raised an eyebrow, pretending to be shocked at Sophie's healthy selection. "A salad? Really? I thought we were celebrating!"

Sophie laughed, her eyes sparkling. "Hey, someone has to keep things balanced!"

Their conversation danced from light-hearted banter to deeper topics, each shared story and joke drawing them closer. They lost track of time, enveloped in their own little world, savouring both the meal and the growing connection. Every laugh felt like a thread weaving their lives together, and both felt an undeniable warmth in each other's presence.

As they polished off the last bites of their meal, Damian leaned back in his chair, a satisfied smile on his face. "That was delicious," he remarked, glancing at Sophie, who nodded in agreement, her expression equally content.

"Would you like to go for a walk?" he asked, his tone casual yet inviting. The idea of continuing their time together in the fresh air seemed appealing, especially after such a lovely meal.

Sophie's eyes lit up at the suggestion. "I'd love that," she replied, her enthusiasm evident. The prospect of strolling together, perhaps exploring the nearby park or waterfront, added an exciting layer to their day.

Damian signalled for the check, and once settled, they both stood, ready to enjoy the next part of their outing. The promise of a leisurely walk together filled the air with a sense of anticipation.

As they stepped outside, the sun cast a warm glow over the bustling streets, and Sophie's excitement bubbled over. She began to skip playfully, her laughter ringing through the air as she ran circles around Damian.

"Catch me if you can!" she called out, her eyes sparkling with mischief.

Damian chuckled, a wide grin spreading across his face as he playfully lunged after her. She darted away, effortlessly weaving, her sundress twirling around her as she moved.

Sophie's carefree spirit seemed to infuse the moment with joy, and Damian couldn't help but laugh at her infectious energy. "You're fast!" he teased, quickening his pace in an attempt to catch up.

"Just a little!" Sophie replied, her voice playful and teasing. She glanced back at him, a triumphant smile on her face as she skipped ahead, her laughter trailing behind her like a melody.

As he finally closed the gap, Damian reached out, lightly grabbing her wrist, pulling her into a gentle spin. "Got you!" he exclaimed, both of them bursting into laughter, the world around them fading away as they revelled in the simple delight of each other's company.

Sophie leaned into Damian's chest, her heart swelling with happiness. "I haven't had this much fun in a long time," she confessed, her voice soft and genuine.

Damian felt a warmth spread through him at her words. He wrapped his arms around her, holding her close as they stood together in the sunshine. The gentle rhythm of their breaths mingled as he felt her relax against him, the tension of the day melting away.

"You deserve it," he replied, his tone sincere. "You work so hard; it's nice to see you enjoy yourself."

Sophie closed her eyes for a moment, savouring the comfort of his embrace. It felt safe and inviting, a stark contrast to the responsibilities that often weighed her down. In that moment, surrounded by the sounds of the city and the warmth of his body, she felt a sense of peace that had been elusive for so long.

Sophie slowly pulled away, the warmth of Damian's embrace lingering in the air between them. As she looked up into his eyes, she could see the reluctance in his expression. He hesitated for a moment before releasing her, his hands slipping from her waist to rest at his sides.

"Don't go too far," he said playfully, a hint of a smile tugging at the corners of his lips, as if he didn't want their moment to end just yet.

Sophie chuckled softly, a flutter of excitement still dancing in her chest. "I won't," she promised, her heart racing from the connection they shared. She felt a mix of warmth and yearning, wishing she could linger in that moment a little longer.

Damian was completely captivated by Sophie, revelling in the laughter and warmth that surrounded them. Every smile she flashed, and every light-hearted comment brought him closer to her, making him forget the world outside their bubble. They strolled leisurely, the sun casting a golden hue around them, enhancing the magic of the moment.

But then, Sophie's phone buzzed in her pocket, breaking the spell. She pulled it out and glanced at the screen, her expression shifting slightly as she realised the time. "Oh no," she said, a tinge of disappointment in her voice. "I better get back. My mum will be expecting me."

Damian felt a pang of regret at the thought of their time together ending so soon. "Of course," he replied, trying to mask his disappointment. "Let's head back then." As they walked, he couldn't shake the feeling of wanting to steal just a few more moments with her, to stretch this beautiful day a little longer.

As they approached the town car, Damian opened the door for Sophie, and she slipped inside, her heart fluttering with excitement. The drive back felt shorter than before, filled with comfortable silence and occasional smiles exchanged in the rearview mirror. Damian couldn't help but steal glances at her, admiring the way the afternoon light danced in her hair.

Upon arriving at Sophie's apartment, Damian stepped out first and came around to help her out of the car. The moment felt electric, the air thick with unspoken words and shared laughter. He walked her to the door, their hands brushing occasionally, igniting sparks of connection between them.

Standing in the hallway, Sophie turned to face him, her heart racing. The evening light framed Damian's face, accentuating his features in a way that made him look almost too good to be true. With a mix of confidence and nervousness, she stepped closer, her breath catching in her throat.

"Thank you for today," she said softly, her eyes locking onto his.

Damian smiled, a warmth spreading through him. "I had a great time too."

In a moment of boldness, Sophie leaned in, pressing her lips against his in a gentle, lingering kiss. It was sweet and tentative, filled with the promise of something deeper. Damian responded instinctively, wrapping his arms around her waist, pulling her closer as he deepened the kiss, savouring the connection they had built throughout the day. When they finally pulled apart, both were breathless, smiles bright on their faces, aware that this might just be the beginning of something special.

Chapter Thirteen

It was Thursday, and Damian found himself lost in thought, reflecting on the lunch he had with Sophie last Saturday. It had gone surprisingly well, much better than he had expected. Sophie had seemed more relaxed, and he had finally met her mother, Marie. From the moment they spoke, Damian had been struck by Marie's quiet strength and sharpness, qualities that reminded him so much of Sophie.

One thing was abundantly clear to him now: if he could win over Marie, he would have a better chance of truly winning Sophie's heart. It was obvious how much Sophie valued her mother's opinion, and their bond ran deep.

But what was the next step? How could he spend more time with both women and show that he wasn't just serious about Sophie, but also deeply respectful of the relationship she shared with her mother?

Then it hit him, an invitation. Something thoughtful, not too formal. Maybe a relaxed dinner at his place where they could all connect on a personal level. But then another idea struck—a day out, something Sophie would love to experience with her mother. A winery tour. Marie might enjoy the peaceful setting, and it would give him more time to show that he truly cared about them both.

Damian's mind raced with possibilities, but the vineyard felt perfect—simple, intimate, and thoughtful. His decision made, he picked up his phone, dialling Sophie's number. His heart thumped in his chest as he waited, the familiar sound of her voice coming through on the other end.

"Hello?"

"Hi, Sophie. How are you today?" Damian asked, trying to keep his voice casual. He hadn't seen her since Saturday, giving her space as she needed it.

"Damian, hey! I'm good, thank you. How about you?"

"I'm doing well, thanks. Actually, I was hoping to ask if you and your mother would like to join me for a small winery tour on Saturday?"

There was a pause, and Damian held his breath, hoping she'd like the idea.

"Oh? A winery tour?" Sophie sounded intrigued. "I'd have to ask Mum, but that sounds really lovely. Can I let you know tomorrow?"

"Of course, take your time. I made sure the tour wouldn't be too strenuous for your mum, and we can arrange a wheelchair if she needs it."

"Wow, thank you, Damian. That's really thoughtful of you," Sophie said, a note of excitement in her voice. "I'll talk to her tonight and let you know tomorrow."

"Perfect," Damian replied, a small smile tugging at his lips. "I look forward to your decision."

As they hung up, Sophie's heart fluttered with excitement. She was already looking forward to the weekend, while Damian felt hopeful, knowing he was one step closer to proving just how much they both meant to him.

Sophie spent the rest of her day feeling a quiet excitement bubbling inside her. She couldn't wait to get home and ask her mother about Damian's invitation. The idea of spending time together outside, in such a beautiful setting, felt like a welcome change. She also couldn't shake how thoughtful Damian had been in considering her mother's comfort, it made the idea even more appealing.

As soon as she stepped through the door that evening, Sophie found her mother resting on the couch with a book in her lap. "Mum?" she called out, her voice carrying a note of anticipation.

Marie looked up, a soft smile on her face. "Hey, sweetheart. How was your day?"

"Good! Actually, Damian invited us to do something this weekend," Sophie began, her heart fluttering a little. "He wants to take us on a small winery tour. He said it won't be too much for you, and we can get a wheelchair if you need it."

Her mother's eyebrows lifted in surprise, her smile widening. "A winery tour? That sounds like fun, sweetheart! I'd love to go."

"Really?" Sophie's face brightened, a sense of relief washing over her.

"Yes, really," Marie replied, giving her daughter a reassuring nod. "It'll be nice to get out for a bit, and it sounds like Damian put a lot of thought into it."

Sophie beamed, excitement flickering in her eyes. "I'll let him know we're in, then!"

Sophie couldn't wait until the next day to give Damian the news. Her heart raced with excitement as she grabbed her phone and dialled his number. The phone rang only once before Damian answered.

"Hello?" his familiar voice came through, warm and curious.

"Hi, Damian," Sophie said, unable to hide the smile in her voice. "We'd love to join you on Saturday."

There was a brief pause, and she could almost picture the relief and happiness on his face.

"That's fantastic," Damian replied, his voice filled with enthusiasm. "I'm really glad you both can make it."

Sophie felt a flutter in her chest. "Mum's really looking forward to it. She thought it sounded like fun."

"Great, I'll make sure it's a special day for both of you," he promised, his tone gentle but full of meaning.

Sophie found herself smiling again. "I'm sure it will be."

After exchanging a few more details about the plans, they ended the call, and Sophie felt a weight lift off her shoulders. The anticipation of the weekend buzzed in her mind, filling her with a sense of excitement she hadn't felt in a while. She smiled to herself, already envisioning the day.

Sophie felt a surge of happiness, knowing her mother would finally get to know Damian better, and they'd have the chance to spend time together outside of their usual routines.

Maybe Damian was serious about her, she thought, a hopeful flicker lighting up in her heart. She had been working at Prescott Design Group for over a month now, and in that time, her feelings for him had only grown. Maybe there was a future with Damian, something real and lasting. The thought both excited and terrified her, but she couldn't deny the possibility anymore.

Damian hung up the phone, a smile tugging at the corners of his lips. Sophie couldn't even wait until tomorrow to let him know—they were coming on Saturday. The thought sent a wave of excitement through him, but also a sense of responsibility. He wanted everything to be perfect, especially for Sophie's mother.

He leaned back in his chair, already planning how he could make the day special. The first thing he needed to do was arrange a wheelchair, ensuring that Marie would be comfortable throughout the winery tour. It had to be easy-going, enjoyable, and relaxed. This wasn't just about impressing Sophie; it was about showing her mother that he cared deeply for both of them.

Damian's mind raced through all the details, he'd make sure the tour was slow-paced, with plenty of opportunities to sit and relax. He'd even have a private tasting arranged, with the best views, and maybe a picnic area where they could enjoy some quiet time together. He wanted this day to be something they both remembered, a day where Marie could see how much Sophie meant to him.

He picked up his phone again, making a few calls to the vineyard to ensure everything would be ready. This wasn't just any day out; it was the chance to show Sophie and her mother just how serious he was.

Saturday arrived with a crisp, clear sky, and Sophie could hardly contain her excitement. Damian had promised to pick them up at 11am, and she wanted everything to be perfect. She carefully helped her mother get ready, making sure Marie had everything she needed, a light jacket in case it got cool, her favourite scarf, and comfortable shoes for the day out. Marie smiled, sensing Sophie's energy, which was contagious.

Sophie herself had chosen a short red sundress that made her feel confident. The dress flowed just above her knees, showing off her legs in a way that made her feel both elegant and playful. She added a touch of mascara, just enough to make her eyes stand out, and smiled at her reflection, pleased with the simple yet thoughtful effort. She wasn't sure why, but today felt special, like a new beginning.

As she finished getting ready, she glanced at her watch. It was almost time. Sophie's heart raced a little faster, not just from the excitement of spending the day with Damian, but because her mother was coming too. She hoped this day would be as perfect as she imagined, a chance for all of them to enjoy each other's company and for her and her mother to see the man Damian really was.

At exactly 11am, a knock echoed through the hallway, and Sophie's heart leaped in her chest. She dashed to the door, trying to contain her excitement, and took a deep breath before swinging it open.

"Hello, Damian," she greeted, her voice warm and bright. He stood there, looking handsome in a crisp shirt and well-fitted pants that highlighted his figure. His hair was neatly styled, and he had a confident, easy smile that made her stomach flutter.

"You look lovely," he said, his gaze lingering on her for a moment longer than usual. Sophie noticed his eyes flicker to the subtle makeup she had applied—something she didn't typically wear. It was nice to see that he appreciated her effort.

"Thank you!" she replied, feeling a blush creep up her cheeks. "I wanted to look nice for our day out."

Damian's smile widened, and he stepped inside, the warmth of his presence filling the entryway. "I think you succeeded," he said, his tone genuine. "Is your mum ready?"

"Yes, just a moment," Sophie said, turning back to call for her mother, her heart racing with anticipation for the day ahead.

Sophie's mother joined them a moment later, her smile warm as she greeted Damian. "Good morning, Damian," she said, her eyes sparkling with excitement.

Damian turned to them both, his expression brightening. "I'm lucky to be escorting two lovely ladies today," he said with a charming grin. "Your chariot awaits."

Together, they made their way downstairs, the anticipation building with each step. When they reached the front of the building, Sophie's eyes widened in delight at the sight of a sleek stretch limousine waiting at the curb. The polished exterior gleamed in the sunlight, making it look like something out of a movie.

Sophie turned to Damian, her excitement bubbling over. "I've never been in a limousine before!" she exclaimed, her voice full of joy.

Damian smiled, a hint of mischief in his eyes. "Well, you better get used to them," he said, his tone light and teasing. He opened the door for them, and Sophie's heart raced as she stepped inside, the plush interior wrapping around her like a warm embrace. This day was off to a perfect start.

Damian gently helped Marie into the limousine, making sure she was comfortably settled in the plush leather seat. He adjusted the seatbelt for her, ensuring she was secure, then slid into the seat next to Sophie. As the door closed behind them, Sophie felt a rush of excitement wash over her.

The driver smoothly pulled away from the curb, the cityscape gradually giving way to sprawling green fields and picturesque vineyards. Sophie leaned back, glancing at her mother, who wore a contented smile, and then at Damian, who seemed relaxed and happy beside her.

"Are you ready for a day of wine and laughter?" Damian asked, his eyes twinkling.

"Absolutely!" Sophie replied, her enthusiasm evident. The conversation flowed easily between them as they made their way outside the city, the landscape becoming more beautiful with each passing mile.

Before long, they arrived at Chateau Montelena, the stunning winery emerging in front of them, surrounded by lush vineyards and rolling hills. The grandeur of the chateau, with its classic architecture, took Sophie's breath away. She felt a thrill of anticipation for the day ahead as the driver parked and opened the door for them.

As they stepped out of the limousine, Damian gestured to the wheelchair that had been arranged for Marie. "Here it is," he said, his tone both reassuring and practical. "If you'd prefer to walk, we can leave this behind and pick it up later. It's completely up to you."

Marie looked at the wheelchair, then at her daughter and Damian. A smile spread across her face. "I think I'll give it a try, but let's see how I feel after a bit of walking," she replied, determination in her voice.

Sophie admired her mother's spirit. "Just take it easy, Mum. We want you to enjoy the day."

Damian nodded, ready to assist in any way. "We can take our time, and if you need a break, the chair is right here." He helped Marie out of the car, offering his arm for support as they made their way toward the entrance of the chateau.

With Sophie walking beside them, the atmosphere felt light and hopeful, the sun shining down on what promised to be a memorable day.

As they entered the chateau, a sense of warmth and elegance enveloped them. The guide led them through the expansive vineyard, explaining the winemaking process with enthusiasm. Sophie listened intently, occasionally stealing glances at Damian, who seemed genuinely engaged and excited to share this experience with them.

Halfway through the tour, Marie began to tire, and she hesitated, glancing at Sophie. "I think I might need to sit for a bit," she admitted, her tone slightly apologetic.

"Of course, Mum," Sophie said gently. "Let's get you settled."

Damian, ever attentive, quickly moved to the wheelchair. "Why don't you take a break? I can push you for a while," he offered, his voice filled with warmth.

Marie nodded gratefully, and with Sophie's help, she transferred into the chair. Damian took hold of the handles, and as he pushed her along the path, he made sure to navigate smoothly over the uneven ground.

"Thank you, Damian," Marie said, her eyes sparkling with appreciation. "You're a gentleman."

"Just doing my part," he replied with a friendly smile, glancing back at Sophie, who beamed with pride.

As they continued the tour, the atmosphere became more relaxed, with laughter and easy conversation flowing between them. Sophie felt a sense of happiness wash over her, watching the bond form between Damian and her mother. The vineyard was breathtaking, and with each sip of information from the guide, they were learning more about the craft that connected them all in this moment.

After the informative tour of the winemaking process, they gathered in a picturesque outdoor area for the wine tasting. Sunlight danced across the lush vineyards, creating a beautiful backdrop. However, Marie surprised them with her request.

"I think I'll pass on the wine tasting," she said, glancing at the sprawling scenery before them. "I'd rather just sit in the sun and enjoy the view."

"Are you sure, Mum?" Sophie asked, a hint of concern in her voice.

"Yes, dear. You go off with Damian for a while. It's a lovely view here, and I'll enjoy it," Marie insisted, her smile reassuring.

Damian felt a wave of gratitude toward Marie for allowing him this chance to have some one-on-one time with Sophie. He glanced at her, his heart swelling with appreciation. "Thank you, Marie, we'll get you settled in a beautiful spot," he said warmly.

As Marie settled into a comfortable spot under a shade tree, Damian turned to Sophie, a playful smile crossing his face. The opportunity for them to connect deeper in this beautiful setting filled him with excitement. The thought of sharing this moment with her, away from the distractions of everyday life, felt almost intoxicating.

"Shall we?" he asked, gesturing toward the tasting area, his eyes sparkling with anticipation.

Damian and Sophie walked toward the private tasting area, the warm sun enveloping them as they settled at a small, rustic table adorned with a spread of elegant wine glasses and a selection of bottles. The soft sounds of the vineyard surrounded them—the gentle rustle of leaves and the distant laughter of other guests, but in that moment, it felt like they were in their own world.

As the sommelier poured the first sample, Damian leaned slightly closer to Sophie, his presence warm and inviting. "I hope you're ready to become a wine connoisseur," he said playfully, raising an eyebrow.

Sophie laughed, her eyes sparkling with excitement. "I'm more of a novice, but I'm willing to learn," she replied, taking in the sight of him. The way he looked at her— intensely yet tenderly—made her heart flutter.

With the first sip, the rich flavours danced on their tongues. "What do you think?" Damian asked, watching her expression with keen interest.

"It's delicious!" she exclaimed, savouring the taste. "I never knew wine could be so complex."

"Just wait until we try the next one," he said, pouring another glass. "Each wine has its own story, just like people."

Sophie nodded, intrigued. "What story does this one have?" she asked, genuinely curious.

Damian leaned back, a thoughtful look on his face. "This one is a bit bold and unexpected—like a surprise in a bottle," he said, a smirk playing on his lips. "It takes a little time to appreciate, but when you do, it's unforgettable."

Sophie felt a warmth bloom in her chest at his words. They both shared a laugh, the atmosphere relaxed and comfortable as they continued to sip and discuss the wines. As they moved from one tasting to the next, the conversation flowed effortlessly, filled with playful banter and deeper exchanges about their lives and dreams.

Every now and then, their eyes would meet, and in those fleeting moments, the world outside faded away. Damian felt a sense of connection that was both exhilarating and profound, while Sophie revelled in the way he made her feel seen and cherished.

"Thank you for today," she said softly, her voice sincere as they finished their last glass. "This is more than I ever expected."

Damian's gaze softened, his heart swelling with affection. "I'm glad you're enjoying it. You deserve moments like this," he replied, the sincerity in his voice making her cheeks flush.

They sat in comfortable silence for a moment, soaking in the beauty of the vineyard, the gentle breeze, and the undeniable chemistry that crackled between them. It was a day that felt a shared experience that neither of them would forget.

After their private wine tasting, Damian and Sophie made their way back to where Marie was sitting under the shade of a large oak tree, enjoying the tranquil view of the vineyard. As they approached, Sophie's excitement bubbled over.

"Mum, you won't believe how amazing the wines were! I tried a bold red that had such deep flavours, and then there was this white that was so refreshing and crisp!" Sophie gushed, her eyes sparkling with enthusiasm.

Marie smiled, though her expression revealed a hint of fatigue. "That sounds wonderful, dear," she said, her voice warm yet weary. "I'm glad you both had a good time."

Damian knelt beside Marie, a look of concern crossing his face. "Are you feeling okay, Marie? We don't want to wear you out."

Marie waved a dismissive hand, but Sophie noticed the slight droop in her mother's shoulders. "I'm alright, just a little tired. It's been a lovely day, but I think I could use some rest."

Sophie exchanged a glance with Damian, who nodded slightly, understanding the unspoken message. "How about we head home then?" he suggested gently. "We can make sure you're comfortable, and Sophie can tell you all about the wines on the way back."

Marie smiled gratefully. "That sounds like a good idea, Damian. Thank you for your thoughtfulness."

As they walked back to the car, Sophie continued to excitedly recount their experiences, detailing the flavours and aromas of each wine they'd tasted, her voice filled with passion. Damian listened intently, his heart swelling with admiration for both women.

Once they settled Marie into the back seat of the limousine, Sophie slid in beside her, leaning against her mother affectionately. Damian took the seat opposite them, ready for the drive back home.

As they pulled away from the vineyard, the gentle hum of the car and the picturesque scenery outside provided a peaceful backdrop to Sophie's animated storytelling. She was grateful for the day, for the opportunity to share it with her mother and Damian, but she couldn't shake the concern she felt for Marie's tiredness.

"Don't worry, Mum," Sophie said, her voice softening. "We'll make it an early night."

Marie smiled at her daughter, her eyes filled with love and appreciation. "No, you should spend some more time with Damian, if he has the time?"

"Are you sure, Mum?" Sophie asked, her brow furrowing with concern.

Marie nodded, her smile encouraging. "Absolutely, sweetheart. I'd love for you two to enjoy some more time together."

Turning to Damian, Sophie bit her lip, her heart racing a little. "Do you want to spend a bit more time together?"

"Only if your mother is settled and okay," Damian replied, his gaze flickering to Marie to gauge her comfort.

Once they arrived home, Damian offered his arm to Marie, helping her up the stairs with a gentle, steadying hand. Sophie followed closely, her heart swelling with gratitude for Damian's kindness. After they reached Marie's room, Sophie helped her mother settle into bed, tucking the blankets around her with care.

"Here are your meds, Mum," she said softly, handing her the small cup of pills. Marie nodded, taking them willingly, and before long, her eyes began to flutter closed. Sophie watched her mother drift off, a peaceful smile on her lips, before quietly closing the door behind her.

Turning back to Damian, she found him waiting in the hallway. "How about we watch a movie?" he suggested, a hopeful glimmer in his eyes.

"That sounds good," Sophie replied, feeling a spark of excitement at the idea of spending more time with him.

Sophie and Damian settled onto the couch, the soft glow of the television casting a warm light around the room. Damian held a large bowl of buttery popcorn, both occasionally reaching for a handful at the same time and sharing amused glances as the film unfolded.

As the movie played, they found themselves laughing at the clever jokes and light-hearted moments, their voices kept at a gentle volume so as not to disturb Marie. Sophie stole glances at Damian, enjoying the way his eyes sparkled with amusement, and she felt a warmth spreading in her chest.

Every now and then, their hands brushed against each other as they reached for the popcorn, sending a delightful jolt of electricity between them. Sophie felt completely at ease, savouring this simple yet intimate moment with Damian. The laughter they shared created a cozy bubble of connection, allowing them to forget the worries of the day and simply enjoy being together.

As the movie credits rolled, the atmosphere shifted slightly. Damian glanced at the clock, realising the time had flown by. "I probably should go," he said, rising from the couch. Sophie felt a pang of disappointment at the thought of him leaving, a slight frown forming on her lips.

Noticing her expression, Damian stepped closer and gently pulled her into his arms. The warmth of his embrace wrapped around her, momentarily easing her sadness. He looked down at her, a mix of tenderness and vulnerability in his gaze. "Can I kiss you?" he asked softly, his voice barely above a whisper.

Sophie's heart raced at his words, and she nodded, feeling a rush of anticipation. Damian leaned in, their lips meeting in a sweet, lingering kiss that spoke volumes of the bond they had built. In that moment, all her worries faded away, leaving only the warmth of his affection enveloping her.

Damian pulled away slowly, his fingers lingering on Sophie's arms as he fought the urge to stay close. The warmth of the moment clung to them, but he knew he had to leave. He took a deep breath, trying to steady himself, as a hint of reluctance shadowed his features.

"Goodnight, Sophie," he said softly, his voice carrying a mix of warmth and regret. Sophie watched him, her heart heavy as he stepped back, creating distance between them.

With one last lingering look, Damian turned and walked toward the door, his footsteps echoing softly in the quiet room. As he opened the door, he glanced back one last time, a flicker of longing in his eyes before stepping out into the hallway. The door clicked shut behind him, leaving Sophie standing in the dim light, feeling the weight of the moment linger in the air long after he had gone.

Chapter Fourteen

On Tuesday morning, Sophie's work phone buzzed, pulling her attention away from the reports scattered across her desk. She picked it up, glancing briefly at the screen before answering. "Hello?"

"Sophie, it's Damian," came the smooth voice from the other end.

Her heart skipped a beat. "Hi, Damian! What can I do for you?"

"I need a favour," he said, a hint of seriousness in his tone.

"Of course! What is it?"

"I have to attend the San Francisco Design Awards next Saturday," he stated matter-of-factly.

Sophie's excitement bubbled over. "Oh, you're lucky! I'd love to go to those. They sound amazing!"

There was a brief pause on the line before Damian replied, "Well, that's what I'm calling about."

Damian's tone shifted, a hint of urgency creeping in. "So, would you consider being my date for the evening?"

Sophie hesitated, her mind racing with mixed emotions. "I don't know, Damian. That's a bit...."

"Please, Sophie," he pressed, his voice smooth yet sincere. "I just need someone I can trust who won't complicate things for me on the night."

She bit her lip, contemplating his request. "But it's a big event. People will see us together and start making assumptions?"

"Who cares? We know the truth, and that's all that matters," Damian continued on the phone, his tone persuasive yet relaxed.

Sophie hesitated, her mind racing with thoughts of the upcoming event. "To be honest, I don't think I would have anything appropriate to wear. It's a black-tie event," she replied, a hint of concern in her voice.

Damian chuckled softly, undeterred. "I'm sure we can find a way to fix that. You'd look great in anything."

Sophie bit her lip, weighing her options. She envisioned the glamorous atmosphere of the San Francisco Design Awards, the elegant gowns, and the creative energy that would fill the room. As much as she tried to maintain her reservations, excitement bubbled within her.

"Well, I would love to go to the awards," she admitted, feeling her resolve waver. After a moment's pause, she finally sighed and said, "Oh, okay. I'll be your date."

"Great! Thank you, Sophie, you're a lifesaver," Damian replied, his voice filled with relief and genuine appreciation. The tension in his tone eased, replaced by a hint of excitement. "I promise you'll have a good time. I'll make sure of it."

Sophie hung up the phone, a mix of excitement and apprehension swirling in her stomach. As she turned to her desk, Ryan leaned against her desk, a curious smile playing on his lips. "So, are you going to the awards on Saturday?" he asked, clearly intrigued.

"Yeah," Sophie replied, tucking a strand of hair behind her ear. "Damian needed a date, so I said yes."

Ryan raised an eyebrow, a playful grin spreading across his face. "A date with the big boss, huh? Sounds interesting."

Sophie smiled, a flicker of excitement dancing in her eyes. "He needed a date," she replied, attempting to mask the nervous flutter in her stomach.

Ryan leaned closer, smirking. "I'm sure he did."

The thought of attending such a prestigious event with Damian made her feel a mix of anticipation and uncertainty. She hoped it would be a memorable night.

Damian hung up the phone, a satisfied grin spreading across his face. "Step one done," he murmured to himself, feeling a surge of triumph. Now, for step two: getting her a dress. The thought of Sophie in something elegant and stunning ignited his determination. He wanted her to feel special, to shine at the awards, and he was more than willing to make that happen. He began brainstorming ideas, mentally cataloguing the boutiques and designers he knew would have just the right look for her.

By Thursday morning, Sophie was a bundle of nerves about Saturday. Damian had insisted on organising the dress for the event, and when she'd initially objected, he'd brushed it off, saying, "You can give it back afterward if it's such a problem. I just want you to look the part and have a great night. You're doing me a favour, so it's only fair I handle that side of things." After some hesitation, she had reluctantly agreed, and Damian told her to expect a delivery by Thursday afternoon.

Sure enough, like clockwork, a knock came at the door that evening, interrupting the light atmosphere in the room. Sophie opened it to find a delivery person holding a large package. "A package for Sophie Highland," they said, handing it over for her signature.

Curious, she sighed and thanked them before carrying the package inside. Her mother looked up from the kitchen, intrigued. "What did you get?"

Sophie set the package on the dining table and opened the envelope. It read:

Dear Sophie, I want you to look your best on Saturday. I hope you like the dress.

With her heart racing in anticipation, she carefully unwrapped the package. As the last layer fell away, she gasped. There lay the most beautiful gown she had ever seen. A wave of excitement washed over her as she imagined wearing it, picturing how stunning she would feel in such a gorgeous piece.

She gazed at the dress in awe; it was a breathtaking piece made from a shimmering bronze fabric that sparkled with every glimmer of light. The one-shoulder design added a contemporary and elegant flair, while the expertly ruched bodice sculpted a flattering silhouette that would accentuate her curves beautifully.

A daring thigh-high split lent a touch of allure, which would reveal a hint of leg with each movement. The luxurious sheen of the material elevated the dress's overall charm, making it an ideal choice for any formal occasion where sophistication was key. The rich bronze hue perfectly complemented Sophie's eyes, making the entire ensemble feel like it was made just for her.

As Sophie continued to explore the package, she discovered a hidden compartment beneath the dress. Excitement surged through her as she pulled out a pair of matching stilettos. The heels were sleek and elegant, crafted from the same shimmering bronze material as the gown.

With a delicate ankle strap and a pointed toe, they exuded sophistication and perfectly complemented the dress. The heels had just the right height to elongate her legs, enhancing the allure of the thigh-high split. Sophie couldn't help but smile, imagining how stunning she would look in the complete outfit, feeling like a true showstopper.

Her mother entered the dining room just as Sophie held up the dress, her eyes widening in delight. "Oh my, it's beautiful!" she exclaimed, a warm smile spreading across her face. "You will look amazing in that, sweetheart."

Sophie beamed at her mother's approval, feeling a rush of excitement. "Do you really think so?" she asked, holding the dress against her frame to get a better look in the mirror.

"Absolutely!" her mother replied, moving closer to inspect the gown. "The colour will highlight your features perfectly, and that design is so elegant. You're going to turn heads at the awards."

Sophie heard another firm knock at the door and quickly made her way to answer it. Upon opening the door, she was greeted by a delivery person holding a smaller package. She signed for it, curiosity bubbling up inside her.

Once inside, she carried the package to the dining room and carefully placed it on the table. With trembling hands, she opened the envelope, revealing a note that read:

With love, Damian.

Her heart raced as she lifted the lid of the box, and her breath caught in her throat. Nestled inside was an exquisite diamond choker necklace, shimmering brilliantly in the light, each facet reflecting a cascade of colours that took her breath away. The delicate choker was adorned with intricately arranged diamonds that sparkled with every movement.

Alongside it, she discovered matching earrings and a bracelet, all equally stunning and radiant. Sophie felt as though her heart might leap from her chest as she took in the luxurious pieces, a wave of disbelief washing over her. "What on earth?" she whispered, marvelling at the unexpected, extravagant gift before her.

Sophie's mother's eyes widened as she caught sight of the dazzling jewellery. "Oh my, that looks expensive!" she exclaimed, stepping closer to admire the piece. The diamonds sparkled brilliantly in the light, casting a mesmerising glow throughout the room. "Did Damian send this to you?" she asked, her voice filled with awe.

Sophie could only nod in disbelief, still processing the gift. She took a deep breath, glancing at her mother, a mix of excitement and apprehension in her eyes. "It's beautiful, isn't it?" she said, trying to sound casual. "He obviously wants me to wear it with the dress for the awards."

Her mother raised an eyebrow, her expression laced with surprise. "It's very extravagant."

Sophie shrugged, letting out a nervous laugh. "I know, but he was pretty insistent on me looking the part. It's just for the night; I'll be giving it back afterward." She hoped her mother would understand that while the gesture felt over-the-top, it didn't mean anything more than the importance of the evening.

Sophie sent a quick picture of the dress to Lizzie, and within seconds, her phone buzzed with a reply:

OMG!

Smiling at the enthusiasm, Sophie dialled Lizzie's number, her nerves buzzing as she waited for her friend to pick up.

"Hey, Soph! OMG?" Lizzie's voice was bright and cheerful.

"Hi, Lizzie," Sophie started, trying to keep her voice steady, though the excitement she felt was clear. "I was wondering… would you help me get ready on Saturday? You know, with the dress and everything."

Before Sophie could finish, Lizzie practically squealed with delight. "Oh my God, yes! I would love to! You're going to look amazing!"

Sophie smiled, feeling a wave of relief wash over her. "Thanks, I just… I feel better knowing you'll be there. You're so good at this stuff."

"Of course!" Lizzie insisted. "And I'm doing your makeup too. I won't take no for an answer!"

Sophie laughed, feeling lighter. With Lizzie's help, she knew she'd feel more confident about the night ahead.

Early Friday morning, while having breakfast, Sophie's phone buzzed as Damian's name lit up the screen. She hesitated for a moment before answering, her heart racing.

"Hey," she greeted, trying to sound casual.

"Hi, Sophie," Damian's voice was warm, with a hint of anticipation. "I just wanted to check; did you get the deliveries? And more importantly, did I make a good choice?"

Sophie couldn't help but smile, though the weight of the gift still lingered. "Yes, I got them, and… they're amazing, Damian. Truly. But I'm a little worried."

"Worried?" he asked, his tone shifting to concern. "About what?"

She hesitated, glancing at the diamond choker on the table beside her. "It's just… it's so expensive. The dress, the jewellery, I've never worn anything like this before. It feels a bit overwhelming."

Damian chuckled softly on the other end. "Sophie, you deserve to look as incredible as you are. I wanted to give you something special for the night, something that shows how much I appreciate you being by my side at the awards. It's just for the night, you don't need to worry about it."

She sighed, still feeling the weight of the gesture but soothed by his words. "Thank you, Damian. I'll try to relax about it."

"I promise you'll feel amazing in it," he said gently. "And I'll be right there with you the whole time."

Sophie hesitated, her voice quiet but sincere. "Okay... I'll trust you on this."

Damian's voice softened, sensing her unease. "I'll pick you up at 6pm sharp, alright?"

"Alright," Sophie replied, her nerves settling just a little.

"See you then," he added, the warmth in his voice easing some of her worries.

"See you," she said, a small smile creeping into her tone despite her reluctance.

They both said their goodbyes, and as Sophie hung up, she thought about the elegant dress and the shimmering necklace, the weight of tomorrow's event lingering in her thoughts.

Saturday afternoon, Lizzie arrived at Sophie's house, her excitement palpable. She practically bounced through the door, her eyes bright with anticipation. "I'm so excited for this!" Lizzie beamed, giving Sophie a quick hug before looking around for signs of the dress.

Sophie smiled, a little more at ease now with Lizzie's contagious energy. "Wait till you see what Damian sent me," she said, leading Lizzie into the living room.

"Show me, show me!" Lizzie urged; her curiosity piqued.

Sophie opened the box and revealed the stunning diamond necklace. The moment Lizzie laid eyes on it, her jaw dropped. "Oh. My. God!" Lizzie exclaimed, her hands flying to her mouth. "Sophie, this is insane! It's absolutely gorgeous!"

Lizzie held the necklace up to the light, watching the diamonds sparkle. "This must have cost a fortune!" she said, her eyes wide with disbelief. "I can't believe you're going to wear this. You're going to look like a queen!"

Sophie chuckled nervously, still a little overwhelmed by the extravagance. "I know, it's a bit much, right?"

"A bit much?" Lizzie laughed. "It's perfect! Damian's really pulling out all the stops. You're going to be the best-dressed woman there." She grinned, holding the necklace up to Sophie's neck. "I can't wait to see the full look together!"

Lizzie was in full-on glam mode, buzzing around Sophie with an infectious excitement. "Okay, first things first, let's get your makeup started!" she said, unpacking her makeup kit onto the vanity. Sophie sat nervously in the chair, feeling the anticipation bubble up inside her.

Lizzie started with the foundation, blending it seamlessly into Sophie's skin. "You've got such amazing skin, Soph. We're going to keep it natural but flawless," she said, her focus entirely on perfecting each stroke. As she added a hint of blush to Sophie's cheeks, she smiled, "You're already glowing, so this is just the finishing touch."

Sophie couldn't help but laugh. "I think I'm just nervous. I've never done anything like this before."

"That's what I'm here for! You're going to be stunning," Lizzie assured her as she moved on to Sophie's eyes, carefully applying a soft, smoky eyeshadow. "This will make your eyes pop, but it's not too heavy. Damian won't know what hit him."

After the eyeshadow, Lizzie expertly applied eyeliner, and mascara, taking a step back to admire her work. "Okay, just a little lipstick, and you're good to go!"

Sophie glanced at herself in the mirror, barely recognising the woman staring back. "Wow," she murmured. "This is... I look so different."

Lizzie grinned, proud of her handiwork. "You look incredible. Now, let's get you into that dress."

As Sophie slipped into the elegant gown Damian had chosen for her, Lizzie stood back, hands on her hips. "The dress, the necklace, the makeup, it all comes together perfectly."

Sophie placed the diamond choker around her neck, fastening it delicately. Lizzie's eyes went wide once again. "You look like a movie star, Soph. Seriously, you're going to turn heads tonight."

Sophie gave one last look in the mirror, feeling more confident with Lizzie by her side. "I can't believe this is me," she whispered.

Lizzie smiled, giving her friend's hand a squeeze. "It's you, all right. Now go knock 'em dead."

As Sophie emerged from her room, her mother was sitting in the living room, flipping through a magazine but glancing up occasionally. When Marie saw her daughter, her eyes widened in disbelief. "Sophie!" she exclaimed, her voice filled with awe. "You look absolutely breathtaking."

Sophie smiled shyly, twirling slightly to showcase the full effect of the gown. The soft fabric swirled around her legs, and the diamond necklace caught the light, sparkling brilliantly against her skin. "Thanks, Mum," she said, her heart fluttering with excitement and nerves.

Lizzie chimed in, beaming with pride. "I'm sticking around until Damian gets here," she announced, crossing her arms confidently. "I want to make sure she's ready to wow him."

Marie's expression softened with appreciation. "Thank you for helping her, Lizzie. It's nice to see her so happy and confident." She leaned forward in her seat, her eyes glistening with a mix of nostalgia and pride. "I can hardly believe how grown-up you look."

Sophie felt a rush of warmth at her mother's words, her nerves slightly easing. "I'm still me, Mum," she reassured, though her heart raced at the thought of seeing Damian soon.

Lizzie nudged Sophie playfully, breaking the moment. "Don't forget, you're not just any 'you' tonight. You're the dazzling woman he's been waiting to take to this awards ceremony!"

Marie chuckled softly, the atmosphere lifting with excitement. "Just remember to have fun, sweetheart. This is a special night for you."

Sophie nodded, her excitement bubbling to the surface again. "I will, Mum. I can't wait to see Damian's reaction."

At exactly 6pm, a firm knock echoed through the house, cutting through the excitement in the air. Lizzie, unable to contain her enthusiasm, darted to the door and swung it open. There stood Damian, exuding charm in a perfectly tailored tuxedo, his hair neatly styled. He looked every bit the dashing date, and Lizzie couldn't help but smile at the sight.

"Good evening, Lizzie!" he greeted warmly, his eyes sparkling with friendliness.

Lizzie grinned back, leaning against the doorframe. "I hope you're ready for this," she teased, her voice laced with excitement as she turned to call out for Sophie. "Sophie! You can come out now!"

As the words left her lips, Sophie appeared from the hallway, her heart racing at the prospect of facing Damian. When she stepped into view, time seemed to slow for both of them. Damian's breath caught in his throat at the sight of her. She was a vision, the elegant gown hugging her in all the right places, and the diamond necklace glimmering delicately around her neck.

His eyes widened in genuine awe. "Wow, Sophie," he breathed, his voice barely above a whisper. "You look absolutely stunning."

Sophie felt a rush of warmth at his compliment, her cheeks flushing. The nervousness that had been building inside her melted away, replaced by a spark of excitement. "Thank you," she replied, her voice soft but filled with a newfound confidence.

Lizzie watched the exchange with satisfaction, stepping back to allow them a moment. "I'll just grab my things," she said, a knowing smile on her face as she slipped away, leaving the two of them to bask in the moment.

Damian stepped into the house; his gaze locked onto Sophie as he approached her. The warmth of her presence drew him in, and he couldn't help but admire the way she carried herself in the elegant gown. Just as he reached her, he turned slightly and noticed Marie standing in the doorway of the living room, watching them with a gentle smile.

"Hello, Marie," he greeted warmly, his voice sincere. "You look lovely this evening."

Marie returned the smile, her eyes sparkling with pride as she took in her daughter and Damian together. "Thank you, Damian. You both look wonderful."

Damian chuckled lightly, grateful for the warm reception. "I thought I better look the part for such a special occasion."

Marie nodded approvingly, her expression turning a bit more serious. "Just make sure to take good care of her, okay?"

Damian's gaze shifted back to Sophie, who was watching him with a mix of anticipation and nervousness. "I promise," he replied earnestly, the weight of her mother's words settling in his mind. He wanted to make this night unforgettable for Sophie, and he was determined to do just that.

After exchanging heartfelt goodbyes with Marie and Lizzie, Damian and Sophie made their way downstairs to the waiting limousine. The driver held the door open, and as they stepped inside, a sense of excitement filled the air. The interior of the limo was luxurious, with plush leather seats and soft ambient lighting that created an intimate atmosphere.

Sophie slid in first, her heart racing with a mix of nerves and anticipation. She settled into the seat, Damian followed her in, closing the door behind him with a soft thud that seemed to mark the beginning of their evening.

As the limousine pulled away from the curb, Damian turned to Sophie, a playful smile on his face. "Ready for an unforgettable night?"

Sophie nodded, her eyes sparkling. "Absolutely. I can't believe we're actually doing this!"

Damian leaned back, his expression earnest. "Let's make it a night to remember, then." With that, the limousine glided smoothly through the city streets, the anticipation of the awards ceremony hanging in the air like electric tension.

Chapter Fifteen

As the limousine pulled up to the venue for the San Francisco Design Awards, they were met with a dazzling scene. The entrance was lined with elegant lights, and the sound of cameras clicking filled the air as photographers captured the glamorous attendees stepping out of their cars.

Damian opened the door for Sophie, offering her his hand as she stepped out onto the red carpet. The moment her heels touched the ground; she felt a rush of excitement mixed with nervousness. She glanced at Damian, who looked impeccably handsome in his tuxedo, his confident demeanour putting her at ease.

Together, they walked hand in hand along the red carpet, the bright flashes illuminating their path. Sophie's heart raced as she caught glimpses of other guests in stunning gowns and sharp suits, the atmosphere buzzing with anticipation and elegance.

As they entered the venue, the grandeur of the ballroom took her breath away. Crystal chandeliers hung from the ceiling, casting a warm glow over the elegantly decorated tables, each adorned with beautiful centrepieces. The buzz of conversations blended with soft music, creating a vibrant ambiance that promised a night to remember.

Damian turned to her, his eyes sparkling with enthusiasm. "Are you ready for this?" he asked, his voice low and reassuring.

Sophie smiled back, her nerves settling as she took in the breathtaking surroundings. "More than ready," she replied, feeling grateful for this opportunity and for the man by her side. Together, they stepped further into the celebration, eager to enjoy the evening ahead.

As Sophie and Damian entered the cocktail reception, the elegant ambiance enveloped them, soft music playing in the background and guests mingling with glasses in hand. Sophie's heart raced with excitement and a hint of nerves, her dress flowing gracefully around her as she walked beside Damian, who looked impeccably polished in his tuxedo.

As they moved further into the room, a tall man with sharp features approached, a confident smirk playing on his lips. Damian's expression shifted slightly, hinting at a rivalry that had been brewing for some time.

"Damian! Good to see you," the man said, his gaze shifting to Sophie. "And who is this lovely lady on your arm? She's absolutely stunning."

Sophie felt a blush creeping onto her cheeks as she glanced up at Damian, whose demeanour remained composed, though a flicker of pride shone in his eyes.

"Hello Brad, this is Sophie," he replied smoothly, a hint of warmth in his voice. "She's someone very special to me."

Brad raised an eyebrow. "Ah, Sophie, beautiful name as well as a beautiful face."

Sophie smiled politely, feeling both flattered and slightly uneasy under the man's scrutinising gaze. Damian, however, didn't miss a beat. "Yes, she is beautiful," he added, protectively wrapping an arm around her waist.

Brad smiled. "Well, it seems you've upgraded, Damian. Enjoy the evening." With that, he turned to mingle with another group, leaving Sophie and Damian standing together, the tension from the encounter lingering in the air.

Sophie looked up at Damian, curiosity mixed with concern. "Is he always like that?" she asked softly.

Damian let out a light chuckle, brushing off the moment. "Just part of the territory. Let's focus on enjoying tonight."

With a reassuring smile, they moved deeper into the reception, ready to embrace the evening ahead.

Damian turned to Sophie, a playful smile on his lips. "Would you like a drink?" he asked, his eyes sparkling with warmth.

Sophie nodded, feeling a flutter of excitement. "Champagne would be lovely," she replied, her heart racing.

"Perfect choice," Damian said with a grin. "I'll be right back." He gave her a reassuring look before weaving through the crowd towards the bar.

Sophie watched him go, her heart fluttering with anticipation. The soft glow of the venue and the elegant atmosphere enveloped her, making her feel as though she had stepped into a dream.

While Damian was away, Clara sauntered over, her heels clicking sharply against the polished floor. With an arched eyebrow and a smug smile, she leaned in, her tone dripping with condescension. "So, you're Damian's flavour of the month?"

Sophie's eyes widened in shock, caught off guard by the bluntness of Clara's remark. She opened her mouth to respond, but Clara continued, "He'll never take you seriously, you know." Her words patronising, leaving Sophie feeling a mix of indignation and disbelief.

Sophie gathered her thoughts, a surge of confidence rising within her. She turned to Clara, meeting her gaze squarely. "That's okay with me," she replied coolly. "Because I'm only using him for sex." Her words were laced with defiance, challenging Clara's condescending demeanour while masking the turmoil beneath. She held her ground, determined not to let Clara's snide remarks undermine her newfound assertiveness.

As Damian returned with Sophie's champagne, he caught the tail end of her bold comment to Clara. A smirk tugged at the corners of his mouth, intrigued by her defiance. Sliding his arm around Sophie's waist, he leaned in slightly, his voice low and playful. "And what amazing sex it is," he remarked, his tone teasing yet warm. The gesture was possessive, drawing her closer as he shot a challenging look at Clara, silently asserting that Sophie was more than capable of holding her own.

Clara's expression shifted from shock to indignation, her mouth slightly agape as she processed Damian's possessive gesture and Sophie's confident reply. Without uttering another word, she turned on her heel, storming away with a haughty toss of her hair, clearly taken aback by the unexpected turn of events.

Once Clara was out of sight, Sophie and Damian exchanged amused glances, laughter bubbling between them. "I guess that put her in her place," Sophie said, a playful grin spreading across her face. Damian chuckled, his eyes sparkling with mischief. "I'd say you handled that rather well."

Damian handed Sophie her champagne, and she took a sip, savouring the bubbly taste. As her curiosity got the better of her, she glanced up at him. "Thank you. But honestly, she's not a very nice person. What did you see in her?"

Damian paused for a moment, looking thoughtful. "I honestly don't know," he admitted. "It was more about the chase."

Sophie raised an eyebrow, a teasing smile playing on her lips. "I told you the first night we met that you need to be pickier. Just remember that for future reference."

Damian chuckled softly. "I don't need to; I've found the one I want," he replied, his gaze locking onto hers. At his words, Sophie felt her cheeks flush with warmth.

Damian leaned closer to Sophie and whispered, "I think it's time for us to find our table."

As they entered the main dining area, the elegant ambiance enveloped them, with soft lighting highlighting the beautifully set tables adorned with exquisite centrepieces. The gentle hum of conversation and clinking of glasses created a warm, inviting atmosphere.

They scanned the room, spotting their assigned table near the front, where they could enjoy a clear view of the stage. Damian led the way, guiding Sophie through the sea of elegantly dressed guests.

Once they reached the table, Damian pulled out a chair for Sophie, a gentlemanly gesture that made her smile. She settled into the plush seat, taking in the scene around her: the vibrant colours of the decor, the carefully plated appetisers already set out, and the buzz of excitement that filled the air.

Damian sat across from her, his eyes sparkling with anticipation as they settled in for the evening. When dinner was served, Sophie and Damian enjoyed each other's company, engaging in light-hearted conversation and sharing laughter as they savoured their meal.

As the time for the awards approached, Sophie turned to Damian, a curious look on her face. "I forgot to ask, are you nominated for any awards tonight?"

"Yes, two: 'Best Commercial Building' and 'Sustainable Design Excellence,'" Damian informed her with a hint of pride in his voice.

"Oh, how exciting!" Sophie exclaimed, her enthusiasm evident.

The Architecture & Urban Design Awards began, with the first category being Best Residential Design. Nominees' projects flashed on the big screen, showcasing their impressive designs. As the winner was announced, the room erupted in applause, and the awardee made their way to the stage to collect their prize.

Next came the Best Commercial Building award. Sophie's smile grew as Damian's name was called among the nominees. When the winner was announced, Damian Prescott, her heart swelled with excitement. She clapped enthusiastically, her eyes shining with pride as Damian stood and confidently made his way to the stage to accept his award.

Damian took a moment at the podium, his expression a mix of gratitude and joy. "Thank you all for this incredible honour. I want to acknowledge the hard work of my team and the vision of everyone involved in this project. Thank you!"

With that, he stepped down from the stage to thunderous applause and returned to his table, where Sophie was practically glowing with excitement. "I'm so proud of you!" she exclaimed, her eyes shining with admiration.

Before they could fully bask in the moment, the next award, Sustainable Design Excellence, was announced. As the nominees were revealed, Sophie felt a thrill of anticipation. When Damian's name was called once more as the winner, she jumped up, clapping vigorously, her excitement spilling over as he made his way to the stage yet again to collect another award.

Damian returned to the table; his second award gleaming in his hand. The pride in Sophie's eyes was unmistakable as she beamed at him. "You did it again! I'm so proud of you!" she said, her voice bubbling with excitement.

With a grin, Damian leaned in and pressed a soft kiss on her lips, a moment that felt electric amidst the celebratory atmosphere. As he settled back down, the warmth of the kiss lingered, and Sophie couldn't help but smile wider, her heart swelling with admiration for the man beside her.

As the final award was announced, a wave of applause rippled through the crowd, signalling the end of the formal ceremony. The lights softened, and the atmosphere shifted, buzzing with excitement as the after-party began.

Guests mingled, laughter and conversation filling the air. Sophisticated music played in the background, enhancing the vibrant ambiance. Sophie's heart raced with anticipation; she felt the thrill of the night still coursing through her veins.

Damian, now relaxed and animated after his wins, turned to her with a grin. "Shall we join the celebration?" he asked, his eyes sparkling with delight.

They moved through the crowd, champagne flutes in hand, and Sophie felt a sense of belonging. She marvelled at the array of dazzling decorations, the twinkling lights, and the elegantly dressed attendees, each one animatedly sharing their experiences of the evening. The air was filled with a heady mix of joy and success, and Sophie knew this night would be one to remember.

As they wandered through the lively after party, Damian's gaze caught a glimpse of a small, dimly lit alcove tucked away from the bustling crowd. He smiled, an idea forming in his mind. Taking Sophie's hand, he gently led her towards it, the noise of the party fading into a soft hum behind them.

Once they reached the alcove, the atmosphere shifted, it felt intimate and private. The shadows danced around them, creating a cocoon of warmth. Damian turned to her, his eyes deep and inviting, and without hesitation, he pulled her into his arms.

Sophie felt her heart race as their bodies came together, and before she could gather her thoughts, Damian leaned in closer. His lips met hers in a tender yet passionate kiss that sent butterflies fluttering through her stomach. The world outside vanished, leaving just the two of them in that magical moment, their bond deepening amidst the soft glow of the alcove.

Finally, when Damian pulled back from the kiss, he rested his forehead gently against hers, his breath warm and steady. "I've wanted to do that all night," he murmured, his voice low and filled with longing.

Sophie smiled softly, her heart racing. "So have I," she whispered, her words barely louder than a breath but full of the same desire. She hesitated for a moment, then asked, "Would you be upset if I asked to go to your place?"

Damian's eyes softened as he looked at her. "No, I wouldn't," he replied, his voice steady, a mix of surprise and warmth in his tone.

Damian took Sophie's hand, his fingers warm and firm around hers, as he guided her through the crowd. They moved with purpose, weaving through the guests at the after-party, their destination undeniable. Sophie's heart raced with anticipation; every step feeling charged with the energy between them.

Once they reached the front of the building, Damian signalled for his limousine. Within moments, the sleek black car pulled up smoothly to the curb. He opened the door for Sophie, who slid inside, the soft leather seats enveloping her in luxury. Damian joined her, and as soon as the door closed, the driver set off.

The city lights flickered outside, but inside the limousine, it was quiet and intimate. Damian leaned back slightly, his hand resting gently on Sophie's knee as the car drove them toward his penthouse. Neither spoke, but the silence was comfortable, filled with an unspoken understanding as the world outside seemed to fade away.

As the limousine pulled up to Damian's apartment building, Sophie felt a flutter of nervous excitement in her chest. The sleek, modern exterior gleamed under the city lights as they stepped out and walked towards the entrance. Damian pressed the button for the private lift, guiding Sophie inside.

The ride to the penthouse was quiet, filled with the soft hum of the elevator. When the doors slid open, Damian unlocked the door and gently pushed it open, stepping aside to let Sophie in first.

Her breath caught in her throat as she stepped into the space. The penthouse was stunning, sophisticated, elegant, and bathed in soft ambient light. Floor-to-ceiling windows lined the living room, offering an incredible view of the city nightscape. The lights of San Francisco twinkled below, stretching out as far as the eye could see, making the room feel like it was floating above the world.

Sophie moved closer to the window, mesmerised by the breathtaking view. "It's beautiful," she whispered, awe evident in her voice.

Damian came up behind her, his presence steady and comforting. "I'm glad you like it," he murmured, his gaze shifting from the view to her, watching the way the city lights reflected in her eyes.

Damian slid his fingers in her long dark hair at her nape and gently drew her head closer to his, giving her a chance to pull back if she wanted to. He lowered his mouth to her lushest lips, cupping her face with his other hand.

Their lips touched in a gentle soft kiss. Desire ripped through his body. His arms tightened around her as he pressed his lips firmly against hers. A fiery, wild heat surged through Sophie, leaving her both stunned and exhilarated.

His kiss was hot, persuasive and demanding. She trembled with each movement of his lips, feeling the heat of his body and the strength of his hands. Overwhelmed by sensation she felt no fear, only an exhilarating boundless desire.

A low moan of pleasure escaped her lips as she slid her hands up his chest around his neck, holding on tightly as he immersed her into a sea of sensation.

Her fingers tugging at the thick silky texture of his hair. Fire, wild scorching flame cascaded through her body.

His tongue gently coaxed her mouth open, eager to taste its depths. She was intoxicating, an elixir of life unlike any woman he had ever kissed before.

Damian was so overwhelmed with desire he felt like he might spontaneously combust.

Sophie was driving him crazy, and she wasn't even trying. The taste, the smell, the touch of her was gloriously potent.

His hands slowly slid down to her hips holding her captive, she moved with mounting pleasure beneath the ardent pressure of his fingers. Everything inside her was aroused, hungry, and the sensual warmth of his lips when he lifted his head to place hot kisses on her neck, they were like a searing flame.

He ran his hands around to her buttocks, cupping her to draw her closer, so she could feel his body's response to hers and understand just how desperately he wanted her.

"Soph, I want you." He said against her mouth. "So much."

"Damian, I want you too…," his lips closed over hers again.

One hand slid around to her breast and cupped it and slowly started to knead it gently.

"Oh, Damian, please."

His thumb slid over her taut nipple, then he squeezed it gently. She whimpered with pleasure.

His lips moved on hers with controlled expertise. She was heated and desperate to have his hands on her. Her body, all yielding curves, pressed to him as time and the kiss spun out of control with desire.

Beneath it all, the shock of lust burning threw her, igniting every nerve and vein so she burned for his touch. Everything within her centred on the raging need within.

His hands moved down her body to rest on her hips pulling her even closer so she could feel his arousal.

His fingers slid the zipper of her dress down her back and slid it off her shoulders, it dropped to the floor in a pool of bronze liquid. He then undid her bra and let it drop to the floor.

He stepped back and gently held her away from him, the moonlight casting a silvery glow on her pale skin, giving her an angelic appearance. His eyes flared as he looked at her body, almost naked and aroused, only for him.

"You take my breath away, you're so beautiful."

She didn't feel self-conscious; she just felt desire and need. Need to have his arms around her again, need to have him spiralling with her. He lifted her effortlessly in his arms, walked to the bedroom and laid her down gently on the bed.

"Have you any idea what you do to me?" His voice low and thick with desire.

"Damian, please…," her breath came on a strangled cry.

Chapter Sixteen

Sometime later, after they had both dressed, Sophie stood by the living room window, gazing out at the cityscape. Damian stepped quietly beside her, his hand gently resting on the small of her back. The soft glow of the city lights bathed them in a warm, intimate hue, casting their silhouettes against the night.

Damian took a deep breath, his thoughts clearly weighing on him, but his voice remained calm and steady. "Sophie," he began, his tone soft but full of intention, "there's something I've been thinking about for a while."

Sophie turned to face him, curiosity flickering in her eyes, waiting patiently for him to continue. The anticipation hung in the air between them, the quiet moment filled with unspoken words.

"I want everyone to know," Damian said, his gaze locking onto hers, "that we're together. Not just in private, but openly, no more hiding, no more guessing. I'm serious about you."

Sophie's breath hitched slightly, the sincerity in his words wrapping around her heart. The vulnerability in his voice, combined with the intimacy of the moment, made her pulse quicken. She looked into his eyes, searching for any doubt, but all she saw was the unwavering confidence that he was ready to take this next step with her.

"I want the world to know you're the woman by my side," Damian continued, his hand now moving to gently cup her face. "And I don't care what anyone else thinks."

Sophie's lips parted, her heart swelling with emotions she hadn't yet fully processed. "Damian, I... I don't know what to say."

His eyes softened as he stepped closer, his voice gentle but firm. "Just say yes," he pleaded. "I don't want to hide it anymore. I want to be able to kiss you, hold you, anywhere and everywhere."

Sophie's mind raced, the weight of the moment settling over her. This is a big risk, she thought, but I love him. I want to be with him. After a brief hesitation, she slowly nodded, a smile tugging at the corners of her lips.

"Thank you," Damian whispered, his voice filled with relief and joy. In a burst of happiness, he picked her up and swung her around, making Sophie laugh as the room spun around them. The world outside seemed to disappear, leaving just the two of them, wrapped in the warmth of each other's embrace.

As Damian set her back on her feet, he flashed a playful grin. "Unfortunately, I have to get you home," he said. "If I don't, your mother will kill me." He laughed, his eyes sparkling with amusement, though a hint of reluctance lingered in his voice as he gently teased her.

Damian walked her to her door, leaning down to plant a soft kiss on her lips. "Thank you for a wonderful evening, Soph," he murmured.

"Thank you, Damian. It truly was magical," she replied, her heart fluttering with the sweetness of the moment.

They said goodnight and Sophie went inside. Damian walking back to the limousine with a big smile on his face. She's mine now, and I want to keep her he decided, nothing going to stand in his way.

Early Monday morning, before leaving for work, Sophie carefully placed the dress, shoes, and jewellery back into the boxes they had arrived in. Everything was beautiful, but far too extravagant for her to keep. She didn't need expensive gifts; all she wanted was him. After all, he had said he was serious. Smiling to herself, she tucked the boxes under her arm and began her walk to work.

Sophie knocked gently on Damian's office door.

"Enter," came his familiar voice.

She opened the door and stepped inside, her smile bright. "Morning, Damian."

"Morning, sweetheart," he replied with a grin, the endearment sending a warm flush across her cheeks.

Sophie returned the smile. "I just wanted to let you know I had an amazing time on Saturday... and the whole weekend, really. All because of you. Thank you, Damian." Leaning in, she kissed him gently on the cheek.

Without hesitation, Damian slid his arm around her waist, pulling her closer. "So did I, Sophie. More than you know," he murmured, his eyes lingering on hers before bending down to kiss her softly on the lips.

Sophie blushed, then gently pulled away with a laugh. "I better get to work. Don't want anyone thinking I get special treatment."

They both chuckled, but the warmth of their connection lingered as Sophie turned to leave his office.

Just then, a knock came at the door, and Damian said, "Enter." He smiled at Sophie, feeling genuinely happy in her presence, she made him feel whole.

As the door opened, a man walked in. Sophie, still giddy with happiness, twirled around and accidentally knocked a folder out of the man's hand, sending papers flying across the floor. Laughing lightly, she apologised, "Oh! I'm so sorry!"

The man smiled warmly at her, "No harm done, Miss Highland."

Sophie froze for a moment. Did she know this man? She shrugged it off and bent down to help him collect the scattered papers. As she picked up one of the sheets, her eyes caught a familiar logo, the logo of her student loan agency. She stared at it for a second too long. It wasn't just any paper. It was a receipt for over seventy thousand dollars, the exact amount of her loan.

Her heart stopped. She slowly looked from the paper to Damian, her mind racing. The man reached for the paper, but Sophie gripped it tightly.

"You paid it," she whispered, her voice barely audible. "You paid my loan."

Damian's face went pale, realising what she had seen. "Soph, it's not what you think."

Sophie's voice trembled as anger and betrayal surged within her. "What do I think, Damian? That you manipulated me? That you lied?"

"Sophie, you don't understand," he started, but she wasn't listening.

She handed the paper back to the man with a quick, "Sorry," before storming out of the room. She barely registered the concerned looks of her colleagues as she hurried to the elevator, making it in just before the doors closed. She pressed the button for her floor, trying to control the panic rising in her chest.

Once she arrived, Sophie marched straight to her desk, gathering her things. Derek, Ryan, Alex, and Mark were preparing for their morning meeting when they noticed her distress.

Ryan was the first to speak, concern etched on his face. "Sophie, are you okay?"

Alex chimed in, "Yeah, you don't look so good."

Mark stepped closer, instinctively reaching out to comfort her.

With tears brimming in her eyes, Sophie met their worried gazes, struggling to keep her voice steady. "I'm leaving. It's been an honour to work with you all." She leaned in, giving each of them a quick kiss on the cheek.

Derek, looking confused, asked, "Why?"

Sophie just shook her head, unable to speak, barely holding back the flood of emotions.

Just then, the elevator doors opened again, and Damian stepped out. The room fell silent as everyone turned to look at him. Their faces were filled with confusion and disapproval.

Damian ignored their stares and walked straight to Sophie. "Please, Soph, let me explain," he pleaded, desperation in his voice.

Sophie refused to let him see her break. Without a word, she snatched the boxes on her desk containing the dress, shoes, and diamond jewellery he'd given her and hurled it at Damian. The box burst open as it hit the ground, scattering its glittering contents across the floor, much like the trust she once had in him.

"Keep it," she spat coldly, her voice filled with finality. "I never wanted anything from you."

She turned on her heel, heading straight for the lift, her hand trembling as she pressed the button. Behind her, the room fell into a tense silence. The diamonds lay strewn across the floor, a stark contrast to the raw emotion Sophie had just unleashed. Ryan, Alex, Marc and Derek exchanged glances, their eyes moving from the glittering jewels to Damian, their expressions hardening into barely concealed disgust.

Damian stood there, frozen, regret flooding his every thought as Sophie waited for the lift doors to open.

"Please, Soph, let me explain," Damian pleaded, his voice thick with desperation.

"I already know, Mr. Prescott," she spat, venom dripping from every word. "It was all about the chase, wasn't it?" Her voice cracked, fury trembling at the surface. "Well, you caught me… or rather, you bought me! Like a cheap whore."

Damian flinched, the words hitting him like a physical blow.

"Thank you, Mr. Prescott," she continued, her tone chillingly cold. "This was all because I walked away that first night. You couldn't stand it, could you? For once, you were on the receiving end. You didn't like it, after years of doing that to women. Well, news flash, Mr. Prescott, women have feelings, too."

Her hand shook as she pressed the button for the lift. "I'll pay you back every single penny. Be sure of that, Mr. Prescott."

The doors slid open. Sophie stepped inside, turning one last time as Damian tried to move toward her, desperation etched across his face. But Ryan and Alex were already there, blocking him, holding him back. Damian struggled, but they stood firm, preventing him from following her.

Sophie met their eyes, tears threatening to spill, and gave them a small, shaky smile. "Thank you," she whispered, her voice fragile but sincere.

As the lift doors slid shut, the dam Sophie had been holding back finally broke, and the tears streamed down her face, silently and uncontrollably.

She made her way through the lobby, her vision blurred by the flood of emotions. Her feet carried her in the direction of home, but she barely noticed her surroundings through the tears. Realising she couldn't let her mother see her like this, Sophie veered off course, stopping at a nearby park. She found an empty bench and sank onto it, trying desperately to get her sobs under control.

After the lift doors closed on Sophie, leaving in tears, Damian shook off Ryan and Alex, who were trying to restrain him from going after her. He sank into a chair, his head falling into his hands, the weight of regret pressing heavily on him.

Mark was the first to break the silence. "I always thought you knew women, Damian. If you thought you could buy Sophie, you know nothing. Sophie is an amazing woman, one I would be honoured to call mine."

Alex nodded in agreement, adding, "Yeah, she's one in a million."

Ryan stepped forward, his expression fierce. "You're a bloody fool, and to be honest, I feel like punching you in the face."

Damian looked up at them, his eyes filled with a mixture of pain and desperation. With a raw voice, he declared, "I love her."

The words hung in the air, and for a moment, the room fell silent as his employees processed what he had just said. They exchanged shocked glances, the gravity of the revelation sinking in.

Derek was the first to break the tension, his tone firm yet encouraging. "Well, you better go tell her."

Damian sprang to his feet, urgency propelling him forward as he pushed past Ryan and Alex, barely registering their surprised expressions. His mind was focused solely on reaching Sophie. He rushed to the lift, pressing the button repeatedly, his heart racing with a singular purpose: to find the woman he loved.

As the lift doors finally slid open, he stepped inside, thoughts consumed by the pain he had seen in her eyes, the tears that had fallen. He couldn't let her walk away without knowing how he truly felt. With every moment that passed, he willed himself to find the right words to express his regret and love.

Bursting into the lobby, he scanned the area, desperation gripping him as he searched for any sign of her. He had to catch her before she disappeared for good.

Damian drove to Sophie's home, his heart heavy with the weight of his actions. He knew he had to face her and beg for forgiveness for manipulating and lying to her, but the thought of the pain he had caused made his stomach churn. As he parked in front of her apartment, he took a deep breath, steeling himself for the difficult conversation that lay ahead.

He knocked on the apartment door, but there was no answer. That struck him as odd; Marie should at least be home. He tried the doorknob, and to his surprise, it turned easily. Stepping into the hallway, he called out softly, "Sophie? It's Damian." Silence met his call, sending a ripple of unease through his gut.

Entering the apartment, he moved toward the living room, catching sight of the photographs of Sophie and her mother. They were a stark reminder of the warmth and love that filled these walls, and the contrast to the current situation made his heart ache.

As he made his way down the hall, a faint, distressed sound suddenly broke the silence. Alarm bells rang in his mind, and he rushed toward the noise, pushing open the door to Marie's room. What he saw froze him in his tracks. Marie sat on the edge of her bed, struggling to breathe, her face pale and glistening with sweat.

"Marie!" he exclaimed, rushing to her side. "What's wrong?"

She looked up at him, her eyes wide with fear. "I can't... breathe," she gasped, clutching her chest.

Damian's heart pounded as he snatched up his phone and dialled emergency services. "I need an ambulance," he said, his voice filled with urgency. "There's a woman here, she's having trouble breathing." After quickly giving the address, he added desperately, "Please, hurry!"

As he spoke, he knelt beside Marie, trying to keep her calm. "You're going to be okay, Marie. Help is on the way," he reassured her, squeezing her hand gently.

Tears welled in Marie's eyes, and she shook her head slightly. "I'm scared, Damian."

"I know," he said softly, trying to mask his own rising panic. "Just focus on my voice. Breathe slowly, in and out. You're strong, and we'll get through this together."

He watched her struggle to follow his instructions, her breaths coming in shallow gasps. Time felt like it was dragging as he continued to talk to her, willing the ambulance to arrive quickly.

Just then, he heard the distant sound of sirens approaching, and a sense of relief washed over him. "Help is here, Marie," he said, glancing toward the door. "Just hold on a little longer."

As the paramedics rushed in, Damian stepped back, his heart heavy with the weight of the situation. He had come seeking forgiveness from Sophie, but now his focus shifted entirely to Marie's well-being. Panic surged within him as he realised, he needed to find Sophie and inform her about her mother's condition. Where could she be?

Marie was carefully loaded into the ambulance, the paramedics working swiftly around her. One of them turned to Damian, his expression serious but calm. "We're taking her to St. Francis Hospital," he said before closing the doors.

As the ambulance pulled away, Damian rushed to his car, his thoughts racing. He still had no idea where Sophie was. He pulled out his phone, hesitating for a moment. Calling wouldn't work—she wouldn't answer, not after everything. But a text? Maybe she would read that. His fingers moved quickly over the screen as he typed.

Your mother, Soph, needs you. Tell me where you are. This is not a ploy to get you to talk to me—it's urgent.

He hit send, hoping she'd see it in time.

Sophie sat on the bench, lost in her thoughts, when her phone buzzed. She sighed, not wanting to talk to anyone, and reached for the phone to turn it off. But as her eyes caught the first words of the message—your mother—her heart froze. In a panic, she quickly read the rest of the text.

Oh no.

Without a second thought, her fingers flew across the screen as she typed where she was and pressed send. Her body moved automatically as she stood up and walked to the curb, waiting anxiously.

Minutes later, Damian's car pulled up. Sophie jumped in, her eyes wide with fear. "What happened?" she asked, her voice trembling.

Damian's grip tightened on the wheel as he explained. "I went to find you… and found her struggling to breathe. I called an ambulance. They're taking her to St. Francis."

Sophie's breath hitched, and she whispered softly, "Please, hurry."

Damian pulled into the hospital parking lot, tires screeching slightly as he found a spot. He and Sophie barely exchanged a glance before leaping out of the car. They rushed across the pavement toward the emergency entrance, Sophie's heart pounding in her chest.

Bursting through the automatic doors, they were greeted by the sterile smell of antiseptic and the low murmur of voices. A nurse at the reception desk noticed their urgency and quickly stepped forward. "You're here for Marie Highland?" she asked, her voice calm but efficient.

Sophie nodded, breathless.

The nurse gestured for them to follow her, leading them down a short hallway before stopping at a waiting area. "Please wait here," she said gently. "A doctor will be out to update you soon."

Sophie and Damian sat down; the air thick with tension as they braced themselves for whatever news was coming.

After what felt like an eternity, though only about ten minutes had passed, the door to the waiting area swung open. A doctor, dressed in blue scrubs and wearing a calm expression, stepped inside. His face was tired but professional.

"Hi, I'm Dr. Keller," he said, offering a reassuring smile as he approached. "I've been overseeing Marie's care."

Damian stood up first, his expression tense but composed. "Damian Prescott," he introduced himself, shaking the doctor's hand firmly.

Sophie remained seated, too shaken to trust her legs to hold her. Her hands gripped the edge of the chair as if grounding herself. When the doctor looked at her, she spoke, her voice soft but steady.

"I'm Sophie, her daughter," she said, trying to maintain control as her heart raced in her chest. She braced herself for the doctor's next words, fearing what might come but desperate to know how her mother was.

The doctor leaned forward, his expression a mix of concern and reassurance. "Sophie, I know this is a difficult time for you, but I want to update you on your mother's condition. We're currently running several tests to assess the extent of her health issues, but I need you to know that she was very lucky Mr Prescott found her when he did."

Sophie's heart raced at the mention of Damian, her mind racing back to the moment he had rushed into her home. "What do you mean?" she asked, anxiety creeping into her voice.

The doctor took a deep breath, choosing his words carefully. "When Mr Prescott arrived, your mother was in a critical state, struggling to breathe. If he hadn't called for an ambulance as quickly as he did, the outcome could have been far more serious. He truly saved her life."

Sophie felt a wave of gratitude wash over her. She turned to Damian, who stood nearby, his expression serious yet relieved. "Thank you," she said softly, her voice trembling.

The doctor continued, "The tests will help us understand the underlying issues and how best to support her moving forward. It's essential we gather as much information as possible to ensure she receives the appropriate care."

Sophie nodded, still processing the gravity of the situation. "I just want her to be okay," she said, her voice barely above a whisper.

The doctor placed a comforting hand on her shoulder. "We're doing everything we can. Your mother is a fighter, and with the right support, we can help her through this."

As the doctor stepped back to make some notes, Sophie glanced at Damian, who offered her a reassuring smile. In that moment, a flicker of hope broke through the heaviness of uncertainty.

Damian took a step closer, opening his arms wide, silently inviting her into his embrace. He let her decide if she wanted his comfort, standing there with a gentle expression, ready to support her in whatever way she needed.

Sophie hesitated for a moment, her eyes locking onto Damian's, searching for reassurance. After a beat, she stepped forward, surrendering to the comfort he offered. His arms wrapped tightly around her, and she felt the warmth of his embrace, as though he was trying to absorb her pain. She leaned into him, allowing herself to be vulnerable, drawing strength from his presence. In that moment, the weight of the world felt just a little lighter.

They sat in the sterile hospital waiting room, their hearts heavy with worry for Marie. The fluorescent lights cast a harsh glow over the scene, contrasting with the warmth Sophie sought in Damian's presence. He sat beside her, a steadfast anchor in the sea of uncertainty, his quiet support palpable.

Whenever Sophie felt the need for comfort, she leaned into him, and he instinctively wrapped his arm around her shoulders, pulling her close. His presence was calming, a reassuring weight against her trembling anxiety. He spoke only when she did, allowing her to guide the conversation, if she wanted one at all.

When she needed silence, he simply held her hand, his grip firm yet gentle, a steady reminder that she wasn't alone in this moment of fear. Each time she squeezed his hand, he responded with a soft, understanding smile, silently urging her to lean on him as much as she needed. The quiet moments stretched between them, filled with unspoken support and shared concern, creating a bond that felt even stronger in the face of uncertainty.

Finally, the doctor entered with a sombre expression, and Sophie's stomach dropped at the sight. He pulled up a chair and sat across from them, his demeanour serious yet gentle.

"Sophie," he began, his voice steady and compassionate. "I wish I had better news. After reviewing your mother's condition, it's clear that her health has deteriorated significantly. The combination of her MS and COPD is proving to be more than she can manage on her own."

Damian's heart ached for both Sophie and her mother. He squeezed Sophie's hand, silently offering support as she processed the words.

Sophie felt a lump form in her throat, her mind racing with the implications. "What do you mean? Is she… is she going to be okay?"

The doctor took a deep breath, his gaze meeting hers with empathy. "Marie will need more support than she can provide for herself. At this stage, we recommend either palliative care or a full-time nurse. This isn't just about her physical health; it's about ensuring her quality of life as well."

Sophie's heart sank further, tears pricking at the corners of her eyes. "But she's always been so independent… I don't want her to feel like she's losing that."

"I understand, and it's important to acknowledge those feelings," he replied softly. "Palliative care focuses on providing relief from symptoms and stress, enhancing her comfort. A full-time nurse can help with her daily needs and ensure she has the proper care."

Sophie swallowed hard, processing the weight of his words. "So, she won't be able to live at home anymore?"

"Not without the proper support," the doctor said gently. "This decision is about prioritising her well-being. We can discuss options for in-home care or facilities that specialise in both MS and COPD patients, where she can receive the necessary assistance."

The reality of the situation crashed down on Sophie. A mix of grief, anger, and helplessness surged within her. "I don't want to make this decision. It feels so final."

"It is a difficult decision, and it's okay to take time to process it," he reassured her. "I can connect you with social workers who specialise in these cases. They can help you navigate the options and find what's best for your mother and for you."

Sophie nodded, a blend of gratitude and despair swirling in her heart. "Thank you… I just want her to be comfortable and happy."

The doctor offered a reassuring smile. "That's all anyone wants for their loved ones. We'll work through this together."

As he stood to leave, Sophie felt the weight of uncertainty pressing heavily on her shoulders. She turned to Damian, tears glistening in her eyes. Without hesitation, he slowly took her into his arms, enveloping her in a warm embrace, trying to ease her pain. She leaned into him, finding solace in his strength as the reality of her mother's situation settled in her heart.

After what felt like an eternity, Sophie and Damian were finally led into the room where Marie lay. The sight of her brought a rush of emotions, relief, concern, and a flicker of hope. Marie was propped up in bed, her face slightly pale but framed by her familiar, gentle smile. An oxygen mask rested over her nose and mouth, a reminder of her fragility, yet she was alert and engaged.

Sophie rushed to her mother's side, her heart swelling at the sight. "Mum!" she breathed, tears welling in her eyes as she gently took her mother's hand. Marie looked at her, her eyes brightening despite the circumstances.

Damian stepped back slightly, giving them space but remaining close enough to offer support. He observed the moment, his heart aching for Sophie but filled with admiration for the strength of the bond between mother and daughter.

"Hey, sweetheart," Marie said softly, her voice slightly muffled but steady. "I'm okay. Just taking it easy."

Sophie leaned in closer, brushing her mother's hair back. "You're going to be just fine, Mum. We're here."

Damian, sensing the depth of the moment, reached for Sophie's hand and intertwined his fingers with hers, a silent pledge to be there for her and her mother. The room, filled with the beeping of machines and the faint hum of hospital life, became a sanctuary of love and resilience as they all settled into the moment together, grateful for the small victories in the midst of uncertainty.

As the hours passed, the comforting atmosphere in Marie's room shifted when a nurse gently entered and informed them that visiting hours were over. Sophie felt a pang of disappointment, not wanting to leave her mother's side. Damian, sensing her distress, squeezed her hand reassuringly as they made their way out.

Once in the parking lot, they walked to Damian's car in silence, the weight of the day hanging heavy between them. He drove carefully, the soft glow of the dashboard lights illuminating the tension that filled the vehicle. Sophie stared out the window, lost in thought, while Damian occasionally glanced at her, his heart aching for her.

When they arrived at her apartment, he walked her to the door, wanting to stay with her, to provide comfort and reassurance. But as he turned to face her, the hurt in her eyes was unmistakable. "Thank you for everything, Damian," she began, her voice trembling slightly. "But it doesn't change what you did. You manipulated me and lied to me."

His heart sank at her words, the sting of her rejection cutting deeper than he expected. "Sophie, I'm so sorry," he replied, desperation creeping into his voice. "I never meant to hurt you."

But Sophie shook her head, tears glistening in her eyes. "I need you to leave. Please, don't come back."

The finality in her tone left him speechless, and he watched as she stepped through her door, retreating into the warmth of her home. Slowly, she closed the door, the soft click echoing in the quiet night.

Damian stood there, staring at the closed door, his heart heavy with regret and longing, feeling the painful distance grow between them as he realised the consequences of his actions.

Chapter Seventeen

It had been a week since Damian last saw Sophie, and the distance felt like a gaping wound that wouldn't heal. He replayed their last conversation in his head endlessly, her words echoing, don't come back. She had been so firm, so resolute, and even though he knew he deserved it, the pain was unbearable.

Every part of him wanted to go back, to beg for her forgiveness, to explain himself once again. He was desperate for another chance, but the weight of her rejection held him back. Sophie wasn't at the office anymore. Derek and the other architects she used to work with gave him icy glares when they thought he wasn't looking. The unspoken hostility was everywhere, and Damian couldn't blame them. He had broken her trust, and everyone around her knew it.

Still, he couldn't shake his connection to her, so he found himself visiting Marie early in the mornings before the official visiting hours started. He'd charmed one of the nurses, convincing her to let him in. Marie was getting stronger each day, and though her physical recovery was promising, her news hit him like a gut punch.

"I've decided to go into palliative care," Marie told him, her voice soft but firm as she sat up in her hospital bed.

Damian felt his stomach drop. "What? Why? You're getting better…."

Marie gave him a sad smile, shaking her head. "Sophie… she's spent so much of her life worrying about me. I don't want her to lose any more of it because of my illness. I'll still see her, but I don't want her to feel trapped by my situation."

Damian swallowed hard, struggling to find words. "She loves you. This will crush her."

"I know," Marie said, her voice thick with emotion. "But I need to let her live. And maybe… maybe this will help her find peace with everything. With you."

Damian's heart clenched at the mention of Sophie. "She won't even talk to me," he admitted, his voice breaking. "I messed everything up."

Marie reached out and took his hand, her grip surprisingly strong. "She's hurt, Damian. But she'll come around. Just give her time. Let her heal."

Damian nodded, though the ache in his chest only deepened. Every fibre of his being told him to go to Sophie, to try again, to fight for her. But all he could do was wait, wait for her, wait for a sign, wait for something to change. And in the meantime, he could only hope that time would heal the wounds he had caused.

Sophie had spent the past week wrestling with a storm of emotions. Damian had been out of her life for seven days, and while she should have felt relief, there was something gnawing at her—a deep ache, a confusing mix of anger and longing. She missed him, despite the betrayal that cut through her like a knife. Every day without him left her conflicted, but her pride, her hurt, wouldn't let her reach out.

But today wasn't about Damian. Today was about her mother. As Sophie walked into the hospital, the weight of her mother's decision hung heavy over her. Palliative care. The words felt so final, so irreversible, and it broke her heart. Marie had tried to explain, insisting that she didn't want Sophie to waste any more of her life worrying, but Sophie didn't see it that way. She loved her mother deeply, and there was nothing she wouldn't do to take care of her. The idea of Marie giving up, retreating from treatment, felt like a defeat Sophie wasn't ready to accept.

With a heavy sigh, Sophie pushed through the door to her mother's hospital room. The familiar scent of disinfectant and the steady beep of monitors greeted her, but what struck her most was the sight of her mother, sitting up in bed, her frailty masked by a gentle smile.

"Hi, Mum," Sophie said softly, her voice tinged with sadness as she walked toward the bed.

Marie looked up, her eyes lighting up despite the obvious exhaustion in her features. "Hi, sweetheart," she replied warmly, reaching out to take Sophie's hand.

Sophie sat down beside her, her fingers intertwining with her mother's, but the unspoken words between them felt like a wall. There was so much Sophie wanted to say, about how unfair this was, about how much she loved her, about how she didn't care if she had to spend every waking moment caring for her. But the lump in her throat made it hard to speak.

Marie's hand tightened slightly around hers. "I know you're upset, Sophie," she said gently. "But this is what I want. I don't want you missing out on your life because of me."

Sophie swallowed, trying to hold back the tears. "You are my life, Mum. I'd do anything for you. Please don't do this because you think you're a burden."

Marie's smile was sad but filled with love. "I know you would. That's why I have to do this."

Sophie looked away, the sting of tears blurring her vision. The room felt too small, too suffocating. She loved her mother more than anything, and the thought of losing her, or even accepting that her mother was ready to let go, was unbearable.

"I'm not ready to lose you," Sophie whispered.

Marie brushed a tear from Sophie's cheek. "I'm not leaving yet love. We still have time."

But for Sophie, the time was slipping away faster than she could bear, and the weight of it was suffocating her.

Marie placed her hand gently over Sophie's. "Sweetheart, I saw Damian this morning."

Sophie's head shot up, her eyes narrowing. "Why?"

"He's been coming to see me every day."

"Really? Why?"

"Because he cares, Sophie," Marie replied softly. She paused; her voice tinged with concern. "He's hurting, badly."

"Well, that's his fault."

Marie sighed. "Sweetheart, don't let what your father did rob you of a man who clearly loves you."

Sophie met her mother's gaze, scepticism flickering in her eyes. "How do you know he loves me?"

Marie's expression softened. "It's obvious to everyone but you. When you walk into a room, all he sees is you. If you ever need help, he's the first one there. He loves you, Sophie."

Sophie hesitated, the words sinking in. "He tried to manipulate me."

"Did he really? Or did he just try to find a way past the walls you've built? If he hadn't done what he did, would you have spent so much time with him?"

Sophie sighed, knowing the truth. "No."

"Exactly. I don't believe for a second Damian would ever intentionally hurt you. He adores you."

Sophie looked at her mother, a hint of doubt lingering. "You like him, don't you, Mum?"

Marie smiled warmly. "Yes, I do. For many reasons, but the most important one is because he loves you. You should give him a chance, Sophie. At least hear him out."

Sophie's voice wavered. "But I've been so harsh to him…"

Marie chuckled softly. "You could do no wrong in his eyes. Go to him, Sophie. Tell him how you feel. I know you love him too. All I've ever wanted is for you to be happy. You've been so strong for so long, and you deserve happiness, darling. I love you."

Sophie's eyes filled with tears as she wrapped her arms around her mother. "I love you too, Mum."

Marie held her daughter tightly, whispering, "I know you do. Now go. Go see Damian."

Sophie lingered in the embrace, then leaned down to whisper, "I'll see you soon, Mum," her voice thick with emotion.

Marie nodded gently, her eyes full of love and reassurance. She gave Sophie's hand one last squeeze, letting her know it was time.

Outside, Sophie hailed a cab, her heart pounding as the city streets flew past. Each turn brought her closer to the office and the man she had been so conflicted about. Anticipation stirred within her, and despite her nerves, the thought of seeing Damian again made her heart race faster.

When Sophie stepped off the lift onto her old floor, she was immediately greeted by the familiar, warm smiles of Ryan, Mark, and Alex. Their faces lit up at the sight of her, and it felt like a reunion she didn't know she needed.

Ryan was the first to speak, his eyes wide with excitement. "Are you coming back?"

"I don't know about that," she laughed, her spirits lifting at the sight of them. It felt good to be around people who knew her so well.

"We've missed you!" Alex and Mark chimed in together, their enthusiasm contagious, and Sophie couldn't help but smile.

Just then, Derek emerged from his office, his expression brightening when he saw her. "Sophie! How's your mum?"

Sophie's smile softened as she answered, "She's getting there. She's a fighter."

Mark grinned and added with a smirk, "Just like her daughter, huh?"

The group laughed, the sound light and familiar, filling the space with a sense of comfort Sophie had missed. They shared a few stories, catching up on the office's latest happenings, and for a moment, Sophie felt like she belonged there again, wrapped in the warmth of their camaraderie.

But her heart hadn't forgotten the real reason she had come. Eventually, she turned to Derek, her pulse quickening as she asked, "Is Damian in?"

Derek nodded, a knowing look crossing his face. "Yes, he is."

Sophie smiled gratefully at them all before making her way to the lift again. As she pressed the button for Damian's floor, her heartbeat quickened with anticipation. When the doors slid open, she stepped out and approached his office, her hand hesitating for a moment before she knocked gently.

"Enter," came Damian's voice from inside, steady but with a hint of tension.

Taking a deep breath, Sophie pushed open the door and stepped inside.

Sophie found Damian seated at his desk, looking serious, his hair slightly tousled as if he had been running his hands through it all day. When he looked up and saw her, his expression immediately shifted to one of concern.

"Sophie… is your mum okay?" he asked urgently, standing up halfway from his chair.

Sophie offered him a small smile, her heart softening at the sight of him. "Yes, she's fine," she reassured him.

Relief washed over Damian's face, and he sat back down, exhaling deeply. "Good," he said, the tension easing from his shoulders. He hesitated for a moment before asking, "What are you doing here?" There was a gentleness in his voice, and the flicker of hope in his eyes was unmistakable.

Sophie took a breath, her nerves fluttering as she spoke. "My mum told me I should hear you out. That I should let you explain."

Damian's expression brightened, a cautious happiness lighting up his face. He gestured for her to sit, and after she did, he moved from behind his desk, settling into the chair across from her. His gaze locked onto hers, filled with intensity and anticipation.

"I… I'm sorry," Damian began, his voice trembling slightly as he tried to gather his thoughts. "I never meant to hurt you. I just wanted to spend time with you. You were always working, so focused, and you never seemed to make time for yourself. I didn't know how else to reach you." He paused, searching for the right words. "You needed to have fun, to be young... and I wanted to be a part of that with you."

He stopped; his breathing uneven as he tried to steady himself. "You made me feel whole," he admitted, his voice softer now, filled with vulnerability. His eyes were searching hers, hoping she could see the sincerity behind his words.

Sophie's voice wavered slightly when she replied, "But you took that decision away from me. You made the choice for me."

Damian's expression softened; regret etched deeply into his features. "I know, and I shouldn't have. You deserved better than that."

He took a deep breath, his heart pounding, knowing he needed to say what had been on his mind for so long. "I love you, Sophie," he said, the words heavy with meaning.

"I think I've loved you since the first moment I saw you in the bar. That kiss we shared... it woke something inside me that I can't let go of. And it would die if you weren't in my life."

His eyes stayed locked on hers, filled with raw emotion, hoping against hope that she could still see something worth saving between them. His words lingered in the air, exposed and vulnerable, as he leaned forward slightly, desperate for her to understand the depth of his feelings.

Sophie looked confused; her brow furrowed as she struggled to process it all. "I... don't know what to do," she said quietly, her voice shaky. "I'm sorry, Damian, I..."

Damian's expression remained calm, though his heart ached with each passing second. "It's okay, Sophie. Take your time to think. Just... just know that I love you." His voice, though gentle, carried an urgency, revealing how much he truly meant it.

Sophie slowly stood; her heart heavy as she looked at him. "I have to go. I'm sorry, Damian, but..."

Damian's composure faltered for the first time, the pain beneath his exterior surfacing in his eyes. "I understand," he whispered. After a pause, he added, "Would you at least think about coming back to work here? Derek wants you back. We all do."

Sophie hesitated, uncertainty clouding her features. "I need time to figure everything out," she murmured, the weight of her emotions making it hard to find clarity.

She walked toward the door, her steps slow and measured. Her hand rested on the handle, but she paused, her heart racing. Without turning back, she spoke softly, "You can't lie to me again. Not ever."

Damian's voice was filled with quiet desperation as he replied, "I won't. I'd never risk losing you again if you came back."

Sophie took a deep breath, feeling the flood of emotions, she'd been holding back rise to the surface. "I love you, Damian."

His breath caught, and he took a step closer, placing his hand gently on her shoulder. His eyes held a glimmer of hope. "You can trust me, Sophie. I promise."

Could she trust him? Sophie wasn't sure, and that doubt still tugged at her heart. But the real question was whether she could live without him. And the truth hit her with startling clarity—she couldn't. Walking away now, after everything, felt impossible. She had fallen for him that very first night they met, and no matter how much hurt had come after, her feelings hadn't changed. She was willing to take the risk, to take that leap.

Turning slowly to face him, Sophie's emotions overwhelmed her. Her voice trembled as she whispered, "I don't want to lose you."

Damian's expression softened, his eyes filled with both longing and determination. "I don't want to lose you either, ever," he said, his voice steady yet vulnerable.

Sophie looked up at him, her heart racing, and for the first time in what felt like ages, a flicker of hope sparked in her eyes. "Well, you better kiss me then," she teased, a small smile breaking through the tension that had surrounded them.

Without hesitation, Damian closed the distance between them, the weight of everything they had been through melting away in that instant. The world seemed to vanish, leaving only the two of them in that fragile, perfect moment. When their lips met, warmth surged between them, reigniting the love that had once felt lost. It was a promise—of new beginnings, of hope, of healing.

Pulling back slightly, Damian whispered, "I love you, Sophie. So much."

He took a step toward his desk; his movements deliberate and opened the top drawer. Sophie watched him, her heart still pounding, her expression confused but curious. When he turned back to her, he dropped down on one knee, a small box in his hand. He opened it, revealing a ring that sparkled like a beacon of hope.

"Sophie," Damian began, his voice thick with emotion, "will you marry me?"

Sophie's gaze flicked from the ring to Damian's face, her heart swelling with disbelief and love. She was momentarily speechless, tears welling in her eyes.

"I bought this when I gave you the necklace," he continued, his voice steady but filled with vulnerability. "I knew back then that you were the one for me. I've loved you more every day since. I couldn't imagine my life without you."

Tears spilled down Sophie's cheeks as she stood there, overwhelmed by the sincerity of his words. Damian looked up at her, his heart in his throat, and with a pleading smile, he added, "Please, put me out of my misery, Soph."

With a shaky laugh and tears still streaming, Sophie nodded. "Yes," she whispered, then louder, "Yes, I will marry you, Damian. I love you."

Damian's face lit up with pure joy as he slid the ring onto her finger, standing up to pull her into a tight embrace. They stood there, holding each other, knowing that this moment was the start of forever.

Epilogue

The wedding was a day filled with love and joy. Sophie had never looked more beautiful, her dress flowing around her like a dream as she made her way down the aisle. Derek, her boss and close friend, had the honour of walking her toward Damian, who stood waiting with a look of pure adoration on his face. Lizzie, her best friend, stood proudly as her bridesmaid, beaming with excitement. The ceremony was simple but heartfelt, a celebration of love that had been hard-won and deeply cherished.

At the reception, the atmosphere was light and joyous. Laughter and music filled the air as friends and family gathered to celebrate the newlyweds. At one point, Lizzie, always the life of the party, sauntered up to Damian and plopped down beside him with a cheeky grin.

"You know, Damian," she teased, her voice playful, "I don't think you've ever properly thanked me."

Damian raised an eyebrow, amused. "Oh? And what exactly should I be thanking you for?"

"I was the one who bought Sophie that dress, and convinced her to go out that night," Lizzie said smugly. "And then I conveniently left her alone for you to swoop in."

With a laugh, Damian leaned over and kissed Lizzie gently on the cheek. "I will be forever grateful, Lizzie," he said sincerely, his eyes sparkling.

Meanwhile, across the room, Sophie stood by her mother, Marie, who looked healthier and happier than she had in years. Marie beamed with pride, her eyes full of love as she gazed at her daughter, who was positively radiant in her wedding gown. Damian's heart swelled every time he looked at Sophie, feeling an overwhelming sense of gratitude that she was his wife now.

Damian had done everything in his power to support Sophie and her mother. He had convinced both of them to hire a full-time live-in nurse, someone who could provide the care Marie needed while allowing Sophie to live her life without constant worry. He even found a small apartment in their building for her mother and the nurse, ensuring that Sophie could remain close to her mother. The nurse, a kind woman just a little younger than Marie, had quickly become a perfect fit, and the arrangement had brought Sophie peace of mind.

Ryan, Alex, and Mark surrounded Sophie; their expressions exaggeratedly forlorn as they playfully bemoaned their fate.

"We're heartbroken, Sophie," Ryan teased, clutching his chest dramatically. "You could have had any one of us, but you had to go and choose Damian."

Alex nodded in mock sorrow. "I thought we had something special."

Mark chimed in, wiping away an imaginary tear. "We'll never recover."

Sophie laughed, her eyes twinkling with affection for her friends. "You'll survive," she teased back, grinning as she playfully nudged Ryan. "Besides, you all know I could never choose anyone else."

Returning to work after Damian had asked her to marry him, Sophie found herself welcomed back into the warm embrace of her close-knit team. They had always been a tight group, but now their bond felt even stronger. The teasing and playful banter picked up right where they had left off, yet something had changed, there was a deeper respect that came with the joy they shared in her happiness.

The cold looks they used to throw Damian's way had vanished, replaced with genuine friendship and a sense of acceptance. No longer was there any resentment or lingering tension, just a shared understanding that Damian made Sophie happy, and that was all that mattered. The office felt more like a family again, with the team working seamlessly together, as if they'd never missed a beat.

As the evening of the reception unfolded, Sophie moved gracefully through the crowd, her eyes searching for Damian. When she spotted him, standing at the edge of the room, her heart swelled with joy. A smile lit up her face, radiating the happiness that she felt deep inside.

Without a second thought, Sophie made her way toward him, her steps light, her heart full. Damian's eyes locked onto hers, and in that moment, it was as if nothing else existed but the two of them. She was glowing, her happiness shining through every inch of her, and Damian's heart soared, knowing she was finally his forever.

"Hello, Mr. Prescott," she said playfully, her voice filled with warmth as she reached his side, a mischievous grin spreading across her lips.

Damian returned her smile, his heart overflowing with love. "Hello, Mrs. Prescott," he replied, his tone soft but filled with joy.

Sophie giggled, leaning in to kiss him sweetly on the cheek. "I like the sound of that," she murmured, her eyes sparkling with affection.

Damian wrapped an arm around her waist, pulling her closer. "So do I," he whispered, his heart soaring as they stood together, surrounded by the people who loved them, knowing that their journey was just beginning.

The End

Hidden Gem

Alison Reid

A complete standalone romance

Previously published individually

Chapter One

Dominic Childs strides through the sleek glass doors of his corporate headquarters, his presence alone commanding the attention of everyone in the bustling office. Conversations falter mid-sentence, heads turn, and a charged silence ripples through the air as he passes. There's a magnetism to him—a quiet, formidable authority that comes with being the undisputed king of his industry.

As the owner and CEO of Childs Incorporated, Dominic oversees a Luxury Brand Management empire that dominates the worlds of fashion, jewellery, and lifestyle. In a city like New York, where luxury is both an art and a weapon, his company reigns supreme. From the glittering lights of red carpets to exclusive boardrooms closed to all but the elite, Dominic's influence is inescapable, shaping trends that reverberate across continents.

At six foot four, he's an imposing figure, his tailored suits framing broad shoulders and a lean, athletic build. Dark hair, meticulously groomed, and piercing blue eyes lend him an air of precision, while his chiselled jawline and unyielding expression project the kind of confidence that commands rooms without a word. Every detail is curated, from the subtle sheen of his Italian leather shoes to the crisp, understated pocket square that hints at his impeccable taste.

His athletic frame is not just for show; it reflects his discipline. Each morning begins with a vigorous run—sometimes on his state-of-the-art treadmill overlooking the glassy waters surrounding his Long Island estate, other times weaving through its forested trails. For Dominic, fitness is more than routine—it's his way of mastering both his body and the restless energy that drives him to the top.

Yet beneath the polished surface lies a man as enigmatic as he is ambitious. Ruthless in business and fiercely private, Dominic's relentless pursuit of dominance stems from more than just ambition. Control is his shield, a way to fortify himself against the vulnerabilities he refuses to acknowledge. In his world, power is everything, and weakness is a luxury he cannot afford.

As he steps out of the lift and into the executive floor's corridor, a hush falls over the space. Staff instinctively step aside, their movements precise, as if choreographed by the gravity of his presence. Dominic acknowledges them with a faint nod—polite but detached, his focus already ahead of him.

Inside his private office suite, the modern elegance of the space exudes the same precision as its occupant: marble desks, chrome accents, and floor-to-ceiling windows offering a commanding view of Manhattan. At the heart of this pristine order sits Diane

Childs, his mother, a woman of grace and quiet steel. Perched at her desk, she glances up, her warm but sharp smile cutting through the cool atmosphere.

"Good morning, Dominic," Diane greets, her voice effortlessly composed as she organises the day's agenda.

"Morning, Mother," Dominic replies, his tone brisk, his steps unhurried but deliberate as he moves toward his office door. "What's on the schedule?"

She glances at her notes. "Meetings are confirmed, and the contracts for the board meeting are ready for your review." There's a pause, and her perceptive gaze lingers on her son. "You're working too hard again."

Dominic doesn't look up as he scans the files she's set aside. "Someone has to." His tone is clipped, matter of fact. "It won't run itself."

It was a routine exchange, one that belied the lingering sting of Sofia's betrayal. She had entered Dominic's life as the ideal personal assistant—efficient, charming, and seemingly devoted. Over time, she became more, effortlessly weaving herself into his personal world. Dominic had allowed himself to believe in her sincerity, even proposing to her. But the truth, when it emerged, was brutal: Sofia wasn't drawn to him but to the glittering lifestyle his wealth provided.

She craved the jewels, designer clothes, and exclusive events, plotting to secure her access to that luxury long after their wedding. Her calculated deceit unravelled weeks before they were to marry, leaving Dominic humiliated and bitter. The experience was a brutal awakening, one that hardened his already guarded nature.

Never again, he vowed. He would not be manipulated, nor would he allow anyone to exploit his trust. Since Sofia, Dominic had adopted an unyielding rule: relationships were strictly temporary, their roles clear and transactional. Love, as far as he was concerned, was a weakness he could not afford.

Diane watched her son with a mother's intuition, keenly aware of the walls he had built. Those walls, painstakingly constructed over years of disappointment and betrayal, had solidified after Sofia's treachery. Though she rarely pressed him on matters of the heart, Diane silently longed for the warmth and openness her son once possessed. The boy who had once dreamed of love and family had become a man consumed by work; his heart locked away behind layers of iron discipline.

But Diane wasn't one to stand idly by. Beneath her composed exterior, she had a plan—a deliberate, gentle strategy to help her son heal and rediscover love. The first step? Finding the right woman. And Diane was certain she already had.

From the moment Diane met Sofia, she had suspected something was off. Sofia's charm felt rehearsed, her affection performative. Polite yet subtly condescending, Sofia spoke to Diane in a way that left no doubt about her true motives. Diane had held her tongue for Dominic's sake, watching as Sofia played the role of doting fiancée. But when the truth came to light, Diane's fury burned quietly alongside her heartbreak for her son.

Now, Diane's attention had turned to Amanda Prentice, the quiet, hardworking secretary who had been hiding her beauty and potential behind a dowdy facade. Amanda was everything Sofia wasn't, kind, ambitious, and uninterested in climbing the social ladder. Diane saw in her the qualities Dominic needed—warmth, integrity, and the ability to look beyond his wealth and power.

It was time to act. Diane knew Dominic wouldn't accept interference in his personal life, but she also knew how to navigate his stubbornness. She had spent years observing him, and she was confident she could guide him toward Amanda without him even realising it.

As Diane followed Dominic into his office, her expression was calm but determined. "I need to talk to you, Dominic," she said, her tone firm yet motherly.

He glanced up from his desk, his sharp blue eyes narrowing. "What is it, Mother?"

"It's time for me to move on," Diane said plainly, folding her hands. "I was only supposed to help temporarily. It's been nine months, and I think it's time you hired a full-time personal assistant."

Dominic sighed, already anticipating where this was going. "Really, Mother? Can't you just stay on? You're good at this, and I don't have time to deal with hiring someone else."

Diane shook her head. "No, Dominic. I've done my part, but I have my own life. You need someone permanent."

Dominic leaned back, crossing his arms. "Fine. But make sure it's a man."

Diane raised an eyebrow, expecting this. "If that's what you want," she replied evenly. "But I think you should keep an open mind. Not all women are like Sofia."

"Mother…" His tone carried a warning, but Diane pressed on.

"No, Dominic," she interrupted gently but firmly. "I understand your hesitation, but you need to trust me to find the right person. I'll handle the hiring process."

"A male," he reiterated, his voice firm.

Diane smiled faintly. "I'll consider all candidates. You've got enough to focus on—I'll take care of this."

Dominic's jaw tightened as he stared at her, clearly weighing his options. Finally, he relented with a curt nod. "Fine. But I have the final say."

"Of course," Diane agreed, already a step ahead. "I'll start interviews this week."

As she left his office, Diane closed the door softly, a satisfied smile playing on her lips. At her desk, she pulled out Amanda Prentice's file, flipping through it with a critical but approving eye.

Amanda's dual bachelor's degrees in business administration and communications stood out, as did the dedication it must have taken to complete them simultaneously. At just twenty-four, Amanda had proven she thrived under pressure, juggling demanding coursework with grace. Yet her intelligence and work ethic weren't what drew Diane most—it was her warmth, humility, and quiet resilience.

Amanda was everything Dominic needed, even if he didn't know it yet. Diane's plan was simple: get Amanda into the role, let her natural charm and competence speak for themselves, and watch as her son slowly realised what he'd been missing.

It wouldn't be easy, but Diane had never shied away from a challenge. Dominic needed someone who could see the man behind the empire—and Diane was certain Amanda was exactly that person.

Chapter Two

Amanda Prentice, a 24-year-old secretary with honey-blonde hair and striking emerald-green eyes, stepped out of her apartment building and breathed in the crisp morning air. The city was already alive with the sounds of New York's early bustle, but for Amanda, it was the quiet calm before her busy day truly began.

"Morning, Miss Prentice," the doorman, Joe, greeted her with a friendly nod as she passed by.

She smiled, shaking her head lightly. "Joe, you know you need to call me Amanda. How long have we known each other?"

Joe chuckled, his face lighting up. "Since you were eighteen, Miss Amanda."

"Well then?" she teased, raising an eyebrow.

Joe shrugged good-naturedly, unable to resist her charm. "Guess I'm just old-fashioned."

Amanda laughed.

"Going for your morning jog?"

"Yep," she replied, adjusting the sleeves of her sweatshirt. "It's too nice to be stuck indoors today."

"Be careful in Central Park, Miss. It's still early, and the city's not quite awake yet."

"I will, Joe. See you soon."

With a nod, she started her run, feeling the familiar rhythm of her sneakers hitting the pavement. As she jogged, Amanda relished the moment of freedom. This was her time to herself, away from the constraints of the office, the expectations of others, and the persona she had crafted for her professional life. Today, like most days for the last six months, she left behind her fake glasses—those bulky, thick lenses that disguised the true beauty of her eyes—and the expensive clothes and jewellery that she was used to.

In truth, she was exhausted by it all. People saw her beauty before they saw anything else, and it had shaped the way she was treated throughout her working life. No one ever cared that she was smart, capable, or hard-working—those traits were overshadowed by the perception of her looks. She was tired of being admired for the wrong reasons. She didn't want to be just another pretty face. She wanted to be valued for her intelligence, her competence, and her abilities. So, to avoid unwanted attention and assumptions, she hid behind clothes that didn't fit quite right, outdated glasses that masked her face, and a plain hairstyle that hid her natural radiance. After her last job and the incident in the break room with her previous boss, she would no longer expose herself to that type of attention.

Joe had known Amanda since she was a teenager, watching her grow into a sharp, capable young woman. Her beauty was undeniable, but six months ago, she'd started hiding it—trading stylish outfits for frumpy clothes and wearing those thick glasses that didn't suit her at all. Joe didn't understand her reasons, but he respected them. Still, he couldn't help but think it was a shame. The woman he knew didn't need to hide from anyone.

He had asked her one day, why she was hiding her beauty behind her tired, frumpy wardrobe. She'd explained in passing that it was for two reasons: First, men at the office kept hitting on her, and she was sick of it. Second, no one ever thought a beautiful woman could have a brain. If she dressed the part—if she blended in—people might actually take her seriously for her skills and not just her appearance.

But Joe didn't quite understand it. He saw through the façade. He saw the woman she truly was, and he knew that anyone who took the time to get to know her would too. But, like so many others, he respected her wishes. If she wanted to dress like an "old maid" as he called it, that was her choice. After all, he had been there to watch her grow up, and he knew the heart of the woman behind the disguise.

As Amanda continued her jog through Central Park, her mind wandered to the day ahead. The office would be waiting for her, the usual routine of answering calls, managing schedules, and working quietly behind the scenes to make everything run smoothly. But today, for just a few moments, she could be herself—free of the pressures of others' expectations. No one here would see her for her beauty, no one would try to tell her how she looked or what she should wear. They'd just see Amanda, the capable secretary, and that was exactly how she liked it.

Forty minutes later, Amanda returned from her morning jog, her breath steady and her mind clear from the calm run through Central Park. She slowed her pace as she approached her apartment building, feeling the familiar sense of comfort and security that came with being home.

As she reached the front entrance, she noticed her father, Henry Prentice, standing outside, chatting with Joe, the doorman. He looked like he had been waiting for her, his sharp eyes scanning the street as he stood tall and composed. Henry, 52, was a man who commanded attention with his presence alone. His dark hair, tinged with grey, and his tailored suit spoke of his success in the world of real estate. Yet, there was a softness to his demeanour when it came to his only daughter, a tenderness that had remained even before his wife, Amanda's mother, passed away five years ago from COVID.

The loss had been devastating for both of them. Henry had lost his partner, the love of his life, and Amanda had lost her mother, leaving a hole in both their hearts. But through the pain, Henry had been an ever-present figure in Amanda's life, doting on her, checking on her often, and trying to make sure she was always okay, even when she insisted, she was fine.

"Here she is now, sir," Joe said, stepping aside with a smile as Amanda appeared, her athletic figure moving with ease toward them.

"Morning, sweetheart," Henry greeted her warmly, his face lighting up at the sight of his daughter. He enveloped her in a tight hug, one that spoke of years of love and care. "How are you this morning?"

Amanda returned the hug, her smile softening as she kissed him on the cheek. "I'm good, Dad. How about you?"

Henry pulled back slightly, his eyes searching her face as though assessing her well-being. "I'm doing alright. But I wanted to see if you'd have breakfast with me this morning."

Amanda's smile widened, but she shook her head gently. "Sorry, Dad, I need to get to work. You know how it is."

He sighed, though there was no real frustration in his voice. "You don't need to work, sweetheart. You know that. You're a very wealthy woman. You don't have to do this."

Amanda rolled her eyes playfully, glancing over at Joe, who had heard this same conversation more times than he could count. She offered him a small, understanding smile, which he returned with a grin.

"I know, Dad, but I like working," Amanda said, her voice light but firm. "It keeps me busy, and I like being able to make my own way. Plus, I get to be part of a team." She shrugged, as though it was no big deal, but it was a part of her independence that her father still found difficult to accept.

Henry gave a small sigh, though he didn't press her any further. "I know you do, sweetheart. But one of these days, you'll realise you don't have to."

Joe, having opened the door for them, held it as Amanda and Henry entered the building. "I'll leave you two to catch up," he said with a respectful nod, knowing well enough that these moments with Amanda and her father were important.

Amanda waved him off with a smile as she led her father inside. "Thanks, Joe, I'll see you later."

"Take care, Miss Amanda," Joe called after them, a knowing smile on his face.

As they entered the lift to her penthouse apartment, Amanda turned to her father, a mischievous glint in her eyes. "Alright, come on up, and we can chat while I get ready.

You know I don't have time to sit down for breakfast, but I can at least listen to you complain about my work schedule for a few minutes."

Henry chuckled softly, a sound that had become rare in the past few years, but still so comforting when it did emerge. "I don't know if I'll complain this time, but I'll certainly try to convince you to take a break from all that work." He followed her from the elevator into her apartment, a little relieved that she was still the same strong, independent woman, even if he wished she would slow down every now and then.

Inside her apartment, Amanda kicked off her sneakers and headed for the kitchen, offering her father a seat at the table as she moved about. "Don't worry, Dad. I'll eat something later. But you can stay here, and I'll make us a coffee, and we can talk about whatever's on your mind."

Henry, always trying to be subtle, couldn't help but voice his concern. "I just don't want you burning yourself out, sweetheart. You've been pushing so hard lately, and I worry about you. You've got everything you need—you don't need to prove anything to anyone."

Amanda met his eyes, her smile softer this time. "I know you mean well, Dad, but I'm not trying to prove anything. I just want to feel like I'm doing something important. You know that."

Henry nodded, but the faint worry in his eyes remained. He wanted to protect his daughter, but he also knew she was more than capable of handling anything life threw her way. Still, the weight of it all, the constant hustle, the sacrifices she made—he hoped she wasn't letting the world take too much from her along the way.

"Amanda," he said softly, his voice tinged with concern, "are you still dressing like a frump for work?"

Amanda's eyes twinkled with mischief as she set the coffee pot down. She knew exactly where this conversation was headed.

"Yes, Dad, and you know exactly why I do," she replied with a playful sigh, her hands moving to tuck a loose strand of honey-blonde hair behind her ear.

"But how am I supposed to have any grandchildren if no one sees how beautiful you are?" Henry pressed, a smile tugging at the corners of his mouth, but the worry in his voice was still there.

Amanda laughed, shaking her head as she leaned against the counter. "Do you want your new son-in-law to only be interested in the way I look?" she said cheekily, raising an eyebrow.

Henry's lips twitched with amusement, but he quickly grew more serious. "You know that's not what I mean," he said, his tone soft but sincere. "I just want you to be happy.

You deserve to be noticed for more than your looks and clothes. You're smart, capable, and beautiful—inside and out. But I worry that by hiding your true self, you're not giving people the chance to see that."

Amanda's smile faltered slightly, her gaze shifting to the floor as she considered his words. She had always struggled with this—balancing her desire to be taken seriously for her intellect and skills while constantly being overshadowed by her appearance. But her father's concern, his gentle nudging, made her pause.

"I know, Dad," she said after a moment, lifting her head to meet his eyes. "But I'm just not interested in any of that right now. I'm only twenty-four. I'm not looking to settle down, and I don't want to be defined by the way I look. I want to be known for what I can do, not for how pretty I am."

Henry studied her for a long moment, his expression unreadable. He had always respected her independence and strength, but he couldn't help but wish she would let herself be seen for the woman she truly was—someone worthy of love and admiration for more than just her achievements.

"I understand, sweetheart," he said, his voice softening. "But just remember, you don't have to hide who you are to prove something to anyone. And there's nothing wrong with letting people see the whole of you—the smart, capable, beautiful woman that I've always known you to be."

Amanda smiled faintly, a warmth spreading through her chest at her father's words. She knew he only wanted what was best for her. "Thanks, Dad. I'll keep that in mind," she said, reaching over to give his hand a reassuring squeeze.

"But still," he added with a teasing grin, "if you happen to meet a nice young man who sees all of you—maybe without the fake glasses and the frumpy clothes—don't push him away too quickly."

Amanda rolled her eyes, her cheeks flushing slightly. "Alright, alright, Dad," she said, laughing. "I'll try to make an exception for the right guy. But no promises."

Henry chuckled, leaning back in his chair, a satisfied look on his face. He knew Amanda was as stubborn as she was independent, but he also knew that deep down, she would one day find a balance between being herself and allowing others to see her for who she truly was. Until then, he would continue to watch over her with the same love and concern he always had, hoping that, when the time was right, she would allow herself to step into the world without hiding behind the walls she'd built.

"I need to get ready for work," Amanda said, glancing at the time on her phone. She had a full day ahead, and her father's visit had interrupted her morning routine.

"When can I come and visit you and see where you work?" Henry asked, leaning back in his chair, his eyes twinkling with curiosity.

Amanda paused, considering the question. She had worked hard to carve out her space at the office, and the thought of her very wealthy father showing up to see where she worked was a little too much. "I've only been there for six months, Dad. I don't need my very wealthy father turning up and making a scene."

Henry raised an eyebrow, his tone playful. "Come on, Amanda. I can be discreet. I know how to blend in."

Amanda shook her head, trying to hold back a smile. She could already picture the scene—her father, larger than life, trying to play the part of a humble, low-key visitor. It would never work. "I'll think about it," she said with a sly grin, "but don't get your hopes up."

She walked toward her bedroom, calling over her shoulder, "I need to shower and get dressed. Will you wait for me? You can give me a lift to the office."

"Okay, sweetheart. At least I'm good for something," Henry replied with a chuckle, clearly delighted by the opportunity to spend more time with her.

Amanda turned and stuck her tongue out at her father, the playful gesture belying the affection she felt for him. Despite their different approaches to life, there was an unspoken bond between them that no amount of money or status could break.

Henry laughed, a deep, genuine sound that filled the room with warmth. As she walked into her room, the sound of her laughter mixed with his, and for a moment, the world outside seemed to fade. In that moment, there was only the shared connection between father and daughter, and it was enough.

Amanda closed the door behind her, and as she began to get ready, her thoughts drifted to her father's earlier question. She wasn't sure if she was ready to let him into that part of her life just yet, but the fact that he cared enough to ask made her smile.

Taking a deep breath, she turned on the shower, letting the warm water wash away the lingering traces of her morning jog and the tension of her father's concern. She wasn't ready for him to invade her work life, but that didn't mean she didn't appreciate his love and support. It was just part of the dance they did, the delicate balance between independence and connection.

As the water cascaded over her, she let herself relax for a moment, thinking about her day ahead. There was work to do, challenges to face, but no matter what, she knew she could handle it. And even if she didn't admit it out loud, having her father by her side, even in small ways, always made it a little easier.

Chapter Three

At lunchtime on Thursday, Diane made her way to the company cafeteria, a place she rarely visited but found perfectly suited for her current mission. Amanda Prentice sat at a corner table, eating a salad while flipping through notes in a leather-bound planner. Her honey-blonde hair was pulled into an unflattering bun, and thick-rimmed glasses obscured the striking green eyes Diane knew were hidden beneath. The shapeless cardigan and drab pencil skirt Amanda wore did nothing to flatter her, but Diane wasn't focused on appearances.

What she saw was a driven, grounded young woman—exactly the kind of person her son needed in his life. But none of that mattered to Diane. What she saw when she looked at Amanda was a smart, hardworking young woman with impressive qualifications and a grounded, family-oriented nature. Exactly the kind of person her son needed in his life—both professionally and, definitely, personally.

"Hello, Amanda. May I join you?" Diane asked warmly.

Amanda looked up, startled. "Mrs. Childs! Of course—please, have a seat."

"Thank you," Diane replied, settling into the chair across from her.

Amanda straightened, a hint of nervousness flickering across her face. Diane's presence was both flattering and a little intimidating. "Is there something I can help you with?"

"As a matter of fact, yes," Diane began, folding her hands on the table. "I've been meaning to speak with you about an opportunity that I believe you're perfect for."

Amanda blinked, clearly taken aback. "An opportunity?"

"Yes," Diane said, her tone calm but deliberate. "As you know, I've been temporarily filling in as Dominic's personal assistant since the previous one left. But it's time to find someone permanent—someone sharp, organised, and level-headed. I believe you're exactly what the role needs."

Amanda's heart skipped a beat, a rush of excitement bubbling inside her. This could be the opportunity she'd been waiting for. "Oh, that would be a wonderful opportunity," she said, her voice steady but filled with genuine interest. "I would definitely be interested in the position."

Diane smiled, nodding approvingly. "I'm glad to hear that. First, though, can you tell me a bit about yourself? I know about your education and work history, but I like to get to know the person behind the resume."

Amanda relaxed into the conversation, feeling more at ease now that the interview was taking a more personal turn. "Of course," she began with a warm smile. "I'm an only child of Henry and Helen Prentice. My mother passed away five years ago from COVID."

Diane's face softened with empathy. "Oh, I'm so sorry to hear that. That period was devastating for so many."

Amanda nodded, her smile turning a little wistful as she remembered her mother. "Yes, it was. But we try to keep going, honour her memory, and make the best of what we have now." She paused, collecting her thoughts. "My father, Henry, is a realtor. We're very close, and he's been a great support to me, especially since my mother passed. He's always been my rock."

"That sounds like a wonderful relationship," Diane said, her voice filled with understanding. She appreciated the depth of Amanda's family connections—especially the way she spoke about her father.

Amanda's eyes brightened as she continued. "I'm 24, single, and honestly, not really interested in settling down just yet. I know my dad wishes I'd find someone, but it's not something I'm rushing into." She let out a small laugh, glancing at Diane with a mischievous smile. "Much to his disgust, I'm perfectly content with my career and my independence for now."

Diane chuckled, enjoying the light-heartedness of Amanda's response. "It sounds like you're focused on building a future for yourself, and that's admirable." She nodded thoughtfully, appreciating Amanda's perspective. "So, tell me, why do you think you'd be a good fit for this role? What draws you to a position of a personal assistant?"

Amanda took a moment to gather her thoughts, then spoke confidently. "I've always been a very organised person, and I thrive in high-pressure environments. I'm detail oriented and I take pride in making sure everything runs smoothly, whether it's scheduling, handling communication, or anticipating needs before they arise. Plus, I'm a problem solver, and I like being able to adapt quickly when things change. I believe those qualities will help me support Mr Childs effectively in this role."

Diane listened intently, nodding in approval as she considered Amanda's answers. "Well, I think you have the right qualities for the job. Let's move forward and see how you handle the more practical side of the position. How soon can you start?"

Amanda's heart raced with anticipation. This was happening—this could be the start of something big. "I can start as soon as you need me to, Mrs Childs."

"Good. I'll have Dominic review everything, but I'm confident you'll be a great fit." Diane stood and extended her hand to Amanda. "I will let you know soon, Amanda."

Amanda shook her hand firmly, feeling a surge of accomplishment. "Thank you. I look forward to your decision."

Diane smiled warmly, her thoughts already turning to the next steps in her plan. She had no doubt that Amanda was the right choice. The beginning of a new chapter had started today—and it would be more than just a professional one.

As Diane walked out of the cafeteria, a sense of satisfaction and excitement swelled within her. Step one of her plans had been executed flawlessly. Amanda Prentice was perfect for the role—now all she had to do was convince Dominic. She knew that wouldn't be difficult. She was confident she could make him see that Amanda was exactly what he needed.

On Friday morning, Diane walked into Dominic's office, her expression lively and full of purpose. She could sense the shift in the air, the opportunity that was within her grasp.

"I've found the perfect candidate for your personal assistant," she announced, her voice steady but with a hint of pride.

Dominic raised an eyebrow, clearly taken aback. "Already? You've only just started looking on Monday."

Diane smiled, unruffled by his surprise. "Yes, I didn't have to look far. She already works here."

"Mother," Dominic sighed, pinching the bridge of his nose. "I specifically said a male."

"Dominic," Diane countered, her tone firm but amused. "At least hear me out before you dismiss her."

She handed him a file, her eyes twinkling as if she knew she had already won. Dominic stared at the file with scepticism but opened it anyway, his eyes scanning the first few lines of the document. Diane continued, her tone now a touch more playful.

"Amanda is extremely intelligent, driven, organised, and best of all, not interested in men at the moment," she added with a cheeky smile, fully aware of what she was implying.

Dominic shot her a look, his gaze narrowing slightly. "I'm listening," he muttered, his eyes scanning the contents of the file again. He flipped through the pages, his mind already beginning to calculate.

"Also," Diane continued, "she is not what you would call conventionally attractive. Which, I'm sure, you'll be happy about."

Dominic glanced at the photo, his lips twitching. Amanda wasn't unattractive, but her thick glasses and plain demeanour ensured she wasn't the type to distract him. Maybe that was exactly what he needed.

He turned back to the file, his curiosity piqued. "She's definitely accomplished for someone so young," he muttered, his fingers idly flipping through the pages as he read.

"Yes, she is. An only child. Her mother passed away from COVID five years ago, but she's very close to her father," Diane explained. "I've checked with her colleagues, and not one of them has a bad word to say about her. They tell me she's hardworking, polite, and extremely helpful. She's been with us for six months now."

Dominic's thoughts began to shift as he read more about Amanda's qualifications and work ethic. She had solid credentials—an impressive combination of intelligence and diligence. There was something about her that intrigued him, even though he wasn't sure exactly what it was. Diane was right about one thing: this wasn't about superficial attraction, which had always caused him so much trouble in the past.

"I don't know, Mother," Dominic said, leaning back, though his tone was less firm. "This is… unexpected."

Diane's smile widened. "I know you're hesitant, but trust me—she's focused on her work, not you. Just give her a chance."

Dominic rubbed his chin thoughtfully. "I have to think about it, of course."

Diane nodded. "Of course. But you could give her a trial and see how she fits. I am confident that once you do, you'll see exactly what I see. She's everything you need in a personal assistant—and nothing you don't."

Dominic finally closed the file and looked at his mother with a new sense of contemplation. "I'll think about it," he said, though there was no denying that the seed of possibility had already been planted.

Diane stood up; her expression satisfied. "You won't regret it. I'll look forward to your decision."

As she left his office, Diane couldn't help but feel a surge of anticipation. She knew that this was just the beginning—and soon, Dominic would come to see that Amanda was exactly what he needed, both in the workplace and beyond.

Chapter Four

Dominic sat back in his sleek, high-backed chair, staring out of the panoramic window of his office. The bustling New York City streets below looked like a living, breathing entity—fast-paced, full of opportunity and danger in equal measure. He'd built his empire here, brick by brick, each decision calculated and precise. Yet, when it came to matters of personal trust, he felt more vulnerable than he ever let on.

He rubbed his temple, recalling the conversation with his mother earlier that morning. She had made a compelling case for finding a new personal assistant, and he couldn't deny that her logic made sense. Diane had been filling in for Sofia ever since the disastrous fallout with his former assistant-turned-fiancée, but even his mother had her limits. She had her own life to live, and as much as he appreciated her presence at work, he knew she couldn't stay forever.

He just didn't trust anyone else.

Dominic's fingers tightened around the edge of his desk. The betrayal Sofia had subjected him to still felt raw, despite the months that had passed since their disastrous breakup. She'd wormed her way into his life, pretending to be the ideal partner, a woman who shared his ambition and vision. But all along, she had been interested in one thing: his wealth and the power his name carried. She had deceived him, manipulated him, and the pain of that realisation lingered long after he'd kicked her out of his life.

"I don't want another female assistant," he muttered under his breath, the words still stinging as if Sofia had betrayed him only yesterday. "A male assistant would be best. No complications. No one trying to seduce me, no hidden agendas."

He leaned forward, fingers tapping restlessly on his desk. It was a simple preference, really. He needed someone capable, someone sharp, someone who wouldn't cross the line. A man wouldn't be trying to seduce him, wouldn't be testing the boundaries of their professional relationship. The last thing Dominic needed was a repeat of Sofia's treachery—someone pretending to care while secretly working to undermine him.

But of course, his mother had other ideas. Diane was insistent that he remain open-minded about the idea of a female assistant, but he just couldn't. The last time he'd allowed someone to get close, it had cost him everything: his trust, his heart, and his sense of security.

He couldn't go through that again.

Dominic's thoughts drifted back to his mother's unwavering insistence that Amanda Prentice, the young secretary, could be the right fit for the job. From what Diane had shared, Amanda seemed to possess a rare combination of qualities that Dominic found hard to dismiss. She was intelligent, professional, and—most importantly—seemed to have no interest in playing the manipulative games that Sofia had. And, to his relief, Amanda wasn't what he would describe as "stunning." In fact, she kept herself fairly plain, a stark contrast to Sofia's polished and seductive allure.

But despite all that, the idea of hiring a female assistant still made Dominic uneasy. He couldn't shake the memory of how Sofia had wormed her way into his life, pretending to be everything he wanted her to be. Her charm had masked the manipulation beneath the surface, and once he'd fallen for it, the lines between their personal and professional lives had blurred beyond repair. It had been a catastrophic mistake, one that had shattered his trust and left him with deep scars.

"I can't let that happen again," he muttered under his breath. He had learned the hard way that employees were off-limits, no matter how professional or capable they seemed. The last thing he needed was another betrayal, another blurred line, another distraction.

Dominic would never forget the moment he arrived home early from a business trip, a simple action that would unravel everything he thought he knew about his fiancée, Sofia. He had planned to surprise her, but what he found instead would haunt him for years.

As he stepped into the foyer, the soft murmur of Sofia's voice carried from the living room. He paused, listening carefully, sensing something was off. Without thinking, he quietly moved closer, staying out of sight as he heard her talking animatedly on the phone.

"Everything's running smoothly," Sofia was saying, her voice dripping with a sweetness that sounded far too practiced. "In three weeks, I'll be Mrs Dominic Childs. Then the world's our oyster."

Dominic's heart sank, but he couldn't move. He was rooted to the spot, frozen by the words he was hearing. She continued, oblivious to his presence.

"He doesn't suspect a thing. The poor thing is so gullible," Sofia continued with a cruel chuckle. "I'm expecting another expensive gift when he gets back tonight. That should seal the deal."

The words hit Dominic like a punch to the gut. His mind raced as he struggled to process the betrayal unfolding in front of him.

Then, her lover's voice came through, laced with possessiveness. "I just don't like him touching you. You're mine."

Sofia's response was casual, almost dismissive. "Of course I am," she said, a self-satisfied tone creeping into her voice. "It won't be long now. I'll slowly pull away from him, I will stop having sex with him after the wedding, even if he divorces me, he'll have to pay big time."

The callousness in her words made Dominic's blood run cold. Every ounce of trust he'd placed in Sofia shattered in that instant. The woman he had believed to be his future wife, the woman he had let into his life, had been playing him all along—using him for his wealth, his power, and his status.

Dominic's fists clenched, his jaw tightening as the realisation settled in. He felt the overwhelming weight of humiliation and anger flood through him, but more than that, he felt a deep, unrelenting sense of betrayal. The woman he had loved, the woman he had been willing to share his life with, had been scheming behind his back the entire time.

Without another word, he turned on his heel and walked out of the apartment, his mind already racing with the steps he would take to end this toxic relationship. But even as he stepped out into the cool night air, he knew one thing for certain: he would never let anyone play him like that again.

He rubbed his hand across his jaw and stared out the window, watching the city hum below him. The decision wasn't easy. His mind kept circling back to Amanda Prentice. Diane had spoken highly of her, and while Dominic wasn't ready to admit it, something about the way Amanda looked intrigued him. Her qualifications were impressive, her work ethic beyond reproach, and from what he'd been told, she seemed to have her head firmly on her shoulders.

Still, there was a nagging doubt. His mother hadn't seen any signs of manipulation in Amanda, but then again, he hadn't seen it in Sofia—until it was far too late. Dominic couldn't afford to be blindsided again. He needed to be smarter this time, to keep his focus on the task at hand and not let any personal feelings complicate things.

But as much as he fought it, Amanda was becoming a persistent thought in his mind. Her professionalism, her dedication—those were qualities he respected. And despite his reservations, he knew it was only a matter of time before he had to make a decision.

He leaned back in his chair, eyes narrowing as he weighed the options. The city continued to pulse outside his office, a constant reminder of the work that needed to be done, but inside, Dominic was lost in thought, contemplating the fine line between trust and caution, between professionalism and something more.

"Maybe I'm being too harsh," he murmured to himself. "She's just a secretary. A professional, just like Sofia claimed to be at first." Then thought about his mother, he trusted his mother with his life. She had never liked Sofia. She never said anything, but he could tell. He should have taken more notice of that.

Dominic's gaze softened for a moment as he thought about the new assistant. If he hired Amanda Prentice, he would be working with her every day. That was a huge commitment. He didn't want to bring someone into his life only to face another betrayal. Yet, as much as he fought it, he knew the final decision rested with him.

The thought of his mother's persistence lingered in his mind, her voice echoing with the quiet certainty that Amanda was exactly what he needed. But was he willing to trust a woman again? Would hiring a female assistant open him up to the same heartbreak he had endured before? Or could Amanda truly be the exception?

"Maybe it's time to take a chance," Dominic finally decided, albeit reluctantly. His fingers brushed over the personnel file his mother had left. According to his mother Amanda was the top candidate.

His eyes narrowed as he thought of what might lie ahead. He would have to be cautious, but he couldn't let fear control his decisions forever. If Miss Amanda Prentice was who his mother believed she was, then perhaps this would be the opportunity for something better.

The city continued to buzz outside his office, but for Dominic, it was silent—his decision hanging in the air like the tension before a storm.

Dominic took a deep breath, the decision weighing on him, but it was time to stop overthinking it. He grabbed his phone and dialled his mother's number, his fingers lingering on the screen for a moment before he hit the call button. It was now or never.

"Hello, sweetheart," Diane answered, her voice warm and inviting, as always.

"Hi, Mum," Dominic replied, his tone surprisingly steady. "Okay, I've made up my mind. I'll give Miss Prentice a chance. But you need to stay with her for at least two weeks, observe how she fits in, and make sure everything is running smoothly. If I don't agree with you by then, we'll reassess and look again."

Diane's heart skipped a beat, and she struggled to suppress the smile that crept onto her face. She'd worked hard to make this happen, and now her plan was falling into place. "That sounds like a good plan, son. I'm glad you're willing to give her a shot. Don't worry, I'll make sure everything goes perfectly."

"She can start on Monday," Dominic said, his voice firm despite the underlying uncertainty.

"Monday it is," Diane agreed, her smile widening in triumph.

Dominic ended the call, leaning back as the weight of his decision settled over him. Monday would bring clarity—or chaos. Either way, there was no turning back.

Chapter Five

Amanda drove up the long, winding driveway of her father's estate in Connecticut, the towering trees on either side casting dappled shadows on the pavement as the sun began its ascent behind the distant hills. It was a sight she'd seen countless times, yet it still filled her with a sense of peace every time she arrived. The estate, nestled amidst acres of lush greenery, was more than just a home—it was a sanctuary for her father, a place where he could retreat from the busy world of real estate and, in his words, "feel closer to your mother."

Five years had passed since her mother's death, but the house still bore her unmistakable touch. An interior designer with an eye for effortless elegance, her mother had turned every corner of the estate into a perfect blend of beauty and warmth. The space, much like her memory, felt alive with her presence.

Amanda often found herself running her fingers along the smooth surfaces her mother had carefully chosen, finding small, bittersweet reminders of her presence in the subtle details—a particular shade of paint, the way the furniture was arranged, the delicate arrangement of flowers on the mantle. It felt like her mother was still there, in every corner, making the house feel like home.

As Amanda parked the car and stepped out, she could hear the creak of the front door opening. Her father, Henry Prentice, stood at the threshold, his tall frame filling the doorway. At 52, he carried himself with a kind of quiet authority, his dark hair just starting to show hints of grey, but his eyes—sharp and intelligent—were as bright as ever.

"Hello, sweetheart," he greeted her warmly, his voice carrying the comforting familiarity she had always loved. "How was the drive?"

"Uneventful, thank goodness," Amanda replied with a smile. "Not like last week when I was stuck in all that traffic. It felt like it would never end."

"You should drive here on Friday night," her father suggested. "The traffic is a lot less. You'd have a nice, relaxing evening when you arrive."

"I need to do my housework sometime," she teased, rolling her eyes as she grabbed her bag from the passenger seat.

Her father quirked an eyebrow, his smirk playful but with an edge of concern. "Sweetheart, why wear yourself out? You know you could hire someone to take care of all that."

Amanda shook her head, smiling fondly at her father. "I know, Dad, but I like doing it. It's just part of the routine."

Henry's expression softened, and he reached out to pull her into a tight hug. "I work hard so you don't have to," he said, his voice a mix of affection and concern.

Amanda pulled back slightly, putting her hands on his shoulders as she looked up at him, her expression serious. "Dad, please. I like having the control over things. You know how I am."

He chuckled, though there was a hint of worry in his eyes. "Okay, okay, I'll stop. You know I'm very proud of you, right?"

Amanda smiled warmly, feeling the familiar rush of love and gratitude for her father. "I know, Dad, and I love you more than anything." She kissed him on the cheek, then hugged him tightly, letting the warmth of his embrace comfort her.

As they stood there for a moment, the quiet of the estate surrounding them, Amanda felt a deep sense of peace. Despite all the challenges she faced in the world outside, moments like this—simple, calm, and full of love—reminded her of what really mattered.

Amanda's phone rang, interrupting the peaceful moment as she and her father stood on the front steps. She fished it out of her bag, her heart quickening when she saw the caller ID. "Hello, Amanda speaking," she answered, trying to sound calm but her voice betraying her excitement.

"Amanda, it's Diane Childs here," the voice on the other end said warmly.

"Oh, hello Diane," Amanda said, her pulse racing. This was the call she'd been waiting for. "What can I do for you?"

"I'm happy to inform you that Dominic has decided to give you a two-week trial period for the personal assistant position. Can you start on Monday?"

Amanda's breath caught in her throat, and a wave of relief washed over her. She had been hoping for this moment, but hearing it confirmed made it feel even more real. "Of course, thank you, Diane. I'm so excited."

"He wants to give you the position with my assistance, just for a two-week trial, and then we'll take it from there," Diane added, her voice full of encouragement.

"That sounds great," Amanda replied, smiling brightly. She turned to look at her father, who was watching her with a curious expression. "I'll see you bright and early Monday morning."

"Yes, you will," Diane said with a chuckle. "I'm confident you won't let me down, Amanda. You're going to do great."

"Thank you, Diane. I'll see you then." They exchanged goodbyes, and Amanda hung up the phone, her hands trembling slightly with excitement.

Henry, still standing in the doorway, looked at his daughter with a raised eyebrow. "What was that about?" he asked, clearly sensing that something big had just happened.

"I got the job!" Amanda burst out, her face alight with joy. "The CEO's personal assistant—I start Monday!" Her words tumbled over each other as she flung her arms around her father, unable to contain her excitement.

Henry stood there for a moment, processing the news. His face lit up with pride, but there was a slight wrinkle of concern in his brow. He was happy for her, of course, but he couldn't help but worry about the pressures of working for a high-powered CEO.

"Congratulations, darling," he said, his voice soft but tinged with concern. He pulled her into a tight embrace, holding her close for a moment longer than usual, as if to reassure himself that she was still his little girl—no matter how successful she became. "But just remember to take care of yourself. It's a big job, and I know how much you already do."

Amanda pulled back slightly, looking into her father's eyes. "I know, Dad. I'll be fine. I've been preparing for this, and it's a great opportunity. I promise I won't let the pressure get to me."

Her father smiled, but his worry remained. "I know you won't. Just… don't let them take advantage of you. And remember, you don't have to prove anything to anyone."

Amanda nodded, a confident smile on her face. "I will, Dad. I've got this. And thank you for always believing in me."

He kissed her forehead before stepping back to admire her. "I'm proud of you, Amanda. You're going to do great things. Just make sure you stay true to yourself."

"I will," she assured him. She then grabbed her bag, ready to start a new chapter in her career, her heart filled with a sense of purpose and the knowledge that her father's support would always be there, no matter what challenges lay ahead.

Amanda spent the entire weekend with her father, soaking in the quiet of his Connecticut estate. It was a much-needed break, a chance to relax and recharge before starting her new job on Monday. The long drive back on Sunday night gave her time to reflect on the opportunity ahead, and as excited as she was, she couldn't ignore the anxious glint she had seen in her father's eyes all weekend.

He'd tried to hide it, but his worry was unmistakable. Every time Amanda mentioned her upcoming role, his gaze would flicker with concern. She could tell he was proud of her, but he also knew the demands that came with working for someone like Dominic Childs. The wealthy CEO was known for his high standards and intense work ethic—both qualities that could be intimidating, even for someone as capable as Amanda.

Amanda, knowing her father's tendency to overthink, had decided to lighten the mood a bit. On Sunday afternoon, as they sat together after lunch, she placed a hand on his arm and smiled. "Dad, I think you should come and have lunch with me on Wednesday. I'll let you know the time, but one condition," she said, her tone playful.

Henry raised an eyebrow, clearly curious. "What's that?"

"You can't show up looking like a wealthy realtor. Promise me," Amanda said with a teasing smile.

Her father's face went slack with shock. "You're serious?"

Amanda nodded, trying not to laugh. "Absolutely. I need you to blend in. You know, no suits, no flashy cufflinks, no Rolex, none of that."

Henry couldn't help but laugh. "Okay, sweetheart. I'll play your game, but only because I get to see where you work finally."

"Exactly," Amanda said, her grin wide. "I'll be happy to show you around."

Henry shook his head, his amusement fading into a soft, proud smile. "Alright, alright. But you'd better warn me if I need to wear something that's not from the 'Dad's been wearing the same thing for the last ten years' collection."

Amanda chuckled, feeling a wave of affection for her father. She could tell he was trying to lighten the mood for her sake, but the worry still lingered in his eyes. "Thank you, Dad. I'll try to put your mind at ease. Just don't make a scene if you are not impressed."

Her father looked at her seriously then, a hint of concern creeping back into his expression. "Amanda, I just want you to be careful. I don't want you getting caught up in something you can't handle."

Amanda met his gaze with a gentle but firm smile. "I'm ready, Dad. I've been preparing for this. You raised me to be strong, and I'm not going to let anything, or anyone make me lose sight of who I am. I'm going to be fine."

Henry nodded slowly, still not fully convinced, but grateful for her confidence. "I know you are. Just don't forget to take care of yourself, okay? You don't have to do everything alone."

"I won't forget, I promise." She squeezed his hand reassuringly. "And now, no more worrying. Let's focus on this lunch and on Wednesday I'll show you just how amazing this new job really is."

With that, the conversation shifted, and they spent the rest of the evening talking about lighter things—memories of her childhood, funny family stories, and even plans for the next visit. But even as they laughed and chatted, Amanda could feel the weight of her father's love and worry hovering over her. She knew he would always be there, watching over her, but now it was her time to show him she was ready to take on the world.

As Amanda drove into the office on Monday morning, a rush of excitement stirred inside her. She had been anticipating this day for so long, and now it was here. She wasn't just eager to prove herself to Dominic Childs—she also wanted to prove to herself, and to her father, that she was capable of handling this new chapter in her life. She had worked hard to get here, and today, she was ready to show that all her preparation had paid off. With a determined smile, she thought to herself, nothing is going to stand in my way now.

She parked her car in the underground staff carpark and took a deep breath, steeling herself for the first day in her new role. As she walked through the front doors of Dominic Childs' sleek, modern office building, the weight of it all settled in. The atmosphere was buzzing with energy, the kind only a high-powered corporate environment could produce.

Amanda's outfit was a calculated choice, a deliberate step toward projecting competence over vanity. Thick glasses framed her face, her least favourite accessory, and her hair was twisted into a severe bun that added to the no-nonsense image she aimed to present.

Her blouse and skirt were shapeless and loose, designed to cover her subtle curves. She didn't want to draw attention to herself; not yet. This was her chance to show what she could do, and she wasn't about to let her appearance distract from her work.

The outer office featured two desks and a small conference table that could seat six. One wall was lined with filing cabinets, while a sofa occupied the opposite side. Dominic's office lay beyond another door, revealing a space that exuded both professionalism and luxury. A massive desk dominated the room, backed by floor-to-ceiling shelves filled with books, memorabilia, and personal items. Another six-seat conference table was situated in the room, along with an oversized sofa along one wall. The overall design struck a perfect balance between functionality and sophistication.

As she entered the office, Diane Childs was already waiting for her, a warm smile on her face. "Good morning, Amanda. Did you have a nice weekend?"

"Morning, Diane. I did, thank you. How about you?"

"Quiet," Diane replied, her smile fading slightly. "Since my husband passed, I don't go out much. What did you do?"

"I spent the weekend with my father in Connecticut," Amanda answered, hoping the mention of her father wouldn't sound like she was over-explaining. Diane gave a soft smile of understanding.

"Oh, how lovely," she said, her tone warm. "Well, we better get stuck in. Dominic likes his day planned as soon as he arrives."

Amanda nodded and followed Diane to the conference table. Diane wasted no time getting straight into the tasks at hand. She outlined the various duties and expectations for the day, and Amanda listened carefully, making notes as Diane spoke. As they went over the schedule, Amanda felt the familiar rush of determination. This was what she had trained for—what she had worked so hard to be prepared for.

As they dove into deeper discussions about Dominic's schedule and upcoming meetings, Amanda's thoughts were sharp and focused. She suggested a few tweaks to the meeting times to optimise Dominic's efficiency, and Diane seemed impressed. The conversation was flowing smoothly when suddenly, the sound of the office door opening interrupted them.

"Good morning, Mother," came Dominic's deep, commanding voice as he strode into the office, his tall frame seeming to fill the room, his sharp suit and confident posture radiating authority. Amanda's heart skipped a beat as she stood, a mix of nerves and excitement swirling within her.

"Morning, Dominic." Diane gestured toward Amanda. "This is Miss Amanda Prentice, your hopeful new personal assistant."

Dominic extended his hand, his expression courteous yet unreadable. "Welcome, Miss Prentice."

Amanda reached out to shake his hand, and the moment their palms met, a spark shot up her arm and settled in her chest, making her heart skip a beat. She glanced up, meeting his piercing gaze. "Good morning, Mr. Childs. It's an honour to be considered for this position. I hope I exceed your expectations."

Dominic stood tall and self-assured, his tailored suit accentuating his commanding presence. He radiated power and control, the kind that made Amanda suddenly hyper-aware of the shift in their dynamic. She had seen him in meetings before, but this was different—this time, she was here to support him, to help him navigate his demanding day.

Diane offered Amanda a subtle, encouraging smile as she handed her two copies of the day's agenda.

"I've already explained what is expected," Diane said in a light but efficient tone. "Amanda, why don't you walk him through today's schedule?"

Amanda took a steadying breath, her nerves calming as she straightened her posture. Handing Dominic a copy of the agenda, she glanced down at her own detailed version and began.

"Your first appointment is at 10am with Mr. White from Glassier Boutiques. The contracts are on your desk for your review before the meeting."

She paused briefly, meeting Dominic's gaze. His sharp eyes radiated intelligence and a calm authority that only heightened her determination to appear composed. She felt the weight of his attention but pressed on confidently.

"After that, you have a lunch meeting with—"

"Everything seems in order," Dominic interrupted smoothly, his tone firm and assured as he skimmed the agenda. He raised his eyes from the papers with a sense of finality. "Thank you, Amanda." Then proceeded into his office, leaving his office door open.

Amanda nodded, trying to keep her composure. "You're welcome."

As the minutes ticked by, Amanda fell into her role effortlessly. She was organised, efficient, and thoughtful, making sure Dominic's day went according to plan without a hitch. Diane watched her carefully, impressed by how quickly Amanda seemed to be settling into the rhythm of the job.

By the end of the day, Dominic hadn't said much, but the slight nod he gave as Amanda handed him the final report for the day felt like a small victory. She knew that today had been just the beginning. She still had a long way to go before she fully earned his trust, but she was determined to prove herself.

As Amanda left the office that evening, the excitement still simmering within her, she couldn't help but feel a sense of accomplishment. This was her chance, and she had taken it. Whatever the future held, Amanda knew one thing for sure: she was ready for it.

The next day went as smoothly as the first. Dominic continued his quiet, no-nonsense routine, speaking only when necessary, and Amanda followed his cues. She was methodical, organised, and always on top of her tasks. She didn't waste a word or time. The office was calm, with an undercurrent of efficiency.

As the morning wore on, Amanda and Diane were deep in conversation, sharing a quiet laugh over something trivial. The sound of their laughter filled the otherwise silent office, light and easy. Dominic, who had been reviewing a few documents at his desk, paused when he heard it.

Dominic's eyes flicked to Amanda, her laughter unexpectedly genuine, breaking through the usual stiffness of the office atmosphere. He hadn't anticipated such a reaction from her—she seemed so put together, so in control, yet in that moment, her laughter was warm and unguarded. He found himself momentarily taken aback, as if he'd glimpsed something behind her carefully crafted exterior.

For a brief moment, he forgot to mask his curiosity. What was it about her that made him want to know more? In the sea of people, he interacted with daily, few stood out the way she did, not just because of her sharp mind, but because of the softness beneath the professionalism. He tried to shake the thought off, but it lingered, gnawing at him. There was a spark there, something Amanda hadn't intended to show, and Dominic was intrigued.

"Amanda?" he said, cutting off his own thoughts. His voice was firm, the way it always was, but his mind was still whirling.

She looked up at him, her expression neutral as she set down her pen. "Yes?"

"I need you to take down some letters. Come into my office."

Amanda nodded and gathered her notebook and pen, following him into his office. She sat down across from him, legs primly together, back straight, poised, and professional. Dominic's eyes involuntarily followed the way she sat. She was so different from Sofia. The contrast hit him in an unexpected way. There were no crossed legs, no suggestive posture, no flirtatious glances. There was just… calm professionalism.

He couldn't help but compare the two women, though he told himself not to. Sofia had always found ways to distract him—whether it was through lingering looks, her coy gestures, or the deliberate way she would position herself. But Amanda… she was different. She wasn't trying to catch his attention. She was just doing her job.

He focused on the task at hand, flipping through some papers as Amanda opened her notebook. He began to dictate quickly, more out of habit than necessity. It was a test, though he didn't realise it at the time. He wanted to see how Amanda would handle the pace.

"Ready?" he asked, almost in a challenge.

"Ready," she replied simply, her voice steady.

He started speaking quickly, each word flowing rapidly as he dictated the letters. He glanced up to see if Amanda was struggling to keep up, but to his surprise, she wrote everything down without hesitation, her pen flying across the paper with remarkable speed.

She didn't flinch or ask him to slow down. Instead, she kept her focus, her eyes on the paper in front of her, her hand moving swiftly and efficiently. Dominic couldn't help but admire how effortlessly she handled the task.

When he finished dictating the first letter, he looked at her expectantly. "You need me to slow down?"

"No need," she replied, without looking up, her voice calm and assured. "All good."

There was something about that response that unsettled him. The way she handled herself with such quiet confidence, the lack of any effort to win his approval or flatter him—he wasn't used to it. Sofia had always known how to play the game, to show him just the right amount of interest at the right times. But Amanda… she wasn't playing any game at all. She was simply doing her job and doing it well.

Dominic found himself feeling a bit put out by her lack of interest. There was no flirting, no subtlety, no attempts to divert his attention away from work. Amanda was focused and professional, and it made him feel… strangely off-balance.

He tried to shake the thought. Focus, Dominic. She's just your assistant, he reminded himself.

But deep down, he couldn't ignore the nagging feeling that something about Amanda was different—more grounded, more serious—and that was precisely why he couldn't figure out why it unsettled him so much.

Chapter Six

Wednesday morning arrived, and Amanda felt a mixture of excitement and apprehension as she prepared for her father's lunch visit. She had warned him not to make a fuss and asked him to dress casually, hoping to avoid drawing attention in the office.

She glanced up at Diane as she entered the office. "My father is coming to have lunch with me today."

"Oh, how lovely!" Diane responded, her face lighting up with a warm smile.

"I just hope he doesn't embarrass me," Amanda said with a hint of amusement, knowing full well how protective her father could be.

Diane chuckled softly, giving her hand a reassuring pat. "He will be fine. And he should be protective. It's a father's job."

Amanda smiled, grateful for Diane's understanding. The morning passed quickly, the usual business routine filling the hours. Amanda had grown used to the rhythm of things now, and while she was still learning the ropes, she felt more confident each day.

Dominic, as always, kept his office door open unless he was in a meeting. She was certain he knew about her father's visit. He didn't seem the type to miss a detail, no matter how small.

Just before lunch, a last-minute issue with a contract surfaced. It was a new clause that needed to be revised before Dominic left for his meeting. Amanda immediately moved to handle it, but Diane noticed her focus and stepped in.

"I'll take care of it, Amanda. You go ahead and enjoy your lunch with your father."

Amanda shook her head, her gaze fixed on the paperwork. "No, Diane. I'll finish this up first. Work comes first."

Diane gave her a knowing look, her eyes softening with understanding, but she didn't press further. She had come to admire Amanda's unwavering dedication to her work, though she couldn't help but notice the slight furrow in her brow. It was clear Amanda was caught in a delicate balancing act—her father's visit pulling her one way, her professionalism anchoring her in the other.

Just as Amanda sat down to type out the revised clause, her father arrived. She heard his familiar voice before she saw him. "Hello, sweetheart."

Amanda looked up and smiled, relieved to see her father had dressed as she requested—casually, without his usual expensive suit. He looked more relaxed, and she appreciated his effort to fit in with the office atmosphere.

"Dad, I'm sorry," Amanda said apologetically. "I can't go to lunch yet. I have to finish this."

Henry's face softened with understanding. "I get it, sweetheart. I'll wait."

Amanda quickly introduced him to Diane, who greeted him warmly. It seemed that there was an immediate connection between them—Diane's warm personality and Henry's charm made for a natural, easy conversation. Amanda felt a pang of relief. She had worried his presence would be awkward, but so far, everything was going smoothly.

Suddenly, she heard Dominic's voice, smooth and confident, cutting through the quiet of the office. He must have heard Henry's arrival. He walked in, his tall frame casting a shadow across the room, his eyes briefly scanning Amanda before they landed on her father. He extended a hand, his expression neutral, but Amanda noticed the slight tightening of his jaw, as if weighing the man before him.

"Mr. Prentice, I'm Dominic Childs. It's a pleasure to meet you."

Henry accepted the handshake with a firm grip. "The pleasure is mine, Mr. Childs. Thank you for allowing me to stop by."

Diane, sensing the situation was settled, said, "You should go to lunch with your father, Amanda. I'll take care of the contract. Don't worry about a thing."

Amanda opened her mouth and protested. "No, Diane. I'll make it up to Dad later. Work comes first."

Amanda smiled at the comment, grateful for Dad's understanding, but she could tell there was more to it. There was something about his tone that made her pause, a hint of admiration she hadn't expected.

"Maybe I could join you for lunch while I wait, Diane?" Henry suggested, his voice sounding casual, but Amanda noticed the subtle undercurrent of genuine interest.

Amanda raised an eyebrow but didn't comment. "That's a good idea," she said, standing up from her desk. "Go ahead, Diane. I'll see you when you get back. Thanks, Dad," she added, walking over to kiss him affectionately on the cheek.

Her father gave her a soft smile, gently guiding Diane by the arm as they walked toward the elevator. Amanda watched them go for a brief moment, her heart warming at how easily they seemed to connect. Then, she turned back to her desk, determined to finish the clause for the contract.

As she resumed typing, she became vaguely aware of Dominic's presence nearby. His steady gaze lingered on her, but she refused to look up. Her focus remained on the task at hand. This was her job, and she prided herself on doing it well, no matter who was watching.

Dominic leaned slightly against the doorframe of his office, arms crossed, his gaze lingering on Amanda. He couldn't quite place it—there was something undeniably captivating about her. It wasn't just her work ethic, though that impressed him. It was the way she moved with quiet confidence, unaffected by anyone's expectations.

Unlike the usual sycophants who tried to win his favour with polished charm, Amanda seemed completely uninterested in impressing him. And that, he realised, made her all the more intriguing.

He replayed the earlier interaction with her father in his mind. The warmth and genuine affection she showed Henry had struck him in a way he didn't expect. Amanda seemed so natural in her relationships, so honest. It was refreshing, especially compared to the calculated personas he often encountered in his world.

She didn't try to win him over with flirtation or flattery. She simply was. And that, Dominic realised, was what intrigued him the most.

As the minutes passed, he found himself growing more curious. Amanda wasn't just efficient or hardworking—there was a quiet strength in her, a sense of dignity and integrity that set her apart.

Dominic straightened, forcing himself to break his gaze. She was his assistant, nothing more, he reminded himself. But even as he returned to his office, the thought lingered: Amanda Prentice was unlike anyone he'd met. She was rare in a way that made him wonder if he'd underestimated not just her, but everything she might bring to his world.

Amanda completed the revised contract clause just in time for Dominic's lunch meeting. She walked into his office, handing him the document. "I've completed the clause," she said.

Dominic scanned the document quickly. "Excellent work, Amanda. Thank you."

"You're welcome. Is there anything else you need before you go?"

"Yes, could you get the Zilton file?"

"No problem." Amanda returned to her office and approached the filing cabinet. The file was in the bottom drawer, so she bent down to retrieve it.

From his desk, Dominic's gaze landed on Amanda as she bent to retrieve the file. For a moment, her typically modest attire revealed a hint of the curves she usually kept hidden, and an unexpected surge of attraction coursed through him. It took him completely by surprise, catching him off guard.

What the hell. Keep it professional, Dominic.

Amanda straightened, holding the file, and approached his desk with her usual professional demeanour. "Here is the Zilton file," she said, her voice calm and efficient.

Dominic accepted the file with a curt nod. "Thank you."

Amanda gave a polite smile before leaving his office. Dominic leaned back in his chair and exhaled slowly, trying to quell the unexpected surge of attraction he'd felt. This wasn't the time, the place, or the person for such thoughts.

Shaking off the distraction, he rose from his desk and methodically gathered the necessary files and paperwork, slipping them into his sleek leather briefcase. With his usual precision, he straightened his tie, grabbed his phone, and headed out the door, ready to refocus on the task ahead. The meeting awaited, and Dominic Childs never let personal feelings interfere with business—at least, not anymore.

Diane and Henry returned from lunch, their laughter echoing down the hallway as they stepped into the office. It was clear they had enjoyed each other's company, and Amanda couldn't help but notice the lightness in her father's expression.

Henry greeted his daughter warmly. "Hello, sweetheart. Can I take you to lunch now?"

Amanda smiled at them both, glancing at Diane, who seemed equally cheerful.

"Yes, off you go," Diane said with a grin. "You've earned it."

"Thanks, Diane," Amanda replied, grabbing her bag. She led her father toward the cafeteria, which was conveniently located within the building.

As they walked, Amanda looked at her father with a playful smile. "So, did you enjoy your time with Diane?"

Henry gave a small chuckle, his tone lighter than usual. "Yes, she's a lovely lady. Very kind, very smart. We had a great conversation about… well, life in general, I suppose."

Amanda tilted her head, intrigued by the sparkle in her father's eyes. "That's good to hear. It's nice to see you connecting with someone new."

He gave her a sideways glance. "Oh, don't start matchmaking, Amanda. I just enjoyed lunch with a delightful person."

She laughed softly. "Fine, I'll behave—for now."

When they reached the cafeteria, Amanda led Henry to a quiet corner. "This place isn't exactly five-star dining, but it's convenient."

Henry waved off her comment. "Anywhere I get to spend time with my daughter is five-star to me."

Amanda rolled her eyes affectionately but couldn't hide her smile. As she ordered her food and settled at the table, she felt a warm sense of contentment. For all her father's protectiveness and occasional meddling, his unwavering support and love always grounded her.

Over lunch, they chatted about everything from her new job to his plans for the weekend, with Henry sneaking in the occasional question about Dominic. Amanda brushed them off with good-natured humour, but she couldn't deny the curiosity lingering in her father's tone.

After lunch, Henry gave her a warm hug before leaving, and Diane headed out to run some personal errands. Amanda returned to her desk, ready to dive back into work, but her thoughts kept drifting. Her gaze occasionally wandered toward Dominic's office, even though he wasn't there.

She leaned back in her chair and let out a soft sigh, her fingers tapping lightly on the desk. It wasn't lost on her how attractive her new boss was. Dominic Childs was the kind of man who turned heads without trying—tall, confident, with sharp features and a presence that commanded attention. He wasn't just attractive; he was magnetic in a way that was hard to ignore.

Amanda frowned slightly, shaking her head at her own thoughts. Get a grip, Amanda, she scolded herself silently. Yes, he was handsome, but he was also her boss. A professional, driven, no-nonsense CEO who likely didn't notice her beyond her work ethic. He probably didn't even notice she was a woman. Even if he did, it wouldn't matter. She had no intention of letting herself get caught up in something that could jeopardise her career—or her dignity.

Still, she couldn't deny there was something about him that drew her in. It wasn't just his looks; it was the way he carried himself, the sharp mind behind those intense blue eyes, and even the rare moments when she caught him watching her with a flicker of something she couldn't quite name.

But she reminded herself of the boundaries she'd set. Acting on even the smallest spark of attraction was just out of the question—it was not possible. Men like Dominic Childs didn't notice women like her, not beyond their professional capabilities. And besides, even if he did, she wouldn't risk everything she'd worked for over a fleeting crush.

Amanda shook off the thought and straightened in her chair, determined to refocus on her tasks. There was no room for personal feelings here. Her job was to assist Dominic and prove her worth, not to entertain foolish fantasies about a man who was entirely out of her league. Keep it professional, Amanda, she told herself firmly, opening her laptop and diving into the next task on her list.

The rest of the week was routine until Friday afternoon. Diane had left early for an appointment, leaving Amanda and Dominic alone in the office.

Amanda, focused on reviewing a file, walking into Dominic's office at the same moment Dominic stepped out of his office, his attention buried in his own paperwork. Neither noticed the other until they collided. The impact nearly knocked Amanda off her feet, but Dominic's quick reflexes saved her. His arm shot out, wrapping around her waist and pulling her against him to steady her.

The moment froze.

Amanda was pressed against him, her hands gripping his shoulders for balance. Dominic's grip was firm but gentle, his hand resting at the small of her back. For a brief second, neither moved, both too stunned to react.

Dominic's mind raced as he registered the feel of her svelte, toned figure against him. She was so petite, yet her presence was commanding. His body betrayed him, an instant reaction he hadn't experienced in a long time.

Control yourself, Dominic, he mentally scolded, but his heart wasn't listening.

Amanda, still in shock, tilted her head back to look up at him, intending to thank him. But as she did, something in his eyes stopped her cold. The words caught in her throat. She had known Dominic was handsome—sharp jawline, intense blue eyes—but up close, he was… magnetic.

His gaze was steady, but there was something in it that flickered just beneath the surface. It was the kind of look that made her heart race before she could even process why. She quickly averted her eyes, her cheeks flushing.

"Are you okay?" Dominic asked, his voice low and concerned.

"I—yes, thank you," Amanda stammered, her cheeks flushing. She tried to step back, but his hand lingered for a moment longer before he finally released her. The absence of his touch felt oddly noticeable.

Dominic cleared his throat and straightened, a slight flush creeping up his neck. He avoided her gaze as he stepped back, mentally chastising himself for the reaction that had caught him off guard. 'I wasn't looking where I was going. My apologies.' The words felt oddly flat, as if they couldn't quite cover the tension in the air.

"No, it's my fault," Amanda said quickly, her hands smoothing her blouse as she avoided his gaze. "I wasn't paying attention."

For a brief moment, silence hung between them, heavy and unspoken. Amanda felt her heart racing, her palms slightly damp. Dominic, too, seemed caught off guard, his usually composed demeanour faltering ever so slightly.

"Well, uh," Dominic began, clearing his throat again, "I'll be in the conference room if you need me."

"Of course," Amanda replied, nodding as she clutched her file tightly, desperate to anchor herself.

Dominic gave her a curt nod before walking away, his movements a touch more measured than usual. Amanda stood frozen for a moment, trying to process what had just happened. Her heart was still hammering in her chest, and her mind replayed the moment his arms had steadied her.

She exhaled slowly and shook her head. *Get a grip, Amanda.* But no matter how hard she tried, the memory of his strong hands and the intensity in his eyes lingered, leaving her more flustered than she cared to admit.

Chapter Seven

Amanda's weekend was quiet. Her father had to work, so their usual Saturday lunch was postponed, and she spent the time catching up with her best friend, Megan.

Saturday afternoon, Amanda was curled up on Megan's couch with a cup of coffee, chatting about work and life when Megan's older brother, Daniel, showed up unexpectedly. Amanda groaned inwardly. Daniel had harboured a crush on her for years, and despite her countless polite rejections, he never took the hint.

"Hey, Amanda," Daniel said with his usual eager grin. "Didn't know you'd be here."

"I'm here most Saturday afternoons," Amanda replied, keeping her tone neutral as she sipped her coffee.

Megan gave her brother a warning glance but stayed quiet. Amanda appreciated her friend's silence amid Daniel's persistent flirtation.

"So, Megan tells me you're working for Dominic Childs now," Daniel said, sitting down across from Amanda. "Personal assistant to the big shot himself, huh?"

"Yes, I started this week," Amanda replied, hoping to keep the conversation short.

Daniel leaned back, his expression turning serious. "You know, you should be careful with him."

Amanda raised an eyebrow. "What do you mean?"

"Well," Daniel began, clearly enjoying the gossip, "his last assistant was used, dumped, and heartbroken. He likes to sleep with his staff."

Amanda frowned. "I didn't know that. But what does that have to do with me?"

Daniel shrugged. "Just saying, the guy is ruthless. He chews people up and spits them out—especially women. He's a player, Amanda. You're better off staying far away from him."

Amanda bristled at his tone. "I'm his employee, Daniel, not his girlfriend. I'm there to do a job, and that's it."

"You're a beautiful woman, Amanda. That's why I'm worried about you. He chews women up and spits them out." Daniel said with a smug smile, clearly enjoying the conversation more than he should.

Megan, sensing Amanda's discomfort, spoke up. "Daniel, enough. Amanda knows what she's doing.'"

Daniel raised his hands in mock surrender. "Fine, fine. Just don't say I didn't warn you."

Amanda forced a polite smile, but inside, she was irritated. Daniel's constant need to insert himself into her life was grating, and his comments about Dominic unsettled her.

She didn't want to think about Dominic in any personal capacity. Yes, he was attractive, but she was determined to maintain professional boundaries. The last thing she needed was someone planting seeds of doubt in her mind about her boss—or her ability to handle the job.

After Daniel left, Megan turned to Amanda with an apologetic smile. "Sorry about him. You know how he is."

"It's fine," Amanda said, waving it off. "But I could have done without the commentary on my boss."

Megan chuckled. "He's always been jealous of anyone who gets your attention, even if it's just professional."

Amanda shook her head and laughed. "Well, he can relax. Dominic Childs is the last person I'd ever get involved with."

But as the words left her mouth, Amanda felt a flicker of doubt. Why did Daniel's comments bother me so much? she wondered. Shrugging off the thought, she focused on enjoying the rest of the afternoon with Megan, determined not to let Daniel—or his opinions—ruin her day.

Sunday morning, Amanda laced up her running shoes and headed to Central Park for her usual jog. The crisp air invigorated her as she weaved through the paths, her thoughts drifting to the upcoming workweek. It had been a good first week, but she knew she had to remain sharp and focused if she wanted to make her mark.

By the time she returned to her apartment building, she was lightly flushed from the exercise, her honey-blonde hair still tied in a ponytail. She spotted Joe, the doorman, starting his shift.

"Hi, Joe," Amanda greeted, tugging her hair tie free and letting her waist-length hair fall loose. She ran her fingers through it to shake out the tangles.

"Morning, Miss Amanda," Joe said with a grin. "Jogging again? You're up early for a Sunday."

"Yep, gotta keep fit," she replied, smiling.

They chatted casually, standing near the entrance. Amanda adjusted her water bottle in the pocket of her leggings as they talked, oblivious to the black limousine slowly cruising past the building.

Inside the limo, Dominic was enroute to a brunch meeting with a potential client. As he leaned back in his seat and glanced out the tinted window, his eyes caught sight of a woman standing outside an apartment building. She was in running gear, her fitted top and leggings perfectly showcasing her athletic figure. Her long honey-blonde hair cascaded down her back, glinting in the sunlight.

Dominic blinked; his interest piqued. There was something familiar about her, but he couldn't quite place it. The woman had a stunning figure—fit, confident, and effortlessly sexy. Is that… Amanda? he thought, the idea catching him off guard. He dismissed it immediately. It couldn't be. Amanda was reserved and always dressed conservatively. This woman had an energy and presence that didn't match the image he had of his assistant.

Still, he couldn't tear his gaze away as the limo continued down the street. His meeting was the last thing on his mind as he replayed the brief glimpse in his head. Could it really be her?

Meanwhile, Amanda finished her conversation with Joe and headed upstairs, completely unaware of the brief, unexpected connection with her boss. She showered, made herself a light breakfast, and settled onto the couch with a book, ready to enjoy a quiet Sunday—oblivious to the fact that Dominic's thoughts lingered on the mystery woman he'd seen that morning.

After Dominic's brunch meeting, he made his way to the upscale restaurant where he had arranged to meet his mother for lunch. As he entered, he spotted her sitting at a table near the window.

"Hi, Mum," he greeted as he walked toward her, his tone warm.

"Hello, Dominic," Diane replied with a smile, standing to give him a quick hug before they both sat down. "How are you?"

"I'm good," he said, settling into the chair across from her. "How about you?"

"Good, good. I'm glad you're here. Now, tell me what you think of Amanda," Diane said, her eyes gleaming with anticipation as she reached for the wine list.

Dominic raised an eyebrow, his lips curving into a small smile. "Straight to it, I see."

Diane didn't miss a beat. "You know I'm not one to beat around the bush, and you've had enough time to form an opinion by now. I'm curious what you really think."

He chuckled softly and ordered a drink from the waiter, his eyes briefly flickering toward his mother before returning to the menu. "I have to agree with you, she's definitely working out."

Diane leaned forward, her voice a little more measured. "I told you; she was the perfect fit. She's organised, driven, and doesn't let anything slip through the cracks. Not to mention, she's focused and independent. I think she'll make an excellent assistant for you."

Dominic nodded, his thoughts drifting back to his time working with Amanda. "You were right. She's reliable. I can count on her, and that's something I don't take for granted. Plus, she's got a good head on her shoulders. Knows what needs to be done, doesn't need constant supervision."

"See? I told you," Diane smiled triumphantly. "But what about the other things? How does she fit in with your ideas of a personal assistant? What do you think of her personality?"

Dominic paused, swirling his drink in his glass as he considered his words. "She fits in well. She's quiet. Do you know where she lives?"

Diane raised an eyebrow, a knowing smile tugging at her lips. "No, why?"

Dominic leaned back in his chair, fingers tapping rhythmically on the edge of his glass. "I thought I saw her at an apartment block on Fifth Avenue."

Diane's smile widened at the mention of the exclusive address. "That's a pretty classy part of town," she mused. "Those apartments cost a fortune. Can't imagine her salary would cover that kind of accommodation."

Dominic chuckled at his mother's surprised tone. "Yeah, you're right."

But Diane didn't mention that Amanda was, in fact, a very wealthy heiress. She'd learned that in a conversation with Henry over lunch on Wednesday. He had been unusually candid with her about his daughter and had even shared a few family details.

"Why does Amanda dress the way she does and hide her beauty?" Diane had asked, intrigued by her new assistant's understated and reserved appearance.

Henry had grinned, clearly pleased that Diane had noticed. "I'm glad you noticed. Amanda thinks people won't take her seriously if she looks the way she really looks." He'd pulled out his phone and shown her a picture of himself and Amanda at a formal dinner.

Diane had been taken aback by the image. "Oh, my lord, she's gorgeous," she had said, her eyes widening in amazement. Amanda was striking—graceful, radiant, and elegant.

"Yes, she is," Henry had responded proudly. "And you've obviously noticed she's very intelligent too."

Diane had nodded. "Yes, I did. She's kind, caring, compassionate… She's got it all."

Henry had smiled, a twinkle of mischief in his eyes. "I just wish she'd settle down and give me some grandchildren."

Diane had leaned back in her chair with a sly grin. "My son wouldn't be able to keep his eyes off her if he knew." She paused for a moment, her voice turning teasing. "I think your daughter would be perfect for my son."

Henry's eyes had widened in surprise. "Really?"

"Yes," Diane had replied, her tone soft but deliberate. "I think they would be a great match. She's exactly what Dominic needs."

Henry had smiled, clearly amused by Diane's matchmaking. "I think I see where this is going, Diane. And I like it."

Diane had laughed, leaning in with a conspiratorial wink. "I'm not rushing anything. But I think they need a little nudge in the right direction. Don't you agree?"

Henry had smiled back, the hint of approval in his eyes. "I'm in."

Back in the present, Dominic spoke again, pulling her back into the conversation. "I guess we'll find out more as we go," he said, tapping his fingers lightly on the edge of his glass. "She's got me intrigued."

Diane smiled knowingly, her eyes twinkling with a quiet confidence. "I think you're already seeing a little more than you realise, Dominic."

The next week unfolded as expected. Dominic was thoroughly impressed with Amanda's work. She was sharp, efficient, and always on top of things—never missing a beat. By Thursday afternoon, he called her into his office.

"Amanda, you've done excellent work here," he said, his tone serious but with a hint of approval. "If you're interested, the job is yours."

Amanda smiled, feeling a mixture of relief and excitement. "Thank you, Dominic. I'd be honoured to work for you as your personal assistant."

Diane, who had overheard the conversation, beamed with satisfaction. She handed Amanda her mobile number when she got back to her office. "If you need anything, don't hesitate to call. Though, I doubt you'll have any issues."

Amanda smiled and thanked Diane, grateful for her support.

But Friday afternoon took an unexpected turn. As Amanda and Dominic were walking out of his office together, the door opened. A voice broke through the quiet atmosphere.

"Hello, I'm looking for Amanda Prentice."

Diane looked up from her desk, catching Amanda's attention as she walked toward her. She smiled at Amanda, "This gentleman is looking for you."

Amanda froze when she saw Daniel standing in front of Diane. He was as charming as ever—handsome, well-groomed, with that familiar smug expression. But what he said next took her by surprise.

"Amanda, what the hell are you wearing?" Daniel exclaimed, his eyes scanning her office attire with apparent distaste. "Why are you dressed like that?"

Amanda, taken aback and irritated, set the papers she was holding down on the desk. "What are you doing here, Daniel?" she asked, her voice laced with disbelief and frustration. She never expected him to show up at her office, let alone criticise her appearance.

Dominic, standing next to Amanda, glanced at Daniel. He was immediately struck by the man's good looks, and an unexpected wave of jealousy surged through him. The familiarity with which Daniel addressed Amanda made Dominic feel uncomfortably possessive, even though he didn't quite understand why.

Amanda, meanwhile, was visibly irritated. She had hoped Daniel would respect her constant refusals for a date, but it seemed he had other plans.

Daniel, undeterred, continued, "I was hoping you'd go out with me tonight. Just the two of us?"

Amanda's irritation was starting to boil over. She glanced at Dominic quickly, embarrassed that Daniel was there, making a scene. Dominic was doing his best to mask the discomfort he was feeling at seeing another man trying to get close to Amanda.

Taking a deep breath, Amanda looked Daniel in the eye. "I appreciate the offer, but I'm busy," she said firmly, her voice cold. "I'm at work, Daniel. This isn't the right time."

Dominic could sense the tension in the room. He wasn't sure who Daniel was to Amanda, but the idea of him showing up uninvited at his office, disrupting Amanda's work, didn't sit well with him.

Daniel raised an eyebrow, clearly not expecting her response. "Busy with him?" He nodded toward Dominic, his tone dripping with jealousy.

Amanda's gaze hardened. "Daniel, this is not the time or the place. I'm busy with work," she repeated, her voice leaving no room for argument.

Dominic, still feeling that strange possessiveness, stepped forward. His posture was authoritative, and his voice cool but polite. "Daniel is it?" he asked. "It's a pleasure to meet you. But I believe Amanda has made it clear she's occupied right now."

Daniel eyed Dominic with surprise, then glanced back at Amanda. His expression faltered, but he didn't back down. "I'll wait for you downstairs," he said with a hint of annoyance before turning to leave. As the door closed behind him, Dominic stood in place, still processing the strange interaction.

Dominic wasn't sure why he felt the way he did. The thought of Daniel getting close to Amanda—now his personal assistant—didn't sit well with him.

He shook his head, trying to dismiss the feelings stirring inside him. This wasn't his problem. Amanda was here to work. But why, then, did the idea of another man—especially someone that looked like Daniel—intruding on his territory make him feel so unsettled?

Amanda returned to her desk, her composure back in place. Dominic went back into his office, but the tension from the encounter lingered in the air.

Diane, who had witnessed the whole exchange, turned to Amanda with a mischievous smile. "Who was that? He's gorgeous."

Amanda rolled her eyes, clearly unimpressed. "And he knows it too."

Diane chuckled softly. "Oh, he's definitely interested in you."

Amanda sighed, clearly exhausted by the attention. "Yes, I know. He's my best friend's older brother."

Diane raised an eyebrow, amusement dancing in her eyes. "And what do you think about that?" she asked, her tone teasing but curious.

Amanda hesitated for a moment before responding. "I don't know. He's persistent, but I'm just not interested."

Diane smiled knowingly. "You say that now," she teased. "But don't be surprised if he keeps trying. Maybe you should give him a chance, you never know until you do. People can surprise you when you get to know them better."

Amanda thought about it for a moment, then glanced up at Diane. "Do you think?"

"Yes, I do," Diane said confidently. "He's gorgeous, obviously successful, and clearly interested in you."

Amanda sighed, her resolve softening. "He is all those things. Maybe I should give him a chance. It's time for me to go anyway." She stood up from her desk, gathering her things. "I'll see you later… Oh, that's right, you won't be here anymore. Well, thank you, Diane. You've been a joy to work with. I hope I see you again soon."

Diane smiled warmly, her expression playful. "Oh, you will, dear. I come and visit Dominic often. Good luck with Mr. Gorgeous." She winked as Amanda walked out.

As Amanda left, Dominic stormed into the outer office, his frustration written all over his face. "What the hell was that?"

Diane, pretending to be surprised, looked up innocently. "What, dear?"

"You, encouraging Amanda to go out with that… that Daniel," Dominic said, his voice tight with irritation.

Diane had to put her head down to hide the smirk threatening to break out on her face. "Why shouldn't she? She's young, single, and he's definitely interested in her. And he's gorgeous, to boot." She shrugged, trying to sound nonchalant.

"She's not interested," Dominic snapped.

"How do you know?" Diane shot back, not missing a beat.

"You heard her," Dominic replied, frustration creeping into his tone.

Diane gathered her bag, preparing to leave. She walked toward the door and turned back to him with a knowing smile. "Dominic, she's single, and she's a lovely girl. She deserves someone who treats her as special as she is. Have a good weekend, dear." She waved goodbye, her grin barely contained.

Dominic watched Diane leave, still fuming. "What the hell!" he muttered under his breath, shaking his head in disbelief as he processed everything that had just happened. Why was he so angry? Amanda had every right to go out with anyone she wanted. So why did the idea of Daniel asking her out rub him the wrong way?

He ran a hand through his hair, trying to make sense of his feelings. It wasn't like he was even interested in Amanda like that—was he? He had always been focused on his work, and Amanda was just his new assistant. But the thought of her with someone else, especially someone as persistent as Daniel, left a knot in his stomach that he couldn't shake.

Meanwhile, as Amanda stepped out of the elevator and into the lobby, she was met by Daniel, who had been sitting in one of the plush chairs, waiting for her. He jumped up immediately, a hopeful look on his face.

"Amanda, come out with me tonight, please," Daniel said, his voice full of charm as he stepped toward her.

Amanda paused, glancing at him, considering the suggestion. She had been hesitant, but after talking to Diane, maybe she should give it a chance. She smiled at Daniel, the decision made. "Okay, Daniel. I'll go out with you."

Daniel's face lit up, clearly thrilled by her answer. "Great! I'll pick you up at seven."

"Okay, I'll see you then," Amanda replied, giving him a small smile as she turned to leave the building.

Daniel watched her walk away; his smile still wide as he mentally planned their evening together.

Back in the office, Dominic stood by his desk, trying to refocus, but his mind kept drifting to Amanda. He cursed under his breath. What was it about this situation that bothered him so much?

Chapter Eight

Amanda took one last look at herself in the mirror before she left her apartment. The red dress hugged her frame in all the right places, the square neckline drawing attention to her shoulders and collarbone. The full skirt swirled gracefully as she moved, giving her a sense of femininity she wasn't used to showcasing. She wore her long honey-blonde hair loose in soft waves that cascaded past her shoulders to her waist. A light touch of makeup enhanced her features without masking them, and the ruby choker around her neck added just the right touch of elegance to complete her look.

At exactly 7pm, the doorman's voice crackled through the intercom. "Miss Prentice, there is a Daniel downstairs for you."

"Thank you, I will be down shortly," she replied.

Amanda paused, adjusting the hem of her dress before heading toward the elevator. She preferred meeting guests in the lobby; her penthouse apartment was off-limits unless they had a keycard. Only her father, who had his own access, was allowed to come straight up.

As she reached the lobby, she spotted Daniel waiting near the entrance. He looked handsome in his dark blue suit, his dark hair neatly styled, and a smile spreading across his face when he saw her. His sharp features contrasted nicely against the smooth fabric of his suit, but as Amanda's gaze lingered for just a moment, she couldn't help but think—Dominic would look so much better in a suit like that. Where did that thought come from?

"Amanda, you look beautiful," Daniel said, stepping forward to take her hand, raising it to his lips and kissing her knuckles in a charming gesture. "I'm glad you are not wearing those horrid glasses."

Amanda smiled, feeling a bit relieved. She didn't actually need glasses; the ones she wore to work were just a prop. Plain glass, nothing more. They hid her true features, just the way she wanted. "Good evening, Daniel, and thank you."

Daniel's eyes lingered on her, and she could see the admiration in them. His attention was flattering, but for some reason, it didn't feel as thrilling as she had anticipated. As they left the building and stepped into his car, Amanda couldn't help but feel a little distracted, her thoughts wandering back to the office, and for some reason, to Dominic.

What was wrong with her? Why did she keep thinking about him? It was just a passing thought. Daniel was nice, and he was clearly interested. This date could be the start of something fun, right?

But as she glanced back at Daniel, who was talking animatedly about the restaurant they were heading to, she couldn't quite shake the thought of Dominic, the way he had looked at her earlier, and the unfamiliar sensation of unease that had been bubbling up inside him when Daniel had shown up at the office. It was confusing, and Amanda was sure she needed to focus on her evening with Daniel, not let her mind wander into places it shouldn't be.

The restaurant was exquisite—sleek, elegant, and buzzing with an air of quiet sophistication. The food was magnificent, each dish more delightful than the last. Daniel was charming and attentive, making sure Amanda had everything she needed, but despite the surroundings, something was missing. Something, or rather someone. Dominic. Why am I thinking about him? Get a grip, Amanda.

Excusing herself, Amanda made her way to the ladies' room to clear her head. She took a moment to compose herself in front of the mirror, but the nagging thought of Dominic lingered, unbidden. When she returned to the dining area, she stopped in her tracks, startled to see Dominic standing by their table, engaged in conversation with Daniel. Daniel was standing tall, his posture confident, while Dominic scanned the room, his eyes searching for someone.

Amanda hesitated, her heart skipping as Dominic turned and left the restaurant with a tall blonde woman at his side. She watched them leave before walking back to the table.

"Dominic was just here," Daniel remarked casually, his eyes flickering toward her.

"Oh," Amanda said softly, trying to mask the sudden rush of emotions that hit her.

"He wanted to wait for your return, but his date got antsy," Daniel added, looking momentarily pleased with himself.

"That's nice," Amanda said flatly, keeping her voice neutral as she forced herself to focus on Daniel. She could feel a hint of annoyance bubbling inside her.

Daniel glanced at her with a look of concern. "He's got his eye on you, you know."

Amanda shook her head, dismissing it with a smile that didn't quite reach her eyes. "Don't be ridiculous. He is my boss. That's all."

Daniel didn't seem entirely convinced, but he let it go. He called for the check, paid with a flourish, and they left the restaurant. The air was cool as they walked outside, and Daniel led her to his car. It was almost 11p.m. by the time they reached her apartment building.

Daniel parked in front of the entrance, his gaze lingering on her as he turned to face her. "I had a really good time tonight, Amanda. I hope we can do this again."

Before she could respond, Daniel leaned in and kissed her. It was gentle, lingering—a kiss that was pleasant but somehow lacking the connection she had hoped for. For a brief moment, Amanda felt no flutter in her chest, and there was no spark. As his lips left hers, a strange thought crossed her mind—one that made her pause. She found herself wondering what it would be like to kiss Dominic. What would it feel like if he was the one leaning in, if his hands were the ones gently holding her face? The thought lingered, and she couldn't shake the feeling that it was him she truly wanted to be with, not Daniel.

"Thank you, Daniel," Amanda said, her voice warm but calm, as she opened the car door. "For a lovely evening. Drive home safe." She gave him a polite smile before stepping out of the car. Daniel nodded and drove off into the night.

As Amanda walked toward the entrance of her building, she saw Joe, the doorman, standing by the door. "Good evening, Miss Amanda," he greeted her with a friendly smile.

"Why are you here at this hour, Joe?" Amanda asked, her tone curious but light.

"Brian's sick," Joe explained, shrugging slightly. "Needed to cover for him tonight. You're looking lovely as always."

"Thank you, Joe," Amanda said, giving him a warm smile as she approached.

Joe's eyes twinkled with a hint of mischief. "So, who was the gentleman?"

Amanda's smile faded slightly as she sighed. "No one important," she replied lightly, trying to keep the mood easy. "I'm not going to see him again. A bit too self-important for my liking." She chuckled, shaking her head.

Joe laughed heartily, clearly amused. "You deserve only the best, Miss Amanda. You're one in a million."

Amanda's smile softened at Joe's words, his familiar warmth easing some of the tension she'd been carrying all evening. She leaned in to kiss him on the cheek, a small comfort after the emotional whirlwind of the night.

"Goodnight, Joe," she said affectionately.

"Goodnight, Miss Amanda," Joe replied, opening the door for her. "Sleep well."

"I will. Night," Amanda responded, giving him a final smile before she entered the building and made her way up to her apartment.

Dominic stood talking to Daniel at his table in the restaurant, waiting for Amanda to return. He had seen Daniel as he was leaving with his date. He had exchanged pleasantries with the man, then Daniel, the smug bastard, had boasted that he had convinced her to go on a date after all. It irritated Dominic more than he cared to admit.

Dominic tried to focus on Monica, but his mind kept drifting back to Amanda. How could a woman like her be so different from the empty-headed women he usually dated? It irritated him that he couldn't stop thinking about her. He needed to understand her—what made her tick. But all he could do was imagine what it would be like to see her outside the office, to know the woman beyond the assistant.

He finally had to leave without seeing Amanda, which annoyed him no end and took Monica home. She had been disappointed when he didn't want to come inside, but truth be told, he wasn't interested. He wasn't even sure why he had agreed to the date in the first place.

The drive back home was quiet, his mind preoccupied. Amanda's face, her laugh, her sharp wit—everything about her lingered in his thoughts. He couldn't seem to shake it.

As he passed the Fifth Avenue apartment building, something caught his eye—a flash of red in the dim light. He slowed the car and glanced toward the entrance. There was a woman talking animatedly to the doorman, her back to him. The doorman looked familiar—the same one he had seen the other day. The woman's red dress gleamed under the streetlights, and as Dominic's gaze moved down, his attention was immediately captured by her legs, long and graceful, her posture exuding confidence and elegance.

Something about her pulled him in, but it wasn't just her appearance. It was the way she moved, the way she carried herself. He watched as she turned slightly, giving him a glimpse of her profile. His heart skipped a beat. Was it Amanda? He couldn't be a hundred percent sure it was her.

His pulse quickened, and without thinking, he parked the car across the street. The lady in red was standing so effortlessly graceful, a vision of radiant beauty. He couldn't tear his eyes away. She kissed the doorman on the cheek before heading inside, completely unaware of Dominic's presence.

The idea of Amanda living here, in such a luxurious building, seemed so out of place. It didn't make sense. But the more Dominic thought about it, the more he realised how little he actually knew about her. What was it about Amanda that kept drawing him in? Why couldn't he stop thinking about her, imagining what it would be like to see more of the woman beneath the professional exterior?

He sat in the car for a while, the weight of his own thoughts pressing down on him. What was it about her that had him so captivated?

Amanda drove to Connecticut for a quiet weekend with her father, savouring the comfort of his company and the peacefulness of the family estate. The two spent the days catching up, reminiscing, and enjoying leisurely walks around the grounds. Her father, Henry, always had a way of making her feel cherished, and she relished these visits with him.

Just as she was about to leave for home on Sunday evening, he approached her with a request.

"Amanda," he began, his tone light but expectant, "I'd like you to accompany me to a charity gala dinner next Saturday."

"Of course," Amanda replied without hesitation. "I'd love to, Dad. I always enjoy spending time with you."

He smiled warmly. "It's very formal, though. I want to buy you a new dress for it."

Amanda frowned, shaking her head. "Dad, I already have formal gowns. You don't need to buy me another one."

"Do you have a green one?" he asked, a glimmer of something mischievous in his eyes.

She raised an eyebrow. "No, I don't. Why?"

"I'd like you to wear a green gown on Saturday," he said matter-of-factly.

"Why green?" she pressed, her curiosity piqued.

He hesitated, a small smile tugging at the corners of his mouth. "Let's just say I saw a dress the other day that I think would look magnificent on you. Please, Amanda, let me do this for you."

Amanda studied him for a moment, sensing how important this was to him. "Okay, Dad," she said with a soft smile. "If it makes you happy. But you know I can buy my own gowns."

"I know you can," he said with a chuckle. "But this one's special. And you must wear your mother's emeralds with it."

Her heart softened at the mention of her mother's jewellery. She hadn't worn the emerald set in years, but she knew how much it meant to her father.

"All right, Dad. I give up," she said, kissing him affectionately on the cheek. "If it means that much to you, I'll wear the dress and the emeralds."

Henry beamed, clearly pleased with her agreement. "Thank you, sweetheart. I promise, you'll be the belle of the ball."

Amanda laughed, rolling her eyes affectionately. "As long as you're happy, Dad."

She left shortly after, her thoughts lingering on her father's insistence. Whatever he had planned, she could tell it was something meaningful.

Dominic had just finished his morning jog on the treadmill, sweat dripping from his brow as he grabbed a towel to dry off. His phone buzzed on the counter. He picked it up, glancing at the screen before answering.

"Hello, Mother," he greeted, his tone warm.

"Hello, Dominic," Diane's voice came through, tinged with an unusual urgency. "I need to ask you a big favour."

"What is it?" he asked, concern creeping into his voice.

"Could you please escort me to a charity gala dinner on Saturday night? It's very important to me, and I don't want to go alone," she said, her tone almost pleading.

"Of course," Dominic replied without hesitation. "I'd be proud to take you."

"Oh, wonderful!" Diane exclaimed, relief evident in her voice. "I was so worried I'd have to go alone."

"Anything to make you happy, Mum. You know I'll be there," he said, his voice filled with affection.

"Thank you, sweetheart. You truly are the best of sons," she said, her happiness radiating through the phone.

Dominic smiled, shaking his head fondly as they exchanged a few more words before hanging up. As he set the phone down, he couldn't help but feel a sense of satisfaction. Making his mother happy always felt rewarding.

He grabbed a bottle of water and stretched his arms over his head, his mind wandering briefly to the upcoming event. A formal gala wasn't exactly his idea of a relaxing evening, but if it meant seeing his mother smile, it was more than worth it. Little did he know just how eventful that Saturday night would turn out to be.

Chapter Nine

Amanda's first week without Diane started smoothly. Dominic was businesslike as always, and Amanda was effortlessly efficient, keeping the office running like a well-oiled machine. She took pride in her work, ensuring that every meeting, email, and phone call was perfectly handled.

But in the quieter moments, when she wasn't busy with tasks, her mind wandered. More specifically, it wandered to Dominic. She tried to ignore it, but the thought crept in uninvited: What would it feel like to kiss him? To be held in his arms?

She shook her head, trying to banish the thought. This is ridiculous. He's my boss, she reminded herself firmly. Yet, the memory of his piercing gaze, the way his suit always fit him perfectly, and the faint scent of his cologne lingered in her mind. Her cheeks flushed at the thought, and she scolded herself for letting her imagination run wild.

Little did she know, Dominic was battling the same distraction. From the moment Amanda had walked into his office on Monday morning, he had found it increasingly difficult to focus. She wasn't like anyone he had ever met—certainly not like any of the women he had dated. There was an effortless elegance to her, a quiet strength that commanded his attention. She didn't need flashy outfits or over-the-top gestures; her intelligence and grace did all the talking.

Dominic caught himself staring more than once that week. The way her hair caught the light, the way her glasses framed her delicate features—it all made him want to know more about the woman beneath the professional exterior.

He told himself it was inappropriate. She was his employee, and he prided himself on professionalism, at least until Sofia had ruined that reputation. But the thought of kissing her—of pulling her into his arms and discovering how she would respond—was becoming harder to ignore.

By Thursday, the tension was undeniable. Every time their eyes met, Dominic felt his pulse quicken. And Amanda couldn't help but notice the way his gaze lingered on her just a fraction too long.

By Friday, Amanda was sure something had changed between them. She caught him watching her when he thought she wasn't looking, and her heart skipped every time he spoke her name.

The air between them crackled with unspoken feelings, but neither dared to acknowledge it. Both were too afraid of what might happen if they crossed the line. But both secretly wondered what it would be like if they did.

Just before five o'clock on Friday afternoon, Dominic finished tidying his desk and was heading out of his office when Amanda rushed into the outer office, her face flushed and her breath uneven.

"Amanda? What's wrong?" Dominic asked, his sharp gaze locking onto her. She looked rattled, and that wasn't like her. Amanda was always composed, no matter the situation.

"It's Daniel," she said, her voice tinged with frustration. "He's here. I just seen him down the corridor coming this way. He won't take no for an answer. All week he's been calling and texting me, and now he's shown up." She glanced nervously toward the door, as if expecting Daniel to burst in at any moment.

Dominic's jaw tightened. His usual calm demeanour shifted, replaced by a simmering irritation he didn't bother to hide. "He's here?" he asked, his tone low and controlled, but Amanda could sense the tension beneath it.

"Yes," she said, her nerves clearly frayed. "I've told him I'm not interested, but he just doesn't seem to get it." She looked around, almost as if searching for an escape route.

Dominic abruptly put his briefcase down, his mind made up before he even realised what he was doing. His instincts took over, and before Amanda could say another word, he closed the distance between them. Gently, yet with purpose, he reached up and removed her glasses, placing them carefully on her desk. Amanda froze, startled, as his hands settled lightly on her arms, pulling her toward him.

"Dominic, what—" she began, but her words were cut off as he cupped her face with his hands and tilted her head slightly upward. Then, without hesitation, he kissed her.

It wasn't a hesitant kiss. It was firm and full of intention, as though he had been holding back for far too long. Amanda's mind went blank for a moment, her breath catching in her throat. His lips were warm and commanding, and the world seemed to tilt as she melted into the moment.

Her initial surprise melted away. Her hands slid up to his shoulders, then into his hair, pulling him closer. Her pulse raced as their lips met, a heady mix of fire and softness leaving her utterly breathless.

The kiss deepened, raw and consuming, filled with an unspoken intensity that made her head spin. His tongue brushed against hers, igniting a fire that sent shivers cascading down her spine. Her breath hitched as a soft moan of pleasure escaped her, unbidden, and her fingers tightened in his silky hair, pulling him even closer. It was unlike anything she had ever experienced—a kiss that left her utterly breathless and completely undone.

"Well, now I know why you haven't been returning my calls," Daniel said from the doorway, his tone sharp with irritation.

Amanda jerked back from Dominic, her face heating as she fumbled for her glasses, slipping them back on as if they might shield her from the awkwardness of the moment. "Daniel…" she began, her voice faltering.

Daniel stepped further into the room, his expression a mixture of anger and disbelief. "So, you're involved with your boss now?"

Amanda opened her mouth to respond, but Dominic moved forward, calm yet commanding. His gaze was icy, his voice steady as he addressed Daniel. "I think it's time for you to leave."

Daniel scoffed, folding his arms. "Oh, so you're the knight in shining armour now, huh? Is this why she's been avoiding me? Because of you?"

"Daniel," Dominic said coolly, his tone brooking no argument, "Amanda's choices are none of your business."

"None of my business?" Daniel snapped, his gaze darting between Amanda and Dominic. "She led me on, and now this?"

"I didn't lead you on," Amanda interrupted, her voice trembling but firm. "I was clear. I told you I wasn't interested in another date."

"Really?" Daniel countered, his anger boiling over. "Because your actions don't exactly match your words, Amanda." His eyes darted back to Dominic. "Or is this your way of climbing the corporate ladder?"

Dominic's jaw tightened, his fists clenching at his sides. "That's enough," he said, his voice low and dangerous. He stepped closer to Daniel, his presence towering. "Amanda has asked you to leave. I suggest you listen before I make you."

Daniel glared at Dominic for a moment, his anger simmering, but he took a step back. "Fine," he spat. "But don't come running to me when this blows up in your face, Amanda."

Amanda's heart raced as Daniel turned and stormed out, slamming the door behind him.

Silence settled over the office, heavy and charged. Amanda stared at the door, her thoughts a chaotic mess. Slowly, she turned to Dominic.

"Are you okay?" Dominic asked gently, his earlier harshness replaced with concern.

She nodded shakily. "I… I think so."

Dominic stepped back, giving her space, though the intensity of the moment still hung in the air. "I'm sorry," he said softly. "I didn't mean to put you in an uncomfortable position."

Amanda shook her head, her voice steadying. "Don't apologise. You were just trying to help."

Dominic's eyes softened, his gaze lingering on her for a moment longer than necessary. "I don't think he'll bother you again."

"No, I don't think he will," she murmured, her thoughts drifting back to the kiss. Her fingers brushed the edge of her desk, as if grounding herself.

"You should go home," Dominic said, his voice quieter now. "Take the weekend to relax."

Amanda nodded, gathering her things in silence. As she moved to leave, she paused at the door, glancing back at him.

"Dominic…" she began, hesitating.

"Yes?"

"Thank you," she said softly, her gaze meeting his.

"You don't need to thank me," he replied, his tone low, almost tender.

She gave him a faint smile and left, her heart pounding—not because of Daniel's confrontation, but because of the way Dominic had kissed her.

And the way she had kissed him back.

As soon as Amanda walked into her penthouse, her phone buzzed in her bag. She pulled it out and saw Megan's name on the screen. She sighed, knowing exactly why Megan was calling.

"Hello, Megan," Amanda greeted, her voice tired but warm.

"Well," Megan began with a laugh, "Daniel just called me, ranting about you. He says you're sleeping with your boss now!"

Amanda couldn't help but laugh. "I'm not," she said firmly. "Dominic only kissed me to make it clear to Daniel that I'm not interested. You know I've told him a million times, but he just wasn't getting the message. I think he finally got it, though."

"Oh, he definitely got it," Megan said with a giggle. "He's fuming. I mean really fuming. He called you every name under the sun, but honestly, he needed that wake-up call."

"I'm sorry, Megan," Amanda said, her tone softening. "I know he's your brother, and I never wanted to cause trouble, but he just wouldn't take the hint."

"I know," Megan said with a sigh. "Trust me, I've been telling him to back off all week, but Daniel doesn't listen to anyone but himself." She paused, her voice growing more mischievous. "So, Amanda, did your boss really only kiss you to get rid of Daniel?"

Amanda froze, her cheeks heating at the question. "Yes," she said quickly, though her voice betrayed a hint of hesitation. "And I have to admit, I'm grateful. It was effective, at least."

Megan let out a laugh. "Sure, sure. But come on, Amanda…spill. Is he a good kisser?"

Amanda groaned, a laugh escaping despite herself. "Megan, seriously?"

"I'm just curious!" Megan teased. "You can't drop a bombshell like that and not share the juicy details!"

Amanda hesitated, biting her lip. She couldn't lie—not to Megan. "Fine," she admitted, a smile creeping into her voice. "Unbelievable. Like… wow. But it didn't mean anything!"

"Oh, Amanda," Megan said, her tone amused. "You might want to tell yourself that, but I have a feeling there's more to this story. Keep me updated!"

"Goodnight, Megan," Amanda said, rolling her eyes but smiling as she ended the call.

As she set her phone down, Amanda's thoughts drifted back to the kiss—Dominic's firm, insistent lips, the way he had held her so protectively. She shook her head, trying to push the memory away, but the warmth it left behind lingered.

"Unbelievable," she whispered to herself, smiling despite her best efforts.

Dominic sat at his desk, his head buried in his hands, trying to make sense of what had just happened. What the hell had he been thinking?

He kissed Amanda.

And it wasn't just any kiss. No, it was the kind of kiss that made his blood run hot and his mind lose all sense of logic. The kind of kiss that left him wanting more, desperate for more.

He groaned, leaning back in his chair and staring at the ceiling. What on earth had possessed him to do it? Sure, he wanted to get rid of that insufferable Daniel, but that wasn't the whole truth, was it?

No.

If he was being honest, Daniel showing up was just the excuse. He'd been wanting to kiss Amanda for weeks now. Her sharp wit, her quiet confidence, the way she could handle him without breaking a sweat—it was intoxicating.

And when he finally gave in? My god, it was incredible. Her lips were soft, warm, and responsive. The way she melted into him, the little moan she let out—it had been everything he'd fantasised about and more.

Dominic shook his head, a frustrated laugh escaping him. "What the hell is wrong with me?" he muttered.

If Daniel hadn't barged in… Dominic clenched his fists, banishing the vivid image that came to mind. Amanda beneath him, her hair a silky halo across her desk, her body arching into his. The sheer intensity of the thought made him groan with frustration.

He was amazed at his own restraint. He'd kissed her, sure, but stopping there? That had taken every ounce of self-control he possessed.

Running a hand through his hair, Dominic let out a heavy sigh. What now? He couldn't take it back, and the truth was, he didn't want to. But Amanda… What was she thinking? How would she react when they faced each other on Monday?

He rubbed his temples, frustration bubbling beneath his skin. He was her boss, for god's sake. Crossing that line was forbidden, no matter how much he'd wanted to.

Yet here he was, unable to focus on anything but how perfect she'd felt in his arms. The memory of her lips lingered, an intoxicating mix of softness and fire. He wanted more—wanted her. To kiss her again, to claim her.

This wasn't like to was with Sofia. What he felt for Amanda in that kiss had eclipsed everything he'd shared with her. And that made it worse. He'd promised himself he wouldn't repeat his past mistakes, wouldn't get tangled up with someone who worked for him.

Dominic inhaled deeply, forcing himself to stand. He walked to the window and stared out at the city lights, hoping the quiet hum of the night would calm him.

But it didn't. Because one thing was painfully clear: Amanda wasn't just anyone. She was his Amanda now. And pretending she was nothing more than his assistant? He wasn't sure he could do that anymore.

Chapter Ten

Amanda woke early on Saturday morning, still reeling from the kiss she and Dominic had shared the day before. The memory of it was impossible to shake—it had lingered in her thoughts all night and even crept into her dreams. She had never felt anything quite like it.

Determined to clear her head, she laced up her running shoes and headed out for a jog. The crisp morning air felt refreshing, but no matter how hard she pushed herself, Dominic's touch, his scent, and the intensity of that moment stayed with her. By the time she returned to her penthouse, she was no closer to forgetting him.

After a long shower, she washed her hair and dressed casually for lunch. Her focus shifted to preparing for the gala later that evening. The dress her father had sent her earlier in the week was exquisite—an emerald-green creation that matched her eyes perfectly. Amanda had to admit, he had impeccable taste. The gown paired perfectly with her late mother's emerald jewellery, which had been left to her along with a significant inheritance. Despite its value, Amanda would have traded it all for just one more day with her mother.

Her father had arranged to pick her up at 7:00pm for the charity gala dinner, which started at 7:30pm. Prompt as ever, her hairstylist, Shelly Agee, arrived at 5.30pm. Amanda greeted her warmly at the lift in her penthouse foyer.

"Hello, Shelly! How are you?"

"I'm well, Amanda. And you? Are you looking forward to tonight?"

"I am. It's been a while since I've had the chance to dress up, so I'm excited."

Shelly set to work, chatting with Amanda as she trimmed and styled her hair. They laughed about old memories and shared updates on mutual friends while Shelly created a timeless look. Amanda's hair was left loose, styled to cascade over one shoulder in soft waves. On the other side, Shelly swept it back with a comb adorned with emeralds, perfectly complementing her gown.

When it was time for makeup, Shelly kept it elegant and understated, enhancing Amanda's natural beauty. The only bold touch was a slightly winged eyeliner that made her striking green eyes even more mesmerising.

"Alright," Shelly said as she stood back to admire her work. "Now for the dress."

Amanda slipped into the emerald silk gown. The strapless design hugged her torso flawlessly, while a tulle overlay shimmered with every movement. The elegant skirt flowed gracefully to the floor, and four-inch heels completed the ensemble.

Shelly beamed as Amanda turned to face her. "You look absolutely stunning. No one will be able to take their eyes off you tonight."

"Thank you, Shelly," Amanda said with a warm smile as her stylist gathered her things and left.

A few minutes later, her father arrived at the penthouse. His sharp tailored tuxedo made him look every bit the distinguished gentleman, but it was clear that his attention was entirely on his daughter.

"You look breathtaking," he said, his voice filled with pride.

Amanda had already donned her emerald earrings and bracelet, but she held up the necklace and smiled. "Would you mind helping me with this?"

"Of course." He stepped behind her and carefully fastened the delicate clasp.

Once the necklace was secure, he stepped back to take her in fully. His eyes softened with admiration. "Your mother would have been so proud of you, Amanda," her father said softly.

A warm smile tugged at her lips, though her heart swelled with bittersweet emotion. "Thank you, Dad. That means a lot."

He offered her his arm. "Are you ready?"

Amanda reached for her small clutch, which held only the essentials—her credit card, phone, and penthouse keycard. She slipped it into her hand and nodded, her voice cheerful. "Ready."

With that, they stepped out together, descending to the waiting limousine that would whisk them away to the gala dinner.

Dominic arrived at his mother's estate in his sleek limousine, dressed impeccably for the evening but still unable to shake the memory of Amanda—or the kiss they'd shared. It played over and over in his mind, a distraction he couldn't afford tonight.

As he stepped out and made his way to the door, he spotted his mother descending the grand staircase, her gown a rich shade of navy blue that shimmered under the lights.

"Mother, you look ravishing," he said sincerely, leaning in to kiss her cheek.

Diane chuckled, her eyes twinkling with mischief. "Oh, stop. I'm sure there will be far more ravishing women at the gala tonight. Women far more suited to catching your eye."

"No one could ever compare to you," Dominic replied with a smirk, offering his arm and leading her to the waiting limousine.

Diane allowed herself a small, secret smile as she murmured, "We'll see about that."

Once inside, Dominic settled into his seat, the hum of the engine a faint backdrop to their conversation. "Do you know who will be at our table tonight?" he asked casually, though his thoughts were clearly elsewhere.

"No, not this time," Diane replied, smoothing the folds of her dress. "Why do you ask?"

"Just curious. You usually know these things."

She shrugged lightly. "It's a thousand-dollar-per-plate dinner, darling. I'm sure we'll know some of the attendees, though who we'll actually sit with is anyone's guess."

Dominic nodded, but his attention was already drifting. The rest of the trip passed in comfortable silence, with Diane gazing out the window and Dominic's thoughts stubbornly circling back to Amanda. The way she had looked at him—soft eyes, parted lips, an unspoken connection—was maddening. The moment lingered, refusing to let go.

As they arrived at the venue, the limousine slowed to a stop in front of a glittering red carpet. Dominic stepped out first, the flash of cameras and the clicking of shutters greeting him instantly. Unbothered by the attention, he turned and offered his hand to his mother, helping her out of the vehicle with the grace and poise that only years of practice could bring.

They walked arm in arm down the red carpet, a striking pair that commanded attention. Dominic's tailored tuxedo fit him like a glove, while Diane's navy gown shimmered elegantly under the bright lights. Admirers whispered and cameras flashed incessantly, but Dominic barely noticed. His thoughts strayed to Amanda, wondering what she was doing tonight. Was she at home, still thinking about their kiss, or was she out with friends, blissfully unaware of how much space she occupied in his mind?

Inside, the reception area buzzed with energy. Guests mingled, sipping champagne and exchanging pleasantries. Dominic plucked two glasses from a passing tray and handed one to his mother.

"Thank you, dear," Diane said, taking a sip. Her gaze swept the room, and she suddenly exclaimed in a surprised tone, "Oh, look, there's Amanda's father!"

Dominic stiffened. "Where?"

Diane pointed subtly across the room. Standing near a cluster of guests was Henry, Amanda's father. Beside him was a woman in a stunning emerald-green gown, her back to them as she conversed with an older gentleman who appeared completely captivated by her.

The woman's honey-blonde hair cascaded in soft waves down to her waist, the kind of hair that lingered in fantasies—spread across a pillow in the throes of passion. It was the most stunning hair Dominic had ever seen, partially pulled back on one side and draped elegantly over her shoulder. He couldn't wait to see her from the front.

The body beneath that exquisite emerald-green gown was nothing short of breathtaking, every curve accentuated in just the right way. No wonder the gentleman she was speaking with seemed utterly entranced. Dominic found himself wondering if her face was as captivating as the rest of her.

He decided he'd have to find out. An introduction was definitely in order.

"Let's go say hello," Diane suggested, already making her way toward Henry.

Dominic followed, his heartbeat quickening. He couldn't tear his eyes away from the woman in green. She moved with grace, the shimmer of her gown catching the light with each slight shift.

"Henry, how nice to see you," Diane greeted warmly as they reached his side. "You remember Dominic."

Henry turned, a broad smile on his face. "Diane, always a pleasure. And of course, Dominic." He extended a hand, which Dominic shook firmly.

"Good to see you again," Dominic said, his tone polite but distracted as his eyes flicked back to the woman in green.

Henry turned slightly, resting a hand on her elbow. "Sweetheart, Dominic is here."

The woman stiffened at Henry's words. She excused herself from the gentleman she'd been speaking with, her movements slow and deliberate. Then she turned.

Dominic's world stopped.

Amanda!

It was Amanda in the green gown. And she wasn't just beautiful; she was breathtaking. No, that wasn't even the word. Gorgeous? Stunning? Exquisite? None of them seemed to do her justice. She was… everything.

"Hello, Diane," Amanda said warmly as she leaned in to kiss Diane on the cheek. "It's lovely to see you." Then, her emerald eyes shifted to Dominic. "Hello, Dominic. Nice to see you."

Dominic stared, momentarily lost for words as his thoughts scrambled to catch up. Her eyes—vivid green, like the gown she wore and the exquisite emeralds adorning her graceful neck—held him captive. It took him a moment too long to gather himself before he finally managed a slightly stiff, "Hello, Amanda."

Her name felt heavy on his tongue, and he wasn't sure if it was because of the kiss, they'd shared or the way she looked tonight—like a vision he couldn't look away from.

Diane smiled warmly at Henry, her eyes alight with a playful glint. "Oh, Henry, there's someone I'd love for you to meet."

Henry, ever the gentleman, offered his arm. "I'd be delighted."

With a knowing smile, Diane looped her arm through his. "These young ones can occupy themselves while we visit," she said cheerfully, casting a brief glance at Amanda and Dominic before leading Henry toward another group of guests.

And just like that, Dominic and Amanda were left standing alone in the midst of the bustling reception room.

Dominic shifted awkwardly, acutely aware of how quiet it suddenly felt between them despite the hum of conversation and clinking glasses around them. Amanda turned to face him fully, and his breath caught.

Her eyes. How had he never noticed how striking they were? Green and vibrant, like emeralds set aflame. They seemed to hold a quiet challenge, mixed with a flicker of vulnerability she couldn't quite hide.

Amanda tilted her head slightly, studying him as though waiting for him to speak.

Finally, Dominic managed to find his voice, though it felt rough, as if it had to climb through the knot tightening in his throat. "You look… stunning."

Amanda's cheeks flushed a delicate pink, and she glanced down for a moment before lifting her gaze back to his. "Thank you," she said, her voice warm and composed. "You look as impeccable as always."

For a moment, they simply looked at each other, the air between them charged with something unspoken. Dominic's heart pounded against his ribs. It wasn't just how beautiful she was—it was the way she carried herself, the quiet strength in her posture, the grace in her every movement.

"You surprised me," he admitted, his voice low.

"Did I?" Amanda's lips quirked into a small smile.

"You did. I wasn't expecting…" He trailed off, unsure how to finish without giving away just how much she'd been on his mind.

Amanda raised a brow, her expression teasing but guarded. "Wasn't expecting me to be here? Or wasn't expecting me to look like this?"

Dominic chuckled softly, shaking his head. "Both, I think."

"Well," Amanda said lightly, her smile widening just a fraction, "life's full of surprises."

Dominic nodded; his gaze fixed on her. "That it is."

Before either of them could say more, a tall, impeccably dressed man strode toward them. His confidence was palpable, and his expensive suit, paired with the glint of a Rolex on his wrist, screamed wealth and privilege.

"Amanda! How wonderful to see you," the man said, his voice smooth and familiar. Before Amanda could step back, he leaned in and kissed her on both cheeks, the gesture lingering just a touch too close to her mouth for Dominic's liking.

Amanda quickly recovered, her composure intact. "Jason," she said politely, her tone warm but distant. "Lovely to see you. Where's Melissa?"

Jason's expression faltered for a moment, a flicker of embarrassment crossing his face. "Melissa and I… we've separated."

Amanda's brows lifted slightly in surprise. "Oh, I'm sorry to hear that."

"I'm not," Jason replied with a charming grin. "Now I can pursue you properly."

Amanda's posture didn't falter, her grace unshaken. "Oh, I don't think that would be wise, Jason. I'm not sure I'm interested in becoming wife number three."

Jason chuckled, unfazed by her sharp remark. "Oh, Amanda," he drawled, closing the space between them. He took her hands in his, brushing his lips over her knuckles with practiced ease. "You're not like the rest. You're a rare gem. I'd keep you safe in my estate, locked away from the world, where your eyes would only ever be on me."

Dominic's jaw tightened, his irritation bubbling dangerously close to the surface. Jason's boldness and Amanda's evident discomfort were grating.

Stepping forward, Dominic placed a hand gently but firmly on the nape of Amanda's neck, his thumb brushing her skin in a gesture that felt both protective and possessive. His voice was calm, but the steel beneath it was unmistakable. "I don't think I'd be so happy about that."

Jason's confident demeanour faltered as his gaze shifted to Dominic, who stood tall and unyielding, his presence commanding.

Amanda glanced up at Dominic, her surprise evident, but she said nothing, letting his silent assertion hang in the air. For a moment, the tension was palpable, the crowd around them fading into the background as the two men locked eyes.

Jason cleared his throat, forcing a smile that didn't quite reach his eyes. "Well, it seems you have a protector, Amanda. I'll leave you to it…, for now."

With a polite nod to Amanda and a barely concealed glare at Dominic, Jason turned and disappeared into the crowd.

Amanda let out a quiet breath, tilting her head to look at Dominic. "That was... unexpected."

Dominic's hand lingered for a moment before he withdrew it, his expression softening as he met her gaze. "I didn't like the way he was talking to you."

Amanda's lips curved into a small, amused smile. "Neither did I. But I think you might have scared him off, for a little while at least."

"Good," Dominic said simply, his voice steady but laced with an intensity that made Amanda's heart skip.

"You seem to be making a habit of scaring men away from me," she teased, a small smile curving her lips. "Not that I'm complaining. Jason has been pursuing me since before he married his first wife—and during both marriages. It's quite unsettling how some wealthy men think women are willing to drop their morals for a diamond necklace or designer clothes."

"Not all men," Dominic replied smoothly, his gaze unwavering. "But by the looks of those emeralds, you don't need a man for that anyway."

Amanda's hand rose to her necklace, her fingers brushing the jewels with a touch that was almost reverent. "My mother had quite a collection of jewellery, which now belongs to me," she said softly, her voice carrying a wistful undertone. "But I would throw it all away if I could have her back, even for just one day."

The weight of her words hung in the air between them, and Dominic's expression softened. He saw the flicker of pain in her eyes, the vulnerability that she worked so hard to mask.

"I'm sorry, Amanda," he said quietly. "I didn't mean to bring up something so personal."

She shook her head gently, a faint, bittersweet smile gracing her lips. "It's all right. Talking about her doesn't hurt as much as it used to. And... it reminds me of how much she loved me."

For a moment, they stood in silence, the hum of the reception fading into the background. Dominic's gaze lingered on Amanda; her beauty more profound now that he saw the depth behind her elegance.

"You seem stronger than most people I know," he said, his voice low but sincere.

Amanda looked up at him, her green eyes searching his. "Strength isn't a choice when life doesn't give you one. But thank you, Dominic."

He took a small step closer, his presence steady and grounding. "For what?"

"For seeing me," she said simply, her voice barely above a whisper.

The words struck him more deeply than he anticipated, and for a moment, he didn't know how to respond. The world around them felt distant, as if they were the only two people in the room.

Dominic cleared his throat softly, offering her a faint smile. "I think it's impossible not to see you, Amanda."

Her breath hitched at the rawness in his tone, and her heart thudded loudly in her chest. The air between them crackled with unspoken emotion, an invisible thread pulling them closer.

Before either of them could speak again, a waiter approached with a tray of champagne, breaking the moment. Amanda took a step back, the spell broken but the intensity still lingering in the space between them.

"Shall we find our parents?" Dominic asked, his voice steadier now, though his gaze hadn't lost its warmth.

Amanda nodded, her composure slipping back into place. "Let's."

Chapter Eleven

All four of them happened to be seated at the same table. Amanda sat between her father and Dominic, while Diane took the seat on Henry's other side. The atmosphere at the table was light and warm, though a subtle tension buzzed under the surface whenever Dominic glanced at Amanda.

As the first course was served, Amanda turned to her father. "Dad, did you know Jason and Melissa have split?"

Henry looked surprised, his fork pausing midway to his mouth. "No, I didn't." Then his brow furrowed as he cast a concerned look at Amanda. "Does that mean you're on the menu again?"

Amanda blinked, caught off guard, before bursting into laughter. "He thinks so."

Diane caught the tightening of Dominic's jaw and the way his grip on his wine glass firmed. She hid her amusement behind a sip of champagne before addressing Henry. "Who is this Jason?"

Henry chuckled, setting his utensils down. "Oh, Jason is a client of mine. From the moment he laid eyes on Amanda, he's been pursuing her—through both of his marriages, mind you. He's been quite relentless, hasn't he, sweetheart?"

Amanda sighed and nodded. "Unfortunately, yes. But Dominic might have scared him off, at least for a little while."

"Oh?" Diane asked, her interest piqued as her sharp eyes flicked between Amanda and Dominic.

Amanda couldn't hide her smile. "Yes, Jason tried to… let's say assert his interest earlier. Dominic stepped in and implied we were together. It scared him off. It was actually pretty amusing." She turned her head to Dominic and smiled warmly.

Diane's lips twitched in amusement as she looked at her son. "Well done, Dominic."

Henry laughed heartily, raising his glass in a small toast to Dominic. "Well done, indeed. Jason's been a bit of a nuisance for far too long."

Dominic's expression softened slightly, though his voice remained even. "It didn't sit right with me, the way he was speaking to her."

Amanda's heart gave a little flutter, but she quickly masked it with a chuckle. "Well, you handled him perfectly. He practically ran off."

Diane's gaze lingered on her son for a moment, a knowing gleam in her eyes, before she turned back to Henry. "I suppose we should keep Dominic around more often if Amanda needs a protector from men like Jason."

Henry grinned. "I wouldn't object. It's about time Amanda had someone looking out for her in situations like these."

Amanda's cheeks warmed, and she quickly reached for her water glass to distract herself. "I can handle men like Jason just fine, thank you very much," she said lightly, though her gaze flickered to Dominic.

Dominic smirked, leaning slightly toward her as he murmured, "I don't doubt it."

The conversation shifted to lighter topics as the courses progressed. Laughter and chatter filled the table, but Dominic's focus remained singular. No matter how much he tried to engage in polite conversation or redirect his thoughts, they always circled back to Amanda.

She was so close—her soft laugh, the delicate scent of her perfume, the way the emeralds at her neck shimmered against her smooth skin. It was maddening. Every time her arm brushed his or she turned slightly toward him, his pulse quickened.

He wanted her.

In the biblical sense.

The raw, undeniable attraction was consuming him, and he could feel the heat pooling low in his stomach. His groin tightened, hard and unrelenting, as thoughts of Amanda filled his mind. Her laughter, her smile, the memory of her lips just inches from his when they'd kissed—he was losing control.

Dominic shifted in his seat, trying to discreetly adjust himself under the table. He clenched his jaw, forcing himself to focus on the conversation at hand. But when Amanda turned toward him, her green eyes bright and curious as she asked him a question, it was nearly his undoing.

"Dominic?" she prompted, a slight tilt of her head.

"Hmm?" He blinked, realising too late he hadn't heard a word she'd said.

Amanda's lips quirked into a curious smile, though there was no teasing in her expression. "I asked if you're enjoying the evening."

He cleared his throat, reaching for his water glass to buy himself a moment. "Of course. The company makes it unforgettable."

Her cheeks flushed faintly at his words, and she quickly turned back to her father, engaging him in conversation.

Dominic let out a slow, measured breath, his hands tightening around the edge of the table. He needed to pull himself together. This wasn't the time or place for these thoughts—or for the overwhelming need coursing through him.

But as the night wore on and the dessert was served, it became painfully clear: Dominic wanted Amanda in every way imaginable. And it was no longer a question of if—but when.

Amanda's thoughts were racing, each one more dangerous than the last. She couldn't help but steal glances at Dominic throughout the evening, her heart pounding whenever their eyes met. There was something about the way he carried himself, the quiet confidence, the raw energy that seemed to radiate from him. And the way he looked at her—sometimes lingering a little too long—made her wonder if he was feeling what she was feeling.

God, I hope not.

The idea that Dominic might notice the attraction she was desperately trying to keep hidden sent a jolt of anxiety through her. He was so effortlessly sexy—every word he spoke, every subtle movement, only made her want him more. She could almost imagine what it would feel like to be close to him, to feel his hands on her, pulling her in, claiming her. The thought was enough to send a flush creeping up her neck and over her cheeks.

Focus, Amanda, she scolded herself. You can't think like this.

But it was hard. So hard. Her mind kept wandering to places it shouldn't, her body reacting against her will. All she wanted, in that moment, was to drag him into the nearest dark corner, away from the prying eyes of the crowd, and have her way with him.

She shifted in her seat, uncomfortable in her dress she was wearing, her nipples hardened and feeling the heat building between her thighs. The mere thought of kissing him— of running her hands over his hard chest, his powerful arms, feeling his lips on hers, his hands exploring her body—was almost too much to bear.

Her breath hitched as the image of being underneath him surged through her mind. His weight pressing her down, the intensity of his gaze as he kissed her, his body moving against hers…

For God's sake, Amanda, get a grip!

She felt her pulse race, her cheeks burning hotter now, and she hastily picked up her wine glass, hoping it would steady her nerves. The glass trembled slightly in her hand, and she forced a smile as she took a sip, willing her thoughts to calm down.

She glanced at Dominic again, catching the way his eyes lingered on her for a second too long, his jaw tightening as if he was fighting something of his own.

No. No, no, no. He's not interested in you like that. You wish he was though, don't you?

But the more she tried to convince herself of that, the stronger the pull between them seemed to become. The attraction was undeniable, like a magnetic force, and Amanda wasn't sure how much longer she could pretend that it wasn't there.

As the meal came to an end, the music began to swell, signalling the start of the dancing. Henry, ever the charmer, extended his hand to Amanda with a warm smile. "Shall we dance, sweetheart?"

Amanda, eager to put some distance between herself and Dominic to cool her flustered nerves, gratefully accepted. She needed a moment to breathe, to regain some composure after the overwhelming sensations that had been swirling through her all evening.

"Are you enjoying yourself, sweetheart?" Henry asked as they glided across the floor, the smooth rhythm of the waltz carrying them in sync with the music.

"Yes, it's been lovely," Amanda replied, trying to keep her voice steady, though the lingering heat of the evening's events still flushed her cheeks. She glanced over Henry's shoulder, her eyes flickering to Dominic across the room. He was engaged in conversation with his mother, and for a brief moment, Amanda allowed herself to breathe again.

Henry's voice broke through her thoughts. "I suppose you don't have to wear your old maid disguise anymore at work," he chuckled. "Now that Dominic has seen the real you."

Amanda's heart skipped a beat at the unexpected comment. She wasn't quite sure how to respond. It wasn't that she didn't appreciate the compliment, but the mention of Dominic seeing "the real her" made her wonder how much he had truly noticed. She wasn't sure what he thought of the sudden change—if he even cared.

"I suppose not," she replied, her voice trailing off as her mind wandered. She wondered how Dominic would react to the transformation in the office. At least she would not need to wear those damn glasses, the ones she'd worn for far too long.

They continued to dance in silence for a moment, the music soothing her nerves slightly, but she couldn't shake the thought of Dominic—his gaze, the way his eyes had lingered on her throughout the evening. She was just starting to feel more like herself, but something told her she wouldn't be able to keep her distance from him for long.

As the song came to an end, Henry escorted her back to their table, where she gratefully sank into her seat. She felt a brief sense of relief, but it was quickly replaced by the all-too-familiar weight of Dominic's presence. He was still on the dance floor, dancing with his mother, a slight smile on his lips as he guided her with smooth, practiced movements.

"Well, I must say, Dominic," Diane said, her voice light and teasing as she looked up at her son. "Amanda's appearance is a complete surprise, don't you think?"

Dominic's smile faltered for a split second before he masked it with his usual composure. "It certainly is," he said, his voice slightly tight. Then, with a more thoughtful tone, he added, "How did we not notice?"

Diane chuckled, her gaze flickering over to Amanda, who was now seated at the table. "I think that was her plan, dear. Apparently, Henry told me she had a few jobs before Childs Incorporated. The male bosses and employees wouldn't stop harassing her." She laughed again, shaking her head. "Henry said he nearly died when he first saw her dressed like an old maid for work."

Dominic's brow furrowed slightly at the mention of the "old maid disguise." It hadn't occurred to him that Amanda had felt the need to hide herself in such a way. He had always seen her as efficient, serious, and reserved—traits that had drawn him in even when she seemed plain. But now, hearing about how she had deliberately concealed her beauty, Dominic couldn't help but feel a surge of realisation. The attraction he had always felt for her, though strong, paled in comparison to what he felt now. She had been captivating before, but now, with her beauty unveiled, his desire for her was stronger than ever.

It was a revelation.

As the conversation continued between his mother and him, Dominic found himself distracted by Amanda, who was now in conversation with another attractive male. The way she carried herself, the elegance she exuded, it was impossible to ignore. He had to admit, he was beginning to see her in an entirely new light. And it was unsettling.

Just as Dominic was guiding his mother back to the table, he saw Amanda being led to the dance floor by the gentleman he had noticed her speaking to earlier. His gaze followed them, a twinge of unease settling in his chest.

Diane, sensing her son's distraction, glanced over at Henry with a knowing smile. "I hope he's not one of Amanda's… Jason's," she asked, her tone casual but laced with curiosity.

Henry sighed, a slight frown pulling at his features. "No, I don't think so," he said, his voice betraying a hint of resignation. "Unfortunately, this means I probably won't see her for the rest of the night."

Dominic looked up sharply, genuinely surprised. "Why?"

Henry shrugged, a slight smile playing at the corners of his mouth. "Oh, as soon as she starts dancing, they come out of the woodwork."

"Really?" Diane said with interest, leaning in slightly as she watched Amanda glide across the dance floor.

"Yes," Henry replied with a touch of amusement in his voice. "With all the handsome men always showering her with attention, I don't understand why she hasn't been snapped up yet."

Dominic's response was almost immediate, his tone more urgent than he intended. "Maybe she doesn't want to be snapped up."

Diane chuckled softly, shaking her head. "Oh, of course she does, Dominic." She turned to Henry with a knowing smile. "She's just waiting for the right man to come along."

"Maybe you're right," Henry agreed, his gaze following Amanda. "She has everything going for her—she's beautiful, intelligent, graceful, wealthy…"

"And more…" Dominic muttered; his eyes still fixed on Amanda. He hadn't meant to say it out loud, but the words slipped from his lips before he could stop them. He didn't even notice the satisfied, almost smug, expressions on Henry and Diane's faces as they exchanged a quiet, knowing glance.

Henry cleared his throat, breaking the moment. "Diane, would you like to dance?"

With a graceful nod, Diane stood, and they made their way to the dance floor, leaving Dominic behind at the table, lost in his own thoughts. His mind was swirling with the realisation of what he had just said—he had spoken the truth, even if he hadn't fully intended to acknowledge it. Seeing her like this, radiant and unguarded, something shifted. Desire merged with something deeper, and for the first time, Dominic wondered if this was more than attraction—it was certainty.

As soon as Amanda was returned to the table, Dominic didn't hesitate. He stood up and offered his hand, his voice low but filled with quiet urgency. "May I have this dance?"

Amanda, still catching her breath from the previous dance, looked up at him and smiled, a hint of warmth in her eyes. "I'd love to."

Without another word, she placed her hand in his, and he gently led her away from the table, his heart pounding slightly faster than usual. As they moved toward the dance floor, the world around them seemed to blur, as though nothing mattered except the two of them.

Once they were close enough, he wrapped his arm around her waist, pulling her gently against him. The moment she was in his arms, all thought left him—completely and utterly. Her body moulded against his as though they were two pieces of the same puzzle, his hand firm yet gentle at the small of her back, guiding her effortlessly with the rhythm. The warmth of her body pressed against his, the softness of her curves, and the intoxicating scent of her perfume filled his senses. Everything else faded away.

He could feel the delicate rise and fall of her breath, the slight sway of her body as they moved together in perfect sync. His fingers brushed against her back, lightly tracing the line of her dress. It was as if the rest of the world had ceased to exist—there was only Amanda. The chemistry between them was undeniable, an electric pull that made his pulse race.

Dominic closed his eyes for a brief moment, just to savour the feeling of holding her, his hand resting on the small of her back, the other gently cupping her hand. His breath was shallow, and for the first time in a long while, his mind was empty of everything but the sensation of this amazing woman in his arms.

Amanda, too, seemed lost in the moment. She tilted her head up slightly to meet his gaze, her eyes reflecting the same unspoken intensity that had been building between them all night. The music around them played on, but it felt as if time itself had stopped. All that mattered was the rhythm of their bodies, the undeniable attraction they shared.

Halfway through their second dance, just as Dominic was beginning to lose himself completely in the sensation of holding Amanda, they were interrupted. Henry and Diane approached them with calm but urgent expressions. Diane looked slightly pale, her hand resting lightly on Henry's arm.

"Dominic, Amanda," Henry began with a polite smile, though his tone was more serious than usual. "I'm afraid Diane isn't feeling well. I have offered to take her home."

Diane smiled faintly, her voice soft but apologetic. "I'm terribly sorry, Amanda, Dominic. I'm afraid I won't be able to continue the evening."

Dominic immediately straightened, concern flickering across his face. "I hope it's nothing serious, mother," he said, his voice warm but with a trace of worry.

"Oh, no, no. Just a bit of a headache," Diane reassured him, though her smile was a little strained. "I'll be fine after a bit of rest."

Henry nodded, then turned to Dominic. "Would it be too much trouble for you to take Amanda home this evening?" he asked, his tone almost a little too casual, but there was an underlying approval in his gaze.

Dominic's heart gave a small, unbidden leap. He turned to Amanda, his eyes brightening. "It would be my absolute pleasure," he said softly, his gaze holding hers just a moment too long. "I'll make sure she gets home safely."

Amanda's gaze met his, her eyes a mixture of gratitude and something else, something more intense. She nodded slightly. "Thank you, Dominic. I'd appreciate that."

Diane smiled and gave a small, gracious nod. "Thank you both for the lovely evening," she said, looking between them both with a knowing, almost mischievous glint in her eyes. "I hope you enjoy the rest of the night."

With that, Henry and Diane departed, leaving Amanda and Dominic standing together on the dance floor, the soft hum of the music giving way to the quiet rhythm of their breaths. The air between them felt electric, the tension growing with each passing second. As the music began again, Dominic gently pulled her back into his arms, their movements seamlessly resuming. His touch ignited a wave of warmth that spread through her, and the world beyond their shared moment faded into nothingness.

As the music faded, Dominic stepped back, his warm smile tinged with hesitation. "Would you like to leave now?" he asked softly, his voice low enough to send a shiver through her.

Amanda nodded, her pulse racing as she placed her hand in his. Without a word, he led her off the dance floor with an elegance that made her heart stumble. They moved toward their table so she could grab her purse, then continued toward the exit. The silence between them wasn't awkward—it was charged, laden with unspoken feelings that neither dared to name.

As they stepped into the cool night air, Amanda felt her pulse quicken further, the rhythmic sound of their footsteps echoing in her chest. The evening wasn't over yet, and the realisation sent a mixture of anticipation and nervous energy coursing through her.

At the entrance, Dominic signalled to the valet, who swiftly brought the sleek limousine to a stop before them. With a slight bow and a teasing grin, he opened the door and gestured gallantly. "Your chariot awaits, m'lady," he said, his voice brimming with playful warmth.

Amanda returned his grin, her heart fluttering as her gaze met his. "Thank you," she murmured, her voice soft yet filled with layers of meaning she wasn't ready to unravel. She stepped into the car, her dress brushing against his hand as she passed. Dominic followed her, the door closing behind them with a gentle click, sealing them in a cocoon of quiet intimacy.

Chapter Twelve

Dominic asked for her address to give to the driver, and when she mentioned Fifth Avenue, he wasn't surprised. The realisation hit him—it had been Amanda in that red dress.

As they pulled up to her apartment building, Amanda turned to Dominic, her voice soft but steady. "Would you like to come up for coffee?"

Dominic's lips curved into a warm smile. "I'd love to."

The car came to a smooth stop, and Joe, the doorman, promptly opened the limousine door, greeting Amanda with a warm smile as she stepped out.

"Miss Amanda, you look absolutely exquisite this evening," Joe said with genuine admiration.

Amanda returned his smile, leaning in to place a quick kiss on his cheek. "You're too sweet, Joe. I take it Brian is still under the weather?"

Joe nodded solemnly. "Yes, poor thing, not at all well."

Amanda's expression softened. "Well, I hope he feels better soon."

Just then, Dominic stepped out of the car and joined her side. Amanda gestured toward him with a small smile. "Joe, this is Dominic Childs—a friend of mine."

Joe's brows rose slightly in surprise before he recovered, offering a polite nod. "Good evening, sir."

"Good evening, Joe," Dominic replied, his tone polite but noticing the doorman's surprise, clearly Amanda did not bring men to her apartment very often—a realisation that pleased him. The doorman opened the door for them to enter the building.

"Have a good night, Miss Amanda," Joe said warmly as they walked through the elegant foyer.

Amanda led Dominic to the elevator, swiping her keycard to activate it. As the elevator doors slid shut, Dominic noted the penthouse button lighting up.

"So, the penthouse," he remarked casually.

Amanda glanced at him, a faint smile tugging at her lips. "Yes, it was my mother's before she married my father, she gifted it to me on my eighteenth birthday."

When they arrived, Amanda stepped into the spacious, beautifully decorated penthouse and turned to Dominic with a soft smile. "Make yourself comfortable while I get the coffee."

He nodded, his eyes following her as she disappeared into the kitchen. The space was impressive but understated, much like Amanda herself. Modern furnishings were paired with warm, personal touches—a cozy throw draped over a chair, fresh flowers on the table, and a gallery of framed family photos on one wall.

Dominic moved to the floor-to-ceiling windows, taking in the stunning view of the city lights. The quiet hum of activity below seemed a world away from the intimate, almost electric atmosphere in the apartment.

Amanda returned a few minutes later, carrying a tray with two cups of coffee, cream, sugar, and a small plate of chocolates. She placed it carefully on the low table between them before glancing up at Dominic. "How do you take it?"

"Black, please."

She handed him his cup with a small smile, then prepared her own, adding a splash of cream and a touch of sugar. Settling into the chair across from him, Amanda tucked her legs to the side, a gesture both elegant and casual. "Thank you for bringing me home," she said softly.

"It was my pleasure," Dominic replied, his gaze unwavering as it lingered on her.

Amanda lifted her cup, taking a sip. The warmth from the coffee wasn't enough to account for the sudden flush on her cheeks under Dominic's scrutiny. She set the cup down and cleared her throat. "This is a first for me, you know."

Dominic raised an eyebrow, curiosity flickering in his eyes. "A first?"

"I've never invited a man up to my apartment before," she admitted, her voice steady but tinged with nervousness. "I think I shocked poor Joe downstairs." She giggled softly, brushing a strand of hair behind her ear.

Dominic's lips curved into a small smile. "I did notice his surprise. I think I might have surprised him too."

Amanda laughed, reaching for one of the chocolates. She popped it into her mouth, her expression turning blissful. "These are my guilty pleasure. I'll run it off tomorrow," she said with a playful shrug.

Dominic's brow quirked, intrigued. "Oh, so you're a runner?"

She nodded. "Yes, every morning—either in Central Park or on my treadmill, depending on the weather. It's my way of clearing my head."

"I wouldn't have guessed," Dominic said, leaning back with his coffee in hand. "You don't strike me as the type who enjoys early mornings."

Amanda chuckled, her green eyes lighting up. "That's because you've only ever seen me at work, half-buried behind my disguise. Trust me, running keeps me sane. It's my quiet time to think."

Dominic tilted his head, a teasing smile playing on his lips. "Do you think I could keep up with you on one of these runs?"

Amanda grinned, the playful energy easing the lingering tension. "I don't know, Dominic. I've been told I'm pretty fast."

"Challenge accepted," he said with a glint in his eye, leaning forward. "I run every morning too. Maybe we'll have to see who can outpace the other."

Her laughter was light, and for a moment, the room felt brighter. But then Dominic's smile faded into something more serious. "Amanda," he began, his voice low and steady, "can I ask you something?"

She stilled, her heart skipping a beat. "Of course."

"Why the disguise?"

Amanda froze for a moment, her fingers tightening around her cup. She took a deep breath before answering. "It seemed… safer."

Dominic nodded; his expression thoughtful as he set his cup down. "Even when you were hiding behind those glasses and severe outfits, there was something about you I couldn't ignore." His gaze softened as it swept over her. "But now, seeing you as you are, I think I understand."

Amanda felt her cheeks burn, though she tried to mask it with a light laugh. "I wasn't exactly trying to be noticed," she admitted. "It's easier to focus on work when people aren't… distracted."

"Distracted?" Dominic asked, his tone both curious and amused. "You mean when men aren't falling over themselves to ask you out?"

Amanda rolled her eyes, though a small smile tugged at her lips. "Let's just say people— men—tend to assume things when you look a certain way. They don't take you seriously."

Dominic's smile faded, replaced by something more sombre. "So, you felt like you had to prove yourself?"

She nodded. "Yes. People didn't think I was capable. All they saw was the way I looked, not the work I was doing. It was exhausting."

"Smart," Dominic said after a moment, his voice laced with admiration. "But Amanda, you don't need to hide anymore. Anyone who doubts you now is a fool."

Amanda's gaze dropped to her coffee, her voice barely a whisper. "Do you really think so? I might shock a few people."

Dominic leaned forward, his tone firm yet gentle. "Amanda, you've proven yourself a hundred times over. Your talent and determination are impossible to ignore. The way you look doesn't define you—but it's okay to let people see all of you."

She met his gaze, her green eyes searching his. "Thank you, Dominic. That means more than you know."

He held her gaze for a moment before leaning back slightly, his curiosity evident. "So, tell me something. It's obvious you don't need to work," he said, gesturing subtly to the elegant apartment, her necklace, and her designer dress. "Why do it?"

Amanda sighed, her expression turning reflective. "My mother came from a wealthy family, and my father is wealthy in his own right. He worked hard for everything he has, and I've always admired that. My mother, even though she had a fortune, chose to study and work hard too. She became a very successful interior designer. She used to tell me, 'It's nice to have money, but the money you earn feels so much better.'"

She shrugged, a wistful smile touching her lips. "I agreed with her. So, when I realised, I was an excellent organiser, I decided to pursue a career as a personal assistant. I was in my first year of a bachelor's degree in business administration when my mum got sick. At the time, I considered quitting altogether. But instead, I started a communications degree as well—it was to distract me, and it kept me busy. Plus, I wanted to make her proud."

Dominic nodded, his expression thoughtful. "I'm sure she'd be incredibly proud of you. Your academic results were very impressive."

"Thank you," Amanda said softly, her gaze dropping to her coffee. She let out a quiet sigh. "After she passed away, my father was utterly lost without her. And I… I buried myself in study, trying to drown in my own grief. I didn't know how else to cope."

Dominic's voice was gentle. "You're very close to your father?"

"Yes," she said, her tone warm. "My mother, my father, and I—we were incredibly close. Losing her was devastating for both of us. Dad was terrified he'd lose me too, the way I threw myself into studying. But eventually, we found a way to move forward together."

She rolled her eyes, a faint smile returning to her lips. "Then, when I started working, no one took me seriously. I was constantly being pursued—for all the wrong reasons.

My last job was the worst. My boss cornered me in the break room one afternoon. That was the final straw—I left that day."

Dominic's jaw tightened, his eyes darkening with anger. "I'm so sorry you had to go through that. No one should have to deal with that kind of behaviour."

She gave him a small, grateful smile. "Thank you. It's why I started wearing the disguise. It was easier to make people focus on my work rather than… other things."

Dominic nodded slowly, his voice steady. "I understand why you did it. But you deserve to be seen and respected for who you are—your talent, your intelligence, your strength and your beauty. You shouldn't have to hide."

Amanda met his gaze, her heart softening at the sincerity in his eyes. "Thank you, Dominic. That really means a lot."

For a moment, the room fell into a comfortable silence, the weight of her story lingering between them. Then Dominic leaned forward, his voice lighter but still warm. "For the record, you don't need a disguise to make an impression. You've been captivating from the start."

Amanda laughed softly, the warmth of his words settling over her like a gentle embrace. "Well, thank you, Mr. Childs. I'll take that as a compliment."

He grinned, his eyes twinkling. "You should. It's the truth."

Dominic stood up, his movements deliberate as he said, "I think it's time for me to leave." His voice was steady, but the conflict in his eyes was undeniable. He didn't want to go—every fibre of his being was urging him to stay. But after everything Amanda had just shared, he couldn't shake the feeling that staying might lead to something she wasn't ready for, and he didn't want to take advantage of her vulnerability.

"Oh… okay," Amanda said, her voice tinged with surprise and disappointment as she rose to her feet.

They walked to the elevator together in silence, the atmosphere charged with unspoken tension. As they reached the door, Amanda turned to him and said softly, "Thanks again for bringing me home."

"No problem," Dominic replied, his gaze lingering on her. Then, almost impulsively, he leaned in to kiss her cheek—a polite, chaste goodbye.

But Amanda turned her head at the last moment, and his lips brushed against hers instead.

Dominic froze, his breath catching as their lips met. For a heartbeat, neither of them moved, the air between them thick with surprise and something far more powerful. Then, as if a dam had burst, heat exploded between them.

Dominic's hesitation vanished as he wrapped his arms around Amanda, pulling her closer. Her hands slid up around his neck, her fingers tangling in his hair as she kissed him back with an intensity that matched his own.

The kiss deepened, raw and urgent, as though they had both been holding back for far too long. Dominic's hand slid up to cradle the back of her head, his thumb brushing against her cheek, while Amanda pressed herself against him, her heart pounding in her chest.

When they finally pulled apart, both of them were breathless, their foreheads resting together. Dominic's voice was hoarse as he whispered, "Amanda…"

She opened her eyes to meet his, her lips slightly swollen from the kiss, her cheeks flushed. "I'm sorry," she murmured, her voice trembling. "I didn't mean—"

He cut her off with a quiet laugh, his hand still cupping her face. "Don't apologise," he said, his tone soft but firm. "I've wanted to do that again since the last time we kissed."

Her lips parted in surprise, her heart racing at the raw honesty in his words. "You have?"

Dominic nodded, his thumb brushing against her cheek. "But I didn't think I had the right to."

Amanda's lips curved into a shy smile as she looked up at him, her hands still resting against his chest. "Well," she said softly, her voice filled with a mix of warmth and nervousness, "I'm glad you did."

He smiled back, leaning down to press a softer, lingering kiss to her lips before pulling back just enough to rest his forehead against hers again. "So am I."

The elevator doors chimed softly behind them, breaking the spell. Dominic stepped back reluctantly, his hand sliding down to hold hers. "I should still go," he said, though his tone was filled with hesitation.

Amanda squeezed his hand, her eyes searching his. "Are you sure?"

Dominic studied her for a moment, his resolve wavering as the warmth in her gaze pulled at him. Finally, he smiled. "Only if you tell me I have to."

Amanda hesitated for a moment before shaking her head. "I don't want you to go," she admitted, her voice barely above a whisper.

Dominic's smile deepened as he took a step closer. "Then I'll stay."

Chapter Thirteen

Amanda took Dominic's hand, her fingers trembling slightly as she led him back to the living area. The city lights outside the massive windows cast a soft glow across the room, painting them both in hues of silver and gold. She stopped in front of the window, hesitating before turning to face him. Her expression was earnest, her cheeks tinged pink.

"Dominic," she said softly, her voice barely above a whisper. "I need to tell you something first."

He tilted his head, concern flickering in his eyes as he searched her face. "What is it, Amanda?" he asked gently.

She turned back to the view taking a step closer to the window, her gaze fixed on the city below as though gathering courage from its sprawling brilliance. "When I said earlier that this is my first…" She trailed off, her hands gripping each other tightly.

Dominic stiffened slightly, his sharp mind piecing the puzzle together before she could explain further. "You're a…" His voice was calm but laced with surprise.

"Yes," Amanda whispered, her blush deepening as she exhaled a shaky breath. "I'm a virgin."

The words tightened something deep in Dominic's chest—not with judgment, but with a surge of unexpected emotions. It wasn't just desire; it was something more profound, more primal. A wave of protectiveness and possessiveness swept through him, anchoring him in the moment.

He stepped closer, his movements deliberate, until he was directly behind her. For a moment, he didn't speak, simply taking in the sight of her silhouetted against the glow of the city lights, her bare shoulders catching the soft reflection from the window.

In one smooth motion, Dominic slipped off his tuxedo jacket and draped it over a nearby chair. Then, without hesitation, he wrapped his arms around her waist, pulling her gently yet firmly against his chest.

Amanda let out a soft gasp at the contact, her body instinctively leaning into his. His embrace was both grounding and electrifying, his warmth chasing away any lingering nerves.

He rested his chin lightly on her shoulder, his breath warm against her skin as they both gazed at their reflection in the glass. "You're stunning," he murmured, his voice low and filled with sincerity.

Amanda's hands moved instinctively to rest over his, her fingers intertwining with his as she leaned her head slightly against him. "You make me feel…" She hesitated, searching for the right words. "Safe. Wanted."

Dominic tightened his hold on her, his voice a gentle rumble. "You are. And with me, you always will be."

They stood there, gazing out at the glittering cityscape, their reflections blending in the glass. Breaking the silence, Dominic spoke, his tone low and steady. "Amanda," he said softly, his lips close to her ear, "we don't have to do anything you're not ready for." His voice was firm, though his heart pounded with the hope she wouldn't change her mind about letting him stay. After a moment, he asked, "I need to know… are you on birth control?"

Amanda blushed again, the heat rising to her cheeks. "Yes," she admitted. "I had to start because of my irregular cycles."

Relaxing slightly, Amanda leaned back into him, letting his warmth soothe her nerves. "I just… I thought you should know about you being my first," she said quietly. "I didn't want there to be any…misunderstandings."

In their shared reflection, she caught the faint curve of a smile playing on his lips. Slowly, he lifted a hand and removed the emerald comb from her hair, tossing it onto a nearby chair. His fingers slid through her glorious, cascading locks, savouring their silkiness before gently sweeping them aside to reveal the delicate nape of her neck. With unhurried precision, he leaned in and pressed a soft, lingering kiss to her exposed skin.

Amanda let out a quiet moan, her body responding instinctively to his touch. She wanted him, and it was undeniable that he wanted her just as much.

Dominic's voice was a husky murmur against her skin. "If you want me to stop, just tell me."

Dominic raised his hand to the zipper at the back of Amanda's strapless dress, his fingers grazing her skin as he slowly, deliberately began to pull it down. The sound of the zipper seemed louder in the quiet room, each inch revealing more of her smooth, bare back. Amanda tensed slightly, her body reacting instinctively to the unfamiliar intimacy, but she made no protest. Instead, she closed her eyes and took a steadying breath, trusting him.

Dominic's movements were unhurried, reverent, as he placed his hands on either side of her dress and gently slid it off her. The fabric glided down her body, pooling at her feet in a shimmering cascade of emerald, green.

Amanda stood before the expansive window, the glittering city lights casting a luminous backdrop to her reflection. She wore nothing but black silk panties, suspenders holding up nude stockings, her four-inch heels and her emerald necklace. Her bare skin glowed softly in the room's muted light, a vision of vulnerability and raw beauty. The weight of the moment pressed heavily on her, yet she felt no urge to retreat. There was no turning back now—and she didn't want to.

Dominic's breath hitched audibly as he gazed at her reflection over her shoulder. His hands rested lightly on her waist, his thumbs brushing the curve of her hips. "My God, Amanda," he murmured, his voice thick with awe and desire. "You're magnificent."

Amanda blushed at his words, the heat creeping up her neck. But instead of retreating into shyness, she felt a thrill unlike anything she had experienced before. This—this moment—was exhilarating, a heady mix of vulnerability and power that made her feel alive in a way she never had in her twenty-four years.

Dominic leaned forward, his lips pressing tenderly against her bare shoulder. The feather-light kisses trailed along her skin, making her shiver as his hands slid upward, wrapping around her ribcage.

Slowly and deliberately, he cupped her bare, perfectly proportioned breasts in his strong hands, his thumbs gliding over the hardened peaks with a tantalising touch.

Amanda's breath caught, her eyes fluttering closed as she let out a soft, unrestrained moan. The sensation was unlike anything she had ever imagined—intense, electric, and completely consuming.

Dominic released her and stepped around to face her, his hands returning to her waist. Amanda stood still, her eyes still closed, and lips slightly parted, waiting for his kiss. But it didn't come. Instead, she felt his gaze on her, heavy and penetrating. Slowly, she opened her eyes to meet his, and the raw desire she saw in his darkened gaze sent a shiver down her spine.

He leaned in slightly, his voice a husky whisper. "You have no idea how much I want you."

Amanda's pulse quickened as her eyes searched his face. Her voice was barely audible, but steady. "As much as I want you," she replied, the truth of her words burning in her chest.

She had never stood this exposed in front of a man before, but she liked it. There was no self-consciousness, no hesitation—just an overwhelming desire to be touched, to be kissed, to be completely his in this moment.

Dominic's head dipped, his lips crushing hers in a fervent, passionate kiss that left no room for hesitation. Amanda's arms wrapped tightly around his neck, her body arching into his as her breasts pressed against the soft fabric of his shirt. The warmth radiating between them sent shivers through her, igniting a fire she couldn't control.

Dominic's hands moved with purpose, sliding up from her waist, his palms skimming over the delicate curve of her ribcage. His touch was both tender and demanding as he captured her breasts once more, kneading them with a reverence that made her gasp against his lips. A low, primal groan rumbled from his chest as he deepened their kiss, his tongue exploring hers with a hunger that left her breathless.

When he broke the kiss, Amanda whimpered at the loss, but the sound turned into a sharp gasp as his lips trailed down her neck. His hot breath fanned over her skin, and he murmured her name like a prayer before his mouth claimed one of her taut nipples.

The sensation was overwhelming, a mix of pleasure and need that made Amanda tilt her head back, her fingers tangling in his hair as she cried out, "Oh… Dominic…" Her body trembled under his touch, the soft pull of his mouth sending waves of heat coursing through her.

Dominic's other hand continued its worship, kneading her other breast as if he couldn't bear to neglect any part of her. The intensity of his movements was matched by the raw desire in his voice when he lifted his head to move to the other nipple. "You're so beautiful," he breathed, his dark eyes meeting hers for a moment before his lips descended again. "It's intoxicating."

Amanda's knees weakened under the onslaught of sensation, but Dominic's arm slipped around her waist, holding her steady against him. His strength was reassuring, grounding her even as he sent her spiralling into a world of pleasure she had never known before.

Her hands roamed over his broad shoulders, her nails digging lightly into the fabric of his shirt as she sought to anchor herself. The city lights outside flickered against the glass, a silent witness to their growing passion, but neither of them noticed.

"Dominic…" she whispered, her voice shaky but filled with longing. She tugged at his shirt, needing to feel his skin against hers, to erase every barrier between them.

He obliged, pulling back just enough to unbutton his shirt, his hands moving with an urgency that matched the pounding of their hearts. When the last button was undone, he shrugged out of the fabric, revealing a chiselled chest that made Amanda's breath hitch.

Her hands traced over the hard planes of his muscles, her touch both exploratory and possessive. Dominic growled low in his throat, the sound vibrating through her as he pulled her closer, their skin finally meeting in a way that felt electric.

"You're incredible," he murmured, his lips capturing hers once more, she surrendered to the moment, to him, and to the desire that burned between them like an unstoppable flame.

Amanda moaned, feeling more alive than ever. Moisture pooled between her legs, making her knees weak. She wasn't sure how much longer they would hold her upright. Never had a man touched her like this, and she revelled in every caress, every sensation.

Soon, he began to kiss his way down her torso, savouring the valley between her breasts before continuing down her flat stomach, kissing, licking, and sucking as he continued. He eventually knelt in front of Amanda, his mouth on the skin just above the top of her panties. His hands glided down her waist, fingers hooking the sides of her panties. With deliberate care, he slid the delicate fabric down her long legs, exposing the most intimate part of her exquisite body while leaving the suspenders and stockings perfectly in place.

Dominic lifted one of her legs and hooked it over his shoulder, giving him better access. Amanda's knee faltered, prompting Dominic to wrap his arms around her for support while is mouth explored the mound in front of him. His tongue explored and licked the sensitive area as Amanda moaned and withered in his arms, encouraging his continued caresses.

It was the most intensely erotic moment of her life—this powerful, masculine man kneeling before her, reverent and devoted, as though worshiping her.

"Oh Dominic… yes… please…" she groaned softly.

He found the precious bud he was searching for and licked it, causing Amanda to buck in his arms. He murmured against her skin, "You taste incredible."

Amanda was experiencing sensations she had never felt before; she never knew she could feel this way. A pressure was building within her, escalating with intensity. Unsure of what it was or where it would lead, she only knew that she wanted, no, needed, to find out, desperately.

Dominic continued to lick and suck the now hardened bud nestled between her slick folds, sensing that she was close. Listening to her moans and cries of pleasure, urging him on.

"Dominic, please… oh!" She cried in pleasure as a powerful orgasm erupted through her. Sensing that her legs could no longer support her, he quickly stood and lifted her up into his arms, cradling her against him as he carried her to the dimly lit bedroom.

Feeling depleted of energy, Amanda wrapped her arms around his neck and lifted her lips to his waiting ones, kissing him hard and tasting her scent on him.

As their lips parted, he gently lowered her to her feet, his hands steadying her as she stood. Kneeling before her once more, he carefully slipped off her heels, his touch tender yet deliberate. One by one, he unfastened her stockings, slowly rolling them down her long, elegant legs, then removed the suspenders, leaving her completely bare before him, except for her necklace. Rising to his full height, he scooped her up effortlessly, cradling her against his chest as he carried her to the bed and gently laid her down. He stood over her, gazing down as her dreamy green eyes locked onto his, her hand outstretched in silent invitation for him to join her.

He quickly stripped off his clothes while she watched, her eyes devouring every inch of him. Her gaze widening as she took in the evidence of his arousal. She had never seen a man naked before, except in books, and they didn't do him justice.

Breathlessly, she whispered, "You're beautiful."

He smiled and replied, "I've never been called beautiful before," chuckling softly, he added, "but I like hearing it from you." Then he joined her on the bed, stretching out along the full length of her body.

His hand slowly slid up from one of her thighs, gliding over the apex of her legs, then over her stomach, moving up to one of her breasts before trailing to her neck. He threaded his fingers into her long, wavy hair and lowered his mouth to hers. Amanda's hands splayed on his chest, roaming over his hardened nipples and down his firm body. Dominic released a moan of pleasure. She had never felt anything so wonderful, so exquisite before, and she wanted to explore his magnificent body.

Amanda slowly pulled back from their kiss, her breath shallow as she gently guided Dominic onto his back. She removed her necklace, placing it carefully on the bedside table before leaning down. Her hands traced the contours of his broad chest, her lips following close behind. She licked his nipples, realising that he liked it when he sucked in his breath and let out a soft groan.

Amanda kissed, licked and nipped at his flesh as she slowly made her way down his body. Although she was a novice and had never done this before, she had read books and magazines, and her girlfriends had confided what their boyfriends liked.

Dominic lay back against the pillows, his body taut with anticipation as he focused entirely on Amanda—on her mouth, her hands, the unhurried confidence with which she explored him. He couldn't recall the last time, if ever, a woman had affected him so profoundly. The intensity of his arousal was almost overwhelming, and as she continued her slow, teasing journey down his body, he wondered distantly how long he could possibly endure the exquisite torment of her touch.

When Amanda finally reached him, she hesitated just a moment, her fingers brushing reverently over his engorged length. Then she leaned in and tentatively licked him from base to tip. The sensation tore a low groan from Dominic's chest, raw and uncontrollable, his hips lifting slightly in encouragement.

Her hand wrapped around him, warm and sure, while her tongue flicked over the bead of moisture at the tip. Then she took him into her mouth, slow and gentle at first, sucking lightly as though learning his response. Dominic's control snapped. His hand flew to her head, fingers tangling in her hair as he moaned her name, thick with desire.

"Amanda…"

The sound emboldened her. She slid her mouth further down him, her tongue moving sensuously against the soft, velvety skin, sending sparks of pleasure racing up his spine. His grip tightened instinctively, his breath ragged, his body on the verge of losing all restraint.

"Enough," he groaned, forcing the word out before he lost himself completely.

Amanda released him and looked up, her eyes sultry and heavy-lidded, lips swollen and glistening. "Don't you like that?" she asked softly, a hint of vulnerability beneath the teasing.

He let out a breathless laugh, his chest rising and falling rapidly. "I like it too much."

Her smile was slow and satisfied as she slid back up his body, her nipples brushing against his skin, sending a fresh surge of desire through him. Dominic cupped her face and pulled her into a deep kiss, his tongue exploring her mouth with unrestrained hunger. A moan slipped from her lips, vibrating against his.

Without breaking the kiss, he rolled them smoothly, flipping Amanda onto her back and covering her with his body. One hand slid between her thighs, finding her already warm and wet. His fingers explored her gently at first, drawing another soft moan from her that he swallowed with his mouth.

He broke the kiss only to trail his lips downward, taking one nipple into the warm cavern of his mouth, his tongue rasping against the hardened peak. Amanda arched beneath him, her fingers clutching the sheets as sensation flooded her.

He slid one long finger into her core, slow and deliberate, while his thumb brushed her sensitive bud in small, teasing circles. Her body writhed beneath him, hips lifting instinctively to meet his hand as he established a steady, unrelenting rhythm. His mouth moved to her other nipple, lavishing it with the same attention.

"You're so responsive," he murmured against her skin, his voice low and thick with desire. "You're driving me insane. You're absolutely incredible."

He took his time, building her pleasure inch by inch, until her breath came in broken gasps and her body trembled beneath his touch. When she cried out his name, desperate and breathless—"Dominic…!"—he knew she was right on the edge.

Her release tore through her moments later, waves of pleasure rippling through her body as she shuddered beneath him. Dominic captured her mouth again, kissing her deeply as his fingers continued their gentle teasing until her tremors finally subsided.

Knowing she was ready, he lifted himself and settled between her parted thighs, positioning himself carefully at her entrance. Amanda tensed slightly, her breath catching as anticipation—and fear—fluttered through her.

Sensing it instantly, Dominic pressed slow, soothing kisses along her neck, lingering over the pulse that raced beneath his lips. "I've got you," he murmured softly.

He eased into her gradually, moving in shallow, gentle motions, giving her body time to adjust. Then, with one deeper thrust, he sank fully into her tight, hot centre. A sharp gasp escaped her lips as sensation flared intensely.

Dominic froze, his concern immediate. "Are you okay?" he asked quietly, his voice tender.

Unable to speak through the ache, Amanda nodded, burying her face against his neck. He kissed along her collarbone and up her throat, his lips brushing her ear as he whispered, "God… you feel incredible. So perfect."

He began to move again, slow and controlled, withdrawing before easing back in, each motion igniting new sensations. The discomfort faded, replaced by something powerful and intoxicating. Amanda's eyes flew open as pleasure surged through her, stealing her breath.

"Yes," she cried, her voice breaking. "Dominic, yes!"

He groaned and captured her mouth in a fierce kiss, his tongue claiming hers as completely as his body claimed her. His pace quickened, thrusts growing deeper, more urgent. Amanda met him instinctively, her body responding to his rhythm, surrendering to the rising tide of pleasure.

They teetered together on the brink before tumbling over the edge in a shared cry of ecstasy. Dominic released himself inside her with a deep, primal groan, feeling her body pulse around him as she climaxed again, milking every last tremor from him. He stayed still, holding her, savouring the intensity of the moment as they rode the final waves together.

He kissed her then—slow, deep, soul-stealing—before finally easing himself free and drawing her into his arms. Amanda settled against his chest, her body heavy and warm, and within moments, sleep claimed her.

Dominic gazed down at her peaceful face, a frown of confusion crossing his features. What was it about this woman? He had never known such completeness, such quiet satisfaction. Not even with Sofia—his intended bride—had he ever felt anything close to this.

He pressed a tender kiss to the top of Amanda's head, holding her close. The questions stirring in his mind could wait. For now, he allowed sleep to take him.

Throughout the night, they came together twice more, each encounter as intense and consuming as the first. By morning, Dominic knew one thing with absolute certainty: he would never tire of her. He never wanted to let her go.

She was special.

And she was his.

Chapter Fourteen

The sunlight streamed softly through the open curtains, spilling into the bedroom and gently nudging Amanda awake. For a moment, she was disoriented, her senses slow to catch up with the new day. Then, like a wave, the memories of the night before came rushing back—flooding her mind with vivid clarity. Her heart raced slightly, a mix of excitement and uncertainty. She felt a rush of warmth on her cheeks, both from the memories and the quiet embarrassment that followed.

Carefully, she began to untangle herself from Dominic's embrace, taking care not to disturb him. His breath was steady and calm, a peaceful contrast to the flurry of emotions swirling within her. She slipped out of the bed quietly, her bare feet making no sound on the cool floor. Moving toward the ensuite bathroom, she washed her face, feeling the cool water help clear her mind. She gently removed her makeup from the night before, the act almost ritualistic as she worked to shed the remnants of the previous evening.

After clipping her hair up out of the way, she stepped into the shower, the warm water soothing her, melting away the tension that had built up over the night. When she finally stepped out, she dried herself off with a plush towel, letting its softness ground her in the moment. She reached for the silk robe hanging on the back of the bathroom door, its cool fabric gliding over her skin as she slipped it on, tying the belt loosely around her waist.

With a sigh, she left the bathroom and moved quietly through the bedroom, glancing over at Dominic's sleeping form. His relaxed expression stirred a mix of emotions within her—part longing, part confusion, but she didn't want to disturb him, so she continued on. She made her way toward the kitchen, her steps soft against the floor as she prepared the coffee, the warmth of the brewing liquid filling the silence of the apartment.

After pouring herself a cup, she carried it carefully to the terrace off the living room. The morning air was cool and crisp, and the city seemed to be slowly coming to life, though it was still early enough to feel like a secret world. Amanda stood at the balustrade, sipping her coffee slowly, her gaze wandering over the view. The quiet hum of the city below felt distant, almost like a lullaby, giving her a brief moment of peace.

Dominic stirred, the sunlight streaming through the open curtains warming his skin. Still half-asleep, he reached instinctively for Amanda, expecting to find her soft warmth beside him. But his hand met only the cool sheets. His brow furrowed as his eyes blinked open, disappointment flickering in his chest. For a moment, he lay there, staring at the ceiling, wondering where she'd gone.

Pushing himself up, he ran a hand through his messy hair before swinging his legs over the side of the bed. He found his underpants and trousers tossed on the floor from the night before and slipped them on with lazy efficiency. Barefoot and shirtless, he padded out of the bedroom, his movements quiet as he searched for her.

The apartment was still and bathed in the soft morning glow. The faint scent of coffee led him toward the living room, and it wasn't long before he spotted her. Amanda stood on the terrace, framed by the morning light, her silk robe fluttering slightly in the breeze. She was looking out over the city, her coffee cup cradled in her hands. Her hair was pinned up, exposing the delicate curve of her neck and shoulders. Dominic paused in the doorway, his breath catching as he took her in.

God, she was beautiful.

There was something about the way the sunlight kissed her skin, the way she stood so still, lost in thought, which made his chest tighten. He couldn't help but smile, a warmth spreading through him that had nothing to do with the morning sun.

Quietly, he stepped out onto the terrace, the sound of his bare feet muffled by the cool tiles. He approached her from behind, his movements slow and deliberate, as if he didn't want to break the spell of the moment. When he was close enough, he slipped his arms gently around her waist, pulling her back against his chest.

"Good morning, sweetheart," he murmured, his voice low and soft, the words brushing against her ear.

Before she could respond, he leaned down and pressed a tender kiss to the exposed curve of her neck, his lips lingering for a moment against her warm skin. Amanda shivered, a tremor running down her spine at the intimate touch. Her breath hitched slightly, and she tilted her head ever so slightly, giving him more access without even realising it.

"You're up early," Dominic said, his tone teasing but affectionate as he rested his chin lightly on her shoulder. "I was hoping to wake up with you still in my arms."

Amanda's lips curved into a small smile as she leaned back into his embrace, her free hand resting over his. "I didn't want to wake you," she said softly, her voice carrying a hint of apology. "You looked so peaceful."

He chuckled, the low, warm sound vibrating through his chest and against her back. "Peaceful or not, I'd much rather wake up with you beside me."

The sincerity in his voice sent a soft flutter through Amanda's heart. She smiled, her fingers brushing lightly over his hand as it rested on her waist. "I'll remember that for future reference," she said, her tone playful but carrying a warmth that matched the quiet morning.

"You'd better," Dominic teased, his voice rich with a touch of mischief. Without waiting for her reply, he gently turned her in his arms, guiding her to face him.

Amanda's breath caught as her eyes met his, the morning light softening his rugged features and casting a golden glow over him. His gaze held hers, lingering as though he was savouring every detail of her face. Then, slowly, he leaned in, his intent unmistakable.

His lips brushed against hers, soft and unhurried, his hand coming up to cradle her cheek with a tenderness that made her knees feel weak. The world around them faded away, the hum of the city and the morning breeze forgotten in the warmth of his kiss. Amanda melted into him, her free hand coming to rest lightly on his chest, feeling the steady beat of his heart beneath her fingertips. The kiss deepened.

When they finally pulled apart, Amanda's cheeks were flushed, her lips curved in a small, breathless smile. "Would you like some coffee?"

He raised an eyebrow, his smile widening, his tone teasing. "If that's all that's on offer."

Amanda laughed softly, the sound light and carefree. "For now," she replied, a playful sparkle in her eyes.

Dominic leaned in again, his intent clear, but before he could close the distance, Amanda slipped quickly out of his arms, her silk robe fluttering behind her as she stepped back with a grin.

"You're going to make me work for it, aren't you?" he said, his voice filled with mock exasperation as he watched her retreat.

"It's more satisfying if you work for it," Amanda called over her shoulder, her voice laced with playful defiance. Her laughter echoed softly as she disappeared back into the apartment.

Standing on the terrace, Dominic watched Amanda retreat into the apartment, her teasing remarks and soft laughter lingering in the air, lighting a fire in his chest. She had a way of captivating him without even trying, making it impossible to look away. Yet, as he stood there, his smirk faltered for just a moment.

Was he really doing this? Was he letting himself get involved with another personal assistant after Sofia had shattered his trust? The memory of that betrayal—the lies, the manipulation—still stung, a reminder of why he had sworn off mixing business and personal life. He could still picture Sofia's calculated charm, how she had wormed her way past his defences, only to leave him feeling like a fool.

But Amanda wasn't Sofia. Deep down, he knew that. There was something different about her—something real. She didn't seek attention or play games. She simply was, and somehow, that was more irresistible than any façade.

He wasn't the kind of man to let doubts paralyse him, and if there was one thing he was sure of, it was that Amanda was special. She made him feel things he hadn't in years, if ever. And maybe, just maybe, she was worth the risk.

With that thought grounding him, he followed her into the kitchen, his steps quiet on the cool tiles beneath his feet.

Amanda stood by the counter, her movements fluid and graceful as she poured another cup of coffee, oblivious to his presence at first. There was something mesmerising about the way she carried herself, like every motion was deliberate but unpretentious.

When she turned and handed him the steaming mug, their fingers brushed. It was just a fleeting touch, but it sent a jolt through him, tightening his chest.

Before he could think it through, the words tumbled out of his mouth.

"Come home with me."

Amanda froze, her brows shooting up in surprise. "What, today? Right now?"

"Yes," he said firmly, his gaze steady on hers. "I need to grab more clothes, and I need to have a run… but mostly, I don't want to leave you. Not even for a day."

Her surprise softened into something unreadable, her eyes flickering with emotions he couldn't quite pin down. She looked at the coffee cup in her hands, as if it might hold the answer, before meeting his gaze again.

"That's… a lot," she admitted, her voice tinged with both hesitation and curiosity.

"I mean it," Dominic said, stepping closer, his words filled with quiet conviction. "This morning, waking up without you—it sucked. I don't want to keep doing that. I want more than just last night or today. I want you."

Amanda's breath hitched, her pulse quickening as his words sank in. She searched his face, looking for any sign of doubt, but all she saw was sincerity. The intensity in his gaze made her chest ache, and for a fleeting moment, she let herself imagine what he was offering—something steady, something real.

"You're serious," she murmured, almost to herself.

"I've never been more serious," he said, setting his coffee aside without a second thought. Reaching out, he tucked a stray strand of hair behind her ear, his touch lingering against her cheek. "I'm not asking for forever right now. Just come with me. Stay a while. We'll figure out the rest as we go."

Amanda hesitated, torn between the temptation of his words and the practicality of her own guarded heart. "And what if I say no?" she asked, her tone light but probing.

Dominic chuckled, the sound warm and deep, wrapping around her like a comforting blanket. "Then I'll keep asking. You said yourself; the best things are worth the effort."

Her lips curved into a reluctant smile, and she shook her head with a soft laugh. "You're impossible."

"And you're deflecting," he teased, stepping closer, his presence overwhelming in the best way. "Is that a yes?"

Amanda exhaled slowly, her playful spark mingling with something more vulnerable. "It's a maybe," she said finally, her voice soft but teasing. "Don't get too confident—I haven't decided if your place is worth staying at yet."

Dominic grinned, victorious. "Then I guess I'll just have to convince you."

Amanda packed a bag, carefully selecting enough clothes for a week while Dominic showered and dressed. Her thoughts raced as she folded her favourite jeans and a few tops, tucking in her toiletries with a mix of excitement and apprehension. The spontaneity of it all left her both thrilled and unsteady, but she couldn't deny the growing pull she felt toward Dominic.

Once ready, they left the apartment together. On the way out, Amanda stopped by the manager's office to inform them she'd be away, keeping her tone casual despite the flutter in her chest. Outside, Dominic waited by the limousine, leaning against it with his hands in his pockets. His relaxed posture contrasted sharply with the nervous energy buzzing through her.

The drive to Dominic's home in Great Neck, Long Island, took just under an hour. They exchanged occasional glances, the quiet between them heavy with unspoken thoughts. As the urban chaos of the city melted into sprawling estates and lush greenery, Amanda found herself growing increasingly curious—and a little nervous.

When the limousine slowed at the entrance to his property, her breath caught. Massive gates swung open, revealing a long driveway lined with flowering trees and meticulously trimmed hedges. At the end of the drive stood a mansion that was both stunning and imposing.

The two-story house was an elegant blend of modern design and timeless sophistication. Wrought-iron balconies graced the upper floor, climbing ivy softening the grandeur. Large arched windows reflected the sunlight, while the stone facade exuded quiet luxury.

"It's beautiful," Amanda murmured, leaning forward as if to take it all in.

Dominic turned to her, his lips curving into a small, satisfied smile. "I'm glad you think so," he said warmly. "I wanted it to be… special."

The limousine came to a stop in front of the house. A fountain bubbled softly in the circular driveway, adding to the serene atmosphere. As the driver opened her door, Amanda stepped out, her eyes roaming over the estate.

"'Like it' might be an understatement," she said, glancing at Dominic as he joined her. "It's breathtaking."

He took her hand, his smile widening. "Come on," he said, lacing his fingers through hers. "Wait until you see the inside."

Amanda let him guide her, her heart pounding with a mix of nerves and excitement. The sprawling mansion before her was breathtaking, but it was the easy confidence in Dominic's stride and the warmth of his hand around hers that steadied her. She had no idea what to expect from this impromptu visit, yet with each step beside him, a strange sense of belonging settled in—a feeling she couldn't quite explain but didn't want to question.

When they stepped through the grand double doors, the interior of the house nearly took her breath away. The first thing that caught her eye was the gleaming marble floors, polished to perfection and reflecting the soft natural light streaming through the massive arched windows. The ceilings soared high above, adorned with intricate moulding and a crystal chandelier that cast a delicate play of light across the entryway.

The space was open and inviting, yet undeniably luxurious. To her right, an elegant sitting room beckoned, its plush furniture arranged around a sleek fireplace. The deep, rich tones of the upholstery contrasted beautifully with the neutral walls, creating an atmosphere that was both sophisticated and cozy.

To her left, a sweeping staircase curved gracefully upward, its wrought-iron railing adding a touch of timeless artistry. Amanda couldn't help but pause, her gaze tracing the elegant design before following the line of the staircase up to the second-floor balcony.

"This is… incredible," she said softly, her voice filled with awe as she turned to Dominic.

He smiled, clearly pleased by her reaction. "I wanted a place that felt like home, but still had a bit of wow factor," he admitted. "Do you like it?"

"Like it?" she echoed, shaking her head with a soft laugh. "It's stunning, Dominic. I don't even know where to look first."

"Well," he said with a teasing grin, slipping his arm around her waist, "let me give you the tour. We've got all the time in the world."

As they moved deeper into the house, Amanda noticed the careful attention to detail in every room they passed. The formal dining room featured a long mahogany table set beneath another glittering chandelier; the walls lined with abstract art that added a modern edge. The kitchen was equally impressive, a chef's dream with sleek granite countertops, state-of-the-art appliances, and a large island perfect for entertaining.

But it was the living room that truly stole her breath. The room was expansive yet inviting, with floor-to-ceiling windows that offered an uninterrupted view of the manicured gardens outside. A plush sectional sofa dominated the space, positioned perfectly in front of a large stone fireplace. Shelves filled with books and personal mementos lined one wall, hinting at a more intimate, personal side of Dominic.

"You live here alone?" Amanda asked, turning to him as they stopped in the living room.

"Yeah," he said, his expression softening. "For now. It's my sanctuary, but sometimes it feels too big. That's why it's nice having you here."

Her heart fluttered at his words, the sincerity in his tone making her cheeks warm. "It's beautiful, Dominic. Truly."

"Thank you," he said, his gaze holding hers for a moment longer than necessary. Then, with a playful smirk, he added, "Wait until you see the terrace and gardens, my favourite part of the house."

As Dominic guided Amanda toward the glass doors that opened onto the sprawling terrace, she found herself increasingly captivated by the elegance of the home and the calm yet inviting atmosphere it exuded. The lush greenery outside came into view, framing the expansive patio with its carefully arranged outdoor furniture and flower-filled planters.

"How long have you lived here?" Amanda asked, her curiosity getting the better of her.

"I've owned it for seven months," Dominic replied, glancing at her with a soft smile. "But I've only been living here for six. It took about a month to finish a few changes before I moved in. I wanted everything just right."

Amanda nodded, admiring the effort he had clearly put into making the place his sanctuary.

"Good morning, Mr. Childs," a cheerful female voice called from behind them.

Both Amanda and Dominic turned to see a woman in a neatly pressed maid's uniform standing in the doorway.

"Hello, Rosa," Dominic greeted warmly. "This is Amanda Prentice. She'll be staying with me for a while."

Rosa's face lit up with a kind smile as she turned her attention to Amanda. "Hello, Miss Prentice," she said politely.

Amanda stepped forward, returning the smile. "Please, call me Amanda," she said, extending her hand.

Rosa accepted the handshake, her expression friendly and welcoming. "Welcome, Amanda. Please let me know if you need anything during your stay."

"Thank you, Rosa," Amanda replied sincerely. "I'll try to be as low maintenance as possible."

Rosa laughed softly. "I hope you enjoy your time here." With a quick nod to Dominic, she excused herself and disappeared back into the house.

"She seems lovely," Amanda remarked, watching Rosa leave.

Dominic's gaze shifted back to Amanda, his expression softening as a playful smile spread across his face. "No," he said, stepping closer to her. "You're lovely."

Before Amanda could respond, he slipped his arms around her waist, drawing her close. His warmth enveloped her, and her breath hitched as he leaned down, capturing her lips in a kiss. It was slow and tender, yet it sent a wave of heat coursing through her.

Amanda felt herself melting into him, her hands finding their way to his chest as his embrace tightened. The world around them seemed to blur, the only thing anchoring her being the feel of Dominic's lips on hers and the steady thrum of his heartbeat beneath her fingertips.

When they finally pulled apart, Dominic rested his forehead against hers, his voice low and filled with affection. "I like having you here, Amanda. It feels… right."

Her heart fluttered at his words, a warmth spreading through her chest. She tilted her head to look at him, a soft smile curving her lips. "You're going to spoil me if you keep saying things like that."

"Good," he replied with a mischievous grin, his eyes twinkling with both playfulness and sincerity. "You deserve it."

Hand in hand, they turned back toward the terrace, the morning sun casting a golden glow over the manicured gardens below. To the left, an infinity pool and tennis court glistened in the light, while the right offered a serene expanse of uninterrupted lawn and lush gardens. Dominic led her toward the railing, and they paused for a moment, taking in the breathtaking view. After a beat, he turned to her with a smile. "Come on," he said softly, "I should show you the rest of the house."

Amanda followed him eagerly as he began the tour, guiding her through the sprawling mansion with pride. Every room seemed more impressive than the last, from the home office lined with bookshelves and a sleek mahogany desk to the state-of-the-art gym with floor-to-ceiling windows overlooking the grounds.

"This place is like something out of a movie," Amanda said, her awe evident as they passed through a corridor lined with modern art.

Dominic chuckled, giving her hand a gentle squeeze. "It's just a house, Amanda. It's who's in it that makes it a home."

Her heart skipped at his words, but before she could respond, he led her to the pièce de résistance—the main bedroom.

Chapter Fifteen

When they stepped inside the master bedroom, Amanda's breath caught. The space was both expansive and intimate, with soft, neutral tones that exuded a serene elegance. A king-sized bed with an upholstered headboard stood as the focal point, its crisp white linens inviting. Floor-to-ceiling windows lined one wall, opening onto a private balcony where sheer curtains billowed gently in the breeze.

"Wow," she whispered, turning in a slow circle. "This is incredible, Dominic."

He watched her with a pleased smile. "I'm glad you think so. This is one of my favourite rooms in the house."

"I can see why," she murmured, drifting toward the balcony doors. The view was breathtaking—lush greenery stretched endlessly before her, with the faint silhouette of the city skyline visible in the distance.

Dominic stepped behind her, his hands resting lightly on her waist. His voice was low and suggestive as he murmured, "I thought we could spend some time here today."

She glanced at him over her shoulder, a teasing glint in her eyes. "I thought you wanted to go for a run?"

He smirked. "Maybe we could find another way to stay… active."

Amanda turned to face him fully, warmth rising to her cheeks as she met his gaze. "And what exactly do you have in mind?" she asked, her voice laced with playful challenge.

Dominic leaned in, brushing his lips against hers in a slow, lingering kiss. When he pulled back, his grin was full of mischief. "I'm sure we'll think of something."

The hours melted away in a blur of passionate kisses, whispered words, and quiet moments wrapped in each other's presence. The world outside ceased to exist as they lingered in the sanctuary of the bedroom, lost in the warmth of one another.

By the time the afternoon light filtered through the curtains, Amanda lay beside Dominic, her head resting against his chest as his fingers traced absentminded patterns along her arm. A deep, unshakable contentment settled over her—something she hadn't felt in longer than she could remember.

"This," Dominic murmured, his voice quiet yet certain, "feels right."

Amanda tilted her head up, meeting his gaze. The sincerity in his expression made her chest tighten, her heart swelling in response. "It does," she whispered, the words barely audible but laced with truth.

Dominic reached out, gently cupping her chin between his fingers. His thumb brushed lightly over her cheek, his touch reverent. "Thank you for coming here," he murmured, his voice carrying both gratitude and something deeper—something unspoken yet impossible to ignore.

As the sun dipped lower in the sky, casting the room in a warm, golden glow, Amanda felt a quiet certainty settle within her. Wrapped in Dominic's arms, she realised she had never felt more at home than she did in that moment.

The rest of the day unfolded like a dream. They spent the afternoon lounging on the terrace, sharing a light lunch between easy laughter and stolen glances. Later, they wandered the sprawling grounds hand in hand, the quiet beauty of the estate mirroring the growing connection between them.

By the time dinner rolled around, they found themselves seated at an intimate table in the dining room, the flickering candlelight casting soft shadows as they talked. The conversation flowed effortlessly, weaving between teasing remarks and heartfelt confessions, creating a world that felt like theirs alone.

That night, as they lay entwined in each other's arms, Amanda couldn't help but marvel at how easily she and Dominic had settled into this rhythm together.

Monday morning, they both rose early, the faint blush of dawn just beginning to light the sky. Dominic suggested a morning jog, and Amanda surprised him by keeping pace effortlessly. They ran side by side through the scenic trails on his estate, the crisp morning air invigorating them both.

When they finally stopped, Dominic bent over slightly, hands on his knees, grinning at her. "Okay, I'm officially impressed. You can keep up with me and run just as far."

Amanda laughed, brushing a strand of damp hair from her face. "What, did you think I'd be dragging behind you, begging to stop?"

"Well, maybe a little," he teased, leaning over to steal a quick kiss.

Their post-run shower was filled with playful banter and stolen touches, Dominic's deep laughter mingling with Amanda's bright giggles. As they got dressed for the day, Dominic shot her a teasing look. "Thank goodness you're not wearing those hideous glasses."

Amanda arched a brow at him through the mirror, a playful glint in her eyes. "Hideous? Those glasses are sophisticated, professional and plain glass."

"Really? You little minx," he laughed, walking over to slide his arms around her waist. "I much prefer seeing those gorgeous eyes without anything in the way."

Amanda rolled her eyes, but her smile gave her away.

When they arrived at the office, they walked in separately. Amanda entered first, with Dominic following close behind. He immediately noticed the way several male employees turned to stare at her—now that she wasn't dressed down and those awful glasses were gone. A flicker of irritation tightened his jaw; he didn't appreciate the attention.

By the time they reached his office, he leaned in and murmured, "Maybe you should start wearing those terrible glasses again."

Amanda laughed, her eyes gleaming with amusement. "I told you I wore them for a reason."

"Hmm," he muttered, not entirely convinced.

Despite the playful exchange, they slipped effortlessly into their professional roles. Their interactions were efficient and respectful, giving no outward hint of the intimacy they shared beyond office walls.

But by Wednesday afternoon, Dominic's resolve began to crack. Amanda had come into his office to drop off some documents, her confident stride and soft smile enough to undo him completely. As she leaned over his desk to point out a detail in one of the files, her scent enveloped him, and he couldn't hold back any longer.

Dominic stood abruptly, the sound of his chair hitting the cupboard behind his desk. He circled the desk, without a word, he moved toward the door, shutting it with a quiet click before hearing the snib of the lock as he turned the key.

Amanda straightened from over the desk, her pulse quickening as she watched him, her eyes widening slightly as she instinctively turned to face him. He came to stand in front of her, his presence overwhelming, his gaze intense.

"Dominic—" she began, her voice tentative, but her words were immediately cut off as he captured her lips in a searing kiss. The world around them seemed to fade away as the tension, carefully contained for days, exploded between them in a rush of passion.

His hands were everywhere, urgent and demanding as they roamed over her body. Papers scattered across the desk, forgotten, as he lifted Amanda effortlessly onto its edge, her legs instinctively parting to make room for him. His kisses were frantic, his lips claiming hers with an insatiable hunger. She melted into him, her heart racing, the room growing warmer as their bodies responded to each other, every touch sending sparks of desire racing through them both.

Amanda's hands tangled in his hair, her breath hitching as his lips trailed down her neck. "This is so unprofessional," she managed to whisper, though her voice was thick with desire.

"We'll call it a much-needed break," Dominic murmured against her skin, his voice low and teasing, before claiming her lips again.

His lips lingered on hers, soft and insistent, as his hands moved to unbutton her blouse urgently. The fabric parted easily under his touch, and he slid his hands beneath her bra, his hands kneading her breasts, his thumbs taunting her hardened nipples.

He murmured against her skin, his breath warm and heavy as he pressed his lips gently to her neck. "I can't get enough of you," he whispered, his voice low and filled with intensity. "You're like a drug I can't do without, something I crave every moment. Every time I'm near you, it feels like I'm drowning in you, and I don't ever want to surface."

His hands traced the delicate curves of her body, moving with purpose as they slowly slid down to her hips, feeling the warmth of her skin beneath his fingertips. The soft fabric of her skirt seemed to cling to her, but he wasn't deterred. With a gentle but insistent motion, he pushed the hem of her skirt up to her hips, exposing the thong she was wearing under her skirt.

Amanda's hands trembled with urgency as she swiftly undid the button of his trousers, her fingers working quickly to pull the zipper down. She barely paused before she pushed them down, along with his underpants, her eyes meeting his for a brief, charged moment. The fabric slid away easily, exposing his engorged erection, and her breath hitched at the sight. She felt a surge of anticipation flood through her as she ran her fingers lightly over his erection, guiding him to her core, "Dominic, I need you now."

He didn't need any more encouragement. With a ragged, impatient breath torn from deep in his chest, Dominic hooked his fingers beneath the delicate straps of her thong and pushed it aside, his touch firm, unhesitating. The barrier between them gone, he surged forward, entering her in one fluid, decisive motion. Her body was impossibly hot, slick and welcoming, and the sheer sensation of it sent a violent shudder through them both.

They gasped together, the sound raw and unguarded, as their bodies reacted instinctively to the sudden, intimate connection. Pleasure surged through Dominic so powerfully that his grip tightened on her hips, his fingers digging into her skin as if anchoring himself.

A low groan escaped his throat, rough and unfiltered. His eyes closed briefly, overwhelmed by the way she surrounded him, by how perfectly she fit. When he spoke, his voice was thick, strained with desire. "Amanda... you feel incredible."

Amanda leaned back, surrendering to the moment, her spine arching as her hands found the solid edge of his desk behind her. The posture opened her to him completely, granting him deeper access, greater freedom. She felt his hands on her hips—possessive, sure—as he began to move, pulling back slowly before driving into her again, each thrust deliberate, powerful, impossible to resist.

The desk creaked faintly beneath them, the room thick with heat and tension as he established a rhythm that made her breath fracture. Each movement sent sparks of sensation rippling through her body, building faster, stronger.

"Dominic… please…" she moaned, the plea spilling from her lips without thought, her voice breathless and desperate, matching the fire igniting between them.

She opened herself to him instinctively, a silent, wordless invitation that urged him deeper. He responded immediately, his movements growing more urgent, more forceful, their bodies finding a shared rhythm that felt inevitable, unstoppable. Every breath they took seemed to fuel the rising intensity, the pressure coiling tighter and tighter within them.

The world narrowed to sensation—to the sound of breath and skin, to the heat and the relentless drive of pleasure mounting beyond control. Then, all at once, it shattered.

The pressure erupted in a blinding flash of white heat, pleasure crashing through them in a powerful surge that stole all sense of time and place. Amanda cried out, her body trembling as waves of ecstasy rolled through her, while Dominic groaned her name, his control breaking as he followed her over the edge.

For a suspended, breathless moment, nothing existed beyond the overwhelming sensation—only pounding hearts, tangled bodies, and the electric aftermath that left them both shaking, clinging to one another as reality slowly returned.

Dominic lowered his head to the valley between her breasts, his breath ragged and uneven, his chest rising and falling with the aftermath of their lovemaking. "That was… amazing," he murmured, his voice rough, as he tried to regain his composure, each breath a struggle against the intensity of what they'd just shared.

Amanda smiled softly, a gentle curve of her lips as she ran her fingers through his hair, her touch tender and soothing. She let the warmth of the moment linger between them, her body still trembling slightly from the intensity. "That's what I call a much-needed break," she whispered, her voice low and filled with a playful afterglow. Her eyes met his, sparkling with a quiet satisfaction.

Dominic was out of the office for most of Thursday, and Amanda had settled into her usual routine when the unexpected happened. She had just returned from a short break when the door to her office swung open, and in walked a tall, strikingly beautiful blonde woman. Confidence radiated from her, and she carried herself with the ease of someone who expected attention—and always got it.

"I'd like to see Dominic, please," the woman said, her tone clipped, laced with both assertion and condescension.

Amanda rose from her desk, taken aback by the unannounced visitor. "I'm sorry, he's out at the moment, but he should be back soon. Can I take a message?"

The woman tilted her head slightly, amusement flickering in her blue eyes. "I'm Sofia," she said smoothly, watching Amanda with thinly veiled curiosity. "Dominic's fiancée."

Amanda's breath hitched. "Oh," she said, grasping for composure. "He… never mentioned a fiancée."

Sofia's smile sharpened. "Well, technically, I'm his estranged fiancée," she admitted with an airy wave of her hand, "but not for much longer." She took a step closer, lowering her voice just enough to make Amanda feel like she was being let in on a cruel little secret. "I hope you haven't fallen for his charm. He has a habit of using women until he gets bored—then he comes back to me."

Amanda stiffened, her stomach twisting at the implication.

"I'm having lunch with him anyway," Sofia added with a dismissive glance toward the door. "Thought I'd drop by before we head to the hotel."

She turned on her heel and walked out, leaving behind a suffocating silence.

Amanda stood frozen, her mind spinning. Fiancée? Estranged fiancée? Why hadn't Dominic told her?

Later that afternoon, still unsettled, she decided to have lunch in the cafeteria, hoping for some solitude to clear her head. Normally, she kept to herself, but today, Jane—a secretary from the floor above—plopped down beside her with a knowing smile.

"So," Jane began, lowering her voice conspiratorially, "I heard something interesting."

Amanda hesitated, wary. "Oh?"

Jane leaned in. "I saw Sofia earlier. She came looking for Dominic."

Amanda's pulse quickened. "Did she?" she asked, keeping her tone neutral.

"Oh, yeah. He left with her just before lunch," Jane continued, stabbing at her salad with her fork. "And they looked very happy together."

A cold weight settled in Amanda's chest. "Happy?" she echoed, her heart pounding. I didn't even know he was back in the office.

"Mm-hmm," Jane nodded. "All over each other—kissing, holding hands. It was like old times. Guess they worked things out. I heard Sofia postponed their wedding and broke his heart, but now she's back. Don't you think that's romantic?"

Amanda forced a tight smile. "Yes. Very romantic."

The words tasted bitter on her tongue.

She barely heard the rest of Jane's chatter, her mind replaying Sofia's words. *He'll use you and then come back to me.*

Was that all Amanda had been? A distraction until Sofia returned.

Just as she was about to head back to her office, her phone buzzed. It was a text from Dominic:

Meeting went longer than expected, having lunch with an old colleague. See you tonight.

Amanda stared at the message, her grip tightening around her phone.

He was lying.

Her eyes flicked over the text again, as if rereading it would somehow change its meaning. There was no mention of Sofia—no explanation, no acknowledgment of the woman who had just upended Amanda's world with a few cutting words. The omission felt deliberate.

A hollow ache settled in her chest as she made her way back to her office. Dominic had never mentioned a fiancée, estranged or otherwise. Not once. Yet Sofia had spoken with such certainty, as if their reconciliation was inevitable. As if Amanda was nothing more than a passing distraction.

She tried to focus on work, but her thoughts spiralled. Just hours ago, she had felt secure in Dominic's presence, in the way he made her feel wanted. Now, doubt gnawed at her. Had she misread everything? Had he ever truly been hers, or had she just been filling the space Sofia left behind?

No matter how hard she tried to push it aside, unease coiled tightly inside her. There were parts of Dominic's life she clearly hadn't uncovered, secrets that now felt like cracks in the foundation of whatever it was they had built. Had they built anything at all?

By the time five o'clock rolled around, Amanda's headache was relentless. She hadn't seen Dominic since that morning, and his absence only made everything feel worse. He didn't even check in. The silence between them was deafening, heavy with unspoken words.

The thought of facing him tonight made her stomach churn. She wasn't ready. She needed space—to think, to breathe, to figure out if she was just fooling herself.

Her fingers trembled slightly as she typed out a message.

Sorry, not feeling well. Going to the penthouse. See you tomorrow.

She hit send, exhaling shakily.

For the first time since meeting Dominic, she wasn't sure she wanted to see him tomorrow.

Without waiting for a response, she powered off her phone, craving the silence. She couldn't deal with anything else tonight—least of all Dominic and Sofia. She needed time to breathe, to think, to feel without interference.

When she arrived at the penthouse, she instructed the manager to turn away anyone who came looking for her—except for her father. The small act of control felt necessary, a shield between herself and the chaos waiting outside.

But the moment she was alone, the walls crumbled.

Tears she had stubbornly held back spilled over, hot and unrelenting. She sank onto the bed, curling into herself as silent sobs wracked her body. The weight of uncertainty, of unanswered questions, pressed down on her chest until exhaustion finally won.

She cried herself to sleep.

Morning came too soon.

Amanda woke feeling drained, her limbs heavy, her head aching from restless sleep. She hadn't gone for her usual jog—a telling sign of just how off-kilter she felt. Every movement was sluggish, mechanical, as she got ready for work. She was running late for the first time in her career, but she barely cared.

As she reached for her phone to check the time, the screen lit up with a slew of unread messages for Dominic. Her stomach clenched as she opened them.

Are you okay?

I've been worried.

Can you call me?

Can I come to the penthouse?

Amanda's chest tightened with guilt. She had shut him out completely, left him in the dark. And yet, his messages weren't defensive or demanding—they were concerned.

That should have reassured her.

But it didn't.

Because concern wasn't the same as honesty. It wasn't the same as trust.

She hesitated, her thumb hovering over the screen. Maybe she should call him, let him explain. Maybe she had overreacted. Maybe it wasn't as bad as she had made it out to be in her head.

Or maybe she was just searching for a reason to believe him.

The thought made her stomach twist.

How easily had she let herself believe Dominic was different? How quickly had she fallen into the comfort of what they had, never questioning what she didn't know? He had never mentioned Sofia. Never given her the slightest hint that there was another woman in his life, estranged or not.

Had she been blind? Naïve?

Was she stupid for trusting him?

Swallowing the lump in her throat, she forced herself to type out a response.

Sorry, running late. Be in soon.

Then she set the phone down, exhaling slowly.

She couldn't let herself get swallowed by this—not now. Work was waiting. Life was waiting. And Dominic...

She would see him soon enough.

Maybe then, she'd get the answers she needed.

Maybe, just maybe, she wouldn't regret hearing them.

Chapter Sixteen

As Amanda arrived at the office, she tried to shake off the lingering anxiety twisting in her gut. But something felt off.

Dominic's office door was closed.

That in itself was strange—he never closed his door unless he was in a meeting or needed absolute privacy. A cold unease crept up her spine as she hesitated outside, her fingers curling into a fist before she forced herself to reach for the handle. She didn't knock.

She was ready to face him. To clear the air. To finally get the truth.

But what she saw inside made her freeze.

Dominic stood in the centre of the room, his hands gripping Sofia's upper arms, holding her close. And Sofia—her arms were wrapped tightly around his neck, her body pressed against his as if no one else in the world existed.

Their lips were locked in a kiss.

The ground vanished beneath Amanda's feet.

Her heart slammed against her ribs; her breath caught somewhere between a gasp and a sob. Heat prickled behind her eyes, and before she could stop them, tears spilled over, hot and unforgiving. She barely registered her own movements as she stepped back, her fingers slipping from the doorknob as she shut the door behind her—quietly, carefully.

She couldn't stay.

She turned on shaky legs and walked away, her vision blurring as she forced one foot in front of the other. Through the office. Out the front doors. Away from the building.

Her car sat waiting in the parking lot, but she didn't stop. She couldn't.

She needed out.

The weight of what she had just seen crashed over her like a tidal wave, each step feeling heavier than the last. The pain in her chest deepened, pressing in until she thought she might break under the sheer force of it.

She had hoped for an explanation, for something—anything—that would make sense of the storm inside her. But now, the truth stood clear and undeniable.

She wasn't a chapter in Dominic's life.

She wasn't even a footnote.

She was nothing more than a fleeting distraction.

A mistake.

Tears streaked down her face as she moved through the streets, aimless and lost. The image of them together was burned into her mind—Sofia's hands in his hair, his lips against hers. It replayed over and over, each repetition cutting deeper than the last.

Had any of it been real? Had she been fooling herself all along?

The belief she had clung to—the belief in him, in them—had crumbled into dust.

And all she was left with was emptiness.

By the time she reached the penthouse, her body felt leaden, her mind numb. The tears had stopped, but only because there was nothing left inside her to give.

She had nothing left.

Nothing at all.

As Amanda approached the apartment building, the familiar sight of Joe, her ever-watchful doorman, stopped her in her tracks. His eyes, sharp as always, immediately zeroed in on the tear-streaked face and the heavy slump of her shoulders.

"Miss Amanda, are you alright?" His voice was soft, concern lacing every word, but Amanda couldn't summon the energy to mask the devastation.

"No, Joe," she choked out, her voice trembling as it broke on the last word. "Not okay. Sorry."

Without waiting for his reply, she turned and nearly ran for the elevator, desperate to escape everything—the world outside, the suffocating weight of her grief, and the truth that felt like it was slowly suffocating her.

The doors closed behind her, and in an instant, the elevator became her sanctuary. Her legs gave way, and she sank to the wall, the sobs tearing through her in ragged waves. She let herself unravel completely, no longer holding back. The tears flowed freely, relentless and unforgiving, as if her body knew no other way to mourn.

Her chest ached, a gaping emptiness where love had once thrived. She had given herself to Dominic without hesitation, without reserve, only to realise—too late—that he had never given her the same. He hadn't loved her. Not like she had loved him.

The weight of that truth crushed her from the inside out. The thought of it, the depth of the betrayal, gnawed at her with a raw, unrelenting pain. Nothing had ever hurt this much, and as the elevator climbed higher, Amanda couldn't escape the suffocating reality of it.

Around thirty minutes after Amanda had arrived home, the soft ding of the elevator pulled her from her sorrowful haze. She wiped her eyes, struggling to regain control of herself, but when the doors slid open, her father's familiar voice filled the silence.

"Amanda, it's your father. Joe called and told me you seemed upset."

Amanda could barely hold herself together. Her voice cracked as she choked out, "In here." Her words trembled, raw with the weight of the emotions swirling inside her.

Her father, Henry, entered the room, his gaze immediately locking onto her slumped form on the sofa. His expression softened with concern, his eyes full of worry as he took in the sight of his daughter—tears streaking down her face, her usual composure shattered.

"What happened, sweetheart?" His voice was gentle, but the depth of his concern was clear.

Amanda couldn't find the words. Not yet. They felt too heavy, too unbearable. She swallowed hard, trying to contain another wave of tears, but they came anyway, uncontrollable.

"I... I can't talk about it yet," she whispered, shaking her head as fresh tears slipped down her cheeks. The betrayal, the loss—it all felt too raw, too much to put into words.

Her father knelt beside her, his strong arms wrapping around her, pulling her into his embrace. "You don't have to, darling. But you don't have to go through this alone." His presence, solid and unwavering, anchored her as the storm of emotions threatened to consume her.

Amanda clung to him, the only man who had ever loved her without condition, the only one who could understand the depth of her pain. After a long moment, she took a shaky breath, wiping her eyes, trying to calm the chaos inside her.

"Dad," she began, her voice small but steady. "I need to get away. Can I go to Connecticut? Stay there for a while?"

Her father didn't hesitate. He placed a gentle kiss on her forehead, smoothing her hair back, his hands soft but firm. "Of course, sweetheart. It's your home, anytime you need it."

Amanda closed her eyes, feeling a small weight lift from her chest, even if just a little. "You can't tell anyone I'm there."

"Not even Dominic?"

"Especially not Dominic," she whispered, her voice faltering at the mention of his name. The pain was still too fresh, and the idea of him knowing where she was, of facing him again, made her stomach twist in anguish. She needed space, time to heal before she could even begin to make sense of it all.

Her father looked at her with deep understanding, his gaze steady and reassuring. "I won't say a word, darling. Whatever you need, I'm here for you."

Amanda sank into his embrace again, letting the steady warmth of his love wash over her. For now, it was enough to know that she wasn't alone, that he would protect her from the pain outside these walls. With her father's promise, she knew she could escape, even just for a while, and find the peace she so desperately needed.

Henry gently helped Amanda pack, ensuring she had everything she might need for her time away. As he zipped up the last bag, he gave her a soft, reassuring smile, though his eyes still held traces of concern. "You'll be alright, sweetheart," he said quietly, his voice warm but firm.

"Thanks, Dad," Amanda replied, her voice still shaky but grateful. She offered him a small, weak smile before stepping toward the door. "I'll be okay. I just… need some time."

He nodded, understanding more than she knew. "I'll be there tonight. Just take it easy. You've got a lot on your mind, but don't worry. We'll figure this out."

Amanda embraced him one last time before heading out to the waiting limousine. As she slid into the back seat, she glanced back to see her father standing in the doorway, watching her leave. The sight of him, unwavering and strong, brought a sense of comfort she hadn't realised she needed. It was a small relief, knowing he would be there for her no matter what.

As the limousine pulled away from the apartment, Amanda's heart weighed heavy with uncertainty. But one thing was certain—she needed this time away. A space to breathe, to clear her mind, and to sort through the tangled mess of emotions inside her.

Dominic's phone lay silent, another text to Amanda going unanswered. He had sent one every twenty minutes, each message more desperate than the last. Where was she? It wasn't like her to be out of touch, especially not like this. His gut twisted with a gnawing anxiety—something was wrong, he could feel it.

The events with Sofia that morning kept replaying in his mind, each moment more disturbing than the last. He couldn't understand how she had behaved, how she had shown up uninvited, how she had kissed him. The moment her lips had pressed against his, a wave of revulsion had gripped him, so strong it made his stomach turn. He had pushed her away instantly, the force of his reaction leaving him shaken. What had he seen in her? What had made him think she was someone worth his time?

That kiss had been a moment of undeniable clarity. It had forced him to confront something he couldn't avoid any longer: the truth of his feelings for Amanda. Thank God Amanda hadn't witnessed it. He hadn't reciprocated, hadn't wanted to, but even so, he knew he needed to tell her about the incident. She deserved to know.

As he thought back, there was one thing that Sofia's actions had made abundantly clear: his feelings for Amanda were deeper, more genuine, and more meaningful than anything he had ever felt for Sofia—or anyone else. What he shared with Amanda wasn't just attraction; it was something far more profound, something he couldn't ignore or deny. It was love—unconditional, unwavering, and real.

The comparison between the two women left no room for doubt. He knew now, without question, where his heart truly belonged.

The outer office door swung open, and Dominic shot to his feet, relief flooding him as he hoped, prayed, it was Amanda. "Amanda? Is that you?" His voice was thick with anticipation, eager to see her and finally confess everything.

But the figure that appeared in the doorway froze him in his tracks. It was Henry—Amanda's father. His presence was a storm, anger radiating from him like an inferno.

"No," Henry spat, his voice icy, like a blade slicing through the air. "It's not my daughter, and you'll never see her again."

Dominic's pulse raced. "What? Why? Is she okay?" Panic surged through him, his thoughts spinning.

Henry's eyes narrowed, his jaw tight with barely restrained fury. "What do you care? After what you did."

Dominic stepped forward, confusion crashing over him like a wave. "What are you talking about? I need to see her. She's not answering my messages. After yesterday—she was unwell—I'm worried about her."

Henry's gaze turned dark, disgust flickering in his eyes. "Worried? Worried?" His voice was low, dangerous. "You're worried after you shattered her heart?"

Dominic's stomach dropped. He couldn't process the accusation, the words hitting him like a physical blow. Shattered her heart? "I would never hurt her," he choked out, his voice trembling with raw emotion. "I love her, Henry."

Henry's face softened for just a moment, but his resolve was steel. "I just saw her, Dominic. She doesn't look like a woman in love. She looks like someone who had her heart ripped out and stomped on."

The words sliced through Dominic, leaving him speechless. The hurt was too deep for any explanation to cut through. The pain was palpable, suffocating. How had he done this?

"Please, I just need to talk to her," Dominic pleaded, desperation in his eyes, his voice thick with fear. "I don't understand. I love her. I've never felt like this before—this is real. Please, just let me see her."

Henry took a step closer, his face hardening, his fists clenched at his sides. "You've lost your chance," he growled, each word heavier than the last. "She's gone. She's in Connecticut, and she doesn't want to see you."

Dominic's heart pounded, his throat tight with panic. "Where in Connecticut?" His voice cracked as he spoke, barely above a whisper.

Henry's eyes blazed with anger. "That's none of your business. If you cared about her, you'd stay the hell away. She needs time, and she sure as hell doesn't need you."

Dominic's legs felt like they would give out beneath him, his chest tight with helplessness. What did I do? What the hell did I do?

"What's going on, Henry? Please," Dominic's voice cracked, the desperation and confusion overwhelming him. "I don't understand."

Henry's gaze softened for a split second, before his brows furrowed again, as if the frustration was boiling over. "You really don't know?"

"No, Henry. I swear," Dominic replied, his voice shaking with sincerity. "I don't know what's happening. I haven't been able to contact her since yesterday. She hasn't answered any is my texts. She hasn't come to work today. I was in meetings all day yesterday. I thought maybe she still didn't feel well, but—"

"She did come to work today," Henry interrupted, his voice sharp. "She left her car here this morning. Joe told me she walked home—what the hell is going on?"

The pieces clicked together, and Dominic's stomach lurched. His hands went to his face, his mind reeling. "Oh no," he whispered, his voice barely audible. "Oh God, no."

Henry's voice rose in alarm. "What's wrong? What's going on?"

Dominic's head dropped as the realisation hit him like a freight train. His voice was barely a whisper. "She must have seen Sofia."

"Sofia?!" Henry roared, fury igniting in his eyes. "Who the hell is Sofia?"

"My ex-fiancée," Dominic muttered, his throat dry. "I was engaged to her, but she turned out to be… manipulative. I called it off just before the wedding. Then this morning, she shows up here, uninvited, trying to rekindle what we had. I pushed her away. I swear to God; I told her to get lost."

Henry's face twisted in confusion. "Why would Amanda care about that? She's not the type to get upset over your past. She's level-headed. Fair."

Dominic ran a hand through his hair, frustration bubbling over. "Because, Henry, Sofia kissed me."

Henry's eyes widened in disbelief. "She did what?"

"I didn't kiss her back," Dominic said quickly, urgency in his voice. "I pushed her away the moment it happened. If Amanda walked in at the wrong time, it must have looked awful. But I swear, Henry, I never wanted that kiss. I was repulsed."

Henry studied Dominic closely, his gaze searching for any sign of deceit. But all he saw was raw desperation and pain. With a heavy sigh, he looked away. "She made me promise not to tell you where she is."

Dominic's chest tightened, his voice cracking as he spoke again, his desperation uncontained. "Please, Henry. I love her. I can't lose her. I swear I'll make this right. Just let me see her. I need to explain."

Henry rubbed his face, torn between anger and concern, his shoulders sagging with the weight of it all. "She's gonna kill me for this," he muttered under his breath. But he nodded, resigned. "I'll give you one chance. Don't screw this up, Dominic. She's hurting right now, and she deserves better than all of this."

Chapter Seventeen

When Amanda pulled up to her father's Connecticut estate, the weight of everything that had happened settled heavily over her like a suffocating blanket. The lush grounds, the grand house—all of it seemed distant and cold, as if none of it could shield her from the storm raging inside her. The housekeeper greeted her with a smile, but Amanda barely registered it. Her reply was soft, almost automatic, "I'm fine, thank you," before she hurried past, her mind too full to even acknowledge the kindness.

Up in her room, she quickly changed into her gym wear, her movements mechanical, numb. She barely looked at herself in the mirror as she tied her sneakers, her reflection foreign, unfamiliar. The girl in the mirror was no longer the same person who had fallen in love with Dominic. That girl had died somewhere along the way.

The home gym was quiet, too quiet, the silence pressing down on her. She didn't even notice the high-end machines, the sleek design—nothing but a blur of chrome and glass. Her thoughts spun as she stepped onto the treadmill, setting it to its highest speed, as if the relentless motion could somehow outrun the pain.

She began to run, each stride faster than the last, her legs burning with effort, her breath ragged. Her heart thudded wildly in her chest, matching the pounding rhythm of her feet on the belt. She pushed herself harder, as though if she could just run fast enough, the pain might disappear.

But the faster she went, the more the tears came, hot and unstoppable. They blurred her vision, stinging her eyes, but she didn't slow down. She couldn't. The ache in her chest was unbearable, suffocating, but the physical exhaustion gave her a distraction, however brief. She focused on the fire in her lungs, the ache in her legs, as if they could drown out the gaping wound in her heart.

She loved Dominic. God, she loved him. She had dreamed of a life with him, of building something real, something lasting. And now, it felt like it was slipping through her fingers. The dreams, the future—they were all just shards of glass now, too sharp to touch.

Her chest tightened, not from the run, but from the weight of the heartbreak. The betrayal. The confusion. How could he have done this? The questions spiralled, but there were no answers. No reason to make sense of the wreckage.

She pushed herself harder, her legs screaming in protest, the treadmill's incline increasing with each passing minute. Her breath came in short, shallow gasps. Sweat poured down her face, but it didn't matter. The physical pain was a release, a way to dull the anguish gnawing at her insides. It was easier to feel the strain, to focus on the burn than to confront the deep, raw hurt lodged in her chest.

Finally, after nearly an hour, her body gave out. She slowed to a stop, her legs trembling with exhaustion. She stumbled off the treadmill and collapsed onto the mat in the corner of the room. Curling into herself, she wrapped her arms around her knees, trembling from the intensity of both her physical and emotional pain.

The dam inside her broke. Her tears came, wild and uncontrollable, falling in torrents as the weight of everything—the lies, the heartbreak, the uncertainty—poured out of her. Each tear felt like a small, aching piece of her soul breaking away.

"I just need to get through this," she whispered hoarsely, her voice cracked and fragile. She clung to the words like a lifeline. "I'll be okay. I have to be."

She stayed there, huddled on the mat, her body wracked with sobs, the quiet of the room wrapping around her like a shroud. The rhythmic sound of her uneven breathing was the only thing that kept her tethered to the moment. For now, she couldn't think beyond the pain. For now, all she could do was run, cry, and hope that, eventually, the ache would fade—though deep down, she knew it might never fully heal.

Henry drove Dominic to his Connecticut estate with a quiet, simmering intensity. His hands were tight on the steering wheel, the knuckles white, but his focus never wavered from the road ahead. Dominic sat beside him, his heart pounding in his chest, his mind a jumbled mess of emotions. He loved Amanda—deeply, irrevocably—and he couldn't bear the thought of losing her. He had to make her understand.

When they arrived, Jenny, the housekeeper, was waiting for them at the door. Her face was drawn with worry, eyes flickering nervously between the two men. "Mr. Prentice," she greeted them, her voice tight. "I'm really concerned about Amanda. She's been in the gym for over an hour, running like the devil is chasing her. I've never seen her like this."

Henry's expression darkened, his frown deepening. "Thank you, Jenny." He turned to Dominic, his voice low and ominous. "I'll take you to her, but listen carefully, Dominic—if I hear her upset, if you make this worse, you're gone. No second chances."

Dominic's stomach dropped, but he nodded, swallowing the knot in his throat. "Understood. Thank you, Henry."

Following Henry's lead, Dominic walked through the house, his steps heavy, each one filled with dread. The silence between them felt like a living thing, thick and suffocating. When they reached the gym, Dominic's nerves were on edge, his mind still racing with everything he wanted to say. But as he stepped inside, he was struck by an unsettling emptiness. The gym was quiet, the machines humming softly, but Amanda wasn't on any of them. Maybe Jenny was wrong. Maybe she had—

A soft sound, broken and desperate, reached Dominic's ears, halting his breath. A muffled whimper. His heart lurched painfully in his chest, and he turned instinctively toward the corner of the room. There, almost hidden in the shadows, he saw her.

Amanda was curled up on the floor, her knees pulled tightly to her chest, her face buried in them. Her body trembled with each wracking sob, and Dominic felt his entire world come crashing down around him. He had never seen her like this—so utterly broken, so vulnerable—and it shattered him in ways words couldn't express.

He moved toward her, each step slow and deliberate, his breath shaky with emotion. He knelt down in front of her, careful not to startle her, and reached out, his hand trembling as he gently touched her hair.

"Amanda," he whispered, his voice thick, breaking under the weight of his regret.

At the sound of his voice, she flinched slightly but didn't look up. Her sobs continued, raw and unfiltered, and the pain in her eyes was almost too much for Dominic to bear.

"I'm so sorry," he said, his voice barely more than a rasp. "Please, tell me what I did. Let me make this right. Whatever it is, I'll do anything."

Amanda's tear-streaked face slowly lifted, her swollen eyes meeting his with a mixture of heartbreak, anger, and disbelief. Her voice was hoarse, fragile, a broken whisper. "Why are you here?" she asked, her words cutting through him like a knife.

Dominic swallowed hard; his chest tight with the weight of everything that had gone wrong. He held her gaze, his heart laid bare for her to see. "Because I love you," he said, his voice steady but filled with raw, unfiltered emotion. "And I can't stand the thought of you hurting like this—especially if it's because of me."

She shook her head, tears spilling over as she looked away, her voice trembling with a mix of hurt and frustration. "I don't want you here."

Dominic's heart twisted, his chest tightening with each word she spoke. He kneeled down in front of her, his hands shaking as he reached out, but he stopped just short of touching her, afraid to push her further away. "Please... just let me make this better," he pleaded, his voice raw with desperation.

Amanda's gaze hardened as she drew in a shaky breath, the pain in her eyes cutting through him like a blade. "You can't," she said quietly, but the words felt like a slap. "I saw you... kissing her." Her voice wavered, filled with both hurt and the sting of betrayal.

"I didn't, Amanda," Dominic said urgently, his voice cracking with the weight of his words. "She kissed me, yes, but I pushed her away the second it happened. I swear to you, it meant nothing. You mean everything to me, Amanda. Only you." His eyes searched hers, desperate for any sign of understanding.

Amanda's breath hitched, her defences faltering but still standing firm. "You didn't even tell me you had a fiancée—not once did you mention Sofia," she whispered, her voice quieter now but laced with pain and accusation. She drew in a shaky breath, trying to steady herself before continuing, "She came to the office on Thursday. She told me you two were getting back together."

Dominic's chest tightened, his jaw clenched, a surge of frustration and anger rising in him. "She lied, Amanda," he said, his voice cold with the truth. "I would never—"

Amanda cut him off, her voice rising with the intensity of her hurt. "Then why did you leave the office with her?" She looked at him, his eyes wide with disbelief, and the pain in her expression made Dominic's heart shatter. "Jane told me she saw the two of you—" her words choked off, "—all over each other, leaving together. And then I get a text from you saying you're having lunch with an 'old colleague.' What am I supposed to think?"

Dominic's entire world seemed to tilt at her words. He hadn't realised how far Sofia had gone to manipulate the situation, to twist the truth until it was unrecognisable. The weight of it crushed him. He took a deep breath, steadying himself before meeting Amanda's gaze. This was it—the moment that could either heal or destroy them.

"Amanda," he said softly, his voice trembling with the depth of his sincerity, "I swear to you, I didn't even see Sofia on Thursday. I was in back-to-back meetings all morning. The only person I had lunch with was an old colleague from the legal team. Sofia wasn't there. She wasn't anywhere near me."

Amanda's gaze softened for a moment, but the walls she had built were still standing, her doubts lingering in the air like an insurmountable barrier. "Then why would Jane say that?" she whispered, her voice breaking under the strain of the confusion she couldn't shake.

Dominic's stomach turned as the realisation hit him. His expression hardened, but his voice remained steady as he answered, "Because Jane is Sofia's best friend," he said slowly, the words bitter in his mouth. "She's been loyal to Sofia for years, Amanda. She would do anything for her. Lie, manipulate, whatever Sofia asked her to do. This… this was their plan, to drive a wedge between us."

Amanda blinked, her gaze flickering with uncertainty, trying to process Dominic's words. The pieces of the puzzle started to click together in her mind, but the lingering pain—the raw hurt—still clouded her judgment. "But why?" she asked, her voice small, almost pleading. "Why would they do this? We didn't even let on that we were together."

Dominic's throat tightened as Amanda's question hung in the air, the weight of it pressing down on him like a physical burden. He had no easy answer, no way to undo the damage that had already been done. He met her gaze, his eyes filled with a mixture of regret and raw determination. "Sofia heard about my beautiful new personal assistant," he began, his voice tight. "She didn't like it. She didn't like you." The words stung, but he pressed on. "But I swear to you, Amanda, I'm not a part of their game. I'm not part of her plan. I love you—only you—and I'm not letting this go. Not without fighting for us."

Dominic sat beside her, his movements slow, measured, as if afraid even the slightest motion might shatter the fragile space between them. Then, without hesitation, he gently pulled her onto his lap, his arms wrapping around her protectively, as though to shield her from the pain she'd been carrying. "I need to start at the beginning," he said softly, his voice thick with emotion. "Will you let me explain everything? Please?"

Amanda didn't respond verbally, but after a long pause, she gave a small nod, her gaze never leaving his. The silence between them seemed to stretch, but the weight of it slowly began to ease.

Dominic exhaled, his breath a little shaky, before he began. "Sofia was my personal assistant before my mother took over the role," he started, the words heavy with the history he wished he could forget. "That's actually why my mother ended up working for me—because Sofia betrayed me so badly, I wasn't willing to trust anyone else."

Amanda tilted her head, curiosity starting to mix with her lingering hurt, her eyes urging him to continue.

He hesitated, then spoke again, his voice tinged with regret. "From the moment Sofia started working for me, she had one goal: to seduce me into thinking she loved me. And I was stupid enough to fall for it. About a year ago, I asked her to marry me. She said yes, of course, because that was always part of her plan."

Amanda's face softened slightly, a flicker of understanding crossing her features, but it was fleeting, replaced by the familiar pain.

"Nine months ago—three weeks before the wedding—I came home early one day to surprise her," Dominic continued, his jaw tightening as he fought to keep the emotions from overtaking him. "When I got to the apartment, she was on FaceTime with someone. I didn't realise at first, but then it hit me... it was her long-time lover."

Amanda gasped, her hand flying to her mouth. "She had a lover, while she was engaged to you?"

Dominic's face darkened, the bitterness in his expression unmistakable. "Yes. I stood there, listening, before she realised, I was home. She was telling him how, after the wedding, they'd be set for life. And when he said he hated the idea of me touching her, do you know what she said?" His voice broke as the memory resurfaced, raw and painful.

Amanda shook her head, her eyes wide with shock, silently urging him to continue.

"She said it was only for a little while longer. That once we were married, she'd stop having sex with me altogether," Dominic said, his voice low, laced with disgust.

Amanda's mouth fell open in shock, her hand trembling as she clutched at his arm.

"She told him that even if I divorced her, they'd still win—because she'd have the name, the connections, and a very large divorce settlement," Dominic added bitterly, his jaw clenching, the pain still fresh despite the time that had passed.

Amanda's voice trembled with outrage. "Oh my God. What a... what a bitch!"

Dominic let out a soft, humourless chuckle, though there was no mirth in it. "I couldn't agree more." He ran a hand through his hair, a nervous gesture that betrayed his frustration. "I left without confronting her. I didn't tell anyone—not even my mother—why I cancelled the wedding and broke things off. I didn't want to give her the satisfaction of knowing how much she hurt me." His voice softened with regret. "Afterward, she kept trying to get me back. That's one of the reasons I bought the house—I didn't want her to know where I lived anymore."

Amanda reached up, her hand trembling as she gently touched his face, her thumb brushing over his cheek. "Oh, Dominic... That's not your fault. Some people are just... really good at manipulation. Look at Jane—she was completely convincing yesterday."

Dominic nodded, his eyes softening at her touch, a warmth filling him despite the lingering hurt. "I know. But I didn't tell you about Sofia because, to be honest, I felt like a fool. Falling for her lies... it's something I'm not proud of."

Amanda's heart ached for him. "You're not a fool," she whispered, her voice full of understanding. "You're human. And people like Sofia take advantage of that."

Dominic closed his eyes for a moment, his forehead resting against hers, and for the first time in what felt like an eternity, he allowed himself to believe in the possibility of healing. "I don't want to be human, Amanda," he whispered, his voice raw. "I want to be better. For you."

Amanda's fingers gently threaded through his hair, her touch soft and comforting, grounding him in that moment.

He gave her a small, grateful smile, the kind that spoke more than words ever could, before continuing. "This morning, when Sofia came to the office uninvited, she said she wanted me back. I told her no way. That's when she started ranting about my new personal assistant. She was jealous—of you, Amanda. She didn't like me being around someone beautiful like you." His jaw clenched as the memory flashed before him. "That's when she kissed me."

He hesitated, his expression darkening with the weight of the confession. "Clearly, she's using every dirty trick in the book to come between us. Yes, she kissed me this morning, but I pushed her away the second it happened. I was revolted by her even getting that close to me. You must have walked in at just the wrong moment. But I swear to you, Amanda, I didn't kiss her back. To be honest, the thought of her being that close to me made me sick."

Amanda studied him for a long moment, her emotions swirling in a storm of confusion. Every word Dominic had spoken rang with such raw sincerity that it was impossible to ignore. Her voice trembled, the vulnerability in it a mix of doubt and longing. "Did you mean what you said about loving me?"

Dominic's gaze softened instantly. Without a second thought, he reached up to cup her face gently in his hands, his touch tender, almost reverent. "Oh, sweetheart," he whispered, his voice thick with emotion. "I love you. With all my heart."

He paused, his eyes locked on hers, willing her to see the truth in them. "The one thing Sofia did for me this morning—if you can even call it a silver lining—was make me realise that what I felt for her was nothing compared to what I feel for you. You are my world, Amanda." His voice cracked slightly, and the vulnerability in it shattered her defences. "I don't want to live without you. I can't live without you."

Amanda's breath hitched, her heart torn between the lingering hurt and a growing flicker of hope. Tears welled in her eyes, but this time, they were different—softer, filled with relief. Slowly, she reached up, her fingers trembling as they brushed over his hands, still cradling her face.

"Dominic, I love you too," she whispered, her voice barely audible but overflowing with conviction. Each word carried the weight of everything she had kept locked inside.

His eyes widened, and the spark of hope that ignited in them was almost palpable. "You do?" he asked, his voice trembling with disbelief, a trace of raw vulnerability lacing his words. "I thought you might, but after everything… I was so scared. Scared that what they did would ruin us. Scared you'd stop loving me, that you'd walk away."

Amanda shook her head slowly, her lips curving into a bittersweet smile, her eyes glistening with unshed tears. "Dominic, I could never stop loving you. Don't you see? That's why I was so upset. I thought… if you didn't love me, if this was all just a dream, then I wouldn't want anyone else. There could never be anyone else."

Her words hit him like a lightning strike, and Dominic's heart swelled with such intensity it felt as though it might burst. Unable to contain himself any longer, he pulled her into his arms, pressing his forehead to hers, his breath mingling with hers. He whispered, "Amanda, marry me. As soon as possible. I don't want to waste another second. I want to spend every moment of my life loving you, protecting you."

Amanda's eyes widened in shock, her breath catching in her throat. "We've only known each other for four weeks," she murmured, her voice barely above a whisper.

Dominic closed his eyes, taking a deep breath, steadying himself. The courage he had gathered poured into his words. "The day I kissed you in the office to scare Daniel away, something changed," he began, his voice low, but steady with emotion. "I thought it was just a tactic, a way to keep him away from you. But when our lips touched, Amanda… I knew. I knew in that moment that losing you would break me. These four weeks don't define what I feel for you—they could never measure it. It's real, Amanda. So real, and I've never been more certain of anything in my life."

His voice faltered as the memory of the previous night resurfaced. "When you didn't come home last night, when your father told me you were gone this morning and didn't want to see me…" His voice cracked, and he shook his head, as if the mere thought of it was unbearable. "It was the worst moment of my life. I felt like the ground had been ripped out from under me. Like nothing mattered anymore."

Taking another breath, his hands trembling as they cupped her face. "Please, Amanda, don't make me go another day—another minute—without knowing you're mine forever. I need you. I love you more than I ever thought it was possible to love anyone. Marry me. Let me spend every moment proving it to you."

Amanda's heart hammered in her chest as his words wrapped around her, raw and unguarded. Her vision blurred with tears as she searched his face, finding nothing but love and unshakable sincerity in his eyes. A sob escaped her lips as she nodded, her voice trembling with emotion. "Yes, Dominic. Yes, I'll marry you. I love you."

Dominic's chest tightened with overwhelming emotion, and before he could say anything else, he whispered, "Thank God," his voice filled with relief, adoration, and pure love. Then, without hesitation, he kissed her—deeply, reverently, as though she were the air he breathed, the only thing that mattered in the entire world. And for him, she truly was.

In that moment, the world seemed to disappear, leaving only the two of them and the unshakable bond that sealed the beginning of their forever.

Chapter Eighteen

Diane and Henry had thrown themselves into planning Amanda and Dominic's wedding with a fervour that left no detail overlooked. With only four weeks to pull everything together, they had chosen Dominic's breathtaking Long Island estate as the perfect setting for their celebration. The sprawling grounds, with their lush gardens and sweeping views of the water, felt like something out of a fairytale. As the big day approached, the estate buzzed with activity, each passing moment bringing them closer to the moment Amanda would walk down the aisle.

Diane, ever the perfectionist, took charge of the décor, carefully curating every element to create a seamless blend of elegance and romance. She selected delicate floral arrangements in soft pastel hues, ensuring that the bouquets and centrepieces complemented the estate's rustic charm. She oversaw the catering with equal precision, choosing dishes that reflected Amanda and Dominic's tastes—sophisticated yet comforting, just like their love for one another.

Meanwhile, Henry handled the logistics with unwavering dedication. From security to seating arrangements, coordinating with local vendors to ensuring every last detail was accounted for, he left nothing to chance. He worked tirelessly, driven by his love for his daughter and his desire to give her the perfect day. Though the long hours left him exhausted, the thought of Amanda's happiness kept him moving forward.

Despite the whirlwind of preparations, Amanda found herself with little time to stress over the details. She stole quiet moments with Diane or Megan, listening as they updated her on the progress. At times, it all felt overwhelming—the sheer magnitude of what was unfolding—but she reminded herself that every effort, every sleepless night, would be worth it when she finally stood beside Dominic as his wife.

With each passing day, the wedding took shape. Invitations had been elegantly designed and sent out, Amanda's dress arrived right on schedule, and the final touches were falling into place. Though Dominic had his own responsibilities to juggle, he made it a point to check in on Amanda, ensuring that everything was exactly as she wanted. His unwavering support only deepened her love for him, reinforcing her belief that she was marrying the right man.

Yet, amid the excitement, Amanda often found herself reflecting on how quickly everything had happened. She thought back to the moment Dominic had proposed—the rush of joy, the flicker of hesitation, the fear of opening her heart so completely. And now, that fear had melted away, replaced by a love so profound it left no room for doubt.

The countdown had begun. In just four weeks, she and Dominic would begin their life together, bound not just by vows but by the undeniable connection that had brought them here.

The final days leading up to the wedding were a blur of dress fittings, venue walkthroughs, and last-minute adjustments. Perfection was the goal, and everyone worked tirelessly to achieve it. Yet, amidst the chaos, Amanda couldn't help but smile. She was about to marry the love of her life in a place that would one day be their home, surrounded by the people who mattered most. And in that moment, all the stress, all the frantic preparations, faded into the background.

Because soon, she would be his. And he would be hers. Forever.

The wedding was now just moments away, and everything had fallen into place exactly as it should.

Upstairs, in a sunlit bedroom overlooking the estate's gardens, Amanda stood before a gilded mirror, surrounded by Megan and Diane as they made the final adjustments to her gown. The delicate lace and intricate beadwork shimmered in the light, hugging her figure with an effortless elegance. Megan, radiant in her emerald-green bridesmaid dress, beamed with pride, while Diane, in a regal violet silk gown, couldn't hide the emotion brimming in her eyes.

"You look absolutely stunning, sweetheart," Diane murmured, her voice thick with emotion.

Amanda's lips curved into a smile. "Thank you. I couldn't have done this without you both."

Megan grinned, her eyes glistening with excitement. "Dominic's going to lose his mind when he sees you."

Amanda let out a soft laugh. "I hope so."

Diane reached for Amanda's hands, squeezing them gently. "Are you ready, my love?"

Amanda inhaled deeply, feeling the weight of the moment settle in her chest—not as fear, but as an overwhelming wave of joy. "More than ready."

With a proud nod, Diane left to inform Henry that his daughter was waiting. The house buzzed with anticipation, the muted hum of voices drifting up from the garden where guests eagerly awaited the ceremony.

Megan turned to Amanda with a teasing smile. "You know, my brother's finally given up on you."

Amanda arched an eyebrow, her lips twitching. "I hope he's happy, Megan. He's a great guy—just not the right guy for me."

Megan chuckled. "Well, he's seeing someone new. I like her. She suits him better."

Amanda smiled, warmth filling her chest. "I'm happy for him. He deserves that."

Before Megan could respond, a soft knock at the door made Amanda's breath catch.

"Come in," she called, her voice steady but filled with anticipation.

The door opened, and Henry stepped inside. The moment his eyes landed on his daughter; his breath hitched. For a long moment, he simply stared, as if trying to imprint this image of her into his memory.

"Oh, sweetheart..." he whispered, his voice thick with emotion. "You look... beautiful."

Amanda's heart swelled as she took in his expression—the awe, the pride, the love. He had always been her rock, but in that moment, she saw just how deeply he felt this day, how much it meant to him.

"You look absolutely stunning," Henry said softly, stepping forward with reverence.

Amanda smiled, her voice shaky with emotion. "Thanks, Dad."

He took her hands, his fingers warm and steady. "You look just like your mother," he murmured, his gaze turning wistful. "She would be so proud of you today."

Amanda's throat tightened. "I wish she were here," she whispered.

Henry squeezed her hands, his voice gentle yet firm. "She is here, sweetheart. She's with you. Every step of the way."

Amanda took a deep breath, nodding as a wave of comfort washed over her. She looked up at him, her nerves beginning to ease. "I'm ready, Dad."

Henry's expression softened, pride and love radiating from him. "Then let's go make Dominic the luckiest man alive."

Megan, watching from the side, grinned. "He already is," she said with a wink.

Amanda laughed, a small, joyful sound escaping her lips.

Just then, Diane reappeared in the doorway, her violet gown shimmering under the soft light. "It's time," she said, her eyes glistening as they met Amanda's.

Henry placed a steady hand on his daughter's shoulder. "Let's get you to Dominic. He's waiting."

As they stepped out into the corridor and descended the grand staircase, Amanda's heart pounded—not with nerves, but with sheer, unfiltered happiness. The soft strains of a string quartet floated up from the garden below, signalling the beginning of the ceremony.

And then, as she reached the terrace, the breathtaking sight of the wedding unfolded before her—rows of guests, the lush floral arrangements, the golden afternoon light filtering through the trees.

Amanda took a deep breath, her fingers tightening around her father's arm.

This was it.

With her father by her side and her heart full of love, she knew she was ready.

Henry gave her hand one final, reassuring squeeze. "Let's go make this official."

And with that, they stepped forward—toward Dominic, toward forever.

Dominic stood at the altar in the garden of his Long Island estate, his heart thrumming with anticipation. The setting was nothing short of breathtaking—lush greenery, flower-lined pathways, and the golden afternoon sun casting a soft glow over the assembled guests. Yet, none of it compared to the woman who would soon be by his side.

He had expected nerves. He had thought there might be a fleeting moment of apprehension. But standing there now, as the soft rustling of leaves and quiet murmurs of guests filled the air, all he felt was a quiet, exhilarating certainty. He was ready. Ready to vow his life to Amanda—the woman who had changed everything, the woman he loved beyond words.

A gentle hush fell over the crowd as his mother made her way down the aisle, her movements slow and graceful, a proud smile lighting up her face. She had been his rock for as long as he could remember, and now she was here to witness this moment—the most important of his life.

The music shifted, and all eyes turned toward the aisle as Megan, resplendent in emerald-green, began her walk. She moved with effortless grace, her presence warm and vibrant. But she was just the prelude—the final act before the moment Dominic had been waiting for.

And then, the flower-adorned doors at the garden's entrance swung open.

Dominic's breath hitched.

Amanda stood there, framed by sunlight, ethereal and breathtaking. The world around him faded into a blur. She was radiant, her wedding gown flowing like liquid ivory, the delicate lacework catching the light. The soft glow of the afternoon sun-bathed her in gold, giving her an almost dreamlike quality. But she was real—more real than anything he had ever known.

His chest tightened as he took her in.

The guests gasped in admiration, but Dominic barely heard them. His entire focus was on Amanda, on the way she stepped forward with quiet confidence, her father at her side. Henry wore a look of profound pride, his smile filled with love and unspoken emotion. The significance of the moment wasn't lost on Dominic. Henry wasn't just walking his daughter down the aisle—he was entrusting her to him, placing her future in his hands.

A nudge at his side pulled him from his trance.

"You lucky bastard," Derek muttered, a teasing grin on his face.

Dominic let out a quiet chuckle, his gaze never wavering from Amanda. His chest tightened with something deeper than luck—something he knew was rare and irreplaceable.

"Believe me," he murmured, his voice thick with emotion. "I know."

Step by step, she drew closer, her smile growing, her eyes shimmering with unshed tears. And with every heartbeat, Dominic felt his love for her deepen.

When she finally reached him, Henry paused, looking at his daughter with a tenderness only a father could possess. He gave her hand a reassuring squeeze before placing it in Dominic's. His grip lingered for a moment—a silent promise, a silent plea. Take care of her.

Dominic met Henry's gaze and gave a solemn nod. Always.

As Amanda's hand slipped into his, warmth flooded through him. The world outside ceased to exist. It was just them now—just the two of them, standing on the precipice of forever.

She looked up at him, and in her eyes, he saw everything—the love, the trust, the unshakable certainty that this was right. That they were meant to be.

The guests rose to their feet, a quiet reverence settling over the garden. The string quartet's soft melody faded into the background as the officiant stepped forward.

"Dearly beloved," he began, his voice warm and steady, "we are gathered here today to witness and celebrate the union of Amanda and Dominic in holy matrimony. Today, they pledge their love, their lives, and their futures to one another, surrounded by the people they cherish most."

Dominic tightened his grip on Amanda's hand, brushing his thumb gently over her knuckles. She responded with a soft smile, her fingers curling around his in silent reassurance.

The officiant continued. "Marriage is not just the joining of two individuals, but the merging of two souls, two dreams, and two lives into one. It is built on trust, respect, and a love so profound it binds you in ways that words alone cannot express."

Dominic swallowed past the lump in his throat, his heart swelling as the officiant turned to him.

"Dominic William Childs, do you take Amanda to be your lawfully wedded wife? To love, honour, and cherish her, in sickness and in health, in good times and bad, for as long as you both shall live?"

Dominic met Amanda's gaze, his voice steady and unwavering. "I do."

The officiant turned to Amanda.

"Amanda Sienna Prentice, do you take Dominic to be your lawfully wedded husband? To love, honour, and cherish him, in sickness and in health, in good times and bad, for as long as you both shall live?"

Amanda's lips trembled as a tear slipped down her cheek. But her voice, though thick with emotion, was filled with absolute certainty.

"I do."

A soft murmur of delight rippled through the guests, the weight of the moment sinking in.

The officiant smiled. "By the power vested in me, I now pronounce you husband and wife."

He barely finished the sentence before adding, "Dominic, you may kiss your bride."

Dominic didn't hesitate. He reached for Amanda, cupping her face between his hands as he leaned in. Their lips met in a kiss that was tender yet electric, filled with the promise of a lifetime.

The moment their lips touched, the guests erupted into applause, cheers ringing through the garden. But Dominic barely heard it. All he could focus on was Amanda—the warmth of her hands against his chest, the way she melted into him, the sheer, uncontainable love in every fibre of his being.

As they slowly pulled apart, their foreheads rested together, their breaths mingling.

"We did it," Amanda whispered, her voice thick with emotion.

A wide, unwavering smile spread across Dominic's face. "We did." He brushed a stray curl from her cheek, his eyes never leaving hers. "And this is only the beginning."

Hand in hand, they turned to face their family and friends, ready to step into their future together.

Side by side. Forever.

Epilogue

The warm glow of candlelight flickered over the elegantly set dining table, casting a golden hue on the faces of those gathered. Laughter and conversation filled the air as Dominic and Amanda hosted a small, intimate dinner party to celebrate their first wedding anniversary. It was a night of love, good food, and shared memories—everything they could have hoped for.

Amanda, radiant despite being nine months pregnant, sat comfortably at the head of the table, smiling as Megan recounted an amusing story about her fiancé, Brian, struggling to plan their honeymoon. Derek and his wife, Penny, chuckled while Diane and Henry—who had grown inseparable over the past year—exchanged a knowing glance.

It had become something of a running joke between them all: if Henry and Diane ever married, Amanda and Dominic would technically become stepsiblings. The thought never failed to amuse their friends, though Amanda and Dominic had nothing but support for their parents' blossoming relationship.

"I mean, just imagine," Derek teased, swirling his wine. "One day, at a future family gathering, we're all going to have to introduce Amanda and Dominic as brother and sister—"

"Stop," Dominic groaned, though his lips twitched with amusement. "That's not happening."

"I don't know," Megan chimed in with a smirk. "Henry and Diane are looking pretty cozy tonight."

Henry, ever composed, merely chuckled as he reached for Diane's hand, squeezing it gently. "Well, when you find someone special, you don't waste time," he said, shooting Amanda a pointed look.

Amanda rolled her eyes, but before she could respond, another sharp contraction rippled through her. She sucked in a slow breath, keeping her expression neutral. She had been feeling them on and off for most of the evening, but she hadn't wanted to alarm Dominic. He was already so protective, always making sure she was comfortable, keeping a hand on the small of her back, checking in with her every few minutes. It was one of the many things she adored about him, but if he knew she was already having contractions, he'd go into full panic mode.

Unfortunately, she didn't have much of a choice in keeping it a secret.

Because just as Diane stood to bring out the dessert, Amanda felt it—a sudden rush of warmth.

She gasped, her eyes going wide.

"Oh," she murmured, looking down in horror as liquid pooled beneath her dress.

The table went silent.

Megan's fork clattered against her plate. Penny's eyes nearly bulged out of her head. Derek swore under his breath.

Dominic, for a moment, just stared. "Amanda?" His voice was calm, but his expression was anything but.

Amanda let out a nervous laugh. "So… my water just broke."

Chaos erupted.

Dominic shot to his feet, knocking over his chair. Megan gasped and rushed to her side. Henry and Diane sprang into action, Henry already reaching for Amanda's coat.

"I—I should call the hospital," Brian stammered, fumbling for his phone.

Dominic, though visibly tense, took a steadying breath. "Okay, let's not panic," he said, more for himself than anyone else. He crouched beside Amanda, taking her hands. "How long have you been having contractions?"

Amanda winced as another one hit. "…Most of the evening."

"Most of the—Amanda," Dominic groaned, pressing a hand over his face before exhaling sharply. "I knew something was off."

She gave him a sheepish smile. "I didn't want you to worry."

"Amanda, I live to worry about you."

Henry chuckled as he draped Amanda's coat over her shoulders. "Alright, lovebirds, let's get moving. The baby's on his way whether we're ready or not."

With swift coordination, Diane and Megan helped Amanda up while Dominic hovered anxiously. The limousine that had brought their guests was quickly repurposed into an impromptu ambulance, with Henry and Diane joining them for the ride to the hospital.

The next three hours were a blur.

Dominic never left Amanda's side, holding her hand through every contraction, murmuring soft reassurances, kissing her temple, and breathing with her when she needed him to. He had never felt more helpless in his life, watching her go through pain he couldn't take away, but she was strong—so unbelievably strong.

And then, finally, the moment came.

With one final push, Amanda's cries of exertion were joined by a new sound—the wail of their newborn son.

The world seemed to stop.

Amanda fell back against the pillows, exhausted, while Dominic let out a shaky breath, his eyes locked on the tiny, wriggling bundle the doctor carefully lifted.

"Congratulations," the doctor said warmly. "You have a healthy baby boy."

Amanda let out a small, breathless laugh, tears slipping down her cheeks as she reached for Dominic's hand. He squeezed it tightly, swallowing past the overwhelming lump in his throat.

Their son.

A moment later, the nurse gently placed the baby in Amanda's arms.

Dominic couldn't move. He couldn't breathe.

All he could do was stare.

Dark wisps of hair peeked out from beneath the tiny blue cap, and his face—soft, pink, and perfect—was scrunched in displeasure as he whimpered in protest at being removed from the warmth of his mother's womb.

Amanda gazed down at him, her eyes full of wonder, and instinctively ran a gentle finger over his tiny cheek.

"Hi, sweetheart," she whispered. "We've been waiting for you."

Dominic exhaled softly, his heart swelling beyond measure. Carefully, he reached out, brushing the back of his finger against the baby's impossibly small hand. Tiny fingers curled around his, gripping tightly.

Dominic let out a choked laugh. "He's got a strong grip," he murmured.

Amanda beamed up at him, exhaustion and love radiating from her in equal measure. "Just like his daddy."

At that, Dominic leaned down and kissed her forehead, then brushed another kiss over their son's soft head. "You did amazing," he whispered.

She smiled sleepily. "We did amazing."

A quiet knock at the door made them both look up.

Diane and Henry peeked in hesitantly, their faces etched with a mix of worry and excitement. When they saw Amanda cradling the baby, relief washed over them.

"Well?" Henry asked. "Do we have a grandson?"

Amanda chuckled. "We do."

Diane let out a soft gasp, pressing a hand over her heart. "Oh, Amanda, Dominic…" Her voice broke.

Henry, clearing his throat, stepped forward. "Have you decided on a name?"

Dominic and Amanda exchanged a look, and then, smiling, Amanda nodded.

"Everyone," she said softly, "meet Ethan Henry Childs."

Henry blinked in shock, his mouth parting slightly. "You—" He shook his head, overcome.

Amanda reached for his hand. "We wanted to honour you, Dad."

For the first time in his life, Henry Prentice was speechless.

Diane wiped at her eyes, sniffling. "I love it," she whispered.

Dominic's gaze swept over the room, settling first on his mother, then on Henry, before resting on Amanda and the tiny miracle in her arms. His family. His home. His entire world.

As Ethan yawned, his tiny fingers curling against Amanda's chest, Dominic felt an overwhelming sense of gratitude settle over him. This moment—this beautiful, quiet moment—was everything he had ever dreamed of and more.

He wrapped his arm around Amanda, pulling her close, and pressed a tender kiss to her temple. "Happy anniversary," he murmured against her skin.

Amanda chuckled softly, her eyes shining with exhaustion, joy, and a love so deep it made his heart ache. "Best one yet."

Dominic glanced down at their son, so small, so perfect, already nestled safely in the arms of the woman he adored. He traced a gentle finger over Ethan's impossibly tiny hand, marvelling at how something so small could hold his entire heart.

"And many more to come," Dominic insisted, his voice filled with love and quiet determination.

Amanda smiled up at him, a knowing glint in her tired eyes. "Think you can handle more of me pregnant?"

Dominic smirked. "I think I handled it pretty well."

Amanda arched a playful brow. "You nearly had a heart attack every time I so much as sighed too heavily."

Diane chuckled from the chair beside them, dabbing at her eyes. "She's not wrong, dear. By the third trimester, I was half expecting you to wrap her in bubble wrap."

Dominic looked momentarily affronted before breaking into a grin. "She's lucky I didn't."

Henry let out a hearty laugh. "Good luck when she tells you she wants another."

Dominic turned to Amanda, his expression softening as he took in the sight of her cradling their son. He knew, without a doubt, that he would want more—more years with her, more laughter, more late nights rocking their children to sleep, more love, more moments just like this.

But for now, this moment was enough.

He pressed a lingering kiss to her forehead, savouring the warmth of her skin, before resting his cheek against her hair. The faint scent of lavender from her shampoo filled his senses as he breathed her in, grounding him in the moment.

The warmth of her body against his, the tiny miracle cradled between them—it was everything. His arms tightened around them both, as if holding onto this perfect, fleeting moment, unwilling to let it slip away.

His voice was steady but thick with emotion as he whispered into her ear, his lips brushing her skin. "You've already given me so much, Amanda, but this… you've made me the happiest man alive—again. I love you, Amanda."

She tilted her head slightly, her tired, tear-bright eyes meeting his. A soft, exhausted smile curved her lips. "I couldn't ask for a better life—you've already given it to me. I love you, Dominic," she murmured, her voice filled with quiet wonder.

Dominic exhaled, his heart full, his world complete. He tightened his embrace, pressing a kiss to her temple as Ethan let out a tiny sigh, his delicate fingers curling against Amanda's chest as he drifted into sleep, oblivious to the world around him.

As the gentle hum of the hospital room wrapped around them, Dominic realised something profound—this wasn't just the best anniversary yet. This was the beginning of everything.

And as he held his wife and son close, he knew—this was only the start of everything he'd ever dreamed of.

The End

279

Trust in Time

Alison Reid

A complete standalone romance

Previously published individually

Prologue

It was Clair's farewell dinner, and the air at the table felt heavy with unsaid words. Her father, Samuel, sat at the head of the table, his eyes glistening with pride as he raised a glass in her honour. Beside him, her stepmother Elizabeth smiled warmly, though Clair knew she was holding back tears. Across from her sat Adam Cross, her father's business partner, a man she had secretly loved for as long as she could remember.

Adam's expression was calm, but his eyes flickered with something deeper each time they met Clair's. He had always been composed, the perfect professional, but tonight was different. The thought of her leaving gnawed at him, though he kept his feelings buried, not wanting to complicate what should have been a celebration. He wondered if she knew, if she had any idea how hard it would be to watch her walk away tomorrow, not knowing if things would ever be the same.

Clair glanced across the table at Adam, her heart pounding in her chest. She had always been good at hiding her feelings but tonight was proving more difficult. Every shared glance, every unspoken moment between them felt charged, but she knew it was too late to confess anything. She was leaving for college in the morning, and their worlds would drift apart for the next four years.

Still, the weight of her love for him sat like a stone in her chest. She wanted to tell him, to reach across the table and hold his hand, to say all the things she'd been too afraid to say. But she stayed silent, forcing a smile as she picked at her dinner, trying to focus on the conversation between her father and Elizabeth.

Adam's gaze lingered on her longer than usual. He had always admired Clair from a distance, keeping his feelings locked away, especially with Samuel as his business partner. But now, with her leaving, the reality of her absence hit him like a blow. Would she think of him while she was away? Did she feel anything for him, or was he just a figure in her life, another part of her father's world?

As the night drew on, laughter and toasts filled the room, but underneath it all, the tension between Clair and Adam simmered quietly. Both of them, locked in their own hearts, felt the ache of unspoken love and the sadness of an impending goodbye.

She would be home for holidays, but the distance, both physical and emotional, felt vast. Tomorrow she would leave, and both would be left wondering what might have been, neither knowing the other's heart.

As the evening drew to a close, Samuel looked across the table at Adam, a thoughtful expression on his face. The night had been full of laughter and goodbyes, but Samuel wasn't ready to let it end just yet. He knew how fond Clair was of Adam, he had seen the way she looked at him when she thought no one was watching. He had never mentioned it, but he could sense there was something unspoken between the two of them.

"Adam," Samuel began, his tone casual but laced with purpose, "why don't you stay the night? That way you can say goodbye to Clair in the morning before she heads off."

Clair's heart leaped at her father's suggestion, but she quickly lowered her eyes, trying to mask her excitement. She busied herself with folding her napkin, hiding the smile that tugged at the corners of her lips. The thought of seeing Adam again before she left, of one more moment shared between them, filled her with a warmth she hadn't expected.

Adam, on the other hand, couldn't help but feel a surge of happiness at Samuel's offer. He had been dreading the end of the night, knowing it would likely be his last chance to see Clair before she disappeared into her new life at college. "That sounds great," Adam replied, keeping his voice steady, though inside he was relieved, and more than a little eager. "I'd love to stay."

Clair glanced up, trying to act indifferent, though her chest tightened with joy. "That's fine," she said, her voice composed, as if the idea was of no consequence to her. But beneath the calm exterior, she could hardly contain the excitement bubbling within her.

Samuel gave a knowing smile, sensing there was more to their shared silence than either was willing to admit. "Great, it's settled then," he said, standing to clear the table, satisfied that Adam would be around for just a little longer.

As the evening wound down, the three of them lingered in conversation, but every moment felt heightened for Clair. She was overjoyed at the thought of seeing Adam again in the morning, even if she had to hide it behind polite smiles and casual conversation. Tomorrow, the goodbye would be bittersweet, but for tonight, she allowed herself to savour the quiet thrill of having him close, even if only for a little longer.

After dinner, the house had grown quiet, with only the soft creaks of the floorboards and the distant hum of the wind outside breaking the stillness. Clair had excused herself early, claiming she wanted to get some rest before the long journey ahead. Adam had watched her retreat to her room, his heart heavy with the unspoken words he should share with her in the morning.

As Adam lingered by the fireplace, sipping the last of his wine, Elizabeth appeared in the doorway, her presence subtle but commanding. She always had an air of grace about her, something that set her apart in any room. Tonight, however, there was something different in her expression, a quiet intensity that Adam couldn't quite place.

"Adam," she said softly, her voice careful, "could you meet me in the study for a moment?"

Adam's brow furrowed slightly, surprised by the request. He had expected the night to wind down peacefully, not for any serious conversation. But the look on Elizabeth's face suggested there was something she needed to discuss, something important. He nodded, setting down his glass and following her down the hall.

The study was dimly lit, its rich mahogany walls and tall bookshelves casting shadows that danced in the low light of the lamp. Elizabeth gestured for him to sit in one of the leather armchairs, leaving the door ajar behind them. She didn't speak right away, instead moving gracefully to the chair opposite him, her movements deliberate.

Adam sat in silence, his gaze steady as he waited for her to speak, unsure of what was coming. Elizabeth's face remained composed, but there was a flicker of something deeper in her eyes, concern, perhaps, or curiosity.

"Adam," she began, her tone measured, "I wanted to speak with you about Clair." She paused, as if weighing her words. "You've known her for quite some time now, and I can't help but notice how much she looks up to you."

Adam's chest tightened at the mention of Clair, but he kept his expression neutral. "I care about her a lot," he replied carefully, unsure of where Elizabeth was leading with this.

Elizabeth's gaze didn't waver. "I know you do. And I believe she cares about you too, maybe more than you realise." Her words hung in the air, laden with meaning.

Adam shifted in his seat, suddenly feeling exposed, as if Elizabeth could see through the carefully constructed walls he had built around his feelings. "What are you getting at, Elizabeth?" he asked, though he suspected he already knew.

Elizabeth leaned forward slightly, her voice soft but direct. "Clair is leaving tomorrow, and I can see there's something between the two of you, something neither of you has spoken about. If you care for her as deeply as I think you do, Adam, then don't let her leave without telling her."

Adam felt his pulse quicken, the truth of her words settling heavily in his chest. He had thought about telling Clair in the morning, but hearing Elizabeth acknowledge what he had been too afraid to admit gave the moment a new weight.

"You think she feels the same?" Adam asked, his voice quieter now, almost vulnerable.

Elizabeth smiled faintly, a knowing look in her eyes. "I do. But you won't know for sure until you ask her, will you?"

Adam nodded slowly, his mind racing. Elizabeth had just confirmed what he had been grappling with all night. Tomorrow, he would tell Clair how he felt, no matter the risk, no matter the outcome.

Elizabeth stood, smoothing her hands over her dress. "Don't wait too long, Adam. You might not get another chance."

With that, Elizabeth gave him a reassuring smile but didn't leave. Instead, she lingered for a moment, her expression shifting slightly, as though something else weighed on her mind.

"There's another matter I'd like to discuss with you," she said, her tone quieter now. "Something personal."

Adam stood, caught off guard by the shift in the conversation. He hadn't expected this, but his curiosity was piqued. "Of course, Elizabeth," he replied, his voice steady. "I'm happy to help however I can."

Elizabeth looked down for a moment, as if gathering her thoughts. When she met his gaze again, there was a vulnerability in her eyes that he hadn't seen before.

It had been late, and Clair, restless, had been wandering the hallways, unable to sleep. The quiet house felt heavy with the weight of her thoughts about leaving for college, her unspoken feelings for Adam swirling in her mind. As she passed by the study, a soft glow spilled out from the slightly ajar door, flickering against the walls like something secretive and hidden.

She paused, curiosity and an odd sense of unease drawing her closer. Through the narrow gap, she saw Adam and Elizabeth standing close together, their bodies nearly touching in the soft light. The intimacy of the moment struck Clair immediately, something about the way they stood, the closeness of their posture, felt charged in a way that unsettled her.

Elizabeth's voice, usually calm and composed, trembled ever so slightly as she spoke. "I'm hoping we have a future together," she said softly, her words barely audible but clear enough to send a shock through Clair's chest.

Clair's heart quickened, her mind racing to understand what she had just heard. A future together? What did Elizabeth mean? The words felt heavy, loaded with a significance that Clair couldn't fully grasp. Was there something between Adam and Elizabeth that she didn't know about?

As if to confirm her worst fears, Adam reached out, placing a reassuring hand on Elizabeth's arm. The gesture, though subtle, felt too intimate, too tender to be mere friendship. It was the kind of touch that spoke of familiarity, of closeness that made Clair's stomach twist in discomfort.

Watching them, Clair felt a pang of something she didn't want to name, jealousy, confusion, and a gnawing sense of betrayal all mixed into one. The way they stood so close, the warmth between them, the gentle way Adam's hand lingered on Elizabeth's arm, it all felt wrong. Too familiar. Too unspoken.

Clair backed away from the door, her breath catching in her throat as she struggled to make sense of what she had seen. Was she imagining things? Or was there something more between Adam and Elizabeth? The scene replayed in her mind, leaving her with a deep, gnawing sense of something unresolved, something that made her question everything she thought she knew.

With a sinking heart, she turned and retreated to her room, unable to shake the uneasy feeling that had settled over her like a heavy, suffocating cloud.

As Adam lay in the guest room that night, the soft hum of the house around him, he couldn't stop thinking about Clair. Her laugh, her smile, the way she had tried to mask her excitement when Samuel invited him to stay, it was all running through his mind, stirring feelings he had kept buried for too long.

He stared at the ceiling, the weight of unspoken words pressing on him. Tomorrow, she would be leaving for four long years, and the thought of her slipping away without knowing how he truly felt was unbearable. He had held back for so many reasons, his partnership with Samuel, her youth, the timing never seeming right, but none of that mattered now. If he didn't tell her tomorrow, he might never get the chance again.

Adam made up his mind. Tomorrow, before Clair left, he would tell her everything. He would tell her how much she meant to him, how he had fallen in love with her without realising it at first, and how the thought of her being so far away tore at him. He didn't care about the obstacles anymore.

He would tell her that he would wait for her, that no matter how long it took, no matter how far she went, he would be there, waiting for her return. It was a risk, and he knew it, but he couldn't let her go without giving her the truth.

As he lay there, Adam felt a strange sense of peace settle over him. Tomorrow might change everything, but for the first time in a long while, he felt certain about what he needed to do. The thought of Clair knowing how deeply he cared, how he would wait for her through all the years of college and beyond, gave him hope.

With that resolution, he finally closed his eyes, anticipation and nerves mingling in his chest. Tomorrow, he would tell her. And maybe, just maybe, it would change everything for them both.

Clair sat on the edge of her bed, her heart shattered by the revelation she had witnessed. Adam's closeness to Elizabeth felt like a knife twisting in her chest, each thought of their intimate conversation piercing deeper. Devastated, she buried her face in her hands, the tears spilling over as the weight of betrayal pressed down on her. She had never expected to feel so profoundly hurt by someone she cared for so deeply.

As the night wore on, Clair's quiet sobs filled the room, mingling with the stillness around her. She cried herself to sleep, each tear a release of the pain that had settled in her heart, leaving her feeling hollow and lost.

When dawn broke, painting the sky in soft hues of pink and gold, Clair woke with a newfound resolve. She couldn't bear to face anyone, not her father, not Adam. The thought of saying goodbye felt unbearable, and she knew that leaving without a word was the only way to shield herself from the heartache that lingered.

With trembling hands, she took a piece of paper and began to write a letter to her father. She expressed her love for him, her gratitude for everything he had done, and her sorrow for leaving without explanation. "I need to do this for myself," she wrote, her heart aching with every word. "Please look after yourself. I love you."

After folding the letter carefully, Clair placed it on her pillow, a silent farewell to the home she had known and the family she cherished.

As the first light of day crept through the curtains, she quietly gathered her things, ensuring everything was ready for her departure. With one last glance at the room filled with memories, she slipped out of the house, her heart heavy yet resolute.

She climbed into her packed car, the engine purring softly as she turned the key. The weight of the past felt suffocating, but as she drove away from the only home she had ever known, Clair felt a flicker of hope amidst the sorrow. This was a new beginning, a chance to escape the hurt and heartbreak left in the wake of Adam's betrayal.

With each mile that passed, she felt the burden lift slightly, a bittersweet relief flooding over her. She was leaving behind the pain, ready to face the unknown, even if it meant facing it alone.

Adam descended the stairs from the guest room, the smell of breakfast wafting through the air, momentarily easing the lingering heaviness in his heart. Caught up in the bittersweet anticipation of Clair's departure for college. As he made his way to the terrace, he expected to see Samuel, Elizabeth, and Clair.

Instead, he found Samuel sitting at the table, his head bowed, a plate of uneaten food in front of him. The warmth of the morning sun streamed onto the terrace, but the atmosphere felt cold and heavy. Adam's stomach dropped at the sight of his friend's sad demeanour.

"Samuel?" Adam ventured, concern flooding his voice. "Is everything okay?"

Samuel looked up slowly, his eyes filled with an emotion that sent a chill through Adam. "No, Adam. It's not." His voice was thick, and he struggled to find the right words. "Clair left for college this morning. Before any of us were up."

The words hung in the air, and Adam felt as if the ground had shifted beneath him. "What do you mean she left?" he asked, disbelief mingling with confusion. "She didn't say goodbye?"

Samuel shook his head, his expression pained. "She wrote a note. Just a short farewell. I didn't even get the chance to talk to her."

Adam's heart sank. A wave of regret washed over him, and he ran a hand through his hair, trying to process what he was hearing. *I was going to tell her how I feel. I thought we had time.*

Samuel sighed heavily, his gaze drifting to the untouched breakfast. "She must have felt she needed to leave without saying anything. I just don't understand why."

Adam felt the weight of regret settle in his chest.

Chapter One

Clair Dawson stood in the middle of her dorm room, the walls now bare and lifeless, a stark contrast to the years of memories that had once filled the space. Sunlight streamed through the windows, casting soft shadows across the boxes stacked in uneven piles around her. She reached up to pull the last poster from the wall, a faded motivational quote about justice and strength that had seen her through long nights of studying case law and criminal codes.

Her friend Lily knelt by the bed, carefully folding a pile of Clair's worn textbooks and stuffing them into a battered box marked "law and justice." Her fingers lingered on the titles: Constitutional Law, Criminal Procedure, Forensic Science. "Hard to believe it's over," Lily said with a soft sigh, her voice tinged with both relief and nostalgia.

Clair gave a quiet laugh, glancing at the half-packed boxes that littered the room. "Yeah, feels like we were just moving in, doesn't it?" She picked up a framed photo from her desk, her and Lily, on their first day of college, bright-eyed and nervous, standing in front of the law school sign. She traced the edge of the frame, lost in thought for a moment before gently wrapping it in a sweater and tucking it into a box.

Lily stood and dusted off her hands. "Ready for the real world, Counsellor?" she teased, nudging Clair's arm.

Clair smiled but didn't answer right away. She glanced around the room, her heart heavy with the bittersweet reality of leaving. "I guess," she murmured, running a hand through her hair. The years had been hard, gruelling classes, sleepless nights, internships at legal firms that had pushed her to the edge, but they had shaped her. This place, this room, had been her sanctuary and her battlefield.

As she zipped up the last suitcase, Lily leaned against the desk. "I'm proud of you, you know," she said softly. "You really did it."

Clair met her friend's eyes and smiled. "We both did. It's time for the next chapter." With one last glance at the empty room, Clair took a deep breath, grabbed a box, and stepped into the hallway, leaving behind the place where she had become more than just a student, she had become herself.

She was going to miss Lily. Lily was heading back to San Francisco, while Clair was bound for Seattle to reconnect with her father and decide what to do next with her life, either Law School or study Criminology. The thought of their paths diverging tugged at Clair's heart as she remembered the day they met.

Clair had stood in the narrow hallway, clutching the handle of her suitcase, her heart pounding in her chest. She stared at the door in front of her, Room 203, the dorm room she'd been assigned to share with someone she'd never met. Her mind buzzed with anxious questions: *What if we don't get along? What if she's messy? What if…?*

With a shaky breath, she turned the knob and stepped inside. The room was half-empty, the other side of the space already decorated with string lights and colourful throw pillows. A girl stood by the window, her back turned to the door as she struggled to balance a large poster of San Francisco against the wall. She had a mop of unruly blonde hair that bounced as she moved, her energy radiating through the room.

"Need a hand?" Clair asked, her voice timid but polite.

The girl whirled around, startled, but her face immediately lit up with a wide smile. "Oh, hey! You must be Clair, right? I'm Lily!" She waved enthusiastically, almost knocking the poster over in the process.

Clair let out a quiet laugh and quickly set her suitcase down, rushing over to steady the poster before it slipped. "Yep, that's me. Nice to meet you, Lily."

"Thanks! I'm terrible at this whole decorating thing," Lily admitted with a playful grin, stepping back to assess her crooked handiwork. "I mean, it's a bit of a disaster, but hey, it's home now, right?"

Clair smiled, already feeling the tension ease from her shoulders. "Looks great to me," she said, glancing at the array of bright, mismatched decorations that somehow made the room feel instantly welcoming. It was the opposite of Clair's neatly packed suitcases, with their organised files and notebooks.

Lily dusted off her hands and plopped down on her bed, pulling a pillow into her lap. "So, tell me everything. Where are you from? What's your major? Do you like pizza? Wait, scratch that. Everyone likes pizza."

Clair blinked, a bit overwhelmed by the rapid-fire questions, but found herself laughing despite the whirlwind of words. "Uh, I'm from Seattle, majoring in Law and Criminal Justice," she started, sitting down on the edge of her bed. "And yes, pizza's pretty much the best thing ever."

"Nice! Future lawyer in the house!" Lily cheered, tossing the pillow aside and leaning forward with wide eyes. "I'm a Psychology major, so I'll probably be analysing your every move from here on out. Just a heads up."

Clair's laugh came more freely this time. "Well, I guess I better watch myself then."

The two fell into an easy conversation, the room soon filled with laughter and stories of high school, hometowns, and awkward family gatherings. Before Clair knew it, the nerves she'd carried with her melted away. There was something about Lily's warmth, her effortless humour, which made the tiny dorm room feel less intimidating.

By the time night fell, they were sitting on the floor, surrounded by half-unpacked boxes and takeout containers, already trading inside jokes and sharing plans for the semester ahead. Clair couldn't help but think that maybe, just maybe, this whole college thing was going to be alright after all.

Clair stood by the curb, the autumn breeze tugging at her hair as she looked at Lily, trying to find the right words. The campus around them buzzed with the sounds of other students moving on, but for a moment, it felt like the world had shrunk to just the two of them. Lily's car was packed to the brim with boxes, posters, and memories of the past four years, and Clair felt a familiar lump rise in her throat.

"Guess this is it, huh?" Lily said, her usual bright smile faltering just a little, as if she were trying to hold onto the last bit of their time together. She shifted on her feet; hands stuffed into her jacket pockets.

Clair nodded, swallowing the tightness in her chest. "Yeah, I guess so."

They stood in silence for a beat, both knowing that this wasn't just goodbye to the dorm, or to college, it was the end of an era. The room that had once been their little world was now empty, and they were heading off in different directions, the future stretched out before them like an endless road.

Clair took a deep breath, her voice soft as she looked at Lily. "You'll come visit me in Seattle sometime, right?" She smiled, though her eyes shone with the weight of the goodbye. "I mean, it's not *that* far. You could use some rain and coffee."

Lily laughed, but it was shaky. "As long as you don't forget about me when you're off winning cases and wearing power suits." She nudged Clair's shoulder playfully, but the sadness in her eyes was unmistakable.

"Not a chance," Clair said, her tone firm. "And you'll need to come analyse all the people I meet, tell me who's trouble and who's not."

"Deal," Lily replied, her voice cracking just a little as she pulled Clair into a tight hug.

For a moment, neither of them said anything, just held on. When they finally pulled apart, Lily brushed a tear from her cheek, trying to play it off with a smirk. "Well, I should go before I turn into a puddle."

Clair smiled, blinking back her own tears. "Drive safe, okay? And seriously, I'm holding you to that visit."

"Yeah, yeah," Lily said, sliding into the driver's seat. "I'll see you soon, Clair. We'll make it happen."

With one last wave, Lily pulled out of the parking lot, her car disappearing down the road. Clair stood there for a moment, watching until she couldn't see her anymore, feeling the ache of saying goodbye. But she knew that no matter how far apart they were, they'd always have those years, and a promise of a visit to Seattle.

Clair slammed the trunk of her car shut, feeling a mix of exhaustion and relief as she surveyed the now-empty parking space. The last box was securely packed, surrounded by her other belongings, all of which were now making the long journey to her father's estate in Seattle. The sun was starting to dip toward the horizon, casting a golden hue over the bustling campus that had been her home for the past few years.

She slid into the driver's seat, taking a moment to appreciate the calm before the drive. The engine roared to life, and as she pulled out of the parking lot, Clair glanced in the rearview mirror at the shrinking dormitory buildings behind her. A sense of finality settled over her. This was truly the end of one chapter and the beginning of another.

The road stretched out before her, a ribbon of asphalt leading toward the Pacific Northwest. The initial hours of the drive passed in a blur of landscapes, rolling hills giving way to the more rugged terrain of the mountains. Clair's thoughts drifted back to the conversations she'd had, the laughter, and the promises made to friends like Lily. The soundtrack of her journey was a mix of classic rock and old favourites, providing a comforting backdrop to the solitude of the open road.

As the hours ticked by, the sun dipped lower, casting long shadows that danced across the highway. Clair stopped occasionally for coffee and a quick stretch, each stop offering a brief respite from the drive and a chance to collect her thoughts. As she approached Seattle, the road signs grew more familiar, and a sense of trepidation filled her.

By the time the city lights of Seattle began to twinkle on the horizon, Clair felt a rush of nervous energy. She navigated through the familiar streets, finally reaching the gates of her father's estate. The grand entrance, flanked by tall, majestic trees, welcomed her home in a way that felt both comforting and bittersweet.

Pulling up to the front of the estate, Clair took a deep breath, letting the serene ambiance of the place wash over her. The sprawling lawns and elegant architecture of the estate stood in stark contrast to the modest dorm she had left behind. She knew that this was where she would begin her next chapter, but it also marked the end of an era of independence and discovery.

Clair sat in the driver's seat of her car, the engine off but the vehicle still humming with the vibrations of the journey she'd just completed. The estate before her was bathed in the soft light of twilight, the grandeur of her father's home casting long, shadowed lines across the manicured lawn. She could see the silhouette of the house through the windshield, its elegant architecture standing as a reminder of both comfort and the complexity of her family's dynamics.

She took a deep breath, her hands gripping the steering wheel tightly. Her gaze wandered to the front door, where she knew her father and stepmother, Elizabeth, were waiting. The thought of reconnecting with them brought a whirlwind of emotions, excitement, apprehension, and a lingering, unsettling anxiety. Elizabeth, who had been a constant presence in her father's life, since she was fifteen, was someone Clair had always felt a bit uneasy around, especially now that she harboured the troubling suspicion about her and Adam.

Adam had been her childhood love; someone she'd shared countless dreams and whispered secrets with. The idea of Elizabeth possibly being involved with him felt like a betrayal, a hidden wound that she'd kept to herself. The knowledge that Adam might have crossed a line that felt so deeply personal made her heart ache but now was not the time to confront this. Not yet.

Clair's eyes focused on the gleaming brass knocker on the front door. The anticipation of seeing her father, whom she had missed dearly, and the unsettling reality of facing Elizabeth, was almost too much to bear. The warmth of the car's interior contrasted sharply with the chill of uncertainty she felt.

She closed her eyes, mentally preparing herself. The weight of her years away from home, her successes, and her unresolved feelings all seemed to converge in this moment. She needed to be strong and composed, to face her father and Elizabeth with the grace they deserved, even if her emotions felt tangled and raw.

Finally, Clair opened her eyes and reached for the door handle. With a deep breath, she stepped out of the car, the crisp evening air meeting her face. The crunch of gravel under her shoes was the only sound as she walked up the driveway, each step echoing the heaviness of the moment.

As she stood before the door, her hand hovering over the knocker, Clair glanced one last time at the familiar home, remembering all the good times she'd shared here. She reminded herself that this was about reconnecting with her father and reestablishing the bond they once had, despite the turbulent emotions bubbling beneath the surface.

With a steadying breath, she raised her hand and brought the knocker down, the sound reverberating through the grand entrance. The moment seemed to stretch into eternity as she waited, her heart racing in her chest. She could only hope that when the door opened, she would find the strength to navigate the complicated emotions that lay ahead, and that whatever lay on the other side would bring clarity and, perhaps, a new beginning.

The deep, resonant sound of the door knocker echoed through the hallway before finally giving way to the creak of the door opening. Clair was met with the warm, polished smile of the estate's butler, Thompson. His neatly pressed uniform and perfectly groomed appearance exuded the kind of dignified warmth that seemed to be a fixture in the grand home.

"Miss Clair!" Thompson exclaimed, his eyes lighting up with genuine delight. "It's wonderful to see you. Your father and Mrs. Elizabeth will be overjoyed!"

Clair offered a tentative smile, feeling a slight relief at the welcoming reception. "Thank you, Thompson. It's good to see you, too."

Thompson stepped aside to allow her entry; his expression full of warmth as he gestured to the foyer. "Please, come in. Your father and Mrs. Elizabeth are out on the terrace. I'll let them know you've arrived."

Clair stepped into the grand entrance hall, taking in the familiar opulence of her father's estate, the high ceilings, the grand staircase, and the elegant furnishings that had always made this place feel like both a refuge and a symbol of her father's success. She glanced around, feeling a mixture of nostalgia and apprehension.

Thompson led her through the house with practiced ease, his steps light and his conduct attentive. As they approached the French doors leading to the terrace, he paused and turned to Clair with a reassuring smile. "They're enjoying a lovely evening outside. I'm sure they'll be thrilled to see you."

"Thank you," Clair said, her voice barely above a whisper. She took a deep breath, trying to steady her nerves. The terrace was just beyond the doors, bathed in the soft glow of lantern light that spilled into the hall.

With a nod, Thompson gently opened the doors and stepped aside. Clair took a hesitant step forward, her eyes scanning the terrace for her father and Elizabeth. The sight that met her was both comforting and bittersweet, her father, with his familiar, warm smile, and Elizabeth, sitting gracefully beside him. They were engaged in an animated conversation, their laughter mingling with the gentle rustle of the evening breeze.

As her presence registered, her father's, face broke into an expression of unmistakable joy, his eyes widening in surprise and pleasure. "Clair!" he called out, rising from his chair with a mixture of astonishment and delight. "You're here!"

Elizabeth looked up; her smile equally genuine but tinged with a hint of apprehension as she took in Clair's arrival. The warmth of the moment was palpable, yet Clair couldn't shake the underlying tension she felt.

Clair took a few steps onto the terrace, her heart pounding as she approached them. Her father's arms opened wide, welcoming her with the embrace she had longed for. "Dad," she said, her voice thick with emotion as she hugged him tightly.

"Welcome home, my dear," he murmured, his voice filled with affection. "We've missed you."

Elizabeth stood as well, offering a more reserved but sincere smile. "Clair, it's wonderful to see you. We've heard so much about your achievements."

Clair nodded, trying to return the warmth of her stepmother's greeting. "Thank you, Elizabeth. It's good to be back."

As the three of them settled onto the terrace, the conversation flowed, and Clair found herself navigating the delicate balance of reconnecting with her father and stepmother while keeping her own turbulent emotions in check. The evening sun dipped below the horizon, casting a golden light over their reunion, and Clair hoped that this moment would be the start of mending old ties and forging a new understanding in her family's intricate tapestry.

Chapter Two

The gentle evening breeze rustling through the well-tended garden below. Her father, Samuel Dawson, was seated opposite her, his expression a mixture of relief and happiness. Elizabeth, gracefully poised in her chair, offered Clair a welcoming smile as she sipped her wine.

"Clair, it's hard to believe it's been four years," her father began, his voice filled with a mix of regret and affection. "We've missed so much time with you."

Clair met her father's gaze, feeling the warmth of his sentiment. "I know, Dad. It's been a long time, and I've missed you both."

Elizabeth leaned forward slightly, her eyes reflecting both curiosity and concern. "We're just so glad you're back. How was the drive?"

"Long," Clair admitted with a small smile. "But I'm here now. I needed a bit of time to think and decide what comes next."

Her father nodded understandingly. "And what does come next? Have you decided?"

Clair took a deep breath, her fingers nervously tracing the edge of her chair. "Actually, I'm taking a couple of months off before I decide if I'll study criminology. I'm considering following in your footsteps and go to law school, but I want to be sure before making any commitments."

His face brightened at the mention of law school, a proud gleam in his eye. "I'm thrilled to hear that. It's a field that can truly make a difference."

Elizabeth's smile was encouraging. "And what will you do in the meantime?"

"I'm going to take some time to settle in and figure things out," Clair said. "I plan to explore some options and reflect on what I really want. I might also get a part-time job to keep myself busy."

He leaned back, his gaze thoughtful. "It's great that you have the opportunity to take your time. But while you're here, don't feel pressured to find a job right away. Just focus on relaxing and enjoying your time with us."

He turned to Thompson, who had been discreetly standing by, waiting for a cue. "Thompson, would you please ensure that Clair's possessions are moved into her old room?"

"Of course, Mr. Samuel," Thompson replied with a nod, ready to carry out the task.

As the butler walked off to attend to the request, Clair looked around the terrace, appreciating the serene ambiance. "Thank you, Dad. I really appreciate it."

He reached across the table and placed a reassuring hand on hers. "We're just glad to have you home, Clair. Take all the time you need. We're here for you."

Elizabeth nodded in agreement, her expression warm. "Yes, take your time. It's good to have you back with us."

Clair felt a surge of gratitude and relief. Despite the underlying tension and uncertainty, the warmth of her father and Elizabeth's support was a comforting foundation. As the evening progressed, they continued to talk, sharing stories and catching up, with Clair feeling a sense of homecoming that made the journey, both literal and emotional, feel worth it.

Clair sank into the plush armchair on the terrace, her eyes heavy with exhaustion. The day had been a whirlwind of travel, emotions, and overwhelming newness, and she found herself struggling to keep her eyes open. She stretched her legs out in front of her and let out a long, tired sigh.

"I'm so tired," Clair admitted, her voice soft and weary. "I think I need some sleep."

Her father, noticing her fatigue, gave her a sympathetic smile. "I understand, Clair. It's been a long day. Before you head off, though, there's something I wanted to mention."

Clair looked up; her curiosity piqued despite her tiredness. "What is it?"

"I've organised a small get-together for you tomorrow," he said, his tone warm and inviting. "It's a chance for you to catch up with some of your old high school friends. Adam will be there as well."

The mention of Adam's name sent a shiver down Clair's spine. It had been years since she last saw him, and the thought of reuniting stirred a blend of longing and apprehension. Adam was the reason she had stayed away for four years. Her mind immediately flickered to her unresolved suspicions, her secret belief that Adam might be involved in an affair with Elizabeth, her stepmother. This hidden burden weighed heavily on her, and the prospect of facing Adam amidst these tangled emotions felt overwhelming.

"Adam? Really?" Clair managed to say, her voice betraying her inner turmoil.

"Yes," he replied with a smile. "He's been following your progress and is very impressed with what you've achieved. He's excited to see you."

Clair's heart sank a little. She had once loved Adam more than anything, but now she was uncertain of how to face him, knowing the potential truth about his relationship with Elizabeth. Her mind raced with conflicting feelings, of seeing the man she had cherished and the complicated reality she suspected.

He continued, seemingly unaware of the storm brewing in Clair's thoughts. "I thought it would be a good opportunity for you to reconnect with friends and perhaps get some perspective on what you want to do next."

Clair forced a smile, trying to mask the turmoil within. "That sounds nice, Dad. I appreciate you organising it."

He gave her a reassuring pat on the shoulder. "Get some rest tonight. You'll feel better in the morning."

As they left the terrace, Clair remained seated, her thoughts a whirlwind of apprehension and nostalgia. The prospect of seeing Adam again, coupled with her unease about Elizabeth, left her feeling uneasy about the reunion. Despite her tiredness, she knew she would need to sort through her emotions and prepare herself for the complex encounter that awaited her. As she finally headed to bed, her mind was already racing with thoughts of what the next day might bring.

Clair pushed open the door to her old room, the familiar creak of the hinges bringing a rush of nostalgia. The room was exactly as she remembered it, walls adorned with old posters, shelves lined with mementos, and the bed neatly made with a quilt she had always loved. The soft, comforting familiarity of the space enveloped her, offering a brief respite from the complexities of her return.

She took a deep breath, savouring the feeling of being back in a space that had once been her sanctuary. As she began to unpack her belongings, her mind drifted to the happy memories she had shared in this room, late-night study sessions, laughter with friends, and the comforting presence of her family. For a moment, the world outside seemed far away.

But then, her thoughts took a darker turn, as they often did when she revisited that last night at home before college. The memory came unbidden, vivid, and unsettling.

Clair had been wandering the hallways, unable to sleep. She had stopped outside the study, a door slightly ajar. The warm light from inside had flickered, casting shadows on the hallway wall. Through the narrow gap, she had seen Adam and Elizabeth standing close together, their bodies nearly touching.

Elizabeth's voice, usually so composed, had trembled slightly as she spoke. "I'm hoping we have a future together," she had said softly. Adam had placed a reassuring hand on Elizabeth's arm, his gesture one of comfort that felt too intimate to be mere friendship.

As the memory faded, Clair stood in her old room, the weight of what she had witnessed settling heavily on her shoulders. The warmth of the room did little to alleviate the cold knot of apprehension in her stomach. The affectionate gestures she had seen between Adam and Elizabeth now felt like a shadow looming over her upcoming reunion. She had harboured a silent suspicion that something was amiss but witnessing their closeness had cast it in a stark and painful light.

Shaking off the unsettling thoughts, she had hoped that coming back home would be a simple return to comfort and familiarity, but instead, it was fraught with complicated emotions and unresolved questions.

Surrounded by unpacked boxes and scattered belongings, Clair couldn't help but wonder what the next day's reunion would bring and how she would navigate the delicate web of relationships.

The day's fatigue weighed heavily on her. Despite her best intentions, sorting through years of accumulated items felt overwhelming. The warm glow of her bedside lamp illuminated the chaos, but it did little to ease her exhaustion.

Her body ached for rest, and her mind was too weary to focus on anything beyond the pressing need for sleep.

She moved slowly to the bed, her movements heavy with fatigue. As she pulled back the covers and slipped beneath them, the softness of the sheets offered a fleeting comfort. She closed her eyes, hoping to push away the lingering unease and the tumultuous thoughts about Adam and Elizabeth. Tonight, she decided, she would allow herself a break from the emotional whirlwind.

Clair took a few deep breaths, allowing the stillness of the room to envelop her. The familiar surroundings of her old room were soothing, even if they were tinged with the complexities of her long-ago suspicions. She promised herself that she would deal with the unpacking and the lingering questions about Adam tomorrow. For now, the exhaustion won over her restless thoughts.

As she nestled into the pillow, the quiet of the house seemed to lull her toward sleep. The day's events, the unsettling memory of the study, and the anticipation of tomorrow all faded into the background as sleep began to take hold. Clair drifted off, knowing that the answers and clarity she sought would have to wait until morning. For tonight, she surrendered to the comforting embrace of rest, hoping that a new day would bring the perspective and strength she needed.

Chapter Three

Clair stirred from a restful sleep; her body initially disoriented as she tried to orient herself in the softness of her old bed. The gentle morning light filtered through the curtains, casting a warm glow across the room. For a few moments, she lay still, the familiarity of her old room mingling with the disorientation of waking up in a place she hadn't called home for years. Then, as she gradually became more awake, the memories of returning home and the comfort of her surroundings came flooding back.

With a sigh, she swung her legs over the side of the bed and sat up. The packed boxes scattered around the room reminded her of the day ahead, one filled with the task of unpacking and settling in. At least she would have plenty to keep her occupied, too busy to dwell on the complexities of seeing Adam again.

Clair shuffled to the ensuite bathroom, the cool tiles a welcome contrast to the warmth of the bed. She stepped into the shower, allowing the cascading water to wash away the remnants of sleep and the anxiety of the previous day. The steam enveloped her, soothing her tired muscles and helping to clear her mind.

After showering, Clair dried herself off with a plush towel, taking a moment to look at her reflection in the mirror. Her hair was damp and tousled, falling in loose waves around her face. Her complexion was naturally fair, with a slight rosy flush from the warmth of the shower. Her eyes, though still a bit puffy from sleep, held a spark of determination beneath their hazel hue. The faintest hint of a tired smile played on her lips as she looked at herself, trying to muster the strength and confidence she would need for the day ahead.

Clair adjusted a few stray strands of hair and took a deep breath, steeling herself for the busy day of unpacking and settling back into her old life. The mirror reflected a young woman on the cusp of new beginnings, ready to face whatever challenges and revelations the day might bring.

She opened her closet and sifted through her clothes, searching for an outfit that would be both comfortable and suitable for a day of unpacking.

Settling on a pair of white shorts and a red blouse, Clair pulled the outfit from the hangers. The white shorts were a crisp, clean cut that fell just above her knees, offering a breezy and casual look. The red blouse, a vibrant shade that contrasted beautifully with the shorts, had a relaxed fit and a light, airy fabric that would be perfect for a day of moving around.

Clair slipped into the shorts first, adjusting the waistband to ensure a comfortable fit. Next, she pulled the blouse over her head, letting it fall gracefully around her torso.

The blouse's soft material brushed gently against her skin, and its bright colour added a cheerful touch to her outfit.

She stood in front of the mirror, smoothing out the fabric and admiring the overall look. The white shorts and red blouse complemented each other well, creating a fresh and summery appearance. The vibrant red of the blouse accentuated her fair complexion and hazel eyes, giving her a lively, energetic look.

Satisfied with her choice, Clair gave herself a final once-over. Her outfit was ideal for the day ahead, casual, comfortable, and suited for the tasks waiting for her. She slipped on a pair of sandals, feeling both confident and ready. With a growing hunger for breakfast, she headed out, eager to enjoy a meal and the day ahead.

Clair descended the grand staircase, the polished wooden steps beneath her feet echoing softly in the quiet morning. The soft morning light streamed through the tall windows, illuminating the opulent interior of the house. She navigated her way down the stairs with a sense of purpose, her thoughts already turning to the day ahead.

As she reached the bottom of the stairs, the scent of fresh coffee and breakfast pastries wafted through the air, guiding her towards the terrace. The doors to the outdoor space were open, inviting in the crisp morning air and the gentle sounds of nature.

Stepping out onto the terrace, Clair saw her father, Samuel, seated at a beautifully set breakfast table. The table was adorned with an array of breakfast items, fluffy croissants, golden-brown pancakes, fresh fruit, and a steaming pot of coffee. He was dressed casually in a crisp white shirt and comfortable trousers, his appearance relaxed as he perused a newspaper.

He looked up as Clair approached, a warm smile spreading across his face. "Good morning, Clair," he said, his voice filled with genuine cheer. "I hope you slept well."

"Good morning, Dad," Clair replied, returning his smile. "I did, thanks. It's nice to see the sun shining."

He gestured to the empty chair beside him. "Come, join me. I've arranged a little breakfast for us. I thought we could start the day together."

Clair took a seat, her eyes taking in the delightful spread before her. As she settled in, he poured her a cup of coffee and placed a plate with a selection of breakfast items in front of her. The warmth and comfort of the meal seemed to ease some of her lingering apprehension.

They chatted casually as they ate, the conversation flowing easily between them. He shared updates on the household and local news, while Clair listened attentively, appreciating the familiar rhythms of their morning routine. The sun continued to climb higher, casting a gentle light over the terrace and creating a peaceful backdrop to their breakfast.

As they enjoyed their meal, Clair felt a sense of calm settle over her, bolstered by her father's warmth and the simple pleasure of sharing a meal together. It was a moment of reprieve from the whirlwind of emotions and decisions awaiting her, and she savoured the comfort of being home with her family.

As Clair neared the end of her breakfast, Elizabeth appeared on the terrace, the soft click of her heels resonating on the tiled floor. She wore a light, elegant summer dress, and greeted Samuel and Clair with a warm, welcoming smile.

"Good morning, Clair," Elizabeth said, her tone cheerful as she joined them at the breakfast table. "I trust you slept well."

"Good morning, Elizabeth," Clair replied, returning the smile with polite warmth. "I did, thank you."

Elizabeth took her seat, and her father poured her a cup of coffee. The conversation continued, light and pleasant, with Elizabeth catching up on the latest family news and sharing her plans for the day.

After breakfast, Clair excused herself and headed upstairs to her room, ready to tackle the unpacking. The sight of the packed boxes, still scattered and unopened, reminded her of the day's task. She began sorting through her belongings, methodically unpacking, and organising her things.

As she worked, her father appeared at the door, noticing her industrious efforts. He walked in with a concerned look. "Clair don't overdo it. There's no rush. We'll be having lunch together later, and I'd like you to take it easy until then."

Clair looked up from her work, wiping her brow with the back of her hand. "I'm almost done here, Dad. I just want to get this sorted out."

He shook his head gently. "It's important to pace yourself. We'll see you at lunch. Make sure to take a break and relax before then."

With a nod, Clair acknowledged his advice. She continued unpacking, but at a slower, more measured pace, knowing she had time to finish before their midday meal. The promise of a relaxing lunch with her family gave her a sense of balance and helped her focus on the task at hand without feeling overwhelmed.

Clair finally finished unpacking her boxes, the room now taking shape with everything neatly in its place. As she surveyed the completed task, she decided that after lunch, she would tackle another project, removing the old posters from her walls. She realised that she wasn't a teenager anymore and wanted to update her space to reflect her new phase in life.

When the time came for lunch, Clair made her way downstairs to the terrace. Her father and Elizabeth were already seated, enjoying the spread laid out before them. The table was adorned with a variety of fresh salads, sandwiches, and fruits, all presented with an inviting elegance.

Clair took a seat and served herself a modest portion, feeling the effects of her earlier work. She picked at her food; her appetite subdued. Her father noticed her small portions and gave her a concerned look.

"You're not eating much," he said, his voice tinged with worry. "Is everything alright?"

Clair looked up, offering a reassuring smile. "I'm fine, Dad. I just didn't eat this much at college. My meals were smaller, and I guess I'm not quite used to a big lunch."

He nodded, though his concern remained evident. Elizabeth offered a supportive smile, and the conversation shifted to lighter topics, aiming to ease Clair's discomfort. As they chatted, Clair appreciated the warmth of the family gathering, even if she wasn't quite ready to fully embrace the meal. The afternoon's task of updating her room awaited, and she was eager to start making her space truly her own.

After Clair finished her modest lunch, she stood up from the table and turned to her father and Elizabeth. "I'm going to update my room this afternoon," she said, her tone determined. "I plan to remove the old posters and give it a fresh look."

He nodded approvingly. "That sounds like a great idea. It's good to make the space your own."

Elizabeth smiled. "I'm sure it will look wonderful. If you need any help or advice, just let me know."

As they spoke, he glanced at the clock and then looked back at Clair. "Oh, and by the way, don't forget the dinner planned for you tonight. Everyone will be here at six o'clock to welcome you and celebrate your return."

Clair's eyes widened slightly in surprise. "Everyone?"

"Yes," he confirmed with a warm smile. "I thought it would be nice to have a gathering in your honour. I hope you're looking forward to it."

Clair nodded; her earlier fatigue replaced by a sense of anticipation. "That sounds lovely, Dad. I'm looking forward to catching up with everyone."

With that, Clair excused herself, ready to tackle the project of refreshing her room. The thought of the evening's gathering added a note of excitement to her afternoon as she prepared to make her space her own and reconnect with old friends and family.

Clair spent the afternoon updating her room, removing the old posters, and rearranging her belongings until the space felt fresh and new. As the clock neared five o'clock, she decided it was time for a relaxing bath before preparing for the evening's dinner.

The warm water enveloped her, easing the tiredness from her limbs and offering a moment of tranquillity. Afterward, she dried herself off and moved to the vanity. With a careful hand, she blow-dried her long honey-brown hair, the warm air adding a silky sheen. She applied a touch of makeup, just enough to enhance her features, a bit of mascara to define her eyes, a hint of blush to accentuate her cheeks, and a delicate lip gloss that highlighted the full, lovely shape of her lips.

Clair slipped into a green satin dress that fit her bodice perfectly, hugging her womanly figure. The dress flared out into a full skirt that ended just above her knees, offering a lively, graceful swing. Paired with high heels of the same shade, the heels added height and elegance, complementing her 5'6" frame.

She adorned herself with gold jewellery, a delicate chain around her neck, matching bracelet, and earrings. The gold accents added a touch of sophistication, enhancing the richness of the green satin.

Standing before the mirror, Clair took in her reflection. Her long hair framed her face beautifully, and she was struck by how lovely she looked. The makeup, though minimal, accentuated her striking eyes and radiant complexion. She felt a surge of confidence, surprised at how the simple act of dressing up made her feel both elegant and self-assured. It was a rare opportunity to dress up after her college days, and she relished the chance to embrace it fully.

With a final glance, Clair smiled at her reflection, feeling both excited and ready for the evening ahead.

Clair descended the grand staircase, each step feeling more exhilarating than the last. The green satin dress swayed gracefully with her movement, its fabric catching the light and accentuating her every step. The high heels clicked softly on the polished stairs, their rhythm blending with the ambient hum of conversation from below.

As she reached the landing on the staircase, she noticed Thompson, the butler, opening the front door to admit a guest. Adam stepped into the foyer, his gaze sweeping the elegant interior before his eyes fell on Clair.

Adam stopped mid-step, his expression shifting from polite acknowledgment to sheer astonishment. He stood there, momentarily frozen, his eyes locked on Clair. The air seemed to crackle with the unspoken recognition between them.

Clair continued her descent, her heart pounding slightly at the sight of the man she loved. When she finally reached the bottom of the stairs, she paused and looked directly at Adam.

Adam was tall and strikingly handsome, with a commanding presence that drew attention. His blue eyes were deep and expressive, often reflecting a mix of confidence and intensity. His well-defined features and strong jawline complemented his overall charm, making him both memorable and captivating. With a hint of a smile, she broke the silence.

"Well, are you going to say hello?" she asked with a sweet smile, her voice a mix of warmth and challenge.

Chapter Four

Adam stood at the entrance, looking every bit the successful professional. He was dressed in a tailored suit, a deep navy blue that contrasted sharply with his crisp white shirt and a neatly knotted tie. His dark hair was impeccably styled, and his deep-set eyes, a striking shade of blue, conveyed a mix of surprise and warmth as they locked onto Clair. His expression softened, though it was tinged with confusion at her disposition.

Adam blinked, as if awakening from a trance, and a smile slowly spread across his face. "Hello, Clair," Adam said, his voice warm and genuine, attempting to bridge the gap that had formed over the years. "It's so good to see you." The moment was charged with the weight of their past and the excitement of their reunion.

Clair's response was cool, her tone measured and distant. "Hello, Adam."

Adam's smile faltered slightly; his confusion evident as he tried to read her expression. The warmth he had intended to convey seemed to meet a barrier, leaving him unsure of how to respond. He remained silent, his brows furrowing in perplexity as he waited for any further exchange. The air between them was thick with unspoken questions, but he chose not to press, respecting the distance Clair had established.

Thompson approached Clair with a courteous nod. "Miss Clair, your father and the other guests are in the library having pre-dinner drinks," he informed her.

"Thank you, Thompson," Clair replied, her tone polite.

She turned and made her way toward the library, her heels clicking softly on the marble floor. Her posture was straight, and her expression remained composed, a sharp contrast to the warm welcome she had offered others.

Adam, still standing near the entrance, watched her go, a look of confusion etched on his face. He hesitated for a moment, then began to follow, his mind racing as he tried to decipher the chill in Clair's manner. The distance between them seemed palpable, leaving Adam to grapple with the uncertainty of their strained reunion.

Clair entered the library, the rich, warm tones of the room creating a cozy and sophisticated ambiance. The scent of aged wood and leather-bound books filled the air. She glanced around, noting the elegant furnishings and soft lighting that set a relaxed mood for the gathering.

Her father was the first to notice her arrival. He rose from his seat with a welcoming smile. "Clair, there you are! It's wonderful to see you."

"Hi, Dad," Clair said, returning his smile and stepping into the room. She was relieved to see the familiar faces of her friends.

Her father then turned to Adam, who had just entered behind Clair. "Adam, it's good to see you too," he said, extending his hand. Adam took it, shaking his hand firmly, still puzzled by the chilly reception from Clair.

As Clair looked around, she spotted six of her school friends, who were gathered in a cluster near the fireplace. Her face brightened at the sight of them.

"Christian, Sofia, Julie, Daniel, Ethan, Grace!" Clair called out; her voice filled with genuine enthusiasm. Her friends looked up, their faces lighting up with recognition and warmth.

"Clair!" Christian Ellis exclaimed, stepping forward to give her a friendly hug. "It's so great to see you!"

Sofia Getty and Julie Winslow followed suit, their excitement evident as they greeted Clair with hugs and smiles.

Daniel Harper and Ethan Williams shook her hand and clapped her on the back, while Grace Hathaway gave her a warm, reassuring smile.

The room soon filled with animated chatter and laughter as Clair reconnected with her friends, the initial tension of the evening melting away in the comfort of their shared memories and friendship.

As Clair chatted with her friends, the conversation flowed effortlessly, filled with laughter and updates on their lives. Christian, standing close by, seemed particularly eager to reconnect. He engaged in the conversation with a relaxed, friendly demeanour, his proximity suggesting a deeper interest. His smiles were warm, and he often found reasons to touch Clair's arm or lean in closer, his intentions clear.

Meanwhile, Clair could feel Adam's gaze on her, a weighty presence that seemed to hover in the background. Though she tried to focus on her friends, the sensation of his eyes tracking her movements was hard to ignore. It created an uncomfortable contrast to the easy warmth of her friends' company.

Despite the ease of her interactions with Christian and the others, Clair was acutely aware of Adam's silent observation. The tension between her cool attitude and Adam's lingering gaze added a layer of complexity to the otherwise joyous reunion with her friends.

Thompson entered the library, his presence marked by the soft rustle of his attire. "Ladies and gentlemen, dinner is served," he announced, his voice clear and inviting.

The group rose and followed Thompson as he led them to the dining room. The space was elegantly set with a long, polished table adorned with fine china, sparkling crystal glasses, and gleaming silverware. Candles flickered softly, casting a warm glow over the room.

Her father took his place at the head of the table, his posture relaxed but authoritative. Elizabeth sat at the opposite end, her appearance graceful and welcoming. Clair followed, taking her seat next to Adam on one side of the table. Christian settled in on the other side of Clair, his proximity further highlighting his intent to rekindle their friendship or perhaps something more.

As everyone took their seats, the conversations resumed with a new focus, dinner, and the pleasures of the evening's company. Clair, seated between Adam and Christian, felt the subtle interplay of her past and present, with Adam's watchful eyes and Christian's attentive proximity adding layers of complexity to the evening.

As dinner began, her father stood up to make a toast, his glass of champagne raised in hand. The room fell into a respectful hush as everyone turned their attention to him.

"It is with immense pride and joy that I welcome my daughter Clair home," he began, his voice carrying warmth and admiration. "After four years of hard work and dedication, Clair has graduated with honours in law and criminal justice. Her accomplishments are a testament to her intelligence and perseverance."

A round of applause erupted from the guests, and Clair felt a flush of warmth spread across her cheeks. She glanced down, her fingers nervously fidgeting with her napkin as she tried to hide her embarrassment. The spotlight on her felt intense, and she shifted slightly in her seat, hoping to deflect some of the attention.

He continued, his smile beaming with pride. "Clair, your achievements have made us all incredibly proud. We're thrilled to have you back and celebrate this wonderful milestone with you."

As he concluded his speech, Clair looked up, offering a shy smile of gratitude. The applause that followed felt both gratifying and overwhelming, leaving her feeling a mix of pride and self-consciousness as she took in the heartfelt acknowledgment from those around her.

Dinner proceeded with a pleasant atmosphere, the clinking of cutlery and soft murmur of conversation filling the room. The meal was a sumptuous affair, with expertly prepared dishes that delighted the guests. The food was served and enjoyed, accompanied by light-hearted discussions and laughter.

Adam, seated next to Clair, made several attempts to engage her in conversation. He started with casual topics, asking about her time at college and her plans for the future. "So, Clair, how was your experience studying law and criminal justice? Any interesting cases or projects you worked on?"

Clair offered brief, polite responses. "It was intense but rewarding. I worked on a few interesting cases, yes."

Adam tried again, shifting to a more personal topic. "Have you thought about what you might do next? Any specific plans or interests?"

Clair gave a short nod, her reply clipped. "I'm still figuring things out."

Despite his efforts to draw her out, Clair's responses remained minimal, and her expression seemed distant. Adam's attempts to mask his confusion were evident as he forced a smile, trying to keep the conversation light and engaging. He occasionally glanced at her, searching for any sign of what might be causing her reluctance to open up. The subtle tension between them created an undercurrent that Adam struggled to navigate, his curiosity about her guarded responses mingling with a growing sense of uncertainty.

Claire's heart felt like a house she had painstakingly built, brick by brick, only to watch it crumble from within. Being in love with Adam had once filled her with warmth, a sense of belonging she hadn't known she could feel so deeply. His smile used to be her safe harbour, his touch the answer to her every doubt. But now, every memory of him carried a shadow.

The betrayal with Elizabeth wasn't just a crack in the foundation, it was as though he had taken a wrecking ball to everything they had. She couldn't reconcile the man she loved with the man who had shattered her trust. Her chest ached with a confusing mix of anger, sorrow, and something she hated to admit, longing. Even now, despite the pain, she still loved him. It was as if her heart hadn't gotten the message that it was supposed to stop.

How could love coexist with betrayal? How could she still yearn for his arms around her when those same arms craved to hold someone else? She felt torn between two versions of herself: one who wanted to guard her heart and never feel this kind of pain again, and another who wanted to forgive, to believe there was still a future with Adam, however impossible that seemed.

Every glance at him now was a reminder of both the man she loved and the one who had broken her heart. And as much as she wanted to hate him, the love she felt was still there, stubborn, and relentless, leaving her caught in a battle between trust and heartbreak.

Adam sat at the dinner party, the hum of conversation and clinking of silverware surrounding him, but his attention was entirely on Clair. She was seated beside him, her posture stiff, her eyes deliberately avoiding his. Every time she spoke to someone else, her voice was light and pleasant, but when she addressed him, if at all, it was clipped, cool, like an icy breeze that left him aching for warmth.

He loved her. He had never told her, never found the right moment or the right words, and now, as she sat mere inches away yet felt miles apart, he regretted it more than ever. He didn't understand why she was being so distant, why her smile never quite reached her eyes when she looked at him. It hadn't always been this way. There were times when her laugh was easy, and her gaze lingered on his just a moment longer, moments when he felt the invisible thread that seemed to pull them together.

But tonight, that thread felt severed. She was cold, polite in a way that made him feel like a stranger. He could feel the weight of everything left unsaid pressing down on him, suffocating him in the middle of a room full of people. He caught her eye briefly, searching for something, anything, that would explain this distance, but she quickly looked away, her face unreadable.

It was killing him, not knowing what he had done, why she was pulling away. He wanted to ask her, to reach out and touch her hand, but the fear of being rejected, of finding out he had already lost her before he ever told her how he felt, kept him still. The warmth in his chest that her presence once brought was now replaced by a cold knot of confusion and heartache.

As dinner drew to a close, the plates were cleared away, and the guests began to settle into a more relaxed mood. Her father stood and addressed the group with a smile.

"Thank you all for a delightful dinner," he said. "We'd like to invite you to join us on the terrace for cocktails and continued conversation."

The guests rose from the table, and the sound of chairs being pushed back mingled with the soft clinking of glasses. The warm evening air beckoned them outside, where the terrace was set up with comfortable seating and an array of cocktails.

Christian, noticing Clair's hesitation as she prepared to leave the table, stepped closer and offered his arm with a charming smile. "May I escort you to the terrace, Clair?"

Clair looked up, slightly surprised but appreciative. She accepted his arm, her fingers lightly resting on his sleeve. "Thank you, Christian," she replied, her tone warm despite the ongoing undercurrent of her earlier tension.

Christian guided her towards the terrace, his presence adding a sense of ease and companionship to the transition from dinner. As they stepped outside, the soft glow of lanterns and the gentle hum of conversation created a welcoming atmosphere, and Clair was glad to have the support of an old friend as she mingled with the rest of the guests.

As the evening progressed and the guests moved to the terrace for cocktails, Adam's confusion began to shift into a simmering frustration. He watched from a distance as Clair and Christian walked arm in arm, the interaction between them seemingly effortless and warm.

Adam's gaze followed Clair more frequently than he intended, his brow furrowing in concentration. Each glance revealed the same cool appearance Clair had maintained throughout the dinner. His attempts to engage her had been met with brief, distant responses, leaving him increasingly perplexed and irritated.

His discomfort grew as he observed Christian's easy interaction with Clair. The sight of them together seemed to amplify Adam's sense of exclusion and frustration. He tried to mask his growing irritation, maintaining a polite facade, but his eyes betrayed his emotions, narrowing with an intensity that suggested a brewing storm of discontent.

As he continued to watch Clair, Adam's frustration morphed into a deeper anger, fuelled by the unresolved tension and his inability to understand her behaviour. He struggled to conceal his feelings; his focus fixed on Clair as he wrestled with the disquieting realisation that he might not fully grasp what had changed between them.

As Adam stood on the terrace, his mind drifted back to the past, unearthing memories that were both poignant and bittersweet. He recalled the way Clair had looked at him with a deep, unspoken admiration during the years before she left for college. Her eyes had always held a special sparkle whenever she was around him, filled with a silent, intense longing that she never quite articulated.

Adam remembered the laughter they shared during those formative years, moments of joy and companionship that had been as effortless as they were fleeting. Their time together had been marked by an easy friendship, filled with shared jokes and warm conversations. Clair had been younger then, her feelings for him evident in the way she followed him with her gaze, hanging onto his every word and gesture.

He recalled the warmth of her presence, how she had always seemed to be just a little bit in awe of him, her feelings evident even if never spoken. There had been a link, a sense of something more that had lingered in the background of their friendship.

As Adam looked at Clair now, the contrast between her past adoration and her current aloofness was stark. The memories of her admiration and the affection they had shared clashed with the coldness she now displayed, deepening his confusion and frustration. The laughter they once shared seemed a world away, and Adam grappled with the sense of loss and the unanswered questions about what had changed in the years since.

As the evening wore on, the terrace grew quieter. The laughter and lively conversation of the earlier hours had faded, leaving behind a more subdued ambiance. One by one, the guests began to depart, leaving only Adam and Clair among the remaining few.

Christian, having lingered to bid his goodbyes, approached Clair with a hopeful smile. "It was really great seeing you tonight, Clair. I'd love to get together again sometime if you're interested. Perhaps a coffee or a meal?"

Clair, still feeling the residual tension from the evening and the weight of Adam's lingering presence, hesitated for a moment. Her cheeks flushed slightly as she looked at Christian, appreciating his kindness. "I'd like that," she replied shyly. "Let's find a time."

Christian's face lit up with genuine pleasure. "Great! I'll give you a call soon. Have a good night."

With a final, warm smile, Christian took his leave, his step light, and his expression cheerful. He departed with the promise of reconnecting, leaving Clair to her remaining thoughts.

Adam watched the interaction from a distance, his expression a mixture of contemplation and unresolved tension. As Christian left, Adam's gaze lingered on Clair, his mind racing with the evening's events and the stark changes in their dynamic.

As the night deepened, her father and Elizabeth excused themselves, their departure marked by a quiet yet polite farewell. Her father, with a final reassuring smile, patted Clair's shoulder. "Good night, Clair. We'll see you in the morning."

Elizabeth offered a warm, albeit slightly reserved, goodnight before following Samuel inside. The soft sound of their footsteps fading away marked the beginning of a quieter, more intimate atmosphere on the terrace.

With the hosts retired for the night, the terrace was left in a serene silence, broken only by the distant hum of night insects and the gentle rustle of leaves in the evening breeze. The soft glow of lanterns cast a mellow light over the space, creating a tranquil setting that contrasted sharply with the earlier bustle.

Clair and Adam remained outside, the departure of the other guests leaving them alone in the dimly lit expanse. Clair sat quietly, her posture slightly tense, while Adam lingered nearby, his expression thoughtful. The silence between them was charged with the weight of unspoken words and unresolved emotions.

As the minutes passed, the stillness between them seemed to grow heavier, both of them wrestling with the lingering tension of the evening.

Chapter Five

Adam settled into a chair across from Clair, the soft glow of the terrace lanterns casting a gentle light over his contemplative face. He studied Clair, his eyes filled with a mix of frustration and concern.

"Clair," he began, his voice steady but tinged with an edge of urgency, "why have you been so cold towards me tonight? It's like you're keeping me at arm's length. Did I do something wrong?"

Clair looked up, her expression weary. "I'm sorry if I've seemed distant. Everything's just been a bit overwhelming tonight. It's a lot to take in, coming back home after so long."

Adam's brow furrowed, clearly unconvinced. "I understand that it's overwhelming, but it feels like there's more to it. Why did you leave for college without saying goodbye? And why haven't you come home at all for the past four years?"

Clair's eyes flickered with a mix of guilt and discomfort. She shifted in her seat, struggling to find the right words. "I... I didn't know how to say goodbye. It felt like too much to handle at the time. And I've been busy, trying to focus on my studies and figuring things out."

Adam leaned forward slightly, his gaze intense. "But it wasn't just about being busy. We were close, and you disappeared without a word. I thought we had something meaningful, and your absence... it was confusing."

Clair looked down, her hands fidgeting in her lap. "I didn't mean to confuse you. It wasn't easy for me either. I guess I thought it was best to keep my distance and focus on my future."

The silence that followed was thick with unspoken feelings. Adam's eyes searched Clair's face, seeking answers to questions that had lingered for years.

Adam's expression hardened with determination as he leaned forward, his frustration palpable. "Clair, you're not answering my questions. I need to understand why you've been so distant. Why did you cut ties so abruptly?"

Clair's shoulders tensed, and her eyes darted away, struggling to maintain her composure. The weight of Adam's scrutiny was pushing her to the edge. The quiet tension between them seemed to crack, the unspoken words finally breaking free.

"Fine," Clair said, her voice trembling slightly. "I'll tell you. I left because I cared about you. I thought you cared about me too. But you betrayed me and my father!"

Adam's eyes widened in surprise, his breath catching for a moment. He opened his mouth to respond, but Clair continued, her voice gaining strength despite the emotional strain.

"I found out about you and Elizabeth. I overheard you both talking that night before I left. The way you comforted her, it was too familiar, and I thought… no, I know you were having an affair with her."

Adam's expression shifted from confusion to shock. "Clair, I cared about you more than you know. You really think I'd do that? There was never anything between Elizabeth and me." His voice was forceful, raw with emotion.

Clair's eyes glistened with unshed tears, her voice now a mix of doubt and sadness. "I couldn't handle it. You'd betrayed me, and it was too much to deal with. So, I left and tried to move on, hoping that distance would make it easier.

The air between them was heavy with the weight of Clair's revelation, the truth laid bare as the night's quiet enveloped them.

Adam's initial shock gave way to a surge of anger. His face flushed, and his voice rose with a mix of hurt and frustration. "I can't believe you'd think that of me, Clair. You knew me better than anyone. How could you believe I'd betray you like that, betray Samuel?"

Clair's eyes flashed with a mix of hurt and defiance. "It wasn't just a suspicion, Adam. It was obvious to me. The way you were with her… there was something going on. And honestly, I like to know if it's continuing."

Adam's anger flared. "That's not fair! You have no idea what's been going on with me or Elizabeth since you left. To think that I would be involved in something like that is infuriating!"

Clair's voice trembled with a mix of frustration and regret. "I didn't know how else to react. I was hurt and confused, and it was the only explanation."

Adam shook his head, struggling to control his anger. "I wish you'd talked to me instead of jumping to conclusions. I'm not the person you think I am. And now, it maybe be too late to undo the damage."

The tension between them crackled with unresolved emotions, each wrestling with the weight of past misunderstandings and current frustrations.

Clair's eyes narrowed with scepticism. "It's hard to just forget what I saw and heard, Adam. It was so real. How am I supposed to believe that nothing happened between you and Elizabeth?"

Adam's anger flared as he leaned closer, his voice edged with frustration. "It's infuriating that you think so little of me. You really believe I'd betray you like that? Samuel is not only my business partner, but also my friend, and I would never do something to hurt him or disrespect our relationship."

Clair's expression remained troubled, the doubt in her eyes not easily dispelled. "It's not just about you and Dad. It's about what I saw and how it made me feel. I'm still struggling to understand it all."

Adam's jaw clenched, his irritation palpable. "It's clear you've made up your mind about me, and that's incredibly painful. I can't change what you supposedly saw, but I need you to know that I never wanted to hurt you. You should have known me better than that."

The conversation left them both on edge, the gulf between past perceptions and present reality widening as they faced the challenge of reconciling their feelings and understanding each other's actions.

Adam stood abruptly, his chair scraping against the terrace floor. His face was a mask of anger and hurt, his eyes blazing with intensity. "I see how you really feel about me now," he said, his voice tight with emotion. "I can't believe that you didn't trust me enough to at least talk to me about this before you disappeared."

Without waiting for a response, he turned sharply and began walking away, his steps heavy and resolute. The anger radiating from him was palpable, the tension in the air almost tangible as he made his way to the door. The finality of his departure left Clair sitting alone, a mixture of regret and unresolved feelings swirling in the dim light of the terrace.

As Adam's figure disappeared into the night, Clair's composure finally broke. She sank further into the chair, her body shaking with the intensity of her emotions. Tears streamed down her cheeks as she buried her face in her hands, the weight of her pain crashing down on her.

Her sobs came in deep, wrenching waves. "I loved you so much," she cried into the empty space, her voice cracking with each word. "I thought you were everything to me. How could you betray me like that?"

The raw hurt of Adam's departure and the unresolved suspicions overwhelmed her. With trembling hands, she stood and made her way upstairs, her heart heavy with sorrow.

In her old room, she moved numbly through the motions of undressing, her movements slow and mechanical. Once in her nightie, she climbed into bed, the familiar surroundings offering little comfort.

As she curled up beneath the covers, her tears continued to flow. She clutched her pillow tightly, trying to stifle the sounds of her weeping. The emotional exhaustion eventually claimed her, and despite the turmoil, sleep finally came, an escape into the darkness, where her pain and heartbreak could only be felt, not shared.

After a restless night of sleep, Clair woke up feeling drained but determined to clear her mind. She slipped into her fitness gear, black leggings, and a matching sports bra, and made her way to the home gym. The early morning light filtered through the windows, casting a soft glow on the equipment.

For two hours, she threw herself into the workout, the physical exertion providing a temporary escape from the emotional turmoil. The rhythmic thud of her steps on the treadmill and the steady clink of weights became a meditation, helping her channel her frustration and sadness into something productive.

Exhausted but slightly calmer, Clair finally finished and went upstairs. She took a long, invigorating shower, letting the warm water wash away the remnants of the night's distress. Afterward, she dressed in a simple red sundress that flowed gently around her knees, its bright colour offering a contrast to her inner turmoil.

She descended the stairs and headed to the dining area, where her father and Elizabeth were already seated for breakfast. The smell of freshly brewed coffee and warm pastries filled the air, but Clair's attention was more on maintaining her composure than on the meal itself. As she joined them at the table, she forced a smile, hoping to navigate the morning with a semblance of normalcy despite the lingering ache in her heart.

As Clair entered the dining area, Elizabeth and her father greeted her warmly. "Good morning, Clair," Elizabeth said with a bright smile. "How did you sleep?"

Her father, looking at her with genuine interest, added, "Good morning, dear. How are you feeling today."

Clair returned their greetings with a polite smile, settling into her seat. Her father, sensing her tentative mood, seized the moment to bring up a topic he'd been considering.

"Clair," he began, his tone thoughtful, "since you mentioned you were thinking about getting a job, I wanted to ask if you'd consider working for me at the firm as a paralegal. We're planning to advertise for the position soon, so it would fit perfectly."

Clair's eyebrows lifted slightly, her scepticism evident. "I appreciate the offer, Dad, but I was hoping to make my own way, not rely on your success."

His eyes softened with understanding, his pride evident in his gaze. "I respect that, Clair. I really do. But think of it this way: you'd be helping me out during a busy time. It's not about relying on me; it's about starting somewhere that's familiar and supportive. You'd be gaining experience while contributing to something important."

Clair considered his words, the conflict between her desire for independence and the practical benefits of the offer warring within her. His offer was genuine, and she could see the sincerity in his eyes.

After a moment of reflection, Clair sighed. "I'll think about it. I want to make sure that whatever I decide is the right choice for me, not just the most convenient option."

He gave her a reassuring smile. "Absolutely, Clair. Take all the time you need. I'm just glad you're home and considering your future."

Clair quickly finished her breakfast, her mind still occupied with her father's offer. She grabbed her keys and mobile phone and decided to take a drive to reacquaint herself with the area. The familiar surroundings promised a welcome distraction and a chance to clear her head.

As she stepped out the door, she glanced at her father and Elizabeth, offering a quick smile. "I'm heading out for a drive to get a feel for the area again. I might not be back until dinner."

Her father nodded, understanding the need for a little time to herself. "Enjoy your drive, Clair. Take your time to think things over."

With a final wave, Clair got into her car and drove off. The road ahead stretched out, promising a day of reflection and reconnection with her old surroundings as she contemplated her next steps.

As Clair drove through Seattle, the city's landmarks flashed by, each one evoking a blend of nostalgia and contemplation. She passed the iconic Space Needle, its needle piercing the sky, and the bustling Pike Place Market, alive with the morning activity. The familiar sights stirred memories of her childhood and the city she once called home.

Despite the beauty and vibrancy of the city, her thoughts were preoccupied with her father's job offer. The idea of working at his firm seemed practical, but she couldn't shake the worry about working so close to Adam. Her mind replayed their last encounter, and the potential for awkwardness or unresolved tension loomed large in her thoughts.

As she drove past the waterfront and through the city's various neighbourhoods, Clair found herself caught between the allure of a new beginning and the fear of reopening old wounds. The drive was both a retreat into her past and a journey toward an uncertain future, leaving her wrestling with the decision that lay ahead.

Clair parked her car at the waterfront, the gentle sound of waves lapping against the dock providing a soothing backdrop as she took a moment to relax. The view of the sparkling water and the distant silhouette of boats created a calming scene, offering a brief respite from her swirling thoughts.

After a while, her phone rang, breaking the tranquil silence. It was Christian. She answered, and they chatted about their respective days, the conversation flowing easily. Clair shared her concerns about her father's job offer, expressing her uncertainty about whether to accept it.

Christian listened thoughtfully before offering his encouragement. "You know, Clair, it might be a great opportunity for you. And if it doesn't work out, you can always quit. Plus, you could use this time to figure things out without too much pressure."

Clair laughed, appreciating his supportive perspective. "You're right, Christian. It does sound like it could be a good fit for now."

Christian's tone brightened as he asked, "How about we go out next Friday night? It would be nice to catch up and have some fun."

Clair smiled; her spirits lifted by the invitation. "I'd love that."

With plans set and their conversation ending on a cheerful note, Christian expressed his happiness before they said their goodbyes. Clair hung up feeling a bit more optimistic, the prospect of a Friday night out with Christian adding a touch of excitement to her day.

Chapter Six

Monday morning arrived with the soft glow of dawn filtering through Clair's curtains. As she stretched and got out of bed, the weight of the day settled in, it was her first day as her father's paralegal. She stood in front of her closet, her mind drifting to the conversation they'd had over dinner the night before. The way her father's eyes had lit up when she accepted the offer was something she wouldn't forget. He had been so genuinely happy, and though she still had reservations, the thought of making him proud brought a small smile to her face.

She selected a professional yet stylish outfit, a crisp white blouse paired with tailored black trousers. As she buttoned the shirt, she felt the anticipation growing. Today wasn't just about starting a job; it was a step into a new chapter, one she wasn't sure she was fully ready for, but knew she had to take.

Looking at her reflection, Clair smoothed down her blouse, pulled her hair into a sleek ponytail, and applied a light layer of makeup. She took a deep breath, trying to calm the nerves fluttering in her stomach. The memory of her father's happiness gave her strength. As much as she wanted to forge her own path, this was a way to connect with him and perhaps figure out what she truly wanted along the way.

With one final glance in the mirror, she grabbed her bag and headed downstairs, ready to face whatever the day had in store.

Clair slid into the driver's seat of her car, adjusting the mirrors and taking a steadying breath. She had politely declined her father's offer to ride in his limousine that morning. As much as she appreciated his gesture, she was determined to make a name for herself without the shadow of her father's influence looming over her every move. She didn't want her colleagues at the firm to think she was receiving special treatment.

The engine hummed to life as she pulled out of the driveway, her fingers gripping the steering wheel a little tighter than usual. The sleek, black limousine her father was in sat idle behind her, its driver watching as she made her own way down the winding road.

As Clair merged onto the city streets, the familiar landmarks of Seattle blurred past her, her thoughts racing with them. She knew her father had only wanted to make things easier for her, but she couldn't help but feel the weight of expectations. Refusing the limousine was her quiet way of asserting independence, a small act to remind herself, and everyone else, that she was more than just the boss's daughter.

With each mile that passed, she felt her resolve strengthen. This job was about proving something, not just to others but to herself. The firm's modern glass building came into view, and Clair inhaled deeply. She parked her car in the employee lot, not the reserved spots up front, and checked her reflection in the rearview mirror.

Today was the first step, and she was determined to take it on her own terms.

Clair stepped out of the car, her heels clicking softly against the concrete as she walked toward the towering glass building that housed her father's firm. The morning air was cool, but her nerves hummed with a quiet energy that kept her warm. As she approached the entrance, she took a deep breath, her eyes momentarily flicking up the sleek façade of the 12-floor structure. Today was the day.

Inside, the lobby was a mix of marble and modern design, its grand space filled with soft echoes of activity. Clair walked up to the security desk in the foyer, the guard giving her a polite smile as she introduced herself. He handed her an ID badge with her name printed neatly beneath the firm's logo.

"Here you go, Miss Dawson. You're all set," he said, his voice friendly but professional.

"Thank you," she replied, fastening the badge to her blouse.

With her ID secured, Clair made her way to the bank of elevators. She pressed the button, waiting for the metallic doors to slide open, her heart beating a little faster with each passing second. When the doors finally parted, she stepped inside, her reflection mirrored in the polished surface.

The elevator began its smooth ascent, climbing toward the top floor, where her father's office, and her new role, awaited. She watched the numbers blink past, the floor count rising. As the elevator neared the 12th floor, Clair adjusted her posture, straightening her shoulders. The soft ding announced her arrival.

This was it, the beginning of a new chapter, one that would test her independence and everything she had worked for.

As Clair stepped out of the elevator, the soft hum of conversation greeted her ears. She glanced to her right and immediately spotted Adam standing by the reception desk, leaning slightly toward the pretty receptionist as they exchanged a few words in hushed tones. The receptionist giggled at something he said, her eyes glancing up just as the elevator doors parted.

Adam turned casually, perhaps expecting another colleague, but his expression shifted the moment he saw Clair emerge. His eyes widened in surprise, and he straightened up instantly, his relaxed posture vanishing.

"What are you doing here?" he blurted out, his voice carrying a hint of disbelief, as though her presence disrupted the easy flow of his morning.

Clair raised an eyebrow, her lips curving into a slight, cool smile. "That wasn't a very pleasant good morning," she replied, her tone calm yet edged with subtle amusement.

Adam blinked, catching himself. "Right… sorry. Good morning, Clair. I just wasn't expecting to see you."

"Clearly," she said, brushing past him with a confident stride toward the receptionist desk to check in. Adam's surprised gaze lingered on her, the awkward tension hanging in the air between them unmistakable.

Clair turned back to face Adam, her expression calm but guarded as she approached the reception desk. "My father asked me to start as a paralegal here," she informed him, her voice measured. "I agreed to help out for now, at least until I decide what my future will be."

Adam's brows furrowed, still processing the unexpected news. "You're going to work here?" His tone was less incredulous this time, but there was a hint of something unreadable in his eyes, perhaps curiosity or even concern.

"Yes," she nodded, a faint smile tugging at her lips. "It will keep me busy while I figure things out." Her words were casual, but there was an underlying firmness, a subtle reminder that this was her decision and her way of maintaining control over her path.

Adam ran a hand through his hair, his gaze not leaving hers. "Well, I guess I'll be seeing you around, then."

"Looks that way," Clair said, her smile never reaching her eyes. She turned back to the receptionist, leaving Adam standing there, still trying to make sense of the shift in their world.

As Clair walked away from the reception desk, her thoughts began to swirl. *Adam is my father's business partner,* she reminded herself. The realisation settled uneasily in her mind. Perhaps her father should have discussed her working at the firm with Adam first. It wasn't like her father to leave something like that unsaid, especially with someone as important to his business as Adam.

Clair glanced back over her shoulder briefly, catching a glimpse of Adam still standing by the reception desk, his expression unreadable. *Did he feel blindsided?* she wondered. It wasn't as if she hadn't expected to run into him eventually, but starting here without any heads-up could complicate things between them even further.

Maybe Dad thought it was best not to mention it, to avoid any awkwardness, she thought, trying to justify it. But another part of her couldn't shake the feeling that Adam should have been more involved in the conversation. After all, they were partners, and her presence could stir up more than just professional tension.

Brushing aside the thoughts for now, she reminded herself why she had agreed to work here: to stay busy and avoid overthinking. Still, the dynamic between her, Adam, and her father loomed in the back of her mind, a silent worry she couldn't ignore.

Clair had barely settled into her new life when her father, appeared in the hallway, his face lighting up at the sight of her. "There you are!" he said warmly, approaching her with a proud smile. He gestured for her to follow him as he led her down the corridor.

"I want to introduce you to the paralegal team you'll be working with," he said, his voice filled with enthusiasm. They entered a spacious office where two people were seated at their desks.

"Clair, meet Emily and Ryan," he said, his eyes twinkling with pride. He gestured to the first paralegal, a shy-looking brunette with wide, doe-like eyes who smiled nervously up at Clair. Emily looked no older than Clair herself, her hair tied back in a neat ponytail, her cheeks flushing slightly as she greeted Clair.

"And this," he continued, turning to the other paralegal, "is Ryan." Ryan stood up and extended his hand with a confident smile, his presence commanding immediate attention. He was strikingly handsome, with dark hair, sharp features, and an easy charm about him. His handshake was firm but friendly, and his green eyes sparkled with curiosity.

Samuel beamed. "My daughter, Clair is here to help with the class action case we're working on. She'll be lending her expertise while she's with us."

Clair smiled politely, though the weight of the introduction made her slightly uncomfortable. *My daughter,* she thought, noticing how the words seemed to hang in the air a little too long, as if they came with expectations.

"Nice to meet you both," Clair said, trying to sound relaxed. Emily nodded shyly, while Ryan's grin widened.

"Looking forward to working with you," Ryan said, his gaze lingering a second longer than necessary.

Her father clapped his hands together. "Well, you're in good hands. Let's dive into this case and get you started."

After her father left, Ryan wasted no time stepping forward, smiling easily as he picked up a thick folder from his desk. "Alright, Clair," he began, his voice professional but tinged with curiosity. He stood just a bit closer than necessary, enough that Clair noticed but didn't feel entirely uncomfortable. His focus was on her, his green eyes studying her with more interest than seemed warranted for a simple introduction.

"The class action case we're working on involves a large number of plaintiffs," Ryan explained, flipping open the folder. His tone was professional, but there was an undeniable energy in the way he spoke, as if eager to impress. "It's a consumer protection case, basically, we're representing a group of people who claim they've been wronged by a major corporation."

Clair nodded, focusing on the information but keenly aware of Ryan's close proximity. His shoulder brushed hers as he laid out a stack of documents on the desk between them. "We're still gathering a lot of evidence," he continued, his voice steady, "but your job will be to help sort through the depositions, review the discovery documents, and assist with organising the plaintiff interviews."

She glanced up at him, catching his gaze lingering on her a moment longer before he shifted his attention back to the case files. Ryan spoke with ease, explaining the legal intricacies, but Clair could feel the subtle undercurrent of his interest, he was professional, yet his body language told another story.

"I'm sure with your background, you'll pick it up quickly," Ryan added, his smile returning as he handed her one of the documents. "If you need anything, I'm right here." The words were spoken lightly, but the meaning behind them wasn't lost on Clair.

Clair gave a polite nod, maintaining her focus on the task at hand, though she couldn't ignore the slightly charged atmosphere between them.

As Ryan continued explaining the case, his shoulder brushing lightly against Clair's, Adam appeared at the doorway, his presence commanding attention without him needing to say a word. His sharp blue eyes swept the room, landing on Clair and then narrowing slightly at the sight of Ryan standing a bit too close.

"Ryan," Adam said, his voice calm but with an edge that made both Clair and Ryan look up. "Keep it professional."

Ryan barely flinched, flashing a confident smile as he stepped back ever so slightly, but still close enough to make a point. "Always, Mr. Cross," he replied smoothly, a playful glint in his eyes as though challenging Adam's subtle reprimand.

Adam's lips tightened into a thin line, his jaw clenching for a brief moment as he held Ryan's gaze. Without another word, Adam turned and continued toward Samuel's office, his expression a mix of irritation and something else Clair couldn't quite place.

As Adam disappeared down the hall, the tension left in his wake was palpable. Ryan, unfazed, simply shrugged and returned his attention to Clair, the easy smile never leaving his face. "As I was saying..." he began again, but Clair couldn't help but notice the flicker of satisfaction in his eyes.

Chapter Seven

Clair's first day at the firm was busier than she expected, but surprisingly pleasant. She dove into the stack of documents Ryan had given her, sorting through case files, reading through depositions, and organising notes on the class action lawsuit. The work was engaging, and it kept her mind off the tension she had felt earlier with Adam.

Throughout the day, Ryan was never far. He stood beside her more often than not, offering advice and pointing out key details in the files. At one point, he leaned in close, his hand hovering just over her shoulder as he explained the nuances of a particularly dense legal document. Clair found herself smiling, appreciating both his help and the comfortable, easy-going way he presented the information. Ryan's proximity wasn't uncomfortable now, just familiar, and his charm made the day go by quickly.

Still, she couldn't help but notice Adam popping his head in now and then. Sometimes he came by to check on something for her father, other times it seemed like he had no real reason at all. Each time, his eyes lingered on Clair, watching her work, noticing how close Ryan stood next to her. He never said much, just gave a curt nod before retreating back to his office.

A few times, when Ryan was standing particularly close, pointing out something in the files with a confident smile, Clair caught Adam's gaze from the doorway. She tried to keep her expression neutral, but there was no denying the mix of curiosity and frustration that flickered across Adam's face before he disappeared again.

By the end of the day, Clair felt accomplished. The work had been challenging but fulfilling, and despite Adam's frequent appearances, she felt more at ease. Ryan's assistance had been invaluable, and she was grateful for the way he made her feel welcome on her first day.

As she packed up her things, Clair couldn't help but reflect on how different the day had been from what she expected. Busy, yes, but in a good way, filled with the kind of challenges she enjoyed and the support that made the work lighter.

The week sped by each day blending into the next with a steady rhythm of tasks and meetings. Clair found herself engrossed in the work, the busy pace both invigorating and exhausting. Emily, with her quiet efficiency, became a dependable ally, while Ryan's help was even more pronounced. His frequent presence, often hovering over her shoulder to offer guidance or pointers, proved invaluable. His enthusiasm and knowledge made the days smoother, and Clair appreciated the support.

By Friday afternoon, Clair was feeling settled into her new role. As she was wrapping up some final tasks, Ryan casually mentioned, "We usually go out for drinks after work on Fridays. It's a good way to unwind after a busy week. You should join us."

Curious, Clair asked, "Who usually goes?"

Emily, who was tidying her desk nearby, answered, "Most of the staff joins in. It's a tradition, really. The only ones who don't come are Mr. Dawson and Mr. Cross."

Clair's eyebrows raised slightly at the mention of Adam's name. "Mr. Cross doesn't go?"

Emily shook her head. "No, he's more of a stay-at-home type, especially after long weeks. And Mr. Dawson, well, he's often busy with other commitments. But the rest of us enjoy it. It's a great way to relax."

The prospect of joining her colleagues for a casual evening out was appealing. Despite the undercurrents of tension she felt around Adam, Clair was looking forward to connecting with her new team in a more relaxed setting. It seemed like the perfect way to end a busy week and perhaps gain a better understanding of the dynamics at the firm.

As Clair considered Ryan's invitation to the end-of-week drinks, she was initially excited about the prospect of unwinding with her new colleagues. However, she suddenly remembered her plans with Christian for the evening. They had agreed to meet up for a date, and she had promised him that she would be ready by 7:30 p.m.

Balancing her desire to socialise with her colleagues and her commitment to Christian, Clair made a quick decision. She would attend the drinks at the bar, join in with the team for a while, and then arranged for Christian to pick her up from the bar to go on their date.

She approached Ryan and let him know that she would be joining them at the bar but would need to leave around 7:30pm. Ryan, understanding but disappointed, assured her it was perfectly fine.

Clair felt a wave of relief as she planned her evening: she would enjoy a few hours with her new colleagues, get a sense of their camaraderie, and then transition smoothly into her evening with Christian.

Clair arrived at the bar and was greeted warmly by her colleagues. Ryan introduced her to a few new faces she hadn't met yet, making sure she felt included in the group. The atmosphere was lively, with laughter and animated conversation filling the space. Clair felt a sense of ease as she mingled, enjoying the relaxed environment after a busy week.

Just as the evening was settling into a comfortable rhythm, the door swung open, and Adam walked in. His presence immediately drew attention. Ryan, glancing over, remarked with a hint of curiosity, "I wonder why Mr. Cross decided to show up all of a sudden."

Adam's entrance seemed to shift the mood slightly, his gaze scanning the room until it landed on Clair. The subtle tension that followed was palpable, though the conversation quickly resumed its previous tempo. Ryan's comment lingered, adding an unspoken question to the air about Adam's unexpected appearance.

Adam made his way over to the group, slipping into the conversation with an ease that suggested he was a familiar presence at these gatherings. He joined the conversation next to Clair, contributing to the lively exchange with his usual charisma. Despite the initial tension Clair had felt, Adam's appearance was relaxed, and he seemed to blend seamlessly into the group.

As the evening progressed, time flew by. Everyone, including Adam, was enjoying themselves, laughing, sharing stories, and engaging in animated discussions. Clair found herself drawn into the camaraderie, appreciating the light-heartedness of the moment.

When Christian arrived to pick Clair up for their date, he found her in the middle of a cheerful conversation. He greeted her with a warm smile, and Clair excused herself from the group, feeling a mix of regret at leaving the fun and anticipation for her evening with Christian. She bid her colleagues goodbye, and as she left with Christian, she glanced back, noting Adam watching her departure with an annoyed expression. Clair chose to ignore it.

As Christian and Clair stepped out of the dimly lit bar, the cool night air greeted them. Christian, with a playful grin on his face, glanced sideways at Clair as they strolled towards his car parked a little way down the street.

"You know," he began casually, slipping his hands into his jacket pockets, "we're going to do something different tonight."

Clair raised an eyebrow, curious but sceptical. "Different how?"

Christian chuckled as they reached the car. He unlocked it with a click and opened the door for her. "Axe throwing."

Clair blinked, her surprise obvious. "Axe throwing? Seriously?"

"Yup," Christian replied, sliding into the driver's seat with a grin that suggested he'd been waiting for her reaction. "Figured we could let off some steam. It's fun, I promise."

Still a bit unsure but intrigued, Clair buckled her seatbelt, a soft laugh escaping her. "It is definitely different."

Christian started the car, the engine purring to life as he shot her a reassuring look. "Trust me, you'll love it."

Christian pulled into the parking lot of the axe throwing venue, the neon lights buzzing overhead as they came to a stop. Clair unbuckled her seatbelt and stepped out of the car, eyeing the building with curiosity and a touch of apprehension. Christian was already rounding the car, grinning as he gestured toward the entrance.

"Ready?" he asked, holding the door open for her.

Clair gave him a half-smile. "As ready as I'll ever be."

Inside, the atmosphere was lively but focused. Wooden targets lined the far wall, each marked with a bold red bullseye. A friendly-looking instructor approached them, axe in hand, and welcomed them with a quick introduction before getting into the basics.

"Alright," the instructor began, demonstrating the technique with smooth precision, "hold the axe with both hands, feet shoulder-width apart, and when you throw, aim for a straight release." He tossed the axe, and it struck the target with a satisfying thud. Clair watched with wide eyes, feeling the weight of expectation settling in.

When it was her turn, she gripped the axe hesitantly and did her best to mimic the instructor's stance. Taking a deep breath, she pulled the axe over her head and threw it forward, only for it to tumble clumsily to the floor, far from the target. A small laugh escaped her as she turned to Christian, shaking her head.

"Not quite as easy as it looks, huh?" she said.

Christian chuckled and stepped closer. "Here, let me help." He moved behind her, gently adjusting her stance. "You need to focus on a smooth release. And keep your wrist firm, like this." His hands briefly guided hers before he stepped back.

Clair took another breath, her grip more confident this time. She raised the axe, focused on the target, and released. The axe sailed through the air and, *thunk!* lodged itself into the target, not perfectly in the centre but definitely on the mark.

A wide smile spread across her face. "I did it!"

Christian grinned back, nodding approvingly. "Told you you'd love it."

After a few intense rounds of axe throwing, Clair and Christian decided to take a break and grab some food. They wandered over to the small concession stand, where the scent of sizzling hotdogs and fresh beer lingered in the air. Christian ordered for them both, two hotdogs loaded with toppings and a couple of beers. They found a spot at a high table, still buzzing from the fun of the game.

"I didn't expect to enjoy this so much," Clair said with a laugh, taking a bite of her hotdog. "It's weirdly satisfying."

Christian grinned, raising his beer in a playful toast. "See? Told you it'd be fun. The secret to a great night is axes and junk food."

They clinked their cups together, sharing a laugh, and continued talking between bites. The lively atmosphere of the place only added to the fun as they joked about their throws, recalling the near-misses and the triumphant hits that somehow felt like little victories.

After finishing their dinner, they played a few more rounds, the competition easing into something more relaxed, just enjoying each other's company. By the time they realised how late it was, they'd both worked up a good mix of laughter and exhaustion.

As the night began to wind down, Christian glanced at the clock. "Looks like it's about that time," he said, nodding toward the door.

Clair nodded, feeling the pleasant weight of the evening settle over her. "Yeah, I guess we should head back."

They hopped into Christian's car, and he drove them back to the bar where Clair had left hers earlier. The streets were quieter now, with only the soft hum of traffic in the distance. When they pulled up beside her car, Christian turned off the engine and got out, walking her the few steps to her driver's side door.

Clair leaned casually against her car, smiling up at him. "Thanks for tonight. I didn't expect to have that much fun."

Christian smiled, standing a little closer, his voice softer. "I'm glad you did. We'll have to do something else next time. Maybe without the sharp objects."

Before Clair could respond, Christian leaned in and kissed her gently, his lips warm against hers in the cool night air. It was soft, unhurried, and when he pulled back, Clair felt a flush creep into her cheeks. She blinked, trying to shake the sudden rush of warmth.

"Goodnight, Clair," Christian said with a smile, his voice low.

Still blushing, she opened her car door and slipped inside, giving him a small, bashful wave. "Goodnight," she echoed softly.

As she started her car, Clair watched Christian walk away, a small smile still playing on his lips. She gave him a final wave as he drove off, unsure of how she really felt about the kiss.

Chapter Eight

It was a quiet Saturday morning, and Clair had started the day with a vigorous workout, pushing herself harder than usual to clear her mind. Afterward, she showered and changed into something more comfortable, deciding to take a leisurely walk around the grounds of her father's sprawling estate. The sun hung low in the sky, casting a warm, golden light across the manicured lawns and lush gardens. Clair found peace in the solitude, letting the sound of birds and the rustling of leaves calm her.

As she wandered through the familiar paths, her thoughts drifted, though she couldn't quite shake the tension she'd been carrying. Something about the quietness of the day felt heavy, as if it were preparing her for something she wasn't ready to face.

By the time lunch rolled around, Clair joined her father and Elizabeth on the terrace. The meal passed in comfortable silence, the gentle breeze making the afternoon feel peaceful, until her father casually dropped the news.

"Adam will be joining us for dinner tonight," he said, almost offhandedly, as if it were just another normal piece of information.

Clair froze, her fork paused halfway to her mouth. Her stomach knotted at the mention of Adam's name. "Adam?" she echoed, trying to keep her voice neutral. "For dinner?"

Her father nodded, taking another bite as though it was no big deal. "Yes, he'll be coming by later. I thought it would be nice."

Clair wasn't thrilled by the idea. In fact, her initial reaction was to find a way to escape it. She'd been doing her best to avoid Adam since things had gotten complicated between them. But she knew there was no easy way out of this. Her father would expect her to be there, and avoiding dinner would only raise questions she didn't want to answer.

She forced a tight smile, her appetite disappearing. "Right. That'll be... nice."

Inside, though, she was already dreading the evening, knowing it would be hard to keep her emotions in check with Adam sitting across from her.

The afternoon passed quietly for Clair as she curled up in a cozy armchair in the sunroom, a novel in hand. The soft light filtered through the large windows, casting a warm glow across the pages. For a while, she managed to lose herself in the story, enjoying the peace of the moment, trying to forget about the evening ahead. But as the clock ticked on, the anticipation of dinner with Adam began to creep back into her thoughts.

Eventually, Clair set the book aside and headed upstairs to get ready. She chose something smart but casual, a soft blouse paired with tailored pants that struck the right balance between put-together and comfortable. As she gave herself one last look in the mirror, she brushed away the nervous feeling that fluttered in her chest.

When she made her way down the grand staircase, her footsteps echoed softly. Just as she reached the landing, she saw the front door open. Thompson, the butler, welcomed Adam inside. Clair's breath caught for a moment as she saw him, his presence instantly stirring the unresolved tension between them.

Adam glanced up at her, his expression cool and distant. "Hello, Clair," he said flatly, his tone indifferent, almost detached.

Clair nodded, matching his coldness. "Adam."

Without another word, Adam turned and made his way toward the terrace, where her father and Elizabeth were already waiting. Clair followed, a small flicker of relief washing over her. *Good,* she thought. *At least he doesn't expect me to be nice.*

When they reached the terrace, Adam's manner shifted. He greeted her father with a warm handshake and Elizabeth with a polite smile, clearly making an effort to charm them both. As if nothing had ever gone wrong between him and Clair.

Her father, smiling as ever, offered Adam a glass of whiskey, which he accepted gratefully. "It's good to see you again, Adam," her father said, clearly pleased with his presence.

Clair watched the exchange, feeling a mix of frustration and indifference. She was soon handed her own glass of whiskey, its smooth warmth offering some comfort as she took a sip, settling into her seat across from Adam. The evening had only just begun, and she already felt the weight of what lay ahead.

As the evening wore on, the soft chime of a bell echoed through the terrace, signalling that dinner was ready. Clair's father rose first, gesturing for everyone to follow him into the dining room. They moved inside, the warm, candlelit atmosphere welcoming them to a long, elegantly set table. Clair took her seat beside Elizabeth, with Adam across from her, and her father at the head.

Dinner was served promptly, several courses of delicately plated dishes that looked as good as they tasted. Throughout the meal, her father and Adam did most of the talking, discussing business, investments, and their shared acquaintances. Clair kept quiet, occasionally nodding when spoken to but mostly focusing on her food, hoping to stay under the radar. Adam seemed completely at ease, his voice relaxed as he engaged her father in conversation, his earlier coldness toward Clair forgotten, or simply ignored.

By the time dessert arrived, a decadent chocolate tart, Elizabeth shifted the conversation. She turned to Clair with a warm smile and said, "Clair, I've been meaning to ask you something. We're organising a charity ball for the homeless next week. It's been in the works for a while now, and your father's firm is sponsoring it. I could really use your help."

Clair looked up, sensing there was more. "Of course, what do you need?"

Elizabeth's smile grew, her tone full of enthusiasm. "Well, we're having an auction at the event to raise money. Several of the ladies will be auctioned off for a date, and I was hoping you'd be one of them. All the proceeds will go to the homeless charity. It's for a wonderful cause."

Clair froze, her fork hovering over her plate. She hadn't expected this. Her mind raced with immediate worry. The idea of being auctioned off for a date in front of all those people made her feel uneasy. *What if no one bids on me?* The thought of standing there, waiting, only for no one to show any interest was mortifying.

She forced a polite smile, trying to hide her discomfort. "Oh... I don't know, Elizabeth. That sounds a bit..." She trailed off, searching for the right words.

Elizabeth, seemingly oblivious to Clair's hesitation, continued, her tone encouraging. "I know it sounds a little daunting, but it's all in good fun. And it's for such a great cause. You'd be helping so many people."

Clair glanced at her father, hoping he might offer her an escape, but he simply nodded approvingly. "It would be good for the charity, Clair," he added, his voice supportive but firm.

Realizing she wasn't going to be able to get out of it, Clair reluctantly nodded. "Alright... I'll do it."

Elizabeth beamed. "Wonderful! I'll add you to the list."

Clair gave a small, strained smile and returned her focus to her dessert, though her appetite had faded. The thought of the auction gnawed at her, and she couldn't shake the worry of being humiliated.

As dessert concluded, Clair pushed her untouched slice of chocolate tart aside, her appetite having waned. She forced a smile, trying to mask her unease about the evening's earlier discussion.

The group moved to the terrace, a favourite spot for them during pleasant weather. The gentle evening breeze and the soft glow of lanterns created a relaxed ambiance. Clair settled into a comfortable chair with a cocktail in hand, the cool drink offering some solace.

They chatted casually, the conversation drifting from topic to topic. Adam, seeming effortlessly at ease, sipped his drink and glanced over at Clair with a nonchalant expression. "So, how was your date last night?" he asked, his tone casual as if discussing the weather.

Clair's heart skipped a beat at the unexpected question. She looked up, trying to gauge his interest. "It was... fine," she replied, her voice steady despite the flutter of nerves. "Nothing too eventful."

Adam nodded, seemingly satisfied with the brief answer. The conversation shifted, and Elizabeth turned to Clair with curiosity. "So, who did you go out with?" she asked.

Clair mentioned Christian's name, and Elizabeth's eyes lit up. "Oh, he's a lovely guy," she said with a smile.

Her father, having overheard, asked, "Where did he take you?"

Clair responded, her tone brightening, "He took me to an axe throwing place. It was a lot of fun."

Elizabeth's curiosity was piqued, and she leaned in, asking a few more questions, intrigued by the unusual choice of date.

As Elizabeth and Clair discussed the details of the date, Adam observed them closely from his seat. Clair animatedly recounted the fun they had at the axe throwing venue, describing the lively atmosphere and the playful competition. Elizabeth listened with interest, her questions revealing genuine curiosity about the unconventional date idea.

Adam's gaze remained steady; his attention clearly focused on Clair as she spoke. Though he offered no comment, his eyes betrayed a hint of contemplation, his expression inscrutable.

As the conversation wound down and the evening drew to a close, Clair felt the weight of the day catching up with her. She excused herself with a polite smile and murmured her goodnights. Rising from her chair, she headed toward the stairs but then decided to stop by the sunroom to retrieve her book. She wanted to unwind in peace before heading to bed.

As she entered the sunroom, she saw Adam coming in behind her. He cleared his throat, looking slightly hesitant. "Clair, could I ask you a question?"

Clair picked up her book, her eyes reflecting a hint of curiosity. "If you must," she replied.

Adam followed her, his expression serious. "Clair," he said, his tone sharper than usual, "if you suspected Elizabeth and I were having an affair, why haven't you told your father?"

Clair looked up, her brow furrowing. "The messenger usually gets shot," she replied calmly. "And I didn't want to hurt my father. Just because I've stayed away for four years doesn't mean I don't love him."

Adam's face tightened with frustration. Before Clair could turn to leave, he stepped forward and put a handout, blocking her path. "That's not really an answer," he said, his voice edged with anger.

Clair met his gaze steadily, her eyes unyielding. "I'm not here to argue," she said firmly.

Adam's gaze lingered, filled with a mix of anger and something else she couldn't quite read. After a tense moment, he pulled her into his arms and kissed her forcefully. Clair was taken aback at first, but for some reason she couldn't understand, she found herself melting into the kiss.

Adam drew Clair closer, wrapping his arms around her with a firm hold. Surprised but not entirely unwilling, Clair instinctively placed her arms around his neck, her fingers tangling in his hair. The kiss deepened and intensified, their bond growing more passionate with each moment.

Clair let out a soft moan of pleasure against Adam's lips, the sound escaping her involuntarily. The sensation of their closeness and the intensity of the kiss overwhelmed her, her body responding to the warmth of the moment.

Adam slowly pulled away from Clair, his gaze lingering on her face with a mix of intensity and contemplation. He studied her for a moment, his expression unreadable. Without saying a word, he turned on his heel and walked away, leaving Clair standing there, her breath still uneven from the unexpected kiss.

Clair stood there, bewildered and frustrated by her own reaction to Adam. Her heart was still racing from the kiss, and she couldn't shake the mix of emotions that surged through her. She felt a sharp pang of annoyance at herself for responding so intensely to Adam, especially since she had felt nothing comparable when Christian had kissed her. The contrast left her grappling with questions about her own feelings and the reasons behind the different responses she experienced with each man.

Clair tried to push the lingering thoughts of Adam from her mind as she made her way upstairs. After changing into her pyjamas and slipping into bed, she pulled the covers around her, hoping to find solace in sleep. However, her mind kept drifting back to the kiss, replaying its intensity and exhilaration. Despite her confusion, she couldn't deny the thrill of the moment she had shared with Adam.

As she lay there, the kiss continued to replay in her thoughts, and she felt a surge of anger at herself. She was frustrated by how easily she had been swept up by Adam's intensity. The thought that he might have kissed Elizabeth with the same passion only added to her irritation. Scolding herself for letting these emotions surface, Clair recognised that her anger was a mix of jealousy and self-reproach. She turned over in bed, trying to find rest amidst the tumult of her feelings.

Chapter Nine

Clair spent a quiet Sunday indulging in her favourite routines. She started the day with a workout, pushing herself through a vigorous session that left her feeling refreshed. Afterward, she curled up with a good book, enjoying the solitude and the peaceful turn of pages.

In the afternoon, she took a leisurely walk through the garden, the serene surroundings and blooming flowers providing a calming escape. She enjoyed the tranquillity, letting her thoughts wander as she strolled among the vibrant colours and gentle scents.

Just as she was settling into the rhythm of her day, her mobile rang. It was Lily. Clair answered with a warm greeting.

"Hi, Clair! I just wanted to check in and see how you're settling back into home," Lily said, her voice cheerful. "And I wanted to let you know how happy I am to be back in San Francisco. It's nice to be home."

Clair smiled, appreciating the call. "It's good to hear from you, Lily. I'm settling in well. It's been a nice, peaceful day. I'm glad you're happy to be back in the city."

Clair's voice softened as she responded, "I miss you, Lily. It's been a bit quiet without you around."

Lily's voice brightened. "I miss you as well! It's just not the same without you. So, what have you been up to lately?"

Clair smiled, settling into a comfortable chair as she chatted. "Not much, really. I've been enjoying some quiet days, working out, reading, and taking walks in the garden. It's been nice to have some time to myself."

Lily laughed lightly. "That sounds lovely. I've been getting back into the swing of things here. Work has been keeping me busy, but I'm also catching up with friends and just enjoying the city."

They continued to exchange updates, sharing snippets of their lives and catching up on each other's news. The conversation flowed easily, filled with warmth and a sense of friendship despite the distance.

Clair settled into the conversation with a relaxed smile. "I've been working as a paralegal at my father's law firm recently," she said. "It's been quite an experience diving into the family business."

Lily's interest was evident. "That sounds fascinating! What's it like working there?"

Clair continued, "It's been both challenging and rewarding. I primarily work closely with Ryan and Emily. Ryan manages many of the firm's major cases, while Emily oversees the administrative side. We've been collaborating on various projects, and while it's a learning curve, I'm really enjoying it."

Lily's voice was filled with curiosity. "That's impressive. It must be nice to have such a close-knit team. How are you managing everything?"

Clair paused for a moment. "It's definitely busy but working with Ryan and Emily makes it easier. They're both supportive and skilled at what they do. Overall, it's been a good experience."

Lily responded with genuine interest. "I'm glad to hear that. It sounds like you're finding your groove."

"Yes, slowly," Clair agreed. They chatted a bit longer before saying their goodbyes and ending the call.

The rest of Sunday passed smoothly, with no interruptions or incidents. Clair enjoyed the quiet and found solace in the peaceful end to her weekend.

Monday morning arrived, and Clair decided to embrace a change. Opting for a more feminine dress, she chose a style that made her feel beautiful and confident. It was a departure from her usual office trousers, but the dress was still perfectly appropriate for work. The decision felt right, and Clair was intrigued by her own desire to wear something different. As she looked in the mirror, she felt a renewed sense of grace and elegance, ready to start the week on a fresh note.

Clair drove to work, the morning sunlight highlighting her new dress as she made her way to the office. She felt a mix of anticipation and excitement about her choice.

Upon arriving and walking through the office doors, Ryan's eyes lit up. He couldn't help but whistle appreciatively and said, "Wow, Clair, you should wear a dress more often. You look great!"

Adam, who was nearby and overheard Ryan's comment, glanced up with a sharp look. He watched Clair's reaction from the corner of his eye, his expression hard to read as he processed the exchange.

Clair blushed at Ryan's compliment, a hint of a flirtatious smile touching her lips. "Thank you, Ryan," she said, her tone warm and slightly teasing. "I'm glad you think so."

Ryan grinned, clearly pleased by her response. "You're welcome. It's always nice to see you switch things up a bit."

With that exchange, Clair settled into her work. Throughout the day, Ryan spent a lot of time assisting her with various tasks, providing support and guidance. His frequent presence by her side did not go unnoticed by Adam, who watched with growing irritation. The sight of Ryan and Clair working closely together seemed to fuel Adam's frustration, his manner becoming increasingly tense.

At lunchtime, Emily and Clair joined Ryan for a meal in the office cafeteria. Ryan, ever the gentleman, took one lady on each arm as they walked, his chivalrous gestures drawing amused smiles from both Emily and Clair. They laughed together at his playful antics, enjoying the light-heartedness of the moment.

As they settled at a table, their laughter continued, blending with the chatter of the bustling cafeteria. They chatted about work and their plans for the weekend, savouring their lunch and the easy camaraderie. The atmosphere was relaxed and enjoyable, and Ryan's attention and gallant behaviour only added to the fun of the afternoon.

Clair worked diligently throughout the week, her focus unwavering as she tackled her tasks. She noticed Adam checking in on her periodically, a pattern that had become increasingly apparent. His frequent visits were hard to ignore, and Ryan, who had been observant, couldn't help but comment.

"Clair," Ryan said with a chuckle, "we've never seen Adam around this much. You must be doing something right."

Clair laughed, brushing off the observation. "Oh, Adam and I have known each other for eight years. It's nothing unusual. He's just checking in."

Ryan raised an eyebrow but accepted her explanation reluctantly. "I suppose that makes sense," he said, though a hint of curiosity lingered in his expression. The comment was dropped, and the focus returned to their work, but the dynamic between Clair and Adam remained a subtle undercurrent in their daily interactions.

Clair's father approached her during a brief lull in her work, his expression thoughtful. "Clair, just a reminder about the charity ball this Saturday. Do you have a formal gown?"

Clair shook her head. "No, I don't."

Her father nodded. "Elizabeth uses a boutique downtown that has some beautiful options. I'll give you the details. And don't forget about the auction, I'm curious to see how much money it will raise for the charity."

Emily, who was nearby, spoke up, "I decided not to volunteer for the auction. I'm just too shy for that kind of attention."

Ryan, overhearing the conversation, added with a grin, "Well, if Clair's up for auction, I'll definitely be bidding on her."

Clair laughed, thinking Ryan was just making a light-hearted joke. "Oh, come on, Ryan. Really?"

Ryan's expression remained serious. "I'm not joking. If you're auctioned off, I'd be more than happy to bid."

Clair's laughter faded into a thoughtful smile as she considered his words, realising he was genuinely interested in participating. "Well, at least I know there'll be one person bidding on me," she said with a light laugh.

After a busy day, Clair joined her work colleagues for Friday drinks at a local bar. The atmosphere was lively, filled with the buzz of end-of-week chatter and laughter. Adam's absence was noticeable, but Clair didn't dwell on it. Earlier in the day, Christian had called to invite her out on Saturday, but she had to decline, citing the charity auction as her commitment.

She enjoyed a few hours with her colleagues, relishing the relaxed vibe and the chance to unwind. As the evening wound down, Clair said her goodbyes and headed home.

Once she was in bed, Clair reflected on the upcoming events and decided she needed to go shopping for a formal gown the next day. With the auction and the charity ball on her mind, she resolved to find the perfect dress to wear, ensuring she would be ready for both the event and any potential surprises.

Saturday morning arrived, and Clair woke up with a sense of purpose. She reviewed the details of the boutique her father had mentioned, noting its location and the hours of operation. She was relieved to find that her father had assured her she could choose anything she liked, with the cost being charged to his account.

Feeling both excited and a bit anxious, Clair prepared for her shopping trip. She dressed casually and made her way to the boutique, eager to find the perfect formal gown for the charity ball. The promise of having the purchase covered by her father's account lifted some of the pressure, allowing her to focus on finding a dress that made her feel confident and beautiful.

At the boutique, Clair was greeted warmly by the staff, who were eager to assist her. The ladies at the store were attentive and listened carefully to her preferences, guiding her through a selection of gowns. They offered thoughtful suggestions and patiently helped her try on various options.

After several fittings, Clair found herself drawn to an exquisite ivory gown. The dress featured a full skirt made of satin and tulle, its elegant draping and soft sheen catching the light perfectly. The staff complimented her choice, and Clair felt a sense of relief and satisfaction as she admired her reflection. The gown was exactly what she had hoped for, and with their assistance, she finally decide it was the perfect dress for the charity ball.

Clair arrived home with the boutique's shopping bag in hand, feeling a mix of excitement and anticipation. As she walked through the door, Elizabeth was waiting in the hallway and immediately noticed the bag.

"Oh, Clair!" Elizabeth exclaimed as Clair revealed the ivory gown. "It's absolutely beautiful! You will look stunning."

Clair smiled, pleased with the reaction. "Thank you, Elizabeth. I'm glad you think so."

The charity ball was set to begin at 7:30 p.m., and Clair's father had arranged for the three of them to leave in the limousine at 7. As the evening approached, Clair prepared for the event, her excitement growing as she envisioned the night ahead.

In the ivory gown, Clair looked nothing short of radiant. The gown's full skirt, crafted from luxurious satin and tulle, cascaded elegantly to the floor, its gentle layers creating a soft, ethereal silhouette. The fitted bodice featured delicate, intricate beading that shimmered subtly under the light, enhancing the gown's timeless grace.

The gown's soft ivory hue complemented Clair's complexion perfectly, and the tulle added a touch of whimsical charm. As she moved, the skirt swayed gracefully, catching the light and creating a captivating effect. Her hair was styled in loose, gentle waves, and the overall look was completed with understated, classic makeup that highlighted her natural beauty.

Clair's reflection in the mirror revealed a vision of sophistication and poise. The gown accentuated her figure while maintaining an air of elegance, and she looked truly stunning, ready to make a memorable entrance at the charity ball.

Clair descended the stairs with a graceful confidence, her ivory gown flowing elegantly with each step. As she reached the bottom, her father and Elizabeth were waiting for her. Their faces lit up with admiration.

"Clair, you look absolutely beautiful," her father said, his voice full of pride.

Elizabeth added with a warm smile, "You're stunning, Clair. The gown looks perfect on you."

Blushing with modesty, Clair thanked them both, her cheeks flushed with pleasure. "Thank you. I'm really glad you think so."

They made their way to the limousine, and as they travelled towards the charity ball, Clair felt a mix of excitement and apprehension. The grandeur of the evening and the significance of the event weighed on her mind. As the limousine approached the venue, Clair's nerves began to surface, making her hesitant about stepping out into the spotlight.

As the limousine came to a stop outside the charity ball venue, Clair took a deep breath, trying to steady her nerves. Her father and Elizabeth exited the vehicle first, offering reassuring smiles as they awaited her.

Clair followed, stepping out gracefully in her stunning ivory gown. The evening air felt cool against her skin, and the glow of the red carpet leading to the venue created an atmosphere of anticipation. She took another deep breath and began to walk along the red carpet, her gown flowing elegantly with each step.

The venue door came into view, and Clair's apprehension slowly gave way to a sense of excitement. The sight of photographers and guests mingling added to the grandeur of the evening, and as she approached the entrance, she felt a surge of confidence. With her father and Elizabeth by her side, Clair walked towards the door, ready to embrace the evening's events.

As Clair entered the grand ballroom, she was greeted by a dazzling scene of elegantly dressed women and dashing men mingling under the shimmering chandeliers. The air was filled with the soft hum of conversation and the clinking of glasses, setting the tone for an exquisite evening.

Her father and Elizabeth led her to their table, situated prominently at the front of the room. As they approached, Clair noticed Adam already seated there. His gaze fell on her, and his expression softened in surprise.

"You look lovely, Clair," Adam said, his voice sincere.

Clair felt a twinge of disappointment at the word *lovely*, which seemed to fall short of the praise she had hoped for. She forced a smile, trying to mask her feelings, and took her seat. The evening's grandeur and the warm atmosphere of the ballroom couldn't entirely dispel her sense of letdown as she tried to enjoy the festivities.

Clair settled into her seat next to Adam, with her father on her other side and Elizabeth positioned next to her father. The table also hosted four male lawyers from the firm, who engaged in lively conversation as the evening began.

Elizabeth leaned in, explaining the schedule for the evening. "We'll start with dinner, and then the auction will follow. Clair, you're the last lady on the list, so it might be a bit of a wait."

Clair felt a flutter of nerves at the thought of being the final participant. She would have preferred to get it over with quickly, but she smiled and nodded, trying to stay composed.

Throughout the dinner, the male lawyers at the table couldn't help but admire Clair. Their compliments were effusive and genuine, far exceeding Adam's earlier remark. They praised her appearance with enthusiasm, calling her stunning and elegant. Each compliment made Clair blush, and she appreciated the more heartfelt attention, though she remained focused on the approaching auction.

Dinner was a pleasant affair, with soft music playing in the background and the clinking of cutlery providing a gentle rhythm to the evening. Clair attempted to enjoy the meal but found herself eating very little due to her nerves about the upcoming auction. She picked at her plate; her mind preoccupied with the anticipation of being the last on the list.

As she looked around the room, she spotted Ryan and Emily at another table. Clair waved to them, and Ryan responded by playfully making a heart shape with his fingers and pointing it in her direction. Clair laughed, appreciating the light-hearted gesture.

However, she noticed Adam stiffen at the sight of Ryan's gesture. His posture became more rigid, and a flicker of annoyance crossed his face before he quickly masked it. Clair, slightly puzzled by his reaction, tried to refocus on the conversation at her table, her nerves still palpable.

As the dinner concluded, the lights dimmed slightly to signal the start of the auction. Elizabeth took to the microphone to explain the evening's proceedings with a warm and inviting tone.

"Ladies and gentlemen," Elizabeth announced, "we'll begin with the auction now. We have five lovely ladies on the list, and each will be auctioned off individually. The highest bidder will have the opportunity to enjoy a dance with his chosen lady. Once each lady has been auctioned, we will move on to the next one."

The crowd's anticipation grew as Elizabeth concluded her introduction, and the first name was called. Clair's heart raced as she prepared for her turn, trying to steady her nerves while watching the excitement unfold around her.

As the auction commenced, all five ladies were lined up on the stage, each seated gracefully on a stool. The atmosphere was a blend of anticipation and excitement, and Clair couldn't help but feel that the whole scene seemed surreal. The spotlight cast a soft glow on them, highlighting their elegance and the evening's grandeur.

The first lady, a petite redhead, was introduced with a flourish. The bidding began at $2,000, and Clair watched in disbelief as the amount climbed rapidly. The bids surged, reaching an astonishing $50,000, leaving the audience buzzing with energy. Clair's heart raced with a mix of anxiety and hope, wishing she would at least receive a bid of her own. The escalating bids for the redhead only heightened her nervous anticipation as she prepared for her turn in the spotlight.

After the bidding concluded, the petite redhead was escorted to the dance floor by her winning bidder. The spotlight followed them as they made their way to the centre of the room, where the soft strains of a waltz began to play.

The gentleman, clearly pleased with his prize, held her gently but confidently, and they began to dance. The redhead moved with grace and poise, her dress flowing elegantly around her as they glided across the floor. The couple's synchronised movements and the romantic ambiance of the waltz created a captivating scene, drawing admiring glances from the guests.

Clair watched the dance with a mixture of awe and apprehension, her turn coming closer as the evening continued.

As the auction continued, each of the three remaining ladies was brought forward one by one, each taking her place on the stage and being introduced to the eager crowd. The bidding for each was brisk and competitive, with the amounts climbing steadily.

The first lady of this round saw the bidding start at $20,000. The excitement in the room was palpable as the bids quickly escalated, showcasing the high stakes of the evening. The winning bidder took her to the dance floor, where they waltzed gracefully together, much to the delight of the onlookers.

The next lady's bidding began at $25,000, and it, too, soared quickly, culminating in another impressive sum. She joined her winning bidder on the dance floor, where they moved elegantly in the spotlight.

Finally, the last of the three was auctioned off with bids starting at $30,000. The competition was fierce, and the final amount was yet another impressive figure. She was also escorted to the dance floor, joining her bidder for a waltz that drew appreciative murmurs from the crowd.

As each of the ladies danced with their winners, Clair's nerves grew increasingly frayed. The escalating bids and the elegance of the dances only heightened her anxiety. The anticipation of her own turn was almost overwhelming as she awaited her moment on stage.

Chapter Ten

Finally, it was Clair's turn. Elizabeth took the microphone with a confident smile and announced, "Ladies and gentlemen, we come to our final lady of the evening. Clair Dawson is not only beautiful but also incredibly intelligent and driven. She has made remarkable contributions in her field and possesses an elegance that truly shines. I'm certain you'll agree she is a remarkable addition to our charity ball tonight."

With Clair introduced, the bidding began at $50,000. Clair's eyes widened in surprise at the high starting amount, her expectations far exceeded. As the bids climbed steadily, the figures quickly surpassed previous records.

The excitement in the room grew palpable as the bids reached $100,000. Then, to everyone's astonishment, Adam raised his paddle with a bid of $150,000. The room fell silent for a moment as all eyes turned to him, including Clair's, who looked at him in shock and curiosity.

Elizabeth called the bid three times before striking the gavel. "Sold to Adam Cross," she announced.

As the bidding concluded, Clair remained stunned when Adam approached to claim his dance. He extended his hand to her, and together they made their way to the dance floor. The spotlight followed them, casting a warm glow around the pair as they prepared to waltz.

Clair turned to Adam and said, "It's been a long time since I've waltzed."

Adam smiled, his gaze steady. "I was the one who taught you when you were sixteen."

As the music began, Adam took her hand and guided her into the dance. The room seemed to fade away as they moved together, their steps perfectly synchronised. Adam's eyes never left Clair's, and his skilled guidance ensured that they danced with a grace and elegance that drew admiring glances from the crowd.

Caught up in the rhythm and the intimacy of the moment, Clair felt as if they were the only two people in the room. The bond between them was palpable, and the dance became a mesmerising escape from the evening's earlier chaos. The elegance of their waltz and Adam's unwavering gaze created a moment of pure, enchanting focus amidst the bustling charity ball.

As the waltz ended, Adam gracefully finished the dance by bowing deeply over Clair's hand and placing a soft kiss upon it. The gesture was both chivalrous and intimate, making Clair blush as she felt the warmth of his touch.

Adam then led her back to the table where her father and Elizabeth awaited. Both were beaming with pride as they watched the pair approach. Elizabeth's eyes sparkled with admiration. "You two were absolutely wonderful on the dance floor," she said. "It was like watching a perfectly choreographed performance."

Her father, equally impressed, nodded in agreement. "You both looked magnificent. It's clear you haven't lost your touch, Adam. And Clair, you danced beautifully."

Clair, still flushed from the dance and Adam's kiss, thanked them both, feeling a mix of pride and lingering surprise from the evening's events.

After the dance, Adam turned to Clair with a smile. "Thank you for the wonderful dance," he said sincerely. "I'll be in touch about the date I just won." His gaze lingered on her for a moment before he moved on to mingle with the other guests.

Clair, still processing the night's events, made her way over to Ryan and Emily. Ryan greeted her with a grin. "I had no hope competing with Adam's bid," he said, his tone light and joking. Clair laughed; her mood brightened by his playful remark.

Ryan then extended his hand with a charming smile. "Would you care for a dance?"

Clair accepted, and they moved to the dance floor together. The change of partners offered a welcome shift from the intensity of her earlier moments with Adam, allowing Clair to enjoy the rest of the evening with a lighter heart.

As the evening progressed, Clair took to the dance floor with her father. They shared a gentle waltz, their movements graceful and filled with the warmth of their father-daughter bond. Her father's supportive presence and loving guidance made the dance feel special.

Next, Clair danced with two of the lawyers from their table. Each dance was a mix of light-hearted conversation and polite, elegant movements, allowing Clair to enjoy the company and add a touch of variety to her evening.

Ryan, who had been a charming and attentive partner earlier, asked Clair to dance several times throughout the night. Their dances were lively and filled with easy camaraderie. Clair appreciated Ryan's friendly air and the relaxed, enjoyable atmosphere he created on the dance floor.

Each dance provided Clair with a different experience, allowing her to enjoy the evening while mingling with the guests and adding a sense of fulfillment to the night.

As the final dance of the evening was about to begin, Adam approached Clair and took her hand with a confident smile. Before she could react, she found herself back on the dance floor with him.

Adam looked at her with a playful glint in his eye. "So, where would you like to go on our date?" he asked lightly.

Clair, caught up in the magic of the night and momentarily forgetting her suspicions, responded with a smile. "Surprise me," she said, her voice filled with anticipation.

Adam's eyes lit up as they danced, the connection between them once again drawing them into a private world amidst the festivities. The evening's enchantment made Clair feel at ease, and she allowed herself to enjoy the moment completely.

As the limousine made its way home, Clair sat quietly with her father and Elizabeth. The soft hum of the vehicle and the gentle glow of the interior lights created a tranquil atmosphere.

Elizabeth, leaning against her father's shoulder, looked content and at ease. Her earlier exuberance and the warmth she exuded while watching Clair and Adam dance made Clair reconsider her earlier doubts. The way Elizabeth nestled into her father's embrace suggested a genuine affection that was hard to ignore.

Clair observed their closeness and the genuine happiness on Elizabeth's face as she spoke about the evening's events. The joy Elizabeth radiated, combined with her heartfelt admiration for Clair and Adam's dance, started to erode Clair's suspicions. Elizabeth's apparent love for her father seemed sincere, and the evening's interactions hinted at a relationship that was more genuine than Clair had initially thought.

As the limousine glided through the night, Clair wrestled with a whirlwind of conflicting emotions. The tranquil ambiance of the ride only intensified her inner turmoil. She replayed the evening's events in her mind, questioning if her suspicions about Adam and Elizabeth had been misplaced.

Clair found herself grappling with doubts about whether she had misjudged her stepmother's intentions and inadvertently overlooked Adam's genuine care for her. Elizabeth's affectionate manner toward her father and her heartfelt reactions throughout the evening began to challenge Clair's suspicions.

However, Clair couldn't easily shake the haunting memories of the unsettling glances exchanged between Elizabeth and Adam, nor could she forget the night she had overheard Elizabeth expressing her hopes, or lack thereof, regarding a future with him. These lingering doubts and the dissonance between her current observations and past impressions left her in a state of emotional turmoil, struggling to reconcile the two conflicting realities.

These recollections gnawed at Clair, creating a sense of unease and uncertainty. She grappled with the possibility that her instincts might have led her astray, even as the troubling memories continued to cast a shadow over her reassessment of the night.

As Clair continued to reflect, she recalled Adam's earlier assurances that he was not having an affair with Elizabeth or ever did, and his sincere expressions of how much he cared for her. The memory of those heartfelt words made her feel a growing unease in her stomach. The possibility that she might have misjudged Adam, and that she had, in turn, dismissed his love and care, filled her with a deep sense of shame. The realisation that her suspicions might have led her to undervalue his genuine affection made her feel remorseful, and she couldn't help but be ashamed of her actions.

Her mind raced with the weight of her doubts as she pondered how she might uncover the truth. The idea of confronting her uncertainties and finding clarity seemed daunting and almost insurmountable. She felt overwhelmed by the complexity of the situation, and the thought of discovering the real nature of Adam's and Elizabeth's relationship felt almost impossible. The task of untangling the web of emotions and conflicting evidence seemed daunting, leaving Clair to grapple with the enormity of the task before her.

Clair wrestled with a troubling realisation. Should she even attempt to uncover the truth, knowing that Adam had once told her that the damage was done? If his words held any truth, then it meant that if he truly cared for her and not Elizabeth, she might have already thrown away any chance of repairing their relationship. The thought weighed heavily on her, making her question whether pursuing the truth would only serve to highlight her own mistakes and missed opportunities.

By the time Clair arrived home, she was emotionally drained. The weight of her thoughts about misjudging Adam had taken a toll on her. As she sat quietly in her room, tears welled up in her eyes. The realisation that she might have misjudged someone who truly cared for her filled her with a deep sense of sorrow. The prospect of having let go of something meaningful because of her own doubts and misunderstandings left her feeling utterly exhausted and heartbroken.

Clair slowly undressed from her elegant gown, the fabric slipping off her with a sigh of relief. She changed into a simple nightie, the soft material a stark contrast to the formal attire she had worn earlier.

As she lay down on her bed, the events of the evening and her swirling emotions weighed heavily on her mind. Despite her exhaustion, sleep eluded her, and she tossed and turned restlessly throughout the night, unable to escape the turmoil that plagued her thoughts.

Clair woke up feeling unsettled on Sunday morning, her mind still tangled with the previous day's events. She spent most of the day on the terrace, alternating between reading and dozing off in the warm, sunlit space.

In the afternoon, Christian arrived, greeted by Thompson, who led him out to the terrace. Christian inquired about the charity ball, and Clair explained that they had raised $395,000 through the auction of five ladies. When Christian asked how much she had been auctioned for, Clair blushed and confessed, "It was $150,000."

Christian's eyes widened in astonishment, but he quickly recovered with a sincere smile. "Well, Clair, you were definitely worth it." His compliment, though surprising, seemed genuine and offered her a small boost of confidence amid her lingering doubts.

Christian looked at Clair with a curious expression. "Who was the winning bidder?" he asked.

Clair replied, a hint of embarrassment in her voice. "It was Adam. You met him at the homecoming dinner."

Christian's initial reaction was one of genuine pleasure, as he offered a warm smile and congratulated her. However, beneath his facade, a flicker of unease flashed across his face. The news that Adam had placed such a substantial bid on Clair stirred a sense of discomfort in him, leaving him conflicted as he tried to mask his true feelings.

Christian looked intrigued and asked, "So, where is Adam planning to take you for the date he won at the auction?"

Clair's expression turned thoughtful as she replied, "I actually don't know yet. I told him to surprise me."

Christian's smile wavered slightly, but he quickly masked his concern with a nod. "That sounds exciting. I'm sure it will be wonderful."

Christian prepared to leave shortly after their conversation. He gave Clair a warm, reassuring kiss on the cheek and said, "I'll call you soon." Clair walked him to the door, her thoughts still swirling from their discussion. As Christian departed, she stood there for a moment, feeling a mix of emotions. She wondered if Christian had future plans with her and felt uncertain if he was the right one for her.

Chapter Eleven

Monday morning at the office was a whirlwind for Clair. As she arrived and settled into her work, she found herself repeatedly interrupted by colleagues eager to comment on the substantial amount Adam had bid for her at the charity ball. Each time someone mentioned it, Clair's cheeks flushed with embarrassment. The comments ranged from congratulations to playful teasing, and although she tried to focus on her tasks, the attention left her feeling both flustered and self-conscious.

Ryan, observing Clair's growing discomfort, approached her with a thoughtful expression. "You know, Clair," he began, "there's something about Adam's interest that seems different since you started working here. I've noticed he comes into this office a lot more than he used to."

Emily, who had joined them, nodded in agreement. "I've picked up on it as well. It seems like Adam's feelings might be more than just friendly."

Clair looked between them, surprised and a bit unsettled by their observations. Ryan's and Emily's comments left her with a mix of emotions as she considered their perspective.

Clair shook her head, laughing softly. "That's silly. Adam and I argue most of the time when he's at my father's house. It's hard to believe he has any deeper feelings."

Ryan shrugged with a wry smile. "You know what they say about love and hate. It's a pity, though, because I was kind of hoping I might have a chance with you myself."

At that moment, Adam walked into the office. His expression darkened as he overheard Ryan's comment, and he glared sharply in their direction, clearly displeased by what he had just heard.

Adam grabbed some paperwork with a tight-lipped expression and, without saying a word, turned and left the office. The door closed behind him with a soft click. Emily watched him go, then turned to Clair with a knowing look.

"See, Clair," Emily said quietly, "it's clear it's not just friendship."

Her tone was both reassuring and pointed, adding weight to the earlier observations about Adam's feelings.

Ryan looked at Clair with a hopeful smile. "So, do I have a chance with you?" he asked, his tone light but earnest.

Clair laughed, shaking her head. "Not until I stop working here. I don't think mixing business with pleasure is a good idea."

Ryan grinned playfully. "Okay, if that's the case, you're fired! Will you go out with me now?"

His joke brought a genuine laugh from Clair, momentarily easing the tension. She appreciated his light-hearted approach but maintained her stance on keeping things professional.

As Thursday afternoon arrived, Clair's father came by her office to see her before she left for the day. With a warm smile, he told her, "I've heard nothing but great things about your work. I'm really proud of you."

Clair felt a surge of gratitude and affection. She leaned in and gave him a gentle kiss on the cheek. "Thank you, Dad. That means a lot to me."

Her father's praise was a comforting end to a busy day. As she was about to step into the elevator to leave, her father rushed over to her with a file in hand. "Could you drop this off at Adam's home? He needs it for court tomorrow, he knows it's on its way. I've put the address on a post it," he said.

Clair glanced at the file and address, feeling a twinge of reluctance but agreed, knowing it was important. She took the file and headed out, preparing for one more task before she could truly unwind.

Clair drove through the city, making her way to Adam's penthouse suite. Upon arriving, she walked up to the door and knocked, waiting for a response. A muffled "Come in" echoed from inside, so she opened the door and stepped into the apartment.

She found Adam at his dining table, which was cluttered with files and papers. His hair was tousled, and he looked deeply engrossed in his work, barely acknowledging her presence as she entered. The scene felt tense and intimate, the disarray of the room a stark contrast to the polished exterior usually associated with Adam.

Adam, absorbed in his work, barely glanced up as Clair entered the room. "Just put the file on the table, and thanks," he said, his voice preoccupied. Clair complied, placing the file down and turning to leave.

Before she could exit, a thought crossed her mind, and she hesitated. "Is everything okay? Do you need help with anything?"

Adam looked up in surprise, realising it was Clair speaking. His expression shifted to one of cautious relief. "Oh, it's you. I didn't realise." He explained that he needed to sort through several files before court the next day. After a moment's consideration, he tentatively accepted her offer of help.

Clair removed her jacket, ready to assist. "Where should I start?" she asked, looking around at the chaotic pile of paperwork.

Adam quickly explained the task: he needed to organise files related to several important cases, locating specific documents crucial for his court appearance the next day. Clair listened attentively and immediately set to work, sorting through the cluttered paperwork.

They worked efficiently and in silence, focused on the task at hand. Two hours later, the files were neatly organised and ready for Adam's review.

Adam looked visibly relieved and turned to Clair with a grateful smile. "Thank you so much," he said. "I really appreciate your help. At the very least, I owe you dinner."

Clair hesitated for a moment, then shook her head. "You don't need to. It's no trouble at all."

Adam, however, insisted, "I really appreciate what you've done. Let me take you out for dinner."

Clair considered his offer, feeling too tired for anything elaborate. "Okay, but just something simple. I'm not up for anything too fancy tonight."

Adam agreed, and they made plans for a casual dinner, both embracing the unexpected evening together.

Adam took Clair to a cozy Italian restaurant he frequented, its warm ambiance and intimate setting perfect for a relaxed evening. Clair was delighted by the choice; Italian cuisine was her favourite. They were shown to a charming table by the window, where soft lighting and the aroma of freshly baked bread created a welcoming atmosphere.

As Claire and Adam sat across from each other, the soft glow of candlelight casting flickering shadows on their faces. The aroma of garlic and herbs filled the air, wrapping around them like a warm embrace, yet there was still a little tension between them. Claire took a deep breath, gathering her thoughts.

"I feel like we need to put the past behind us and try to move forward," she said, her voice steady but laced with vulnerability. She looked into Adam's eyes, searching for understanding, hoping for a glimmer of hope.

Adam paused, his gaze dropping to the table for a moment before meeting hers again. "I would like that," he replied, sincerity colouring his words. The weight of their shared history hung between them, but in that moment, a fragile thread of possibility began to weave through the air, hinting at a new beginning.

They both smiled, realising that moving forward was more important than dwelling on the past. With that, the tension eased, and they decided to enjoy each other's company.

Throughout the meal, they enjoyed delicious pasta dishes and shared a few light-hearted conversations. The evening was filled with laughter and genuine friendship, the stress of the day fading away. The simple yet charming restaurant provided the perfect backdrop for them to unwind and enjoy themselves. By the end of the night, both were grateful for the unplanned yet pleasant evening together.

As they left the restaurant, Adam chuckled and said, "You know, that dinner doesn't count as the date I won at the auction."

Clair smirked and teased, "It could be, if you wanted it to."

Adam shook his head, smiling. "No, I think I'll save that for something special."

Clair nodded, feeling a bit of relief and amusement. "Okay, fair enough."

Adam drove them back to his apartment, the comfortable silence between them a contrast to the earlier tension. When they arrived, Clair suddenly remembered, "Oh, I left my coat inside."

Adam glanced at her with a playful grin. "Then I guess you have to come back up." They both got out of the car and made their way inside, still riding the lightness of the evening.

Clair and Adam rode the elevator up to the penthouse in silence, the atmosphere between them more relaxed after their dinner. When they reached his door, she quickly slipped inside to collect her coat. Just as she was about to leave, Adam's voice stopped her.

"Do you want to stay for a coffee before you go?" he asked, a touch of hesitation in his tone as though he wasn't sure how she'd respond.

Clair paused, coat draped over her arm, her bag slung over her shoulder. She considered it for a moment, then, with a small smile, she nodded. "Yeah, sure," she said, setting her bag and coat back down on a nearby chair.

Adam seemed relieved by her decision, and he moved to the kitchen to make the coffee while Clair settled in, feeling the shift in their dynamic as the evening stretched on.

Adam handed Clair a steaming cup of coffee, the warm aroma filling the room as she wrapped her hands around it. They sat down on the sofa, the city lights glittering through the large windows behind them. After a few sips of coffee and a moment of silence, Adam glanced over at her.

"Were you worried about the auction the other night?" he asked casually, though his eyes betrayed genuine curiosity.

Clair took a deep breath, her fingers tracing the rim of the cup. "Terrified, actually," she admitted, letting out a small, nervous laugh. "I honestly thought no one would bid on me. I mean, all those other women..."

Adam's expression shifted to one of disbelief. "Are you kidding?" he interrupted, his voice firm. "You were the most beautiful woman there, Clair."

She blinked, taken aback by the sincerity in his words. Adam's gaze never wavered, and for the first time that night, Clair found herself struggling to meet his eyes. The compliment lingered between them, and suddenly, the room felt warmer than just a moment before. "You said I looked lovely. That's not beautiful," she replied, her voice barely above a whisper.

Adam hesitated, his brow furrowing slightly as he searched for the right words. "I wasn't sure you'd want to hear that kind of compliment for me," he admitted, his tone softening. He leaned back slightly, the warmth in his eyes giving way to a hint of vulnerability. "I didn't want to make you uncomfortable or overstep any boundaries." There was a sincerity in his voice, a desire to respect her feelings while still wanting her to know how he truly saw her.

Clair's cheeks flushed at his words, and she looked down shyly, a soft smile playing on her lips. "Thank you," she said quietly, her voice barely above a whisper.

After a brief pause, she mustered the courage to ask the question that had been nagging at her since the auction. "But... why did you bid so much? It seemed a bit excessive."

Adam leaned back slightly, his expression thoughtful but unwavering. "There were three reasons," he said, his tone steady and sincere. "It was for a good cause, I thought you were worth it, and more importantly, I didn't want anyone else winning your date."

His words hung in the air, and Clair could feel her heart race just a little faster. She had expected some teasing or a more casual answer, but the way he said it, with such certainty, left her speechless for a moment.

Clair felt the warmth rush to her cheeks again and, in an attempt to make light of the moment, she laughed softly. "You really need to stop making me blush," she teased, glancing up at him with a playful smile.

Adam chuckled, leaning forward slightly. "I didn't realise I had that effect on you," he said, his tone just as light but with a hint of something deeper behind his words.

Clair shook her head, trying to keep the mood casual. "Well, you do," she admitted, still smiling, though her heart fluttered at the sincerity in his gaze.

Adam leaned back in his chair, a small smile tugging at the corner of his mouth. "I'm glad," he said softly, his eyes never leaving hers. After a pause, he changed the subject, his tone becoming more casual. "So, do you like working at the firm? And how's Ryan? He hasn't been too much of a pest, has he?"

Clair chuckled, shaking her head. "No, Ryan's harmless. A bit cheeky sometimes, but nothing I can't handle." She smiled, then added, "As for the firm, it's been a good experience. Busy, but I'm learning a lot."

Adam nodded thoughtfully. "Good, I'm glad you're settling in. Just let me know if Ryan ever gets out of line." His tone was light, but there was a protectiveness behind his words that Clair couldn't help but notice.

Clair leaned forward slightly, laughing as she recounted the story. "Actually, Ryan did try to ask me out," she said with a smirk. Adam's eyebrows raised in surprise, but he didn't interrupt. "I told him I didn't like mixing business with pleasure, so you know what he did. He pretended to fire me, just so he could ask me out!"

Adam's expression softened into a grin, though there was something flickering behind his eyes. "Really?" he asked, his voice low but amused.

Clair nodded, still chuckling. "Yeah, it was pretty funny. I mean, I wasn't expecting it at all. Of course, I told him no, but he did make me laugh."

Adam's grin faded slightly as he leaned back in his chair. "Well, I'm glad you handled it." There was a hint of tension in his voice, but he quickly masked it with a smile. "But if anyone's going to pretend to fire you, it should probably be me."

Clair laughed, feeling the warmth between them settle into a comfortable silence for a moment.

Clair leaned back, taking a sip of her coffee. "You know," she began with a playful smile, "if anyone fires me, dad might have something to say about it."

Adam chuckled softly but raised an eyebrow as she continued, her expression growing a bit more serious. "Actually, I've been meaning to apologise. The way dad handled hiring me... he really should've talked to you about it first. It wasn't fair for him to just place me there without your input."

Adam's eyes softened as he listened, shaking his head slightly. "Clair, you don't need to apologise for that. Your dad's always been... well, protective. And honestly, you've proven yourself more than capable. It's not like you haven't proved your worth."

Clair looked down at her coffee, feeling a mix of relief and lingering guilt. "Still, I didn't want you to think I was there because of any... special treatment."

Adam leaned forward, his gaze intent but kind. "I've never thought that. You're good at what you do, Clair. And if anything, the way you've handled yourself has made it clear you deserve to be there."

She smiled softly, grateful for his understanding.

Clair shifted slightly in her seat, setting her empty coffee cup down with a soft clink. "I should probably get going," she said, glancing at her coat and bag.

Adam, who had been watching her carefully, leaned forward a little. "Do you have to?" he asked quietly, his voice low and sincere.

Clair felt her cheeks warm instantly, and she looked up at him, eyes wide. "Why would you say that?" she stammered, her heart skipping a beat.

Adam's gaze remained steady, though there was a hint of something deeper behind it, something vulnerable. "Because I'm enjoying your company," he replied simply. "And I don't want the night to end just yet."

Clair blushed deeper, caught off guard by his honesty. She wasn't sure what to say, and for a moment, all the emotions she had been trying to suppress came flooding back, confusion, curiosity, and something else she wasn't ready to name.

Clair looked away, trying to compose herself before meeting Adam's gaze again. She gave him a soft smile, attempting to ease the tension. "You really should get some sleep," she said gently. "You've got court tomorrow, remember?"

Adam chuckled, leaning back in his chair. "Always the voice of reason," he said with a smirk. "But you're right."

Clair stood up, gathering her coat and bag once more. "Thanks for dinner, and the coffee," she said with a smile. "Good luck in court."

Adam rose from his seat, a determined look on his face. "I'll walk you to your car," he insisted.

Clair shook her head. "There's no need. I'm fine."

Adam gave her a reassuring smile. "I insist."

Reluctantly, Clair allowed him to accompany her. They walked together to her car, the evening air crisp around them.

As Clair reached her car, Adam gently pulled her into his arms. For a moment, they stood there, wrapped in a quiet embrace. The warmth of his body contrasted with the cool night air, and Clair felt a flutter of emotions as she rested against him. Adam's touch was reassuring, and the gesture was filled with unspoken words and feelings.

Adam leaned in, his gaze softening as he tilted his head. He placed a gentle kiss on Clair's lips, the touch tender and lingering. It was a brief but intimate moment, leaving a warm sensation that lingered long after the kiss ended. The kiss was gentle, full of unspoken affection, and it left Clair feeling both cherished and intrigued.

Clair's cheeks flushed a deep pink as she pulled back from the kiss. She managed a soft, "Goodnight," before sliding into her car. As she drove away, her mind was a whirlwind of conflicting emotions. The warmth of the kiss lingered, mingling with her uncertainty and curiosity about what it meant for them. The drive home was filled with a mix of excitement and confusion as she grappled with the implications of their fleeting but meaningful moment.

Chapter Twelve

On Friday afternoon, Clair was immersed in her work when everyone at the office was called to the reception area. She joined Ryan and Emily, her curiosity piqued as they made their way to the gathering. Her father stood at the centre of the crowd, his expression proud and beaming. The lift doors opened, and Adam stepped out, prompting an enthusiastic round of applause from the office staff.

Her father patted Adam on the back and said, "Congratulations on winning your big case!" The room buzzed with admiration for Adam's achievement as he acknowledged the applause with a humble nod, clearly touched by the recognition.

Adam took the floor, his expression appreciative as he addressed the gathered crowd. "Thank you all for the warm congratulations," he said, his voice sincere. "I'm truly grateful for the praise, but I want to emphasise that this was a team effort. It wouldn't have been possible without everyone's hard work and dedication."

As he spoke, Adam's gaze shifted toward Clair. His eyes lingered on her with a mix of warmth and intensity, acknowledging her presence amid his gratitude. His focus on her didn't go unnoticed, adding a personal touch to his acknowledgment of the team's collective effort.

As the end of the workday approached, the office buzzed with the anticipation of the weekend. Ryan, glancing at Clair as she gathered her things, asked, "Are you coming to drinks after work?"

Clair nodded with a reassuring smile. "Yes, I'll be there."

With that settled, Clair continued to pack up her desk, organising her files and tidying her workspace. She was ready to enjoy the weekend, the promise of a social evening ahead adding a touch of excitement to her end-of-week routine.

Ryan, Emily, and Clair arrived at the bar, their casual Friday evening plans taking shape. They walked in, and since they were the first to arrive, they took charge of organising the space. Ryan surveyed the bar area, selecting a large table in a central spot to accommodate the group. Emily helped arrange chairs and set up a few menus, while Clair assisted with adjusting the seating to ensure there was enough room for everyone. The trio worked efficiently, creating a welcoming space where they could relax and enjoy their evening with colleagues.

Adam walked into the bar with a group of office staff, engaged in casual conversation and laughter. As they made their way to the area Clair, Ryan, and Emily had set up, Adam navigated through the crowd with ease. He skilfully positioned himself next to

Clair, taking a seat beside her with a friendly smile. The group settled in, and Adam's presence next to Clair was a subtle but noticeable shift in the evening's dynamics.

The group was enjoying a lively evening, sharing light meals and drinks while revelling in each other's company. Laughter and conversation filled the air, creating a warm and relaxed atmosphere. Clair decided to take a break and headed to the bathroom.

As she left the restroom, a man in the hall approached her. His behaviour was forward as he asked for a kiss. Clair, taken aback, politely declined and attempted to sidestep him to continue on her way. However, the man reached out and grabbed her arm, trying to prevent her from leaving. Clair's heart raced, her initial surprise turning into fear as she struggled to free herself from his grasp.

Clair struggled to pull her arm free from the man's grasp, her heart pounding as she tried to avoid his unwanted advances. His attempts to kiss her were frighteningly aggressive, and she felt a surge of panic. Desperately she wrenched her arm and attempted to push past him, but his grip tightened.

"Please don't," Clair said, her voice trembling with desperation.

"I've been watching you all night," he replied, his tone laced with malice. "I think you could be a lot of fun."

"Please stop!"

Just then, Emily rounded the corner and saw the scene unfolding. She hurried over, trying to intervene. "Hey, let her go!" She demanded firmly. The man turned to Emily, his expression hostile. "Mind your own business," he snapped refusing to release Clair. The situation was escalating, and Clair's fear deepened as she continued to struggle.

Emily's sudden disappearance heightened Clair's panic. Her heart raced as she struggled to free herself, but the man's grip only tightened. The terror only heightened as he forcefully pinned her against the wall, his intentions clear. Clair's mind raced, desperately searching for an escape as she felt the cold pressure of his body against hers.

She twisted and kicked, her foot aiming for his shin in a desperate attempt to break free from him. Her heart raced, adrenaline coursing through her as she fought against the hold that felt both constricting and suffocating. The situation seemed hopeless, and the fear of not knowing if help would arrive only added to her distress.

Just as the man's lips touched Clair's, he was abruptly thrown across the room, crashing against the wall with a thud. Clair dropped to the floor, her heart pounding in her chest as she scrambled away from the scene. Her vision was blurred by tears, but she quickly noticed Adam standing between her and the man, a fierce determination in his eyes. The danger had passed, but the shock and relief left Clair shaken on the floor, trying to regain her composure.

As Adam confronted the man, Ryan rushed to Clair's side, helping her to her feet with a concerned expression. He quickly assessed her, making sure she was okay before glancing over at Adam, who was now forcefully restraining the assailant. Adam's anger was evident as he dealt with the man, delivering a sharp, controlled blow to his face, to keep him subdued. Ryan's presence provided Clair with immediate comfort, his protective stance a stark contrast to the chaos that had just unfolded.

Ryan's face was etched with worry as he gently asked Clair, "Are you okay?" His voice was laced with desperation as he guided her away from the chaotic hallway. Once they were in a quieter area, he carefully helped her onto an empty table, his arm resting reassuringly around her shoulders. Clair was visibly shaking, her breaths coming in quick, shallow bursts. Ryan's presence was a steadying force amidst her fear, his concern palpable as he tried to offer her as much comfort as possible in the aftermath of the frightening encounter.

Adam emerged from the hallway, his expression a mix of anger and concern. The man was nowhere in sight. Without hesitation, Adam rushed over to Clair, his eyes filled with worry. He knelt beside her, his voice soft and urgent as he asked, "Clair, are you alright? Did he hurt you?" His hands hovered near her, wanting to offer comfort but unsure of how to do so without overwhelming her. The intense concern in his gaze spoke volumes, his usual composed appearance replaced by a raw, genuine anxiety for her well-being.

Clair looked up at Adam, her eyes brimming with tears. Her voice trembled as she managed to say, "No, I don't think so." She was visibly shaking, her breath coming in uneven gasps. The distress of the encounter was evident in her tear-streaked face and the way her body shook with each breath. Despite trying to remain composed, the fear and shock of the incident were overwhelming.

Adam turned to Ryan with a firm expression. "I'm taking Clair home," he said decisively. Ryan, understanding the gravity of the situation, nodded in acceptance. "Good idea. Clair, make sure to look after yourself," he advised gently. Ryan's concern was palpable, and he gave Clair a reassuring nod before Adam guided her out, his protective manner evident in every step they took.

Adam carefully helped Clair into the passenger seat of his car, his touch gentle yet firm. Clair was still too shaken to fully grasp what was happening, her movements slow and disoriented. As he closed the door and walked around to the driver's side, Adam's concern was evident. He got in and started the car, his gaze frequently shifting to Clair, who was staring blankly ahead, trying to process the trauma she had just endured.

Adam drove through the city, his focus solely on Clair, who sat quietly in the passenger seat, her mind still racing. When they arrived at his penthouse, Adam guided Clair inside with careful, reassuring gestures. It wasn't until they were settled in his lounge, with its calm and dim lighting, that Clair fully realised where she was. The plush furniture and tasteful decor of Adam's penthouse seemed to envelop her in a strange comfort, but her shaken state made it hard to appreciate. Adam, sensing her disorientation, moved to make her a cup of tea, hoping it would help soothe her nerves.

Adam handed Clair a steaming cup of sweet tea, his expression filled with concern. Clair accepted it with trembling hands, her fingers still shaking despite the warmth of the cup. She took a cautious sip, the soothing sweetness providing a small measure of comfort. Adam watched her quietly, giving her space while keeping an eye on her, wanting to ensure she felt as secure as possible in the aftermath of the frightening incident.

After a long, quiet moment, Clair finally looked up at Adam, her voice barely above a whisper. "Thank you," she said softly, her eyes still reflecting the lingering fear from earlier.

Adam gave her a small, reassuring nod, his gaze never leaving her. "You don't need to thank me, Clair," he replied gently. "I'm just glad you're safe."

Clair spoke softly, her voice trembling slightly. "I've never been in a situation like that before," she admitted, her eyes distant as if reliving the moment. "I'd heard stories about girls getting attacked in college, but I always avoided those kinds of situations... I didn't go out much, so I thought I'd never have to worry about it."

Adam watched her carefully, his expression softening with concern. "You shouldn't have to worry about it at all," he said firmly, his voice full of quiet resolve.

Clair continued, her voice still soft, almost as if she were speaking to herself. "In college, I just... avoided men altogether. I kept my head down, focused on my studies. My friend Lily was the same. We stuck together, always at the library or in our dorm. She used to joke that we were the least adventurous people on campus. But honestly, it was easier that way... safer."

Adam sat beside her, listening quietly, his gaze steady but compassionate. He didn't interrupt, just letting her talk, giving her the space to process everything. His presence was calm, reassuring, as if he knew she needed someone to just be there without judgment or pressure.

Clair sighed, her words spilling out in a quiet stream. "It's not that I didn't have guys ask me out. I did. I just said no... all the time. Some of them would get frustrated, calling me stuck up, saying I thought I was too good for them." She paused, staring down at her hands wrapped around the cup of tea. "But it was easier to just avoid it all. Less complicated."

Realising she was rambling, Clair suddenly stopped and glanced up at Adam, her cheeks warming. "Sorry... I'm babbling."

Adam shook his head slightly, offering her a gentle smile. "You don't need to apologise, Clair." His voice was soft, understanding. "You've been through a lot tonight."

Clair placed her teacup carefully on the coffee table, her fingers still trembling slightly as she pulled her hands away. She hesitated for a moment, her eyes searching Adam's face, before speaking softly. "Adam... could you... could you just hold me for a minute?"

Her voice was fragile, almost uncertain, but her vulnerability was clear. Adam didn't hesitate. He gently reached out, wrapping his arms around her, pulling her close. Clair rested her head against his chest, closing her eyes as his warmth enveloped her. For a moment, the world outside disappeared, and all that remained was the quiet comfort of being held.

Clair stayed nestled in Adam's arms for quite a while, feeling the steady rise and fall of his chest. The warmth of his embrace slowly soothed her, and gradually, the trembling that had gripped her since the incident began to subside. Adam's arms remained securely around her, offering silent reassurance as the minutes passed.

With each breath, the fear and panic seemed to drain away, leaving Clair calmer than she had felt all night. She didn't say a word, nor did Adam, but the quiet comfort between them was enough. The safety she felt in his arms was undeniable, and slowly, the tension that had held her body tight began to melt.

After what felt like a long, comforting silence, Clair finally felt her nerves settle enough to pull away. Slowly, she lifted her head from Adam's chest and loosened her grip on him, drawing a deep breath as she eased herself back.

Her hands gently slid away from him, and she offered a small, grateful smile as she met his eyes. Though she felt more stable now, the vulnerability lingered in her expression. She whispered, "Thank you," her voice soft but steady, before moving a little further from him on the couch, allowing herself some space.

Adam leaned back slightly, his gaze steady on Clair as he spoke. "I'm just glad I was there," he said quietly, his voice laced with a protective edge. "When Emily came running to the table and told Ryan what was happening, my blood ran cold." He shook his head, his jaw tightening briefly at the memory.

"I couldn't get to you fast enough." His expression softened slightly as he looked at her. "That guy's going to have a very bad headache tomorrow," he added with a wry smile, trying to lighten the mood, though the intensity in his eyes showed just how serious he had been in defending her.

Clair looked up at Adam, her voice still a bit shaky. "I really appreciate you saving me, Adam. That guy... he really scared me. I thought no one was going to get there in time." Her fingers fidgeted nervously in her lap as she continued, her eyes clouding with the memory. "When Emily came, I was so relieved, but then she just...

disappeared. I didn't know what to do. I tried to get away, but he was too strong. I've never felt so trapped."

Her voice wavered slightly as she admitted how vulnerable she had felt. "He said that he'd been watching me all night and that he wanted to have some fun with me. I thought it would only get worse. But then you showed up." She gave him a small, grateful smile, the weight of the fear still lingering but softened by his presence.

Clair shifted in her seat, glancing down at her hands before looking back at Adam. "I should go," she said softly, her voice laced with exhaustion but a quiet resolve. She stood up slowly, her legs still feeling unsteady beneath her. "You've already done so much... I just need to get home and try to forget what happened."

Her eyes met his, filled with gratitude, but also the lingering remnants of the night's fear. She wrapped her arms around herself, almost as if trying to shield herself from the events that had transpired.

Adam stood up and reached out, lifting one hand to gently touch Clair's cheek. He slid the back of his fingers tenderly down her face, his touch soft and reassuring. Clair, feeling a surge of boldness, turned her face slightly and pressed a gentle kiss to the back of his hand. The moment was filled with a quiet intimacy, and Adam's eyes softened as he watched her.

Adam's voice was soft and earnest as he leaned closer to Clair. "I don't want to frighten you, Clair," he said quietly, "but may I kiss you?" His eyes were filled with a mix of vulnerability and hope, awaiting her response with a tender gaze.

Chapter Thirteen

Clair nodded slightly, her eyes meeting Adam's with a mixture of trust and anticipation. Adam gently pulled her into his arms, his hands cradling her face as he lowered his lips to hers. The kiss was tender and reassuring, a soft brush of affection meant to comfort and connect in the aftermath of the evening's events.

Clair placed her hands gently on Adam's chest, feeling the steady rise and full of his breath. As she leaned in, she kissed him back with equal tenderness, her lips moving softly against his. The kiss was a mutual exchange of reassurance and warmth, offering solace and a moment of shared intimacy amid the lingering tremors of the evening's events.

Adam deepened the kiss, his arms pulling Clair closer as his lips pressed more firmly against hers. The kiss grew more passionate, conveying a profound mix of relief, affection, and protection. The world outside seemed to fade away as the intensity of their union enveloped them both, providing a comforting and intimate escape from the night's earlier fears.

Clair wrapped her arms around Adam's neck, drawing him closer as she kissed him more passionately. Her fingers tangled in his hair, pulling him into the kiss with a fervent intensity. The warmth of the moment surged between them, and their kisses became more urgent, expressing the deep relief and affection that had been building. Each touch and press of their lips was a silent testament to their shared attraction.

Adam sat on the lounge gently pulling Clair onto his lap, his arms encircling her waist as he continued to deepen their kiss. As she settled comfortably on his lap, their closeness intensified the bond they were sharing. His hands rested on her back, holding her securely as their lips moved together with increasing passion. The world outside seemed to fade away, leaving only the shared warmth and intimacy of their embrace.

Adam's hands slowly and cautiously slid from Clair's back to her sides, his touch gentle and exploratory. As his hands moved, he maintained a careful respect for her boundaries, aware of the intimacy of the moment. The atmosphere between them remained charged with the mutual affection and trust they had built.

Clair, her voice soft and filled with a mix of vulnerability and desire, asked Adam to touch her. Her eyes were filled with a longing that matched the warmth of the embrace.

Adam's hand, guided by a mix of tenderness and intent, slid carefully to her breast. His touch was gentle, exploring with a softness that matched the intimacy of the moment. Clair responded to his touch with a mixture of anticipation and pleasure, her breath catching slightly as their connection grew more profound.

Clair moaned softly with pleasure as Adam's touch continued, her body responding to the gentle caress. His breath was warm against her lips as he whispered her name, "Clair," with a deep, husky tone. The intimate sound of his voice only heightened the sensations between them.

Clair instinctively pressed herself closer into Adam's hand, her desire for deeper contact evident in the way she moved. Her body responded to his touch with a heightened sense of urgency, seeking more from the intimate bond they were sharing.

Adam carefully pulled Clair's blouse out from the waist of her skirt, his fingers tracing a path up her bare stomach. He slid his hand beneath her bra, his touch exploring the soft, warm skin as he gently cupped her breast.

Clair moaned softly, her voice trembling with pleasure as she whispered, "Adam." She followed it with a breathy, "Yes," expressing her eagerness and desire.

Clair could feel the evidence of his arousal pushing into her thigh, which was just making her more desperate for his touch.

Adam gently pulled back, his expression serious and conflicted. "Clair," he said softly, "I think we should stop. This isn't right." His concern was evident as he looked at her, wanting to make sure they were both comfortable and fully aware of what was happening.

Clair's cheeks flushed with embarrassment, but her voice was firm as she looked into Adam's eyes. "I'm sorry," she said softly, "but I don't want to stop. I want this." Her hands remained on him, and her gaze conveyed both her desire and her vulnerability.

Adam's expression was etched with concern as he searched Clair's face, his hands resting lightly at her waist as though afraid to move too quickly. "Are you absolutely sure?" he asked gently. Though his body responded unmistakably to her closeness, his voice carried a quiet apprehension. He needed to know—needed to be certain—that this was what she truly wanted.

Clair lifted her chin and met his gaze without hesitation. Her eyes were steady, luminous with resolve and trust. "Yes," she said softly, but there was no wavering in her voice. "I want you." The words were simple, yet they carried the weight of choice and intention.

Adam drew in a slow breath, the tension in his chest easing as her certainty washed over him. "I want you too," he admitted, his voice low and thick with emotion, as though the confession itself altered something between them.

With deliberate tenderness, Adam lifted Clair from his lap, cradling her close as if she were something precious. He carried her down the hallway toward his bedroom, each step unhurried yet purposeful. The dim light spilling from the hallway lamps cast soft shadows across her face, illuminating the warmth in her eyes as she looked back at him, her arms instinctively tightening around his neck.

Inside the bedroom, Adam gently set Clair on her feet beside the bed. For a moment, neither of them moved. Then slowly, almost reverently, he reached for the buttons of her blouse. One by one, he eased them free, his fingertips brushing her skin with every motion. Clair mirrored him, her hands trembling slightly as she worked at the buttons of his shirt, the intimacy of undressing one another making her pulse quicken.

Their clothes slipped from their shoulders and fell forgotten to the floor. Adam reached behind her and unfastened her bra, letting it slide away. He paused then, taking her in fully. In the muted glow of the room, her skin looked impossibly soft, her curves inviting and real. His fingers curled slightly at his sides, aching to touch her. "You are beautiful," he murmured, the words spoken with quiet reverence.

Clair smiled, warmth blooming in her chest. "I was just about to say the same to you."

Adam's hand slid into her hair, fingers threading through the soft curls as he tipped her head back, exposing the delicate line of her throat. He kissed her there—slow, lingering kisses that made her breath falter—while his other hand found her breast, teasing and exploring with careful, practiced ease. Soft gasps escaped her lips as sensation rippled through her.

His mouth drifted lower, into the pale valley between her breasts, and with a low groan of satisfaction, he closed his mouth over one tight, rosy nipple. Heat flared instantly through her, a jolt so intense it stole her breath. His tongue rasped gently before circling, the sensation sending her spiralling.

Clair writhed against him, arching instinctively, her fingers clutching at his shoulders as she pleaded breathlessly for more.

Adam reached for the fastening of her skirt and let it fall to the floor. At the same time, Clair's hands moved to his trousers, undoing them with growing confidence, sliding the fabric from his hips. Their urgency grew, fuelled by mutual need and trust.

He lifted her once more and placed her carefully on the bed, arranging her against the pillows before removing the last of his own clothing. When he joined her, he did so slowly, his gaze never leaving hers.

Holding her eyes with a smouldering intensity, Adam traced a path down her stomach, his fingers stroking, teasing, learning her reactions. When his touch drifted lower, skimming the top of her panties, he leaned in to kiss her, slow and sweet, as though grounding her even as he unravelled her.

Her breath hitched sharply, a soft moan slipping free as his fingers slid to the apex of her thighs. His mouth claimed hers again, deeper this time, his tongue moving with intent as his hand explored the soft, yielding warmth beneath his touch.

Clair sobbed softly into his mouth, overwhelmed by the sensations building inside her. His fingers moved with confident ease now, sliding through the tender, moist folds of her most sensitive centre. Pressure built steadily, unfamiliar yet intoxicating, until she wasn't sure what she was seeking—only that she needed more.

Then pleasure exploded through her, blinding and powerful. She cried out his name, screaming it into his mouth. "Adam!"

He broke the kiss only to trail his lips down her neck, his body following as his mouth found her breast again. He took her nipple into his hot, wet mouth, sucking and licking while his fingers continued their intimate teasing. Clair trembled beneath him, sobbing with ecstasy as sensation coursed through her, her body surrendering completely to his touch.

Adam's mouth drifted lower, trailing warm, lingering kisses over her ribs until he reached her flat stomach. His hand slid upward, cupping and kneading her breast, his thumb circling slowly until her breath caught. She shivered beneath his touch, every nerve alive as his lips continued their unhurried descent.

He hooked his fingers into the waistband of her panties and eased them down her legs with deliberate care, baring her to him. Replacing the fabric with his mouth, he settled between her thighs, his tongue gliding through the wet, heated folds at her core. The intimate contact sent a sharp gasp tearing from her lips.

Clair's body arched instinctively, her hips lifting as Adam focused on the sensitive nub that made her cry out. His mouth worked her patiently, licking and sucking with practiced ease, drawing her higher and higher until sensation crowded out all thought.

"Adam… please!" she cried, her fingers tangling in his hair as pressure built relentlessly inside her.

He didn't stop. His mouth continued its slow torment until her body could no longer contain what he'd awakened. Pleasure burst through her in powerful waves, stealing her breath, her cry echoing his name as her body convulsed beneath him.

Only when her trembling subsided did Adam lift his head. His mouth moved back up her body, lingering over her breasts, capturing one nipple between his lips, rasping it gently with his tongue before giving the other the same exquisite attention. Clair whimpered softly, her body still sensitive, still aching.

When he finally positioned himself between her legs, she opened to him willingly, feeling the unmistakable heat of his arousal against her soft inner thighs. Adam kissed her neck, his breath warm against her skin as he whispered, low and intimate, "Clair, you're so beautiful. You're driving me crazy. I want to take you."

"Yes… please, Adam," she pleaded, her voice trembling. "Make me yours."

He aligned himself with her entrance, lingering just long enough to make her ache before easing into her slowly. She was tight, unbelievably warm, and he groaned at the sensation. Clair clung to him, uncertain but trusting, her body tense as he moved gently, giving her time to adjust.

Back and forth he moved, shallow at first, until the tension in her body eased, until her muscles softened and she began to arch against him, her need growing unmistakable. Then, with a deeper thrust, he sank fully into her, claiming her completely.

Clair's eyes flew open as a sharp cry escaped her lips. "Oh!"

Adam froze instantly, concern flickering across his face before tenderness replaced it. He smiled down at her softly, brushing his thumb along her cheek. "Now you're mine," he murmured, and began to move again, slowly, carefully, overwhelmed by her yielding warmth and innocence.

She wrapped herself around him as he lowered his mouth to hers, capturing her lips in a deeply erotic kiss. His tongue explored her mouth with the same intensity as his body explored hers, their movements finding a shared rhythm that swept Clair into a spiral of breathtaking sensation.

The tension built again, faster this time, until she cried out, her body shuddering as wave after wave of pleasure washed over her. Adam stiffened, a low, animal growl tearing from his throat as he followed her over the edge, climaxing with her.

After a while, he rolled onto his side, taking Clair with him, her body fitting perfectly along his. She rested against his chest, wrapped in the warmth and safety of his embrace. Exhausted and deeply content, the steady rise and fall of his breathing lulled her, and she drifted into a peaceful, bliss-filled sleep.

As Adam held Clair close, his thoughts turned inward. The realisation that she had been a virgin struck him deeply. He'd known she was inexperienced, but not untouched. The trust she had placed in him, the vulnerability she had offered so freely, filled him with awe and an unexpected sense of responsibility. Holding her now, he understood the significance of what they had shared—and felt the undeniable weight of how profoundly it had changed them both.

Clair woke up in an unfamiliar bed, the room dim and silent. As her mind began to clear, the events of the previous night came rushing back: the intense bond, the passion, and the profound intimacy she had shared with Adam. A mixture of realisation and emotion washed over her as she lay there, feeling both vulnerable and reflective.

She sat up, clutching the bed sheet tightly across her chest to cover her exposed breasts. Her heart raced as she glanced around the room, her thoughts a tangled mix of confusion and regret. The bed's warmth contrasted sharply with the cold realisation of what had happened. Clair struggled to piece together her emotions and understand the full impact of the night, her mind racing with the weight of her choices and their consequences.

Adam entered the room, wearing just a pair of shorts, with two cups of coffee in his hands, a gentle smile on his face. "You're awake," he said softly. "I thought you might like some coffee." He sat down on the edge of the bed and extended a cup toward her. The warmth of the coffee contrasted with the cool morning air, offering a small comfort as Clair took the cup from him.

She took the cup from Adam with a quiet "thank you" and brought it to her lips, savouring the warmth and the comforting aroma. As she sipped the coffee, her gaze flickered shyly toward Adam, her cheeks still flushed from the previous night. She felt a mix of gratitude and nervousness, unsure how to address the intimacy they had shared and what it meant moving forward.

Adam watched Clair with a concerned expression, gently setting his cup on the bedside table. He reached out, his hand brushing lightly against her arm. "Are you okay?" he asked softly, his tone filled with genuine worry. He studied her face, searching for any signs of discomfort or distress, hoping she was managing the whirlwind of emotions that followed their night together.

Clair looked up at Adam, her voice tinged with uncertainty. "I'm not really sure. This is all new to me." She took a hesitant sip of her coffee, her gaze flickering between him and the room.

Adam nodded understandingly, his expression softening. "I know," he said gently. "I understand it can be overwhelming. If you need anything or want to talk, I'm here." His reassurance was meant to comfort her, acknowledging the intensity of the situation without pressuring her.

Clair's voice was soft but tinged with concern. "Did I… pressure you into making love to me?" Her eyes met his, searching for the truth. The vulnerability in her question highlighted her need to understand if their intimacy had been driven by her actions or desires.

Adam's expression softened as he looked at Clair. "No," he said gently, "I wanted it as much as you did. It wasn't just you; I was just as eager and willing." His words were meant to reassure her, affirming that their shared experience was mutual and heartfelt.

Clair took a deep breath and looked up at Adam, her eyes filled with uncertainty. "I'm not sure how to act now," she admitted softly. "Everything feels so different, and I don't know what comes next or how to handle this." Her voice was tinged with vulnerability, struggling to find the right words, feeling both exposed and unsure in the aftermath of their night together.

Adam gazed at Clair with warmth and sincerity. "I hope we can do this again sometime," he said, his tone conveying genuine affection and a desire for continued connection. His words were meant to offer comfort and reassurance, suggesting that he valued what they had shared and was open to more.

Clair looked at Adam with a mixture of vulnerability and curiosity. "Really?" she asked softly. "I didn't think I was very good at it." Her self-doubt was evident, revealing her uncertainty about her performance and her longing for reassurance.

Adam's eyes were earnest as he responded, "Are you mad? You were amazing. I'm still in awe of how incredible it was." His words were intended to comfort her, highlighting his appreciation for their experience together.

Clair's cheeks flushed with a soft pink. "It was pretty great," she admitted shyly, her eyes meeting Adam's. "Well..., you were," she added with a small smile, her gratitude and affection clear in her expression.

Adam looked at Clair with a tender smile. "You know," he said softly, "I really think last night was incredible, and I feel like we have something special." His tone was warm and sincere, expressing his belief in their bond and the potential for something meaningful between them.

Clair looked down, her fingers nervously gripping the edge of the bed. "I'm not sure," she said softly. "I need to think about everything." Her voice was hesitant, reflecting her need to process the emotions and implications of their night together. She needed time to reflect on what it all meant for her and for their relationship.

Adam's expression softened, and a hint of disappointment flickered across his face. He nodded slowly, trying to mask his feelings. "Okay," he said gently, his tone supportive despite the subtle sadness in his eyes. He respected her need for time and space, even as he wished for a different outcome.

Clair looked at Adam with a mix of hesitation and resolve. "Adam," she began softly, "I think you might have to fire me." Her voice trembled slightly as she continued, "Given what's happened, it might be best if we keep our professional and personal lives separate." The words felt heavy, but she was trying to navigate the complexities of their situation with as much clarity as she could muster.

Adam asked, his voice steady yet tinged with concern, "Would you be more open to a relationship with me if I fired you?" His question was direct, seeking to understand if their professional dynamic was influencing her feelings.

Clair looked thoughtful, her gaze shifting as she considered the question. "I'm not sure," she finally replied, her voice soft and uncertain. "I need some time to figure things out." Her words reflected her confusion and the complexity of her emotions in the wake of their recent experiences.

Clair looked at Adam with a serious expression. "Can we keep this between us?" she asked softly. "I really don't want anyone at work to know about what happened."

Adam nodded, his face reflecting understanding. "I agree," he said. "It's probably best for now that we keep this private." His tone was reassuring, and he seemed to respect her desire for discretion, offering her a semblance of control over the situation.

Clair gave a small, nervous laugh, and added, "Does this mean I can start walking around in front of you naked?" Her attempt at humour was light-hearted, a way to ease the tension and regain some sense of normalcy after their intense conversation.

Adam chuckled softly and replied, "I wouldn't mind, as long as it's just the two of us in the room." His tone was playful yet reassuring, showing his comfort with their intimate relationship and his willingness to be open with Clair.

Clair placed her coffee cup on the bedside table and stood up from the bed, her movements slow and deliberate. She walked around the bed to Adam; her gaze filled with warmth and affection. As she reached him, she leaned in and pressed her lips to his in a passionate, lingering kiss. The kiss was full of the intimacy and rapport they had shared, a heartfelt gesture that spoke volumes about her feelings and the closeness they had achieved.

Adam's eyes twinkled with a playful glint as he pulled back slightly from the kiss. "If you keep doing that," he said with a smirk, "I might just have to give you a repeat performance." His tone was teasing, yet warm, as he made light of their intimate moment, hinting at the strong bond and attraction that still lingered between them.

Clair smiled; her cheeks flushed with a playful glow. "I wouldn't mind," she replied, her voice soft but filled with a hint of mischief. Her eyes met Adam's with a twinkle of affection, clearly enjoying their light-hearted exchange and the closeness they shared.

Adam reached out, pulling Clair gently onto his lap. He held her close, his hands resting on the small of her back as he looked up at her with a mixture of affection and desire. His embrace was warm and strong, making Clair feel secure as she nestled into him. Adam's lips brushed her forehead before he whispered, "You have no idea how much I want you right now."

"Almost as much as I want you." Clair whispered back.

With a shared look of desire, Adam and Claire tumbled together back on to the bed. Their bodies moved in sink as they fell into the soft sheets. Adam's arms wrapped tightly around Clair as they both laughed softly, the tension between them replaced by a warm, growing passion. The moment felt effortless as they sank into the mattress, their lips finding each other in the deep, lingering kiss. The world outside faded away, leaving only the two of them lost in the closeness of their embrace.

Chapter Fourteen

It was late in the afternoon when Adam finally drove Clair back to her car. The sun had dipped low in the sky, casting a golden hue over the city streets as they made the quiet drive. The atmosphere between them was warm but contemplative, the weight of the morning still lingering between their shared glances and comfortable silences.

When they arrived at the bar where Clair had left her car the night before, Adam pulled up next to it, turning off the engine. He looked over at her, a soft smile tugging at his lips. "Here we are," he said gently.

Clair smiled back, her heart fluttering with a mix of emotions, gratitude, uncertainty, and something deeper she couldn't quite name. "Thanks for everything," she said, her voice soft.

Adam nodded. "Anytime." He paused for a moment, as if he wanted to say more, but instead, he simply leaned over and pressed a lingering kiss on her forehead. Clair smiled as she got out of his car and moved to her own, glancing back one more time before slipping behind the wheel. As she drove away, her mind was swirling with thoughts of Adam and the new uncertainty between them.

Clair pulled into her driveway, the familiar sight of her home grounding her after the whirlwind of emotions from the past twenty-four hours. She stepped out of her car, feeling the weight of the day settling on her shoulders as she made her way inside.

As soon as she entered, the quiet calm of the house washed over her. She sighed softly and headed upstairs to her bedroom. Once there, she glanced at her reflection in the mirror, her hair slightly tousled and her eyes betraying the exhaustion of everything that had transpired.

Without hesitation, she moved to her closet and grabbed a fresh set of clothes, then walked to the bathroom. The sound of the shower turning on filled the room with steam as she let the warm water cascade over her. It felt soothing, washing away the stress, the tension, and the lingering traces of the emotions she had been wrestling with.

Clair closed her eyes, letting the water flow over her face, her thoughts still on Adam and their time together. She wasn't sure what came next, but for now, she focused on the simple relief of being home, clean, and wrapped in the quiet solitude of her own space.

After her shower, she changed into comfortable clothes and padded back to her room, feeling refreshed but still carrying the weight of unanswered questions in her heart.

Clair descended the stairs, the soft sound of her footsteps echoing in the quiet house. Her stomach growled, reminding her that she hadn't eaten much all day. The kitchen was still and familiar as she entered, the late afternoon light streaming through the windows, casting a warm glow on the countertops.

Clair opened the fridge, scanning its contents with little interest at first, still preoccupied with the swirl of emotions and thoughts from her time with Adam. Finally, she settled on a simple snack, some fruit and yogurt. As she prepared the small meal, the repetitive actions of slicing the fruit and mixing the yogurt helped soothe her mind, offering a momentary distraction from everything that had happened.

She carried her food to the kitchen table and sat down, taking small bites. The quiet of the house was a stark contrast to the whirlwind of emotions she was still trying to sort through. As she ate, her thoughts kept drifting back to Adam, the way they had connected, and the uncertainty of what that involvement meant for them moving forward. The simplicity of her snack, though comforting, didn't ease the complexity of her feelings.

Finishing her meal, Clair leaned back in her chair, the weight of the day still pressing on her. But for now, at least, she was home, with a moment to herself to breathe and think.

As Clair sat quietly at the kitchen table, the remnants of her small meal in front of her, her thoughts drifted back to the night with Adam. She couldn't help but wonder if Adam had known she was a virgin. The way he had been so gentle, so patient, it was as if he sensed her inexperience. She hadn't expected it to happen like that, not at nearly twenty-three, but she hadn't been particularly concerned about it either.

What surprised her more was the feeling of contentment that settled over her when she thought about Adam being the one who introduced her to the art of love. Despite the whirlwind of emotions, she felt a deep sense of peace knowing that it had been with him, someone who cared enough to make the experience special.

Clair wasn't naïve; she understood that relationships could be complicated, and what they had now might become even more so. Yet, she couldn't help but smile softly at the thought of Adam, how he had held her, kissed her, and made her feel truly wanted. The uncertainty of what lay ahead lingered in her mind, along with her suspicions about him and Elizabeth. Still, she couldn't deny the joy that came from knowing her first experience had been with someone like him. It felt right in a way she hadn't anticipated.

As Clair stood from the table and stretched, she glanced around the quiet house. The stillness told her that her father and Elizabeth must be out for the evening. The thought brought a sense of relief, she didn't feel like answering any questions or making conversation right now. All she wanted was a moment to herself, to process everything that had happened, and to rest.

Her body ached in ways she hadn't experienced before, a gentle reminder of the intensity of the previous night and morning with Adam. Every muscle seemed to hum with a mixture of exhaustion and satisfaction, making her long for the comfort of her bed.

Deciding that an early night was exactly what she needed, Clair made her way upstairs, each step a reminder of the new sensations that had overtaken her body. The exhaustion was more than physical; it was emotional too. The weight of everything that had changed between her and Adam was pressing down on her, and sleep seemed like the best way to escape it for a little while.

She entered her room, the familiar space bringing her a sense of calm. Without overthinking it, she slipped out of her clothes, feeling the soreness in her limbs as she moved, and crawled into bed. The sheets were cool against her skin, and as her head hit the pillow, she closed her eyes, grateful for the quiet and the chance to rest.

Tomorrow would bring more questions, more things to consider, but for now, sleep was all she wanted.

The next morning, Clair woke feeling refreshed, her body no longer aching from the events of the day before. The sunlight streamed through her curtains, filling the room with a soft, warm glow. For the first time in what felt like days, she felt ready for the day ahead.

After a quick workout in the home gym, she indulged in a long, hot shower, letting the water wash away any lingering tension. Wrapping herself in a soft robe, she moved with a newfound lightness, as though the weight of her thoughts had eased overnight.

Dressed and ready, Clair made her way to the terrace where the familiar sound of her father's voice and the clinking of breakfast plates greeted her. Her father, Samuel, sat at the head of the table, a newspaper in hand, while Elizabeth, sipped on her tea. The morning air was fresh, and the scent of coffee and warm pastries filled the space.

Clair leaned down and kissed her father on the cheek. "Good morning, dad," she said, her voice bright and cheerful.

He father smiled at her, folding his paper. "Good morning, sweetheart. You're up early."

Clair then turned to Elizabeth and greeted her with equal warmth. "Good morning, Elizabeth," she said, offering a smile.

Elizabeth returned the smile with a nod, her eyes observing Clair as she sat down at the table. "Good morning, Clair. You seem in a good mood today."

Clair nodded, feeling surprisingly at ease. "I slept well," she replied simply, though her mind briefly flickered back to the events with Adam. But for now, she was content to enjoy breakfast and the easy rhythm of the morning.

Her father, Samuel, leaned back in his chair, sipping his coffee as he looked across the table at her. His expression was relaxed, but there was a subtle curiosity in his eyes.

"So, where did you disappear to yesterday?" he asked, his tone casual, as if he were asking about the weather. His gaze, however, lingered on her, studying her reaction with the quiet attentiveness only a parent could have.

Clair shifted in her seat, trying to keep her composure. She knew this question was coming but had hoped to avoid it. With a quick smile, she shrugged. "Just spent some time with a friend."

Her father raised an eyebrow slightly, not pressing her but clearly not fully satisfied. He nodded slowly, taking another sip. "Alright, just wondering." His words hung in the air, gentle yet probing.

She took a deep breath, forcing a casual smile. "I, uh, drank a bit too much on Friday," she admitted, her eyes flickering up to meet his for a second before quickly looking back down. "I ended up staying at a friend's house. And, well... we decided to make a day of it."

He leaned back slightly, his expression calm but thoughtful. He didn't speak right away, simply nodding as he processed what she'd said. His silence made Clair's stomach tighten, but she kept her tone light. "It wasn't anything crazy, just... you know, one of those spontaneous things."

Her father raised an eyebrow, his lips twitching into a subtle smile. "A bit too much, huh?" His voice was easy, not judgmental, but there was a hint of something knowing behind his words.

Clair laughed nervously, shrugging. "Yeah, just a bit. But it was fine, really." She tried to sound convincing, hoping to put an end to the conversation.

He nodded again, his smile lingering. "Alright, just wanted to make sure you're okay. I'm glad you had fun." He took another sip of his coffee, letting the subject drop, but Clair could tell from the look in his eyes that he wasn't completely satisfied with her answer. Still, he let it go for now, giving her the space she needed.

After breakfast, Clair excused herself and made her way upstairs to her room, her footsteps soft against the familiar creak of the floorboards. Once inside, she closed the door gently behind her, leaning against it for a moment. The weight of everything that had happened on Friday night with Adam was still pressing on her, and the conversation with her father had only added to her unease.

She crossed the room, her eyes scanning for her mobile phone, which lay on her bedside table, half-hidden under a book. Grabbing it, she sat on the edge of the bed, her fingers brushing across the screen as she unlocked it.

Lily. Her best friend. Clair's thoughts drifted to her, knowing that if anyone could help her make sense of the mess in her head, it would be Lily. She'd know how to listen, how to ask the right questions, without making Clair feel judged.

As she scrolled to Lily's name in her contacts, Clair paused. A part of her wasn't sure she was ready to talk about Adam, about what had transpired Friday night, the confusion still so raw. But maybe that was exactly why she needed to. She sighed, her thumb hovering over the call button. *I need to talk this through,* she thought. *I can't keep it bottled up.*

Finally, she tapped the screen, the phone ringing softly in her hand.

The phone barely rang twice before Lily's familiar, cheerful voice filled the line.

"Hey, Clair! What's up?" she greeted brightly. "I'm just having a quiet day at home. Nothing too exciting, what about you?"

Clair gripped the phone tighter, her heart pounding in her chest. She had rehearsed what she might say a hundred times, but now, with Lily on the other end, her thoughts tumbled out in a rush, unfiltered.

"I lost my virginity on Friday night."

There was a pause on the other end. The air seemed to still as Clair's words hung between them. Lily, always quick with a response, was momentarily silent, the cheerful tone from moments before fading into something more serious, more grounded.

"Wait, what?" Lily finally said, her voice softening with concern. "Clair... are you okay?"

Clair could hear the concern in Lily's voice and quickly rushed to reassure her. "Yes, yes, I'm okay," she said, her voice steadier now. "Really, I am."

She took a breath, trying to find the right words to explain. "It wasn't... I mean, it wasn't bad at all. It was actually kind of... a beautiful experience. A woman's needful experience, you know? Something I felt I was ready for. And Adam, he was really gentle, Lily. He didn't rush me, he was patient, and..." She hesitated, a small smile tugging at the corners of her mouth. "He was passionate. In a way that made me feel safe."

Lily was quiet for a moment, absorbing what Clair was saying. "Okay," she finally replied, her tone soft, but no longer filled with the same urgency. "If you're sure you're alright, Clair. That's what matters most."

Clair nodded to herself, feeling a small sense of relief. "I am," she repeated, more confidently this time. "It was right for me, in that moment."

Lily's initial concern quickly shifted into curiosity, her tone brightening as she leaned into the conversation. "Really?" she asked, a playful edge creeping into her voice. "So, was it actually *good*? Like, worth the wait? I mean, you always said you'd know when the time was right, but did it live up to what you imagined?"

Clair could almost picture the mischievous grin on Lily's face. Before Clair could respond, Lily continued, half-joking but clearly intrigued. "Because, honestly, I've been thinking about it too. If I found a guy, I'd feel comfortable enough with, someone who'd make me feel safe like that... maybe I'd be ready, you know?" Her voice softened, a hint of seriousness returning. "I guess I'm just trying to figure out if it's really as special as everyone says."

Lily's openness made Clair smile. She understood the mix of curiosity and vulnerability her friend was feeling.

Clair leaned back against her pillows, her eyes drifting as she remembered the moment. A soft, dreamy smile crossed her face as she spoke.

"It was... actually beautiful, Lily," she said, her voice almost a whisper, as if reliving it all over again. "More than I expected, honestly. It wasn't just about the physical part, it was the way he looked at me, the way he made sure I felt safe and... cherished." She paused, her smile deepening, her heart fluttering a little. "And yeah... you definitely want to do it again. You know?"

There was a warm, almost wistful tone in her voice, as if she was savouring the memory, letting herself fall back into the feelings that had overwhelmed her that night. "It's not just about the act itself. It's everything around it that makes you want to experience it again."

Clair let out a small laugh, feeling a little shy for being so open, but knowing Lily would understand.

Lily's curiosity seemed to grow with every word Clair shared. She hesitated for a moment, then asked, "Did you... did you do it again?" Her voice was tentative but eager, a blend of genuine interest and concern.

The question hung in the air between them, and Clair felt her cheeks flush slightly. She took a moment to gather her thoughts before answering, her heart racing a bit from the directness of Lily's inquiry.

Clair took a deep breath before replying, "Yes," she said softly, her voice almost shy. "We did it multiple times the next morning."

She chuckled softly, her nerves easing as she spoke. "It felt right, and it was... just so wonderful. We were both really in tune with each other, and it felt like the right way to start the day."

There was a pause, and Clair could almost hear Lily processing the news, her curiosity momentarily satisfied but perhaps replaced with even more questions.

Lily's reaction was a mix of admiration and practicality. "Wow," she said, her tone reflecting genuine surprise and a touch of envy. "You're really lucky you chose a guy who was gentle and caring like that."

Her voice took on a more serious note as she continued. "But I have to ask, are you on the pill? Or using some other form of birth control? I mean, it's important to be safe."

There was a hint of concern in her question, underlining her genuine care for Clair's well-being.

Clair nodded, grateful for Lily's concern. "Yeah, I'm on the pill," she replied, her tone reassuring. "I had to start it last year because my periods were too erratic."

She leaned back, feeling a mix of relief and pride in being prepared. "I was glad I was because I didn't have to worry about that." She smiled, knowing that she had taken the necessary steps to feel secure in her choices.

Lily let out a relieved sigh, her voice brightening. "Good! That's a relief to hear," she said, clearly feeling more at ease. "So, tell me about this Adam. Who is he? Is he handsome? How old is he?"

Clair could hear the excitement in Lily's tone, and she felt a rush of energy thinking about Adam. "Well," she began, her smile returning as she thought of him. "He's really attractive, definitely my type. And he's not too old; I think he's around thirty-two years old. He has this charming vibe that just draws you in."

Clair's enthusiasm was palpable as she continued, eager to share more about the person who had made such an impression on her.

Lily's interest piqued, and she replied, "Thirty-two, huh? An experienced guy then."

Clair took a deep breath, the excitement in her voice shifting to uncertainty. "Actually, Adam is my dad's business partner," she admitted, a hint of apprehension creeping in. "So now I'm not sure what I should do about work."

She glanced out the window, her mind racing with the implications of their involvement. "I mean, it's all so complicated now. I don't want it to affect anything professionally, but it feels... different. I really like him, but I also have to consider how it might look."

Her expression turned thoughtful as she pondered the potential fallout of their relationship intertwining with her immediate career.

Lily's eyebrows furrowed slightly as she processed Clair's words. "Do you work closely with this Adam?" she asked, her tone a mix of curiosity and concern. "I mean, how often do you see him at the office?"

Clair nodded, feeling the weight of the question. "Yeah, I do. We have a few interactions together, and I've been in meetings with him a few times. It's not just a casual connection." She paused, considering how much to reveal. "I guess that makes everything a bit more complicated."

Clair continued, her tone brightening as she spoke about work. "You know, I actually like the job more than I thought I would," she admitted. "At first, I was worried everyone would just see me as the boss's daughter, but no one has treated me that way. The job really challenges me in a good way."

Lily nodded, her voice encouraging. "You know, if you like the job, don't give it up just yet," she advised. "See how things pan out. He might be really professional about it, and I know you will be. Just play it by ear and see what happens."

Her tone was reassuring, as if she were trying to help Clair navigate the complexity of her feelings and the workplace dynamics. "You deserve to enjoy both your job and your personal life, so don't rush into any decisions."

Clair smiled, feeling a sense of relief wash over her. "Yeah, you're right. Thank you, Lily. I knew I could count on you to help me clear my mind."

They continued to chat a bit longer, discussing everything from work to their plans for the rest of the weekend, the conversation flowing easily as it always did. Eventually, they wrapped things up, and Clair felt a lightness in her heart.

"Alright, I'll talk to you later," she said, her tone warm.

"Bye, Clair! Take care!" Lily replied before they both hung up, leaving Clair feeling more grounded and hopeful about what lay ahead.

After hanging up, Clair tucked her mobile phone into her pocket, a sense of calm settling over her. She stood for a moment, gathering her thoughts before heading downstairs. The soft sunlight filtered through the windows as she made her way to the door.

Once outside, she stepped onto the path that wound through her father's estate. The grounds were lush and beautifully maintained, with vibrant flowers lining the walkway and the gentle sound of birds chirping in the background.

As she walked, Clair breathed in the fresh air, letting the peaceful surroundings soothe her mind. She felt a sense of freedom in the open space, allowing her thoughts to drift as she took in the beauty of the estate, feeling more centred with each step.

As Clair walked along the path, lost in her thoughts, her mobile phone suddenly buzzed in her pocket, jolting her back to the moment. She fished it out and saw Adam's name on the screen. A flutter of excitement mixed with nerves coursed through her as she answered.

"Hello?" she said, trying to keep her voice steady.

"Hi, Clair," Adam's voice came through, warm and familiar. "I just wanted to check in and see how you're doing. Hope everything's okay?"

Clair felt a smile spreading across her face at the sound of his voice. "Yeah, I'm good, just taking a walk," she replied, her heart racing a little. "How about you?"

Adam chuckled softly on the other end. "I was actually just thinking about you," he said, a hint of warmth in his voice. "I went to the gym earlier, and now I'm just catching up on a bit of work."

Clair felt a flutter of happiness at his words. "That sounds productive," she replied, feeling a bond growing as they chatted. "How was the gym?"

"It was good," he said, his tone playful. "It helps clear my head. What about you?"

Clair replied, "Oh, not much. I worked out for a while, had breakfast, chatted with my best friend, Lily, took a walk, and now I'm talking to you... not much, really."

"Sounds relaxing," Adam replied, his voice light. Then, with a shift in tone, he added, "But honestly, I actually miss you."

Clair felt a warmth spread through her at his words, a mixture of happiness and longing. "I miss you too," she said, her heart racing as she realised just how much she missed him.

Adam let out a cheeky laugh. "I might have to fire you," he joked, a playful glint in his voice. "I'm not sure I'll be able to stay away from you at work!"

Clair couldn't help but laugh along, feeling a lightness in their banter. "Well, I guess that's a risk we'll have to take!" she replied, her heart fluttering at the thought of their playful relationship.

They chatted for a bit longer, their conversation flowing easily as they joked and shared stories. Clair felt completely at ease, the earlier tension melting away while talking to Adam.

Eventually, he sighed, a hint of reluctance in his voice. "As much as I'd love to keep talking, I should probably get some work done," he said, sounding slightly disappointed. "I'll try not to let you distract me too much."

Clair smiled, knowing he was only half-joking. "Okay, but don't work too hard!" she replied, wishing the conversation could continue a bit longer.

They exchanged goodbyes and hung up, leaving Clair with a lingering warmth from their chat.

Clair spent the rest of the day in a peaceful haze, enjoying the tranquillity of her surroundings. She took her time with simple tasks, savouring a book in the garden and preparing a light dinner for herself. As the sun began to set, she reflected on her conversation with Adam, the warmth of their connection still lingering in her mind.

When evening arrived, she settled into her cozy bed, the soft sheets wrapping around her like a comforting embrace. A smile danced on her lips as she replayed their playful banter and the way he had expressed how much he missed her.

Feeling content and happy, Clair closed her eyes, letting the gentle sounds of the night lull her into a restful sleep, her heart light with possibilities for tomorrow.

Chapter Fifteen

As Clair arrived at work on Monday morning, she was met with a caring atmosphere. Ryan and Emily approached her, their faces filled with concern.

"Clair, are you okay?" Ryan asked, his voice low and sincere. "We were really worried about you after what happened on Friday night."

Emily nodded, her eyes wide with worry. "Yeah, we just wanted to check in. It must have been really frightening."

Clair took a moment to absorb their concern, feeling a mix of gratitude and anxiety. "I'm okay, really," she replied, forcing a reassuring smile. "It was a scary situation, you all helped me, thank goodness, and Adam got me home safely."

Ryan and Emily exchanged a glance, clearly still unsure. "If you need to talk or anything, we're here for you," Emily said gently.

Clair appreciated their support, knowing it would help her navigate the week ahead. However, they didn't realise that her relationship with Adam was the one thing weighing heavily on her mind at the moment.

Ryan approached Clair quietly, his expression serious as he studied her face. "Clair, are you really okay?" he asked softly, his concern evident in his eyes. The weight of his worry hung in the air, and Clair could tell he was genuinely troubled by her well-being. She appreciated his thoughtfulness, knowing he was someone she could lean on during a difficult time.

Clair smiled gently at Ryan, sensing his concern. "I'm really okay," she reassured him. "Adam got me home safe and sound after everything that happened."

She could see a hint of relief wash over Ryan's face, and she continued, "It was a scary situation, but I'm handling it. Thank you for checking in on me." Her words were sincere, and she hoped to ease some of his worry.

Ryan nodded, his expression softening. "Good, because I was worried about Adam too," he said quietly. "When he heard someone was hurting you, he looked like he was going to kill that guy. He looked like the devil himself."

His words conveyed the depth of his concern, and Clair could see how much he truly cared about her. She appreciated his protective nature, even as a twinge of unease crept in at the thought of Adam's intense reaction.

Clair took a deep breath, trying to find the right words. "Adam has known me for a long time," she explained. "And I think if my dad knew he was there when I got hurt, it wouldn't go down well. He understands that."

She glanced away for a moment, feeling the weight of the situation pressing on her. "I just want to forget it ever happened," she added, hoping Ryan would grasp her desire to move on.

Ryan nodded, accepting what Clair was saying. "I get it," he replied, his tone supportive. "Just know I'm here for you if you need anything."

With a reassuring smile, he turned to head back to his desk, leaving Clair feeling grateful for his understanding and support as she prepared to tackle the rest of her day.

Clair focused intently on her work, immersing herself in the tasks at hand. She made a conscious effort not to look up when Adam walked into the office to grab some paperwork.

She could sense his presence nearby, feeling his gaze on her, but she kept her eyes fixed on the screen, trying to push aside the swirl of emotions and thoughts about their recent encounter. The sound of papers rustling, and the faint scent of his cologne lingered in the air, yet she remained determined to stay concentrated, hoping to avoid any unnecessary interaction.

Adam finally broke the silence, his voice cutting through the tension. "So, have you recovered from Friday?" He made sure Ryan and Emily could hear; his tone casual yet concerned.

Clair glanced up to meet his gaze. "Yes, I'm okay. Thank you for taking me home," she replied, feeling a mix of gratitude and anxiety.

Adam nodded, then asked, "You managed to get your car back?"

"Yes, thanks. Thompson helped me out," Clair answered, trying to keep the conversation light while navigating the unspoken complexities between them.

"Good," Adam said, his expression softening for a moment before he turned to leave the office, the weight of the moment lingering in the air.

The rest of the day passed without any further incidents, the routine of work helping Clair to push aside her lingering thoughts. As the clock neared five o'clock, her desk phone rang, pulling her attention away from her tasks.

"Hello?" she answered, recognising Adam's personal assistant's voice on the other end.

"Clair, Adam would like to see you in his office," Craig said.

Clair felt her heart skip a beat, but she kept her tone calm. "Oh, okay." She couldn't shake the feeling that this might take longer than she expected.

Thinking about Ryan and Emily, she turned to them and said, "Have a good night!"

"Good night," they replied, watching her leave the office with a mix of curiosity and concern as she headed toward Adam's office.

Clair found Craig packing up for the day as she entered the office. He looked up and smiled. "Go straight in," he instructed, gesturing toward Adam's office.

Taking a deep breath, Clair approached the door and slowly opened it, slipping into the room and closing the door. To her surprise, Adam must have been pacing near the entrance, as he quickly stepped forward, grabbing her and pulling her into his arms. Without hesitation, he kissed her, the intensity of the moment catching her off guard and sending a rush of warmth through her.

Clair melted into the kiss almost immediately, surrendering to the warmth and familiarity of Adam's embrace. They shared the kiss for a while, the union between them deepening as he held her tighter.

Eventually, he pulled back reluctantly, still keeping her in his arms. "I've been wanting to do that all day," he said, a hint of a smile on his lips.

Clair laughed softly, her heart racing. "So have I," she replied, feeling a rush of joy at their shared moment.

Adam looked at Clair, his expression hopeful. "Can I see you tonight?"

Clair pretended to ponder the question, feigning deep thought. "Mmm, maybe. I'll have to check my calendar," she replied playfully.

Adam squeezed her gently, then quickly kissed her cheek. "Don't torture me," he said with a teasing grin, his eyes sparkling with anticipation. Clair couldn't help but smile, enjoying the light-hearted banter between them.

Clair looked up at Adam, her smile fading slightly as she added, "I'll need to let my father know first. He worries, you know."

Adam nodded, understanding the importance of her father's concern. "Of course," he replied, still holding her gaze. "But yes?"

Clair smiled again, feeling a rush of excitement. "Yes," she confirmed. "I'd love to see you tonight."

Adam let out a relieved sigh. "Thank goodness!" he exclaimed, swinging Clair around playfully.

Clair squealed in surprise, laughter bubbling up as she wrapped her arms around his neck, caught off guard by his sudden burst of joy. The moment felt carefree and exhilarating, bringing a smile to her face that she couldn't shake.

Clair giggled and asked Adam, "Okay, can you put me down now?" He obliged, giving her another quick kiss on the lips before setting her back on her feet, releasing her gently.

"Do you want me to meet you at your place?" she asked, her heart racing with anticipation.

"Yes," he replied, his eyes brightening. "Is it okay if we order takeout and watch a movie?"

Clair beamed at him. "That sounds lovely," she said, feeling a wave of excitement.

With a big smile on her face, she turned and left Adam in his office, the prospect of the evening ahead lighting up her thoughts.

Clair returned to her office to pack up, noticing that Ryan and Emily had already left for the day. Once she gathered her things, she made her way to her father's office.

Karen, his personal assistant, looked up with a friendly smile. "He's free," she said. "You can go straight in if you like."

Clair thanked her and took a deep breath, preparing herself before walking into her father's office, ready to update him on her plans for the evening.

Clair stepped into her father's office and greeted him with a warm smile. "Dad, I just wanted to let you know I won't be home for dinner. I'm going out with a friend."

Her father raised an eyebrow, curiosity evident in his expression. "Is it the same one from Friday night?" he asked, his tone hinting at concern.

Clair felt a slight flutter in her stomach but nodded. "Yes, it is," she replied, gauging his reaction. She hoped to reassure him as she shared this new development.

Her father's expression softened, and he looked a bit more relaxed. "Okay, sweetheart, have a good time," he said with a smile. "It's just that Elizabeth thinks you have a boyfriend."

Clair felt a wave of heat wash over her. "Does she? Why?"

"She says it's woman's intuition or something like that," he replied dismissively.

Clair shrugged, trying to maintain her composure. "No, no boyfriend yet," she said, feeling a pang of guilt for lying to her father.

"Okay, sweetheart, I'll see you tomorrow," her father said with a playful grin. "We'll probably be in bed before you get home. Us oldies don't have as much stamina as you young ones," he laughed, easing the mood.

Clair couldn't help but chuckle along, appreciating his humour. "Have a good night," she replied with a smile before turning and leaving.

Clair stepped into the lift, her mind already swirling as she descended to the ground level. The quiet hum of the elevator did little to soothe her thoughts. Once the doors slid open, she walked briskly to her car, unlocking it and sliding into the driver's seat.

For a moment, she just sat there, hands resting on the steering wheel, letting her thoughts run wild. Her feelings for Adam were undeniable, strong, deep, and complicated. She had harboured them since she was sixteen, a crush that had evolved into something much more over the years. But now, she was unsure of just how strong his feelings were for her.

And then there was Elizabeth. The suspicion that Adam had been involved with her gnawed at the back of Clair's mind. She didn't believe it now, not really, but it had cost her so much, years of strained relationships with her father and Adam. That nagging suspicion, though, the possibility that nothing ever happened between Adam and Elizabeth, made her feel the weight of wasted time. Time she could never get back.

Her chest tightened as she thought about what that meant for the future, for her feelings, and for the relationship she was now daring to explore with Adam.

Clair's mind drifted back to the moment she had confronted Adam about her suspicions. It had been a tense conversation, her voice shaky as she told him she believed he had been having an affair with Elizabeth or at least had one.

Adam's reaction had been immediate, shock flickering across his face, quickly followed by anger. "You really think I'd do that?" he had asked, his voice low but filled with hurt. His eyes had searched hers, as if trying to understand how she could even entertain such a thought.

In that instant, Clair realised she might have been wrong. She remembered the weight of guilt settling over her as she sat there, feeling small and ashamed for doubting him. His reaction was too genuine, too raw. Now, she believed him, fully and completely. The years of mistrust, the emotional distance she had created between them, all of it seemed foolish now. She was sure she had been wrong all those years ago.

But even with that clarity, the regret of what she'd lost lingered.

Chapter Sixteen

Clair took a deep breath, started her car, and pulled out of the parking lot. As she drove through the city streets, her thoughts were still tangled in everything that had happened between her and Adam. The familiar route to his apartment block felt different this time, more charged with anticipation.

She arrived at his sleek apartment building and parked, her heart beating a little faster as she walked inside and took the lift to the penthouse. The ride up felt like an eternity, the soft hum of the elevator doing nothing to calm her nerves.

When the doors slid open, she stepped out, walking the short distance to Adam's door. She hesitated for a moment, then knocked softly.

Within seconds, the door swung open, revealing Adam standing there with a warm smile. "Hey," he said, his voice soft but laced with something more, relief, or perhaps excitement. Clair couldn't help but smile back.

Clair smiled softly as she said, "Hi," and leaned in to give Adam a quick kiss on the cheek as she stepped inside. The familiar scent of his cologne filled the air, instantly making her feel at ease.

As Adam closed the door behind her, he asked, "So, what do you feel like for dinner?"

Clair turned to him, a playful glint in her eyes. "You," she teased, slipping her arms around his neck with a mischievous grin. The warmth of her touch and the flirtatious energy between them sent a spark through the air, making Adam chuckle.

"You're trouble," Adam murmured, his hands settling on her waist as he leaned in. Clair tilted her face up toward him, her lips parting slightly, silently inviting him to kiss her. The tension between them crackled, and Adam didn't hesitate, closing the distance and capturing her lips in a slow, lingering kiss.

Adam pulled away reluctantly, his forehead resting lightly against hers as he looked into her eyes with a serious expression. "Clair," he began, his voice low and sincere, "I don't want you to think all I want from you is sex."

His gaze softened as he spoke, clearly wanting her to understand. "There's so much more to this, to us, than just that."

Clair smiled up at Adam, her eyes full of trust. "This is all new to me," she admitted softly. "I really haven't thought much about what you want. I'm just going with the flow and doing what feels right."

Her smile widened slightly, and she added with a playful warmth, "And I like you touching and kissing me."

Adam's face lit up, a mixture of happiness and relief washing over him. "I'm glad," he said with a grin. "Because I like touching and kissing you too, maybe a little too much."

His tone was playful, but there was an underlying sincerity that made Clair's heart flutter. The weight of the moment lifted, leaving them both smiling, content in the unspoken connotation between them.

After a moment of shared smiles, Adam cleared his throat, returning to his earlier question. "So, what do you feel like for dinner?" he asked, his tone light but curious, eager to hear her response. He leaned back slightly, giving her his full attention as he awaited her answer, the playful atmosphere still lingering between them.

Clair disengaged gently from Adam, a teasing smile still on her lips as she walked over to the lounge and settled onto the couch. She looked back at him playfully. "I still like my first response, but if you insist, I choose food, how about Chinese?"

Her tone was light, and she felt a spark of excitement at the idea of sharing a meal with him, the atmosphere buzzing with easy rapport. Adam chuckled, clearly enjoying her playful spirit.

Adam nodded, a grin spreading across his face. "Okay, Chinese it is! I'll go ahead and order it," he said, moving toward his phone.

As he paused, he turned back to Clair. "Do you like or dislike anything in particular?"

Clair shook her head, her smile reassuring. "No, anything will be fine," she replied, feeling relaxed as she settled into the cozy atmosphere of his apartment. Adam smiled, clearly pleased with her easy-going nature, and began placing the order.

Adam finished placing the order for the Chinese food, then turned to Clair with a warm smile. "Would you like a glass of wine?" he asked.

"Yes, I would," she replied, her eyes brightening at the suggestion.

He moved to the kitchen, quickly pouring two glasses before returning to the lounge. Handing one to her, he settled onto the couch beside her. They both took a sip, the rich flavour of the wine adding to the relaxed atmosphere. As they sat together, the room felt filled with a comfortable intimacy, their earlier conversation lingering in the air.

Adam took a sip of his wine and glanced at Clair. "So, how was your day?" he asked, genuinely curious.

Clair shrugged lightly, a smile playing on her lips. "Uneventful, really. Just busy, but I like being busy," she replied. The rhythm of her day kept her grounded, and she appreciated the feeling of productivity. Adam nodded, understanding that sense of fulfillment as they continued to enjoy each other's company.

Clair turned to Adam, a playful glint in her eyes. "So, how was your day?" she asked, genuinely curious.

Adam leaned back, a smile on his lips. "It was good, just the usual work stuff."

Clair tilted her head, her expression mischievous. "Win any more big court cases?"

He chuckled, shaking his head. "Not today, just the usual legal battles." The playful exchange added a light-heartedness to their evening, making them both feel at ease.

Clair's phone rang in her bag, pulling her attention away from Adam. "Sorry," she said, digging it out and answering, "Hello?"

"Hi, Clair! It's Christian," came the familiar voice.

"Oh, hi Christian! How are you?" she replied, a hint of surprise in her tone.

He asked if she had a good day, and she answered, "Yes, it was nice, thank you."

Christian then inquired if she was free on Saturday, causing Clair to blush slightly. "I'm not sure; I'll have to get back to you," she said, trying to keep her voice steady.

"Okay," he replied. They exchanged goodbyes, and Clair hung up, feeling a mix of emotions as she turned back to Adam, her heart racing a little.

Clair took a deep breath, turning to Adam with a slightly serious expression. "That was Christian," she said, her tone honest. "He was asking if I was free on Saturday."

She paused, gauging his reaction. "I want to be upfront with you about it," she continued. "I don't want anything to come between us." Her eyes met his, seeking understanding as she laid her cards on the table.

Adam's expression shifted slightly, a hint of jealousy creeping into his voice. "I hope you're going to tell him you're not free," he said, his brow furrowing.

Clair sensed the tension in his tone and felt a warmth spread through her. "Of course I am," she replied, wanting to reassure him. "But I want to explain that it was never going to happen. I knew that the first time he kissed me. I don't want to be cruel about it, though, because he really is a nice guy."

Adam relaxed a bit, his shoulders easing as he nodded. "Fair enough," he said, though a hint of curiosity lingered in his voice. "But why was it never going to happen? Just curious, he is a good-looking guy."

Clair met his gaze, understanding the underlying tension. "He is," she admitted, "but I just didn't feel anything when he kissed me. When you kissed me that first time, even though you were angry at me, I felt something." She waved her hand between them, emphasising the connection. "It was different. There was a spark."

Adam smiled, his expression turning soft and sincere. "I've wanted to kiss you since you turned eighteen," he said, a hint of playful nostalgia in his voice. The warmth in his eyes made Clair's heart flutter, and she felt the weight of those unspoken feelings hanging between them, rich with possibility.

Clair looked at Adam, her brow slightly furrowed in curiosity. "Why did you kiss me that night when you were angry with me?" she asked, her voice steady but tinged with intrigue. She leaned in slightly, eager to understand the complexity of that moment and the emotions that had driven him to act against his feelings of frustration.

Adam took a deep breath, his expression thoughtful. "I was frustrated with you," he admitted, running a hand through his hair. "But in that moment, I just felt like it. There was so much tension, and despite my anger, I couldn't help myself. It was like all the feelings I'd been pushing aside just came rushing to the surface." His gaze held hers, revealing the depth of his emotions behind the frustration.

Clair smiled softly, her eyes sparkling with appreciation. "Well, I'm glad you did," she said. "Because if you hadn't kissed me, I don't think I would have noticed anything *different* about Christian kissing me." She paused, reflecting on how that moment had changed everything for her, highlighting the relationship she truly desired.

Adam nodded, a smile spreading across his face. "I'm glad too," he replied, his voice warm. "I felt something *different* as well." He met her gaze, the sincerity in his eyes conveying how meaningful that moment had been for him. The air between them buzzed with unspoken understanding, deepening the bond they shared.

Clair, feeling the moment shift, put her glass on the coffee table and grinned. "In that case, I think it's about time you did it again."

Adam laughed, his eyes sparkling with mischief. He set his glass down as well, then pulled Clair onto his lap, drawing her close. Their lips met, and the kiss deepened, igniting the familiar spark that had brought them together in the first place.

Just as the kiss intensified, a knock at the door broke the moment. Adam's expression shifted to annoyance, clearly irritated by the interruption. Clair slid off his lap, a hint of disappointment in her eyes as she watched him rise. He sighed, running a hand through his hair, and walked toward the door, trying to mask his frustration as he opened it.

Adam opened the door to find the delivery boy holding a bag of steaming Chinese food. He exchanged a quick thanks and took the food, bringing it into the kitchen. Clair got up to join him, excitement bubbling in her chest as she grabbed plates and cutlery from the drawers. Together, they set the dining table, the tantalizing aroma of the food filling the air and momentarily distracting them from the earlier interruption.

As they settled down at the dining table, the atmosphere became lively. Clair and Adam dug into their meal, sharing bites and flavours while engaging in light-hearted conversation. Laughter filled the room as they playfully teased each other about their food choices and past experiences. With each shared story and playful jab, their relationship deepened. Before long, they were both stuffed, leaning back in their chairs, unable to eat another thing, their plates nearly empty. The warmth of their shared moments lingered as they exchanged satisfied smiles.

After finishing dinner, Clair and Adam cleared the table together, stacking plates and packing away the leftover food. Once the kitchen was tidy, they settled onto the couch, the cozy atmosphere wrapping around them.

Adam turned to her, curiosity in his voice. "What do you want to watch?"

"Anything with action," she replied, a playful glint in her eye.

He raised an eyebrow, surprised. "Really? I was expecting a romcom."

Clair laughed, shaking her head. "I do like them, but I prefer to watch those alone and dream." Her smile was infectious, and Adam couldn't help but chuckle at her honesty.

Adam leaned back; his curiosity piqued. "So, what do you dream about?" he asked, a teasing smile on his face.

Clair paused, contemplating her response. "Well, it varies," she said thoughtfully. "Sometimes it's about having a successful career, but to be honest, you're probably going to laugh at me." She glanced at him, a hint of vulnerability in her eyes.

He assured her he wouldn't.

Taking a deep breath, she continued, "I dream of having a family, like, a dreamy husband one day and having babies." She blushed, her cheeks warming. "I know it sounds silly, but I really think being a mother could be the most rewarding thing you can do."

Adam raised an eyebrow, genuinely surprised. "Why would you think I'd find that silly?"

Clair shrugged, her gaze shifting as she spoke. "Well, in this day and age, everyone seems so focused on their careers," she said. Then she looked at him sideways, a hint of hesitation in her voice. "I've never told anyone that."

Her confession hung in the air, revealing a side of her that she rarely shared. Adam's expression softened, appreciating her honesty.

Clair's voice trembled slightly as she spoke. "My mother was the most wonderful mother. She told me she loved me every day and was always there when I needed her." Tears began to form in her eyes, but she fought to keep them at bay, not wanting to show her vulnerability to Adam. "She used to say that love is the most powerful thing in the universe, so when you find it, treat it with the respect it deserves."

Her words carried a weight of emotion, revealing the deep impact her mother had on her understanding of love and relationships. Adam listened intently, his expression shifting to one of empathy and admiration for her strength.

Adam's expression softened as he asked, "When did you lose her?"

Clair's voice quivered as she replied, "I was thirteen. I was devastated. She was on her way home from the market when a truck hit her car. She was in a coma for two weeks before Dad had to turn off the machines." Tears began to fall, and she wiped them away with frustration. "I was with her when she took her last breath. I didn't think I would smile again." She attempted a small smile, but the sadness lingered. "But time heals people. Dad was devastated; they loved each other deeply. But I was surprised when he told me, when I was fifteen, that he met someone and was going to marry her. He never introduced her to me until he was sure."

She took a deep breath, her eyes reflecting the complexity of her emotions. "Elizabeth has always been nice to me, but she's not my mother, you know?"

Adam's gaze turned serious as he shared, "Yes, I know. I lost my parents when I was twenty-two." His voice was steady, but the pain lingered beneath the surface. "It was sudden, an accident. I had to grow up fast after that." He paused, remembering the weight of that loss. "I understand how hard it can be to see someone else stepping into that role. It's a complicated feeling."

Clair took a deep breath, her voice softening. "Yeah, you want to be happy for them, but part of me, maybe I shouldn't say this," she paused, searching for the right words. "I was angry with my father. It felt like he was moving on too quickly, like he was forgetting my mom." She glanced at Adam, hoping he understood the mix of emotions swirling inside her.

Adam nodded, his expression empathetic. "I understand. It's natural to feel that way," he said softly, pulling her into a warm hug. The embrace felt comforting, a silent acknowledgment of their shared pain and loss. Clair relaxed in his arms, grateful for his understanding and support.

Clair wiped away the remnants of her tears, a light laugh escaping her lips. "Now I need some action...," she began, realised what she had said. Giggling, she quickly added, "That came out wrong!"

Adam chuckled, the tension easing between them. With a playful grin, he reached for the remote and turned on the television, ready to dive into something exciting that would shift the mood.

As the opening scenes of *San Andreas* filled the screen, Clair and Adam settled into the couch, the energy between them lightening. They exchanged comments and laughter at the action-packed moments, both drawn in by the thrilling plot and The Rock's charismatic presence.

Clair found herself leaning into Adam, sharing popcorn and playful jabs about the outrageous stunts. Each explosive scene brought them closer, their enjoyment palpable as they revelled in the adrenaline of the movie. Time slipped away as they laughed and gasped together, both completely immersed in the shared experience.

As the credits began to roll, Adam glanced at the clock on the wall, a hint of surprise in his voice. "Wow, it's nearly ten o'clock," he said, his brow raised. "Time really flies when you're having fun." He turned to Clair with a smile, the warmth of their evening lingering between them. "Did you enjoy it?"

Clair smiled and replied, "Yes, I've seen it multiple times."

Adam's eyes widened in surprise. "I thought you hadn't seen it!" he exclaimed.

She shrugged playfully. "It's one of my favourite movies."

Adam raised an eyebrow. "Is it because of The Rock?"

Clair laughed. "He's alright, but he has too many muscles! I'd feel like he'd crush me." She giggled, imagining the scenario, and Adam couldn't help but chuckle along.

Clair turned to Adam with a cheeky grin, her eyes sparkling with mischief. "So, what do you want to do now?" she asked playfully, leaning back on the couch and crossing her arms, clearly inviting a bit of fun.

Adam smiled, shaking his head slightly. "You're real trouble aren't you?" he said, amusement dancing in his eyes as he leaned closer, clearly enjoying her playful energy.

Clair wrapped her arms around Adam's neck, pulling him closer as she looked into his eyes, a playful smile on her lips. "So, what do you think?" she murmured, inviting him in for a kiss. The warmth between them crackled with anticipation.

Chapter Seventeen

It was 11 o'clock by the time Adam walked Clair down to her car, the night air cool around them. They paused at the door, and he leaned in, giving her a tender kiss goodnight that lingered, filled with unspoken promises. Clair felt a warmth spread through her as she got into her car, glancing back at him before driving home, her heart still racing from their evening together.

Clair arrived at her father's estate, the familiar surroundings bringing her a sense of comfort. She quietly made her way upstairs, the soft carpet muffling her footsteps. After a quick shower, she felt refreshed, the warm water washing away the day's emotions. Once dry, she slipped into bed, the cool sheets enveloping her as she settled in, savouring the peacefulness of the night and the lingering thoughts of Adam.

Clair woke up feeling refreshed after a restful night's sleep. She quickly got ready for work, her mind still lingering on the previous evening. After a short drive, she arrived at the office, surprised to find she was the first one there.

As she settled at her desk, her father walked by and noticed her. He stepped into the office with a warm smile. "Good morning, sweetheart. Did you have a good time last night?" he asked, his curiosity evident.

Just as Clair was going to answer her father's question, Adam walked in, clearly having overheard. Clair smiled and said, "Yes, we had dinner and then watched a movie." Adam listened intently, a hint of amusement in his eyes.

Her father, still unaware of Adam's presence, asked, "Maybe you should invite your friend over so I can meet her." Clair felt a flush rise to her cheeks, trying to maintain her composure.

At that moment, Adam stepped closer, greeting them both with a casual, "Good morning, you two." He turned to her father, adding, "Samuel, could I speak with you for a minute?"

Her father looked at Adam, distracted from the conversation with Clair, nodded to Adam. "Sure, come into my office."

As they walked away, Clair exchanged a grateful glance with Adam. Her father absentmindedly said, "Have a nice day, sweetheart," before they both left the room.

As Clair settled back into her work, a wave of guilt washed over her. She hated lying to anyone, especially her father, who had always been so open and trusting. The thought of not being honest about her relationship with Adam weighed heavily on her conscience. She felt torn between protecting her father's feelings and embracing her own happiness. Each time she brushed off the truth, it felt like a small betrayal, and she wished she could be completely open with him.

Clair's week flew by, with work keeping her busy and her relationship with Adam progressing smoothly. They had spent Wednesday night together, sharing a meal and laughter, and with each passing day, her feelings for him deepened. Thinking about that night brought a soft smile to her face.

At 5 o'clock, her work phone rang. Adam's voice came through, warm and inviting. "Hey, would you like to go to a seafood restaurant tonight?"

"That would be fine," Claire replied, a smile creeping into her voice, though her tone remained slightly reserved.

Noticing her businesslike response, Adam's curiosity piqued. "Are Ryan and Emily still there?" he asked, a hint of mischief in his playful tone, suggested he was ready to tease her about it.

"That's correct," Claire confirmed, her heart racing a little.

"I want to kiss you all over," he said with a laugh, the playful tone making her cheeks flush.

"That sounds great," Claire replied, trying to match his light-heartedness.

Adam chuckled. "I want to hear something inappropriate, Miss Dawson."

Claire couldn't help but grin. "I think that's not going to happen."

"Meet me at my apartment car park."

"Yes, certainly. Have a nice afternoon, goodbye."

As she hung up, Ryan noticed her smile. "Who was that?" he asked, raising an eyebrow.

"Oh, no one important," Claire replied, blushing as she tried to play it cool.

When Claire met Adam in the car park of his apartment that evening, she looked at him with mock anger. "You're not playing fair," she said, her tone teasing yet playful.

He laughed, swinging her around effortlessly. "You know what they say: all's fair in love and war."

Claire giggled, squirming a bit. "Put me down, you monster!"

Adam smirked playfully. "Yeah, but you love it."

Claire met his gaze, a playful glint in her eyes. "Yes, I do."

She glanced around, her playful behaviour shifting slightly. "Ryan was getting suspicious," she said, lowering her voice as if the walls might hear her. Her eyes darted back to Adam, a mix of amusement and concern in her expression.

Adam feigned a look of remorse, placing a hand over his heart. "I'm sorry," he said, his voice dripping with mock sincerity. "I promise, I'll be good." A playful smile tugged at the corners of his mouth, clearly unable to hide his amusement as he leaned closer for a kiss.

Claire flung her arms around Adam's neck, pulling him close as she kissed him passionately. Adam wrapped his arms around her, drawing her in tightly, savouring the moment as they lost themselves in each other.

As they arrived at the seafood restaurant, the inviting scent of salt and spices filled the air. The hostess led them to a secluded table tucked away in a cozy corner, offering a sense of intimacy that made Claire's heart flutter.

They settled in, the soft glow of candles flickering between them as they perused the menu. After deciding on a seafood basket for two, they leaned back in their chairs, anticipation buzzing in the air.

The conversation flowed effortlessly, laughter spilling from their lips as they shared stories and playful jabs. At one point, Adam playfully fed Claire a piece of shrimp, their eyes locking in a moment that felt both tender and electric. She giggled, returning the favour with a piece of crab, their shared meal turning into a delightful dance of connection. Each bite was seasoned with joy, and time seemed to slip away as they enjoyed each other's company, surrounded by the warmth of the restaurant and their blossoming bond.

As they indulged in their seafood feast, Claire accidentally smeared a bit of sauce on her lips. She laughed, reaching for a napkin, but before she could wipe it away, Adam leaned in closer.

With a playful glint in his eyes, he brushed his thumb gently over her lips, his touch sending a shiver down her spine. Then, without hesitation, he leaned in and kissed the sauce away, his lips soft against hers. The moment was charged with warmth and intimacy, and Claire felt her cheeks flush as she met his gaze, their laughter mingling in the air.

As they finished their meal, Claire took a breath, a hint of nervousness in her voice. "I bought some clean clothes, if you wanted me to stay the night...," she said, looking up at Adam with a hopeful smile.

His face lit up with eagerness. "Yes! I'd love that," he replied, the excitement evident in his tone. The warmth of his response filled her with relief, and she couldn't help but grin back at him.

Claire glanced down, a hint of shyness colouring her cheeks as she asked, "I hope you don't mind..." Her voice was soft, barely above a whisper, as she met Adam's gaze with a mixture of hope and uncertainty. The vulnerability in her expression made her look even more endearing, and she waited for his response, heart racing in anticipation.

Adam smiled warmly, his eyes sparkling with affection. "I wish I had thought of it first," he said, his tone light yet sincere. "It's a great idea." He leaned a little closer, his enthusiasm palpable as he added, "Having you in my arms all night would make my night so much better." The warmth of his words wrapped around Claire, easing her nerves and filling the space between them with a shared excitement.

The next morning, Claire awoke to a sense of comfort that enveloped her like a warm blanket. Everything felt natural, as if they had been in sync for much longer than just a few days. The soft light filtering through the curtains cast a gentle glow in the room, and she could hear the faint sound of Adam moving around the kitchen.

As she stretched and took in the cozy atmosphere, a smile tugged at her lips. The easy rhythm of their conversation from the night before echoed in her mind, and she felt a quiet joy at how seamlessly they had bonded. It was as if they had crossed a threshold, stepping into a shared space that felt both familiar and exhilarating. She realised that this was more than just a fleeting moment; it was the start of something deeper, and the thought filled her with a sense of hope.

As they stood in the car park, Adam smiled at Claire, his eyes warm with gratitude. "Thank you for staying the night," he said softly, his hand brushing hers. "We should do this more often."

Claire returned his smile, a soft blush colouring her cheeks. "I'd like that," she replied, her heart fluttering slightly at the thought.

Adam leaned in, pressing a gentle kiss to her lips, lingering for a moment longer than usual, as if savouring the union between them. "See you at the office," he murmured with a grin as he pulled away, his eyes still locked on hers.

With a final wave, they both headed to their cars, the morning sun rising behind them as they made their way to the same office, the memory of the night before still lingering between them.

By Friday, things felt effortless between them, and Clair realised with certainty that she had fallen in love with him again.

She didn't like being away from him, and even when they were apart, thinking of him made her feel special. She wanted to make him happy, and he made her feel the same.

Yes, she was definitely in love. But she hadn't told him yet, unsure if he was ready to hear those words from her.

When Ryan asked if she was going to join for after-work drinks, she shook her head. "No, I'm taking a break for a bit," she said. Ryan gave her a knowing nod, not pushing her to explain further.

As the clock ticked past five, the office had mostly emptied for the weekend. Clair lingered at her desk, enjoying the quiet, methodically finishing up her tasks. She had plans to see Adam again tonight, and the thought of it sent a little thrill through her as she prepared to meet him in his office.

Clair stood from her desk, grabbing her bag, and made her way to Adam's office. The building was eerily quiet, everyone else having left for the weekend. As she approached Adam's office, she noticed his door was slightly ajar, so without thinking much of it, she pushed it open.

The scene that greeted her felt like a punch to the gut.

Elizabeth was there, her arms draped around Adam's neck, her head nestled on his shoulder. "Oh, Adam, I love you," Elizabeth said happily, her voice brimming with promise. To Clair's utter disbelief, Adam responded by wrapping his arms around Elizabeth in what seemed like a comforting embrace.

For a few seconds, Clair just stood there, frozen in shock and pain, unable to process what she was seeing. Her mind raced, her heart sinking deeper into despair. The world seemed to crumble around her.

Then Adam saw her. His eyes widened in surprise, guilt flashing across his face. "Clair!" he began, but she didn't want to hear anything he had to say.

Without a word, she turned on her heel and fled, her vision blurred with unshed tears. She ran to the stairwell, knowing he would try to catch her at the lift. But he didn't see her slip away down the stairs. He didn't follow.

Clair bolted down the stairwell, her heart pounding in her chest, tears blurring her vision. She didn't stop until she reached the sixth floor, her legs giving way beneath her as she collapsed onto the cold concrete steps.

The sobs came uncontrollably, deep and raw, tearing through her like never before. She buried her face in her hands, the betrayal cutting through her like a knife. Every emotion she had tried to hold in came crashing out, and she wept like she had never wept before, the sound echoing in the empty stairwell.

Clair sat on the steps for what felt like an eternity, her tears eventually slowing, though the ache in her chest remained. In reality, only half an hour had passed. She took a few deep breaths, trying to collect herself. Wiping her eyes and straightening her clothes, she slowly made her way down the rest of the stairs to the ground floor.

As she entered the lobby, the bright lights and normalcy of it all felt jarring. The security guard at the front desk looked up, spotting her. "Oh, Miss Dawson, Mr. Cross was looking for you, I think he is waiting near your car, he seems very determined to talk to you," he said with casual concern.

Clair forced a small, tight-lipped smile, giving a brief nod to the security guard before quickly making her way to the side door. Her heart pounded as she fumbled through her bag for her phone, her hands trembling. Without thinking too much about it, she dialled Christian's number. She had forgotten to call him back about Saturday, but right now she needed an escape, somewhere, anywhere.

As the phone rang, her mind raced. She couldn't face Adam, not now, maybe not ever. And Elizabeth? The thought of her sent a fresh wave of pain crashing over her. When Christian answered, Clair's voice came out small but steady. "Christian, can you pick me up?" she asked, trying to hold herself together. "I just need to get away."

Christian's voice immediately filled with concern. "Clair? Are you okay? What's wrong?"

Clair swallowed hard, trying to keep her emotions in check. "I don't really want to talk about it right now," she said softly, her voice shaky. "I just… I need to get away. Can you come get me?"

"Of course," Christian replied without hesitation. "Where are you? I'll be there as soon as I can."

Clair exhaled a shaky breath, grateful for his response. "I'm at the office, on the side street. Don't go to the front entrance. I'll wait there."

"I'm on my way," Christian replied, his voice steady with concern. "Just hang tight, okay?"

Clair nodded, even though he couldn't see her, and whispered, "Thank you."

Clair stood beneath the shadow of a large tree, keeping herself out of sight from the office building. Her heart raced as she anxiously scanned the quiet street. Before long, Christian's car pulled up, the headlights casting soft beams across the pavement. Without a second thought, Clair hurried to the car, jumping into the passenger seat.

As soon as the door closed behind her, she turned to him, her voice trembling. "Please, just drive."

Christian glanced at her; concern etched on his face. "Is my place okay?" he asked gently.

"Yes, please," Clair replied, her voice barely above a whisper.

The drive was enveloped in silence, punctuated only by the soft hum of the engine. Tears continued to slide down Clair's cheeks, each one a reminder of the heartache she was trying to escape. She stared out the window, lost in her thoughts as the world blurred by.

When they arrived at Christian's modest yet inviting apartment, he gestured for her to come inside. The space was cozy, filled with warm lighting and simple decor.

"Take a seat," he said gently, guiding her to the couch. Clair sank into the cushions, grateful for the momentary comfort.

Christian disappeared into the kitchen, the sounds of clinking glasses and running water filling the air as he prepared a sweet tea for her. She appreciated the effort, knowing it was a small gesture meant to soothe her. As she waited, she took a deep breath, trying to steady her racing thoughts.

Christian returned with the tea and handed Clair the cup. She took it carefully, her hands trembling, and thanked him before taking a sip.

With a concerned look, Christian asked softly, "What happened, Clair?"

Clair took a deep breath, her heart heavy as she began, "You're going to hate me. But I've been seeing someone."

Christian's expression shifted, a knowing look crossing his face. "It's Adam, isn't it?"

Clair met his gaze, surprised and a bit taken aback. "Yes, how did you know?"

Christian leaned back slightly, a hint of frustration in his eyes. "I could see it coming from a mile away. You don't spend $150,000 for a woman you are not interested in, no matter how rich you are."

Clair looked down, her voice barely above a whisper. "I'm sorry, Christian."

He softened, giving her an understanding nod. "It's okay. But what's wrong?"

Tears brimmed in her eyes again as she struggled to find the words. "I just... saw something that hurt me." She took a deep breath, her voice trembling. "I saw my stepmother and him together."

Christian frowned, concern etched on his face. "What do you mean, together?"

"In each other's arms," she replied, her voice breaking. "And she was telling him she loved him."

"Oh, Clair, I'm so sorry."

Clair set the teacup on the coffee table and buried her face in her hands, the tears flowing freely as the pain overwhelmed her. Christian moved closer, wrapping his arms around her in a comforting embrace. He held her tightly, offering silent support as she cried, letting her emotions spill out. He gently stroked her back, murmuring soothing words, creating a safe space for her to let go of her hurt.

Clair's phone rang, and she fished it out of her bag, her heart sinking when she saw Adam's name on the screen. She handed the phone to Christian, her voice trembling. "Can you answer it?"

Christian looked at her, concern etched on his face. "Do you want *me* to answer it?"

"Yes," Clair said, her eyes pleading. "Tell him not to call again. If I don't answer, he'll just keep trying."

Christian answered the phone, his tone steady. "Adam? It's Christian. Clair doesn't want you to call her." He paused, taking in Adam's response. "She's upset and needs space right now. If you cared, you wouldn't have hurt her like this." Another pause followed. "This isn't the right time. I don't know when that time will be but let her decide. Don't call again." His expression remained resolute as he hung up, determined to protect Clair.

Clair took a shaky breath and whispered, "Thank you," to Christian. She then dialled another number. "Thompson, it's Clair. Can you let my father know I won't be home this weekend?" After a brief pause to listen, she added, "Thank you," before hanging up. A slight weight lifted off her shoulders as she turned her phone off, seeking a moment of silence from the outside world.

Clair looked up at Christian, her expression serious. "Can you drive me to a motel?" she asked, her voice steady but laced with urgency. She needed a place to collect her thoughts after everything that had happened.

Christian shook his head, concern etched on his face. "You can stay here. I have a spare bedroom."

"Are you sure? I probably won't be good company," Clair replied, a hint of vulnerability in her voice.

Christian smiled reassuringly. "What are friends for? Let me just make up the bed. I'm sure I have some track pants and shirts that'll fit you. Then we're all set." He turned to head toward the spare room, his behaviour lightening the mood as he glanced back at her.

As Christian worked away, making the bed and searching for clothes, Clair sipped her tea, feeling the warmth seep into her. She watched him, her heart swelling with gratitude for his unwavering friendship. In this moment, she felt a sense of safety and comfort, knowing she could rely on him during such a painful time.

Christian suggested a light-hearted movie, and as they settled onto the couch, Clair began to relax. The familiar banter and shared laughs with him eased some of the heaviness in her heart. For a while, the movie distracted her from the turmoil she felt inside. But when she finally retreated to the spare bedroom, the weight of her emotions crashed down. Alone in the quiet, she curled up in the blankets and cried herself to sleep, letting the tears flow as the pain of the day washed over her.

The next morning, Christian offered to take Clair to retrieve her car. Once that was done, she climbed into the passenger seat of Christian's car.

"Ready for breakfast?" he asked, flashing her a reassuring smile.

"Definitely," Clair replied, grateful for his company. They chose a cozy diner nearby, and as they settled in, the aroma of freshly brewed coffee enveloped them. Their conversation flowed easily, touching on light-hearted topics, and Christian's easy-going nature gradually lifted Clair's spirits.

As they enjoyed pancakes and eggs, she found herself laughing and savouring the moment, a much-needed distraction from the chaos of the past few days.

The day passed quietly at Christian's apartment. They spent the afternoon watching movies, sharing stories, and enjoying each other's company. Christian's presence provided a comforting distraction, but as evening fell, Clair felt the weight of her emotions creeping back in.

After dinner, they settled on the couch, but Clair couldn't shake the heaviness in her heart. As the night wore on, she felt herself retreating inward. Christian tried to lighten the mood with jokes, but Clair's laughter felt forced.

When they finally said goodnight, she slipped into the spare bedroom, and as soon as the door closed, the tears came. Alone in the dim light, Clair cried herself to sleep, the ache of her heartbreak spilling over as she longed for the stability and love she had lost.

The next morning, Clair woke up feeling a mix of determination and anxiety. She knew she needed to confront her father about everything that had happened. After getting ready, she found Christian in the kitchen making coffee.

"I need to talk to my dad," she said, her voice steady. "He has a right to know."

Christian nodded, his expression supportive. "I agree. You should."

Clair took a breath, grateful for his presence. "You've been wonderful through all of this. I really appreciate it. I just wish things could be different because you're a great guy."

Christian offered a gentle smile. "Maybe once everything settles, anything could happen."

Clair met his gaze, feeling the weight of his words. "Yes, anything is possible," she replied, not wanting to commit to anything just yet. She needed to focus on herself and the challenges ahead.

Clair smiled at Christian, feeling a mix of gratitude and warmth. She stepped closer and leaned in, giving him a soft kiss on the cheek. "Thank you for everything," she said, her voice filled with sincerity.

Christian smiled back, his eyes reflecting understanding.

With a final nod, Clair turned and headed for the door, her heart pounding as she made her way to her father's estate. She took a deep breath, steeling herself for the conversation ahead, determined to face whatever came next.

Clair arrived at her father's estate, her heart racing as she stepped inside. Thompson greeted her with a warm smile, but his expression shifted to concern when he saw her.

"Good morning, Miss Clair. You're back early," he said.

"Hi, Thompson. Where's Dad?" she asked, trying to keep her voice steady.

"On the terrace with Mrs. Elizabeth," he replied, gesturing toward the back of the house.

Clair took a deep breath, steeling herself for what lay ahead. She walked through the elegant halls, each step feeling heavier, until she reached the terrace. As she approached, she could see her father and Elizabeth sharing a moment, laughter mingling with the gentle breeze.

Gathering her courage, Clair stepped forward, ready to confront the truth.

Chapter Eighteen

As Clair stepped onto the terrace, Elizabeth turned, her face lighting up with relief. "Oh, Clair! Thank goodness you're okay!" she exclaimed, rushing over to hug her.

Clair stood stiffly, unsure how to respond, and Elizabeth noticed the tension in her embrace but tried to maintain her warmth.

Her father's expression shifted to something more serious. "I'm glad you're home, Clair. We need to talk," he said, his voice grave.

Clair's stomach dropped as she met his gaze, sensing the weight of the conversation that lay ahead.

Clair settled into a chair, facing her father and Elizabeth, her heart racing. Her father cleared his throat, his expression serious. "We know you were seeing Adam," he began.

Clair felt a pang and quickly corrected him. "I was," she said softly.

Her father nodded, seemingly undeterred. "Well, we'll see about that. Anyway, I know what you saw on Friday," he continued, glancing at Elizabeth. He took her hand, and she squeezed it gently, offering him support.

Clair felt a knot tighten in her stomach, bracing herself for the conversation that was about to unfold.

Her father continued, "It wasn't what you thought it was." Clair opened her mouth to protest, but he raised a hand to stop her.

"Adam was doing some work for Elizabeth," he added, his tone firm.

Clair felt a surge of frustration. She glanced at Elizabeth, convinced that she had somehow manipulated her father into this narrative. The disbelief simmered within her as she struggled to process his words, feeling the weight of the situation bearing down on her.

Elizabeth began, "The night before you went to college, I was engaging Adam to help find my daughter, Sara."

Clair's mouth fell open in disbelief.

"I had a daughter when I was sixteen and put her up for adoption. I asked Adam to help me find Sara, but there are a lot of legal complications, so Adam agreed to assist. I'm not sure what you saw that night, but I was hoping to build a relationship with her. I admire the bond you have with your father, and I felt I needed to at least try to reach out to Sara." She attempted a small smile.

Clair's mind raced, recalling Elizabeth's earlier words, "I'm hoping we have a future together." A knot twisted in Clair's stomach, a mix of confusion and betrayal flooding her senses as she struggled to reconcile the new information with her feelings.

Elizabeth continued, her voice tinged with a mix of hope and sorrow. "It's been a long battle, with many hopes raised and dashed multiple times over the past four years. But on Friday, Adam confirmed he finally found Sara, and she has agreed to meet me."

Clair's mind raced, a whirlwind of emotions flooding her. She turned to her father, searching for answers.

He nodded, his expression serious. "Yes, I knew. We didn't tell you until we were certain she might become part of the family." The weight of his words hung in the air, leaving Clair grappling with the implications of everything she had just heard.

Elizabeth continued, her tone earnest. "What you saw on Friday was my utter relief at Adam's news. Yes, I hugged him, and yes, I told him I loved him, but not in the way you think. Your father and I are extremely fond of Adam; he has been a constant in our lives."

Clair felt a mixture of confusion and anger. "So, it was all just about your daughter?" she asked, struggling to reconcile her feelings.

Elizabeth nodded, her expression softening. "It's complicated, Clair. I understand how it looked, but my feelings for Adam are about gratitude and support, not romance. I hope you can understand that."

Clair's mind raced, caught between disbelief and confusion. She turned to her father, searching for confirmation. Elizabeth smiled gently at Clair. "I know you think Adam betrayed you, but he didn't," she said softly.

Clair's heart ached, torn between the pain of what she'd seen and the possibility that there was more to the story. "Then why didn't he tell me?" she asked, her voice trembling.

Her father sighed, his expression a blend of sympathy and concern. "You should understand, Clair. Attorney Client privilege. He couldn't tell you."

The truth began to dawn on Clair, the pieces of the puzzle clicking into place. She felt a wave of shame wash over her as she realised how she had treated Adam, reacting out of jealousy and hurt without understanding the full context. The weight of her assumptions pressed heavily on her, and guilt tightened in her chest as she thought about how unfairly she had judged him. The thought of pushing him away when he had been trying to help made her heart ache.

Clair stood up abruptly, determination surging through her. "I need to talk to Adam," she declared, her voice steady despite the turmoil within. She felt a deep urgency, knowing she had to clear the air and apologise for her misunderstandings. Turning to Elizabeth, she added sincerely, "I'm so sorry for misjudging you all these years. I can't excuse my behaviour, but I truly am sorry."

Elizabeth stepped forward and enveloped Clair in a tight hug. This time, Clair embraced her back, feeling a wave of warmth and love.

Clair leaned down to kiss her father gently on the cheek. "I love you both," she said, glancing back over her shoulder as she moved toward the door. "But I really need to speak to Adam." With that, she left, her heart set on making things right.

Clair hurried to her car, her heart racing with determination. She fumbled with the keys as she unlocked the door, sliding into the driver's seat and starting the engine with a quick turn of the key. The tires screeched slightly as she pulled away, her mind focused on Adam.

The drive felt like a blur, her thoughts swirling with regret and urgency. She navigated the familiar streets, her heart pounding in rhythm with the rush of adrenaline. As she arrived at Adam's apartment building, she parked quickly, barely waiting for the engine to die before she jumped out and raced toward the entrance.

Clair stepped into the elevator, her heart pounding as it ascended. The brief ride felt endless, each floor passing slowly. Finally, the doors slid open, and she made her way to Adam's door, her nerves tightening with each step.

She knocked, her hand trembling slightly, and moments later, the door swung open. Adam stood there, an unreadable expression on his face. "What are you doing here, Clair?" he asked coolly, and her heart sank at the distance in his voice.

"I need to talk to you," she replied, her voice steadier than she felt, hoping to bridge the gap that had grown between them.

Adam stepped aside, gesturing for her to enter. "Well, you better come in then," he said, his tone still guarded. Clair hesitated for a moment, uncertainty swirling in her mind.

"Thank you," she finally replied, stepping inside and glancing around the familiar space. As she waited for him to close the door, she felt the weight of the moment pressing down on her, both anxious and hopeful for what was to come.

Clair took a deep breath, her voice steady. "Elizabeth told me everything. I'm sorry I misjudged you." She watched him closely, searching for a hint of understanding in his expression.

Adam's gaze remained cool. "Thank you, but that's not good enough."

Her heart sank. "What do you want from me?"

"A partner that trusts me," he replied, his tone firm. "And right now, you're just not it. I'm glad you and Elizabeth can mend your fences, but I can't reconcile your behaviour toward me. Every time something happens, you run and think I am in the wrong."

Clair felt a mix of regret and frustration, realising the depth of the rift between them.

Clair's voice trembled slightly as she replied, "I'm sorry. I was hurt. I thought…"

"I know what you thought," Adam interrupted, his eyes filled with disappointment. "And that hurts the most. I thought we were close, Clair. I thought you knew me. You didn't even give me a chance to defend myself, you just thought the worst of me, just like four years ago. I could overlook it the first time, but I just can't this time."

His words hung heavy in the air, amplifying her sense of regret. She felt the weight of their fractured relationship, realizing how easily trust can be shattered.

Clair took a deep breath, trying to maintain her strength. "Is there anything I can say or do to change how you feel?"

"No, I'm done, Clair. I can't keep being hurt by you."

As she processed his words, a painful realisation washed over her: he truly didn't want to hear what she had to say. She turned, her heart heavy, and began to walk toward the door. Tears streamed down her face as she opened it, glancing back at Adam's silhouette.

"Adam, I'm sorry. I understand how you feel. I'm not going to try to change your mind because I can see you won't…" Her voice faltered, the weight of her emotions almost too much to bear. "Just know one thing… I love you; I always have."

With that, she stepped out of the apartment, feeling the finality of her words echoing in the silence as she walked away for the last time.

Clair stepped into the lift, her heart heavy and her eyes brimming with tears. As the doors slid shut, she felt the weight of her situation crashing down on her. She climbed into her car, the familiar interior now feeling foreign and suffocating. With shaking hands, she started the engine and pulled away, not knowing where she was headed, just needing to escape.

As she drove, sobs wracked her body, the realisation of what she had thrown away hitting her like a tidal wave. Each tear that fell felt like a reminder of Adam's love, and the ache in her chest deepened with every passing moment.

At a stop sign, she hesitated, but the pain in her heart pushed her forward. Blurred vision made it hard to see, and as she entered the intersection, she didn't notice the approaching truck. In an instant, everything went dark.

Adam stood frozen, the weight of Clair's final words echoing in his mind: "I love you; I always have." The revelation struck him like a lightning bolt, she loved him, yet she had hurt him once more. A whirlwind of emotions surged through him: anger, confusion, and an undeniable ache for what could have been.

He felt the sting of betrayal mix with the flicker of hope her confession ignited. How could someone he cared for so deeply keep pushing him away? As the door swung shut behind her, he was left grappling with the complexity of his feelings, caught between wanting to forgive her and the pain of her repeated misunderstandings. Each moment stretched into eternity as he fought against the urge to call her back, knowing that the hurt ran deep.

For hours, Adam found himself lost in memories of the fun times he had shared with Clair, the way her laughter lit up a room, how her eyes sparkled when she smiled, and the warmth of her kisses that came lingered long after. The way she felt in his arms, the way she responded to him when they made love. Each recollection was bittersweet, reminding him of the bond they once had and the joy she brought into his life.

Just as he began to savour the fleeting moments, his phone rang, cutting through his reverie. He glanced at the screen, not recognising the number. A wave of irritation washed over him; he didn't want to talk to anyone right now. Instead, he let the call go to voicemail, turning his phone off, returning to the whirlpool of his thoughts. He needed to process everything, to untangle the mess of emotions swirling in his heart.

As Adam sat in the silence of his apartment, the weight of his thoughts pressed heavily on him. Then, suddenly, it hit him like a freight train: he still loved Clair, he couldn't let her go, he had loved Clair since she was eighteen, it hadn't changed. The realisation washed over him, flooding his chest with a mix of exhilaration and despair.

All the laughter, the tenderness, the way she made him feel alive, it all merged into one undeniable truth. He had pushed her away, yet his feelings had only deepened. The thought of losing her for good twisted painfully in his gut. He couldn't let it end this way.

Adam glanced at his watch; it was late, but he felt a sense of hope for tomorrow. As soon as he got to work, he would talk to her. He would tell her that he loved her and that he didn't want to lose her, not ever.

Chapter Nineteen

Adam arrived at work, heart racing with anticipation to talk to Clair as soon as she walked in. He scanned the parking lot but noticed her car wasn't there yet, he was thirty minutes early. As he entered his outer office, he overheard Craig on the phone.

"Okay, Karen, I'll let Mr. Cross know," Craig said.

Waiting for Craig to end the call, Adam asked, trying to keep his impatience in check. "What do you need to let me know?"

"Mr. Dawson won't be in the office for the foreseeable future," Craig replied. "You need to allocate his cases to some of the other associates."

"Why?" Adam asked, annoyance creeping into his voice, why hadn't Samuel spoken to him directly? Then he remembered the voicemails on his mobile. He really didn't have time for this; he needed to talk to Clair today.

"Because his daughter had an accident, and it doesn't look good," Craig informed him.

Adam's heart sank as the weight of the news settled in.

Adam's heart raced as he processed Craig's words. "What do mean? What accident? When? How?" he blurted out, disbelief flooding his voice.

Craig gave him a puzzled look, then replied, "She had a car accident on Sunday morning. Apparently, a truck hit her car."

The gravity of the situation hit Adam like a punch to the gut. He felt his breath quicken, and a wave of concern washed over him. "Is she… is she going to be okay?" he asked, the worry lacing his voice.

"I don't know," Craig said, his expression turning serious. "Apparently Mrs. Dawson called Karen last night to let her know Mr. Dawson was in a state, and he wouldn't be in until Miss Dawson was out of danger. But by the sounds of it, it's pretty serious."

Adam's mind raced with thoughts of Clair. He needed to see her, to be there for her.

Then he heard Craig continue, "I feel so sorry for Mr. Dawson. You know he lost his wife the same way."

The weight of Craig's words sank in, amplifying Adam's urgency. He couldn't bear the thought of losing Clair, not after everything they had been through.

Adam turned to Craig, urgency in his voice. "You need to get Greg and Thomas to handle any issues that come up. I have to go." Without waiting for a response, he rushed out of the office, ignoring Craig's confused protest of "But... Mr. Cross."

In the lift, adrenaline coursing through him, Adam listened to the voice messages he hadn't had the chance to check.

The first was from Elizabeth: "Adam, Clair has had an accident. She's at the local hospital."

The second message from Elizabeth followed, her voice trembling. "Adam, you need to get to the hospital... She's in a bad way... she's unconscious ...." Her voice trailed off into sobs before the message cut out.

The third message was from a furious Samuel: "Adam, what the hell did you say to my daughter... to make her drive into the front of a truck? She's... I can't believe you aren't answering your phone..."

Confusion gripped Adam. What did Samuel mean by that? His heart raced as he thought of Clair, desperate to get to her before it was too late.

Adam jumped into his car, his hands gripping the steering wheel tightly. He accelerated without a second thought, weaving in and out of traffic as he must have broken every road rule on the way to the hospital. Red lights blurred past him, and the sounds of sirens filled his ears, but nothing registered except the urgency to reach Clair.

His heart raced with each passing moment, anxiety building as he imagined the worst. The hospital loomed ahead, and he pushed the gas pedal harder, determined to be by her side. Nothing mattered now but getting to Clair and hoping it wasn't too late.

Adam burst into the emergency department, his heart pounding as he scanned the room. Elizabeth spotted him first, her eyes narrowing in warning. Samuel, already on edge, turned to see Adam and his fury erupted. "You...! Get out...!" he shouted, his voice shaking with anger and desperation.

Elizabeth quickly intervened, stepping between them. "Samuel, you need to calm down," she urged, her tone soothing but firm.

"How can I calm down when my daughter is laying in there like..." Samuel's voice faltered, the weight of his words hanging heavy in the air as he struggled to contain his emotions. Adam's chest tightened, guilt flooding through him as he realised the gravity of the situation.

Adam's heart sank at Samuel's words. "How is she?" he asked, desperation creeping into his voice.

Samuel shot him a furious glare. "You have no right to ask! Get out!"

Elizabeth intervened, her voice steady. "Samuel, please calm down. You aren't going to be any use to Clair if you end up in hospital yourself."

Adam pressed on, urgency in his tone. "What happened?"

Samuel's voice broke as he replied, "You happened! She went to talk to you…, she was leaving your place then…" His sobs overwhelmed him, and he sank into a nearby chair, unable to continue.

Elizabeth looked at Adam, her expression grave. "The police are saying she drove out in front of a truck on purpose. They have dash cam video." The weight of her words hit Adam like a physical blow, leaving him reeling as he processed the devastating implications.

Elizabeth continued, her voice trembling as she gently rubbed Samuel's back. "The doctors are still evaluating her… one of her arms is broken… there's swelling on her brain… they said the airbags saved her life, but with the impact from the truck, her injuries are severe… She hasn't woken up since the accident… that's all we know for now…"

Samuel's face crumpled, and he whispered, "I can't lose her too… not like this…"

Adam felt a weight settle in his chest, unable to articulate the guilt that churned inside him. "I didn't know she…" His words faltered, choking him as he struggled to face the gravity of the situation. All he could do was stand there, consumed by regret and fear.

Adam turned to Samuel; his voice unsteady but filled with sincerity. "I love your daughter," he began, the weight of his emotions evident in every word. "I never meant to hurt her. That was never my intention."

Samuel glared at him; anguish etched on his face. "Why did she try to kill herself then? If you loved her, why was she that upset? Did she see you? Did she talk to you?"

The accusation hung in the air, and Adam felt a sharp pang of guilt. "Yes, but…"

"What did you say to her, Adam?" Samuel interrupted, his voice raw with emotion. "Why would she intentionally drive into the path of a truck? What did you say to her? Why would she want to die?"

Adam could only shake his head, the weight of their misunderstandings pressing down on him. "I don't know… I just don't know."

The doctor approached Samuel with a serious expression. "Mr. Dawson," he said, catching Samuel's attention.

"Yes?" Samuel replied, anxiety creeping into his voice.

The doctor began, "Let's sit," and waited for everyone to be seated before continuing. "Your daughter has suffered a serious traumatic brain injury. Right now, she's in a coma, which means her brain isn't responding consciously due to the swelling from the trauma of the accident." He paused, letting the gravity of his words sink in.

"We attempted to relieve the pressure on her brain with medication, but it wasn't effective, so we had to take her into surgery early this morning."

"We performed a burr hole drainage procedure, where we drill small holes into her skull and attach drainage tubes to allow blood and cerebrospinal fluid to escape, alleviating the pressure on her brain. She's currently on a respirator to assist with her breathing, and we'll keep monitoring her intracranial pressure closely."

His tone softened as he explained further, "At this point, it's difficult to predict her long-term outcome. With TBIs, there's a wide range of potential outcomes, from full recovery to lasting impairments. I need to be clear that some patients recover slowly, while others may not regain consciousness at all."

He took another moment, watching their reactions. "We will conduct neurological exams and imaging tests to assess brain activity and look for signs of improvement, but these need to be spaced out to give us the most accurate information. The next few days will be critical for understanding the severity of her injury."

"It's important for her to be surrounded by familiar voices and support," the doctor added. "Talking to her, playing music she loves, or simply being present can sometimes make a difference in these situations."

Then, with a heavier tone, he said, "While we remain hopeful, I must be honest, it's possible she may not regain consciousness, or there could be lasting effects from this injury. We're also concerned she may have attempted to do this to herself. If that's the case, she may not fight, and right now, fighting is what your daughter needs to do."

He paused, allowing them to absorb the gravity of the situation. "We'll keep you updated regularly and adjust her care as we gather more information. Do you have any questions?"

Samuel's voice was tight with emotion. "Can I see her?"

"Yes, of course," the doctor nodded but cautioned. "But you need to prepare yourself. What you're about to see is very confronting."

Elizabeth wiped her tears, looking at the doctor. "Can we all see her?"

The doctor turned to Samuel. "If her father agrees."

Adam's heart raced, hoping Samuel would allow it.

Before Samuel could respond, Elizabeth interjected firmly, "Yes, he agrees."

To Adam's relief, Samuel remained silent, not objecting.

Gratitude washed over Adam as he prepared to face the reality of Clair's condition, knowing this was a chance to be there for her.

The three of them were led into the intensive care unit, and the sight that greeted them was devastating. Clair lay in the hospital bed, still and vulnerable, her fragile state almost unrecognisable.

Her body was motionless, surrounded by a maze of medical equipment. A ventilator tube extended from her mouth, rhythmically expanding her chest as the machine did the work of breathing for her. Her head was heavily bandaged, with tubes protruding, one side swollen and bruised from the impact of the accident. Her face, marred by the aftermath of the crash, was swollen and disfigured, with cuts and abrasions crisscrossing her features, likely from the shattered glass. Both eyes were bruised and swollen shut, giving her face an almost haunting quality.

One of her arms lay immobilised in a cast, resting gently at her side, while other parts of her body were covered in stitches and bandages where her skin had been torn or cut.

Wires and monitors snaked across her body, attached to machines that tracked her vital signs, heart rate, oxygen levels, blood pressure, each reading carefully monitored by the steady beeping of the machinery. The ventilator hissed softly, the only sound breaking the quiet as the machines worked tirelessly to keep her alive.

Adam's heart clenched painfully as he stared at Clair, the weight of the situation crashing down on him. He ached to reach out to her, to tell her that he was there, that he loved her, but all he could do was stand frozen, watching the rise and fall of her chest, praying for a miracle.

Elizabeth wrapped her arms around Samuel, holding him tightly as he broke down. Tears streamed down his face as he whispered, "She looks exactly like Helen did. I can't lose her too…" His voice trembled with despair, the weight of grief crashing over him like a wave. Elizabeth's heart ached for him, feeling his pain as she held him, wishing she could take it away. She brushed her fingers through his hair, murmuring soothing words, trying to offer comfort in the midst of their shared heartbreak.

Adam stood frozen, his gaze fixed on Clair as memories flooded back, her haunting words echoing in his mind: *I was there when she took her last breath.* The weight of her pain crushed him, and his breath hitched as tears filled his eyes. He felt helpless, the reality of her fragile state piercing through his heart like a sharp knife. Each shallow breath she took felt like a reminder of the love and bond they had shared, now overshadowed by fear and regret. He longed to reach out, to hold her hand and tell her that he loved her, but he felt paralysed by the gravity of the moment.

The nurse entered the room quietly, her presence bringing a sense of calm amidst the chaos. She moved to Clair's bedside, checking the monitors that beeped rhythmically, noting the fluctuations in her heart rate and breathing. With gentle hands, she examined the IV in Clair's arm, ensuring everything was functioning properly.

After a brief moment, she turned to Adam, her voice soft yet professional. "I'll bring in another seat," she said, recognising the need for more space for everyone. Adam nodded, unable to find his voice, his heart heavy with the weight of uncertainty. All he could do was watch as the nurse stepped out, leaving him alone with his thoughts and the stark reality of Clair's condition.

As Samuel, Elizabeth, and Adam sat in the room, their eyes fixated on Clair, an oppressive silence enveloped them. Each heartbeat echoed in their minds as they desperately searched for any sign that she would pull through. Hours passed like an eternity, filled only with the steady hum of machines and the occasional shuffle of nurses outside.

Eventually, a nurse entered, breaking the stillness. "I'm sorry, but we need to ask you to step out for a while so we can perform some tests."

Adam's heart sank, but he understood the necessity. As they moved into the waiting room, he turned to Samuel, his voice earnest. "Samuel, you must know I wouldn't do anything to cause Clair to try to hurt herself. I really do love her."

Samuel's expression hardened; anguish etched deeply into his features. "Love isn't enough if it leads to this, Adam." The words hung heavy between them, a painful reminder of the chasm that now lay in their relationship.

Elizabeth gently rubbed Samuel's back, her voice soft yet firm. "None of this is fair, but we all have to be strong for Clair. When she wakes up, and if she really did try to hurt herself, she's going to need all of us to make her feel loved and protected."

Samuel sighed heavily, his shoulders sagging under the unbearable weight of the moment. "Yes, I know you're right," he muttered, his voice laced with sorrow and helplessness. His eyes dropped to his hands, which fidgeted restlessly, as if searching for something, anything, to hold onto.

Without hesitation, Adam reached out and gently took one of Samuel's hands in his own.

Samuel glanced up at Adam, his eyes brimming with pain and uncertainty.

Elizabeth, seeing the exchange, placed both her hands over theirs and softly said, "We need to be strong together, Clair will pull through." Her voice wavered but held a quiet determination, a glimmer of hope amid the sorrow.

Chapter Twenty

Three days had passed, and Clair was still in a coma. Her swollen and bruised face had slowly started to heal. The cuts and the bruising had started to fade. Her bandages were still wrapped around her head, though much less bulky now, revealing more of her soft hair. She was beginning to look like the beautiful woman Adam had fallen in love with.

Adam sat beside her, holding her hand gently in his. He had spent countless hours at her side, reading to her, hoping she could hear him somehow. His voice was steady, though there was always a tremor of emotion beneath it, as if willing her to wake up with every word he spoke. As he read aloud, he occasionally glanced at her face, searching for the slightest flicker of movement, any sign that she might return to him.

Periodically, the physical therapist would come in to perform exercises on her, aiming to reduce the likelihood of muscle atrophy.

That morning, the doctors had conducted a brain activity scans, and Adam anxiously awaited the results. To his surprise, Samuel had permitted him to receive updates from the medical team, signalling that his anger toward Adam was beginning to soften.

As Adam sat in her room, he felt a mix of hope and dread. Samuel's earlier hostility had lessened, replaced by a shared sense of concern for Clair's well-being. They both understood the gravity of the situation, and although the distance between them still existed, it felt less insurmountable in that moment.

When the doctor finally entered her room, Adam's heart raced, bracing for the news that could determine Clair's fate.

The doctor started, "I'm pleased to report that Clair's scans this morning show high levels of brain activity. This is a positive sign, indicating that her brain is processing information and responding to stimuli. However, I want to stress that it doesn't guarantee Clair will wake up, but it is certainly a step in the right direction."

Adam took a deep breath, feeling a surge of hope. "Thank you, Doctor," he said earnestly before turning to Clair, as the doctor left the room. With his heart full of emotion. "I knew you would fight," he murmured, squeezing her hand gently. "You have to come back to me. I want to hear your voice again. I miss you, sweetheart." His voice trembled as he leaned closer, his gaze fixed on her serene face, wishing for the moment she would wake up.

Just then, Christian walked in, a hopeful smile lighting up his face. "How is she today?" he asked, glancing between Adam and Clair. Adam felt a wave of gratitude for Christian's unwavering support. Adam had called him about Clair's condition, knowing she would want him there.

"Her scans showed high levels of brain activity," Adam replied, his voice filled with cautious optimism. "It's a good sign."

Christian nodded, concern replacing his smile. "That's great to hear. I know she's a fighter." He stepped closer to Clair's bedside, his disposition respectful and caring. Leaning down, he whispered to her, "It's time to wake up, love. Everyone will think you're lazy." Tears welled in his eyes as he gently kissed her forehead, a tender gesture filled with hope.

Christian turned to Adam, a serious expression crossing his face. "And how are you?"

Adam replied, "I'm fine," though the words felt hollow. He could sense the weight of the situation pressing down on him, but he pushed it aside, focusing on the flicker of hope that Clair's progress had sparked.

Christian sat by Clair's bedside for a little while longer, sharing light-hearted stories and reminiscing about when they went axe throwing, trying to infuse the room with warmth. He glanced at Adam, gauging his emotions, then turned back to Clair.

As he stood up, he leaned down and gently kissed her forehead. "I'll be back tomorrow, expecting to see your beautiful eyes," he said softly, a hint of hope in his voice. He then nodded a goodbye to Adam before stepping out of the room, leaving behind a lingering sense of care and warmth.

Not long after Christian left, Ryan and Emily walked in, their presence bringing a fresh energy to the room. "Hey, Adam," Ryan said with a warm smile, then turned to Clair, his expression softening. "Hey, Clair. We're here for you."

Emily echoed his sentiments, "Hi, Clair. You've got a lot of people rooting for you."

They weren't surprised to learn that Clair was seeing Adam. Adam recalled Ryan chuckling and saying, "I knew something was up by Clair's second day at the firm. I saw more of you in those two days than I had the entire year before!"

Adam managed a small smile, appreciating the solidarity as they settled in, their support filling the room with a sense of hope.

Ryan glanced around the room before asking, "When did Mr. Dawson leave?"

Adam, still sitting by Clair's side, responded softly, "Not long ago. He has to pace himself... it's not easy on him."

Ryan nodded, understanding. "Yeah, I can only imagine. This must bring back some really bad memories of his wife," he said, his voice filled with sympathy. Then, with renewed confidence, he added, "But Clair's going to pull through. I know it. She's tough."

Adam looked up at Ryan, grateful for his unwavering belief in Clair's strength.

Ryan and Emily left soon after, offering Adam a few final words of encouragement before heading out. As the door closed behind them, the room fell into a familiar quiet. Adam turned his gaze back to Clair, his heart heavy but hopeful.

"So many people love you, sweetheart," he whispered, gently squeezing her hand. "You need to make them proud. You need to come back and make me smile again."

Just as the words left his lips, he felt a faint movement in his hand. His heart skipped a beat. Was it real? Or was he just imagining it, desperate for any sign?

Adam's breath caught in his throat as he waited, barely daring to hope.

Adam's eyes locked onto Clair's hand, watching it intently, every nerve on edge. Then, there it was, another slight movement. His heart raced. It was real.

"Clair, can you hear me?" he asked, his voice barely above a whisper, filled with a mix of disbelief and hope. Her fingers twitched again in response.

His grip on her hand tightened gently. "Clair, it's Adam," he said, his voice trembling now. Another movement. This time, it was unmistakable. She was trying to respond.

Tears welled in his eyes as hope surged through him. She was coming back to him.

Adam quickly pressed the call button, his heart pounding in his chest. Within moments, the nurse rushed in, her expression calm but alert.

"She squeezed my hand," Adam said, his voice filled with excitement and urgency. "Twice."

The nurse's eyes widened slightly, her professional conduct slipping into a hopeful smile. "That's a very good sign," she said as she moved toward Clair's bedside to check her vitals and monitor her responses. Adam watched anxiously, his heart lifting with cautious optimism.

The nurse looked at Adam with a smile of quiet reassurance. "I need to call the doctor," she said softly, glancing at the monitors to ensure everything was stable. "I'll be back soon."

Adam nodded, his eyes never leaving Clair as the nurse quickly stepped out of the room. His heart raced with hope, his grip on her hand tightening slightly, willing her to wake up.

Adam leaned in closer, his voice tender and full of emotion. "I love you, Clair. You and I are one." He felt another faint squeeze of her hand, and his heart swelled with hope. "I know you can hear me, I love you, Clair."

Just then, the doctor rushed into the room, followed closely by the nurse. He quickly began checking Clair's vitals and responses. "Clair, can you hear me?" he asked gently, performing a few tests. Though the movements were small, Clair responded to each one, her hand giving slight squeezes and her eyes fluttering just faintly.

The doctor looked up at Adam, a glimmer of optimism in his eyes. "She's responding," he said. "It's a good sign."

Adam, filled with a mix of relief and urgency, said, "I need to call her father." He quickly stepped into the waiting room, his hands trembling as he turned his phone on and pressed Samuel's contact.

Thompson answered after a couple of rings, his voice tight with worry. "Thompson, I need to speak to Samuel," Adam said quickly. "She's responding."

There was a brief pause, then Thompson's voice softened in gratitude. "Oh, thank God," he muttered, clearly overwhelmed.

A moment later, Samuel was on the line, his voice shaky but hopeful. "Adam? What did you say?"

"She's responding," Adam repeated, his heart racing.

"We'll be there soon," Samuel said without hesitation, and the call ended.

Samuel and Elizabeth arrived at the hospital shortly after, their faces a mixture of hope and fear. Adam met them just outside Clair's room and quickly told them what had happened. "She squeezed my hand, Samuel," Adam said, his voice filled with emotion. "She's responding."

Samuel didn't waste a second, rushing into the room. He took Clair's hand gently, his voice soft and filled with love. "Sweetheart, it's Dad. Can you hear me?"

A soft squeeze of her hand answered him. Samuel's eyes filled with tears. "Oh, Clair, thank God," he whispered, his voice breaking. "We love you, sweetheart."

Another faint squeeze followed, and Samuel let out a shaky breath of relief, his heart swelling with hope.

Elizabeth had followed Samuel into the room but stood back, her eyes fixed on Clair, tears streaming silently down her face. She watched as Samuel spoke to his daughter, her heart aching at the sight of Clair responding, however faintly.

The emotions overwhelmed her, relief, fear, and love all at once. As Clair squeezed Samuel's hand, Elizabeth brought her hand to her mouth, stifling a sob, her tears falling freely now. She didn't say a word, just stood there, watching her stepdaughter with a mixture of hope and grief in her eyes.

Samuel stayed by Clair's side until Elizabeth eventually insisted, her voice gentle but firm. "You need to rest, Samuel. Come back in the morning, she's going to need you strong." Reluctantly, Samuel nodded, kissed Clair's forehead, and left, leaving Adam in the quiet room.

Not long after, the doctors came in, explaining they were going to turn off the respirator to see if Clair could breathe on her own. Adam, still seated by her side, held her hand tightly, his heart pounding in his chest. He barely dared to breathe himself as he watched the doctor adjust the machine, his eyes fixed on Clair's chest.

The seconds felt like hours, but then, slowly, her chest rose on its own. She was breathing.

Adam exhaled sharply, overwhelmed with relief as tears filled his eyes. He tightened his grip around her hand. "You're doing it, sweetheart," he whispered. "You're coming back to me." A small laugh escaped him. "You have to come back; you owe me a date, remember?" Clair squeezed his hand in response.

Adam refused to leave that night; no one could convince him to go. If Clair woke up, he wanted to be the first person she saw. Hours passed, but Adam felt a flicker of hope he hadn't experienced since the accident.

Around three o'clock in the morning, he had fallen asleep in the chair, his head resting on her bed next to her hand. Suddenly, something stirred him awake. He felt a gentle hand running through his hair, soft and reassuring.

Chapter Twenty-One

Clair slowly emerged from the fog of her coma, disoriented and unsure of her surroundings. As her eyes fluttered open, she noticed the sterile room and the machines beeping softly around her. Then she caught sight of a head resting next to her hand. The familiar tousled hair was unmistakable. It was Adam.

With considerable effort, she lifted her hand and gently placed it on his head, running her fingers through his hair in a tender gesture.

Suddenly, Adam's head shot up, his eyes wide with disbelief and tears streaming down his cheeks. "Clair, oh Clair, you're back," he exclaimed, his voice filled with a mixture of relief and joy.

Clair blinked slowly, trying to make sense of her surroundings. The room was bright and filled with unfamiliar sounds, the beeping of machines and the faint scent of antiseptic. Confusion washed over her as she took in the sight of Adam, his face streaked with tears, a mix of joy and concern etched into his features.

Where was she? Why was she here? The last thing she clearly remembered was finishing work and walking to Adam's office, excitement bubbling inside her. Then, a blank void followed. How did she end up in this hospital room, with Adam beside her, looking so emotional?

Her heart raced as she struggled to piece it all together, the fog in her mind thickening. She wanted to ask him what had happened, to understand how she had come to be here, but the words felt trapped in her throat. All she could do was gaze at him, searching his eyes for answers.

Adam looked at her with an overwhelming wave of love, his heart swelling as he whispered, "I love you, Clair."

Clair attempted to smile, but even that felt like a monumental effort. She opened her mouth to respond, wanting to express her feelings, but as she tried to speak, the words got stuck. "I lo…" she managed, but her throat felt raw and sore, preventing her from forming the words completely. Frustration flickered in her eyes as she looked at Adam, wishing she could tell him how much he meant to her. Instead, she simply held onto his gaze, hoping he could feel the depth of her emotions without needing to say a word.

Adam leaned closer, his eyes shimmering with emotion. "I know, sweetheart," he said softly. "Don't try to talk just yet. The doctor warned me your throat would be very sore." He paused, a smile breaking through his worry. "Just seeing your beautiful eyes open is enough for me right now." His heart swelled with relief, and he gently squeezed her hand, savouring the moment after so much uncertainty.

Clair's brow furrowed in confusion as she tried to process her surroundings. The beeping machines and sterile smell were foreign and unsettling. Why was she here? Why was Adam so upset? She glanced at his tear-streaked face, but the effort of trying to understand was too much. Just as a wave of exhaustion washed over her, pulling her back, her vision blurred and faded, sending her back into the comforting darkness.

Adam felt a pang of disappointment as Clair's eyes fluttered shut once more. He understood it must have taken immense effort for her to open them in the first place, but the fleeting moment of connection had filled him with hope. He brushed his fingers gently along her hand, willing her to fight through the confusion that had clouded her expression. The distress in her eyes before she succumbed to darkness weighed heavily on his heart, but he clung to the hope that she would awaken again, stronger, and clearer.

At around six in the morning, Adam stirred from his light sleep, feeling the warmth of Clair's hand resting on his hair. He lifted his head, the soft light of dawn illuminating her face.

"Adam," she whispered, the sound barely audible, but it was music to his ears.

A rush of emotions flooded through him, relief, joy, and an overwhelming sense of love. "Clair," he breathed, his voice thick with emotion. "You're back." He couldn't believe it; she was speaking to him, even if it was just a soft murmur. The moment felt monumental, a turning point in their journey together.

Adam pressed the call button, anticipation coursing through him. The nurse entered swiftly, her eyes lighting up when she saw Clair's eyes open. "Welcome back, Clair! It's so good to see you," she said with a bright smile.

Clair looked at the nurse, confusion flickering in her eyes, but she managed a small, tentative smile in return.

The nurse then turned to Adam, her manner shifting to one of professionalism. "I'll go get the doctor," she said, sensing the urgency in the room.

Adam nodded, thankful for her swift action as she hurried out to fetch the doctor, leaving him alone with Clair, his heart brimming with hope.

Adam sat by Clair's side, gazing at her in awe as he gently kissed her hand. Just then, the doctor entered, a warm smile on his face. "Oh, it's good to see you, young lady," he said. Clair smiled softly, though confusion was evident in her eyes.

The doctor continued in a gentle tone, "You were in a car accident. You sustained head injuries, but you're on the mend. It's important not to overdo it; let your body guide you on what you can and can't do. Your throat will be quite sore for a few days, making it hard to talk. We'll be doing some more tests to check for any lingering effects from the accident. Do you understand, Clair?"

Clair nodded slowly, taking in his words as Adam watched, heart full of hope.

As the doctor stepped out, he spoke to the nurse about what tests to order, ensuring Clair would receive the best care. Adam turned his attention back to Clair, slowly bending down to kiss her gently on the lips. "I love you, sweetheart," he whispered, a warm smile spreading across his face. "I need to call your dad, okay?"

Clair nodded in response, her eyes reflecting both confusion and comfort. Adam's heart swelled with hope as he prepared to reach out to Samuel, eager to share the good news.

Adam stepped into the hallway, his heart racing with excitement as he dialled Samuel's number. The phone rang only once before Samuel answered, his voice filled with concern. "Adam? What's going on?"

"Samuel, she's awake," Adam said, trying to keep his voice steady. "Clair is awake! She opened her eyes and spoke my name."

There was a moment of stunned silence on the other end, then Samuel's voice broke with emotion. "Thank God! Is she... how is she?"

"She's confused but stable," Adam replied quickly. "The doctor just seen her and is ordering some tests, but she's responding. I think she'll be okay."

"I'll be there as soon as I can," Samuel said, urgency creeping into his tone. "Thank you for calling me."

Adam hung up, a wave of relief washing over him. He returned to Clair's room, ready to share the good news with her.

Adam leaned closer to Clair, his heart swelling with emotion. "Your father is on his way, Clair. He'll be here soon," he said softly.

She looked at him, her eyes glistening, and whispered, "Thank you."

A smile spread across Adam's face at her words, but it widened even more when she added, "I love you."

His breath caught in his throat, overwhelmed with joy. "I love you too, Clair," he replied, his voice full of warmth.

The day unfolded in a blissful haze of happiness and hope. Clair's father, Elizabeth, Christian, Ryan, and Emily all came to visit throughout the day, their faces lighting up the room with excitement at seeing her awake. Each of them took turns sharing stories and offering encouragement, their joy palpable. Though Clair dozed off frequently, a testament to her body's need for rest, everyone understood and cherished the moments she was alert.

As the sun began to set, the visits dwindled, and soon, only Adam remained by her side. He had taken the opportunity to go home, shower, and change while her father and Elizabeth were there, returning refreshed and eager to be with her again. With the room quiet and the faint hum of the machines in the background, Adam settled into his chair, his heart full of gratitude for her recovery.

As Clair slowly opened her eyes, the familiar sight of Adam brought a flicker of warmth to her heart. She felt a rush of emotions and a strong desire to talk. With a deep breath, she tried to form the words, but her throat felt dry and raspy. "How did I have an accident?" she whispered; her voice barely audible.

Adam's heart ached at the sound, but he smiled reassuringly. "You were in a car accident, Clair. But you're safe now, and you're going to get better." He leaned closer, his eyes filled with love and concern.

Clair's brow furrowed as she tried to process his words. "But…" she began, her voice trailing off.

Adam quickly interjected, "There will be time for explanations later. The doctor said you might not remember everything from the days leading up to the accident." A wave of concern washed over him, fearing she might recall the painful words he'd spoken to her just before the accident.

He leaned in closer, his expression earnest. "Just know this: I love you, and you love me. We are one, Clair. I'm not going anywhere. Do you understand?" He searched her eyes for reassurance, hoping to anchor her amidst the confusion.

Tears filled Clair's eyes as she whispered, "Okay." A playful spark flickered in her gaze, and she attempted a cheeky grin before adding softly, "Well, I think it's time you kissed me again."

Adam laughed, feeling a rush of warmth. "You are trouble," he said, leaning in. He kissed her gently, being careful not to hurt her, savouring the sweet moment that felt like a promise of brighter days ahead.

In the days that followed, Clair's recovery became a remarkable journey of resilience. Doctors were encouraged by her progress, noting that she seemed to have no lingering effects from the accident. Each day, she grew stronger, and her determination was palpable.

By the third day, she took a monumental step: with the help of her physiotherapist, she got out of bed and walked a short distance. The sight of her moving, albeit slowly, filled the room with a sense of triumph. The doctors exchanged impressed glances, marvelling at her speed of recovery. Adam watched, his heart swelling with pride and joy, knowing that Clair was reclaiming her life one step at a time.

It became evident that Clair's memory wasn't fully intact; moments from her life from the Friday afternoon were completely absent. The doctors explained that recovery varied from person to person, and while some memories might return over time, others might not. They emphasised the importance of being gentle with her if she began to recall any traumatic events, urging Adam and her family to guide her through any confusion with patience and support. Clair's progress was promising, but the uncertainty surrounding her memory lingered, casting a shadow over her otherwise bright recovery.

It had been two weeks since the accident, and Clair had made remarkable progress. Everyone was incredibly proud of her, and Adam was in awe of her strength and determination. But he couldn't reconcile the idea that she had wanted to harm herself. Though he knew he had hurt her deeply before the accident, the thought that she might have considered something so drastic was hard for him to believe.

That afternoon, Clair sat across from the psychologist, aware that this was the last hurdle before she could finally go home. Though she didn't fully understand why everyone seemed so concerned about her well-being, she realised the doctors had her best interests at heart. Her hands rested in her lap, fidgeting slightly as she worked to stay composed.

The psychologist, a calm woman with kind, understanding eyes, leaned forward slightly, her tone gentle yet direct, ready to guide Clair through the final assessment.

"Clair," she began softly, "before you're discharged, I need to ask you a few questions, just to make sure you're feeling mentally and emotionally ready to go home. This is a safe place, so please be honest."

Clair nodded, her heart racing slightly, but she remained focused. She knew this was important.

The psychologist continued, "Since the accident, have you had any thoughts of harming yourself or felt that life wasn't worth living?"

Clair took a moment to reflect, then shook her head. "No," she replied, her voice steady. "I haven't felt like that."

The psychologist smiled gently. "That's good to hear. What about before the accident? Did you ever feel overwhelmed or like things were hopeless?"

Clair hesitated for a second, vaguely remembering an emotional turmoil she had been in before the accident. "I was upset," she admitted quietly, "but I never thought about hurting myself."

"Thank you for sharing that with me," the psychologist said, her voice soft but professional. "It's normal to feel overwhelmed, especially when we go through difficult times. I just want to make sure you feel safe within yourself now."

Clair nodded, more confidently this time. "I do. I want to go home. I want to move forward."

The psychologist studied her for a moment, then smiled warmly. "That's exactly what I wanted to hear. You've made incredible progress, and as long as you continue to communicate and reach out for support when you need it, I believe you're ready to go home."

Clair exhaled, relief washing over her. "Thank you," she said softly.

The psychologist stood, extending her hand. "You're strong, Clair. You're more than ready for this next step. Just remember, we're always here if you need us."

With a small but grateful smile, Clair shook her hand, feeling a renewed sense of hope.

While Clair was undergoing her psychological assessment, the doctors reviewed her progress and approved her release for the next morning if the psychologist cleared her. However, they needed to confirm her post-discharge living arrangements. In a discussion with her father, Elizabeth, and Adam, the doctor emphasised the importance of continued support. Clair would still need assistance for a while, and her recovery would rely heavily on everyone's patience and understanding.

Her father, Samuel, immediately said, "She'll be well looked after at my home."

But Adam interjected firmly, "No, she's coming home with me."

Tension built as the two men exchanged sharp looks, their disagreement escalating into a heated argument. Sensing the rising conflict, the doctor raised his hand. "This isn't going to help Clair," he said calmly. "A discussion needs to be had."

Elizabeth, ever the voice of reason, quickly stepped in. "Why don't we compromise? Adam can move into the estate until Clair is fully recovered. That way, she has both of you nearby, and you both get what you want."

The doctor nodded approvingly, waiting for Samuel's response.

Samuel looked at Adam, his expression serious. "Would you agree to that?"

Adam nodded. "Yes, I agree."

Samuel relaxed slightly and said, "It's settled then."

The doctor smiled, clearly pleased with the compromise. "I'm glad you've come to an agreement," he said. "Clair will be discharged tomorrow morning. Make sure everything is prepared for her comfort at home, and we'll provide you with the necessary instructions for her continued recovery."

He glanced between Samuel and Adam, reassured by their cooperation, before nodding and leaving the room.

When Clair returned to her room, everyone was waiting for her. As the nurse wheeled her in, she smiled and announced, "I think I can go home tomorrow."

Her father nodded and added, "Adam will be moving in while you recover, so we'll all be here for you."

Clair's eyes lit up as she turned to Adam. "Oh, thank you," she said, her gratitude evident.

He took her hands and kissed them gently, replying, "There's nowhere else I'd want to be." And he truly meant it.

Chapter Twenty-Two

Once Clair was back home, she still needed assistance during her recovery. Her father had hired a nurse to be with her during the day, ensuring she had the support she needed. Although she appreciated the help, Clair insisted that both her father and Adam return to their jobs full-time.

"I've taken enough of your time," she stated firmly, even as they both argued against her decision. Their concern was palpable, but Clair's determination prevailed, making her feel slightly empowered in the process. It was a small victory, but it reminded her that she could still assert herself, even amidst her healing journey.

Clair still couldn't piece together the days leading up to the accident; the transition from walking to Adam's office to waking up in the hospital remained a blur. Some days, she found herself straining to remember, giving herself headaches in the process.

Despite the confusion, she loved having Adam by her side. He was with her every night, and she insisted on having him in her bedroom, much to her father's dismay. Yet, Samuel ultimately wanted his daughter to be happy, so he conceded to her wishes.

Every night, Adam would hold her close until she drifted off to sleep, providing a sense of comfort and safety that helped ease her worries, even as she wrestled with her memories.

Three weeks had passed since the accident, and Clair was slowly reclaiming her independence. The bruises were fading, though a few cuts still marked her skin, and her arm remained in a cast. Still, she could now walk up and down the stairs on her own and even shower, occasionally needing the support of a chair. That afternoon, as she headed toward the terrace, she overheard Elizabeth on the phone.

"I'm really looking forward to you meeting Clair and Adam. I'll let you know when it can be arranged. Bye, Sara."

The name struck a chord, and a rush of memories flooded Clair's mind, making her dizzy. Elizabeth noticed her disorientation and rushed over. "Clair, are you okay?"

"I remember," Clair said, tears welling in her eyes. "Adam told me to leave."

"What?" Elizabeth's voice was filled with concern as she helped Clair into a seat on the terrace.

Clair looked at her in despair. "He didn't want to be with me."

Elizabeth rushed to reassure Clair, her voice gentle but firm. "No, Clair, that's not true. Adam cares about you deeply. He would never want you to feel that way."

Clair shook her head, her eyes filled with anguish. "But it was because he told me to leave. That's why I had the accident."

Elizabeth paused, taking a deep breath. "Clair, did you do it on purpose?"

Clair's response was immediate and filled with distress. "No! I must have not seen the truck because I was crying so much. I shouldn't have driven; it was because Adam told me to leave."

Elizabeth's heart ached for her stepdaughter understanding the weight of her emotions. "Clair, accidents happen. It wasn't your fault. You were in a difficult place, but you're here now, and that's what matters."

Clair looked at Elizabeth, her voice trembling with uncertainty. "Does Adam really want to be here? Or is he with me because he feels guilty?"

Elizabeth leaned closer, her expression earnest. "No, Clair, Adam loves you. He's here because he wants to be, not out of guilt."

Clair's brow furrowed, doubt still clouding her eyes. "Does he? How can I be sure? He told me to leave."

Elizabeth took a moment, gathering her thoughts. "People say things in the heat of the moment. It doesn't change how he feels about you. You've both been through so much. Just give him a chance to show you."

Clair's voice quivered as she spoke, "I don't want him to be here because he feels responsible. I want him to be here because he truly wants me." Her eyes shimmered with vulnerability, revealing her fear of being a burden rather than a partner. She looked down, the weight of her emotions pressing heavily on her chest.

Clair took a deep breath, her voice steady yet soft as she said, "I need to rest and think." She offered Elizabeth a faint smile before turning away. Carefully, she made her way up the stairs, each step a small victory. As she reached her room, she closed the door gently behind her, seeking solitude. The quiet enveloped her, allowing her thoughts to swirl and settle in the stillness, giving her a moment to process everything weighing on her heart.

Clair lay on her bed, feeling numb. Did he really love her? Did he feel guilty? She replayed his words: "No, I'm done, Clair. I can't keep being hurt by you."

She pondered this for what felt like an eternity, until exhaustion took over and she drifted off to sleep, tears soaking her pillow.

Adam was seated at his desk, focused on his work when Craig's voice interrupted. "Mrs. Dawson is on the phone for you."

A wave of concern washed over him at the thought of Elizabeth calling. Had something happened to Clair? "Put her through," he said, steeling himself for whatever news awaited him.

When the line connected, he answered, "Hello?" His voice was steady, but inside, anxiety churned as he worried about Clair.

"Adam, Clair remembers what happened," Elizabeth said, her tone serious.

Adam froze; this was the news he had been dreading. "Is she okay?"

"She thinks you're here because you feel guilty."

"That's ridiculous," he replied, his voice rising with frustration.

"I know, Adam. I just wanted you to be prepared for her feelings."

He thanked her, and after a brief goodbye, they hung up. Adam's mind raced with concern; he needed to get home to Clair.

Adam left the office and drove to her father's estate, where he was currently staying with Clair. His mind raced as he hurried up the stairs, uneasy about the conversation that lay ahead.

"Clair," Adam said softly, placing a gentle hand on her shoulder as he sat on the edge of the bed. His presence was warm and reassuring, pulling her from the depths of her thoughts. She slowly opened her eyes, taking in his worried expression and the concern etched on his face.

Adam took a deep breath, his heart racing. "We need to talk," he said, his tone serious.

"Yes, we do," Clair replied, her voice steady but tinged with anxiety.

Adam began, "Clair, you need—"

"Stop! Please." she interjected, her eyes locking onto his. "No, you need to hear what I have to say first."

He felt a knot tighten in his stomach, dreading the words that might come next. He nodded, bracing himself for whatever she was about to share.

Clair sat up in bed, propping herself against the pillows, determination etched on her face. "Adam, I remember the accident. I remember how it happened and why." She paused, gathering her thoughts. "I didn't do it on purpose, like everyone seems to think."

Adam felt a wave of relief wash over him at her words.

Clair continued, her voice steady but laced with regret. "It happened because I was stupid enough to drive when I couldn't see through my tears."

"Clair, I—" Adam began, wanting to reassure her.

"Please, Adam, let me finish," she pleaded, her gaze unwavering.

He nodded, a knot of worry tightening in his chest, unsure of what she would say next.

"I remember the words you said to me before I left your apartment," Clair began, her voice steady.

Adam braced himself, anticipating the weight of her accusation.

Clair sat nervously, her hands twisting in her lap, heart racing as she tried to gather the words that had been lodged in her throat for so long. The weight of years spent misunderstanding him, the regret of pushing him away, pressed down on her, heavier now than ever. Taking a deep breath, she steadied herself, her voice soft but filled with emotion.

"Adam, I need to tell you something I should have said long ago," she began, her eyes lifting to meet his, searching for any glimmer of hope. "I've been wrong about you, about us... all these years." She hesitated for a moment, the weight of her confession causing her voice to crack. "I know now that you're trustworthy, loving, and honest. You've always been. And I—" she faltered again, her words thick with emotion, "I didn't trust you when I should have. I let my own fears and insecurities cloud everything, and I'm so sorry for not believing in you."

She paused, gathering her courage. "You were right. I did hurt you, and you didn't deserve that."

That was not what Adam had expected to hear. His breath caught in his throat as her words settled over him.

"I ran four years ago," Clair continued, her voice trembling slightly, "because I didn't believe what I already knew of you. I knew you were always honest with me, and I still doubted you. I was stupid, Adam. I shouldn't have disappeared, but... I loved you back then. And I was hurt."

Adam smiled gently at her, a wave of relief washing over him. "I loved you too. I was going to tell you the next day before you left, but you were gone before I had the chance. I wanted to tell you I'd wait for you. But then you never came home, you always had a reason not to."

She swallowed hard, tears threatening to spill over as she confessed the truth she had kept buried for so long. The silence between them hung heavy, but for the first time, Clair felt like she could finally say everything that needed to be said.

Clair's eyes shimmered with tears as she pressed on, her voice thick with emotion. "Then on that Friday, I ran again because I doubted you. But that's not true, I *do* trust you. I love you, Adam."

She paused, her voice trembling as the weight of her words sank in. "Today, when I remembered everything, my first thought was, 'Did you really love me, or did you stay because you felt guilty?' I found myself doubting you again, and I hated that. But you're the most honest, loving person I've ever known, and I feel privileged that you actually love me."

A small, tentative smile played on her lips as she looked up at him. "I never meant to hurt you. I'm truly sorry." Her hand tightened around his, her eyes pleading for understanding. "Will you please forgive me?"

"Clair…" he said quietly, his voice thick with emotion. "I thought… I thought you were going to say you believed I was only here because of the accident, because I felt guilty. But that's not true. I'm here because I love you. I've always loved you. And yes… I forgive you."

His hand reached up to cup her cheek gently. "I've never stopped believing in us, even when it seemed impossible. I'm just glad you finally see it too."

Clair let out a breath she didn't know she'd been holding, relief flooding her as Adam's words sank in. She leaned into his touch, her heart swelling with gratitude and love.

"I see it now," she whispered, tears falling freely. "I trust you, Adam. I'm so sorry it took me so long."

Clair's eyes shimmered with unshed tears; her vulnerability laid bare before him. Adam felt his heart soften in ways he didn't expect. All the frustration, all the misunderstandings seemed to dissolve in the face of her heartfelt apology. He realised in that moment that she wasn't doubting him anymore. She was offering him her heart, fully and without reservation.

Adam felt a wave of relief wash over him as he pulled Clair into a tight embrace. "Oh, Clair, I love you. You are my world," he whispered into her hair. "That day of the accident, after you left, it hit me like a sledgehammer, I couldn't stop loving you. But it was late, and I didn't go to you. I came to work on Monday to tell you I was an idiot." He shuddered at the memory. "Then I found out about the accident. I thought I was going to lose you, and it terrified me."

He held her close, feeling the warmth of her presence, and knew in that moment that they could overcome anything together.

Holding her tight, knowing they had finally broken through the walls that had kept them apart for so long. They had found their way back to each other, and nothing would stand between them again.

For a long time, she clung to him tightly, filled with gratitude for his unwavering love.

She pulled back and smiled at him, a playful glint in her eyes. "You know, I'm starting to feel like my old self again," she teased, her voice taking on a sultry edge. With a cheeky grin, she added, "And it's been way too long since you've shown me just how much you love me. How do I make that happen? Maybe I should just walk around in front of you naked?"

He smiled back, fully aware of her teasing. "Seriously, you are trouble," Adam murmured.

Adam gently pulled her into his arms, his hands cradling her face as he lowered his lips to hers. The kiss was tender, a declaration of love.

Clair leaned in, returning his kiss with equal tenderness, her lips softly brushing against his. "I've missed you so much," she murmured against his lips.

Adam whispered back, "You have no idea how much I want you."

Clair smiled, her voice barely audible as she whispered, "Almost as much as I want you."

Adam deepened the kiss, his arms pulling Clair closer as his lips pressed more firmly against hers. The kiss grew more passionate, conveying a profound mix of passion and love.

Clair wrapped her arms around Adam's neck, drawing him closer as she kissed him more passionately. Her fingers tangled in his hair, pulling him into the kiss with a fervent intensity. The heat of the moment surged between them, and their kisses became more urgent, expressing their love and desire for one another.

A long while later, they made their way downstairs, hand in hand, smiles lighting up their faces as they entered the dining room.

Her father glanced up and said, "Oh, there you are. How are you feeling tonight, sweetheart?"

Clair smiled warmly at him. "I feel wonderful, Dad. Thank you for asking."

Elizabeth gave Clair a knowing smile, her eyes twinkling. "I see you two... talked."

Clair blushed, trying to sound casual. "Yes, we had a long talk." She shot a smile at Adam, squeezing his hand affectionately.

Adam smiled down at her as he helped her into her seat at the dining table. Clearing his throat, he added, "Yes, a very good talk."

Her father, unaware of the subtle undertones in the conversation, beamed. "Wonderful. I'm so glad you're happy, and I'm relieved you remember how the accident happened. Elizabeth told me you said it was a complete accident."

Clair nodded. "Yes, dad, it was. I didn't try to hurt myself. I was just... careless for driving when I shouldn't have."

Samuel sighed with relief. "Well, you will know better next time."

Before Clair could respond, Adam interjected, his gaze fixed on her with firm resolve. "There won't be a next time."

Clair met his eyes and softly agreed, "No, there won't."

They all had a cheerful dinner, laughter filling the room as they enjoyed each other's company. Later, they moved to the terrace, where the warm night air felt comforting. Clair sat in an armchair next to Adam, her father and Elizabeth settled on the settee nearby, quietly enjoying the peaceful evening.

Suddenly, Adam stood up, his movement catching Clair's attention. He knelt down in front of her, something he'd done frequently in the past weeks to check on her comfort. But this time, there was a seriousness in his expression that made Clair's heart skip a beat.

Adam's voice was steady as he spoke, though his gaze was fixed solely on her. "Clair, I have loved you for a very long time. You are my world, and I never want to be without you."

Clair's eyes widened, her breath catching as Adam pulled a small box from his pocket. "Will you do me the honour of becoming my wife?" He opened the box, revealing a stunning diamond solitaire. "Will you marry me?"

Tears welled up in Clair's eyes, completely taken by surprise. She nodded, unable to speak at first, overwhelmed with emotion. Finally, she managed to whisper through her tears, "Yes... yes."

Adam stood, pulling her into his arms, kissing her deeply and holding her tightly.

Elizabeth and her father leaped to their feet, their faces lighting up with joy as they rushed over to congratulate the newly engaged couple. Laughter and hugs followed; the night now even more special as they celebrated together.

Later that night, alone at last in their room, Adam lay next to Clair, her warm body nestled in the crook of his arm. She had a wide grin on her face, her eyes fixed on the sparkling ring on her finger.

"I didn't expect this," she said softly, her fingers gently tracing the band.

Adam chuckled, "Really?"

She turned to him, her expression sincere. "No, I just wanted to be with you, forever."

Adam smiled softly, tightening his grip on her hand. "I've wanted to be with you since you were eighteen," he said, his voice filled with warmth, he chuckled. "You've always been the one, Clair. I've never wanted anyone else."

"Remember that night we watched that movie with The Rock? You told me your dream was to have a family, a *dreamy* husband, and babies. I knew right then... I was going to marry you."

Clair's eyes widened, surprised. "Really!"

"Yes, but I wasn't sure if I fit the profile of a dreamy husband," he laughed, teasing her.

Clair kissed him, her lips soft against his. "Believe me, you definitely fit that profile."

Epilogue

It was Clair and Adam's first wedding anniversary. The time had flown by, but it had been pure bliss. If anything, Adam loved his wife more with each passing day. Clair felt the same. She had some exciting news for him tonight and could hardly contain her excitement, nearly bursting at the seams to tell him.

Clair was just finishing her makeup when Adam walked into their bedroom.

"Clair, you look beautiful," he said.

Clair laughed softly. "You said that last night when I had nothing on," she teased, flashing a cheeky grin. "Make up your mind!"

Adam chuckled, leaning in to kiss her cheek tenderly. "If I had a choice, I'd pick last night in a heartbeat."

Clair stood from the stool, wrapped her arms around his neck, and kissed him passionately on the lips. Pulling back slightly, she gave him a sultry look and whispered, "Well…?"

Adam shook his head, trying to clear the fog. "You really are trouble, Mrs. Cross," he said with a grin.

Clair hugged him tightly, her eyes bright. "I love it when you call me that."

"If you keep looking at me like that, we'll never make it to your father's place," Adam teased, wrapping his arms around her waist.

"Would that be so bad… hmm?"

Adam laughed, giving her a playful pat on the bottom. "Move it, Mrs. Cross," he urged, ushering her out of their bedroom.

"You're no fun," Clair pouted.

He laughed and said, "I promise I'll make up for it when we get back tonight."

"Promise?" She asked.

They left the penthouse, their home since the wedding, which held a special place in Clair's heart, and made their way to her father's estate, for the dinner party Elizabeth had organised to celebrate their wedding anniversary.

Upon arrival, they found all the people they loved gathered to celebrate with them, Samuel, Elizabeth and Sara, Elizabeth's daughter, who had become a cherished part of the family. Clair took an instant liking to Sara; she had been raised by kind and decent parents and was a joy to be around. It was wonderful to see how deeply Elizabeth adored her.

Clair and Elizabeth had grown very close as well, Clair's past suspicions long forgiven and forgotten.

Lily, her bridesmaid and best friend, was there with Ryan, of all people. The two had hit it off at Clair and Adam's wedding and had been inseparable ever since. Clair was thrilled when Lily announced she was moving to Seattle to be with Ryan.

Emily was there too, with Christian, who had been smitten with her since their first meeting at the wedding. It took Emily a while to come out of her shell, but Christian's patience paid off; now they were engaged, and Clair and Adam couldn't be happier for them.

Clair decided to stay at the firm, and she and Adam agreed they could remain professional as long as they went home together. There were a few moments in the photocopy room that perhaps shouldn't have happened, but they managed to make it work.

As they sat at the dining table, Thompson poured wine for everyone. When he reached Clair, she placed her hand over the glass and said, "No, thank you, Thompson. I'm fine with water." Adam glanced at her curiously, but she smiled reassuringly, and he returned her smile.

Dinner was a joyful affair, filled with lively conversations, laughter, and love. Surrounded by friends and family, Clair felt truly blessed.

As dessert was being served, Adam stood up to make a toast. "To my wonderful, loving wife," he said, "may we have many years together. I love you, Clair." He leaned down and kissed her softly on the lips. Clair blushed, her smile radiant with love in her heart and eyes.

As Adam sat down, Clair stood up, drawing curious looks from all the guests. Clair had never been comfortable being the centre of attention but tonight was special. She turned to Adam; her voice steady but filled with emotion. "I just want to say, I love you too, Adam." Then, shifting her gaze to the groups, she added warmly, "I'm so glad you're all here tonight. I truly feel blessed to be surrounded by friends and family. But next year," she glanced back at Adam, her smile widening, "you'll need another chair, or at least a highchair."

Adam looked at her, hope lighting up his eyes. "Are you saying what I think you're saying?"

Clair smiled softly. "Yes, sweetheart. We're going to be blessed with a little one in about six months. I wanted to wait until I passed the twelve-week mark to tell you."

In an instant Adam sprang out of his chair, scooping Clair into his arms and spinning her around. "That's wonderful! Oh, thank you, Clair!"

Clair smiled and whispered, "No, thank you, Adam," before they kissed, her feet still dangling as he held her off the ground.

The room erupted in cheers as everyone stood up gathering around Clair and Adam to offer their congratulations. It was a beautiful moment. Adam looked so proud, gazing at Clair with awe and love in his eyes.

Her father wrapped Clair in a hug, saying, "I'm finally going to be a granddad!" He smiled down at his daughter. "I love you, sweetheart."

"I love you too, dad. Always."

Later that night, as they lay in bed, Adam asked, "How did you keep it a secret for so long?" His curiosity was evident.

"It was hard," Clair admitted. "I was sick a lot those first few weeks. I honestly thought you'd guess, but I hid it well," she replied, looking up at him with a cheeky grin.

"Yes, you did," he said, smiling as he kissed her gently on the lips.

Then Clair grew serious, her eyes soft as she gazed at Adam. "Thank you, sweetheart."

"For what?"

"For making all my dreams come true."

The End

Thank you for reading Cautious Hearts!

If you enjoyed this collection of cautious hearts and irresistible connections, be sure to watch for more upcoming romance collections by Alison Reid, including:

Alpha Kings - *A Billionaire Alpha Male Romance Collection*

Dark & Dangerous - *Brooding Heroes Romance Collection*

Final Surrender - *Alpha Heroes Yielding to Love Collection*

Forbidden Hearts - *A Forbidden Love Romance Collection*

Forever Mine - *A Longing-for-Love Romance Collection*

Guarded Hearts - *A Surrender to Love Romance Collection*

Hearts & Secrets - *Small Town Romance Collection*

Hearts in Peril - *A Suspenseful Romance Collection*

Hidden Truths - *A Secret Identity Romance Collection*

Lies & Hearts - *A Lies, Secrets & Betrayal Romance Collection*

Love After Regret - *A Second-Chance Redemption Romance Collection*

Misjudged Hearts - *A Love After Judgement Romance Collection*

Torn Between Hearts - *A Love Triangle Romance Collection*

All of Alison Reid's books feature standalone stories, swoon-worthy heroes, and guaranteed happily-ever-afters.

Books by Alison Reid

A Billionaire for Christmas

A Heart in Florence

After The Storm

Always You

Before I Fell

Before the Thaw

Beneath the Lies

Billionaire Bodyguard

Billionaire Rancher

Blueprints of the Heart

Branlow

Collide

Echoes of Deception

Falling for the Billionaire

Forever Yours

Heart of the Outback

Hearts on the Line

Hidden Gem

Kept Promises

Mended Hearts

Mistaken Hearts

New Year's Eve Kiss

Quiet Danger

Reckless Hearts

Reflections of Deception

Second Glance

Shadows of the Past

Shattered Dreams

Shattered Hope, Stolen Kisses

Still Yours

The Billionaire's Accidental Legacy

The Billionaire's Bargain

The Billionaire's Mistake

The Billionaire's Regret

The Billionaire's Secret Baby

The Billionaire's Unexpected Heir

The Blood Debt

The Playboy's Surrender

The Wrong Sister

Trust in Time

Undercover Billionaire

Until you Loved Me

Vows of Vengeance

Wife in Name Only

Find all my books on Amazon:

https://www.amazon.com/author/alisonreid1970

About the Author

Alison Reid writes contemporary and small-town romance filled with heart, passion, and second-chance love stories. Her novels often feature strong heroines, irresistible heroes, and the happily-ever-afters readers adore. When she's not writing, Alison enjoys reading, spending time with her family, and imagining new love stories. She hopes her books give readers a few hours of escape, joy, and swoon-worthy romance they won't forget.